HINDUISM

HINDUISM

From Rig Veda to the Republic

RAM VARMA

RUPA

Dedicated to my daughters,
Vandana, Jyotsana and Upasana

First published by
Rupa Publications India Pvt. Ltd 2024
7/16, Ansari Road, Daryaganj
New Delhi 110002

Sales centres:
Bengaluru Chennai
Hyderabad Jaipur Kathmandu
Kolkata Mumbai Prayagraj

P-ISBN: 978-93-5702-175-3
E-ISBN: 978-93-5702-169-2

First impression 2024

10 9 8 7 6 5 4 3 2 1

Printed in India

CONTENTS

PART SEVEN

INTRODUCTION

Hinduism, which evolved in India, is one of the oldest living religions in the world. About 83 per cent of India's population is Hindu. In later times millions of Hindus have migrated to other countries, taking their faith and culture with them. The word 'Hindu' is of ancient Persian origin. The Persians or Iranians were fellow travellers of the Rigvedic people, who are believed to have migrated to India from Central Asia. The people of Sindh–Baluchistan had used the word 'Hindu' to describe those who migrated beyond and settled on the river Indus in India, which was called the 'Sindhu'. It is assumed that the Iranians pronounced '*sa*' as '*ha*', and therefore, 'Sindhu' as 'Hindu'.

In his book *Hindu History*, historian A.K. Majumdar observes as follows:

> With the possible exception of the Chinese, Hindus are the oldest nation in the world. Their national existence and civilization date from the dawn of human history. The Egyptians, Assyrians, Greeks, Romans, and Persians are 'history' now. It is the Hindus alone who have stood the test of time; with but slight changes, they are still the same people as they were thousands of years back.[1]

Majumdar adds a quotation from Edward Thorton's *History of the British Empire in India, Vol. 1*:

> Ere yet the pyramids looked down upon the valley of the Nile; when Greece and Italy—those cradles of European civilization—nursed only the tenants of the wilderness, India was the seat of wealth and grandeur.

Majumdar's profound observation reminds me of some lines from poet Iqbal's famous poem:

[1]Majumdar, A.K., *Hindu History,* Rupa Publications, New Delhi, 2008, p. 4.

Aye aaberoode Ganga, woh din hai yaad tujhko,
Utara tere kinare, jab karvaan hamara? (...)
Yunaan-o-misr-o-rooma, sab mit gaye jahan se,
Kuchh baat hai ki hasti mit-tee nahin hamari.

[O Ganga of milk-white waters, do you remember the day
when our caravan had arrived and camped on your shores?[2]
Iran, Egypt, Rome—all have vanished from the world.
But there is something unique about us, that our existence
remains perennial in the world.]

As a matter of fact, the Aryans had reached the shores of the Indus initially, and had taken a few centuries to reach the shores of the Ganga. But Ganga being considered the most sacred among the Indian rivers, Iqbal hails their momentous arrival on her shores!

[2]The Aryans had landed on the bank of the Indus and reached the shores of Ganga much later.

PART ONE

THE INDUS VALLEY CIVILIZATION

Excavations in the Indus Valley revealed the existence of the world's first civilization, which flourished between 3000 BC and 2000 BC at Mohenjo-daro and Harappa, now in Pakistan. Until the mid-nineteenth century, no one knew about the Indus Valley Civilization. During the British rule, when a railway line was being laid out from Karachi to Lahore, heaps of old baked bricks were unearthed in a mound near the railway track. The British engineers John and William Brunton began using these as ballast for the railway line. He told Alexander Cunningham of the Royal Engineers about the discovery of brickbats, who then visited the site and collected several artifacts from the ruins. This site was in Harappa.

Some years later, in the 1920s, Sir John Marshall, director-general of the Archaeological Survey of India, carried out excavations in Harappa and revealed this amazing civilization. After two years, R.D. Banerji discovered Mohenjo-daro. Since then, hundreds of sites of this civilization have been found.

The heart of the civilization was the vast flood plain of the Indus and Hakra rivers. The Hakra (also known as the Ghaggar or Saraswati), which once flowed east of, and parallel to, the Indus, had dried up later on.

It has been estimated that this civilization developed out of farming and herding communities and began flourishing about 4,500 years ago. In time it grew to cover a large portion of the present-day Pakistan, parts of northern India and of what is now Afghanistan. The geographical area of the Indus Civilization covered about 1.3 million sq. km—stretching south from the Himalayan foothills of Punjab, down to the mouth of the Indus and from there eastward and westward along the sea coast—eastward from Gujarat up to Bhagatrav at the mouth of the river Narmada, and westward along the Makran Coast up to Sutkagen-dor on the river Dasht. The dates of the mature phase of the Indus Valley Civilization, modified on the basis of radiocarbon dating, are roughly from 2500 BC to 1700 BC, when the Aryans probably destroyed this civilization.

Thick layers of silt were found deposited in the upper strata of Mohenjo-daro. The ever-shifting course of the Indus would have been a major threat to these riverine settlements. The long-term effects of geological changes like tectonic disturbances were even more serious, resulting in the eastward diversion of some of the rivers that flowed through Punjab, Rajasthan and Sindh, and the eventual drying up of the river Saraswati leading to the gradual salination of the soil.

The people of the Indus Valley Civilization planned their cities carefully. They built their buildings on mud-brick platform, thereby protecting them from seasonal floods. Indeed, the cities of Mohenjo-daro and Harappa had a planned grid pattern on which were built houses of baked or sun-dried bricks. The bricks had roughly three standard sizes. Each house was connected to an efficient drainage system. There were amenities of good water supply and drainage, baths and public buildings. On the eastern side of the two towns there were powerful fortifications with a strong citadel. The living quarters of the rich covered a larger area while the poor lived in one- or two-room tenements. There was great emphasis on personal hygiene. Even the two-room tenements had a bathroom. The water supply to the cities was from community wells, while the rich had wells in their houses.

The 'Great Bath'of the Mohenjo-daro citadel had a residence for a high official or head priest with a large hall with 20 pillars. Explorer Koshambi had speculated that 'it was part of the ritual for men not only to bathe in the sacred water but also to cohabit with the female attendant representatives of the mother goddess to whom the citadel complex belonged. This is not far-fetched. The temples of Ishtar in Sumer and Babylon had similar practices.' I understand that the temple dancers of our great South Indian temples too were at the beck and call of the priests in earlier times.

In major cities there were large buildings that may have been used for grain storage or some other purpose. The one at Mohenjo-daro covered over 1,000 sq. m. At Harappa, the granary was built outside the citadel. At Lothal, in Gujarat, a dockyard and a wharf have been excavated, alongside a high platform for granaries.

The most tantalizing source of information about the religion of the Indus Valley Civilization are the seals. The seals have letters inscribed on them, but their script remains undeciphered. However, the figures engraved on the seals are of strong religious significance. There are depictions of wild animals like tigers, elephants and rhinoceroses. A seal found in a tomb at Mohenjo-daro shows a *peepal* tree and heads of horned animals. Whether by sea or land, the products of the Indus reached Mesopotamia as a number of seals have been found in Sumer at levels dating between about 2300 BC and 2000 BC. About three-quarters of the Indus terracotta figurines represent animals, mostly the humped bull, but also the buffalo, the rhinoceros, the monkey and the elephant. The unicorn is the most remarkable animal seen in Mohenjo-daro artefacts, generally shown with a sacred brazier next to it, signifying its hallowed nature.

The most striking deity of the Harappa culture is the horned god. He is a three-faced, ithyphallic god who, according to Marshall, 'is recognizable at once as a prototype of *Shiva*'.[1] Wearing an elaborate head-dress, necklaces and a girdle, he sits naked, in a typically yogic posture, his arms laden with bangles. Surrounded by many animals, he is of a ferocious visage and looks like a depiction of Shiva as Pashupati (Lord of the Beasts). Indeed, he has much in common with God Shiva of later Hinduism. He is sometimes depicted with three faces and in his most important aspect is a fertility deity. On the largest of the seals, he is surrounded by four wild animals—an elephant, a tiger, a rhinoceros and a buffalo—and beneath his stool are two deer, as in the representations of the Buddha preaching his first sermon in the Deer Park in Benaras, now Varanasi.

There is ample evidence of music and dance, wine and revelry in the cities; one seal shows a man beating a drum and

---

[1]Marshall, Sir John Hubert, *Mohenjo-Daro and the Indus Civilization: Being an Official Account of Archaeological Excavations at Mohenjo-Daro Carried out by the Government of India between the Years 1922 and 1927, Vol.1*, A Probsthain, London, 1931, p. 52.

people dancing. Hunting was also common; engravings show men shooting antelopes and goats with bows and arrows.

Both men and women wore a lot of ornaments—both wore necklaces, fillets, armlets and finger-rings; in addition, women wore girdles, ear-rings and anklets. The rich had ornaments of gold, silver, ivory, faience and semi-precious stones, but the poor had to make do with copper, shell, bone and terracotta. Women covered their entire left arm with bangles, usually made of shell, but wore only a couple of bangles on the right (working) arm. A vast jewellery hoard of gold and semi-precious stones—nearly 500 pieces—was found hidden in a hole in Harappa.

The best-known sculpture found in Mohenjo-daro is the 18-cm-high steatite bust of a stout, heavy-jowled, middle-aged man—often described as the priest-king—wearing an embroidered robe of trefoil design and a smug, faintly disdainful expression. Besides, there is a bronze statue of a nude, Proto-Australoid nymphet, with budding, tumescent breasts and a slender body. Her left leg is slightly raised, perhaps, as Marshall thought, to beat time to music. She strikes a saucy, sullen pose, her right arm placed impudently on the hip and her head thrown back. She is totally naked, except for a short chain with heavy pendants around the neck, a large number of bangles on the left arm and a couple of them at the wrist and elbow of the right arm. The statue, without feet or ankles, just 11.5-cm high, is not beautiful in the conventional sense, but has a strangely sensuous charm.

The most astonishing thing about the Indus Valley Civilization is in maintaining a near-absolute uniformity throughout the Indus region in the making of pottery vessels and stamp seals, in the dimensions of bricks used in the houses, the system of weights and measures, and in urban planning, for many centuries.

Giving a narration of the Harappa culture, A.L. Basham says[2]:

> The area covered by the Harappa Culture extended for some 950 miles from north to south, and the pattern of its civilization was so uniform that even the bricks were usually

[2]Basham, A.L., *The Wonder That Was India: A Survey of the Culture of the Indian Sub-Continent Before the Coming of the Muslims*, Rupa & Co, 1954, pp. 14–24.

> of the same size and shape from one end to the other. At Mohenjo-daro nine strata of buildings have been revealed. As the level of the earth rose from the periodic flooding of the Indus, new houses would be built almost exactly on the sites of the old houses. There is no doubt that they had contact with Mesopotamia. (...) Standardized burnt brick of good quality was the usual building material for dwelling houses (...) The bathrooms were provided with drains, which flowed to sewers covered throughout their length by large brick slabs (...) It was the most impressive of their achievements.

In his report on the excavations at Mohenjo-daro, Sir John Marshall maintained that some two centuries or more had elapsed between the fall of the Indus cities and the invasion of the Aryans. However, many competent authorities, led by Sir Mortimer Wheeler, now believe that Harappa was overthrown by the Aryans.

The Aryan migrants did not overwhelm the Indus valley in one fell swoop. It was a slow inundation. This threat to the cities came from the west. The Indus people had no great military tradition and do not seem to have maintained a strong army.

The final onslaught was sudden, at least in Mohenjo-daro, and caught people unaware. The people fled in terror, but many were cut down in the streets, in their homes, at a public well. Harappa seems to have been spared such a gory end, probably because the people there had fled before the attackers arrived. The only sign of violence there is a mass of human skulls of about 20 people at the outskirts of the city.

Despising the urban lifestyle, Aryans did not even care to occupy the cities they overran. Often, they simply set fire to Indus settlements—the Rig Veda repeatedly glorifies Agni for burning down the settlements of the dark-hued people. Some of the Indus people seem to have fled even to the west probably to take refuge with the Dravidian-speaking people of Baluchistan.

As a Rigvedic hymn says:

The foolish, faithless, rudely-speaking niggards,
Without belief or sacrifice or worship,
Far away hath Agni chased those Dashyus,
In the east hath turned the godless westward.

Southern India was probably the original home of the Dravidian people and would remain their domain, but for many centuries they would remain prominent in northern India too, where there were substantial Dravidian communities as late as the Mughal times. The Indus cities thus became ghost cities, and in time acquired their present name signifying their blighted fate: 'Mohenjo-daro' in Sindhi language and 'Lothal' in Gujarati are said to mean 'the place of the dead'.

PART TWO

THE RIGVEDIC CULTURE

Curiosity arose in my heart to read the Rig Veda, after my retirement in August 2000. I had read the *Ramacharita Manas* composed by the great Hindi poet, Tulsidas, during my school days, which had referred to the Vedas and Puranas with utmost reverence. After my retirement from government service, a wish was born to read the Vedas.

I had gone to Jaipur where my brother lived. In his company I bought a full set of a bilingual Rig Veda in four volumes—in original Sanskrit with Hindi translation and commentary by Bhagavati Devi Sharma, a disciple of Pt Shri Ram Sharma. From Delhi I bought Ralph T.H. Griffith's English translation, *The Hymns of the Rigveda*. Besides, I bought the Atharva Veda (in two volumes) translated by Devi Chand.

Keeping the Atharva Veda aside, I began taking an occasional dip in the Rig Veda, comparing Ralph Griffith's English translation with Bhagwati Devi Sharma's Hindi rendition. It felt like a tentative immersion into a vast ocean!

At that time my daughter Jyotsana was working as deputy secretary in the Department of Economic Affairs, Ministry of Finance. She was living in a flat in Khan Market area, in front of Khushwant Singh's house. Khushwant kept an open house, and once or twice when I visited Jyotsana, I accompanied her to Khushwant's place in the evening. I had been an ardent admirer of Khushwant's, having been an avid reader of the *Illustrated Weekly of India*, which he had edited for a number of years, and which during his editorship had gained considerably in popularity and circulation.

Khushwant Singh's drawing room was like the salon of an English nobleman. He entertained an eclectic circle of visitors and regaled them with his inimitable wit and humour. The conversation was in English but Khushwant would quote Urdu couplets of our celebrated poets, from his inexhaustible memory, interspersed with choicest bits of English poetry. Jyotsana too was well-versed in English as well as Urdu poetry and offered lively comments, in keeping with the courtly environment of the *majlis* (private gathering, Arabic for 'sitting room'). Khushwant Singh's son Rahul Singh looked after the few guests and filled up their glasses. Khushwant would be dressed informally; I remember him wearing just a kurta and a *kuchchha,* his loose shock of hair without a turban.

Once, in Jyotsana's bookshelves I found a Penguin Books's paperback edition of Wendy Doniger O'Flaherty's translation of 108 selected hymns of the Rig Veda (which would be about one-tenth of the number of hymns in total). The book had been published in England; Jyotsana must have picked it up from London. Rather than embarking on the gigantic task of translating the entire Rig Veda, Wendy Doniger had made a thematic selection of the most important hymns and produced a slim, reader-friendly volume for people like me, who did not know Sanskrit. This book, authored by the eminent Vedic scholar from Oxford, opened for me the portals of a long-vanished world. Indeed, I experienced a thrill akin to what the British archeologist Howard Carter must have felt on discovering the dazzling gold treasure of King Tutankhamen!

~

The Rig Veda is considered a monument of Indo-European mythology. Six hymns in the Rig Veda are dedicated to *Dhyava–Prithvi*. '*Dhyava*' or '*Dhyaus*' corresponds to the Greek god Zeus, who was a personification of the sky. In fact, Sir William Jones, a polymath of Greek and Latin, who had been sent to India as a High Court judge by the East India Company and had learnt Sanskrit here, had discovered that the language of the Rigvedic people had common ancestry with Greek and Latin. He had made this profound observation:

> The Sanskrit language, whatever be its antiquity, is of a wonderful structure; more perfect than Greek, more copious than Latin, and more exquisitely refined than either; yet bearing to both of them a stronger affinity, both in the roots of verbs and the forms of grammar, than can possibly

> have been produced by accident; so strong, indeed, that no philologer could examine them all without believing them to have sprung from some common source, which perhaps no longer exists. There is similar reason though not quite so forcible, for supposing that both the Gothick [Germanic] and Celtic, though blended with a different idiom, had the same origin with Sanskrit; and the old Persian might be added to the same family.[3]

The hymns of the Rig Veda are pristine soulful prayers composed and recited by the nomadic hordes of the Indo-European people in praise of their gods. They came down from Central Asia, probably from the steppes north of the Caspian Sea at the divide of Europe and Asia, in search of a homeland. While one branch went over to Anatolia, another crossed into Iran. From there, over several centuries, they advanced into the Middle East and India and overwhelmed the ancient and decaying civilizations there.

Of these diverse tribes, the group that settled in the Iranian plateau, called themselves 'Aryans'—the only branch of the Indo-Europeans known to take that name—and they called their land 'Ariana,' the home of Aryans, which later came to be called 'Iran.' The term Aryan was probably a tribal name initially, but in time it came to mean 'nobleman' or 'master' in contradistinction to the indigenous people whom the Aryans subjugated.[4]

The ancient Aryans spoke the same language and shared the same culture. We should therefore assume that the ancient Aryans, apart from having a common language—the proto-tongue that was the mother of Sanskrit, Persian, Greek, Latin, Celtic, Teutonic and Slavic—also belonged to a common racial stock.

They were conscious of being ethnically and culturally distinct. But as the race split and the tribes scattered, intermixing with diverse local people, through the slow process of physically adapting to their new environments, they began to diverge genetically and culturally. They came from distant arid areas, mounted on horses

[3]Keay, John, *India Discovered*, Harper Collins, 1988, p. 30.
[4]Erali, Abraham, *Gem in the Lotus: The Seeding of Indian Civilization*, Penguin India, 2000, p. 64.

or riding horse-drawn carriages, bringing their herds of cows along, in search of pastures, with 'sun and water and grass'.

Indeed, the Iranian and Indian Aryans were kinsfolk; they shared a common culture, spoke dialects of the same language and worshipped common gods like Indra, Varuna, Mitra, Savitr, Soma and Agni. However, they split again in the closing centuries of the third millennium BC due to some differences, and moved eastward into Afghanistan and Baluchistan. Pressing on, they squeezed through the narrow passes of the Hindu Kush and the Suleiman Range and entered the Indus Valley around 1700 BC.

Abraham Eraly says that India was not a conscious destination for them—they could not have had any clear prior knowledge of the land they were moving into and were not in any case an organized political power deliberately seeking conquest. Thus, there was no planned Aryan invasion of India, only a haphazard migration spread over several centuries.

Their conquest and destruction of the settlements in Mohenjo-daro and Harappa has been described in the earlier section. Having overwhelmed the orderly but decaying civilization, they moved on to the greener pastures in the Punjab and settled on the salubrious banks of the Sindhu River (which later came to be called the 'Indus') and her tributaries, and in a long time, reached the Saraswati River.

∽

The form of worship during Rigvedic times was the *yajna* (fire ritual). The Rigvedic sages organized yajna in the morning, offered *ghrita ahuti* (oblation of ghee) in fire, invoked the gods and chanted the hymns they had composed in their praise.

Agni was the principal god of the Rigvedic people. One can easily surmise why. A thick pall of darkness fell at night in the densely forested land that India was over 3,500 years ago, when the Rigvedic people reached here. Only fire rescued them from the terrors lurking in the dark, comforted them and gave them a sense of security in their bounteous newfound land.

But making the fire was quite an ordeal for them; there were no match-sticks then. They fashioned two sticks of wood for kindling fire, called *arni*—one larger, shaped like a man, the other smaller, shaped like a woman. They would stand around the *yajna vedi* (the altar or place for the ritual), rub the 'male arni' against the 'female arni' on a heap of dry *kusha* grass, reciting their sonorous hymns in praise of Agni. As sparks fell from the rubbing of the sticks, smoke arose, and then, lo and behold, God Agni appeared miraculously, in person, in answer to their prayers—golden-haired, fierce, burning bright, demanding to be fed, like an infant calf craving for its mother's milk.

The *rishi*s (saintly learned persons) exulted and prostrated before the golden apparition and fed him dollops of *ghrita* (ghee or clarified butter), which excited and aroused the fiery god, who brightened and expanded. Then they offered him the fermented Soma juice to drink, which inflamed him. They joyously sang his praise and offered him juicy chunks of well-cooked meat. God Agni exulted and radiated on receiving the oblations.

Agni was a living god, easy to access, as father to his sons. They made him their messenger and mediator to their heavenly gods. Indeed, Agni acted as their principal *purohita* (priest) and *hotr* (the priest who invokes the gods in the yajna) as well as their messenger to celestial gods—Indra, Rudra, Varuna, Soma et al—to come to their yajna vedi to receive oblations. There was the carpet of soft *durva* grass, for the gods, who alighted and sat around the yajna vedi, and were fed to satiety, through the agency of Agni. While offering rich oblations, the rishis sang eulogies to the gods and exhorted them to use their infinite prowess to exterminate their enemies and bless them with prosperity and progeny (mainly sons).

Such were the Vedic people; such was their faith. They were a hardy, happy people who lived in their paradisiacal world, enjoying the toil that life entailed and the fruits that the bounteous Mother Earth afforded them. Their minds were free, still uncluttered by the theories of the 'hereafter' and 'rebirth'.

I have cited the attributes of Agni from the very first hymn of the first *mandala* or 'book' of the Rig Veda, which was believed to be composed by Rishi Madhuchhanda, son or descendant of the famous Vedic sage Vishvamitra, and will quote the hymn a little later.

Seven mandalas of the Rig Veda, from the second to the eighth, are compositions of seven principal rishis, namely Vishvamitra, Vasistha, Bharadwaj, Atri, Gritsmada and their *shishya*s or their descendants. The first and the tenth mandalas are an amalgam of hymns composed mostly by later rishis. The ninth mandala is special; it is exclusively dedicated to God Soma—the heady drink which was also regarded as a celestial deity. It contains hymns composed by several rishis, singing Soma's glory.

The Soma plant was said to grow on mount Mujavant, a peak on the southwest of the valley of Kashmir. Ralph Griffith says that:

> The plant called Soma was gathered by moonlight, the word also means the Moon. It was crushed after stripping the leaves. The juice was sprinkled with water and placed on a sieve or strainer. The acidic juice trickled into a vessel and was mixed with flour, etc. and was left to ferment. Thereafter it was offered in libations to the Gods and also drunk by the priests.[5]

Unlike the other major religions of the world such as Buddhism, Christianity and Islam, Hinduism was not founded on the teachings of one godly person. As we have seen, its origins go back to the hymns of the Rig Veda from where it gradually evolved over thousands of years. Many sects arose within Hinduism and each developed its own philosophy and form of worship.

Numbering over a thousand, these vedic hymns are mankind's first poetic salutations to the dim-descried deities and the forces of the universe. These hymns are the fountainhead of mankind's oldest surviving religion that has come to be called 'Hinduism'.

The Rigvedic hymns were composed around 1700 BC–800 BC. The Sama Veda, Yajur Veda and Atharva Veda were composed afterwards. The Rig Veda is referred to as *shruti* (that which is heard), as the *rishi*-poets who composed the Vedic hymns were too modest or shy of claiming themselves as their authors. They felt that they 'heard' the faint murmurings of the sacred syllables

[5]Griffith, Ralph, *The Hymns of the Rigveda*, Motilal Banarasi Das, Delhi, p. 1.

and turned them into hymns. To my mind when, under a golden-hued firmament, they performed yajna at dawn, the rishi-poets were aware of the presence of their Gods, and words bubbled up from their charged mind and *richa*s (verses of the Rig Veda) formed in psychic exultation.

Indeed, every poem is shruti in a way. When the poet is inspired, his mental firmament receives the poem in tiny slivers, as it were, like snowflakes descending from the sky, which he shapes into a poem.

They memorized these hymns and passed them on to their sons or disciples. Writing was unknown at that time, so for many centuries, the Rigvedic hymns were stored by the rishis in their memory and were verbally passed on to their sons and disciples. As such, in any case the Rigvedic hymns were shruti. They were 'written down', indeed inscribed on palm leaves, a few centuries before Christ, whereafter the pundits kept them close to their chest. Only during the British rule, people like Max Müller and other scholars from Europe got access to them and translated them.

Max Müller had paid a handsome tribute to India, calling her 'a very paradise on earth'. He had said, 'If I were to look over the whole world to find out the country most richly endowed with all wealth, power and beauty that nature can bestow—in some parts a very paradise on earth—I would point to India.'[6]

On the other hand, the great Hindi poet, Sumitra Nandan Pant, had surmised that mankind's first poet must have been a *viyogi*—one suffering from the pangs of separation of his beloved, that his plaintive sighs formed into a mournful song, and poetry flowed out involuntarily, like tears from his eyes, in silence:

Viyogi hoga pehla kavi, aah se upja hoga gaan,
Nikal kar aankhon se chup-chap, bahi hogi kavita anjaan.

But the epithet 'viyogi' does not fit the Aryans in the least, who were India's, rather mankind's, first prolific and profound poets. Rather than being haunted by the separation of their beloved, they were indefatigable family men with wives and kids, possessing

[6]Müller, Friedrich Max, *India: What Can It Teach Us*, Rupa & Co, 2010.

large herds of cows. They had been on the move for several years, escaping from a harsh climate, in search of a congenial habitation, which they found in India.

∽

The Rig Veda is a collection of 1,028 hymns in all. The hymns were composed by more than a hundred poets, called rishis[7] and are arranged in 10 chapters called mandalas. They are addressed to the gods of the Aryans like Indra, Varuna, Rudra, Soma, the Maruts, Agni, etc. and were meant to be recited by the rishis during ritual sacrifices. Each hymn is a complete poem by itself. They open a window on 'the timeless world of myth and ritual', as Wendy Doniger[8] observes. She candidly confesses that her rendering of the hymns into English is anything but perfect, and quips good-humouredly: 'A translation is like a woman; if it is beautiful, it cannot be faithful; and if it is faithful, it cannot be beautiful'.

For the hymns not included in Wendy Doniger's selection, I gleaned the sense from Ralph Griffith's painstaking English translation as well as their Hindi version by Bhagavati Devi Sharma. Bhagavati Devi considers the hymns as something akin to '*Brahma vakya*', voice of saintly oracles, and in her translation attempts to give religious and reverential coating even to secular and bawdy hymns.

Yes, there are some bawdy, down-to-earth 'hymns' in the Rig Veda!

∽

INDIA, THAT IS BHARAT

The Hindus were migrants in India. The Indian subcontinent has been formed from what was once a part of the Gondwana landmass, also called as Gondwanaland. It was connected to Madagascar, Africa and Australia. The Indian subcontinent moved northwest due to the plate tectonic movements for several million

[7]There are a few *rishikas* too, female hymn composers.

[8]Doniger, Wendy, *The Rigveda*, Penguin Books, London, 1981, p. 16

years till it collided with Eurasia. This thrust finally resulted in the creation of the world's highest mountain range from the Tethys Sea, viz. the Himalayas. With time this extensive mountain range got covered with snow, giving India a majestic crown of sparkling snow that stretched from the east to the west, providing protection from enemies and cold dry winds of Central Asia. The Himalayan mountain range is the progenitor of the great river systems of the Indus and its tributaries—the Jhelum, the Chenab, the Ravi, the Beas and the Sutlej; the Ganga and its tributary the Yamuna; the Brahmaputra; and the Mekong. India takes her name from the Indus.

The Bharatas, who gave their name 'Bharat' to the country, were the most important Rigvedic tribe. They were settled at that time between the rivers Saraswati and Yamuna. The Bharatas and the Tritsus were allies and were enemies of the Purus. King Divodas of the Tritsus clan was a great conqueror who had successfully fought against the Purus and Yadus on the one hand, and against the Dasa king, Shambara and the Panis on the other.

In post-Rigvedic times, however, the Bharatas coalesced with the Purus and became the Kuru people of later times.[9] However, in the traditional genealogy of the Kuru chiefs, both Bharata or Purus occur as names of their ancestors, and they are indiscriminately described as 'sons of Bharata' or sons of 'Puru.'

The Rig Veda reminds me of the lines in Thomas Gray's 'Elegy Written in a Country Churchyard':

> Full many a gem of purest ray serene
> The dark unfathomed caves of ocean bear.

The Rig Veda is verily an ocean, full of rare, lustrous gems. I have selected a few gems of varying hues and lustre which we see in the next chapter.

[9]Majumdar, R.C. (ed.), *The Vedic Age*, Bharatiya Vidya Bhavan, 1996, p. 249.

SELECTED HYMNS FROM THE RIG VEDA

Cattle, particularly the horse and the cow, played a predominant part in the lives of the Vedic Aryans. However, A.L. Basham points out that,

> ...there is no evidence that they were held sacred at this time—the cow in one or two places was given the epithet 'not to be killed,' but this may only imply her economic importance. In any case it is quite clear that both oxen and cows were slaughtered for food.
>
> The horse was almost as important as the cow, though mainly for military purposes. The Aryans, harnessed to light chariots, must have terrified the people of the Indus valley.[10]

A.L. Basham quotes verses from the Rigvedic hymn, IV. 38, composed by Rishi Vamdev Gautam, which eulogizes a divine horse, Dadhikra.

Hymn IV. 38. Dadhikra

2. You mighty Dadhikra, impetuous, swift and colourful like a hawk, are brave like a King, whom everyone must honour.

3. You rush swiftly down a precipice, rejoicing the hearts of Purus, earning their praise. Springing forth like a brave-heart for battle, whirling the chariot and flying like the tempest.

4. You gain precious booty in combats, chasing the cattle, winning spoils. You shine in bright colour, making the boorish people run in fright.

6. Eager to be first, you dart amid the ranks of the chariots, happy as a bridegroom wearing garlands, spurning the dust and champing at the bit.

8. At your deep neigh, like thundering clouds, the foemen tremble in fear. You fight against thousands, and none can resist

---

[10]Balsham, A.L., *The Wonder That Was India: A Survey of the Culture of the Indian Sub-Continent Before the Coming of the Muslims,* Rupa & Co, 1954.

your terrible charge.

10. Dadhikra has overwhelmed the foes with vigour. May the strong Steed who wins thousands, requite with sweetness these my words of praise.

~

In Western usage, Rig Veda usually refers to the Rig Veda Samhita (the collection of hymns). But appended with the Samhita are the Aitareya and Kaushitaki Brahmanas, which provide useful commentary on the hymns.

The Sama Veda is a guide for singing the verses of Rig Veda. It puts them to a musical measure and illustrates musical rendering of Rigvedic hymns.

The Yajur Veda, as the name suggests, deals with the methodology of conducting the yajna-sacrifice in which the hymns were recited. Appended with it are two Brahmanas, the Aitareya and the Shatpath Brahmana, which explain sacrificial rituals, their symbolism and methodology. Shatpath Brahmana gives diagrams of construction of complex fire-altars. Indeed, the trinity of the Rig Veda, Sama Veda and Yajur Veda is bound by a common thread and forms a whole.

Some important Upanishads also form part of Shatapath Brahmana like the Brihad-Aranyika, Ishopanishad, Kathopanishad, etc. In Kathopanishad the boy Nachiketa meets the god Yama and holds a dialogue with him on life and death.

Besides, the Shatpath Brahmana gives the origin of the Puranic myths regarding the avatars of Vishnu—*Kurma* (tortoise), *Matsya* (fish), *Varaha* (boar), *Narasimha* (man-lion) and *Vamana* (dwarf). The Kurma avatar is linked with the legend of the churning of the ocean by the gods and demons. In Matsya avatar Vishnu appears to Manu in the form of a fish and warns him of the impending deluge. The Matsya grows to an enormous size and guides Manu's ship to safety at the peak of a mountain where Manu re-establishes life through the performance of Vedic sacrificial rites.

The pre-eminent Hindi poet Jaishankar Prasad had composed his epic poem 'Kamayani' on the theme of the cosmic deluge. Its opening verse is:

> *Himgiri ke uttung shikhar par, baith shila ki sheetal chhanh,*
> *Ek purush bheege nayanon se dekh raha tha parlay pravah.*
> [On a high peak of the Himalayas, sitting in the cool shade of a cliff, a man[11] watched with misty eyes the swirling waters of the deluge.]

Interestingly, the story of Noah in the Hebrew Bible bears a striking resemblance with Vishnu's Matsya avatar. Yahweh, the god in Judaism, decided to flood the earth because of mankind's sinful state. Yahweh tells Noah to build an ark in order to preserve human and animal life. Noah boards the ark with his family along with the representatives of all animals. All life outside the ark perishes. After the flood recedes, a rainbow forms in the sky and all those aboard the ark disembark, and life begins anew.

∽

Generally, most Hindus believe in the authority of the Vedas and have deep regard for the later philosophic writings of the Upanishads, written around 700 BC. They also accept the teachings of the Dharmashastras, the ancient law books, like Manusmriti.

The Bhagavada Gita is revered by the Hindus like the Bible. It is believed to have been spoken by Shri Krishna to Arjun on the battlefield of the Mahabharata war between the Kauravas and the Pandavas, at Kurukshetra, currently in the state of Haryana. But the book contains 18 chapters; Shri Krishna couldn't have possibly spoken them in the battlefield! Actually, this universally acclaimed, splendid poetic and religious creation was a joint venture of erudite pundits in later centuries.

Historian John Keay observes that 'for Hindus the traditions of Sanskrit literature are still sacrosanct. Vedic prayers are still said, televised serializations of the Sanskrit epics can bring the entire Indian nation to a hushed standstill. The compositions of the ancient arya are not just history; they are the nearest thing to revelation.'[12]

---

[11]'Man' may have referred to Manu.

[12]Keay, John, *India: A History*, Harper Collins, India, p. 19.

Indeed, the vedi made in Hindu marriage ceremonies by the priests is a replica of the Vedic yajna vedi. The Brahmin priests invoke Agni in the vedi and virtually install a few gods around it, chanting *shlokas* (Sanskrit verses). They make the wedding couple go round the vedi seven times, reciting a few verses from the famous Rigvedic hymn that celebrates the wedding of the Sun's daughter Surya. They offer *purna-ahuti* (final oblation) then, inviting important guests to offer incense in the yajna vedi.

Gods come down to witness the Hindu wedding ceremony, and as the plume of the holy smoke rises from the *yajna mandap*, they depart, having blessed the nuptials.

Wendy Doniger opens her selection with a hymn dedicated to Vishvadevas (Gods of the world), and I would do the same. The rishi who composed it was diffident in claiming its authorship. The hymn is ascribed to Manu Vaivastat (son of Vivasvan—the Sun).

Hymn VIII. 30. Vishvedevas

1. Not one of you, ye Gods, is small, not one is a feeble child. All of you are truly great.

2. Therefore you are worthy of praise and sacrifice, you thirty-three gods of Manu, arrogant and powerful.

3. Protect us, help us and speak for us; do not lead us into distance, far away from the path of our father Manu.

4. You gods who are all here and who belong to all men, give far-reaching shelter to us and our cows and horses.

Cows and horses were the most prized possessions of the Rigvedic people, as the hymn declares. Indeed, the cows were a kind of currency for the Rigvedic people.

There are many other hymns eulogizing the Vishvadevas. The one authored by Sage Vihavya Angirasa invokes many of the 33 Hindu gods by name.

Hymn X.128. Vishvadevas

1. Let me win glory, O Agni, in our battles: enkindling thee,

may we attain power and strength. May the four regions bend and bow before me; with you for guardian, may we win in combat.

2. May all the Gods be on my side in battle, the Maruts led by Indra, Vishnu, O Agni. May god Vayu blow, favouring these my wishes.

3. May the Gods grant me riches; may the blessing and invocation of the Gods assist me. Foremost in battle be the *hotar* priests of the Gods: may we have brave fighters around to protect us.

5. You, six Divine Expanses[13] and Vishvadevas grant us victory over our foes; protect our progeny and ourselves. O King Soma, never let us be vanquished by our enemies.

7. Lord of the universe, Creator of creators, O God Brihaspati and both Ashvins, shelter this sacrifice and the sacrificer from evil.

8. All pervasive and most invoked, let the all-powerful bull Indra, afford us wide protection. May the lord of bay horses, Indra, bless our progeny; harm us not.

9. Let our foes stay afar from us: with Indra and Agni's help we will drive them off. O Vasus, Adityas, Rudras, make us mighty: glorify us as thinkers and sovereign lord.

In Verse 7 above, Brihaspati is addressed as the 'creator of creators'. Brihaspati is also the husband of the goddess of speech '*Vak*'. Wendy Doniger says that in fact the literal meaning of his name 'Brihaspati' is 'the lord of sacred speech.'[14] I quote a hymn, X. 71, on the origins of sacred speech. This hymn is ascribed to Brihaspati and dedicated to the deity *Gyan* (knowledge). Ralph Griffith considers it a 'very difficult hymn'. He adds that the famous fourteenth century scholar and commentator of the Vedas, Sayana, considers it to contain *param brahma-gyan* (the ultimate knowledge of the Supreme Brahma).

Hymn X. 71. The Origins of Sacred Speech

1. When the poets and sages first set in motion the beginnings of Speech, giving names to all things, they revealed the perfectly guarded secrets of the world. They were prompted by love.

[13]Heaven, Earth, Day, Night, Water and Plants.

[14]Doniger, Wendy, *The Rigveda*, Penguin Books, London, 1981, p. 62.

2. When the poets and sages fashioned Speech out of thought, sifting words as grain is sifted through a sieve. They designed speech as a channel of love.

3. Through holding yajna-sacrifice, they traced the path of Speech and found it harbouring among the rishis. Together the seven sages praised it.

4. Some who looked did not see Speech; some listened to it but could not understand it. But to some it revealed herself as a loving wife undresses, and reveals her body to her husband.

7. Even those who can see and hear goddess Speech are not equal in their flashes of insight, as there are ponds just knee-deep and others deeper; a few plunge in to a good depth for a refreshing bath.

8. When friendly Brahmins sacrifice together with their mind and heart, some are left behind for lack of knowledge, while some knowledgeable Brahmins surpass them with their power of veneration.

10. All friends rejoice in the victory of a friend who wins fame in the religious assembly. He saves them from dishonour and their food-provider (the organizer of the yajna). He is worthy of going forward and winning acclaim.

11. One (priest) sits bringing to blossom the flower of the verses, another sings verses in the Shakvari metre. One proclaims the truth of ancient ways; another lays out the measure of the sacrificial arena.

~

There is yet another mysterious hymn, X. 125, dedicated to Vak, the goddess of speech. Speech is herself the speaker of this hymn, though her name does not appear in it.

Hymn X. 125. Vak

1. I travel with the Rudras and the Vasus, wander with the Adityas and all the gods. I hold aloft both Varuna and Mitra, Indra and Agni and both the Ashvins.[15]

---

[15]She means to say that all these gods will be 'speechless' without her.

5. I announce and utter the words that give joy to gods and men. Those who are famous for their wisdom owe it to me, Whom I love I make exceedingly mighty; I make him a sage, a wise man, a Brahmin.

6. I stretch the bow for Rudra so that his arrow will strike down the hater of prayer and devotion. I rouse and incite the people for battle. I have pervaded the earth and the sky.

8. I am the one who prevails like the wind, embracing all creatures. Beyond the sky, beyond the earth, I am supreme in my grandeur.

Besides Wendy Doniger's book, I have also benefitted immensely from Bhartiya Bhavan's book, *The Vedic Age.*[16] Dr B.K. Ghosh calls the Rigvedic hymns, 'lyrical poems adapted to the purpose of ritual.'[17] The Rigvedic poets, he says, 'were deeply affected by the apparently mysterious working of the awe-inspiring forces of nature. Their hymns reflect in places that primitive attitude of mind which looks upon all nature as a living presence ... The luminaries (the sun, moon, the stars) who follow a fixed course across the sky are *deva*s (lit. the shining ones) or gods.'

According to Dr Ghosh the hymns addressed to Heaven's daughter *Usha* (Aurora as her Roman equivalent) are perhaps the oldest and certainly the most beautiful. They are inspired by the sight of the sunrise over the snow-clad peaks of the Himalayas.

I quote a hymn composed by Rishi Gautam Rahugana, dedicated principally to Goddess Dawn, Usha. The poet calls her a 'dancing girl'. The hymn also eulogizes the Ashvins in the last three verses; the Ashvins are horse-faced gods who carry the chariot of Vivasvan, the Sun.

Hymn I. 92. Usha and the Ashvins

1. Look how Usha has raised her banner in the eastern half of the sky, adorning and anointing herself with Sun's shining rays.

[16]Majumdar, R.C. (ed.), *The Vedic Age*, Bharatiya Vidya Bhavan, 1996.
[17]Ibid. 346.

Unleashing herself like an impetuous warrior, her rays advance like golden cows.

2. Readily have the purple beams of light shot up, yoking the golden cows for spreading the glowing light in the path of the Sun.

3. Her beams sing their song like women coming from afar, bringing refreshments day after day to the liberal sacrificer, and the worshipper who pours the Soma juice.

4. Like a dancing girl, she puts on bright ornaments; she bares her bosom as a cow reveals her swollen udder. Creating light for the whole universe, Usha emerges from darkness as cows break out from their enclosed pen.

5. Usha's brilliant flame spreads and drives back the formless dark abyss. As one sets up the stake in the sacrifice, the Sky's daughter spreads her many-splendoured light, anointing and adorning it with colourful ornaments.

6. Radiant Usha has crossed to the farthest bank of darkness, spreading her wings. Smiling like a lover who wishes to win his way, she shines forth with her lovely face and awakens us to happiness.

7. The Gotamas have praised Heaven's radiant daughter, the leader of the charm of pleasant voices. O Usha, confer on us strong men as offspring and as victory prizes; let your rewards begin with cattle and culminate in horses.

8. O beauteous Usha, who shines in wondrous glory, let me obtain riches, renowned and ample, in brave sons and troops of heroic men, famed for horses.

9. Gazing out over all creatures, the Goddess shines from the distance facing straight towards every eye. Awakening into motion everything that lives, she inspires and admires the verses of her adorers.

11. She has awakened all beings, uncovering the very edges of the sky, pushing aside her sister (the night).

12. Spreading out her rays, like a river in full flood, she shines from distance. Never transgressing the divine commandments, she reveals herself by the rays of the Sun.

13. O Usha, enriched with holy rites, yoke to your car the purple steeds, empower us to gain and nourish sons and grandchildren.

14. Usha, resplendent giver of gifts, showers the riches of kine and horses upon us here and now.

15. Harness your red-gold horses now, O prize-giving Usha, and bring all good fortune to us.

16. O Ashvins, who work wonders, turn your chariot towards us that brings cattle, that brings gold, and come back to us.

17. You Ashvins, who give a shout from heaven (to wake people at sunrise) and make light for mankind, bring us strength.

18. Hither may they bring the two gods, Vivasvan and Usha, who wake at dawn, moving on paths of gold to drink the Soma, working wonders and giving joy.

~

Reading this enchanting hymn, I was reminded of the opening lines of a poem by our greatest modern poet, Jai Shankar Prasad, in praise of India:

Arun yeh madhumaya desh hamara.
Jahan pahunch anjaan kshitij ko milta aik sahara.
Arun yeh madhumaya desh hamara.

By calling our country 'madhumaya' he was probably describing the beauty of India at dawn. '*Madhu*' means sweet, delicious or delightful. So'*madhumaya*' would mean 'permeated or suffused with sweetness and light'. Like Rishi Gautam Rahugana, he too was mesmerized by the beauty of the golden dawns in India.

Jai Shankar Prasad goes on to mention in the second line another mysterious quality of India: 'Where an unaware horizon meets a destination.' Was he pointing to travellers finding a destination, like the Rigvedic people, the Aryans, who after leaving their arid Arctic habitation and traversing thousands of miles on horse-back or horse-drawn chariots, crossing high mountain passes, found a home in India. Or was he hinting at the continental shift I had referred to earlier—resulting in the miraculous creation of India by joining with what was called 'Gondwanaland'?

~

The Rigvedic poet is enchanted by not only the radiant beauty of the dawn but also the mystic beauty of the night. There is a hymn dedicated to *ratri* (the night)—X. 127—composed by Rishi Kushik Saubhar who was a predecessor of the famous sage, Vishvamitra. This, according to Wendy Doniger, is the only hymn in the Rig Veda dedicated to the goddess of the night, the sister of Dawn.

Hymn X. 127. Ratri

1. The goddess Ratri has drawn near; looking about on many sides, with her eyes—the stars—she is bedecked with all her glories.
2. The immortal goddess has filled the wide space between the sky and the earth, the depths and the heights. She stems the tide of darkness with the light of her stars.
3. The goddess has drawn near, pushing aside her sister, the twilight.
4. O Ratri, as you came near to us, we have turned homeward to rest, as birds go to their nests in a tree.
5. People who live in villages have gone home to rest, as have the animals with feet and animals with wings, even the ever-searching hawks.
6. Ward off the she-wolf and the wolf from us, O Gramya (the goddess who resides in villages), keep the thief away and be easy for us to pass.
7. Darkness, palpable, black, but glittering in star light, has come upon me. O Dawn, come and banish it from me like a debt.
8. O Ratri, I have driven this hymn to you as the herdsman drives cows. Choose and accept it, O, Daughter of the sky, like a song of praise for the conqueror.

Hymn I. 50 eulogizes the Sun. It was composed by Praskanva Kanva, son of Sage Kanva, one of the seven most eminent rishis who composed the Rigvedic hymns. In this hymn the Sun is described as riding a chariot driven by seven mares, his rays (his daughters). The Sun is also identified with Varuna, the guardian of the moral law, who keeps a vigilant eye on mankind.

Hymn I. 50. The Sun

1. His brilliant rays bear the god Jataveda (Agni) aloft, the knower of all creatures, so that everyone may look on him.

2. The starry constellations, along with the night, steal away like thieves, when the Sun appears, who fixes His gaze on everyone.

3. His refulgent rays are his banners, which herald him from a distance, shining over mankind like blazing fires.

4. Traversing vast space, O Sun, you are the maker of light. Worshipped by all, you illumine the whole wide realm of space.

5. You visit the three realms of the Gods, of Fathers and of mankind, so that they can all behold your light.

6. You are the eye with which the purifying God Varuna looks upon the busy race of man.

7. You go across heaven and the vast realm of space, O Sun, measuring days by nights, looking upon living beings.

8. Seven golden mares with radiant hair carry you in your chariot, O far-seeing God Sun.

9. O Sun, ensconced on your chariot of seven multi-coloured daughters, you proceed, surveying all.

10. We have come out of darkness, O Sun, bringing your lofty light; the God among the gods, the Light most excellent!

11. As you ascend in the Sky today, O benevolent Protector, cure me of my heart disease and my yellow pallor.

12. Let us place this yellow pallor among parrots and starlings; let us give this yellow pallor to tree leaves and vines.

13. With his conquering vigour, this Aditya has gone up high, hurling down my hateful enemy into my hands. Let me not fall into my enemy's hands.

There is a group of gods connected with the Sun in various ways. Dawn is a goddess incarnate, related to the Sun. The Ashvins, the horse-faced gods who carry his chariot, are sons of Vivasvan, the Sun. God Pushan is his charioteer and is therefore associated with journeys on the roads and travellers. Indeed, Pushan presides over roads and journeys and protects the travellers. There is a hymn, I. 42, dedicated to Pushan, which was composed by Kanva Ghor.

Hymn I. 42. Pushan on the Road

1. Shorten our ways, O Pushan, remove the obstructions in our path. O cloud-born God, go close before us!

2. O Pushan, chase away from our road the wolf; the wicked, vicious wolf who threatens us.

3. The notorious highwayman, the robber who plots in ambush, drive him far away from the track.

4. Trample under your foot the wicked firebrand, the double-tounged rascal, whoever he may be.

5. O wonder-worker Pushan, possessing great wisdom, we beg you for that help which you provided to our Forefathers.

6. You bestow every good fortune and are the bearer of the golden sword. Make riches easy for us to win.

7. Lead us past our pursuers; make our paths pleasant and easy to travel. Bestow on us the power of understanding ourselves.

8. O God Pushan, lead us to pastures rich in grass; let there be no sudden fever on the journey. Bestow on us the power of understanding.

9. Using your powers, O Pushan, give fully and lavishly to fill our bellies. Bestow on us the power of understanding.

10. Never do we forget Pushan; we sing his glory with well-worded hymns. We pray to the worker of wonders to give us riches.

The Indian countryside was densely forested at that dawn of civilization when the Rigvedic people reached here. There is a pretty hymn (X. 146) addressed to the goddess *Aranyani,* guardian deity of the forest, that evokes the spirit of the pristine environment. It was composed by Rishi Devmuni.

Hymn X. 146. Aranyani

1. O Spirit of the Forest, you seem to be averse being sighted. How is it that you do not seek the village? Are you not afraid of living alone in the wilderness?

2. When the little birds, singing *chi-chi-chi,* take up the refrain from the droning cricket, are they singing your praise like tinkling

bells?

3. O Spirit of the Forest, look the cows are grazing over there, a dwelling place appears to be shrouded by the creepers over there. Carts rumble carrying grass and timber.

5. O Spirit of the Forests, you don't harm anyone. You eat sweet fruits and lie down wherever you please.

6. I pray to the Vana Devi, sweet scented, redolent. Mother of wild beasts and all sylvan beings; she tills not herself but reigns in plenty.

There is a hymn, X. 75, called 'Nadi Stuti', in praise of the rivers of India, esteemed as deities by the Rigvedic people. About 21 rivers find mention in this celebrated hymn which sings a full-throated panegyric of the river Sindhu, the lord and leader of the 'Flock of Rivers'. It was on the banks of the Sindhu that the Aryans had first settled. The hymn was composed by Sage Sindhukshit Angirasa. I have mainly followed Ralph Griffith's translation. It mentions the Ganga, although the Aryans had reached the Ganga basin much later. In later times Ganga came to be considered as the most sacred river.

Hymn X. 75. Nadi Stuti

1. O ye Rivers, let me sing your grandeur that is beyond compare. You flowed in groups of seven from the Sky and the Heaven[18] to the Earth. River Sindhu surpasses in might all the mighty streams that flow.

2. God Varuna cut the channels for your forward course, O Sindhu, when you ran to win the race, you speeded over the precipitous ridges of the earth. You were the Lord and Leader of these running streams while hurtling down.

3. Your tumultuous roar resounds in the sky and reaches the heaven. O Sindhu, you rush on bellowing like a bull, like torrents of rain that fall thundering down.

[18]A group of seven rivers flowed from three different sources; 'three times seven' = 21, in all.

4. Like mothers to their calves, like milch kine with udders full of milk, your tributaries run to you roaring, O Sindhu. Like a warrior king, you lead the swift streams like the wings of your army.

5. Favour this my prayer, O Ganga, Yamuna, Saraswati; O Shutudri, Stoma, Parushni; O Asikini, Marudvridha, Vitasta, Arjikiya with Sushoma, hear my call.

6. O Sindhu, you were eager to flow first with Trishtama, then with Susartu and Rasa and with Shvetya. You ride your chariot taking Kubha, Gomati, Krumu and Mehatnu in your train.

7. Flashing and gleaming white, O mighty Sindhu, you prance like a dappled mare, beautiful and fair to behold.

8. Rich in good steeds is Sindhu, clad in regal robes, driving a grand chariot, wearing golden ornaments. She is lovely like an ever-young damsel, abounding in evergreen plants and flowers, exuding sweet fragrance.

9. Sindhu has yoked her chariot drawn by steeds and shall win booty in this fight. So have I praised the glory and power of this mighty and unrestrained Lord of Rivers!

This remarkable hymn mentions the Ganga and Yamuna but mainly glorifies the Indus. River Gomati of Verse 6 above is Gomal, Shutudri is the modern Sutlej and Drishadvati the modern Chutang. 'Vipash' (fetterless) is the Beas, Parushni is the modern Ravi and Vitasta is Jhelum. Asikini is the modern Chenab, which is also called the Chandra-Bhaga.

Apart from the rivers in the Indus basin, this hymn mentions the Ganga, Yamuna, Saraswati and Sarayu. River Saraswati comes between the Yamuna and Shutudri, and has been identified with the modern Sarsuti, which was lost in the desert at Bhatner later on.

The Saraswati is a river par excellence and appears most frequently in the Rig Veda. At that time, it used to reach the Arabian Sea and was as large as the Sutlej. In Hymn II. 41, the Vedic poet Gristmad Angiras addresses her as '*Ambitame, Naditame, Devitame Saraswati*' (The best of mothers, the best of rivers and the best of goddesses). Besides, two other hymns of the Rig Veda, VI. 61 and VII. 95, are solely dedicated to her and sing her glory.

Hymn VI. 61, dedicated to the river Saraswati, was composed

by Bharadwaj Baryaspatya. I quote Verses 2, 8, 12 and 14 from this hymn:

Hymn VI. 61. River Saraswati

2. She with her might hath burst with her strong waves, slicing the ridges of mountains as easily as uprooting lotus stalks.

8. Her limitless flood, swift moving with a rapid rush, comes forward with tempestuous roar.

12. Seven-sistered, she sprung from three-fold source.[19] She brought prosperity to the Five Tribes[20] and must be invoked when celebrating every mighty deed.

14. Guide us. O Saraswati to glorious treasure, refuse us not your milk, nor spurn us from you! Gladly accept our friendship and obedience; let us not go from you to distant countries.

Ralph Griffith had wrongly believed that the Saraswati was a minor river. In fact, he could not accept that this hymn pertained to the Saraswati at all. In his notes to the hymn, he had commented: 'The description given in the text can hardly apply to the small stream generally known under that name; and from this and other passages that occur, it seems probable that Saraswati is also other name of Sindhu or the Indus.'[21] What an awful blunder from an eminent scholar!

There is yet another hymn, VII. 95, dedicated to the Saraswati River composed by Rishi Vasishta Maitravaruni. In its first verse the word '*sindhuranya,*' meaning 'mighty rivers,' occurs.

Hymn VII. 95. River Saraswati

1. The river Saraswati with fostering current comes forth, our sure defence, our fort of iron. She comes driving her chariot, her waters surpassing in majesty all other rivers (sindhuranya).

Griffith was probably misled by the word 'sindhuranya' in this hymn, which he takes to mean the river Sindhu [Indus], and

---

[19]Research has shown that in olden times, even the Sutlej and the Yamuna were tributaries of the Saraswati; they changed their courses later, possibly due to volcanic upheavals.

[20]Brahmin, Rajanya, Vaishya, Shudra and Ati-Shudra.

[21]Griffith, Ralph, *The Hymns of the Rigveda*, E.J. Lazarus, 1889, p 323.

comments that 'Sindhu or Indus appears to be intended under this name.'

The second verse of this hymn describes River Saraswati to be flowing from the mountains to the ocean:

2. River Saraswati alone flows, with her pure waters, from the mountains to the ocean. [*Ekachetat Saraswati nadinam shuchiryati giribhya aa samudrat.*]

The Saraswati thus appears to have been both a river and a deity to the Rigvedic people, what river Ganga (which is only twice named in the Rig Veda) became to their descendants in the course of time.

∽

The entire territory known to the Vedic settlers was divided into a number of tribal principalities, ruled by different kings. 'The din of battle is always in the background of the Rigvedic stage,' says Dr B.K. Ghosh,[22] and quotes Hymn III. 33, describing an important historical event—the battle of ten kings (*Dasha-Rajya*). The armies of King Sudas had to cross the rivers Vipash (Beas) and Shutudri (Sutlej), and the celebrated Sage Vishvamitra Gathin requested the rivers to lower their levels to let the armies pass. Vishvamitra was the purohita of King Sudas and was leading his army.

However, King Sudas dismissed Vishvamitra later on and appointed Sage Vasishtha in his place, resulting in a long and bitter rivalry between the two celebrated priests. In fact, they both figure in the Ramayana as well. Probably their sons or grandsons had adopted their names.

On his dismissal Vishvamitra led a tribal confederacy of ten kings against the Bharatas. They included five well known tribes—Puru, Yadu, Turvasha, Anu and Dhruyu. A bloody and decisive battle took place on the banks of the Parushni River (Ravi). Again, the Bharatas emerged victorious. There was another battle that King Sudas had to fight in which the non-Aryan tribes united against him under King Bheda. This battle took place on the southern bank of Yamuna. Again, they were defeated and King

[22]Majumdar, R.C. (ed.), *The Vedic Age*, Bharatiya Vidya Bhavan, 1996. p. 348.

Sudas was victorious.

Hymn III. 33. Battle of Ten Kings

1. [Vishvamitra] Flowing from the bosom of the mountains, eager as two swift mares with loosened rein, like two bright mother-cows who lick their infant calves, speed down their waters.

2. O Rivers, you flow impelled by Indra, and move, as it were, on chariots to the ocean; O radiant streams, flowing together, swelling in currents, you go to the ocean.

3. I implore most maternal Shutudri and entreat the broad and blessed Vipash, who are flowing homewards to the ocean, licking their calves.

4. [The Rivers reply] We rivers, flow untiring to home which Gods have made for us, nourishing everyone. Why is Brahmin Vishvamitra singing our praise?

5. [Vishvamitra] Linger a little at my friendly bidding; rest, O holy rivers, for a moment in your journey. Kushika's son, with hymn sublime, solicits your favour.

6. [The Rivers] Indra who wields the thunder dug our channels: he smote down Vritra who stayed our currents. At Indra's bidding we run overflowing, unhindered.

7. [Vishvamitra] That heroic deeds of Indra must be lauded for ever; he rent the demon Ahi in pieces. He smote the obstructors with his thunder, and eager for their course flowed the waters.

8. [Rivers] Never forget this word of thine, O Singer, which future generations will re-echo. In hymns, O Bard, show us thy loving kindness. Humble us not, to you we honour!

9. [Vishvamitra] Listen, O kind Sisters, to the bard who comes to you from far away with chariots and wagons. Bow down, O kind Sisters; be easy to traverse, keep your waters below our axle.

10. [Rivers] Yea, we will listen to your words, O Singer, with wagons and chariots you come from far away. Lowing like a nursing mother we'll bend and yield, like a maiden to her lover.

11. [Vishvamitra] O Rivers, as soon as this warrior band of the Bharatas, urged on and sped by Indra, have gone across, then let your flow be in rapid action. I crave your favour who deserve our worship.

12. The warrior host, the Bharatas, crossed over; the bard won the favour of the Rivers. Now swell with your currents, go hurriedly pouring riches. Fill your channels fully and roll swiftly onward.

The military prowess of the Bharatas was matched by the superiority of their cult and ritual practices. Sage Vishvamitra was not a Brahmin; he was a Rajanya (Kshatriya) and had belonged to the Kushika clan of the Bharatas.

The Dasas or Dashyu have been described as the enemies of the Vedic people, sometimes characterized as demonic. Though in many passages in the Rig Veda the term Dashyu is applied to supernatural enemies, there is no doubt that in several passages the term designated human foes. In fact, they were human foes of the Aryans. They are said to be black-skinned *(krishnat-vach)*, noseless or flat-nosed (*a-naas*) and evil-tongued (*mridhra-vach*). In the Rig Veda, Dasa is not so reproachful as Dashyu. Dasa in later literature became a synonym for slave and dasi for a slave girl. It can plausibly be assumed that originally the term was applied to captives in war who were enslaved.

The main difference between the Dashyus and the Vedic Aryans appears to be religious. The Dashyus did not hold Vedic sacrifices; they were rite-less (*a-karman)*, indifferent to the gods (*a-devayu*), without devotion (*a-Brahma*), lawless (*a-vrata*), following strange ordinances (*anyavrata*), reviling the gods (*deva-piyu*), etc. Some of these epithets have been applied to the Dasas as well. To the Rigvedic bards, there was not much difference between the two.

The Dasas or Dashyu may have been the survivors of the Harappa culture along with the Tamil-speaking kindred peoples of the Punjab and the North west. They too were rich in cattle, and dwelt in fortified places called *pur,* which the Aryan God Indra had destroyed. The hymns were composed many years after the great battles and were misted over with legend.

The other enemies of the Aryans were the Panis, described as wealthy people who probably refused to patronize the Vedic priests, and who stole the cattle of the Aryans. The identity of the Panis is uncertain. However, the words Panik or Vanik, Panya and

Vipani, found in Sanskrit, suggest that the Panis were merchants and non-Aryan caravan traders. They were not so strongly hated as the Dasas, and their settlements seem to have survived.

The word Rakshasa does not indicate any definite tribe. It normally refers to demons in early Vedic literature, and the word is applied to human foes only metaphorically. The Pishachas likewise are not a tribe in Vedic literature, though in later literature it is the designation of a tribe.

∽

The offering of flattering prayers and ritual sacrifices to please the deities, in the hope of obtaining gifts of material prosperity and brave sons from the celestial deities, for the both *yajman* (the sacrificer) as well as the priests, is the most outstanding characteristic of the Vedic hymns.

All Vedic hymns were composed for recitation while performing the yajna-sacrifice. The word 'yajna' has been translated as 'sacrifice' in English. Sacrificing conveys a sense of forfeiting something precious. In Rigvedic sacrifices, animals, mainly bulls, were slaughtered and meticulously cooked, and then offered to Agni in the yajna. Translating the word as 'sacrifice' was probably correct. But in later usage, the word 'yajna' does not denote animal sacrifice. Most Hindus who now perform yajna are largely vegetarian; animal sacrifices are confined to a few occasions, for select deities like Kali or Durga.

∽

During this era, the priest's job was very attractive as he received huge *dakshina* (donation). Interestingly, there is a hymn that eulogizes 'liberality' as a deity and advises wealthy people to give generous donations particularly to wise Brahmins. The hymn was composed by Bhikshu Angiras. He belongs to the celebrated clan, Angirasa, of Vedic priests. The appellation '*bhikshu*' suggests that he had fallen on hard times, and probably had to go abegging sometimes like poor ascetics.

Hymn X. 117. Liberality

1. The gods have not ordained hunger to be the cause of our death; even to the well-fed man death comes in various forms. The wealth of the liberal is never exhausted but the stingy person never finds a friend.

2. He who possessing food refuses a morsel to the begging destitute, approaching him, and hardens his heart against him even though he had served him before, he too, likewise, never finds a friend.

3. He indeed is a patron who gives to the beggar, wandering and thin, longing for food; who readily responds to his call to alms, and also thenceforward becomes his friend.

4. He is no friend who does not give to the friend—to the comrade asking for food. Let him turn away from him, with him there is no shelter; rather seek shelter with a generous stranger.

5. Let the wealthy be generous to the applicant; let him take a longer view. For life rolls on like the wheel of a chariot; wealth comes now to one, now to other.

7. Only by ploughing does the plough-share produce food; only by walking can a distance be covered. A Brahmin who can sing verses is preferable to the one who cannot; a liberal friend is better than an illiberal one.

There is another hymn eulogizing dakshina, the payment or presents made to the priests, who performed yajna-sacrifices for the yajman. Ralph Griffith calls dakshina 'guerdon' or a reward. The hymn, X. 107, dedicated to dakshina, was composed by Divya Angirasa, another member of the celebrated family. He accords dakshina the status of a deity!

Hymn X. 107. Dakshina

1. The whole world has been filled with a brilliant light because of the great bounty of dakshina offered by the yajman to the priests; its darkness removed. Our forefathers had installed this goddess Dakshina and had opened the spacious path of donation.

2. The givers of dakshina attain high seats in heaven. Those who donate horses, dwell with the refulgent Sun forever; those giving gold are blessed with life eternal, while those gifting clothes are rewarded with a long, prosperous life.

3. They please the gods who respectfully and liberally offer dakshina, as it is a form of worshipping gods; not the niggardly who give because they dread dishonour.

5. Those giving dakshina are the first citizens, chiefs of clans and habitations; those who offered it first of all were the rulers of men.

6. Those who gave dakshina first of all, were the knowers of the Self, of supreme Bramha, of Saman-chants; they knew the brightly-shining God's—Agni's—three forms.

7. Those who offer horses, cows, gold, money and life-giving grain in dakshina, are covered with an armour that protects them from life's travails.

10. Bounteous givers are offered decked steeds to ride; a well adorned damsel awaits their pleasure. His home is like a lake with lotus blooms, adorned like palaces of gods.

11. Excellent steeds carry the liberal dakshina giver. The gods assist him in battles and he conquers his foes in combat.

There is also a dismal and shameful hymn called, 'Dana Stuti', by the poet Kakshivant, belonging to the celebrated priestly family of the poet Dirghatamas. Kakshivant praises his liberal donor, King Svanaya Bhavayya and greatly exaggerates the presents that he had received.

Hymn I. 126. Dana Stuti

1. No bad hymns am I offering by exerting my intellect in praise of King Bhavya, ruling on the Indus; the incomparable king, desirous of fame, who assigned to me a thousand sacrifices.

2. A hundred gold pieces from the fame-seeking king, together with a thousand horses have I received. I, Kashivant, obtained a hundred cows from my master, who thereby exalted his fame up to heaven.

3. Dark horses were given by King Svanaya, and ten chariots carrying slave-girls fell to my share; followed by a herd of sixty thousand cows. All this fee did Kakshivant receive at the end of the session of yajna-sacrifice.

4. Forty ruddy horses of the set of ten chariots are heading the column of a thousand cows; fiery steeds decorated with pearls have the Kakshivants and Pajras received.

The last two Verses, 6 and 7, have not been translated by Griffith, considering them too obscene. Verse 6 is spoken by King Svanaya, describing his well-endowed queen. The queen replies in the next verse: 'Come unto me, touch me with love; I am soft like a lamb on the slopes of Gandhar.'

Agni, being the messenger of the hymns and oblation to the gods, is of prime importance to the Vedic people, and rishis vied with each other in composing hymns lauding Agni. As I mentioned in the beginning, the very first hymn of the first Mandala is dedicated to Agni. It is composed by Rishi Madhuchhanda, descendant of the famous rishi Vishvamitra.

Hymn I. 1. I Pray to Agni

1. I pray to Agni, the household priest who is also the God of the sacrifice, the one who chants and invokes and brings most treasure.

2. Agni earned the prayers of the ancient sages, and of those of the present, too; he will bring the Gods here.

3. Through Agni one may win wealth and prosperity, waxing day by day, and gift of heroic sons.

4. O Agni, the sacrifice protected by you on all sides (from Rakshasas and fiends) verily goes to the Gods.

5. May Agni, the wise Priest, truthful, most gloriously great, come hither with the Gods.

6. Whatever blessings Agni will grant to us worshippers, that, O Angiras,[23] come true through you.

7. To you Agni, the dispeller of darkness, we come day by day, bringing our homage.

8. To you, Ruler of sacrifices, radiant guardian of the Law eternal, residing in your heavenly abode.

[23]Angirasa was progenitor of an ancient family of priests.

9. O Agni, be to us easy of approach, like a father to his son. Abide with us Agni, for our happiness.

I quote another hymn to Agni, similar to the first hymn, composed by Medhatithi Kanva, a descendant of Rishi Kanva.

Hymn 1. 12. Agni

1. We choose Agni the messenger of gods, master of the subtleties of sacrifice, who brings the gods to our sacrifice.

2. We invoke Agni, inviting the Lord of the House; most beloved oblation bearer to the gods.

3. Bring the Gods hither, O Agni, born for him who strews the sacred grass; thou art our herald; most worthy of praise.

4. Wake up the willing Gods, O Agni, be our ambassador; Come and sit on the sacred grass with the Gods.

5. O Agni, Radiant One, to whom the holy *ghrita* is poured; burn up our demonic enemies whom the fiends protect.

6. By Agni, sacrificial fire is inflamed; taking the ladle in his mouth, He bears the gift to the Gods.

7. O Sages whose ways are ever true, praise Agni in the sacrifice, the God who drives calamities away.

9. Who so, O Agni, calls you respectfully with sacred gifts to the feast of Gods, favour him.

11. O Agni, lauded by our newest song of praise, shower opulence on us; give us brave sons.

12. O Agni, by your effulgent flame, by invoking all the Gods; show pleasure in this laud of ours.

Wendy Doniger's selection contains nine hymns dedicated to Agni. One of them is the celebrated hymn, 'Apam Napat' (Child of Waters). Agni has been called 'the child of waters' as he is imagined to be born in the form of lightening from the waters of the 'aerial ocean' (the firmament). Wendy Doniger adds that in the Avesta, the sacred book of the Zoroastrian religion, Agni appears as an Asura who lives deep in the waters, surrounded by females, driving swift horses. Indeed, all gods were called 'Asura' then, but the Rigvedic people, who parted company from the Iranian folk, called their gods 'Sura.'

This hymn plays upon the simultaneous unity and non-unity of the earthly and celestial forms of Agni and the Child of Waters. It was composed by Rishi Gritsmada Angirasa.

Hymn II. 35. Apam Napat

1. Striving for the victory prize, I have set free my eloquence; let the god of rivers gladly accept my songs. Surely the child of the waters, urging on his swift horses, will adorn my songs, for he enjoys them.

2. We would sing to him this prayer well-fashioned from the heart; surely, he will recognize it. With his divine energy, the child of the waters has created all noble creatures.

3. Some flow together, while others flow toward the sea, but the rivers fill the same hollow cavern (the ocean). The pure waters surrounded this pure, radiant child of the waters.

4. The young women, the rivers, flow around the young god, making him shine and gazing solemnly. With his clear strong flames, he shines riches upon us, wearing his garments of ghrita, blazing without fuel in the waters.

5. Three Goddesses[24] wish to give food to the god so that he will not weaken. He has stretched forth in the waters; he sucks the new milk of mothers who have given him birth for the first time.

6. In his birth he leaps out like a horse or like the Sun. He guards our patrons from falling prey to malice or violence. When far away in fortresses of unbaked bricks, hatred and falsehood shall not reach him.

8. True and inexhaustible, he shines forth in the waters with pure divinity. Other creatures and plants, his branches, are reborn with their progeny.

9. Clothed in lightning, the upright child of the waters has climbed into the lap of waters as they lie down. The golden-hued women flow around him, bearing with them his supreme energy.

---

[24]The three godmothers of Agni, according to Griffith are Ila, Sarasvati and Bharati, the personifications of sacred prayers and worship. Agni dwelt within the waters as their unborn babe.

11. With his fair name and radiant aspect the Waters' son grows in secret; when the young maidens kindle him thus and feed him golden hued ghrita.

12. To him, the closest friendly god to men among many, we would offer worship with sacrifices, obeisance, and oblations. I (the priest) rub Agni's back with ghrita: bring him food; I praise him with verses.

13. Being a Bull, he makes the waters potent. He sucks them as an infant and the waters lick him. The child of the waters whose colour never fades, enters another body here (on the earth, as sacrificial fire).

14. He dwells in his sublime state, resplendent with never-perishing rays. The young waters, bringing ghrita to their child, cover him in their folds.

15. O Agni, I gave good shelter to the people, have given a goodly composition to the princes. Bless us with brave sons as progeny and power to speak in Assembly.

There is yet another hymn to Agni, ascribed to Daman Yamayan. Wendy Doniger explains that in this hymn Agni appears in two distinct roles; in the first part (Verses 1–8) Agni is the 'cremation fire', who carries the oblation as well as the dead man to the Fathers (dead ancestors). He is asked to burn the corpse gently but not too much, to temper it to perfection and to send it to Fathers without destroying it. In the second part (Verses 9–12) Agni is called Jatavedas, who has to take the oblations to the gods and lead the dead man to God Yama. Thus, the first fire is associated with the corpse and the Fathers, and the second fire, Jatavedas,[25] is associated with offering oblation to the Gods. The funeral fire is extinguished in Verses 13–14.

Hymn X. 16. Funeral Fire and Jatavedas

[25]Jatavedas is one of Agni's names, which means 'knower of creatures'.

1. Do not burn him entirely, O Agni, or engulf him in your flames. Do not consume his skin or his flesh. When cooked perfectly, O Jataveda, only then send him to the Fathers (*pitradeva,* who reside in heaven).

2. When he is cooked perfectly, O Jataveda, then give him over to the Fathers. When he goes on the path that leads away the breath of life, he will be led to the will of the Gods.

3. [To the dead man] May your eye go to the Sun, your life's breath to Vayu. Go, according to your dharma, to Earth, or Heaven. Or go to the waters, if that is your fate; take root in the plants with your limbs.

4. [To Agni] The goat is your share, burn him with your heat, your brilliant light and flame. O knower of creatures, carry this man to the world of those who have done good deeds.

6. [To the dead man] Whatever the black bird has pecked out of you, or the ant, the snake or even a beast of prey, may Agni who devours all, heal it, or let Soma purify it.

7. Shield yourself with cow's flesh against the flames of Agni and cover yourself with fat and marrow, so that Agni will not consume you with his impetuous heat in his passionate desire to burn you up.

8. O Agni, do not burn this bowl[26] that is dear to the Gods and to those who love Soma; a bowl which is fit for the Gods to drink from, in which the immortal Gods carouse.

9. I send the flesh-eating Agni far away. Let him go to those whose king is Yama, carrying away all impurities. But let Jatavedas carry the oblation to the gods, since he knows the way.

12. O Jatavedas, joyously would we kindle you. now joyously bring the joyous Fathers here to eat the oblation.

13. O Agni, now let this spot of earth cool, which you have scorched. Let tender durva grass, leafy herbs and water lilies grow here.

[26] A wooden bowl that the dead man had used in life to make Soma offerings to the gods and to the Fathers who love Soma was placed at the corpse's head, filled with ghrita.

How were the Vedic gods born? It's a riddle—as the Hymn X. 72, explains. 'Aditi', is in reality the earliest name invented to express the Infinite—the visible Infinite, the endless expanse beyond the earth, beyond the clouds, beyond the sky.

Hymn X. 72. Aditi and the Birth of the Gods

1. Let us now speak with wonder of the births of the gods—so that someone may see them when the hymns are chanted in later ages.

2. Brahamanspati[27] produced these gods like a smith with blast and smelting,[28] when existence was born from non-existence.

3. In the earliest Age of the Gods, existence was born from non-existence. After this the quarters of the sky were born from Aditi[29] who crouched with her legs spread.

4. The earth was born from her, and from the earth the quarters of the sky were born. From Aditi, Daksha[30] was born, and from Daksha, Aditi was born.

5. O Daksha, Aditi was born as your daughter, and after her were born the blessed Gods, the kinsmen of immortality.

6. When you Gods stood, close-clasping one another in yonder deep, then from your feet a thickening cloud of dust-like mist arose, as from dancers' feet.

7. When you Gods, like ascetic Yatis, caused the world to swell, you drew forth the Sun that was hidden in the ocean.

8. Eight sons are there of Aditi, who were born of her body. With seven she went forth among the gods, but she threw Martanda (the Sun) aside.

9. So with her seven sons Aditi lived into the remote age. She bore Martanda so that he would in turn beget offspring like a mortal.

Explaining the last verse, Wendy Doniger says that Aditi bore

---

[27]Brahamanspati is the supreme creator, who fashioned and gave birth to the world and the gods.

[28]'Blast and smelting', the phrase sounds like the latter-day scientific phrase 'Big Bang.'

[29]Aditi is a primal, archetypal generative force.

[30]Aditi is the infinity or the infinite and Daksha is force or power personified.

eight sons, but only seven were called Adityas (sons of Aditi). The eighth, Martanda, was later shaped by the Adityas into the Sun.

One of the most beautiful hymns in the Rig Veda is Hymn X. 85, celebrating the marriage of the Sun's daughter, Surya. Hindu marriages are modelled on this hymn. Griffith says it's one of the latest hymns in the Rig Veda. The composer has shied away from revealing his name. It is ascribed to 'Surya-Savitri', i.e., to Surya herself, who is also the deity of the hymn. I have changed the sequence of the hymns and joined those concerning her deflowering.

Hymn X. 85. The Wedding of Surya

1. The Earth is propped up by Truth; the sky is propped up by the Sun. Through *Rta*[31] the Adityas stand firm and the Moon is placed in the Sky.

2. Through Soma (the drink) the Adityas are made strong; through Soma the Earth is mighty. Soma (the Moon) has been set in the lap of the constellations.

3. One thinks he has drunk Soma[32] when they press the Soma plant. But, Soma that the Brahmins know no one ever eats.

5. When they drink you, who are a God, then you are filled up again. Vayu is your guardian; the Moon is the one that shapes the years.

6. The Raibhi metre was Surya's companion during the nuptial ceremony, and the Narashanshi metre accompanied her to her husband's home. Her bridal robe was adorned by hymeneal[33] songs.

7. Sweet thoughts were the pillow of her couch; sight was the unguent for her eyes. Heaven and Earth were her hope-chest when Surya went to her husband's home.

8. Hymns of praise were the shafts of her chariot, Kurir metre was the diadem and coiffure. The Ashvins were the first suitors

[31]'Rta' means the order that governs the Universe.
[32]Verses 3 and 4 are a eulogy of Soma, the celestial drink.
[33]Hymen is the god of marriage in Greek mythology. Hymen is also a membranous fold of tissue partly or completely blocking the vaginal external orifice at birth. It usually ruptures spontaneously before puberty.

of Surya and Agni led the train.

9. Soma (the Moon) became the bridegroom while the two Ashvins had wooed her. As Savita gave his daughter, she said 'yes' in her heart.

10. Her spirit was her chariot and the Sky was its canopy. Bright were both the Steers that drew it when Surya approached her husband's house.

11. The two Steers were yoked by verses and *Saman* chants; they went in accord. Surya's longing was driving the wheels of chariot, when the path stretched on in the sky.

12. Luminous were the wheels of her chariot, the wind was its axle. Carried by her heart's chariot, Surya went to her husband's home.

13. The wedding procession of Surya went forward as Savita sent it off. In Magha month the oxen were slain, in Phalgun the bride was brought to the husband's home.[34]

14. When you Ashvins came to the wedding in your three-wheeled chariot, asking for Surya for yourselves, the Gods gave their consent and Pushna chose you as his two fathers.

15. When you two lords of lustre came as suitors of Surya, where was one wheel of your chariot? Where did you stand for her sire's command?

19. The Moon becomes new again as he is born, going in front of the dawns as the banner of the day. As he arrives, he apportions the gods their share and stretches out his long span of life.

20. Mount the golden-hued, light-rolling chariot, O Surya, adorned with *kinshuk*[35] and *shalmali*[36] flowers, and enter the world of immortality: Prepare for an exquisite wedding voyage to your lord.

21. 'Go away from here! For this maiden has a husband.' I implore Vishvavasu[37] thus as I bow to him. 'Look for another

[34]Magha and Phalgun are the eleventh and twelfth months of the Hindu calendar. Verses 16, 17 and 18 have been omitted being superfluous.

[35]Also known as Palash, *Butea frondosa*.

[36]Silk-cotton tree.

[37]Vishvavasu is a Gandharva who is supposed to possess maidens before their

girl who is ripe and still lives in her father's house. That is your birthright.'

22. 'Go away from here, Vishvavasu, we implore you with reverence. Look for another girl, willing and ready. Leave this bride to unite with her husband.'

23. May the path be straight and thorn-less on which the newly-weds go courting. May Aryaman and Bhaga lead them together. O Gods, make the union of wife and husband perfect.

24. I[38] free you from the noose of Varuna and release you from the parental bond; I place you unharmed in the wedding altar and in the world of virtuous action.

25. I free you from here but not from there (the husband's home). I have bound her firmly there, so that by the grace of Indra she will have fine sons and be fortunate in her husband's love.

26. Let Pushan lead you from here, taking you by the hand; let the Ashvins carry you in their chariot. Go home to be mistress of the house with the right to speak commands to members of the household.

27. May you be happy and prosper in your children. Watch over the household as mistress of the house. Mingle your body with your husband's, and even when you are grey with age, you will have your rights.

28. The purple and red appears;[39] the stain is imprinted by a magic spirit. Her family prospers and her husband is bound in marital bonds.

29. Give away the tainted gown and distribute wealth to the Brahmins. The stain becomes a magic spirit walking on her feet and, like the wife, draws near the husband.

30. The husband's body becomes pale and unlovely if the husband covers his sexual limb with his wife's robe.

31. The diseases that come from her own people following the bridal procession, may the gods send them back whence they came.

34. The bridal robe burns, it bites; it has claws and is dangerous

marriage.

[38]Savita, the father, frees the daughter from committing any sin by her marriage.

[39]Verses 28–30, 34 and 35 concern the deflowering of the bride and the staining of the bridal gown. This blood becomes a magic spirit, Kritya, potent and dangerous.

as poison. Only the priest who knows the Surya hymn is able to receive the bridal gown.

35. Cutting, carving and chopping into pieces—are the colours of Surya's blood stains, which the priest alone purifies.[40]

32. Let no highwayman, lying in ambush, fall upon the wedding couple. Let them go safe on the path. Let all demonic powers run away.

33. This bride has auspicious signs; come and look at her. Wish her the good fortune of her husband's love, and depart, each to his own house.

36. I take your hand for good fortune, so that with me as your husband you will attain a ripe old age. Gods Bhaga, Aryaman, Savita, Purandhi[41] have given you to me to be the mistress of the house.

37. May Pushan[42] rouse her to be most eager to please, the woman in whom men sow their seed, so that she will spread her thighs in her desire for us and we, in our desire will plant our seed in her.

38. They first of all led Surya to the gods,[43] while circling in bridal procession. Give her back to her husband, O Agni, now as a wife with progeny.

39. Agni has given her with long life and beauty. Let her have a long life-span, and let her husband live for a hundred autumns.

40. Soma first possessed her, and then the Gandharvas. Agni was your third husband and the fourth, the son of a man.

41. Soma gave her to the Gandharvas, and the Gandharvas gave her to Agni. Agni gave her wealth and sons.

42. Stay here and do not separate. Enjoy your whole life-span playing with sons and grandsons and rejoicing in your home.

---

[40]Literally, this verse describes the cutting up of the bridal robe, but it might refer to the cutting of sacrificial animal. There is a further overtone of the physical injury due to the defloration itself, the sacrifice of the maidenhead on the altar of marriage.

[41]Purandhi is the bringer of abundance.

[42]Pushan is invoked here not as the son of the Ashvins, as in Verse 14, but as the god of safe roads and journeys and as the one who prepares the bride for sex.

[43]It refers to Soma, the Gandharvas and Agni, who possess the bride first (in Verses 40 and 41.)

43. Let Prajapati bless you with progeny; let Aryaman anoint you. Free from inauspicious signs, enter your husband's world. Bring good luck to the biped and quadruped animals of the family.

44. Have no evil-eye; do not be a husband-killer. Be good-tempered and glowing with beauty. Bringing forth strong sons, prosper as one eager to please and beloved of the gods.

45. Gracious Indra, give this woman fine sons and the good fortune of her husband's love. Place ten sons in her and make her husband the eleventh.[44]

46. Be an empress of your husband's father, an empress over your husband's mother; be an empress over your husband's sister and empress over your husband's brothers.

47. Let all the gods and the waters together anoint our two hearts. Let Matarishvan, together with the Creator and goddess Deshtri, join the two of us together.

Hymn I. 164. is among the most mysterious hymns in the Rig Veda. Composed by Rishi Dirghatamas Auchathya in the form of a series of riddles about the Universe, it gives words to the poet's wonder at the form and expanse of the Universe, at the perfectly orderly, ceaseless motion of the Sun, the Moon and the stars.

The deities for the first 41 verses of the hymn are the Vishvedevas; for the rest are goddesses and gods like Vak, Soma, Agni, Sun, Vayu, Saraswati, Parjanya, etc. In translating it I have taken help from Wendy Doniger, Ralph Griffith, W.D. Whiney, as also Bhagwati Devi Sharma's Hindi translation.

Hymn I. 164. The Riddle of the Universe (Asya Vamashya)

1. I have seen the beloved world sustainer, Lord of All Tribes (the Sun) with his seven sons (Sun's seven-hued rays). This Lord has a radiant companion, Lightening, who lives in mid-sky, and a distant brother, Agni, with ghrita on his back.

2. His one-wheeled chariot (*Kaal-Chakra*)[45] is drawn by seven

[44]Let her take care of her husband as she cares for her sons.
[45]The Wheel of Time.

divine horses of all colours. All existences rest on the Sun's ageless and unstoppable chariot that has three naves (Sky, Earth, Firmament).

3. Seven horses draw the seven sons who ride on this seven-wheeled chariot. Seven sisters call out to the place where the seven names of the cows (*gavaan*)[46] are hidden.

4. Who saw the Primal God in the process of birth, the one with a Form who was brought forth by the formless one?[47] Where was the breath, the blood and soul of the Earth? Who shall go to ask from someone who knows?

5. Unripe in mind, in spirit undiscerning, I ask about the hidden footprints[48] of the Gods. Over the young calf (Sun) how do the Gods spread the seven hued rays?

6. Unknowing, ignorant, I ask for knowledge about it from the wise who know: What is the One who, though unborn, propped apart these six realms of space?

7. Let him who really knows proclaim, where the beloved bird (Sun) securely founded his station. The Solar rays like cows, shower milk from the Sky, and (in Summer) drink water with their feet.

8. The Mother[49] mated with the Father in accordance with *Rta* (Universal Order), embraced him in mind and spirit. The coy Dame recoiled when she was pierced and was filled with dew prolific. The reverent came in adoration.

9. The Mother Earth was harnessed to the chariot pole of the cows; the infant rested in the dark bed of clouds. Then the calf lowed and looked for the many-coloured cow in the three distances.[50]

10. The One, bearing three mothers and three fathers, stood

[46]Cows (gavaan) may perhaps mean Vaani, which has seven musical notations.

[47]The newborn sun has a form (the male element) though it is born from the formless void—the Big Bang.

[48]'The footprints of the gods' may be the sacrificial laws.

[49]The Mother may mean the Earth who is pierced by Father Sun. Recoiling from incest, she nevertheless does what must be done, in accordance with the Universal Order, and is praised for this.

[50]'The calf lowed'—the cloud thundered; in three directions—heaven, mid-air, and earth.

upright: they never make him weary. On the back of the distant heaven they speak of Speech, who knows all, but does not move all.

11. The twelve-spoked wheel of *Rta* rolls round and round the sky and never ages. O Agni, seven hundred and twenty sons in pairs[51] rest on it.

12. Some say that the Father, with his five feet and twelve shapes, dwells in the farther half of the Sky. But others here say that the Far-seeing One in the seven-wheeled, six spoked chariot, moves in the near half.

13. All living creatures rest and depend upon this five-spoked wheel that rolls around and around. Though heavily laden, its axle does not get hot, nor has it ever broken in its naves.

14. The wheel revolves, un-wasting, with its felly; the ten yoked horses draw it up the outstretched path. All the worlds are kept in motion on the eye of the Sun that moves on, though shrouded in dark space.

15. They say that besides those born in pairs there is a seventh born alone,[52] the six set of twins are like the sages born from the Gods. The sacrifices for them are firmly set, but they change their forms and waver as he stands firm.

16. The sun-rays, being women, they declared to me to be men; he who has eyes may see, the blind will not distinguish. The Son who is a poet[53] has understood it; who knows it rightly is his father's Father.

17. Beneath what is above, and above what is beneath, the cow went upward, holding her calf by the foot.[54] In what direction

---

[51]The wheel formed with 12 spokes is the year with 12 months. The 720 sons, joined in pairs, are the days and nights of the year, 360 of each.

[52]In Vedic mythology, Aditi gives birth to the immortal Adityas in pairs, while she rejects the sun, Vivasvan, born alone. In the ritual, there are 12 paired months and one odd one, the intercalary month which interrupts the sequence and causes the other months to 'change and waver'.

[53]The Sun is to be considered as the father of the rays of light, which again in their collective capacity, being the cause of rain, are the fosterers or parents of the earth. The Sun is, therefore, the father of the father. Similarly, an intelligent son may be called a parent of an ignorant father, being superior in knowledge. Wordsworth had wisely proclaimed: 'The child is father of the man!'

[54]The cow Dawn, between the Sky (above) and the Earth (below), has her calf, the Sun, at her heels.

and to what half of the Sky has she gone away? Where did she give birth? Not within the herd.

18. Whoever here knows his father beneath what is above and what is beneath—who with such mystical insight can here proclaim the source from which the mind of God was born?

19. Those that are in the future they say they are in the past; those that are in the past they say are in the future. The things that you and Indra did, O Soma, still pull the axle pole of space as though yoked to it.

20. Two birds, like friends joined together, sit on the same tree. One of them eats the sweet fruit; the other looks on and eats not.[55]

21. Where the fine birds sing unblinkingly about their share of immortality among the wise, there the shepherd of all existence (*visvashya, bhuvanashya gopa*[56]), the wise one, entered me—the fool.

22. On what tree the honey-eating birds all settle and give birth—what they call the sweet berry at its top—no one who knows not the Father eats that.

23. Only those gain immortality, who know that the Gayatri hymn is made from the Gayatri foot (metre),[57] the Trishtup hymn from Trishtup metre and the Jagati hymn from Jagati metre.

24. With the Gayatri foot they fashion a hymn, with the hymn a chant (the *Sama*[58]), with the Trishtup a strophe (a stanza); with the strophe of two feet or four foot they fashion a speech. With the syllable they fashion the seven tones.

25. With the Jagati he fixed the stream in the sky. In the Rathantara chant he discovered the Sun. They say the Gayatri[59]

---

[55]The eleventh-century Vedic commentator Sayana says that the two birds are the Vital and Supreme Spirit, dwelling in the body. The Vital spirit enjoys the fruit or rewards of actions while the Supreme Spirit is merely a passive spectator.

[56]The Lord of the Universe, *Parmatma*.

[57]Gayatri metre (or foot) has eight syllables, Trishtup has 11 syllables and Jagati 12 syllables.

[58]A chant or 'Sama' is the melody for singing a hymn. The Sama Veda contains the chants for singing the Vedic hymns.

[59]Verse 10 of Hymn 62 of Book III, composed by Sage Vishvamitra, is called the celebrated Gayatri Mantra: 'May we attain that excellent glory of Savitar the God; May He stimulate our prayers.' It forms part of the daily devotions of devout Hindus.

has three kindling-sticks, and so its power and magnificence excels.

26. I call to the cow[60] who is easy to milk, so that the milker with clever hands may milk her. Let Savita[61] inspire us with the finest vigour. The pot of milk is set on the fire—this is what I happily proclaim.

33. The sky is my father; here is the navel that gave me birth. This great earth is my mother, my close kin. The womb for me was between the two bowls stretched apart; here the father placed the embryo in the daughter[62].

34. I ask you about the farthest end of the earth; I ask you about the navel of the universe. I ask you about the semen of the stallion bursting with seed; I ask you about the final abode of Speech.

35. This altar is the farthest end of the earth; this yajna is the navel of the earth. This Soma is the semen of stallion bursting with seed and Supreme Brahma[63] is the final abode of Speech.

36. Seven half-embryos[64], the prolific seed of existence, their functions are determined at Vishnu's command. Endowed with wisdom, intelligence and thought, they surround us on all sides.

37. I do not know just what I am! Mysteriously I wandered about, wrapped in thoughts. But when the first born of *Rta* approached me, I won a share of this Speech.

38. Backward and forward, seized by *svadha*[65], the imperishable soul, takes birth in mortal bodies; the two, body and soul, constantly going apart—people perceive the one, they do not perceive the other.

39. The undying syllable[66] of the song is final abode where all

---

[60]'Cow' is the rain cloud; Vayu, the milker calf, is the world longing for the rain to fall.

[61]Savita is the embodiment of twilight.

[62]The sun impregnated his daughter, the earth.

[63]Brahma (or Brishapati) is as the husband of Speech as in Hymn X. 109, quoted earlier.

[64]Griffith notes that the 'The Seven, according to Sayana, are the solar rays, and Vishnu is said to be the Sun.'

[65]'Svadha'—the offering to the manes, the heavenly fathers.

[66]Griffith adds a note: 'The syllable is the Pranava, the mystical, sacred syllable Om.' Griffith adds that 'the syllable is set forth in the Upanishads as the object of

the gods reside. What can one who does not know this do with the song? Let only those who know sit together here.

40. May you be well-proportioned, O inviolabe cow, be happy eating in green meadows and make us happy. Eat green grass and drink clean water, wandering all over, as you graze.

41. The Gau (literally Cow, meaning Poetic Speech) creates waves in the waters (hearts of men) shaping into one-footed, two-footed, four-footed, eight or nine footed verses, gathering a thousand syllables, resounds in the firmament.

42. The quarters of the sky live on the oceans that flow out of her in all directions. The whole universe exists through the undying syllable that flows from her.

43. I saw from far away the smoke of fuel with spires that rose on high and beneath it. The Gods have roasted the dappled bull. These were the first ritual laws.

44. The three long-haired ones reveal themselves at the right moment. The One (Agni) shears the vegetation when the year is ended; One (Sun) whose powers the world acknowledges; of One (Vayu) the sweep is seen, not his figure.

45. Speech has been measured out into four divisions; the inspired Brahmins know it. The three kept in close concealment cause no motion; the fourth part of Speech is what men speak.

46. They call it Indra, Mitra, Varuna, Agni, and it is the heavenly bird, Garutman (the Sun), that flies. To what is One the sages give many a title; they call it Agni, Yama, Matarishvan.

47. The golden birds clothed in waters fly up to the sky on the dark path. They have now returned from the seat of Rta, and at once the earth was drenched with ghrita.

48. Twelve fellies, one wheel, three naves—who has understood this? Three hundred and sixty spokes are set on it that do not loosen.

49. Your inexhaustible breast, O Saraswati,[67] a veritable spring of pleasure, feeds choicest things; freely bestowing treasure and things beautiful—bring that here for us to suck.

---

profound religious meditation, and the highest spiritual efficacy is attributed to it.'

[67]Saraswati as goddess of speech; as also the river in the Sky and on the Earth.

50. The gods held a yajna to celebrate yajna; these became the first ritual laws. They dwell in the dome of heaven with the *Sadhyas*.

51. The same water travels up and down day after day. While the rain-clouds enliven the earth, the yajna flames enliven the sky.

52. The great heavenly bird (Sun) with wonderful wings, the beautiful embryo of the waters and the plants, that delights us with rains overflowing—I call to him for help.

Rigvedic Hinduism is considered a polytheistic religion as there are several gods who are paid homage in the Rig Veda. But Verse 46 probably sums up the Vedic philosophy:

> They call it Indra, Mitra, Varuna, Agni, and it is the heavenly bird, Garutman (the Sun), that flies. To what is One the sages give many a title; they call it Agni, Yama, Matarishvan.

There is a mystifying hymn, X. 136, entitled 'Keshi', the long-haired ascetic. The hymn is dedicated to three gods, Agni, Surya and Vayu. It consists of seven verses, composed jointly by the seven sons of Rishi Vatarshan, named—Juti, Vaatjuti, Viprajuti, Vrishanak, Karikrat, Aitash and Rishyashring—every son contributing one verse of the hymn. It portrays the ascetic Keshi with long hair. He is the stallion of the wind and a friend of the gales. He drinks a hallucinatory drug, other than Soma, in the company of God Rudra, who is excluded from the Soma sacrifices.

Hymn X. 136. The Long-Haired Ascetic

1. He with the long loose locks holds Agni, Heaven and Earth, and possesses a poisonous drug. He has the whole sky to traverse. He reveals the Sun and declares the light.

2. The ascetic, a descendent of Rishi Vatarshan, is girdled with Vayu and wears soiled, yellow-coloured garments. Following Vayu's swift course, he goes where the Gods have gone before.

3. 'In ecstasy we sail with the wind. You mortals see our

natural bodies only and no more.'[68]

4. He flies through the regions of air, looking down on all things below. He is friend to this God and that God, being their associate in sacred acts.

5. The stallion of the Wind, the ascetic, is friend of the Gales and is impelled by the Gods. He lives in two oceans, on the east and on the west.

6. Long Hair moves with the *Apsaras*, the nymphs of heaven, and Gandharvas and sylvan creatures. He is their sweet and most delightful friend.

7. Vayu has churned it up, Kunannama[69] has prepared it, Long Hair sups the poison potion, sharing the bowl with God Rudra.

Let's now have Hymn IX. 168 that eulogizes '*Vata*', the Gale Wind, which was composed by Rishi Anil Vatayan.

Hymn IX. 168. The Gale Wind

1. O, the power and the glory of the chariot of the Gale Wind! It breaks things into pieces as it passes by, making a sound like thunder. Touching the Sky as it moves, it makes the regions red; passing over the Earth, it creates dust-storms.

2. The Tempests[70] race together after the Gale; they come to him like women to a rendezvous. Yoked with them to a single chariot, God Gale Wind, king of the whole universe, passes by.

3. Moving along his paths in the middle realm of space, he does not rest for a single day. Where was he born, this friend of the waters? What was he created from, the first born of Rta?

4. Breath of the Gods, embryo of the universe, this God wanders wherever He please. His sounds are heard but his form is not seen. Let us worship the Gale with oblation.

---

[68]Spoken by Keshi, the ascetic.

[69]A female deity who appears only here.

[70]The Gale Wind is masculine while the Tempests are feminine beings, companions of the Wind, whirlwinds or downpours.

HYMNS ON INDRA

In the Rig Veda, Indra is the King of the gods. Aditi, who has been praised earlier in Hymn X. 72 as the mother of the Earth as well as of the seven Adityas and Martanda (the Sun), is the mother of Indra.

How Indra was born is most unusual. Hymn IV.18 describes the birth and childhood deeds of Indra. It is composed by Rishi Vamadeva Gautama. It's a curious dialogue hymn; the dialogue takes place between the mother Aditi and the baby Indra as he is coming out of her womb!

Hymn IV.18. The Birth and Childhood Deeds of Indra

1. [Aditi] This (my womb) is the ancient, proven path by which all the gods were born and moved upward. By this very path the baby should be born when he has grown great.[71] He should not make his mother perish in that way.

2. [Indra] I cannot come out by that path; these are bad places to go through. I will come out cross-wise, through the side. Many things yet undone I must do; one (Vritra) I will fight, and with one (Vishnu) I will speak.

3. [Narrator] Indra watched his mother as she went away after his birth; 'I cannot help following; I will follow her. In Tvashrta's house Indra drank the Soma worth a hundred cows, pressed in two bowls.

4. Why has she pushed him away, whom she carried for a thousand months and many autumns? For there is no one his equal among those who are born and those who will be born.

5. As if she thought he was flawed; his mother hid Indra though he exceeded many in manly strength. Then he stood up and put his garment on himself; as he was born, he filled the two world-halves (Earth and Firmament) with radiance.

6. [Aditi] These waters flow happily, shouting 'Alalaa!'; the waters were screaming together like righteous women. Ask them what they are saying, from what encircling mountains the waters

[71]Indra did not come out of the mother's womb as a baby but as a grown-up man!

burst apart?[72]

7. Are you speaking words of praise and invitation to him? Do the waters wish to take on themselves the flaw of Indra[73]? With his great weapon my son killed Vritra and set these rivers free.

8. Still a young woman, I did not throw you away for my sake; nor did the evil spirit Kushva tried to swallow you up for my sake. But for my sake the waters were kind to the child, and for my sake Indra stood up at once.

9. Nor for my sake the shoulder-less one (Vritra) wound you, brave Indra, and strike away your two jaws; though wounded, you overpowered him, and with your weapon you crushed the head of the Dasa.

10. [Narrator] The heifer gave birth to the firm, strong, unassailable bull, the stout Indra. The mother let her calf wander un-licked to seek his own ways himself.

11. And the mother turned to the bull: 'My son, the gods here are deserting you.' Then Indra, wanting to kill Vritra, said, 'Vishnu, my friend, step aside as far as you can[74] (and let me kill Vritra on my own).'

12. Who made your mother a widow? Who wished to kill you when you were lying still or moving? What God helped you when you grabbed your father by the foot and crushed him?[75]

13. [Indra] Because I was in difficult straits, I cooked the entrails of a dog, and I found no one among the gods to help me. I saw my mother dishonoured. Then the eagle brought the Soma for me.

---

[72]Aditi is obviously referring to the waters that were released when Indra killed Vritra. This event couldn't have happened immediately after Indra's birth. Griffith is right when he says: 'This hymn appears to be made up of somewhat incoherent fragments.'

[73]The flaw of killing the demon Vritra.

[74]As translated by Griffith.

[75]Griffith mentions that Vyamsha was Indra's father, though he does not disclose the source of this information. To my mind, if Aditi was his mother, Daksha should be his father. According to me, this verse has been erroneously added to this hymn, when the hymns were committed to writing. Nowhere else in the Rig Veda is there any mention of Indra committing patricide.

Indra is the principal deity of the Vedic people. He had performed unique heroic deeds. To him are dedicated the maximum number of hymns. Let me quote a few verses from Hymn III. 30, composed by the eminent Rishi Vishvamitra Gathin.

Hymn III. 30. Indra

1. O Lord of the the fast-running bay[76] horses, for you the mid-air's loftiest regions are not very far. Made for the firm, valorous and vigorous God like you are these libations. The pressing stones are set and the fire is kindled.

4. O Indra, you go forth alone for overthrowing and destroying the demon Vritra, who had never been assaulted and shaken before. For those who worship and follow you—the mountains, the Earth and Heaven—you stand firmly established.

6. Forthwith your Bay steeds go down the steep, O Indra, your thunder-bolt goes forth crushing your foemen, slaying those who confront you as well as those who flee and those who follow. You make all you promises come true, all accomplished.

8. O much-invoked Indra! You crushed to pieces Kunara, the handless fiend who dwelt with Danu.[77] O mighty Indra, you smote dead the hateful footless Vritra as he vexed in vigour.

Hymn III. 32, also composed by Vishvamitra Gathin, again sings Indra's praise.

Hymn III. 32. Indra

1. O Indra, Lord of Soma, drink this Soma, the draught of noonday which you love; O impetuous, bounteous Giver, loose you two Bay Horses and rejoice, puffing your cheeks.

4. The Maruts who were there, they excited with song the meath-created strength of Indra. By them impelled to act, he reached the vitals of Vritra, who imagined that none might wound him.

[76]Horses of reddish-brown colour.

[77]Danu is Vritra's mother; she lived with the demon Kunaru.

6. O Indra, When, having smitten godless Vritra with your flying weapon, you freed the streams to run as if races in the swift contest; he lay there, who had kept the goddesses encompassed.

17. We salute Maghavan, auspicious Indra, the best hero in this fight where spoil is gathered; the mighty God who listens, who gives aid in battles, who slays Vritra and wins and gathers riches.

Another hymn composed by Rishi Gritsmada Angirasa, belonging to the celebrated Bhrigu clan of rishis, chants the glories of Indra:

Hymn II. 12. Who Is Indra?

1. Just after being born, the God of lofty spirit, who by his power and might became the chief protector of Gods; before his hot breath the two world halves trembled—He, my people, is Indra!

2. He who made fast the tottering earth, who made still the quaking mountains, who measured out and extended the expanse of the air, who propped up the sky—He, my people, is Indra!

3. He who slew the Dragon and loosed the seven rivers[78], who drove out the cows that had been pent up by Vala, who gave birth to fire between two stones, the winner of booty in combats—He, my people, is Indra!

4. By whom the universe was made to tremble, who chased away the Dasas, who like a gambler gathering the winnings, seized the foe's riches. He, my people, is Indra!

5. Of whom they ask: 'He the Terrible, where is?' Or they say, 'He does not exist.' Believe in Him! Who sweeps away the foe's possessions—He, my people, is Indra!

6. He who strengthens the weary and the sick, and the priest who is in need; helps the man who harnesses the stones to press Soma. He who has lips eager for drinking—He, my people, is Indra!

7. He under whose command are horses and cows and villages and all chariots. Who gave birth to the Sun and the Dawn, and led out the waters. He, my people, is Indra!

[78]Sapt-Sindhu—the collective name of the river Indus and her tributaries, in which region the Vedic people had settled to begin with.

8. He who is invoked by the two armies, both locked in combat. He who is invoked separately even by two men standing on the very same chariot. He, my people, is Indra!

9. He, without whom people cannot conquer; He, whom they call for help when they are fighting, who is the Lord of everything, who shakes the unshakeable. He, my people, is Indra!

10. He who killed with his weapon all those who had committed a great sin, even when they did not know it, he who does not pardon the arrogant man for his arrogance, the slayer of the Dasyus. He, my people, is Indra!

11. He who in the fortieth autumn discovered Shambara living in the mountains, who killed the violent serpent, Danu, who lay there. He, my people, is Indra!

12. He, the mighty bull, who with his seven reins let loose the seven rivers to flow; who with his thunderbolt in his hand furled down Rauhina as he was climbing up to the sky. He, my people, is Indra!

13. Even the Sky and Earth bow low before him, and the mountains are terrified of his hot breath; he who is known as the Soma-drinker with the thunderbolt in his hand, He, my people, is Indra!

14. He who helps with his favour the one who presses and the one who cooks, the praiser and the preparer, he for whom prayer is nourishment, for whom Soma is the special gift. He, my people, is Indra!

15. O Indra, You, who furiously grasp the prize for the one who presses and the one who cooks, you are truly real. Let us be dear to you, Indra, all our days, and let us speak as men of power in the sacrificial gatherings.

There are hundreds of hymns eulogizing Indra. Vedic rishis vied with each other showering encomium on him. Let me quote another hymn, X. 89, composed by Rishi Renu, also a son of the celebrated Sage Vishvamitra.

Hymn X. 89. Indra

1. I will extol most heroic Indra who with his might forced the Earth and Sky asunder. The great upholder of mankind, he surpasses the rivers and seas in his greatness.

2. Heroic like the Sun, he turns the regions like wheels of a chariot. Like ever prancing dazzling horses, he destroyed the black-hued darkness.

3. O sages, let us together chant new eulogies of him which are unique in Heaven and Earth. He longs for an enriching acclaim, as he is keen to vanquish foes and protect friends.

4. Chanted vigorously, the eulogies to Indra, send rains from the Sky to the earth. For he has fixed the Earth and Sky to his chariot's axle.

5. Impetuous Soma, with his rousing draughts, nourishes Indra to destroy dreaded foes; other similar plants growing in the forest shall not deceive Indra.

6. Soma has flowed to him, whom nothing can equal, Heavens nor the Earth, the firmament nor mountains. In his rage he shatters the firm and breaks the strong.

7. As an axe fells the tree, he slew Vritra, destroyed his strongholds and dug out the rivers. He cleft the mountain like a newly made pitcher and released the cows.

8. You are punisher of guilt, O Indra, you smite the sinner—men who violate the lofty Laws of Varuna and Mitra.

9. Men who lead sinful lives, break agreements and injure Varuna, Mitra, Aryaman; against these foes, O Mighty Indra, you sharpen your thunderbolt.

10. Indra is Sovran Lord of Earth and Heaven, of waters and mountains, of the sages and wise men. Invoke him with lauds for rich rewards.

11. Vaster than the heaven and earth, vaster than the firmament, wider than the ocean's and the wind's expanse, Indra's power exceeds them all.

12. Forward, as herald of refulgent Usha, O Indra, let your insatiate thunderbolt fly and pierce with hottest blaze the men who love deception.

13. When you appeared, O Indra, the moon, the mountains, forests, plants and herbage followed you. The Sky, Earth and the

waters followed.

14. Where is your terrible weapon that slays the Rakshasas, when these fiends would lie on the ground in the place of immolation.

15. Those who are in enmity against us, O Indra, and are waxing in might, let blinding darkness follow them, turning their bright nights into blight.

16. May these plentiful libations offered by the yajman (the sacrificer) and the soulful prayers sung by us rejoice you, O Indra, and you come to us, who praise you.

17. O Indra, extend your protection to us, give us new favours and fortune; we of Vishvamitra's generation, who weave ever new hymns in your glory.

18. We invoke Maghavan, auspicious Indra, the best warrior in the fight where spoils are gathered; the Slayer of Vritra, who bestows riches on his worshippers.

About one-fourth of the Rigvedic hymns eulogize Indra. Homage to him may remain inadequate even after quoting many more hymns. Yet I want to quote a hymn, VIII. 91, authored by a Rishika Apala, daughter of the celebrated Vedic rishi Atri. This young girl had remained 'unwed' despite being married. Her husband shunned her as she was probably infected by a skin disease. She pressed Soma for Indra and invited him to a drink—and was 'blessed' by him.

Hymn VIII. 91. Apala and Indra

1. A maiden going for water found Soma by the way. She brought it home and said, 'I will press it for you, O Indra; I will press it for you, O mighty Lord!'

2. O invincible Indra, you who visit homes of devotees, I offer you this Soma I have pressed with my teeth, together with grain and gruel, cakes and prayers.

3. My offerings may not be able to satisfy you, yet I wish to make an attempt. Slowly and gently, ever more gently, flow for Indra, O drop of Soma!

4. 'Surely, He is able, surely He will do it, surely He will make us more fortunate. Surely, we who are hated by our husbands should flee and unite with Indra'.

5. 'O Indra, make these three places sprout—my father's barren head and our field, and this part of my body below the waist'.

6. 'Make that field of ours (grow crops), and this part of my body, and my father's head—make them grow hair'.

7. In the nave of a chariot, in the nave of the cart, in the nave of the yoke, O Lord Indra of a hundred powers, you purified Apala three times and made her skin shine.

In thoroughness of research none can compete with A.L. Basham. He has found a long hymn in the Rig Veda, VIII. 46, eulogizing Indra, which was composed for a sacrifice organized by Balbootha, a Dasa chieftain. Balbootha had come to terms with the Aryan conquerors and had embraced the Vedic religion.[79]

The hymn's author is Vash, son of Ashva, who, like Kakshivan, greatly exaggerates the quantum of dakshina he has received. Griffith comments that 'the hymn appears to be composed of two or more originally separate hymns.' The long hymn is devoid of lyrical beauty but is significant in being sponsored by a Dasa chieftain. I quote a few selected verses from the hymn. The poet has indeed outdone Kakshivan.

Hymn VIII. 46. Indra

1. O, Indra, our Protector, Lord of ample wealth, we depend on thee, Thou driver of tawny steeds.

2. O, Hurler of the Bolt, we know you as our nourisher and giver of wealth.

4. Full protection has the mortal man whom Mitra, Aryaman and the Maruts guide.

7. In Indra are enshrined all powers of protection. Let His swift reddish-brown steeds bring him to us and to Soma juice

[79]Basham, A.L., *The Wonder That Was India: A Survey of the Culture of the Indian Sub-Continent Before the Coming of the Muslims*, Rupa & Co, 1954, p. 32.

for his carouse.

10. Responding to our wish for cows, for steeds and chariots, be gracious. O Greatest of the Great!

11. O Victorious Hero, your munificence is boundless. O Bolt-armed Maghavan, protect us, your worshippers!

21. Poet Vash, son of Ashva, has obtained untold wealth in this glorious dawn, from Kanita's son Pruthushrava.

22. Steeds sixty thousand and ten thousand kine, and twenty thousand camels have I received, of red and brown hue.

23. Ten black steeds with tails long and fair, turn with swift whirl my chariot wheel.

24. The gifts which Pruthushrava, Kanita's munificent son gave—a chariot wrought in gold—and won himself most lofty fame.

32. Hundreds of cows, steeds, camels have we received as Dasa Balbootha and Taruksha's gifts. These are thy people, O Vayu, who rejoice with Indra and gods as Protectors.

33. And now these donors have presented to Vash, son of Ashva, this young girl, adorned with ornaments of gold.

Indra's famous generosity when he becomes exultant, particularly after imbibing copious draughts of Soma, emboldens the poet to imagine himself in Indra's place in hymn, VIII. 14, which was composed by two descendants of Rishi Kanva—Gosookti and Ashvasookti. The hymn is in the nature of Daan Stuti, imploring Indra to shower riches on his worshippers.

Hymn X. 14. If I Were Like You, Indra!

1. If I were like you, Indra, the single Sovereign of all wealth, the man who praised me would be rich in cows.

2. I would do my best, O Lord of Power, to enrich and strengthen the sage, were I the Lord of cattle.

3. For the one who sacrifices and presses Soma, your opulence showers herds of cows and steeds on them.

4. There is no one, neither God nor mortal, O Indra, who hinders your munificence when you are praised and you wish to give rich gifts.

5. The yajna-sacrifice makes Indra grow greater when he rolled back the earth and made himself a diadem in heaven.

6. We seek help from you, O Indra, you who have grown great and have won all treasures.

7. In Soma's ecstasy, Indra extended the firmament and realms of light, when he cleft demon Vala, limb from limb.

8. He drove out the cows for the Angirasas, bringing to light those that had been hidden, and hurled Vala down headlong.

9. By Indra were the luminous realms of heaven established and secured, firm and imovable from their position.

10. Like the exhilarating wave of the waters, your praise, O Indra, hastens along; bright shine the drops of Soma that gladden you.

11. The hymns of praise, the chants of your glory, make you grow great, O Indra, and you shower happiness on the singer of the praise.

12. Let the two long-maned reddish brown horses bring Indra, the giver of rich gifts, to drink Soma juice here at the sacrifice.

13. With the foam of waters, Indra, you tore off the head of the demon Namuchi, when you conquered all challengers.

14. You whirled down the Dashyus who wanted to climb up to the sky, O Indra, when they had crept up using their magic spells.

15. You scattered to every side the ones that did not press Soma; as Soma-drinker you are Supreme!

~

Indra's pre-eminent adventure was the killing of the dragon Vritra and release of the cows and the pent-up waters. It established him at the head of pantheon of the Rigvedic gods. Curiously, in the discovery of Vritra's stronghold and of the Panis who had stolen the cows of Angirasas, Indra's dog, Sarama, had played an important part.

The Panis lived on the other side of river Rasa, a minor tributary of the Indus. The tribal Panis were inimical to the Vedic rishis like the Angirasas. They had stolen the cows of the rishis and hidden them in mountain caves. The dog Sarama followed the trail of the cows and succeeded in reaching their hiding place, where she held a dialogue with the Panis. The story of Sarama's spying is contained in Hymn X. 108, in which she talks to the Panis. A poet from the Angirasa clan might have composed it.

Hymn X. 108. Sarama and the Panis

1. [The Panis] With what desire has Sarama come to this place? The road stretches far into distant lands. What is your purpose with us? How did you find your way here? And how did you cross the waters of Rasa?

2. [Sarama] I have journeyed here, sent here as the messenger of Indra, and I am looking for your great treasures, O Panis. Because the river feared my Lord Indra, she let me cross the waters and I came.

3. [Panis] What is Indra like, Sarama? What is his appearance, who sent you here as his messenger from afar? If he comes here, we will make friends with him, and he will be the herdsman of our cows.

4. [Sarama] I know him as one who cannot be tricked. Indeed, He who sent me here as his messenger from afar, tricks others. Deep turbulent rivers cannot come in his way. You Panis will lie here slain by Indra.

5. [Panis] These are the cows you desire, O lovely Sarama; having flown beyond the ends of the sky, we would release them without a fight? And mind you, we have sharp weapons.

6. [Sarama] Your words, O Panis, are no armies. Your wicked bodies might survive the arrows, the path to your hiding place may be impregnable. But Brihaspati's wrath will not spare you.

7. [Panis] Sarama, this enormous hiding cave, full of cows, horses and riches is set firm in cliffs of rocks. We Panis, who are good sentinels guard it. You have come in vain on this secluded path.

8. [Sarama] The sages—Ayasas, Angirasas and Navagas—roused by Soma will share this enclosed cave of cattle among them. Then you Panis will spit back these words.

9. [Panis] Sarama, since you have come here, compelled by the force of gods, we will make you, our sister. Do not go back, lovely Sarama; we will give you a share of the cattle.

10. [Sarama] I know no brotherhood, nor sisterhood. Know that Indra, who inspires terror; and Angirasas, when I left them, they were desirous of gaining the cattle. O Panis, run far away from here.

11. Run into the distance, Panis. Let the cattle come out by the right path and go, the cattle which Brihaspati and the inspired sages, the pressing stones and Soma, found where the cows had been hidden.

Hymn I. 32 is composed by Hiranyastoop Angiras, on the slaying of Vritra by Indra. Vritra is generally supposed to be a fiend, though also called *Ahi* (serpent).

Hymn I. 32. The Killing of Vritra

1. Let me now sing the heroic deed of Indra, the first that the thunderbolt-wielder performed. He killed the dragon and pierced an opening for the waters; he split open the bellies of mountains.

2. He killed the dragon who lay upon the mountain; Tvshtra[80] fashioned the roaring thunderbolt for him. Like lowing cows, the flowing waters rushed straight down to the sea.

3. Wildly excited like a bull, he took the Soma for himself and drank from three bowls in the three-day ceremony. The generous Indra seized his thunderbolt and hurled it as a weapon; he killed the first-born of dragons.

4. Indra, when you killed the first-born of dragons and by your magic overcame the dragon's magic, at that very moment you brought forth the Sun, the Sky and Dawn. Since then, you have found no enemy wishing to conquer you.

5. With his great weapon, the thunderbolt, Indra killed the shoulder-less Vritra, his greatest enemy. Like the trunk of a tree whose branches have been lopped off by an axe, the dragon lies flat upon the ground.

6. For, muddled by drunkenness like one who is no soldier, Vritra challenged the great hero who had overcome the mighty and

[80]Tvashtra is an artisan of the gods.

who drank Soma to the dregs. Unable to withstand the onslaught of his weapons, he found Indra an enemy to conquer him and was shattered, his nose crushed.

7. Without feet or hands he fought against Indra, who struck him on the nape of the neck with his thunderbolt. The steer who wished to become the equal of a bull bursting with seed, Vritra lay broken in pieces.

8. There as he lies like a bank-bursting river; the waters taking courage to flow over him. The Dragon lies beneath the torrents which Vritra had encompassed.

9. Then ebbed away the vital energy of Vritra's mother Danu,[81] for Indra had hurled his deadly weapon at her. Above was the mother, below was the son; Danu lay down like a cow with her calf.

10. In the midst of never-ceasing currents of water, their bodies were hidden. The waters bear off Vritra's nameless body; the foe of Indra sank into eternal darkness.

11. As the Panis had imprisoned the cows, the waters were husbanded and protected by the dragon Dasa.[82] When Indra killed Vritra, he split open the outlet of the waters that had been closed.

12. When Vritra smote your thunderbolt, you parried it as a horse whisks flies with his tail, O brave Indra, you are an unparalleled god! You won back the cows; you released the seven streams so that they could flow.

13. No use was the lightning and thunder, fog and hail that Vritra had scattered about, when Indra fought the Dragon. Indra remained victorious for all time to come.

14. O avenger of the Dragon, Indra! What did you see, that fear entered your heart when you had killed him? Then you crossed the ninety-nine streams like the frightened eagle crossing the realms of earth and air.

15. Indra, who wields the thunderbolt in his hand, is the king of that which moves and that which rests, of the tame and horned animals. He rules the people as their king, encircling the

[81]Danu is Vritra's mother and of other demons who were called Danavas.
[82]Another name for Vritra.

mall as a rim encircles spokes.

~

There is a naughty and bawdy hymn, X. 86, with a refrain: 'Indra Supreme Above All!' It is replete with sexual banter concerning Indra and Indrani, which Renou has called 'the strangest poem' in the Rig Veda. Apart from Indra and Indrani, there are two more characters in the hymn, 'Vrishakapi' and 'Vrishakapayi'.The word 'Vrishakapi' literally means 'the monkey bursting with seed', with obvious innuendo of the male sexual organ. Vrishakapayi is Vrishakapi's wife.

In the hymn Indrani complains to her husband Indra that Vrishakapi has been taking undue sexual liberties with her, which was vexing her. The verses of the hymn end with the refrain 'Indra Supreme Above All!'

Hymn X. 86. Indra Supreme Above All!

1. [Indrani] O my Lord Indra, they no longer press Soma for you, nor do they think of you as God, as my friend Vrishakapi has been gorging himself on the nourishments that rightly belong to you. Indra Supreme Above All!

2. My lord Indra, you seem to approve the erring ways of Vrishakapi. No, you will not find Soma to drink in any place. Indra Supreme Above All!

3. [Indra] What has this tawny animal, this Vrishakapi, done that you complain against him and begrudge his nourishing on my wealth? Indra Supreme Above All!

4. [Indrani] O Indra, your beloved Vrishakapi, whom you protect—let that dog who attacks the pig bite his ear! Indra Supreme Above All!

5. The ape has defiled my precious, well made, anointed things. I will cut off his head and I will not be good to that evil-doer. Indra Supreme Above All!

6. No woman has finer loins than I, or is better at love making. No woman thrusts against a man better than I, or raises and spreads her thighs more. Indra Supreme Above All!

7. [Vrishakapi] O little mother, so easily won, as it will surely

be. My loins, my thigh, my head seem to thrill and stiffen, little mother! Indra Supreme Above All!

8. [Indra] Your arm and fingers are so lovely, your hair so long, your buttock so broad. You are the wife of a hero—so why do you attack our Vrishakapi? Indra Supreme Above All!

9. [Indrani] Vrishakapi assaults me as if I have no one to protect me. But I have a real man, for I am wife of Indra and the Maruts are my friends. Indra Supreme Above All!

10. I am Indra's queen who attends public festivals and meeting places. There I am respected and praised as upholder of *Rta*. Indra Supreme Above All!

11. [Vrishakapayi] Indrani is the most fortunate[83] among women, I have heard; her husband will never die of old age. Indra Supreme Above All!

12. [Indra] Never, Indrani, have I enjoyed without my friend Vrishakapi, whose offering of oblation is heavenly and goes to the gods. Indra Supreme Above All!

13. [Vrishakapi] O Wife of Vrishakapi, you are rich in wealth, and in your sons. Let Indra eat your bulls and the oblation that is so pleasing and so powerful. Indra Supreme Above All!

14. [Indra] They have cooked for me fifteen bulls, and twenty, so that I may eat the fat as well. Both sides of my belly are full. Indra Supreme Above All!

15. [Vrishakapayi] Like a sharp horned bull, loud bellowing amid the herds, O Indra, sweet to your heart is the brew that she who tends you pours. Indra Supreme Above All![84]

18. O Indra, this Vrishakapi has found a slain dead animal, a sword, a basket, a new pot and a cart loaded with firewood.[85] Indra Supreme Above All!

19. [Indra] I am coming forward, looking about and

[83]Wendy Doniger explains that the word 'Subhaga', occurring in the verse, denotes a woman who is beautiful, therefore, loved by her husband, and therefore, fortunate in the most important way for a woman—her husband will live long!

[84]Verses 16 and 17 have been omitted by Ralph Griffith, saying he cannot translate them into decent English. I do the same.

[85]These are all items used in a sacrifice of expiation for one who has violated a vow of chastity.

distinguishing between the indigenous inhabitant and noble Aryan ally. I am drinking with the one who has prepared simple brew; I am looking for one who would offer Soma sacrifice. Indra Supreme Above All!

20. How many miles separate the desert and the ploughed land?[86] Let's go home, Vrishakapi. Indra Supreme Above All!

21. [Indrani] Come back, Vrishakapi, and we two will meet in agreement.[87] Come again on the homeward path, although you destroy my sleep. Indra Supreme Above All!

22. [The Poet] As you went home to the north, Vrishakapi, where was the beast of many sins? To whom, O Indra, the inciter of Indrani go? Indra Supreme Above All!

23. Manu's daughter, Pershu, delivered twenty children at birth. She was greatly delighted, although her womb felt the pains. Indra Supreme Above All!

Indra defends Vrishakapi in the hymn and tries to pacify Indrani. In Verse 21, Indrani invites Vrishakapi to meet in agreement. However, there is some confusion and controversy about the identity of Vrishakapi. Sayana says Vrishakapi is a son of Indra as he addresses Indrani as '*ambe*' (mother). That is clearly unacceptable as no son will take sexual liberties with his mother.

Obviously, the word 'Vrishakapi' is a pun on Indra's own sexual organ. In Verse 12, Indra tells Indrani, 'Never have I enjoyed without my friend Vrishakapi.' 'Vrishakapayi', wife of Vrishakapi, who speaks the eleventh and fifteenth verses, is a pun on Indrani's genital organ too. Indeed, Indrani is probably jesting and teasing Indra for his excessive indulgence in love-making. Indra Supreme Above All!

~

There is an interesting hymn dedicated to Shachi Paulomi, X. 159, which expresses a woman's triumphant conquest of her husband and banishing of her rival wives. In Matshya Purana, Shachi

[86]Indra may be referring to the contrast between a barren woman and one who has given birth.

[87]Indrani is reconciled now and invites Vrishakapi.

Paulomi is said to be daughter of the chief of demons, Puloma, who was son of Daksha's daughter Danu.

Hymn X. 159. Shachi Paulomi

1. There the sun rises, and here my *Bhaga* (good fortune) has arisen. Being a clever woman, I as conqueror have won my husband as mine own.

2. I am the banner and the head. I am the formidable one who has the deciding word. I am triumphant and my Lord shall be submissive to my will.

3. My sons are slayers of the foes; my daughter is a ruling queen and I am completely victorious. My voice is supreme in my husband's ears.

4. The oblation that Indra made and so became glorious and supreme, this is what I have made for you, O Gods, I have become truly without rival wives.

5. Without rival wives, a killer of the rival wives, victorious and pre-eminent, I have seized for myself the attraction, as it were, of flirtatious women.

6. I have conquered and subdued these rival wives, so that I may rule as empress over this Hero, my husband, and over the people.

Indra is intimately connected with Parjanya, the Storm God, who is also called a bull like him. Rain was most important to the Vedic pastoralists and there is beautiful hymn composed by Rishi Atri Bhaum in veneration of God Parjnaya.

Hymn V. 83. Parjanya the Bull

1. I summon the powerful god Parjanya, praise and pay homage to him. The bellowing bull, freely flowing with luscious drops, places his seed in the plants as an embryo.

2. He shatters the trees and slaughters the demons; he strikes terror into every creature with his enormous deadly thunderbolt. Even the sinless tremble before the bull-like God—when Parjanya strikes the evil-doers.

3. His messengers of rain appear like a charioteer lashing his

horses with a whip. The Sky resounds with lions' roars when his rain-bearing clouds come.[88]

4. Winds blow, lightenings fly, plants surge up, the Sky swells, the Sun overflows. The sap of life quickens in every creature when Parjanya refreshes the Earth with his seed.

5. Under your power the Earth bends low, hoofed animals quiver, plants of all forms bloom. O Parjanya grant us safe shelter by your powers.

6. Send us rain from Heaven, O Maruts. Make the streams of seed-bearing stallion overflow as they swell. Come here with your thunder, pouring waters, for you are our father, O bright Sky-God.

7. Roar and thunder, sow your seed, come circling around the world in your chariot, full of water. Turn downward the leather-bag. Let the hills and valleys become level.

8. Draw up your enormous bucket and pour it down. Let the streams flow forth, set free. Let Heaven and Earth be drenched with ghrita. Fill up the ponds for our cows.

9. O Parjanya, when you bellow loudly and thunder and slaughter the evil-doers, the whole world and all living creatures rejoice.

10. You have sent the rain; now withhold it. You have made the deserts fit for travel, made the plants to grow food and have earned prayers from living creatures.

Professor B.K. Ghose observes that 'hymns of this type are unique in world literature, for nowhere else are the deification of natural phenomena so clearly perceived.'[89] He adds that the martial spirit of the Vedic people is reflected in Hymn VI. 75, which is not a war song, but rather a magical incantation supposed to secure victory in battle. The hymn was composed by Rishi Payu Bharadwaj, belonging to the famous dynasty of Rishi Bharadwaj—one of the seven most celebrated Rigvedic rishis.

Hymn VI. 75. The Weapons of War

[88]This verse reminds me of Rama telling Lakshman when going on Sita's trail: '*Ghana ghamand nabha garajata ghora; Siyaheen darpata mana mora*'.

[89]Majumdar, R.C. (ed.), *The Vedic Age*, Bharatiya Vidya Bhavan, 1996, p. 348.

1. The thunder cloud becomes like the mailed warrior, when he plunges into the thick of battle. May you be victorious without being injured in body; may the strength of the armour protect you!

2. By the bow he'll win the cattle; by the bow shall we win the mighty struggles. The bow destroys the enemy, by the bow shall we conquer the regions.

3. The bow's string nears the ear as if to whisper, holding in embrace its dear friend (the bow). Stretched on the bow this string lisps like a girl, that helps on to victory.

HYMNS ON VARUNA

God Varuna, who is also an Aditya (Aditi's son), is the supreme guardian and ruler of the moral law, has but a few hymns dedicated to him. Varuna's name bears a striking similarity with the Greek word *Ouranos* (Sky). Professor V.M. Apte observes that 'Varuna is the upholder of the physical and moral order symbolized in *Rta*. He is more intimately connected with *Rta* than any other god.'[90]

Hymns dedicated to Varuna are predominantly ethical and devout in tone. He is supposed to maintain a roving troupe of spies. They keep a constant vigil on the mortals; none can deceive God Varuna. Neither god nor a mortal being may violate Varuna's ordinances. He holds the *pashas*, the fetters with which he binds the sinners. In every hymn to Varuna there is a prayer for forgiveness of sin.

He also regulates the seasons which make the rivers flow. He is invoked with Mitra as a bestower of rain. It is due to Varuna's regulation that the ocean does not overflow, although the rivers constantly pour into it. Besides, he fixes the paths of the luminaries across the sky. He stands out as the moral governor among all the deities.

Hymn II. 28, composed by Sage Koorma Gartsmada, is

[90]Ibid. 368.

dedicated to Lord Varuna. The sage begins with a prayer for riches but soon modifies his tone.

Hymn II. 28. Varuna

1. May this (hymn) addressed to Aditi's son, who is wise and self-supreme, excel all the existing (hymns) in greatness. I beg renown of Varuna the Mighty, the God whom it is exceedingly pleasant to worship, of that affluent Varuna do I beg glorious fame.

2. Having extolled thee, O Varuna, with thoughtful care may we have high fortune in thy service, singing thy praises day after day, in the hope of being rich in cattle.

3. May we be in thy keeping, O wide-ruling Varuna, Lord of the Gods! O Son of Aditi, pardon us for our sins and admit us to your friendship.

4. Aditi's son unleashed the rivers and started them on their paths. They course along in obedience to Varuna's ordinance, feel no weariness, nor cease from flowing; like birds they swiftly fly in never-ending course.

5. Loosen the bond of sin like a girdle, O Varuna; we shall fully conform to the rule of equity you have ordained. May not the thread snap while I am still weaving my prayer-song, may not the measuring rod strike out of season.

6. Avert terror from me, O Varuna, be kind to me, as a righteous ruler. Release me from anguish, as a calf from the rope; not even for a moment can I live away from you.

7. Do not strike us, Varuna, with your weapons; O Asura, destroy those who commit sin in your search. May we not have to bid adieu to light; loosen the hold of the envious on us.

8. O mighty Varuna, now and hereafter, even as of old, will we venerate and worship you. O invincible God, your statutes, never to be altered, are fixed as on a mountain.

9. Move far from me any sins I might have committed. O King, let me not suffer from guilt of others. Full many a morn remains to dawn upon us; in these, O Varuna, direct us while we live.

10. O Varuna, your glories we sing in sacrificial assemblies. May I not live, to witness my wealthy, liberal friend's—destitution. O King, may I never lack well-ordered riches.

~

In Hymn, II. 28 above, Varuna has been called an 'Asura'. That needs explaining. The record of treaties between the Hittite king Shubbiluliuma and the Mittani king Mattiuaza, dating about 1600 BC, was discovered at Boghaz-koi. In these treaties the names of four Vedic gods, Mitra, Varuna, Indra and the Nasatyas, had occurred. It proved beyond a shadow of doubt that the Aryans who later found refuge in India had branched out from them.

Indeed, Hittites were the earliest known inhabitants of what is now Turkey. They began to control the area in about 1900 BC. They later conquered parts of Mesopotamia and Syria and by 1500 BC had become a major power in the Middle East. A Hittite princess was married to King Ramses II when, in 1285 BC, a Hittite king, who had fought a war with Egyptian forces, was defeated.

It has been established that a group of Indo-Iranian people inhabited the plains of rivers Oxus and Jaxartes in Iran in 1400 BC onwards. Professor Ghosh explains that the primitive Indo-European religion recognized only nature-gods (sky, sun, wind, etc.) and a fire-cult. But already the undivided Indo-Iranians knew a Soma-cult beside the older fire-cult and abstract deities as well as the older nature-gods.[91]

However, the old Indo-European '*deivo*' was considered inappropriate for the new abstract and ethical deities, and a new term, Asura, came to be used for them. Varuna was the chief of these ethical deities just as Indra was the chief of the nature-gods. This caused a schism and the more vigorous and adventurous followers of Deiva-religion advanced further east, braving the hardships of the forward march, and reached India.

As far as the Aryans who stayed back in Iran are concerned, the reformer Zarathustra's advent in 1000 BC substantially changed the original religion. In his Gathas, Zarathustra protested effectively against ceremonial slaughter of animals, as the Buddha did in India four centuries later.

~

[91]Majumdar, R.C. (ed.), *The Vedic Age*, Bharatiya Vidya Bhavan, 1996, p. 223.

In another hymn addressed to Varuna, VII. 86, the Sage Vasishtha Maitravaruni, entreats Varuna in an apologetic tone to forgive him if he had committed some wrong.

Hymn VII. 86. Varuna

1. Glorious is the birth of Lord Varuna. He propped apart the two world-halves even though they are so vast; pushed away the dome of the Sky to make it high and wide and set the Sun and the stars on their journey, and spread out the Earth underneath.

3. O Varuna, I have enquired from several wise men as to what is my sin? All of them say the same thing: 'Surely, Lord Varuna is angry with you.' I want to ask you the reason of your anger.

4. What O Varuna, is the terrible sin, what my transgression, that you would slay your friend who sings your praises? Tell me, O Unconquerable Lord, and immediately I would approach you with my homage.

5. Free us from the sins of our ancestors and those wherein we have ourselves offended. O King, the thieves are absolved of their crime when they feed grass to the cattle. Set Vasishtha free from sin like a calf set free from a rope.

6. Not our own will betrayed us, but seduction and thoughtlessness, O Varuna—wine, dice or anger. The elderly lead astray the younger. Not only during wakeful state, we commit sins even in our dreams.

7. Slave like shall I serve you, O bounteous Lord; serve you free from sin. Give wisdom to us, the ignorant. Lead us to riches who sing prayers in your glory.

8. O Lord Varuna! May this prayer lodge in your heart. May we succeed in our endeavors! Preserve us evermore with your blessings.

In yet another hymn dedicated to Varuna, VII. 89, Sage Vasishtha prays to this terrible deity not to send him to the House of Clay (the grave).

Hymn VII. 89. House of Clay

1. Let me not go to the house of clay, O King Varuna—not yet. Have mercy, spare me, O Mighty Lord.

2. If I seem to stumble and tremble like a wind-blown goat-skin; O Thunderer, have mercy, spare me, O Mighty Lord.

3. O Bright and Powerful God, through want of strength I erred and went astray. Have mercy, spare me, O Mighty Lord.

4. Thirst had come upon me, though I stood in the midst of abundant waters. Have mercy, spare me, Mighty Lord.

5. O King Varuna, whatever the offence may be, which we humans commit against heavenly gods, or through carelessness have violated your laws, do not injure us, O Mighty Lord, for that inequity.

ᔑ

There is another hymn, I. 24, dedicated to Varuna, composed by poet Shunah-Shepa, son of Rishi Agigarta. Curiously, the name 'Shunah-Shepa' means 'dog-tailed'. He was adopted by Sage Vishvamitra and was saved from being offered as a sacrificial animal. Griffith, in his introductory note, narrates the Shunah-Shepa story:

> This hymn, addressed to Varuna, Prajapati, Agni, Savitr and Bhaga, is the first of a series attributed to Shunah-Shepa, the son of Sage Agartha. The legend is told in full detail in Aitariya Brahmana. King Harishchandra of Kashi, worshipped Varuna in order to obtain a son, promising to sacrifice to him his first-born (in the hope of having more than one son in the bargain). A son is born, named Rohita; but the king delays the sacrifice until Rohita grows up, when his father communicated to him his intended fate. Rohita refuses submission, and spends several days in the forest away from home.
>
> There, at last, Rohita meets Rishi Agigarta, in great financial stress. Rohita persuades him to part with his second son Shunah-Shepa to be offered as his substitute to Varuna. Agigarta sells Shunah-Shepa to the king, father of Rohita. Vishvamitra, who was the chief officiating priest of the

king of Kashi, was childless; he adopts Shunah-Shepa. At the *yajna*-sacrifice, Rishi Vishvamitra appeals to the Gods against the boy's sacrifice and Shunah-Shepa is liberated. He becomes a sage, composes hymns and comes to be called 'Devrat Vaishavamitra'.

Let me now quote the hymn Shunah-Shepa composed:

Hymn I. 24. Varuna and Other Gods

1. Who now is he, what God among Immortals, of whose auspicious name we may recall? Who shall restore us to Mighty Aditi, that we may see our Father and Mother?
2. God Agni, the first among Immortals, his auspicious name let us recall. He shall to Mighty Aditi restore us, that we may see our Father and Mother.
3. O God Savitr, the Lord of precious riches, help us in receiving our share.
4. O God Bhaga, you hold wealth, highly lauded, unenvied, beyond reproach or hatred.
5. Through your protection and largesse, O Bhaga, we might obtain the height of affluence.

~

Shunah-Shepa's hymn is quite pedestrian! I had included it as I wanted to tell his strange story.

~

Singing praise of Indra, who got the waters released from Vritra; propitiating the rain-god Parjanya; and satiating themselves with the celestial drink, Soma, the Rigvedic people had forgotten the travails and hardships of wandering for years in search of a homeland. They remind me of Faiz Ahmad Faiz, who had declaimed:

Aaye kuchh abra, kuchh sharaab aaye,
Phir aaye jo azaab aaye!

[Let there be some rain, and let there be some wine;

Thereafter, let whatever catastrophy strikes me!]

It struck me that Faiz would have been happy living with the Rigvedic rishis—writing poetry, drinking Soma and eating fire-cooked beef!

~

Like the pre-eminent god Indra, who has the largest number of hymns dedicated to him, Soma Pavaman, as this elixir was called, had the distinction of being eulogized in a large number of hymns. There is a merry hymn composed by Shishu Angiras, with a refrain 'Flow O Soma, for Indra!'. I quote this hymn from Wendy Doniger's selection.

Hymn IX. 112. Soma Pavaman

1. Diverse indeed are our callings, different are the tasks of men. The carpenter seeks what is broken, the physician a fracture, and the Brahmin priests, greedy for yajna sacrifices, look for a sacrificer. Flow O Soma, for Indra!

2. With seasoned timber and bird feathers (for making arrows), with gold and precious gems for ornaments, the smith seeks a rich patron, ready with his furnace. Flow O Soma, for Indra!

3. A bard I am, my father a physician and my mother grinder of barley. With diverse thoughts and actions, we all seek wealth, as a cow seeks green grass. Flow O Soma, for Indra!

4. The harnessed horse longs for a light cart; seducers long for a woman's smile; the male organ for two hairy lips and the frog for water. Flow O Soma, for Indra!

This hymn indicates that the Rigvedic society was without rigid compartments of class or caste. It was a composite society wherein professions were not hereditary and sexual relations without a taint of obscenity.

~

There is an entertaining hymn composed by Rishi Pragath Kanv. It celebrates the effects of drinking Soma, particularly the feeling of being set free, being released into boundless open space and getting a whiff of immortality.

Hymn VIII. 48. We Have Drunk Soma

1. I have tasted the sweet drink of life; knowing that it inspires good thoughts and joyous expansiveness to the extreme; all the Gods and mortals seek this *madhu*.[92]

3. We have drunk the Soma and have become immortal; we have attained the light, discovered the Gods. O immortal Soma, what can hatred and malice of a mortal do to us now?

4. O drop of Soma, absorbed into the heart be sweet and kind as a father to his son, thoughtful as a friend to a friend. Far-famed Soma, stretch out our life span so we may live longer.

5. The glorious drops I have drunk have set me free in wide space. They have bound me together in my limbs as thongs bind a chariot. Let the drops protect me from stumbling and falling in ecstasy.

7. We would enjoy you, pressed with a fervent heart, like riches from a father. O King Soma, stretch out our life-spans as the Sun stretches the spring days.

9. For you, Soma, are the guardian of our body; you have settled down in every limb of mine. Even if we break your laws, have mercy on us like a good friend and make us better.

10. Having imbibed you, I feel close to the Lord of bay horses, Indra. With the Soma that is lodged in us, I approach you, Indra, to stretch out our life-span.

12. The drop that we have drunk has entered our hearts, an immortal inside mortals. Let us serve Soma as oblations to Fathers to let them abide in His mercy and kindness.

13. Uniting in agreement with the Fathers, O drop of Soma, you have extended yourself through Sky and Earth. Let us serve Soma with oblation and be masters of riches.

15. O Soma, enter into us as we soar to the Sun, watching over men. O drop of Soma, summon the divine host and protect us now and forever.

[92]Not to be taken for a product of bees.

This following hymn from the tenth Mandala is dedicated to the Pressing Stones of the Soma plant which are also considered deities. The hymn is ascribed to Rishi Arbud Kadraveya. He calls the pressing stones—bulls, eagles, draft animals, horses and playful children.

Hymn X. 94. The Pressing Stones

1. Let the stones raise their voices, and let us raise our voices. Speak our speech to the stones that speak. When you, stones, you, mountains, full of Soma, rush to bring the rhythmic sound to Indra.

2. They speak in a hundred ways, a thousand ways, howling with their green jaws. Working busily to do the good work, the stones have succeeded in eating the oblation even before the priest of the oblation—Agni.

3. They speak: they have found the honey. They growl and gnaw on Soma plant's flesh. As they snap at Soma's branches, the bulls who have grazed well, begin to bellow.

5. These eagles have sent their cry up to the sky. Hearing it the female dear danced ardently in the meadow. The Stones plunge deep for their rendezvous with the lower stones; they infuse the lower stones with floods of the seeds of sun-bright Soma.

7. Sing to these bulls that have ten girths, ten yoke-straps, ten harnesses, ten reins that never wear out, to them that are yoked ten times to bear ten shafts.

8. The stones are swift horses; their bridle with ten thongs fits them comfortably. They have tasted the filtered juice of the first pressing of the Soma juice, milked from the stalk.

9. These Soma eaters kiss Indra's pair of reddish-brown horses. As they milk the stalk they sit upon the ox.[93] When Indra has drunk the honey they have milked, he grows great and acts like a bull.

11. Porous or not porous, the stones never tire, never die; they are never sick or old or shaken by passion; nicely fat, they are free from thirst and desire.

12. Your fathers[94] are entirely firm in age after age; peace-

[93]The soma stalks are placed upon an oxhide.

[94]Mountains—the father of stones—as in Verse 1.

loving, they do not budge from their spot. Untouched by age, companions of tawny Soma, you are tinged yellow like a saffron tree; you have made the sky and earth listen to your uproar.

14. They have raised their voices for the sacrificial juice, like playful children jostling a mother. Set free the inspiration of the one who presses Soma, and let the stones that we hold in awe return to being stones (be de-sanctified after finishing the holy task of grinding Soma).

∽

I am tempted to include another delightful hymn, X.119, composed by Sage Laba Aindra; its verses have a refrain: 'Have I not drunk Soma?' '*Laba*', it appears, is also the name of a bird. Verily, the poet's imagination takes a fanciful flight! The hymn has a refrain—'Have I not drunk Soma?'.

Hymn X.119. The Soma Drinker Praises Himself

1. This, yes, this is my resolve: to own a cow or a horse. Have I not drunk Soma?

2. Like impetuous winds, the drink has lifted me up. Have I not drunk Soma?

3. The drink has lifted me up, like swift horses bolting with a chariot. Have I not drunk Soma?

4. This hymn has come to me as a lowing cow comes to her darling calf. Have I not drunk Soma?

7. The two world halves[95] aren't a patch against a single wing of mine. Have I not drunk Soma?

8. In my grandeur have I surpassed Heaven and the spacious Earth! Have I not drunk Soma?

9. Yes! I will place the Earth here, or perhaps there. Have I not drunk Soma?

10. I will thrash the Earth soundly, here or perhaps there. Have I not drunk Soma?

11. One of my wings is in the Sky; I have trailed the other below. Have I not drunk Soma?

---

[95]Sky and Earth.

12. I am greater than the greatest, I'm lifted into the firmament. Have I not drunk Soma?

13. I seek the worshipper's abode; I am oblation bearer to the Gods. Have I not drunk Soma?

The preceding hymn shows that the Rigvedic poets had a robust sense of humour. There is a delightful hymn, VII. 103, dedicated to the frogs, who begin singing during rains as if imitating the Rigvedic poets singing their hymns. The Rigvedic people loved the rains, so did the frogs. The rishis chanted their hymns, expressing their joy of living in their new-found monsoonal habitat, so did the frogs who started singing joyfully in chorus when it rained.

Ralph Griffith quotes Max Müller's comment on this hymn: 'The hymn ... which is called a panegyric of the frogs, is clearly a satire on the priests; and it is curious to observe that the same animal should have been chosen by the Vedic satirists to represent the priest, which by the earliest satirist of Greece, Aristophanes, was selected as representative of the Homeric heroes.' Bhagwati Devi Sharma gives philological meaning of the Sanskrit word '*mandook*' for a frog, and says that the word's roots are *mund* (bathing), *mud* (joy), *maad (masti)*—one who remains happy being in water and enjoys it.

VII. 103. The Frogs

1. After lying still for a year, the Brahmins who were keeping a vow of silence, and the frogs,[96] have raised their voice that Parjanya has inspired.

2. The frogs had dried out like a leather bag, lying in a pool, when the heavenly showers came upon them. The frogs began their music then, joined in chorus, like the lowing of the cows with calves.

3. As soon as the season of rains begins, and it rains upon them who are longing and thirsting for it, one frog approaches another and calls to him, 'Akhkhala'[97] as a son approaches his father.

[96]After hibernation.

[97]Wendy Doniger quotes the sacred chant in *The Frogs of Aristophanes:*

4. One frog greets the other as they revel in the waters that bursts forth; the frogs leap under the falling rain, the speckled frog mingling his voice with the green frog.

5. When one of them repeats the speech of the other, as a pupil that of the teacher, they chant with fine voices, their limbs revived after being parched.

6. One lows like a cow, one bleats like a goat; one is speckled, one is green. They bear one common name (frog), but differ in form and modulate their voices diversely.

7. Like Brahmins at the night-long yajna, who chant around the full bowl of Soma, so frogs around a pool celebrate the rainy day.

8. The frogs raise their voices like Brahmins with Soma while performing year-long yajna, and come out heated like the Adharvyu[98] coming out sweating after sitting by cauldrons. None remain hidden.

9. The frogs, like the ritual-dedicated men, remain in the year-long discipline of *Rta*. When the season of rains has come after a year, the hot fires (of the yajna) come to an end.

10. O speckled and green frogs, who bleat and low like goats and cows, give us riches. Let the frogs give us hundreds of cows and lengthen our lives in this most fertilizing season.

Five hymns of a poet named Kavash, son of Iloosh, who had served as a purohita of King Kurushravana, find place in the Rig Veda. One of these, X. 34, the 'Gamester's Lament' is the most famous. It's dedicated to the nuts of a tree called Vibhidaka (*Terminalia bellerica*). These nuts were used as dice. The poet declares, in the opening verse of the hymn, that 'the cheering Vibhitaka has brought me joy, like the draughts of Soma from mount Mujavant.'

Incidentally, Dr A.D. Pusalkar points out that in Mohenjo-daro 'dicing was a common pastime as indicated by the large number of dice unearthed. Both cubical and tabular specimens are found,

'Brekkekkekkek koax koax koax'.
[98]Head Priest.

the latter being more common.'[99] Let me also add that the root cause of the battle of the Mahabharata was Yudhishthir's addiction for playing dice!

Hymn X. 34. Gamester's Lament

1. The dangling nuts, born where the wind blows the lofty tree,
   Delight me with their rolling on the board.
   The cheering Vibhitaka has brought me joy,
   Like a draught of Soma from mount Mujavant.
2. She did not scold me, or lose her temper,
   She was kind to my friends and me.
   Because of a losing throw of the dice
   I have driven away my devoted wife.
3. Her mother hates me; my wife repels me
   A man in trouble finds no one to pity him.
   They say, 'I find a gambler as useless
   As an old horse that some one wants to sell'.
4. Other men fondle the gamester's wife, his
   Possessions coveted by the plundering dice.
   His father, mother, brothers say: 'We don't
   Know him, tie him up and take him away.'
5. I am left behind by my friends as they depart.
   But when the brown dice raise their voice,
   I run at once to the rendezvous with them,
   Like a woman to her lover.
6. The gambler goes to the meeting-hall, asking
   Himself 'Will I win?', trembling with hope.
   But the dice run counter to his hopes,
   Giving his opponents the winning throws.
7. The dice goad like hooks and prick like whips,
   Coated with honey, they enslave, deceive and torment;
   They give and take it back again.
   They have an irresistible power over the gambler.
9. Down the dice roll, and up they spring,
   Unarmed, they master the man with arms.

[99]Majumdar, R.C. (ed.), *The Vedic Age*, Bharatiya Vidya Bhavan, 1996, p. 179.

Like unearthly coals strewn over the gaming board,
Though cold to touch, they burn out the heart.
10. The deserted wife of the gambler grieves,
The mother grieves for her son who wanders
Homeless, in debt, in fear, in need of riches;
He goes by night to the other men's home.
11. It torments the gambler to see his wife
The woman of other men, in their homes.
In the morning he yokes the brown steeds,
In the evening he sinks by the fire, an outcast.
12. This is what the noble Savitr shows me:
'Play no longer with the dice; till your field!
Enjoy your gain, and deem that wealth sufficient.
There are your cattle, and there is your wife, O gambler!

HYMNS ON VISHNU

In post-Vedic times, Indra faded out from the religious firmament of Hinduism and Vishnu and Shiva emerged as the most prominent deities. This was surprising as in the Rig Veda there were only three hymns dedicated to Vishnu. The following brief hymn, I. 154, composed by Rishi Dirghatama Auchathya is probably the basis of the later myth of Vishnu's Vamana (Dwarf) avatar.

Hymn I. 154. Three Strides of Vishnu

1. Let me now sing the mighty deeds of Vishnu, who has measured apart the realms of the Earth, who propped up the highest dwelling-place (Heaven), striding forth three times.

2. They praise Vishnu for his heroic deeds who dwells in the mountains like a ferocious wild beast, in whose three wide strides all creatures reside.

3. Let this song of inspiration go forth to Vishnu, the wide-striding Bull living in the mountains, who alone, with but three steps measured apart this vast, far-reaching earth.

4. His three footprints were inexhaustibly filled with honeyed

sweetness. Alone, He supports threefold the Earth and the Sky and all creatures.

5. May I attain His well-loved mansion where men devoted to the Gods rejoice. For there one draws close to the wide-striding Vishnu; there, in His highest footstep, is the fountain of honey.

6. We wish to reach your dwelling places, O Lord Vishnu, where there are untiring, many-horned cattle. For there shines upon us the wide-stepping Bull's sublimest mansion!

God Shiva as such is not known to Rig Veda; but there is Rudra, father of the Maruts. Though in the Rig Veda, Rudra and Vishnu are not as important as Indra, in later mythology Rudra emerges as Shiva, and is a part of the 'Trinity' of Brahma, Vishnu and Mahesh (Shiva). While Brahma and Vishnu are Rigvedic gods, Shiva resembles the ithyphallic fertility god of the Harappan culture who was called 'Proto-Shiva' by Sir John Marshall.

The Rigvedic Rudra has braided hair and a brown complexion. He wears golden ornaments and a glorious necklace (*nishka*). He is the father of the Maruts whom he brought forth from the shining udder of the cow Prishni. He is fierce like a terrible beast and is called a Bull, a ruddy boar of Heaven. Although Rudra is a luminal figure in the Rig Veda, exalted and mighty, yet is not invited to regular Vedic sacrifices.

He is venerable and auspicious ('*shiva*') but in many passages he is also looked upon as malevolent. As the embodiment of wildness, unpredictable danger and wrath, he is addressed more with dread and with the hope of keeping him at bay. Rudra is a harbinger of disease as well as a healer. The cult of the Goddess Kali in later Hinduism is probably his legacy. There is a hymn to pacify and placate him, composed by Rishi Gritsmada Angiras.

Hymn II. 33. Rudra, Father of the Maruts

1. O Father of the Maruts, send your blessings to us. Do not cut us off from the sight of the Sun. May you be gracious to spare our horses. O Rudra, let us be born again through our children.

3. O Rudra, armed with the thunderbolt, most glorious and

strongest of all born are you. Carry us safely to the farther shore of anguish; ward off all attacks on us and injury.

4. We would not wish to anger you, O Rudra the Bull, by invoking you together with another God. Protect our people with your purifying powers; of all healers you are the best.

5. May I with laudatory hymns win Rudra's favour, who is worshipped with gifts and invocations. Never may the gracious, tawny god suspect us and subject us to his anger.

6. The Bull with the Maruts inspired me with his vital energy when I was in need of help. I long to win the kindness of God Rudra, as I would like to reach the shade unharmed in the heat of the Sun.

8. To him, the strong, tawny, fair-complexioned Rudra, I utter this hymn of praise. I bow low in homage to the Radiant One. We sing praise of the dreaded name of Rudra.

10. Rightly you carry the arrows and bow, O Rudra; rightly you wear the precious golden necklace shaped with many forms and colours; rightly you extend this terrible power over everything. There is nothing more powerful than you, O mighty Rudra!

12. As a son bows to his father, so I bow to you, O Rudra! I sing to the giver of plenty, the true Lord!

13. Your healing powers, O Maruts, so pure, so strengthening, so comforting, which our father Manu chose. O mighty Maruts, I desire these, and happiness and health from God Rudra.

14. Let Rudra's dreadful missile turn aside and spare us; may the wrath of the impetuous God avoid us. Turn your strong bow from our generous patrons, O bounteous God! Have mercy on our children and grand-children.

There is a short hymn addressed to Soma-Rudra, VI. 74. Composed by Bharadwaj Brihaspatya, grand son of Bharadwaj Angiras, who was also said to be the priest of King Divodas.

Hymn VI. 74. Soma-Rudra

1. Hold fast your God-like sway, O Soma-Rudra, let these our sacrifices quickly reach you; placing in every house your seven

great treasures, bring blessings to our quadrupeds and bipeds.

2. O Soma and Rudra, chase in every quarter the sickness that has visited our dwelling. Drive *Nir-riti* (diety of decay and death; from the meaning 'devoid of rta' or disorder) away into the distance, give us riches; May we live happily with ample food!

3. Provide, O Soma-Rudra, all needful medicines for our bodies to heal and cure us. Set us free and drive away the sins we have committed; unbound us.

4. Armed with keen shafts and weapons, O Soma-Rudra, be gracious unto us. Release us from the noose of Varuna; keep us free from sorrow in your tender and loving kindness.

Speculation on the origins of the cosmos—how the creation of the universe took place—forms the subject matter of several hymns in the Rig Veda. Before we go to them let us visit Hymn X. 130, which is said to have been composed by a son of Prajapati named *Yagya*, as mentioned in Harivansha Purana. Clearly, it's a pseudonym. The hymn is based on the celebrated 'Purusha Sookta', which we will see shortly.

Hymn X. 130. The Creation of the Sacrifice

1. The sacrifice that is spread out with threads on all sides, drawn tight with a hundred and one divine acts, is woven by the heavenly Fathers as they come near: 'Weave forward, weave backward' they say, as they sit by the loom that is stretched tight.

2. The Man (*Purusha*) stretches the warp and draws the weft; the Man (*Purusha)* has spread it out upon the dome of the Sky. These are the pegs that are fastened in place; the Gods made the melodies into the shuttles for weaving.

3. What was the original model, and what was the copy, what was the connection between them? What was the butter, what the enclosed wood? What was the metre, what the invocation and the chant, when all the gods sacrificed to the gods?

4. The Gayatri metre was the yoke-mate of Agni; Savita joined with the Ushni metre, and with Anushtubh metre was Soma, that reverberates with the chants. The Brihati metre resonated in the

voice of Brihaspati.

5. The Viraj[100] metre was the privilege of Mitra and Varuna; the Trishtubh metre was part of the day of Indra. The Jagati entered into all the Gods. That was the model for human sages.

6. That was the model for our Fathers, when the primeval sacrifice was born. With the eye that is the mind, in my thought I see those who were the first to offer this sacrifice.

7. The rituals harmonized with the chants and the metres; the seven divine sages harmonized with the original model. When the wise men looked back along the path of those who went before, they took up the reins like charioteers.

Another mysterious hymn, X. 129, which is also called the Creation Hymn, is dedicated to the supreme un-manifested Soul of the universe, and is ascribed to Prajapati Parmeshti. The rishi who composed it remains unknown.

Hymn X. 129. Creation Hymn (Nasadiya)

1. There was neither non-existence nor existence then; there was neither the realm of space nor the sky which is beyond. What stirred? Where? In whose protection? Was there water bottomlessly deep?

2. There was neither death nor immortality then. There was no distinguishing sign of night or day. That One breathed, windless, by its own impulse. Other than that, there was nothing beyond.

3. Darkness was hidden by darkness in the beginning; all around was water, flowing bottomlessly deep. That One, the indestructible life-force covered with emptiness arose through the power of '*tapa*'.

4. *Kama*[101] possessed that One in the beginning; the seed was produced and planted. The Poets, seeking in their heart, found the bond of existence in non-existence.

5. The heat rays of desire bound the seed-placers and

[100]Viraj, the female cosmic principle, is here merely a metre.
[101]Power of procreation.

receivers—were they below, were they above? There was impulse below; there was giving forth above.

6. Who really knows? Who will here proclaim it? Whence was *Shristi* (the Universe) created? The gods came afterwards, with the creation of this universe? Who then knows whence it has arisen?

7. Whence had this creation arisen? Perhaps it formed itself, or perhaps it did not—the One who looks down on it, in the highest heaven, only He knows, or perhaps He does not know.

Whoever composed this hymn, it gives words to the ineffable!

Another charming Hymn on Creation, I. 160, is dedicated jointly to Dhyava–Prithvi (Sky and Earth), parents of the Sun. It is composed by Rishi Dirghatama Auchathya. I have gone by Wendy Doniger's translation.

Hymn I. 160. Sky and Earth

1. Sky and Earth, these two who bestow prosperity on all, are upholders of Rta and bear the Poet of the Space (the Sun). Between the two Goddesses, the two noble bowls, the fulgent God Sun travels, following the laws of nature.

2. Wide and capacious, strong and inexhaustible, the Sky and Earth, protect the universe. The two world-halves are two bold and wonderful damsels[102] whom their father[103] dresses in shapes and colours.

3. The son of these parents,[104] their clever charioteer with the power to make things clear, purifies the universe by magic.[105] From the dappled milk-cow and the bull with spilling seed, every day he milks the milk that is his seed.

4. Most skillful of the skillful gods, he[106] gave birth to the two world-halves which bring prosperity to all. He measured the

[102]These two are the two goddesses mentioned in the previous verse.
[103]The Creator—Vishwakarma.
[104]The Sun, child of Sky and Earth.
[105]The Sun's magic dispels darkness, thus purifying and clarifying world.
[106]The Creator.

two realms of space[107] with his power of inspiration and fixed them in place with un-decaying pillars.

5. Sky and Earth, you mighty pair, whose praises we have sung, grant us great fame and sovereignty, by which we may extend our rule over the people for ever. Bestow us with enormous power.

Two other hymns on creation, joined together, are dedicated to God Vishvakarma, the World Creator, who is imagined as a sculptor, a smith, a carpenter and who is assisted by seven celestial sages. The hymns are ascribed to Vishvakarma Bhauvan, which appears to be a pseudonym. However, in Aitereya Brhamana, 8. 21, there is a story that Rishi Kashyap had anointed Vishvakarma Bhauvan, who had conquered the Earth and had organized Ashvamedha Yajna! It appears to be a fanciful tale woven by Rishi Kashyap's descendants!

Hymn X. 81. Vishvakarma (The World Creator)

1. The sage, our father, who took his place as priest of oblation, seeking riches through prayer, entered into those who were to come later, and concealed those who went before.

2. What was the base, what was the raw matter, and how was it done, when Vishvakarma, casting his eye on all sides, created the Sky and Earth and revealed the Sky in its glory?

3. With his eyes, mouths, arms, feet on all sides, God Vishvakarma created the Sky and Earth, fanning them with his arms.

4. From what wood, taken from what tree, did he carve the Sky and Earth? You deep thinkers, ask yourselves in your own hearts, what was the base he stood on when He set up the world?

5. Those forms of yours that are highest, those that are lowest, and those that are in the middle, O Vishvakarma, help your friends to recognize them as they offer oblation. You who follow your own laws, had sacrificed your own body, making it grow great.

6. O Vishvakarma, grown great through oblation, you sacrificed

[107]Between Sky and Earth.

to the Sky and Earth yourself. Let other men go astray, let us have a rich and generous patron.

7. Vishvakarma, the Lord of sacred speech, *Vak*, swift as thought—we will call to him today to help us in the contest. Let Him, who is the maker of good things and is gentle to everyone, rejoice in our invocations and help us.

Hymn X. 82. Vishvakarma (The World Creator)

1. The Father of Eye (the Sun), who is wise in his heart, created these two worlds that bend low as ghrita.[108] As soon as their ends had been made fast in the east, at that moment the Sky and Earth moved far apart.

2. Vishvakarma is vast in mind and vast in strength. He is the one who created it all, who set the world in order, and who is the highest. The Seven Sages (*Sapt Rishis*), the first sacrificers, let them rejoice where they dwell.

3. Our Father, who created and set in order, and knows all worlds, who alone gave names to the Gods. He is the one to whom all creatures come for knowledge.

4. To him the ancient sages together sacrificed riches, who created it all when the realm of light was still immersed in the realm without light.

5. That which is beyond the Sky and beyond this Earth, beyond the Gods and the Asuras—what was that first embryo that the waters received, where all the Gods saw it?

6. He was the One from whom the waters received the first embryo, when all the gods came together. On the navel of the Unborn was set the One on whom all creatures rested.

7. You cannot find Him who created these creatures; the veil of ignorance blinds you. Those who recite hymns are glutted with the pleasures of life; they wander about wrapped in mist and stammering nonsense.

[108] Ghrita is symbolic of primeval creative matter—the seed of the Creator—as well as the sacrificial oblation. The Creator churns the chaos with ghrita.

Hymn X. 121 is a mysterious hymn, dedicated to *Ka?,* the Unknown God. Ralph Griffith takes 'Ka' to mean '*quis*', 'Who?', that is, the Unknown God, meaning, Prajapati. Wendy Doniger says that Max Müller dubbed it '*Deus Ignotus*'. She adds that the creator in this hymn is called *Hiranyagarbha*, (a truly pregnant term) 'Golden Embryo'. Bhagwati Devi Sharma says Hiranyagarbha means '*Avinashi Jyoti*', Eternal Light!

The Hymn has a refrain at the end of every verse: 'Who is the God whom we should worship with this oblation?'

Hymn X. 121.'Ka?'—The Unknown God—The Golden Embryo

1. In the beginning the Golden Embryo arose. Once he was born, he was the one Lord of Creation. He held in place the Earth and the Sky. Who is the God whom we should worship with this oblation?

2. He who gives life, who gives strength, whose command all the gods obey. His shadow is immortality—and death. Who is the God whom we should worship with this oblation?

3. He who by his greatness became the one king of the world that breathes and blinks, who rules over his two-footed and four-footed creatures. Who is the God whom we should worship with this oblation?

4. He who through his power owns these snowy mountains and the ocean, they say, together with the River Rasa.[109] He has the quarters of the Sky as his two arms. Who is the God whom we should worship with this oblation?

5. He by whom the awesome Sky and the Earth were made firm, by whom the dome of the Sky was propped up, and the Sun, who measured the middle realm of space. Who is the God whom we should worship with this oblation?

6. He to whom the two opposed masses looked with trembling in their hearts; supported by His help, on whom the rising Sun shines down. Who is the God whom we should worship with this oblation?

7. When the high waters came, pregnant with the embryo that

[109]River Rasa is a mythical stream that flows round the atmosphere and the earth.

is everything, bringing forth fire, He arose from that as the life breath of the Gods. Who is the God whom we should worship with this oblation?

8. He who in his greatness looked over the waters, which were pregnant with Daksha,[110] bringing forth the sacrifice.' He was the one God among all the gods! Who is the God whom we should worship with this oblation?

9. Let him not harm us, He who fathered the Earth and created the Sky, whose laws are true, who created the high, shining waters! Who is the God whom we should worship with this oblation?

10. O Prajapati, Lord of progeny, no one but you embrace all those creatures. Grant us the desires for which we offer you oblation. Let us be lords of the riches!

Hymn X. 90, Purusha Sookta, is the most famous Creation Hymn which expounds that the world was created when the Gods dismembered the cosmic giant, *Purusha*, the primeval male, and held a cosmic sacrifice, offering His limbs in oblation. It is a late hymn. Wendy Doniger reveals that the dismemberment of the Norse giant Ymir or Hymir is in the same genre.

It is also the solitary hymn in the Rig Veda, in which the concept of caste, of the four varnas, has been introduced, which cast the composite Aryan society into four graded divisions.

Hymn X. 90. Purusha Sookta

1. A thousand[111] heads had Purusha, a thousand eyes, a thousand feet. He pervaded the Earth on all sides and extended beyond by ten fingers.

2. This Purusha is all that is visible, whatever has been and whatever is to be. He is the ruler of Immortality, when he grows beyond everything through food.[112]

3. Such is his greatness, and the Purusha is yet far greater than

[110]Daksha represents the male principle and was identified with Prajapati.
[111]Meaning innumerable.
[112]Through sacrificial offerings.

this. All earthly creatures are a quarter of him; his three quarters are what is immortal in Heaven.

4. With three quarters the Purusha rose upwards; one quarter of him still remains here. From this quarter he spread out in all directions, into that which eats and that which does not eat.

5. From him *Viraj*[113] was born, and from Viraj came the Purusha. When He was born, He ranged beyond the Earth, in its front and behind.

6. When the Gods prepared the sacrifice with Purusha as the offering

7. In this yajna held at the beginning of time, the Gods anointed the Purusha upon the sacred grass. With Him the Gods, the *Sadhyas*[114] and the sages held the sacrifice.

8. From this vast sacrifice stretched out on the Earth, the dripping fat was collected. From it were created animals that live in the air, in the forest, and in the villages.

9. From that sacrifice were born the Rig-Vedic verses and metres, Saman chants and the Yajur formulae.

10. Horses were born from it, and other cattle that have two rows of teeth; cows were born from it, and from it the goats and sheep were born.

11. When they divided Purusha, into how many parts did they apportion him? What do they call his mouth, his two arms and thighs and feet?

12. The Brahmin was his mouth; both his arms were made into Rajanya.[115] His thighs became the Vaishya[116]and from his feet the Shudra[117] were born.

13. The Moon was born from his mind; from his eyes the Sun was born. Indra and Agni came from his mouth and from

---

[113]The active female creative principle, or the female counterpart of Purusha as Aditi of Daksha in X. 72, 4, 5. Viraj is said to have come in the form of an egg from Adi-Purusha, who then entered into this egg which he animates as its vital soul or divine principle. Viraj was later replaced by *Prakriti*, the mate of Purusha in Sankhya Philosophy.

[114]Sadhyas = those who are yet to be fulfilled—the demi-gods or saints.

[115]Rajanya = The ruling or the military class.

[116]Vaishya = The trader and agriculturist class.

[117]Shudra = Slaves and labourers.

his vital breath the Wind was born.

14. From his naval the middle realms of the space arose; from his head the Sky evolved. From his feet came the Earth and the quarters of the Sky from his ear. Thus, they set the worlds in order.

15. There were seven enclosing sticks for him, and thrice seven fuel sticks, when the Gods, spreading the sacrifice, bound Purusha as the sacrificial victim.

16. The Gods sacrificed Purusha in this sacrifice; from it evolved the ritual laws, the yajna dharma. They reached the dome of the Sky where they dwelt with the Sadhyas.

∽

A careful reading of this seminal hymn shows that the Verses 11 and 12 are fake and superfluous and are later additions. They were probably inserted at the time when the hymns were committed to writing. The hymn is complete without these two spurious verses. In fact these two fake verses contradict verses 13 and 14, which proclaim that Indra and Agni came from his mouth (not the Brahmin) and from his feet came the Earth (not the Shudra).

Historically, the Rigvedic people were a caste-less society. In the prevalent social order, the Rajanya were supreme. However, in Verse 12, the Brahmins have usurped for themselves a place even higher than the Rajanya to whom they were beholden, as the Rajanya mainly sponsored the yajna sacrifices. In this seminal hymn, they fraudulently inserted these two verses which divided the Rigvedic society into four varnas, divisions.

The hymn, as it exists now, suffers from blatant contradictions as pointed out above. The verse succeeding these sprurious additions holds that Indra and Agni came from his mouth, *not Brahmins*; and 'From his feet came the Earth', *not the Shudras*! However, the saving grace is that the redactor did not dare to efface any part of the original hymn.

Most probably this preposterous interpolation was inserted when the Rig Veda was committed to writing and compiled into mandalas. The fact remains that the interpolation is a hoax and was a deliberate mischief on the part of the Brahmins.

~

Writing about the condition of the people as described in the early Vedas, A.K. Majumdar[118] says: 'The Aryans knew the use of various metals such as gold, silver or iron. There were blacksmiths, potters, carpenters, sawyers, barbers, sailors, physicians, priests, goldsmiths, and weavers.

There were libations of Soma juice, invocation of gods with earnest, sincere and simple prayers. Animals were killed in sacrifice. The Aryans partook of the offered meat.'

Significantly, he adds that 'the Aryans of Central Asia knew no caste. The Indo-Aryans also in the first two centuries of their Indian life knew it not. The only Rig-Vedic hymn that distinctly refers to the four classes is X, 90.12 which is in fact a much later composition ... Certain it is that the caste system as we have it now, or as appears from the Code of Manu did not exist in the Vedic age.'

Professor Max Müller too holds: 'If then, with all the documents before us, we ask the question, does caste, as we find in Manu and at the present day, form part of the most ancient religious teaching of the Vedas? We can answer with a decided "No".'[119]

However, A.L. Basham observes: 'When the Aryans entered India there was already a class distinction in their tribal structure. Even in the earliest hymns we read of the *Kshatra*, the nobility, and the *vish*, the ordinary gentleman, and the records of several other early Indo-European peoples suggest that a tribal aristocracy was a feature of Indo-European society even before the tribes migrated from their original home.

As they settled among the darker aboriginals, the Aryans seem to have laid greater stress than before on purity of blood, and class divisions widened, to exclude those Dasas who had found a place in the fringes of Aryan society, and those Aryans who had intermarried with the Dasas and adopted their ways. Both these groups sank in the social scale.'

---

[118]Majumdar A.K., *Hindu History,* Rupa Publications, New Delhi, 2008.
[119]Müller, Freidrich Max, *Chips from a German Workshop*, Vol. II, 1867, p. 307.

I was reading Mahatma Gandhi's *India of My Dreams*—a collection of his writings. In an article titled 'The Gospel of Bread Labour' Gandhiji wrote:

> I have felt for years, that there must be something radically wrong, where scavenging has been made the concern of a separate class in society. We have no historical record of the man who first assigned the lowest status to this essential sanitary service. Whoever he was, he by no means did us a good.[120]

Generally, there are class divisions in all civilized societies, but the rigid and abominable caste system introduced in this hymn does not exist anywhere. The 'untouchables' are only found in India! Besides, a fifth caste of *Ati-Shudra* or *Chandala* had also cropped up.

∽

Wendy Doniger finds bias against women in the Rig Veda. 'The *Rigveda'*, she says, 'is a book by men about male concerns in a world dominated by men; one of these concerns is women, who appear throughout the hymns as objects, though seldom as subjects.'[121] In my opinion that's rather unfair; there are several goddesses like Aditi, Yami and Urvashi, who appear as subjects. Besides, there are wives of gods like Indrani, and of rishis like Lopa Mudra, who speak frankly about sexuality.

There is a delightful dialogue hymn dedicated to both Yama, son of Vivasvan (the Sun) and his twin sister Yami, in which Yami initiates the dialogue. Yama and Yami, son and daughter of Vivasvan, who were considered the first 'human' (mortal) pair, are the deities of the hymn.

Wendy Doniger suggests that in the Avestan mythology, the primeval incest of the twins remains an important episode in the procreation of the human race, whereas in India, Yama rejects the erotic solicitations of his twin-sister Yami in the Rig Veda.

---

[120]Gandhi, M.K., 'The Gospel of Bread Labour', *India of My Dreams*, Navajivan Publishing House, Ahmedabad, p. 57.
[121]Doniger, Wendy, *The Rigveda*, Penguin Books, London, 1981, p. 242.

Hymn X. 10. Yama and Yami

1. [Yami] Would that I might draw you into intimate friendship, my mate,[122] now that our father has gone far across the ocean. A man of foresight should receive a grandson from the father, thinking of what lies ahead on earth.

2. [Yama] Your *'sakha'* does not desire such relationship with one of his own kin-ship. We are progeny of the mighty Asura,[123] who sees far and wide.

3. [Yami] The immortals desire this, that offspring should be left by you—the first mortal. Let your mind unite with my mind and you enter my body as a husband.

4. [Yama] Shall we do now what we have never done before? Shall we who spoke truth out loud, now whisper falsehood (*anrita*)?[124] Vivasvan and the Dame of Waters—such is our bond, our lofty heritage.

5. [Yami] Even in the womb, God Tvashtra, the creator and impeller, shaper of all forms, made us consorts. No one disobeys his commands; Earth and Sky are our witnesses for this.

6. [Yama] Who was witness of that first day? Who has seen it? Who can proclaim it here? Great is the law of Varuna and Mitra; what you say, wanton woman, violates the moral order.

7. [Yami] Desire for you, O Yama, has come upon me, the desire to lie with you upon the same bed, as a wife to her husband. Let us roll about together like the wheels of a chariot!

8. [Yama] These spies of the Gods, who wander around us do not blink their eyes. Wanton woman, go away fast to another man, not cling to me. Roll about with him like the wheels of a chariot.

9. [Yami] I would deceive the eye of the Sun for the instant of the blink of an eye. We kindred pair would commingle like the Heaven and Earth. Let Yami behave toward Yama as if she were not his sister.

10. [Yama] Later ages may come, indeed, when blood relatives

---

[122]Yami uses the word 'sakha' meaning 'friend'.

[123]The Rigvedic people were kinsmen of the Avestans of Iran from whom they had separated. The gods in Avesta are called Asura.

[124]The word 'anrita' has been used—something that violates the moral order!

would act as if they were not related. Make a pillow of your arm for some bull of man. Seek another husband, lovely lady, not me.

11. [Yami] What good is a brother, when the sister has no protector? What good is a sister when the brother dies sonless—causing *nir-riti?*[125] Overcome with desire, I whisper this again and again: mingle your body with my body.

12. [Yama] Never will I mingle my body with your body. They call a man who unites with his sister a sinner. Arrange your lustful pleasures with some other man, not with me, lovely lady. Your brother does not want this.

13. [Yami] Alas! What a weakling you are, Yama! There is no trace of heart or spirit in you. Some other woman will surely embrace you like a girth embracing a harnessed stallion or a creeper clinging a tree.

14. [Yama] You too, Yami, find another man and he will embrace and entwine you like a tree. Win his heart and let him win yours. Join with him in blessed harmony.

~

There is another engaging hymn consisting of a dialogue between the earthly lover Pururava, the son of Ida, and his heavenly mistress, the water-nymph Urvashi. The story is narrated in Shatapath Brhamana. Urvashi loved him and married him on condition that he might make love to her three times a day, but never against her will. Besides, she should never see him naked.

She lived with him for four years and became pregnant. Then the Gandharvas said to one another: 'This Urvashi has been living too long among men! We must find a way to get her back!'

One fateful night, as they slept, the Gandharvas descended from the sky. Urvashi kept an ewe with two lambs tied to her bed. The Gandharvas carried off the two lambs tied to her bed, and she cried out, 'They are taking away my babies as if there is no man here!' Pururava sprang out of the bed. At that moment the Gandharvas produced a flash of lightning and she saw him naked. Instantly she vanished.

---

[125]Nir-riti (Sanskrit)—chaos, destruction.

Grieved by her departure, Pururava wandered all over Kurukshetra where he lived. There was a lake full of lotus flowers called Anyatahplaksha. While he was walking on its banks, he saw nymphs swimming in it in the form of swans. Urvashi was among them; she noticed him and said: 'That's the man with whom I lived! Let's show ourselves to him.' The nymphs said: 'Very well'. They appeared to him in their true form. Their dialogue at the lotus lake is enshrined in the following hymn:

Hymn X. 95. Pururava and Urvashi

1. [Puruarva] O my wife, turn your heart and mind to me. Stay here, you fierce-souled woman, and let us talk. If we do not speak out these thoughts of ours, it will bring me no comfort, even until the most distant day.
2. [Urvashi] What use to me are these words of yours? I have left you, like the rays of dawn. Go back to your dwelling, Pururavas, I am hard to catch and hold, like the wind.
3. [Pururava] Or like an arrow shot from the quiver, or like a racehorse winning cattle. The Gandharvas made the lightning flash to trick us.
4. You brought me your surpassing wealth and came to my dwelling whenever I craved for you, accepting my embraces day and night.
5. [Urvashi] Indeed, thrice in a day I accepted your fond caresses; you filled me even when I had no desire. To your desires I yielded as you were the king of my body.
6. [Pururava] The Apsaras, Sujurni, Shreni, Sumanaapi, Hrideychakrashurn, Granthini, Charanyu—they have all slipped away like the red colours of Dawn.
7. [Urvashi] When he (our son) was born, the Apsaras encircled him and nurtured him with milk. And then, Pururavas, the Gods empowered you for battle, to destroy the Dashyus.
8. [Pururava] When I, a mortal man, courted you, the celestial nymph who had laid aside her raiment and shied away like a frightened gazelle.
9. [Urvashi] When a mortal man, wooing the immortal nymphs, consorts with them, they show the beauty of their bodies like

swans and bite and nibble in love play.

10. [Pururava] You of the waters, flashed like lightning and brought me the pleasures of love. From you was born a noble manly son. Let Urvashi lengthen his life span by nurturing him.

11. [Urvashi] You have to give him protection, O Pururava. I had warned you I would leave you if I saw you naked. Why do you talk in vain?

12. [Pururava] Why will the son born of you seek his father? He will shed tears, sobbing, when he learns about his mother deserting him. Who would separate a man and wife of one heart, in whom the fire of love still blazes? But the Gandharvas tricked us and made the lightning flash.

13. [Urvashi] As for the son, I will answer: he will shed tears, crying, sobbing for mother's tender care. But I will send him away as he is yours. Go home, you will never have me now.

14. [Pururava] What if your lover should vanish today, never to return, go to farthest distance? Or if he should lie in the lap of Destruction, or the ferocious wolves eat him?

15. [Urvashi] Pururava, do not die; do not let the vicious wolves eat you. For there are no lasting friendships with women; they have the heart of jackals.

16. When I wandered among mortals and dwelt with you for four years, thrice each day I swallowed your ghrita, and even now I am sated with that.

17. [Pururava] I, your lover, O Urvashi, long to draw you to me, though you fly in the air and measure the middle realm of space. I ask you to return and reap the reward for a good deed. For fire consumes my heart.

18. [Urvashi] This is what we heavenly nymphs say to you, son of Ida. Since you are kinsman of death, your descendants will sacrifice to the Gods with the oblation. However, you shall taste the joy in Heaven.

There is a post-script in the *Shatapath Brahaman* to explain the cryptic end of last verse of the hymn—'but you shall taste the joy in Heaven':

Urvashi's heart melted for him, and she said: 'Come on the last evening of the year when your son was born, you shall lie for one night with me.'

Pururava came on the last night of the year, and there stood a golden palace. They told him to enter, and brought her to him.

She said: 'Tomorrow the Gandharvas will grant you a boon and you may ask a boon'. He said: 'You tell me what to ask.' She answered: 'Say, "Let me become one of you."'

In the morning the Gandharvas gave him a boon, and he asked: 'Let me become one of you.'

'There is no divine fire among men,' they said, 'so holy that a man becomes one of us by sacrificing with it.' So, the Gandharvas put divine fire in a pan, and said: 'By sacrificing with this you will become one of us.'

He took the divine fire with his son, and went homeward. On the way he left the fire in the forest and went to a village with the boy. When he came back the fire had vanished. In the place of the fire there was a peepal tree and in place of the pan there was a mimosa tree.[126] So, he again went back to the Gandharvas.

They said, 'For a year you must cook rice enough for four. You must make the upper firestick and the lower firestick of peepal wood, and the fire you get from them will be divine fire.'

He sacrificed with it for a year and became a Gandharva and joined with Urvashi.[127]

There is an entertaining hymn, I. 179, about the venerable Rishi Agastya and his wife Lopa Mudra. Agastya had taken a vow of self-abnegation. Lopa Mudra seeks to turn him away from asceticism and beget a child upon her. Rati, the consort of Kamadeva, god of love, is the deity of this hymn. It is ascribed to Rishi Agastya and his ascetic wife Lopa Mudra.

Hymn I. 179. Agastya and Lopa Mudra

---

[126] A flowering species like acacia.

[127] *Shatapath Brahamana*, XI, 5, 1.

1. [Lopa Mudra] For so many autumns past have I toiled, night and day, and each dawn has brought old age closer. Age impairs the beauty and glory of our bodies. Virile[128] men should go to their wives.

2. For even the men of the past, who acted according to *Rta* (Moral Order) and had enunciated eternal statutes, had broken off (found time) to have progeny. Women should unite with virile men.

3. [Agastya] Not in vain is all this asceticism which Gods encourage. But we two must strive together for progeny, and merging together as a couple prolong the race, by all means.

4. [Lopa Mudra] Desire has come upon me for the bull who roars and is held back. Desire is engulfing me from this side, that side, all sides.

[The poet] Lopa Mudra draws out the virile bull; she sucks dry the panting wise man!

5. [Agastya] By this Soma which I have drunk, in my innermost heart I say: Let Him forgive us if we have sinned, for a moral man is full of many desires.

6. Agastya, digging as with a spade, wishing for progeny and strength, succeeded despite his ascetic ways, for he was a powerful sage. He found fulfillment of his worldly hopes as also his godly aspirations.

To Sage Agastya has been ascribed a hymn, I. 185, on the theme of creation of Dhyava–Prithvi *(Dhyu-Loka and Bhoo-Loka)*, which has great philosophic depth. It has the refrain, '*Dhyava rakshtam Prithvi no abhvaat*', meaning 'O Sky and Earth, guard us from *adhvam*'. The mysterious word '*abhvam*,' says Wendy Doniger, designates 'a dark, bottomless, enormous and terrifying abyss.'

Hymn I. 185. Guard Us from the Monstrous Abyss

1. Which of these two, Heaven and Earth, came first, which later? How were they born, O poets, who really knows? These two by themselves support all existing things. The two halves,

[128]The word '*vrishan*' (Sanskrit) means 'shedding seed or rain'.

Heaven and Earth, like day and night, roll past each other like two wheels.

2. These two who have no feet, they do not seem to move, but uphold a teeming offspring that have feet and are moving, like a natural son in the parents' lap. O Heaven and Earth, guard us from the monstrous abyss.

3. I call upon Aditi's unrivalled bounty, celestial and awe-inspiring, that dispels evil and repels assault and saves us from violent death. O Heaven and Earth, guard us from the monstrous abyss.

4. We pay homage to the two world-halves whose sons are the gods; these two gods, with revolving halves of the days, free us from suffering and help the helpless. O Heaven and Earth, guard us from the monstrous abyss.

5. The two young women, twin sisters, are lying in the lap of their parents, sharing common space and kissing the navel of the world. O Heaven and Earth, guard us from the monstrous abyss.

6. With truth I call upon the two wide and mighty Parents, who gave birth to the gods; these two who are lovely to behold, who have received immortality. O Heaven and Earth, guard us from the monstrous abyss.

7. With reverence I pray to the blessed Pair, who are wide, vast, and enormous, with distant boundaries: Having received immortality, bring us good fortune and dispel evil. O Heaven and Earth, guard us from the monstrous abyss.

8. Whatever wrong we have ever done to the Gods, or to an old friend or the master of the house, for all these let this hymn serve as an apology. O Heaven and Earth, guard us from the monstrous abyss.

9. Let both Heaven and Earth, who are benevolent to man, bless and preserve us. May there be plenty for the patron of the sacrifice! Let us be happy, O Gods, and be invigorated by the drink of ecstasy.

10. I have in my wisdom spoken the truth to Heaven and Earth: Be near us and protect us like father and mother from reproach and trouble.

11. Let my prayer be fulfilled, O *Dhyava-Prithvi*, Father and

Mother, let us be closest of the Gods. May we find the drink whose luscious drops give strength and ecstasy.

There is another mysterious hymn, X. 165, about an ominous bird who is a messenger of Nir-riti, the goddess of death and destruction. The ominous dove is required to be driven out of the house. The poet who composed it is named Kapot Nairrt. It is said that the poet had placed his foot on the sacrificial fire and had composed these verses in atonement of his sin. The deities of the hymn are the Vishvadevas, the poet prays to them to drive the ominous bird away.

Hymn X. 165. The Dove of Death

1. O Gods, a dove has come here, messenger of the deity Destruction, seeking someone. For that we will sing the hymn to perform expiation. Let all be well with our two-footed creatures and our four-footed creatures!

2. O Gods, Let the dove who has been sent here be kind to us; let the bird be harmless in our houses. Let the inspired Agni relish our oblations; let this winged-spear spare us.[129]

3. Do not let the winged-spear, who settles by the fireplace in the kitchen, attack us. Let all be well with our cows and with our men. O Gods, do not let the dove harm us.

4. Just as the screeches of an owl are in vain, may the settling of the dove by fire be in vain too. I bow before Yama, the God of Death, in supplication, who sent this dove as his messenger.

5. May the Dove be driven out; I am pushing her away by singing this verse. Let the Dove rejoice in the oblation I offer! I lead the cows around to wipe out all the dove's evil traces. Let it fly away, flying at its best, and leave us with the strength to live.

In common perception Rigvedic verses are regarded as Veda vakya and are considered holy and sacred by the Hindus. Very few

[129]The dove is likened to a missile flying on wings.

people had access to the Vedas as they were preserved orally and were kept secret by the families of the composer rishis. Even after they were reduced to writing, around the Buddha's time, literacy was minimal and their language had become archaic.

Sexuality is openly discussed in the Rigvedic hymns, without any taboo, which might be shocking to us now. However, we must remember that at the dawn of civilization, when the Vedic sages were composing their hymns, the sexual act had no trace of profanity about it; it was indeed considered sacred—a prime obligation of man, his raison d'être—reason for existence!

As an example, we may take the hymn X. 101, attributed to Rishi Budh Saumya, in which the sexual act is allegorically described as ploughing the earth and reaping the harvest, or drawing water from an inexhaustible natural fountain, which sounds bawdy to us. Bhagwati Devi Sharma has translated it in a garbled and misleading fashion. Indeed, translations done under the guidance of the Arya Samaj leader Dayanand Saraswati suffer from this malaise—they falsely try to cover the Vedic sexuality with a fig leaf.

Wendy Doniger, however, bravely sticks to the original. Hymn X.101, it becomes evident as one moves on, is an allegory of the sexual act.

Hymn X. 101. The Sacrificial Priests

1. Wake up with one mind, my friends, you who share the same nest (lodging), and kindle the fire. Along with Indra, I call Dadhikra, Agni and Goddess Dawn.

2. Make your thoughts harmonious; stretch them on the loom; make a ship whose oars will carry you across; keep the weapons ready and set them in place. O my friends, drive the ship forward.

3. Harness the plough and stretch the yoke on it; sow the seed in the prepared womb. And if the sound of our song is weighty enough, then the ripe crop will be ready for the scythes.

4. The inspired poets who know how to harness the plough and stretch the yokes on either side shall win favour among the Gods.

5. Make the buckets ready and fasten the straps well. We must draw water from the fountain that is easy to draw water

from, flowing freely, inexhaustible.

6. I draw water from the fountain whose buckets are in place with good straps, easy to draw water from, freely flowing and inexhaustible.

7. Keep the horses happy and you will win the stake. Make your chariot into the vehicle of good fortune. Drink at the fountain that has Soma-vats for buckets, a pressing-stone for its wheel, a consecrated goblet for its casing; this is the fountain where men drink.

8. Make an enclosure, for this is drink for men. Stitch the breast-plates thick and broad. Make iron forts that cannot be breached; make your goblet strong so that nothing will flow out.

9. O Gods, turn your attention toward our cause; let your divine thought be disposed toward the sacrifice. Let the great cow give us milk in thousands of streams of milk, as if she were walking in a meadow.

10. Pour the tawny one into the lap of wood; carve it with knives made of stone. Embrace it all around with ten girths; yoke the draft animal into the two shafts.

11. Now the draft animal is pressed tight between the two shafts, like a man in bed with two women. Stand the tree up in the wood; sink the well deep without digging.

12. The penis, men, take the penis, and move it and stick it in to win the prize. Inspire Indra, Nistigri's (Aditi's) son, to come here to help us and to come eagerly to drink Soma.

∽

The Vedic Aryans came on horseback or driving chariots drawn by horses. Wendy Doniger observes that the horse in the Rig Veda is at least three things at once: a real animal whose domestication enabled them to conquer the Indo-European world; a race-horse that ran in profane and sacred contests; and a precious sacrificial victim. Indeed, the horse looms large in the Rig Veda, and many Gods are called horses—Indra, Surya, Agni, Soma.

On important occasions like the coronation of a new king, the king's stallion was made the sacrificial victim, instead of a bull. It would facilitate comprehension of the nuances of the complex

Vedic ritual, 'yajna', if we read hymns dedicated to horse sacrifice. Hymn I. 163 was composed by Rishi Dirghatama Auchathya:

Hymn I. 163. Hymn to the Horse

1. You whinnied for the first time when you were born with the wings of an eagle and the forelegs of an antelope, coming from the celestial source through an ocean of air. That, Swift Runner, was your great and awesome birth.

2. Yama had gifted him and Trita had harnessed him; the Vasus fashioned him out of the Sun. Indra was the first to mount him and a Gandharva grasped his reins.

3. O Swift Runner, through a secret design, you are Yama, you are Aditya, you are Trita. You are like Soma and yet unlike him. You have bonds in Heaven with these three Gods.

4. They say you have three bonds in the sky, three in the waters, and three within the ocean. And to me you appear, O Swift Runner, like Varuna. It is said to be your highest birth.

5. These are the places where they groomed you; there are traces of your hooves where they put you down. Here I saw your lucky reins, which the Guardians of the Order keep safely.

6, From afar, I beheld thy form like a Bird that flew from below through to Heaven. I saw your head soaring upward on the paths pleasant to travel, unspoiled by dust.

7. Here I saw your glorious form at the altar, eager for nourishment where a man brings you and you swallow the plants, O greedy eater!

8. Following you, came the King's chariot, a martial procession and the charm of maidens. The Gods entrusted virile power to you.

9. Horns made of gold hath he, his feet shine like bronze. He is swift like thought, faster than Indra who was the first to mount the Swift Runner. The Gods have come to partake of the oblation.

10. The celestial coursers (mounts of Gods) fly in line like wild geese, their ends held back while the middle surges forward, revelling in their strength in the Sky's racecourse.

11. Your body flies, O Swift Runner; your spirit rushes like wind. Your mane spreads in many directions, flickers and jumps

about in the forests.

12. The racehorse has come to the slaughter, pondering with his heart turned to the Gods. The goat who is his kin is led before him;[130] behind him come the poets and the singers.

13. The Steed has come to the noblest mansion, to his Father Dhyava and Mother Prithvi. May he go to the Gods today and be most welcome, and then ask them for the things that the worshipper wishes for.

There is another hymn, I. 162, also composed by Rishi Dirghatama Auchathya, which is strikingly concrete in its details.

Hymn I. 162. Horse Sacrifice

1. Mitra, Varuna, Aryaman, Indra, the ruler of the Ribhus and the Maruts! Let them not fail to heed us when we proclaim in the assembly the heroic deeds of the racehorse who was born of the Gods.

2. When they lead the firmly grasped offering (the goat) in front of the horse, that is covered with cloths and heirlooms; the dappled goat goes bleating straight to the dear dwelling of Indra and Pushna.

3. This goat is led forward with the racehorse as the share of Pushna. When they lead forth the welcome offering with the charger, Tvashtra urges him on to great fame.

4. When, as the ritual law ordains the men circle three times, leading the horse that is to be the oblation on the path of the gods, the goat who is the share of Pushna goes first, announcing the sacrifice to the Gods.

5. The *Hota* (singer of the hymn), *Adhavyu* (officiating priest), the atoner, the fire-kindler, the holder of the pressing stones, the reciter—all fill your bellies with this well-prepared sacrifice.

6. The hewers of the sacrificial stake and those who carry it and those who gather together the things to cook the charger—let their approval encourage us.

[130]A goat is slaughtered before a horse sacrifice.

7. The horse with his smooth back went forth into the fields of the Gods, just when I composed my prayer. The inspired sages exult in him. We have made him a welcome companion at the banquet of the Gods.

8. The charger's rope and halter, the reins and bridle on his head, and even the grass that has been brought up to his mouth—let all that stay with the horse even among the Gods.

9. Whatever of the horse's flesh the fly has eaten, or whatever stays stuck to the stake or the axe, or to the hands or nails of the slaughterer—let all that go with the horse to the Gods.

10. Whatever food remains in his stomach, sending forth gas, or whatever smell there is from his raw flesh—let the slaughterers make that well done; let them cook the sacrificial animal until he is perfectly cooked.

11. Whatever runs off your body when it has been placed on the spit and roasted by the fire, let it not lie there on the earth or on the grass, but let it go to the Gods who long for it.

12. Those who see that the racehorse is cooked say: 'It smells good! Take it away!' and those who wait for the doling out of the flesh of the charger—let their approval encourage us.

13. The testing fork for the cauldron that cooks the flesh, the pots for pouring the broth, the cover of the bowls to keep it warm, the hooks, the dishes—let all these attend the horse.

14. The place where he walks, where he rests, where he rolls, and the fetters on the horse's feet, and what he had drunk and the fodder he has eaten—let all of that stay with him even among the Gods.

15. Let not the fire that reeks of smoke darken you, nor the red-hot cauldron split you into shreds. The Gods receive the horse who has been sacrificed—worshipped, consecrated and sanctified with the cry of '*Vashat*!'[131]

16. The cloth that they spread beneath the horse—the upper covering, and the golden trappings on him, the halter and the

[131]Vashat!—an exclamation uttered by the Hotri priest at the end of the sacrificial verse. On hearing this, the Adharvyu priest casts the oblation offered to the deity into the fire.

fetters on his feet—let these things that are his own bind the horse even among the Gods.

17. If someone riding you has struck you too hard with heel or whip when you shied, I make all these things well again with prayer, as they do with oblations ladle in sacrifices.

18. The axe cuts through the thirty-four ribs of the racehorse who is the companion of the Gods. Keep the limbs undamaged and place them in the proper pattern. Cut them apart, calling out piece by piece.

19. One is slaughterer of the horse of Tvashtra; two restrain the horse. This is the rule. As many of your limbs as I set out, according to the rules, so many balls I offer into the fire.

20. Let not your dear soul burn as you go away. Let not the axe do lasting harm to your body. Let no greedy, clumsy slaughterer hack in the wrong place and damage your limbs with his knife.

21. You do not really die through this, nor are you harmed. You go to Gods on paths pleasant to go on. The two bay stallions,[132] the two roan mares are now your chariot mates. The racehorse has been set in the yoke.

22. Let this racehorse bring us good cattle and good horses, male children and all-nourishing wealth. Let Aditi make us free from sin. Let the horse with our offerings achieve sovereign power for us.

[132]The two bay stallions are the horses belong to Indra, the two roan mares to the Maruts while the donkey is the mount of the Ashvins.

PART THREE

THE ATHARVAVEDIC CULTURE

Besides the Hindi translation of the Atharavaveda by Bhagwati Devi Sharma, I had bought *The Atharvaveda*, an English translation by Devi Chand, published by Munshiram Manoharlal of Delhi. In the meanwhile, my dear friend Dr Raghuvendra Tanwar, emeritus professor, Kurukshetra University, had sent me a copy of William Dwight Whitney's translation called *Atharva-Veda-Samhita*, from the Harvard Oriental Series, immensely enriching my resources. Indeed, it was Dr Raghuvendra Tanwar who had also sent me *The Vedic Age* published by Bhartiya Vidya Bhavan, from which I have been quoting extensively in the Rigvedic section; this book also covers the Atharva Veda. Besides these, Dr Raghuvendra Tanwar had also sent me books on the Bhagavada Gita, Manusmriti and on Kautilya.

In her introduction to the Atharva Veda, Bhagwati Devi quotes Sayana who had observed that while the Rig Veda is '*Par-lokik*' (other-wordly), the Atharva Veda is '*Aiha-lokik*' (this-worldly). She quotes the Nirukta to explain that the root '*tharva*' actually means '*kutil*' (crooked, dishonest, fraudulent). She also stated that while the descendents of the Atharvan and Angiras sages were its main composers, the Gopath Brahmana gives credit for its popularity and propagation to Rishi Bhrigu, a disciple of Sage Angiras.

It has been estimated that about one-seventh material of the Atharva Veda is drawn from the Rig Veda but the *Rik-mantras* (mantra from the Rig Veda) appear with significant variants. Dr B.K. Ghosh holds that:

> The typically Atharvanic charms and incantations are the product of a primitive culture not far removed from the dawn of human civilization. The *mantras* of *Atharvaveda* were meant for application at the humbler *Grihya* sacrifices of the common people which evolved round the simple primitive fire-cult. Besides, there were not many sponsors of the elaborate Rigvedic sacrifice in the Hindu society. In the

> meanwhile, the priestly class had increased manifold. So, they got the control of the non-Brahminical *Gribya* sacrifices, and compiled a *Mantrapaath* for these. This *Gribya Mantrapaath* is the *Atharvaveda*.[133]

Indeed, magic and cult both have an identical aim at the origin—the control of the transcendental world. The ritual texts describe sacrifices to incorporate exorcism formulae and there were magic rites whereby the priest can destroy 'the enemy whom he hates and who hates him'. The Manusmriti sanctions the use of exorcism against enemies.

According to Dr V.M. Apte:

> The oldest name of *Atharvaveda* is 'Atharvangirasah'—the Atharvans and Angirasas. They denote two kinds of magic formulae: Atharvan is 'holy magic bringing happiness' to the sacrificer, while *Angirasa* is 'hostile or black magic' bringing ruin to the enemy. The former includes formulae for the healing of diseases and the latter include cures against enemies, rivals, malicious magicians, etc. These two kinds of ancient magic formulae form the chief contents of the *Atharvaveda*.[134]

The names of gods in the Atharva Veda are the same as in the Rig Veda but they are now mainly treated as destroyers of the demonic and human enemies. Even the philosophical hymns have been given a magical twist. The principal aim of the Atharva Veda appears to be to appease the demons. It was not liked by the priesthood to begin with, and they initially excluded it from the sacred triad of the Rig Veda, Yajur Veda and Sama Veda.

However, in the Atharva Veda one comes across a hymn like IV. 16 dedicated to Varuna, which describes the power of the

---

[133]Ghosh, B.K., 'Chapter XX', *The Vedic Age*, R.C. Majumdar (ed.), Bhartiya Vidya Bhavan, p. 411.

[134]Apte, V.M., 'Chapter XXII', *The Vedic Age*, R.C. Majumdar (ed.), Bhartiya Vidya Bhavan, p. 442.

omniscience of God Varuna with such impressive beauty as rarely found in the Vedic literature. However, the second part of the hymn is an exorcism formula against liars:

Hymn IV. 16

1. The mighty ruler of the world beholds as though from close at hand. He is protecting the whole world; the learned know this trait of His.

2. If a man stands alone or walks and acts covertly; when two men whisper as they sit together, God Varuna is present as the third.

3. This wide Earth as well as the High Heaven are Varuna's kingdoms. The oceans are Varuna's loins, and this small drop of water, too, contains Him.

4. If one should flee beyond the Heaven, he cannot be free from Varuna's clutches. God Varuna's thousand-eyed spies are roaming all over in this world.

5. King Varuna watches all between Heaven and Earth and beyond. He counts the twinklings of men's eyes; He throws down the sinners as a gambler throws dice.

6. Your fatal snares, O Lord Varuna, like seven beams of light, catch the man who tells a lie and let the man pass unharmed whose words are truthful.

7. O Lord Varuna, who keeps vigil on all mankind for their noble and ignoble deeds, snare them with a hundered nooses who tell lies, don't let them escape. Let such villains fall to the ground and (be) crushed.

Atharvavedic religion became an amalgam of Aryan and non-Aryan cultures when the Aryans came across uncivilized tribes worshipping snakes and spirits. Rudra became the dreadful Bhootapati. In the Rig Veda, nir-riti is a place of darkness, it became *Narak-Lok* (Hell) in Atharva Veda. Now the idea of reward and punishment, after death, in exact correspondence to the good and bad deeds, gained a firm hold.

The Atharva Veda enumerates quite a large variety of diseases and the demons who were supposed to cause them. *Takman* (a kind of fever) is frequently mentioned in the Atharva Veda. Many other diseases like consumption, dysentery, ulcers, jaundice, rheumatism, snake-bite etc are mentioned.

There are several insights we gain and things that we get to know through the Atharva Veda. Such as, that a normal house was large enough to contain not only a large family, but also pens for cattle and sheep; and that there was a special place for the *Grihyapatya* fire.

The caste distinction had outstipped its proper limits and invaded the field of civil and criminal law. For manslaughter the system of wergeld[135] was in force. But the crime of murdering a Brahmin was considered too heinous to be expiated by a wergeld. The wergeld for killing a Kshatriya was 1,000 cows, 100 cows in the case of a Vaishya and 10 cows for killing a Shudra.

Mixed caste marriages were sanctioned by Dharma-Sutra. The *Anuloma* was a type of marriage where a member of the higher caste taking a wife or wives of the lower castes was permitted. Yet *Pratiloma* marriages, where the husband's caste was lower than that of the wife, were not rare. However, the Vasishtha Dharma-Sutra holds that the offspring of a Shudra male and a Brahmin female becomes a Chandala, who were treated as out-caste. This effectively prevented Brahmin women from marrying a Shudra.

Manusmriti (IX. 81) says that, 'A barren wife should be abandoned in the tenth year; a wife who bears only daughters should be abandoned in the twelfth year and one whose all children die, in the fifteenth year. But one who is quarrelsome should be abandoned without delay.'

The general principle was enumerated that the males were masters of the women: 'The father protects them in childhood, their husband protects them in youth, and their sons protect them in old age: a woman is never fit for independence.'

However, the Upanishads give a glimpse of some exceptioal

[135]A price set upon a man's life on the basis of his rank and paid as compensastion by the family of the slayer to the kindred or lord of the slain man to free the culprit of futher punishment or obligation.

cases like the story in the Chhaandogya Upanishad of Satyakama Jabal, who was born in a low caste. Kshatriya kings like Janaka were famous for their learning. The famous dialogue between Yajnavalkya and his wives, Maitreyi and Gargi Vachaknavi, shows the height of intellectual and spiritual attaiments to which women could rise.

Dr B.K. Ghosh observes that there is a fundamental distinction between Rigvedic hymns with those of the Atharva Veda. He says, 'From the view-point of contents, there can be no doubt that the typically Atharvanic charms and incantations are the product of a primitive culture ... They were meant for application at the humbler *Grihya* sacrifices of the common people which evolved round the plain and simple primitive fire-cult.'

The Strauta Mantrapaath, i.e., the Rig Veda, was composed by the priests for priests, and partly for their social supporters, the princes and potentates. The tone of the Rig Veda, therefore, even where the mantras are not directly addressed to the gods, is mainly one of begging and persuading. But the tone of the Atharva Veda is altogether different. Here the Brahmina priest is addressing his social inferiors from whom he need not turn off the shady side of his character.

Thus, in the Atharva Veda the original Rigvedic hymn, X. 109, on the 'Brahmin's wife' (*Brahmajaya*), has been amended in the Atharvedic hymn, AV. V. 17. The priest has demanded remarkable privileges for his class in the amended version. The first seven verses of this hymn constitute the Rigvedic verses.

Hymn AV. V. 17

8. Even though there were ten non-Brahmin previous husbands of a woman, the Brahmin alone becomes her husband if he seizes her hand.

(Curiously, in his translation, Devi Chand transforms 'woman' into 'Vedic knowledge' and renders this verse as: 'A Brahmin, who takes into his hand the task of propagating Vedic knowledge, he alone is her true guardian.')

9. The Brahmin indeed is the husband, neither *Rajanya* nor *Vaishya*. This the Sun goes on proclaiming to the five tribes of men.

Hymn AV. V. 18

In the next hymn, AV. V. 18, the Brahmin's property was sought to be protected.

9. Brahmins have sharp arrows and missiles, the volley they hurl is not in vain; pursuing with fervour and fury, they cast him down from afar who take his property.

10. They that ruled a thousand, and were ten thousands, those Vaitahavyas were defeated for having devoured a Brahmina's cow.

(I had taken the above translation from Ralph Griffith. Devi Chand, in his translation, has added a footnote chastising Griffith for incorrect translation. Devi Chand comments: 'Griffith considers Vaitahavyas as a tribe of people in the north, who were descendants of Rishi Vaitahavya. This explanation is unacceptable, as there is no history in the Vedas. The word means "persons who rob the sages of their foodstuffs". They who destroy and burn the library of a Vedic scholar are finally ruined.')

Hymn AV. III. 28.2

In Hymn AV. III. 28.2, the Brahmin's claim becomes ridiculous when, in all seriousness, it is suggested, as a way of averting the ill omen of a twinning animal,[136] that one of the twin calves should be made over to a Brahmin.

Most amusing, however, is the long Hymn AV. XII. 4, in fierce denunciation of those who fail to bestow their barren cows to Brahmins. A barren cow could only serve one purpose—improve the quality of food in the Brahmin's household!

Evidently, the Brahmin's supposed privileges have been shamelessly asserted in the Atharva Veda, and of his obligations there is hardly any mention.[137]

[136]Any animal, like a cow, giving birth to two calves.

[137]*The Prehistoric Age*, Bharatiya Vidya Bhavan, Mumbai, 1996, p. 412.

SELECTED HYMNS FROM ATHARVA VEDA CHAPTER 1

What baffles me is why Devi Chand is steadfast in not disclosing the names of the Vedic gods in his translation. Hymn VII of Chapter 1 is dedicated to Agni. I quote Verse 4:

Agnih poorva aa rabhataam preIndro nudatu bahumaan.
Braveetu sarvo yatumaanaYamasmityetya.

[Let Agni begin the task of destroying the Asuras and let the all-powerful Indra provide support;
the Asuras would then be ready to accept their guilt.]

Devi Chand translates it as follows: 'May a learned preacher first take in hand the work of reforming a sinner; may a strong-armed king then impel him to be virtuous. Let every wicked person consequently come hither and say, here am I.'

In his translation he has converted Agni into a 'learned preacher,' Indra into a 'strong-armed king' and Yama a 'controller of wicked persons', without disclosing their real names. However, in his footnote he explains:

Brihaspati: a preacher who possesses the knowledge of the Vedas.
Agni: A learned person resplendent with knowledge like fire.
Soma: Chief among the preachers, as Soma is chief of medical herbs.

His explanation appears even more confounding to me!

Verse 4 of the next Hymn VIII is again addressed to Agni:

YatreshaamaAgne janimaani vaittha guhaa satamatrinaam Jaatvedah.
Taanstvama brahamanaa vaavridhano jahyeshaam shatatarhamaAgne.

[O Agni, Source of benevolent Light! Reach out to the erratic, wayward people in their dark caves, show them the right path of betterment and remove their distress.]

Devi Chand translates it as follows: 'As thou, O learned preacher, knowest the descendants of these secret greedy beings, so strengthened by the knowledge of Veda, O preacher, ameliorating them morally, destroy their sins thorough a hundred devices.'

It is not translation; it's transformation! I don't think Swami Dayananda Saraswati wanted that the names of the Vedic Gods should not be disclosed.

~

Hymn XII of Chapter 1 relates to the eradication of *yakshma*, body ache, headache, etc. I quote Verse 3:

Muncha sheershaktyaa uta kaas ainam
parushparuraaviveshaa yo ashya.
Yo abhrajaa vaataja yashcha shushmo
vanaspateenatsachataam parvataanshcha.

[O Health-giving Sun, relieve us from headache and cough and destroy the disease-carrying germs from the body. Remove the diseases caused by rains and hot and cold weather; let the herbs found in the hills and forests cure us.]

Devi Chand has translated the first half correctly but the second half incorrectly: 'O physician, do thou release this man from headache, free him from cough which has entered into all his limbs and joints. One should resort to forests and hills for relief from diseases resulting from excessive rains, severe wind and intense heat.'

Besides incorrectly translating the latter half, he chastises Sayana in his footnote: 'Sayana translates the latter half of the verse, "that diseases occurring from rain and wind and heat should go to forests and hills." This interpretation is illogical and irrational.'

Sayana was trying to explain that the rishi who composed the hymn was banishing the disease to the mountains by the power of his mantra! 'How illogical and irrational!' exclaims Devi Chand, correcting even the rishi.

~

While translating **Hymn XIV**, which relates to a maiden (*Bhagmashah*), he upbraids both Sayana and Griffith. I quote **Verse 1**:

Bhagamashyaa varcha aadishadhi vrikshadiva srijam.
Mahaabudhna eva parvato jyok pitrishvaastaam.

[We acknowledge this virgin's beauty and splendour as people admire the loveliness of a flower. As a mountain stands fearlessly, let her live in my house without any apprehension.]

Devi Chand translates it as follows: 'As from the tree a wreath, have I assumed her fortune and her fame among my kinsfolk she might dwell for long, like a mountain broad-based.'

He adds a footnote: '"I" refers to the bridegroom, and "her" refers to the bride. Sayana interprets this verse as a misfortune, that the girl remains unmarried in the house of her parents. This is illogical. A girl is expected to remain firm and steadfast in her domestic life, after marriage, in the house of her father-in-law, and not that of her own parents.'

∽

Verse 4 is as follows:

Asitashya te brahamana Kashyapashya Gayashya cha.
Antahkoshamiva jaamayoapi nahyaami te bhagam.

[O maiden, we protect your viginity by the power of mantras of rishis like Asita, Kashyapa and Gaya, just as women protect their jewellery by keeping it in a box.]

In his translation, Devi Chand obliterates the existence of celebtates sages like Asita, Kashyapa and Gaya and asserts that these words denote the qualities of God! I don't think Swami Dayananda would approve. He translates it as: 'Through the Vedic knowledge of the unrestrained, All-seeing and all-sustaining God, I preserve thy knowledge, dignity and virtues, as ladies preserve their ornaments and clothes in a box.'

He adds a footnote: 'Griffith wrongly considers Asita, Kashyapa and Gaya as ancient rishis. These words denote the qualities of

God. "I" refers to the bridegroom. "Thy" refers to the bride.'

∽

In **Hymn XVIII, Verse 4** is as follows:

> *Rishyapadim vrishdateen goshedham vidhamaamut;*
> *Vileedhyam lalaamyamay taa asamannaashayaamasi.*
>
> [A woman whose feet are like a deer's, teeth like those of an ox; whose gait is like a cow and speech coarse; we remove these adverse features by the power of mantras.]

Devi Chand's translation: 'We should always refrain from marrying girls who are unsteady and have feet of an antelope, mighty-toothed like a bull, pigmy-sized like a cow, blowing hot with anger like the bellows, ever licking something, however beautiful, charming and lovely they may be.' He adds a footnote: 'Griffith interprets "*rishyapadeem*", etc. as names or epithets of sorceresses, witches or female fiends of various forms. This is far-fetched and inappropriate explanation. The verse refers to girls who should not be accepted in marriage.'

∽

In **Hymn XIX, Verse 1** the poet makes a fervent prayer to Indra to ensure that the enemy arrows don't reach them:

> *Maa no vidan vivyaadhino mo abhivyaadhino vidan;*
> *Aaraachharavya asmadvishoocheerIndra paatay.*
>
> [O Lord Indra, let not the hostile archers overcome us, nor let those who attack us on all sides approach us. Make the enemy arrows flying in different directions fall far from us.]

Devi Chand fights shy of disclosing Indra's name and translates 'Indra' as the 'Commander of the army'!

∽

Hymn XX, Verse 1 is dedicated to Vedic gods, Soma and the Maruts:

Adaarsrid bhavatu deva Somaasmin yagye Maruto mridataa nah;
Maa no vidadbhibhaa mo ashastirmaa no vidad vrijinaa dveshaa yaa.

[O refulgent god Soma, don't let enmity or disunity be created amongst us. O Maruts, don't let the enemy advance towards us, nor let infamy or defeat touch us.]

Without disclosing Soma's name, Devi Chand calls him 'Refulgent God' and the Maruts, 'Pure Souls.'

∽

Next, the **Verse 2:**

Yo addya senyo vadhoaghaayoonaa mudeerate;
Yuvam tam MitraVarunavasmad yaavayatam pari.

[O Mitra-Varuna, keep away the deadly weapons with which our enemies are attacking us; pray don't let them touch and harm us!]

Devi Chand translates it as follows: 'O Prime Minister and King, Ye twain, turn carefully away from us, the deadly massacre of the sinners, which is being conducted today by the valiant soldiers of the army!'

To my mind it is massacre of the original meaning of the verse!

∽

The last hymn of Chapter 1, **Hymn XXXV**, is composed by Rishi Atharva. It is a prayer for Long Age (*Deerghayu*). I quote the first and third verse:

Yadaabadhnan Dakshyaayanaa hiranyaam Shatanikaay sumanashyamaanaah.
*Tat te badhnaamyaayushe varchase balaaya deerghaayutvaaya shatashaaradaaya.*1.

[O man, wishing for long life, we tie the pleasure-giving golden wrist-band to your hand which the *rishis* of Daksha

> had bound to King Shataaneek. It will enhance your physical prowess and you will enjoy life for a hundred autumns.]

Devi Chand translates it as follows: 'The yogis, who live for the purity of soul, full of noble thoughts, preserve the precious semen of the body, that it may last for a hundred years, so I, thy preceptor, O pupil, advise thee to preserve it for longevity, glory, strength and a long life of a hundred autumns.'

He adds a footnote: 'In the opinion of Griffith, Daksha in the Veda is a creative power associated with Aditi (infinity or eternity) the mother of Adityas. This interpretation is illogical as there is no history in the Vedas. Dakshayana means self-controlled yogis and noble persons, who preserve their precious semen.'

This is plain denial of truth and a blatant assertion of untruth.

In **Verse 3** of this hymn the word 'Indra' occurs; Devi Chand translates it as *'Brahmachari'*—a celibate! That is probably the best joke about Indra!

Leaving aside the garbled, evasive and misleading translation by Devi Chand, the stark fact remains that the tenor and content of the Atharva Veda is radically different from that of Rig Veda. Atharvavedic prayers are mostly magic spells for eradicating diseases like headache, body ache, pain in joints, malarial fever, leprosy, bronchitis, diabetes, boils, wounds, blood-letting, even sorcery and witchcraft.

SELECTED HYMNS FROM ATHARVA VEDA CHAPTER 2

Hymn II, Chapter 2 is composed by Rishi Maatrinaamaa. It is dedicated to the Gandharvas and the Apsaras. We had met the Gandharvas and the Apsaras in the Rig Veda, in company of Pururuva. I quote its first and last verses.

> *Divyo Gandharvo bhuvanashya yaspatirek aiva namashyo vikshhveeedya;*
> *Tam tva yomi Brahmanaa divya deva namaste astu divi te sadhastham.*1.

[The radiant *Gandharvas* and *Apsaras* are among the lords of the universe; we pay our homage to these hevenly apparitions and pray to them.]

Ya klandaast misheechayo akshyakaamaa manomuhah;
Taabhyo Gandharvapatneebhyo apsaraabhyo akaram namah.5.

[We pay our homage to the Apsaras who are charming to behold; they satisfy the desire of the eyes, but make the heart desirous.]

∽

Hymn IV, Chapter 2 is composed by Rishi Atharva and addressed to 'Long Life'. The first verse is as follows:

Deerghaayutvaaya brihate ranaayaarishanto dakshamaanaah sadaiva;
*Manimah vishkandhadooshanam jangidam bibhrimo vayam.*1.

[In order to attain long life and enjoy a disease-free, invigorating existence, we keep the '*Jangid-mani*'[138] close to the body.]

Devi Chand misleads by translating '*Jangid-mani*' as 'God': 'For length of life, the success in life's struggle, uninjured, ever exerting, may we accept God, the Praiseworthy Devourer of sins, and the Averter of obstacles.'

He also adds a footnote: 'Sayana interprets "jangid" as a tree found near Benaras. This explanation is illogical, as it savours of history, but the Vedas are free from history. The word means God, who devours all sins. Griffith explains the word "jangid" to mean 'a plant frequently mentioned in the *Atharvaveda* as a charm against demons and a specific for various diseases. This interpretation too is irrational.'

Indeed, Devi Chand is an averter of meaning!

[138] '*Mani*' means a jewel, while '*jangid*' means a produce of forests. It appears to be produced from some herb.

The next **Hymn V** is authored by Sage Bhrigu and is a eulogy to Indra. The third verse of the hymn is as follows:

Indrasturaashyaanimatro Vritram yo jaghaan yateerna;
*Bibheda Valam Bhrigurna sasahe shatroon made Somashya.*3.

[Indra is a friend of all people but he swifly attacks the enemies. Having fortified himself with Soma, he destroyed the demon Vritra, who had enclosed the the waters. He also killed the demon Vala who had taken away the cows of Angirasas, ancestors of Sage Bhrigu.]

Devi Chand translates it as follows: 'The Swift-conquering king is the friend of his subjects. Just a Yogi, the observer of *Yamas* and *Niyamas*, overcomes ignorance, lust and anger, foes to his meditation, so does the king destroy the enemy of his state. Just as the Sun disperses the cloud, so does the king shatter the forces of the enemy, and quell his foe in the rapturous joy of power.'

He adds a footnote: 'Griffith describes Bhrigu as a Rishi, regarded as the ancestor of the ancient race of Bhrigus. This is unacceptable as there is no history in the Vedas.' He even denies the identity of the celebrated Sage Bhrigu who is a historical figure! 'There is no history in the Vedas!' is his *amogha shashtra* (a trusty weapon).

Hymn XII is a '*Shatru Naashan Sookta*,' to vanquish foes, authored by Rishi Bharadwaj. It is dedicated to Dhyava–Prithvi, Indra, etc. **Verse 2** is as follows:

Idam Devaah shranut ye yagyiyaa stha Bharadwajo mahyamukthani shansati;
*Paashe sa baddho durite ni yujjataam yo asmaakam mana idam hinasti.*2.

[O Gods, listen to the ardent prayer of Bharadwaja: Bind in strong fetters the inimical desires, lust and anger, which degrade the soul, and throw them far away from me.]

Hymn XIV, authored by Rishi Chatan, relates to vanquishing the evil spirits. **Verse 2** of the hymn is as follows:

Nirvo goshthaadjaamasi nirakshannirupaansaat;
*Nirvo Magundyha duhitaro grihebhyashchaatmahe.*2.

[O evil daughters of Magundi, we drive you out of our cow-pens. We chase you away from our grain-stores and other lodgements of yours.]

Devi Chand adds a footnote: 'Magundi has been interpreted by Griffith as a female evil spirit. This explanation is illogical as there is no history in the Vedas. The word means ill desire that destroys our happiness.'

Asso yo adharaad grihastatra santvaraayah;
*Tatra sedinyurchyatu sarvaashcha yatudhaanyah.*3.

[Let the evil-spirit Aaraayi who causes poverty, and demonic Sedi who spreads pestilence, be driven out and sent to the underworld to live there for ever.]

As usual, Devi Chand adds a footnote to chide Griffith: 'Griffith translates Araayaas as female fiends and night hags. The word means calamities and mishaps.'

Hymn XXX. Kamini Mano: 'Abhimukhikaran Sookta' is a romantic hymn, ascribed to God Prajapati; it is dedicated to a lovely maiden.

Yathedam bhhoomya adhi trina vaato mathayati;
Aiva mathnaami te mano maan kaminashyo yatha
*mannapagaa asah.*1.

[O Kamini (maiden), As a gust of wind lifts a straw lying on the ground and makes it whirl in the air, let me stir and agitate your heart, so that you may long for me and don't ever go away from me.]

Sam chennayaatho Ashvina kaamina sam cha vakshathah;
*Sam vaam bhagaso agamat sam chittani samu vrita.*2.

[O Ashvins, send her, whom I desire, to me, so that our body organs, our hearts and desires move in unison.]

Yat suparna vivakshavo anameeva vivakshavah;
*Tatra me gachhataadadhvam shalya iva kulmalam yatha.*3.

[Like the ardent call of a colourful bird for his mate and a youthful lover's invite for a rendezvous, my love-laden sharp-edged dart shall pierce her.]

Yadantaram tad baahyam yad baahyam tadantaram;
*Kanyaanaam vishvaroopaanaam mano gribhaayoshadhe.*4.

[Maidens with a fair outer looks and pure inner heart; let this potent charm capture such flawless damsels.]

Aiyamagan patikaamaa janikaamo ahamaagamam;
*Ashva kanikrdad yathaa bhagenaaham sahaagamam.*5.

[Desirous of a husband, this maiden has come to me, and like a horse neighing in pleasure, I entwine her.]

∽

Hymn XXXIII provides an antidote against consumption (yaksham). It's a typical Atharvavedic hymn designed to equip Brahmins with ritual charms to cure body ailments.

Aksheebhyaam te nasikaabhyaam karnaabhyaam
chhubukaadadhi;
Yaksham sheershanyam mastishkaajjivyaayaa
*vi vrihaami te.*1.

[O patient, from both your eyes, nostrils, ears and your chin, as from your brain and tongue, I root out consumption seated in your head.]

Greevaabhyast ushnihaabhyah keeksabhyo anookyaaat;
Yaksham doshanya manssaabhyaam baahubhaam vi
*vrihaami te.*2.

[O sick man, from the arteries of the neck and the nape, from the spinal cord, arms and shoulder-blades, I root out consumption from your arms.]

Hridiyaat te pari klomno halikshyanaat paarshvaabhyaam,
*Yaksham matsnaabhyaam pleenhano yaknaste ve vrihamasi.*3.

[O diseased man, from your heart, lungs and gall-bladder, from kidneys, spleen and liver; I eradicate consumption from all these organs.]

Antrebhyaste gudaabhyo vanoshthorudaraadadhi;
*Yaksham kukshibhyaam plaashernaabhya ve vrihaami.*4.

[From your bowels and intestines, rectum and the belly, from all organs of your digestive system, I root out consumption.]

Ooroobhyam te ashtheevadabhyaam paaribhyaam prapadaabhyaam;
*Yaksham bhasadhyam shribhyaam bhaasadam bhansaso vi vrihaami te.*5.

[From your thighs and knees, heels and foreparts of feet, from your loins and hips, from urinary canal and faecal parts, I eradicate consumption.]

Asthibhyaste majjabhyah snaavabhyo dhamanibhyah;
*Yaksham paanibhyaam ungalibhyo, nakhebhyo ve vrihaami te.*6.

[From your bones and bone marrows, tendons and veins, from hands, fingers and nails, I banish consumption.]

Ange-ange, lomni-lomni yaste parvaniparvani;
*Yaksham tvachashyam te vayam kashyapashya veebrahen vishvancham ve vrihaamasi.*7.

[From every organ of the body, every hair, every joint wherein it lies, I root out consumption.]

SELECTED HYMNS FROM ATHARVA VEDA CHAPTER 3

Hymn I has been composed by the eminent Rishi Atharva. It exhorts Indra, Agni and the Maruts to fight and bewitch the Enemy Army. I quote Verses 1, 3 and 6.

Agnirnah shatroon pratyetu vidvaan pratidahannabhishasti maraatim;
*Sa senaan mohayatu pareshaam nirhastaanshcha krinavajjaatavedaah.*1.

[O Agni, delude the enemy army; make them throw away their arms. Then you march forward burning their body parts.]

Amitrasenaam Maghavannasmaachchhatrooyatimabhi;
*Yuvam taanIndra VratrahannaAgnishcha dahatam prati.*3.

[O glorious Indra, you destroyed the demon Vritra. Now You and Agni together diminish our enemy army and burn them.]

Indrah senaam mohayatu Maruto ghnantvojasaa;
*ChakshoonshAgniraa dattaam punaretu parajitaa.*6.

[O Indra, you delude the enemy army and let the Marutas destroy them. Let Agni take away their eye sight. Let the enemy army return thereafter.]

∽

Hymn II, also composed by Rishi Atharva, is similar to Hymn 1. The first three verses pray to Agni and Indra to delude and destroy the enemy army. The Rigvedic people composed hymns in praise of their gods but fought real battles with their enemies. Rishi Atharva is hoping to vanquish enemies by praying to the gods to march against them!

Agnirno dootah pretyetu vidvaan
pratidahannabhishastimaraaatim;
Sa chittani mohayatu pareshan nirhastaanshch
*krinavajjaatavedah.*1.

[May the messenger of the Gods, Agni, march against our enemies, scorching them. Let him delude the enemy army and disarm them.]

Indradra chittani mohayannarvaadaakootya char;
*Agnervatashya dhraajyaa taan vishoocho vi naashaya.*3.

[O Indra grace us with a visit, come deluding the army of our foes. Destroy them by Agni and Vayu's terrible, astounding power.]

Verse 5 exhorts the dreaded disease *Apve* to annihilate the enemies:

Ameeshaam chittaani pratimohayanti grihaanaangaanyApve paarehi;
*Abhi prehi nirdah hritsu shokairgrahyaamitranstmasaa Vidhya shatroon.*5.

[O Apve![139] You delude our foemen and enter their bodies, singe their hearts with grief, and destroy them by clutching them in your grip.]

~

Hymn IV was also composed by Rishi Atharva, who congratulates King Samvarana for regaining his throne.

Aa tva gan raashtram saha varchasodihi praad visham patirekraat tvam vi raaj.
*Sarvaastvaa raajan pradisho havyantoopsadyo namashyo bhaveh.*1.

[O King, you have regained kingship. Be crowned in splendour, shine as leader and ruler of the people. Let the people bow before you in reverence.]

Ashvina tvagre Mitra-Varunobha Vishvedeva Marutastva hriyantu.
*Adha mano Vasudevaya krinushva tato na ugro vi bhaja vasooni.*4.

[139]Apva—female deity who presided over sin (Sayana).

> [O King, let Ashvins, Mitra, Varuna, Vishvedava, the Maruts recognize you and bless you. Then turn your thoughts to charity, give gifts according to deserts and to us.]

Devi Chand translates this verse as follows: 'O King, first shall the Commander-in-chief, and the speaker of the Assembly, head of the Police Department and the C.I.D. head, all learned persons, all soldiers and businessmen, accept thee as their sovereign. Then turn thy mind to giving gifts of treasure, thence, mighty one, distribute wealth among us!'

He has transformed the hymn by bringing in the Constitution and the Penal Code. Such blatant distortions and impositions!

~

Hymn XII describes the '*Shala*', the living cottage of those days which also had a compound for the cattle. I quote **Verses 3–6** here:

> *Dharunyasi shale brihachchhandaah pootidhaanyaa;*
> *Aa tva vatso gamedaa kumaar aa dhenavah saayaamaaspandamaanaa.*3.

> [O *Shala*, you have a high ceiling and all kind of grains are stored within. Children play within your precincts and calves reside. At eventide the milch cows come running homeward.]

> *Ima shaalaam Savita VayurIndro Brihaspatirni minotu prajaanan;*
> *Ukshantoodnaa Maruto ghriten Bhago no raajaa ni krishim tanotu.*4.

> [May the Gods Savita, Vayu, Indra, Brihaspati bless this Shalaa, and the Maruts provide us with ghrita and water. May God Bhaga make our ploughing fruitful.]

> *Maanashya patni sharanaa Shyonaa Devi devebhirnimitaashyagre;*
> *Trinm vasaanaa sumanaa asastvamathaasmbhayam sahveeram raendaah.*5.

> [O Shala, you are an embodyment of the wife of Vastupati, the protector of grains. The Gods constructed you in the

beginning of the world. Pure in heart, you are clad in the robes of grass. O Shala, give us valiant sons and prosperity.]

Riten sthoonamadhi roha vanshogro viraajannap vridakshva shatroon;
Maa te rishannupasattaaro grihaanaam shale shatam jeevem sharadah sarvaveeraah.6.

[O *Vansha* (bamboo pole, '*baans*' in Hindi)! You stand firm in the centre of the Shala and keep the terrible enemies away. Let not the people who dwell within be wounded; afford them protection and let them live a hundred years with their sons!]

To my mind, this hymn captures the essence of the Vedic people's lifestyle in the sylvan surroundings of India about 3,500 years ago.

∽

Hymn XIX is ascribed to Rishi Vasishtha and dedicated to Vishvedeva. It's a battle song. Battle was an occasional happening in the life of the Aryans. I quote its **Verses 1 and 4,** sung by the proud purohita:

Sanshitam ma idam Brahma sanshitam veerya balam;
Sanshitam kshatramajarvastu jishnuryeshaamasmi purihitah.1.

[Sharpened be this prayer of mine, may the manly strength of our army be irresistible. Sharpened and irresistible be the Ruler's valour, whose victorious Purohita am I.]

Teekshneeyaansah parshorAgnesteekshanataraa uta;
Indrasha vajraat teekhneeyaanso yeshamasmi purohitah.4.

[Sharper than the axe and sharper than the flame; sharper than the thunderbolt of Indra is the King whose *Purohita* am I.]

∽

Hymn XXIII is ascribed to God Brahma and is dedicated to the female *yoni* (vulva, the external female genitalia). It is intended to promote fertility and banish sterility among women and prepare them to produce male progeny. I quote its first four verses:

Yen vehad babhoovith naashayaamasi tat tvat.
*Idam tadanyatra tvadap doore ni dadhnasi.*1.

[O woman, we banish and expel from your body the disease of sterility, caused by some sin commited by you. We lay this dreaded disease apart and throw it far away from you, so that it may not affect you.]

Aa te yonim garbha aitu pumaan baana eveshudhim;
*Aaa veeroatra jaayataam putraste dashmaashyah.*2.

[O woman, as arrows enter a quiver effortlessly, we place a male embryo in your *yoni*; let this embryo lodge there for ten months and be born as a valiant son.]

Pumaansam putram janaya tam pumaananu jaayataam;
*Bhavaasi putraanaam maataa jaataanaam janayaashcha yaan.*3.

[O woman, give birth to a male son. Then bring forth another male son after him. You shall be the Honoured Mother of the sons you have delivered and those you would deliver in future.]

Yaani bhadraani beejaanyarishbhaa janayanti cha;
*Taistavam putram vindasva saa prasoordhenuka bhava.*4.

[O woman, as the cows get impregnated by the insuperable semen of bulls and give birth to male calves, you too be a fruitful mother-cow of potent, heroic sons.]

Devi Chand, in his translation, has translated the word '*vrishabha*' (Bull) occurring in the first line of the verse as 'the herbs named '*Rishbhak*' !

Hymn XXV is composed by Rishi Bhrigu and is dedicated to '*Kama Bana*' (Arrow of the God of Love). I quote **Verse 2:**

Aadheeparnaa Kaamashalyaamishum sankalpakulmalaam;
*Tam susannataam kritvaa Kaamo vidhyatu tva hridi.*2.

[O woman, the resolute arrow of *Kama Deva* is equipped with the wings of desire; let God *Kama* place the arrow on his bow and pierce your heart!]

Devi Chand has converted the arrow of Kama Deva into the arrow of desire for knowledge, and says: 'Let desire for knowledge, having truly aimed, shoot forth and pierce thee, O Ignorance, in the heart!'

∽

Hymn XXVIII is ascribed to God Brahma and is devoted to animal upkeep and well-being of cattle. In its opening verse it refers to '*Yamini*' the creative power, which sometimes turns into flesh-eating *Kravya*. These ill omens result in birth of twinning animals (producing two calves).

Aikaykayesha shrishtaya sam babhoova uatra gaa asrijant bhutakrito vishvaroopah;
*Yatra vijayate yaminyapartuh saa pashoon kshinaati riphati rushati.*1.

[When the world came into being, the Creator created the Earth-Cow. The creative power of the womb, Yamini, however, degenerates into Kravya sometimes and creates complications.]

Aisha pashoontsam kshinaati kravyaad bhootva vyadvari;
*Utainaam Brahamane dadhyaata tathaa shyonaa shivaa shyat.*2.

[The ill omen of a twinning cow should be averted by giving the cow and one calf to a Brahmin.]

Devi Chand translates this verse as: 'That chaos, destroying each and every one, and being flesh-devourer, ruins common ignorant persons. At such a critical time, the chaos in the society should be handed over to a highly learned person, who knows the Vedas, for the restoration of peace and happiness'.

∽

Hymn XXIX is composed by Rishi Uddaalak. Its seventh verse is dedicated to God Kama, which is fascinating:

Ka idam kasmaa adaat Kaamah Kaamaayaadaat;
Kamo daataa Kaamah pratigriheetaa Kamah samudramaa vivesh;
*Kaamen tva prati grihanaami Kaamaitat te.*7.

[Who bestowed this boon of *Kama* (sexual desire)? Sexual desire produces longing in the heart and the heart surrenders to it. I accept this boon of Kama; I am all yours! (A young girl is called *'Kamini')*.]

SELECTED HYMNS FROM ATHARVA VEDA CHAPTER 4

Hymn I, authored by Sage Vain, celebrates the creation of the universe (*Brahmaand*) and sings the glory of the all-pervading Brahma! I quote **Verses 3 and 4:**

Pray o jagye vidvaanashya bandhurvishwaa devanaam janimaa vivakti.
*Brahama brahman ujjabhaar madhyaanneechairuchyai: svadhaa abhi pra tasthee.*3.

[The knower who is related to the divine powers, may explain how the divine powers were created. The all-pervading Brahma has created the universe—the lower, upper and the middle parts—as well as the forces of nature that nurture the plants and creatures.]

Sa hi divah sa prithivya ritastha mahi ksemam rodasi askabhaayat.
*Mahaan mahee askabhaayad vi jaato dhyaam sadma paarthivam cha rajam.*4.

[The God created *Dhyava–Prithvi*, Heaven and Earth, and pervades in them. He supports the two worlds and the atmosphere.]

Hymn II is a retelling of the Hymn X. 121 of the Rig Veda—Ka: 'What God Shall We Adore With Our Oblation?' It recalls the emergence of 'Hiranya Garbha'—the 'Golden Embryo'.

Hymn III is **composed** by Rishi Atharva. It reverts to the standard Atharvedic invention of destruction of man's enemies by magic chants. I quote **Verses 2, 3 and 4**:

Parenaitu patha vrikah parmenota taskarah;
*Paren datvati rajjuh parenaadhaayurarashatu.*2.

[Let the wolf go on a distant path, and the thief on the most remote pathway. Let the *datvati rajju* (female serpent—'rope with teeth') go on the far road, and the sinful foes on a distant route.]

Akshau cha te mukham cha te vyaaghra jambhayaamasi;
*Aat sarvaan vinshatim nakhaan.*3.

[O tiger, we pierce both your eyes with the power of this mantra, and crush your head to pieces. We break your jaws and all twenty claws.]

Vyaaghram datvataam vayam prathamam jambhayaaamasi;
*Aadu shtenamatho ahim yaatudhaanamatho vrikam.*4.

[Let us first of all kill the tiger among the animals with sharp teeth. Thereafter we kill the thief and robber, and then the snake and the jackal.]

Hymn IV, composed by Rishi Atharva,[140] is dedicated to a medicinal herb, *Vrisha*, which enhances the virility of men.

Yaam tva Gandharvo akhanad Varunaay mritbhraje;
*Taam tva vayam khanaamashaudhim shapeharshaneem.*1.

[140]Devi Chand, in a foot note, says 'Atharvan means God who is Non-violent.'

[O Medicinal Herb! The Gandharvas dug you up for Lord Varuna. We also dig up you for enhancing the power of the male genitals.]

UdUshaa udu Soorya udidam maamakam Vachah;
*Udejatu Prajaapatir vrisha shushmen vaajinaa.*2.

[Let Goddess Dawn and the Sun and my mantra enhance the strength of the herb. Let Prajapati strengthen the vigour of the herb vrisha.]

Yatha sma te virohatoabhitaptmivaanit;
*Tataste shushmavattaramiyam krinotvoshadhi.*3.

[O man! When engaged in coition, this herb will endow you with greater vigour.]

Uchchhushmaushadheenaam saar rishabhaanaam;
*Sam punsaamIndra vrishnayamasmin dhehi tanoovashin.*4.

[Of all potency enhancing medicines this is the most efficacious. O God Indra, master of human bodies, lend this man the vigour of a powerful man.]

Apaam rasah prathamjoatho vanaspatinaam;
*Ut Somashya bhraataashutaarshamasi vrishnyam.*5.

[O *Aushadhi*, you are the first born during the churning of waters. You are God Soma's sister and was created by the mantras of Rishis.]

AdhyaAgne adhya Savitaradhya Devi Saraswati;
*Adhyaashya Bramanaspate dhanuriva taanayaa pasaha.*6.

[O Agni, O Savita, O Saraswati, O Brahamanaspate, strengthen and stretch this man's genitals like a bow.]

Devi Chand does not know how to purify the verse of its prurience in which even Goddess Saraswati has been requested to stretch and strengthen a man's genitals. He does not disclose the names of the Vedic Gods and says: 'O Preceptor, O Father, O Knowledge, O God, extend today the rule of this brave man like a bow'.

Aaham tanomi te paso adhi jyaamiva dhanvani.
*Kramasvavarsha iva rohitamanavaglaayataa sadaa.*7.

[O man, We extend your genitals like a bow stretched with an arrow. Now mount with full force to perform the sexual act.]

Devi Chand's translation: 'O man, I extend thy kingdom, like the rope in the bow. Unfatigued attack thou the foes, as a tiger attacks a deer!'

Ashvashyaashvatarashyaajashya petvashya cha;
*Atha rishabhashya ye vaajaastaanasmin dhehi tanoovashin.*8.

[O *Aushadhe*, provide this man the potency of a horse, a wild ass, a he-goat, a ram, a bull!]

∽

Hymn XVI is ascribed to God Brahma and dedicated to Varuna. It has been quoted in the introductory part in the beginning.

∽

Hymns XVII, XVIII and XIX are dedicated to herb *apaamaarga*. It is proclaimed to be a wonder herb, particularly efficacious against diseases related to sterility and malfunctioning of sexual organs. Actually, it was supposed be a 'cure all'. Besides, it would help in driving away the foes as well as the '*yatudhaan*'—male and female Pishaach or Rakshasa. Indeed, the Brahmins administered the herb and recited these verses and probably afforded psychological relief to the credulous folk.

∽

Verse 2 of **Hymn XIX** mentions the name Rishi Kanva, son of Nrishad:

Brahmanen paryuktaasi Kanven Narshaden;
Senevaishi tvisheematee na tatra bhayamasti yatra
praapnoshoshadhe.

[O Sahadevi (another name of *Apamaargaa*), the Brahmin Kanva, son of Nrishad, has sung your glory. You go to protect your worshipper like a fierce army. Wherever you go, there is no fear of any disease.]

As usual, Devi Chand resents Griffith's mention of the name of Rishi Kanva in his translation and chides him: 'Griffith translates Kanva as a rishi, son of Nrishad. This interpretation is unacceptable, as there is no history in the Vedas. Kanva means a learned person.'

Indeed, Griffith is not 'interpreting' at all; he is guilty of correct translation!

∽

Beginning with **Hymn XXIII**, there are seven hymns addressed to all deities, for eradication of sins. They are all repetitive in nature. They are said to be composed by Sage Mrigaar. **Hymn XXVIII,** however, mentions his name as 'Mrigaar' meaning 'Atharva'.

I will quote the first verse from these hymns to convey their sense:

Hymn XXIII

Agnermanve prathamashya prachetasah paanchajanyashya bahudhaa yamindhate;
*Vishovishah pravishivaamsameemahe sa no munchatvahasah.*1.

[God Agni, who is generally ignited by fuel, we invoke that most venerable God by prayer and bow to him. He inheres in all things in the world; we pray to him to free us from our sins.]

∽

Hymn XXIV

Indrashya manhahe shasvadidashya manmahe Vritraghna stomaa upa mem aaguh;
*Y daashushah sukrito havameti sa no munchatvahasah.*1.

[We are very well aware of the boundless glory of Indra; of

the supreme prowess of the slayer of Vritra. We know the hymns that are chanted in His praise. God Indra who comes to the aid of the sacrificer, may He free us from all our sins!]

∽

Hymn XXV

Vayoh Saviturvidathaani manmahe yaavaatmnvad vishatho yau cha rakshathah.
*Yau vishvashya paribhoo badhoovathustau no munchatamhasah.*1.

[We are well aware of the tasks performed by the Sun and Vayu without waiting for anyone's prayer. O god Savita, O god Vayu, you are present in all living beings and activate them; you protect the whole world. We pray to you to free us from all our sins!]

∽

Hymn XXVI

Manve vaam Dhyava-Prithivi subhojasau sachetasau ye aprathethaamamitaa yojanaani;
*Pratishthe hyabhavatam vasoonaam te no munchatamhasah.*1.

[O *Dhyava-Prithivi*, we pray to you, knowing your exalted renown. You are spread out on infinite space and are the prime source of the wellbeing and wealth of men and of the gods. We beseech you to free us from all our sins!]

∽

Hymn XXVIII

Marutaammanve adhi me bruvantu premam vaajam vaajasaate avantu;
*Aashooniva suyamaanahva ootaye te no munchatamhasah.*1.

[We are aware of the untold power of the Marutas. We pray to them to count us as their devotees. We call them for our safety. O Marutas, we beseech you to free us from all our sins!]

~

Hymn XXXVIII

Bhavaasharvau manve vaam tasya vittam yayaurvaamidam pradishi yad virochate;
*Yaavasheyshaathe dvopado yau chatushdastau no munchatamhasah.*1.

[O Gods Bhava and Sharva, we know your greatness; this entire world is lighted by your power. You are the lord of all mankind and animals. Pray, You together free us from all our sins!]

~

Hymn XXIX

Manve vaam MitraVaruna vritaavadhau sachetasau druvhano yau nudethe;
*Pra satyaavaanamavatho bhareshu tau no munchatamhasah.*1.

[O *Mitra* and *Varuna*, You are both of the same mind and intent, who take care of the waters enclosing the Earth. You remove the evil-minded and and protect those who tread the path of truth. We sing your glory. Free us from all our sins!]

~

Hymn XXXIV is composed by Rishi Atharva and dedicated to an imaginary deity, Brahmodana, meaning the generative power of the Supreme Brahma. I quote **Verse 5,** which mentions the existence of a mysterious egg in man's body that develops into a lotus:

*Aish yagyanaam vitato vahishtho vishtaarinam paktvaa divamaa vivesh. Aandeekam kumudam sam tanoti bisam shaalookam shafko mulali. Aitaastvaa dhaaraa upa yantu sarvaah swargeloke madhumat pinvamaanaa upa tvaa tishthantu pushakarineeh samantah.*5.

[This yajna is the best of all and so are those who perform it to enter the gates of Heaven. This yajna expands the egg placed at the base of man's bottom like the tubuler stem supporting the lotus buds. May you be blessed by the celestial streams of Heaven!]

Hymn XXXV, ascribed to Prajapati, refers to '*Yamodana*' and claims to conquer Death. I quote **Verse 6:**

Yasmaat pakvaadamritam sambabhoova yo Gayatryaa adhipatirbabhoova.
*Yasmin Vedaanihitaa vishwaroopaastenaudanenaati taraani mrityum.*6.

[From the properly prepared *Yamodana* was created the celestial nectar. This celestial nectar became the deity of the *Gayatri mantra*, which is the essence of the principal verses of Rig Veda as well as of *Yajur* and *SaamVeda*. From *Yamodana* we escape Death.]

Hymn XXXVI, composed by Rishi Chatan, bestows power to overcome Pishachas. I quote its last verse:

Abhi tam Niritirdhattaamashvamivaashvaabhidhaanyaa.
*Malvo yo mahyam krudhyati sa u paashaanna muchchate.*10.

[As a horse is tied with ropes, let deity *Nir-riti (Destruction)* siege upon my enemy and bind him in her cord. Let my enemy who is enraged with me not be freed from Destruction's cord.]

Hymn XXXVII is composed by Rishi Baadaraayini and is intended to destroy disease-causing germs. **Verse 3** mentions five herbs which are helpful in overcoming diseases—*Gugglu, Pila, Naladi, Aukshagandhi* and *Pramadani.*

ᔑ

Hymn XXXIX is composed by Sage Angira.

> *Prithivi dhenustashyaa Agnirvatsah;*
> *Saa meAgninaa vatseneshamoorjam kaamam dehaam;*
> *Aayuh prathamam prajaa posham rayim svaahaa.*2.
>
> [The Earth is a cow and Agni is her calf. Let the Earth and her calf Agni provide us food, long life, progeny, strength and plentiful wealth. We offer oblation to them.]

In similar fashion the venerable sage prays to the firmament, the Sun, the Moon. The last verse is addressed to Jataveda Agni:

> *Hridaa pootam mansaa Jatavedo vishwaani Deva vidvaana;*
> *Saptaashyami tava Jaatavedastebhyo juhomi sa jushasva havyam.*10.
>
> [O *Jaataveda* Agni, knower of all beings, who posseses seven mouths; we offer you the oblation, purified by our innermost mind and soul. Oblige us by acceping the oblations!]

ᔑ

Hymn XL is ascribed to Shukra, designed to destroy the enemies. It prays to Jataveda Agni to destroy the enemies coming from East, West, North or South and not spare those who attack from the netherlands or from the sky. Those who come from above should be scalded by the Sun. I quote the last hymn:

> *Ye dishaamantardeshebhyo juvhati Jatavedah sarvaabhyo digbhyoabhidaasantyasmaan;*
> *Brahmartvaa te paraancho vyathantaa pratyagenaan pratisaren hanmi.*8.

[O Jaatavedaa Agni, destroy the enemy attacking with an intent to destroy us from the main direcions; but let the enemies attacking from intermediate regions be punished by the supreme Brahma!]

SELECTED HYMNS FROM ATHARVA VEDA CHAPTER 5

Hymn I, authored by Rishi Atharva, is dedicated to Varuna.

Ridhanmantro yonim ya aa
vabhoovaamritaasuvardhamaanah sujanmaa;
*Adabdhaasubhraajamaanoaaheva trito dhartaa daadhaar treenee.*1.

[*Trita*, the deathless Spirit who is refulgent like daylight, who upholds the manifested three worlds and is their guardian and supporter and inheres in them. He takes birth from time to time for mankind's wellbeing.]

Devi Chand explains that 'Trita' means 'guardian, protector.' He added that 'Griffith considers Trita to be a mysterious ancient deity, frequently mentioned in the Rig Veda, principally in connection with the Maruts, Vayu and Indra. His home is in the remotest heaven, and he is called *Aptya*, the Watery, that is, sprung from, or dwelling in, the sea of cloud, and vapour. This explanation is unacceptable, as there is no history in the Vedas.'

Hymn III is also composed by Rishi Atharva who offers a fervent prayer to Agni, Indra, Vishnu, the Maruts, Vishvedeva, Savita, Rudra, etc., for protection against foes, to bewilder the foes so that they run away from the field. **Verse 7** is addressed to three Goddesses, which I quote:

Tistro Devirmahi nah sharma yachchhata prajaaye nastanve yachcha pushtam.
*Maa haasmahi prajayaa maa tanoobhirmaa rathaam dvishate Soma rajan.*7.

[O Three Goddesses (Bharati, Prithvi and Saraswati,)[141] you ensure our full wellbeing. Give nourishment and food to us and our people. We should not lack in offspring and cattle. O King Soma, we should not be troubled by our enemies.]

∽

Hymn IV is authored by Rishi Bhrigu Angira. It's a prayer for safety against diseases like *kushtha* (leprosy), takman (malarial fever), cough, etc.

∽

Hymn V is composed by Rishi Atharva in praise of a herb called '*Silaachi*', which is described as follows:

Raatree maataa Nabhaha pitaa Aryaman te pitamahah;
*Silaachee naama vaa asi saa Devaanaamasi svasaa.*1.

[Night is your mother (as you are nourished by moon rays), the Sky is your father (as you are born from rain water) and Aryaman your grandfather. You are *Silaachee*, sister of the Gods.]

Silachee is a flowery creeper, and the first part of **Verse 3** compares it romantically with a nubile lass:

Vrikashamavrikshamaa rohasi vrishanyanteeva kanyalaa.
*Jayanti pratyaatishthantee spranee naam vaa asi.*3.

[Like a nubile lass desiring union with a male you cling to a tree. You are liable to be conquered and are upward moving, therefore you are known as *Sparni.*]

∽

Hymn VII was also composed by Sage Atharava. It offers a grudging tribute to a malevolent deity, Araati (Poverty). Let's see why:

[141]According to Bhagwati Devi Sharma.

Aa no bhar maa pari shtha Araate maa no
raksheerdakshinaam neeyamaanaam;
*Namo veertsaayaa asamridhye namo astvaraatye.*1.

[O *Devi Araate*, Pray fulfill us by bestowing prosperity on us, and do not prevent us from earning *Dakshina*. O goddess of poverty and enemy of prosperity, we bow to you from afar]

Maa vanim maa vaacham no veetraseerubhaavIndraAgni aa
bhartaam no vasooni;
*Sarve no adhya ditsantoaaraatim prati haryat.*6.

[O *Araate*, do not obstruct our speech and our worship. Let Indra and Agni shower prosperity on us from all directions. May all Gods enrich us and act against our foes]

Paroaapehyasamridhye vi te hetim nayaamasi;
*Veda tvaaham nimeevanteem nitudantimaraate.*7.

[O Goddess of Poverty! Go far away from us, we turn your harmful dart aside. We know you to be a source of agony and sorrow.]

∽

Hymn VIII is aimed at destroying the enemies as in earlier chapters. **Hymn X** seeks to obtain an armour of stone which would not be destroyed by the enemy coming to attack from all quarters.

∽

Hymn XIII is composed by Sage Garutmaan and seeks to avert death by snake-bite.

Dadirhi mahyam Varuno divah kavirvachobhirugrairni
rinaami te visham;
Khaatamkhhatamuta saktamagrabhamireva dhanavanni
*jajaas te visham.*1.

[God Varuna has given me a boon, by the power of His sacred words I remove your poison, O Snake! I withdraw your poison that has entered the body. As water gets lost in sand, I destroy the poison in your body.]

Chakshushaa te chakshurhanmi vishen hanmi te visham;
*Ahe mriyasva maa jeeveeh pratyagabhetu tva visham.*4.

[O Snake, I destroy the power of your eyes with the power of my eyes and destroy your poison with poison. O Snake, you should die; don't remain alive. Let your poison go back in your body.]

Asitasya taimaatashy babhrorpodakashya cha;
*Saatraasaahashyaaham manoravya jyaamiv dhanvano vi munchaami rathaam eva.*6.

[Of black and brown snakes that live in wet places and of those that live away from water, we remove the poison of these wrathful and powerful snakes, as easily as the string from the bow, or the horses from chariots.]

Taabuvam na taabuvam na dheta tvamasi taabuvam;
*Taabuvenaarasam visham.*10.

[You are not Taabuva, indeed you are not Taabuva! your poison gets ineffective because of Taabuva.]

Tastuvam na tastuvam na ghet tvamasi tastuvam;
*Tastuvenarasam visham.*11.

[An object worthy of censure cannot be free from censure. O serpent, you are worthy of censure. Let your poison be removed by the medicine *Tastuva*!]

It's pure abracadabra, mumbo jumbo, to delude and defraud the simple, illiterate folk!

~

Hymn XIV is ascribed to Shukra and is dedicated to an imaginary herb to protect people from *Kritya*, a deadly disease.The first verse describes the herb:

Suparnastvaanvavindat sookarastvakhanatrasaa;
*Dipsaushadhe tvam dipsantamav krityakritam jahi.*1.

[O celestial herb, an eagle had sighted you and a boar had dug up you with his snout. O potent medicine, those who wish to kill us by *Kritya*'s help, you kill them.]

Ava jahi yatudhaanaanav krityaakritamjahi;
*Atho yo asmaan dipsati tamu tvam jahyoshadhe.*2.

[O wonderous medicine, you destroy the violent Rakshasas and those wish to kill us by using *Kritya* against us. Those who desire to kill us, you kill them.]

Yadi vaasi Devakrita yadi vaa purushaih krita;
*Taam tvaa punarnayaamseeIndrena sayuja vayam.*7.

[O *Kritya*, whether you have been directed by gods or men, know that we are God Indra's friends and are sending you back to destroy the senders.]

Udeyneeva vaaranyabhiskandam mrigeeva;
*Krityaa kartaarmrichchhatu.*11.

[Just as a female elephant and a female deer jumps at her assailant, O *Kritya*, you assail those who directed you against us]

Hymn XV is said to have been composed by the eminent Sage Vishvamitra; it is dedicated to a medicine, *Maadhulaushadhi.* It seeks to eradicate diseases by Madhulaaushadhi, which, like mead, was fermented from honey. The medicine is also called '*Rritajaata*'—'born from Rta'.The hymn has a poetic refrain, *Rritajaata rritaavari madhu mey madhulaa karah!*

Aika cha mey dasha cha meyapavaktaara aushadhe;
*Rritajaata rritaavari madhu mey madhulaa karah.*1.

[O Medicine, those denouncing us may be one or ten, you were born from *Rta* and are suffused with *Rta*.]

Dve cha mey vinshatishcha meyaapavaktaar aushadhe;
*Rritajaata rritaavari madhu mey madhulaa karah.*2.

[O Medicine, those denouncing us may be two or twenty; you were born from *Rta* and are suffused with *Rta*.]

Tistrashchya mey trinshachcha meyaapavaktaar aushadhe;
*Rritajaata rritaavari madhu mey madhulaa karah.*3.

[O Medicine, those denouncing us may be three or thirty; you were born from *Rta* and are suffused with *Rta*.]

In this fashion, the hymn goes on in sing-song manner till it comes to the last verse:

Shatam cha mey sahastram chaapvaktaaraushadhe;
*Rritajaata rritaavari madhu mey madhulaa karah.*11.

[O Medicine, those denouncing us may be hundred or thousand; you were born from *Rta* and are suffused with *Rta*.]

∽

The next **Hymn XVI,** is also composed by Rishi Vishvamitra. In those good old days, it was a necesssity to encourage men to procreate progeny—a reverse of Indira Gandhi's Family Planning programme, which aimed at '*Hum Do, Hamaare Do*' (We Two, Our Two). This hymn categorizes men by a measure of potency called '*vrisha,*' meaning 'a semen-spilling bull'. It seems to grade men for their procreative power by arithmetical progression or regression.

*Yadhdhekavrishoaasi srijaarasoaasi.*1.

[(O man!) If you are endowed with one unit of *Vrisha,* you should procreate more, lest you are considered lacking in procreation.]

*Yadi dvivrishoaasisrijaarasoaasi.*2.

[(O man!) If you are endowed with two units of *Vrisha,* you should procreate more, lest you are considered lacking in procreation.]

The hymn goes on in this manner till it comes to the **Verse 11**:

> *Yaddheykaadashoaasisoaapodakoaasi.*11.
>
> [(O man!) if you are devoid of the above mentioned ten measures of *Vrisha*, and are the eleventh, you are lacking in '*udaka*'—the power of erection!]

This hymn seems to aim at '*Hum Do, Hamaare Sau!*' like Dhritrashtra!

∽

Hymn XVII, dedicated to '*Brahmajaya,*' is an extended version of the Hymn X. 109 of the Rig Veda: 'Rape and Return of Brahmin's Wife'. Dr. Ghosh had referred to it in his exposition of the nature of the hymns of Atharva Veda, which I have quoted earlier.

∽

Hymn XVIII is dedicated to '*Braham Gavi*' (Brahmin's Cow) and predicts dire punishment for those taking her away. Dr Ghosh had also quoted two **Verses 9 and 10,** from this hymn in his exposition. **Verse 9** proclaims: 'The Brahmins possess sharp arrows and missiles; the volley they hurl never misses its target. Pursuing with fervour and fury, they cast him down from afar.'

Before I quote a few verses from it let me add that Devi Chand refuses to accept that the hymn is about a Brahmin's cow. He holds that the hymn is about Brahma-Vedic Knowledge, which is the preserve of the Brahmins.

> *Akshadrugdho Raajanyah paapa atmaparaajitah;*
> *Sa Brahamanashya gaamadhyaadadhya jeevaani maa shva.*2.
>
> [A voluptuous, sinful, spiritually degraded King, who eats a Brahmin's cows, shall only live today, not tomorrow.]
>
> *Aavishtitaaghavishaa pridaakooriva charmanaa;*
> *Saa Brahamanashya Raajanya trishtaisha gauranaadhyaa.*3.
>
> [O King, the Brahmin's cow is like a terrible snake covered under skin, charged with lethal poison; none may kill it and live.]

Jihvaa jyaa bhavati kulmalam vaannaadeekaa dantaastapasaabhidigdhaa.
*Tebhirbrahamaah viddhyati Devapeeyoon hridvalairdhanurbhirdevajootaih.*8.

[The Brahmin's tongue acts as a bow-string, his voice as the arrow and his teeth, sharpened by penance, act as arrow-heads. The arrows that he sends pierce the foe from afar, never miss their target.]

~

Hymn XIX is aimed at ensuring the safety of the Brahmin's cow or property, his honour and his progeny. It predicts dire destruction of the whole country if a Brahmin is troubled, tortured or insulted.

Ugro Raja manyamaano Brahmanam yo jighatsati;
*Paraa tat sichyate raashtram Brahmano yatra jeeyate.*6.

[The King who, considering himself powerful, makes a Brahmin angry by his acts, and the country where a Brahmin is miserable, that kingdom or country is sure to degenerate.]

Tad vai rashtramaa sratavato naavam bhinnaamevodakam;
*Brahmaanam yatra hinsati tad raashtram hanti duchchhuna.*8

[The country in which a Brahmin is killed shall be destroyed by physical calamities. As water engulfs a broken boat, the country shall perish because of the sin of killing a Brahmin.]

Verse 9 invokes the legendary Sage Narada who lives in heaven:

Tam vrikshaa apa sedhanti chhaayaam no mopagaa iti;
*Yo brahamanashya sadhvanmabhi Narada manyate.*9.

[O Narada, even the trees would repel people who take away a Brahmin's property, treating it as their own. The trees would drive them away from their sheltering shade.]

Devi Chand takes exception to Griffith calling Narada a celestial sage who visits Earth to report what is going on in Heaven and returns with his account of what is happening on Earth. 'This explanation is unacceptable', exclaims Devi Chand, 'as it savours of history in the Vedas. The word "Narada" means king, the leader of men.'

Na varsham MaitraVarunam brahamajyamabhi varshati;
*Naasmai samitih kalpate na mitram nayate vasham.*15.

[The rain produced by Mitra-Varuna does not fall in a country where the Brahmins are oppressed. The king of such country does not get the Samiti's approbation and even his friends do not support him.]

Hymn XXII, composed by Rishi Bhrigu Angira, relates to the eradication of Takman, the malarial fever, like several such hymns before. I would quote only the first and the last verse.

Agnistakmaanmapa baadhataamitah Somo Graavaa Varunah pootdakshaah;
*Vedirbarhih samidhah shoshuchaanaa apa dveshaanshamuyaa bhavantu.*1.

[Let Agni, Soma, Gravaa, Varuna, Indra, the *yajna vedi*, the oblation, the *kusha* grass banish the takman fever; let our foes go away far from here.]

Devi Chand in his translation has transformed the Vedic Gods, Agni, Soma, Varuna into 'venerable physicians'!

The last **Verse 14** is also interesting:

Gandhaaribhyo moojavadabhyoaangebhyo Magadhebhya;
*Praishan janamiva shevadhim takmaanam pari dadhasi.*14.

[Just as a man is sent to far off Gandhaar, Anga and Magadha to control the treasury, we banish you to distant lands.]

Devi Chand, as usual, is critical of Griffith mentioning that Gandharis are inhabitants of Gandhar, a country to the west of the Indus and to the south of Kabul River, called Kandhara now, asserting that there is no history in the Vedas. He gives no reason why he is averse to disclosing the names of Vedic gods or historical sages and the places which occur in Vedic hymns.

~

Hymn XXIII is composed by Sage Kanva. The sage attempts to destroy worms *(Krimi)* by reciting its verses. I quote the four verses:

> *Otey mey DyhaavaaPrithvi otaa Devi Saraswati';*
> *Otau ma IndrashchaAgnishcha krimim jambhayataamiti.*1.
>
> [May the Sky, the Earth, Goddess Saraswati, Indra and Agni combine to destroy the worms.]

Devi Chand renders it as follows: Sun and Earth are interwoven for me, divine knowledge is meant for me, electricity and fire are intermingled for me. May these destroy the worms. This is my prayer.

> *AsyeIndra kumarashya krimeen dhanpate jahi;*
> *Hataa vishvaa araatay ugren vachasaa mam.*2.
>
> [O opulent Indra, destroy the inimical worms torturing this boy. Let our ardent prayer destroy the dangerous worms.]
>
> *Saroopau dvao viroopo dvao krishanau dvao rohitao dvao;*
> *Babhushcha babhrukarnashyacha gridhrah kokashacha te hataah.*4.
>
> [Two worms of the same shape, two of different shapes, two of black colour, two of red, one of brown colour, one of brown ears, a vulture and a wolf; all have been killed by the power of my hymns.]
>
> *Atrivid vah krimayo hanmi KanvavajJamadagnivat;*
> *Agastyashya brahamana sam pinashyaham krimeen.*10.
>
> [O worms, as *Rishis* Atri, Kanva and Jamadagni had destroyed you, we do likewise; we crush you by the power of Agastya's *mantras*.]

Hymn XXV is a '*Garbhaadhaan Sookta*', ascribed to God Brahma, aiming at safe pregnancy.We have read a similar hymn earlier. It invokes goddesses Sinivali and Saraswati to help protect the male seed in the females. Besides the two goddesses, it calls on all the Vedic gods to render assistance. The last five verses exhort gods like Tvashta, Savita, Prajapati to ensure that the pregnant woman is blessed with a male child! The last four verses have a refrain: '*Pumansam putarama dhehi dashme maasi sootave!*'(Let a male child be born in the tenth month!).

I quote a few verses:

Garbha dhehi Sinivaali garbha dhehi Saraswati;
Garbha te Ashvinobhaa dhattaama pushkarstraaja.3.

[O Sinivali, render help in conception; O Saraswati, you protect the womb.]

As usual, Devi Chand adds a footnote to chastise Griffith: 'Griffith considers Siniwali to be the goddess of the day of the new moon and also of fecundity and easy birth. This explanation is unacceptable, as there is no history in the Vedas. The word means a woman who is careful and regular in her diet.'

Vishnuryonim kalpayatu Tvashta roopani pinshatu;
Aa sinchatu PrajapatirDhata garbha dadhatu te.5.

[Let Vishnu equip women to conceive, let Tvashta duly shape her limbs and joints; let Prajapati protect the womb and Dhata develop the child.]

A male child was of prime importance to the Vedic sages!

Adhi skand veerayasva garbhamadhehi yoniyaam;
Vrishaasi vrishnayaavan prajaaye tva nayaamasi.8.

[Arise, O young man, you are powerful and possess manly strength; plant your semen within the womb. We urge you to procreate and produce progeny.]

Dhatah shreshthena roopenaashya narya gaveenyoh;
*Pumaansam putramaa dhehi dashme maasi sootave.*11.

[O God Dhata, establish in the womb of this beautiful maiden a charming male child to be born in the tenth month of conception.]

∽

Hymn XXVIII, composed by Rishi Atharva. prays for a long life; we have already seen a similar hymn earlier. I quote **Verse 8**, which invokes the sacred syllable '*Om*':

Trayah suparnaastrivrita
yadaayannekaaksharmabhisambhooya shakraah.
*Pratyauhanmrityumamriten saakamantardhanaa duritaani vishvaah.*8.

[When the sacred syllable is formed with three rays (a, u, m), it transforms into nectar; which eradicates all infirmities and confers immortality.]

∽

Hymn XXIX is composed by Rishi Chatan and is dedicated to Jataveda Agni. It prays for protection against diseases. I quote a couple of verses.

Tatha tad Agne krinu Jatavedo vishwebhirdevai saha samvidanah;
*Yo no dideva yatmo jaghaasa yathaa so ashya paridhishpataati.*2.

[O Jataveda Agni, try to ensure in consultation with all gods that the fort wall of such a disease falls down which torments us and wishes to consume us.]

Kravyadamagne rudhiram pishacham manohanam jahi Jatavedah;
*TamIndro vaji vajrena hantu chhinattu Somah shiro ashya dhrishnu.*10.

[O Jataveda Agni, slay the flesh-devouring, blood-sucking, mind-destroying *Pishachas*. Let invincible Indra kill them with his thunderbolt; let powerful Soma behead them.]

Hymn XXX is a pedestrian composition seeking long age. I quote two verses:

Ma bibherna marishyasi jardashtim krinomi tva;
*Nirvochamaham yakshamamangebhyo angajwaram tava.*8.

[O man, tormented by illness, have no fear; we will ensure that you live in this world till old age. We will drive out *yakshma* and other ailments from your body.]

Angabhedo angajvaro yashcha te hridayamayah;
*Yakshmah shyena iva prapaptad vaachaa saadhah parastaraam.*9.

[The pain that troubles you, the fever that torments you, the disease that has lodged in your heart and the consumption that consumes you, I shall remove them all like a hawk that has fled far away.]

Hymn XXXI is an antidote against Kritya. We had encountered Kritya earlier.

Yaam te chakruraame paatre yam chakrurmishradhanne;
*Aame maanse krityaa yam chakruh punah prati haraami taam.*1.

[Our enemies have enclosed Kritya in a clay pot, mixed it in grains or in raw meat; we send this *Kritya* back to our enemies.]

Yaam te chakruh krikavaakaavaje vaa yam kureerini;
*Avyaam te krityaam yam chakruh punah prati haraami taam.*2.

[The enemies have administered Kritya on our cocks, goats, rams and ewes; we return it to those enemies.]

Yaam te chakruh sabhayaam yam chakruradhidevane;
*Aksheshu kritya yaam chakruh punah prati haraami taam.*6.

[Kritya which the enemies have sent to the Assembly and to the dice court used in gambling, we send it back to the enemies.]

Yaam te krityaam koope avadadhuh shamshaane vaa nichakhnuh;
*Sadhyani krityaam yaam chakruh punah prati haraami taam.*8.

[The enemies have thrown Kritya in the wells and buried it in the graveyards and sent it to our homes; we remove it and return Kritya to the sender.]

Krityaakritam valaginam moolinam shapatheyyam;
*Indrastam hantu mahataa vadhenaAgnirvidhyatvastayaa.*12.

[May Indra slay our secret, slanderous, low-bred enemies with his mighty bolt; may Agni scorch them in his flames.]

SELECTED HYMNS FROM ATHARVEDA CHAPTER 6

The Atharvedic hymns that claim to cure all kinds of maladies and act as effective antidote against evil spirits and demons, snakes and vermins, were churned out by the Brahmins, who had won the confidence of the public and established a reputation of being godly people.

Hymn VI is composed by Rishi Atharva and dedicated to Brahmanaspati. The sage was invited by the Rajanya for offering sacrifice to ensure enemy destruction.

YosmanBrahamaspate devo abhimanyate;
*Sarvam tam randhayaasi me yajamaanaay sunvate.*1.

[O Brahmanaspte Deva, our evil, atheist enemies who are designing to vanquish and destroy us, make them subservient to this devotee of yours who performs this *yajna,* offering Soma juice.]

Yo nah Soma sushanshino duhshansha aadideshati;
*Vajrenaashya mukhe jahi sa sampishto apaayati.*2.

[O Lord Soma, these spiteful people wish to enslave us; smite them with your thunderbolt, crush their faces to pieces and make them run away.]

Yo nah Somaabhidaasati sanaabhiryashcha nishtayah;
*Apa tashya balam tir maheev Dhyautvadhatmanaa.*3.

[O God Soma, whoever are our enemies, belonging to our tribe or otherwise, you smite them like the lightening from the sky, destroy their might and their armies.]

Two short **hymns, VIII and IX,** composed by Rishi Jamadagni, are dedicated to the God of Love—*Kama* (Eros).They express a passionate desire for Kamini—a beautiful maiden!

Hymn VIII:

Yathaa vriksham libujaa samantam parishasvaje;
*Aivaa pari shvajasva mam yathaa mam kaaminashyo yathaa mannaapagaa asaha.*1.

[As the creeper clings to, and throws her arms around the tree, hold me in tight embrace, desiring me, O my beloved, never to depart.]

Devi Chand cannot permit such profanity in the Vedas as directed by his guru, Swami Dayananda Saraswati. He translates 'kamini' as 'knowledge' and entreats her: 'Just as the creeper throws her arms on every side around the tree, o shouldst thou. O Knowledge, hold me in thine embrace, that thou mayset be in love with me, my darling, never to depart.'

Yathaa suparnah prapatan pakshau nihanti bhoomyaam;
*Aivaa ni hanmi te mano yathaamam kaaminashyo yathaa mannaapagaa asaha.*2.

[As the Eagle soaring high, presses his wings downwards to the Earth, I fix my thoughts on you, O my darling, hold me in tight embrace, desiring me, never to depart.]

Yatheme DhyaavaaPrithivee sadhyah paryeti Sooryah;
*Aivaa paryemi te mano yathaa mam kaaminyasoyathaa mannaapagaa asaha.*3.

[As at dawn, the Sun encompasses the Heaven and Earth in his golden glow, so do I envelop you, my love. Come, hold me in tight embrace, desiring me, never to depart.]

Hymn IX:

Vaachchha me tanvam paadau vaachchhakshau vaachchha sakthyau.
*Akshyau vrishanyantyaah keshaa mam te kaamen shushantu.*1.

[Love me and desire me, O my doting Sweet-heart, love my body, my eyes, my thighs; Your curling hair, craving eyes and parched lips make me thirst for love.]

Mama tva doshanishrisham krinomi hridayashrisham;
*Yathaa mama krataavaso mama chittamupaayasi.*2.

[I take you in my arms and lodge you in my heart, so that you comply with my wishes and grant my desire.]

Yaasaam naabhiraarehanam hridi samvananam kritam;
*Gaavo ghritashya maataroamoom sam vaanayantu mey.*3.

[Whose navel is attractive and heart overflowing with love, let this maiden, docile like a cow, and brimming with *ghrita,* incline to love me.]

∽

Hymn XI is ascribed to Prajapati and is dedicated to *Retas,* sexual union. It's called *'Punsavana Sookta'*. Bhagwati Devi Sharma explains that a hymn composed for wishing a male child is called Punasavana Sookta, while that composed desiring a daughter is called '*Straishooya Sookta*'. I have not come across any hymn wishing for a daughter in Atharva Veda or Rig Veda!

> *Shameemashvattha aaroodhastatra punsuvan ktitam;*
> *Tad vai putrashya vedanam tat streeshvaa bharaamasi.*1.

> [As the Ficus religiosa riding a young peepal tree, produces a manly baby tree; thus, when virile men spill semen into a maiden's womb, a boy is born.]

> *Punsi vai reto bhavati tat striyaamanu shichyate;*
> *Tad vai putrashya vedanam tat Prajaapatirbraveet.*2.

> [When man's potent sperm irrigates a woman's womb, a son is born, Lord Prajapati has so ordained.]

> *PrajaapatirAnumatih Sinivalya cheeklirpat;*
> *Straishyooyamanyatra dadhat pumaansamu dadhadiha.*3.

> [In other circumstance, when Lord Prajapati and Goddesses Anumati and Siniwali will it, a girl is born.]

Devi Chand fires the salvo of 'no history in the Vedas' at Griffith in his footnote: 'Griffith considers Anumati and Siniwali as deities presiding over different phases of the moon and associated with conception and child birth. This explanation is unacceptable, as there is no history in the Vedas.'

Hymn XII is composed by Rishi Garutmaan. It offers a remedy for snake bite, a common occurrence in India.

> *Pari dhyaamiv Suryoaheenam janimaagamam;*
> *Ratree jagadivaanyadamdhasaat ten te vaarye visham.*1.

> [As the Sun knows the Heaven, we know the snakes. As the night separates the Sun from the Earth, we remove snake poison from your body.]

> *Yadbrahamabhiryadrishtbhiriyad devairviditam pura;*
> *Yad bhootam bhavyamaasanvat tenaa te vaaraye visham.*2.

> [The Gods, the rishis and the Brahmins had known this cure from early times and will remain knowledgeable in future. I

am going to remove snake poison from your body by reciting this mantra.]

Madhva prinche naddya1: parvataa giriyo madhu;
*Madhy Parushni Sheepaalaa shamaasne astu sham hride.*3.

[We treat you with this madhu (sweet potion) found in the hills on the banks of River Parushni (Ravi), which induces sleep as it cures the poison and comforts the heart and the mouth.]

Devi Chand even takes exception to Griffith pointing out that Parushni is a river in Punjab which is called Ravi now. He repeats parrot-like: 'This explanation is irrational, as there is no history in the Vedas. The words are names of medicines.' Very funny! There may not be any history in the Vedas, but geography is certainly there.

~

Hymn XIV, authored by Rishi Babhrupingal seeks to drive away a disease named '*Balaasa*': He has dedicated the hymn to the disease!

Asthistramsm parustramsamaasthitam hridayamayam;
*Balaasam savam naashayaangeshthaa yashcha parvasu.*1.

[O dire disease Balaasa, you have penetrated the bones, the joints, the lungs and the heart, tormenting the entire body.]

Nirbalaasam balaasih kshinomi pushkaram yathaa;
*Chhinadyashaya bandhanam moolamurvaarvaa eva.*2.

[We remove Balaasa as easily as uprooting stalks of lotus from a pond; we disconnect it from the body as ripe cucumber falls off the plant.]

Nirbalaasetah pra pataashungah shishuko yatha;
*Atho ita iva haayanoapa drahyyaveerhaa.*3.

[O dreadful infirmity Balaasa, exit this body as a young deer bolts, and like the last year, never return.]

The largest number of hymns in Chapter 6 deal with the problem of diseases. **Hymn XV** was composed by Rishi Uddalak in praise of the Palasha tree which gets laden with bright yellow flowers.

Uttamo ashyoshadheenaam tava vrikshaa upastayah;
*Upastirastu so smaakam yo asmaan abhidaasati.*1.

[You are the best of all the trees, all other trees are your subordinates. The diseases that wish to dominate us, let them be subservient to us.]

Sabandhushchaasabandhushcha yo asmaan abhidaasati;
*Teshaam saa vrikshaanaamevaaham bhooyaasamuttamh.*2.

[As this tree is the best among the trees, likewise we along with our brethren should be supreme over those that want to harm or injure us.]

Yathaa Soma aushadheenaamuttamo Havishamkritah;
*Talaashaa vrikshaanaamivaaha bhooyaasamuttamh.*3.

[Just as Soma is the best of oblations amid the medicinal plants, the *Talasha* (or Palasha)[142] tree is the best among flowering trees.]

Hymn XVI, authored by Rishi Shaunaka, is dedicated to the Moon. It mentions several herbs, probably because these herbs thrive in moonlight.

Aabayo anaabayo rashasta ugra aabayo;
*Aa te karambha madhyasi.*1.

[O *Aabaya*,[143] your juices are both sweet and sour. This mixture that I have made is the best.]

[142]Acharya Sayana had suggested that the tree mentioned as 'Talasha' was in fact Palasha.
[143]Sayana has suggested that 'Aabaya' refers to mustard.

Vihalho naam te pitaa Madaavati naam te maataa;
Sa hi na tvamasi yastvamaatmaanmaavayah.2.

[Your father's name was Vihalva, your mother's *Madaavati*; this mixed juice is different from them both.]

Tauvilikeaavelayaavaayamailab ailayeet;
Babhrushacha babhrukarnashchaapehi niraal.3.

[O *Tauvilike* (Herbal medicine), you give us energy and cure our illness. Make this ailment in the eyes called '*Ailab*' disappear. Let the diseases called *Babhru* and *Babhrukarna* leave the body, and let the disease *Niraal* be cured.]

Alsaalaasi poorvaa silaanjaalaashuttaraa;
Neelaagalsaalaa.4.

[O *Alsaalaa*, as you remove laziness; you are called '*Poorvaa*' and are the first to be administered. O *Shalanjalaa*, you reach out to the body cells and are called '*Uttaraa*'; to be administered at the end. O *Neelaagalasaalaa,* you are to be administered in the middle.]

Devi Chand translates these hymns, calling the herbs and medicines as all-pervading, refulgent God.

Hymn XVIII, composed by Rishi Atharva, is aimed at eradicating Jealousy from the mind of man.

Irshaayaa dhraajim prathamaan prathamashyaa utaaparaam;
Agnim hridayyam1 shokam tam te nirvaapayaamasi.1.

[O Envious Man, we eradicate for ever the first effects of jealousy and its subsequent effects as also the mental anguish and the fire of anger that burns within the heart.]

Yathaa bhoomirmritamanaa mritaanmritamanastaraa;
Yathota mamrushyo mana aiveshyormritam manah.2.

[Just as the earth is devoid of all feelings, so is the envious man more senseless than a dead man; like a corpse he loses all sensibility.]

Ado yat te hridi shritam manaskam patayishnukam;
*Tatasta eershyaam munchaami nirushpaanam driteriva.*3.

[O jealous man, I drive out jealousy from your mind as the blacksmith drives hot air out of the bellows.]

~

Hymn XX is composed by Rishi Bhrigu Angira. It is dedicated to the deity who controls the diseases yakshma or takman, high malarial fever, as in an earlier hymn, or jaundice.

Agnerevaasashya dahat aiti shushimana utaiva matto vilapannapaayati;
*Anyamashyadichchhatu kam chidvratastapurvadhaaya namo astu takmne.*1.

[Like the fierce burning fire this fever torments the body, making the affected person rant and rave. I bow to dreadful takman!]

Namo Rudraay namo astu takmane namo raagye Varunaay tvisheemate.
*Namo dive namah Prithivyai nama aushadheebhya.*2.

[I bow in reverence to Rudra and bow to takman; I pay homage to radiant King Varuna and to Prithvi and the herbs.]

Ayam yo abhishochayishnurvishvaa roopaani haritaa kranoshi.
*Tasme te-aarunaaya vabhrave namah krinomi vanyaay takmane.*3.

[I salute you, O red and brown coloured takman that spreads in forested areas, causing acute pain and distress, making the body pale yellow, draining all energy.]

~

Hymn XXI is composed by Sage Shantati and addressed to an 'Aushadhi' that gives the gift of long hair to women. I quote the last verse:

Revateernaadrishah sishaasavah shishasatha.
*Uta stha keshandrihaniratho ha keshavardhini.*3.

[O powerful medicinal herb, you grant good health to all and never cause hurt. Be merciful and grant the boon of long and lustrous hair to our women.]

Devi Chand has translated this verse as follows: 'O wealthy, non-violent, charitable subjects, long to give your gifts freely. Thou art the strengthener and augmentor of glory and renown.' He calls it translation!

~

Hymn XXIV, also composed by Sage Shantati, is a prayer to '*Aapah*' (Waters), praising the rivers coming down from snow-clad mountains.

Himvatah prasravanti sindhau samaha sangamah;
*Aapo ha mahyam tad deveerdadan hriddyotabheshajam.*1.

[O Waters, originating from snow-clad mountains, you rivers flow into the ocean; provide us medicines alleviating fever and assuaging our hearts.]

Sindhupatneeh sindhuraagyeeh sarvaa yaa naddhya1 sthana.
*Datta nastasya bheshajam tenaa vo bhunjaamahai.*3.

[You are wives of the ocean; the ocean is your King. O perennially flowing streams, relieve us from painful ailments, so that we enjoy strength-giving food.]

~

Hymn XXV is composed Shunah-Shepa, adopted son of the renowned Rishi Vishvamitra, to eradicate diseases like '*Mannya*' which caused painful swelling of veins in the neck and shoulders. It has a refrain—'*Itastaah sarva nashyantu vaakaa apachitaamiv*' (Let them be ineffective like lustful words to a chaste wife!).

Panch cha panchaashachcha sanyanti Mannya abhi;
*Itastaah sarva nashyantu vaakaa apachitaamiv.*1.

[The fifty-five boils or tumours that appear in the upper part of the neck; let them be ineffective like lustful words to a chaste wife.]

Sapta cha yaah saptatishcha sanyanti graivyaa abhi;
Itastaah sarva nashyantu vaakaa apachitaamiv.2.

[The seventy-seven boils or tumours that appear in the neck; let them be ineffective like lustful words to a chaste wife.]

Nava cha yaa navatishcha sanyanti skandhaa abhi;
Itastaah sarva nashyantu vaakaa apachitaamiv.3.

[The ninety-nine boils or tumours that appear on the shoulders; let them be ineffective like lustful words to a chaste wife.]

Hymns XXVII, XXVIII and XXIX have been composed by Rishi Bhrigu and are dedicated to Yama, the god of death as also to Nir-riti, the goddess of chaos or destruction. An ominous pigeon or dove, who is the messenger of Nir-riti, has been sighted. The rishi pays homage to this messenger, offers *havvya* in a yajna and prays to the bird to depart without harming the family and the cattle stock. He also invokes Agni to ensure that no harm is caused due to the dove's ominous visitation.

Hymn XXVII

Shivah kapota ishito no astvanaagaa Devah shakuno graham nah;
Agnirhi vipro jushataam havirnah parihetih pakshini no vrinaktu 2.

[O Gods, this pigeon who has come to our house, may he be for our well-being, and cause no harm to our family. O wise Agni, please accept this oblation and save us from being ruined.]

Hymn XXVIII, also composed by Sage Bhrigu, makes a similar prayer to the ominous Dove to depart from the family's grain storage. In this hymn, too, the rishi seeks assistance of Lord Yama:

Richa kapotam nudat pranodamishm madantah pari gaam nayaam;
*Sanlobhayanto duritaa padaani hitva na oorjam pra padaat pathishthah.*1.

[O Gods, Send this ominous Dove to some far distance. Let this Dove leave our grain store and fly off. We remove the marks left by the Dove and take our cows, fed with grains, for a walk.]

Yah prathamah pravatmaasasaad bahubhyah panthaamanupasyashanah.
*Yosyeshe dvipado yashchatushpadastasmai Yamaaya namo astu mrityave.*3.

[O God Yama, you are foremost and most exalted among gods, the lord of the world of bipeds and quadrupeds; You award people according to their deserts at death. We pay homage to you to protect us.]

In **Hymn XXIX,** besides a dove, an owl has also been sighted. Rishi Bhrigu prays to Nir-riti:

Yau te dootau Nir-riti idmetoaaprahitau vaa graham nah;
*Kapotolookaabhyaampadam tadastu.*2.

[O goddess Nir-riti, weather the Dove and Owl are your messengers or not; Pray, don't let them stay in our dwelling.]

Hymn XXX has been composed by Rishi Uparibabhrav, singing praise of *Yava* (barley) and the *Shami* (Palaash) tree:

Deva imam madhunaa sanyutam yavam Sarswatyaamadhi manaavacharkrishuh;
*Indra aaseet seerapatih Shatakratuh keenaashaa aasan Marutah sudaanavah.*1.

[When the Gods gifted the sweet savoury 'yava' (barley) to men near the River Saraswati, Indra was the master of the plough and the Maruts became cultivators.]

Brihatpalaashe[144] *subhage varshavriddha rritaavari;*
*Maatev putrebhyo mrida keshebhyah shami.*3.

[The fortunate *Shami* tree, bearing broad leaves, is nourished by rain; may it have a hundred branches for it affords us pleasure, like a mother to her sons.]

∽

The next **Hymn XXXI** is ascribed to Brahma and addressed to *Pappman,* the deity of sin. The rishi tells this evil deity to leave him and go to people who adopt untruthful ways, else he will leave it at the cross-roads.

Yo nah Paapman na jahaasi tamu tva jahimo vayam;
*Pathaamanu vyaavartane-anyam Paapmaanu padyataam.*2.

[O Sin, if you do not leave us, we will leave you at the turning of the paths; so that you might find someone else and go with him.]

∽

Hymn XXXII was composed by Rishi Chaatan and is dedicated to Agni, Rudra, Mitra, and Varuna. It is designed to destroy the *Yaatudhaanas;* the rishi prays to Agni to destroy them:

Antardaave juhutaa svetadyaatudhaanakshyanam ghriten;
*Aaraad Rakshansi prati daha tvam Agne na no grihaanaamup teetapaasi.*1.

[O Priests, offer oblations of *ghrita* and let us pray to Agni to destroy these violent *Yaatudhaana* (Rakshasa, Pishacha, germs of diseases.) O Agni, save our households from grievous harm.]

---

144 The tree Brihatpalaash, called 'Shami' here, is probably related to the Palaasha tree we have seen earlier.

Rudro vo greevaa ashrait pishachah prishteervoaapi shrinaatu yatudhaanah;
*Veerud vo vishvatoveeryaa Yamen samajeegamat.*2.

[O *Pishacho*, Rudra has broken your neck; let Him now break your ribs. O *Yatudhano*, my powerful prayer has sent you to the abode of Yama.]

Hymn XXXIV, composed by Rishi Chatan, is much the same as the foregoing hymn, praying for destruction of the Yaatudhaanaas.

ᔑ

Hymn XXXV, composed by Rishi Kaushik is addressed to *Vaishvaanar*, the benevolent Agni. I quote the first and the last verse:

Vaishvaanaro na ootaya aa pra yaatu paraavatah;
*Agnirnah sushtuteeroopa.*1.

[Let God Agni, benefactor of all mankind, come from far distance to protect us and hear our prayer.]

VaishvaanaroAngirasaam stommuktham cha chaaklirpat;
*Aishy dhyumnam svaryamat.*3.

[Vaishvaanar Agni has rendered these verses capable, and by revealing the secrets of obtaining fame and food, has enabled me to experience the joys of heaven.]

Hymn XXXVI, composed by Rishi Atharva is also dedicated to Vaishvaanar.

Sa vishvaa prati chaaklrip rritoorutam srijate vashee;
*Yagyashya vaya uttiran.*2.

[Vaishvaanar Agni provides sustenance to all people. Agni carried oblations to the Gods and regulates the seasons as the Sun.]

ᔑ

Hymn XXXVII, is also composed by Rishi Atharva; it is intended for destruction of those who hurl curses.

Upa praagaat sahastraaksho yuktvaa shapatho ratham;
*Shaptaaramanvichchhan mama vrik evaavimato graham.*1.

[May the thousand-eyed Indra come to us riding his chariot, and destroy those who curse us, as the wolf kills sheep.]

Yo nah shapaadashapatah shapato yashchya nah shapaat;
*Shune peshtramivaavakhaamam tam pratyashaami mrityave.*3.

[We don't curse anyone, but if someone curses us, we throw him to Death as one throws a piece of bread to a dog.]

∽

Hymn XXXVIII, also composed by Rishi Atharva, is a prayer to be endowed with Energy or Power!

Sinhe vyaaghra uta yaa pridaakau tvishirAgnno Brahamane Soorye yaa;
*Indram yaa Devi Subhagaa jajaan saa na aitu varchasaa samvidaanaa.*1.

'Whatever energy or power the lion, tiger, adder, the burning fire, God Brahma, the Sun and Devi Subhaga have, and the power with which Indra was born, grant us the same power.'

Hymn XXXIX, also authored by Sage Atharva, seeks glory like Indra, Agni and Soma.

Yasha Indro yasha Agniryashah Somo ajaayat;
*Yasha vishvashaya bhootashyaahamasmi yashastamh.*3.

[Indra and Agni seek glory; Soma too was born wishing for glory. As they were glorious, I too long and wish for glory!]

∽

Hymn XL, again authored by Rishi Atharva, offers a prayer to Dhyava-Prithvi, Soma, Savita (the Sun), Sky, the Seven Stars (Saptarshi) and Indra.

Abhayam Dhyavaa-Prithvi ihaastu no-abhayam Somah Savita krinotu;
*Abhayam no-astoorva antariksham Sapt Rishinaam cha havishabhayam no astu.*1.

[O Dhyavaa-Prithvi, let your protection make us fearless. May the Sky, the Moon and the Sun fill us with courage! May the oblation offered to the Seven Stars (Saptarshi) free us from fear!]

Asmai graammaya pradishchatastra oorjam subhootam svasti Savita nah krinotu;
*AshtrivIndro abhayam nah krinotvanyatra raagyaamabhi yaatu manyuh.*2.

[O Savita, bless us so that we grow ample grains in our village and live safely; with blessings of Indra, let our benign king protect us so that we have no fear from our enemies.]

Anamitram no adharaadanmitram uttaraat;
*Indraanmitram nah pashchyaadanamitram puraskridhi.*3.

[O Indra, be pleased to make us free from enemies from the north and south and from east and west!]

∽

Hymn XLI is a prayer for being blessed with long life. The author has not disclosed his identity; the hymn has been ascribed to Brahma. It prays to the Moon in the first verse and to Saraswati in the second verse. In the last, third verse, it prays to the constellation of the Seven Stars (Saptarshi), which I quote:

Maa no haashishurrishiyo daivyaa ye tanoooa ye nastanvastanoojah.
*Amartyaa matyaanrabhi nah sachadhvamaayurdhatta prataram jeevase nah.*3.

[May the celestial Seven Stars (*Saptarshi*) protect us; may our family members don't forsake us. May the Immortal Seers protect us mortals and award us an excellent long life.]

Hymn XLII is authored by Rishi Bhrigu Angira and is dedicated to *Manyu* (Anger). In the first two verses it promises to eradicate anger from the heart as easily as a man removes a bow-string from the bow or throws off a heavy stone he is carrying. I quote the third verse:

Abi tishthaami te Mannyum paashnryaa prapaden cha;
*Yathaavasho na vaadisho mam chittamupaayasi.*3.

[O generator of anger, *Manyu,* I trample on your anger with my heal and toe so that you yield to my will and don't utter wrathful words.]

Hymn XLIII is also authored by Bhrigu Angira. It praises the durva grass that grows in the plains as also the herb of multiple roots that grows near the sea shore as effective remedies against anger. I quote the last verse which promises to control the tongue to calm the nerves and erase redness from the face caused by anger:

Vi te hanayaam sharanim vi te mukhyaam nayamasi;
*Yathavasho na vaadisho mabha chittamupaayasi.*3.

[O man, we would control your tongue in your mouth, which creates anger and animosity; you would not be able to utter angry words then and remain subservient to my will.]

Hymn XLIV was composed by Sage Vishvamitra, it promises to cure blood-letting.

Asthaad dhyaurasthaat Prithivyasthad vishvamidam jagat;
*Asthurvrikshaa oordhvasvapnaastishthaad rogo ayam tava.*1.

[Just as this Sky with the planets and stars, and the Earth, stand firm and the trees stand still while asleep, let this blood flowing out of the veins stop and be still.]

Shatam yaa bheshajaani te sahastram sangataani cha;
*Shreshthamaastraavbheshajam vasishtham roganaashanam.*2

[O patient, of all your hundred remedies and other thousand cures, this one that I give is the most effective.]

Rudrashya mootramashyamritashya naabhih;
Vishaanka naam vaa asi pitranaa mooladutthitaa
*vaateeritnaashanee.*3.

[The urine of Rudra is like nectar and this medicine 'Vishaanakaa' that I have is the most potent against the malady of breaking wind.]

The poet probably means 'rain water' by the phrase 'Urine of Rudra'—a vulgar, unbecoming simile!

∽

Hymns XLV and XLVI offer a cure against bad dreams, which are followed by those for long life and protection against forest fire.

There is another hymn seeking long life, **Hymn XLVII**, authored by Rishis Angiras and Pracheta. The first verse prays to Agni to grant sons, grandsons, prosperity and long life. The second verse prays to Indra and the Maruts to grant a long life. I quote the third verse:

Idam triteeyam savanam kaveenaamriten ye
chamasamairyant;
Te saudhanvanaah sva raanshaanaah svishtim no abhi vashyo
*nayantu.*3.

[The son of Angiras, Ribhu Sudhanva, who had made a chariot and a wonderful container (*chamasa*) for drinking Soma juice and had succeeded in achieving salvation, even Godhood.[145] May the Ribhus bestow on us excellent rewards and long life!]

∽

Hymn L, composed by Rishi Atharva, is a prayer to the Ashvins—requesting them to kill rats in his fields!

---

[145]It's a tall claim! Rishi Angiras and his descendents are famous for making such absurd claims.

Hatam tardam samankamaarvrumAshvina chhinta shiro api prishteeh shrneetam.
*Yavannedadaanapi nahyatam mukhmathaabhayam krinutam dhaanyaaya.*1.

[O Ashvins, Pray destroy these destructive rats and protect our green barley fields; cut off the heads of the rats and crush their ribs!]

∽

Hymn LI, composed by Rishi Shantaati, sings the glory of the elixir Soma.

Vayoh pootah pavitrena pratyan Somo ati drutah;
*Indrush yujyah sakha.*1.

[The ethereal Soma juice, fanned and made sacred by Vayu, quickly inflames all my limbs and reaches the navel. The Soma is a friend of Indra.]

Devi Chand translates it as: 'The pure internal soul, cleansed through the ennobling contemplation of God, soon attains to salvation, and becomes His friend through yogic.' He has a license to mislead in the name of Swami Dayananda Saraswati!

∽

Hymn LII is a prayer similar to many others against the *Yatudhaans* and Pishachas, while **Hymn LVI** praises dreams, who have the consort of Varuna as their mother and who soothe and afford solace to man in sleep. It prays to dreams to guard man from nightmares assigns them to their foes.

Hymn LVII, composed by Sage Shantati, seeks Lord Rudra's blessing for protection against diseases. I quote the last verse:

Shan cha no mayashcha no maa cha nah kim chanaamamat;
*Kshmaa rapo Vishwam no astu bheshajam sarvan no astu bheshajam.*3.

[O God Rudra, grant us protection from mental and physical anguish caused by diseases; let my progeny and cattle be from them. Forgive my sins and make me free from the maladies.]

Hymn LX is a charming composition by Rishi Atharva dedicated to Rigvedic God Aryaman.

Ayamaa yaatyaryamaa purastaad vishitstupah;
*Ashya ichchhannagruvai patimut jaayaamajaanye.*1.

[Aryaman is rising in the East. He is rising with intent to provide a bride to a single man and a husband to a nubile lass.]

Devi Chand translates this verse as: 'Here comes the illustrious father of the bride, seeking a husband for this bride, a wife for this unmarried man.'

AsharamadiyamAryamannanyaasaam samanm yatee;
*Ango nvAryamannashyaa anyaah samanmaayati.*2.

[O Aryaman, these young damsels, craving for a husband, are dejected, not having found one. Other maidens are in the same plight.]

Dhaataa daadhaar Prithivim dhaataa dhyaamut Sooryam;
*Dhaataashyaa agruvai patim dadhaatu pratikaamyam.*3.

[May *Dhata Deva*, who upholds the Earth, the Sky and the Sun in their stations, provide meet husband to these maidens.]

Hymn LIV is composed by Rishi Atharva and dedicated to Vishvedeva..Its theme is living in harmony.

Sam jaaneedhvam sam prachtadhvam sam vo manaansi jaanataam.
*Devaa bhaagam yathaa parve sanjaanaanaa upaasate.*1.

[As from olden times, the Gods partook of their shares of oblations, O man, you should acquire knowledge with one accord; live together and share ideas in unison!]

Samaano mantrah samitih samaanee samaanam vratam sah chittamesham.
*Sammanen vo havishaa juhomi samanam cheto abhismvishadhvam.*2.

[O men, let your thought processes, principles and ideals be in unison. I will sanctify your lives with a *mantra* and offer oblations in common on your behalf.]

Samaanee va aakootih samaanaa hridayaani vah;
*Samaanamastu vo mano yathaa vah sushaasati.*3.

[O men, let your hearts beat in unison; let your thoughts flow in one direction towards a common goal so as to accomplish, and succeed in, your tasks together.]

Hymns LXV, LXVI and LXVII address vanquishing enemies. All three have been composed by Rishi Atharva. I quote one verse from each.

Hymn LXV

Nirhastebhyo nairhastam yam Devaah sharumasyatha;
*Vrishchyaami shatroonaam bahoonanen havishaaham.*2.

[O Gods, the arrows that you use to slay your enemies; with the same arrows we will slash the arms of our enemies by offering oblation to you.]

Hymn LXVI

Nirhastaah santu shatravoangaishaam mlaapayaamasi;
*AthaishaamIndra vedaansi shatsho bhajaamahai.*3.

[O Indra, Drain the strength of our foes from their hands and from every part of their body. Let us obtain their wealth in hundreds and thousands with your assistance.]

Hymn LXVII

Aishu nahya vrishaajinm harinasyaa ghiyam kridhi.
*Paraadamitra aishatvarvaachee gauroopeshatu.*3.

[O Indra! You shower joys and prosperity on us. Gird our soldiers with black deer's skins to strike terror in the hearts of our enemies and make them desert the field. Let us obtain the wealth and the cows of the defeated foes.]

∽

Hymn LXX, composed by Rishi Kankaayan, is dedicated to the cow. It gives a curious analogy for the intense love the cow has for her calf:

Yatha maansam yathaa suraa yathaakshaa adhidevane,
yathaa punso vrishanyata streeyaam nihanyate manah;
*Aivaa te aghne manoadhi vatse ni hanyataam.*1.

[As a meat-eater loves meat, a wine-drinker loves wine, the dice-player loves the dice and a lustful man loves women, the cow loves her calf.]

There is no way Devi Chand will allow correct translation of such a verse. He translates it as: 'Just as knowledge, prosperity, various dealings are associated with kingship, just as a strong man's desire is firmly set upon a dame, so let thy heart and soul, O unassailable subjects, be firmly set upon the All-pervading God!'

∽

Hymn LXXII, authored by Sage AtharvaAngira is dedicated to *Shepa*, the male genital organ. I quote the last verse:

Yaavadangeenam paarasvatam haastinam gaardabham cha yata;

Yavadashvashya vaajinstaavat te vardhtaam pasah.3.

[Just as the forest dwelling animals, elephants, horses, donkies and the rest keep their sexual organs strong and in good shape, let the organs of this man be strong and powerful to perform the sexual act.]

∽

Hymns LXXIII and **LXXIV** composed by Rishi Atharva are similar to his Hymn LXIV quoted above; they seek harmony among people. Hymns seeking long life, fame, physical strength and protection against diseases were in great demand and many of these short, three-verse quickies were composed to satisfy it. They are devoid of any freshness.

The theme of **Hymn LXXXI,** composed by Rishi Atharva, is *garbhaadhaan* (conception). I quote Verse 2:

Parihasta vi dhaaraya yonim garbhaaya dhaatave;
Maryaade putramaa dhehi tam tvamaa gamayaagame.2.

[May the Gods protect the genital organ of this woman and her foetus. May she conceive a son and may she impel the child to come out at the right time.]

∽

Hymn LXXXII is ascribed to Bhaga, the god of nuptial relations; it is dedicated to Indra. It gives voice to a young man's desire to get a wife. I quote the second verse:

Yen Soorya SavitrimAshvinohatuh pathaa;
Ten maamabraveed Bhago jaayaam vahataaditi.2.

[God Bhaga told me: 'The way the Ashvins obtained Soorya-Savitri, you too obtain a wife the same way.' The poet is referring to the Rigvedic hymn which describes the wedding of Sun's daughter Surya.]

∽

Hymn LXXXIV is dedicated to Nir-riti, similar to the ones we have seen earlier, while **Hymn LXXXV** seeks to avoid diseases like tuberculosis. **Hymn LXXXVII** is eulogy to a king at his accession ceremony:

Hymn LXXXVII

> *Ihevaidhi map chyoshthaah parvativavichaachalat;*
> *Indra iveha dhruvastishtheha raashtramu dhaaray.*2.
>
> [O King, may you be firmly established on the throne and stay firm like the mountains. As Indra rules in heaven, you rule here and lead the nation.]

∽

Hymn LXXXIX, authored by Rishi Atharva, seeks to kindle the flame of love in a maiden's heart. I quote the last two verses:

> *Shochayaamasi te haardi shochayaamasi te manah;*
> *Vaatam dhoom iva sadhryan maamevaanvetu te manah.*2.
>
> [I kindle the thoughts of love in your heart, O pretty maiden; As smoke is drawn towards the wind, let your heart be drawn to mine.]
>
> *Mahyam tva MitraVarunau mahyam Devi Saraswati;*
> *Mahyam tva bhoomya ubhavantau samashyataam.*3.
>
> [Let Mitra-Varuna, Goddess Saraswati, even the Earth's two ends and the middle part promote our union; may your love for me increase forever!]

∽

Hymn XC11, also composed by Rishi Atharva, is dedicated to *Vaajin*, the horse, the most loved animal of the Vedic people. I quote the first verse:

> *Vaatrambaa bhava vaajin yujjyamaan Indrashya yaahi prasave manojavaa;*
> *Yujjantu tva Maruto vishvavedas aa te Tvashtaa patsu javam dadhaatu.*1.

[O Horse, you run fast like wind, when yoked to a chariot. Inspired by Indra, you reach the destination with the speed of mind. May the Maruts and Tvashtra add swiftness in your feet.]

Devi Chand does not want to disclose that the hymn is addressed to the horse. He translates the verse as follows: 'O powerful king, with full consciousness, be as fast as wind. Go forth as swift as thought at god's behest. May wealthy, ennobling learned persons yoke thee to royal administration. May god lay swiftness in thy foot.'

I knew he has an aversion to revealing names of Vedic gods but I could not understand what objection he might have to a eulogy to a horse. I got the answer when I looked at his footnote: 'The verse has been applied to *Praana* by Pt Jaidev Vidyalankar and to the horse by Sayana and Griffith. Pt Jaidev Vidyalankar has translated *Vajin* as breath while Pt Khem Karan Das Trivedi has translated *Vajin* as a strong king.'

Devi Chand's high regard for his gurus makes him give short shrift to the correct meaning of the Sanskrit word 'vajin.'

∽

Hymn CI, authored by Sage Atharv-Angira, is similar to Hymn V of Chapter 4. It prays for strengthening of the male genital organ.

Aa vrishaayasva shvasihi vardhasva prathayasva cha;
*Yathaangm vardhataam shapastena yoshitamijjahi.*1.

[O man, be potent like the seed-spilling bull. Let your organs be strong to consummate your union with a woman.]

Aaham tanomi te paso adhi jyaamiv dhanvani;
*Kramasvarsha iva rohitmanavaglaayataa sadaa.*3.

[You are equipped like the arrow placed on a fully stretched bow; go to your mate as a bear attacks a deer.]

∽

Hymn CVI, composed by Rishi Pramochan, offers an idyllic description of a Vedic sage's cottage, surrounded by the flowering green grass.

> *Aayane te paraayane doorvaa rohatu pushpineeh;*
> *Utso vaa tatra jaayataam hrido vaa pundareekavaan.*1.

> [In front and behind the cottage, the green, flowering '*durva*' grass grows. There is a pond in front in which the lotus blooms.]

(The Sanskrit word '*durva*' has become '*doob*' in Hindi.)

∽

Hymn CVIII is composed by Shaunaka and addressed to *medha* (intellect). I quote the second verse:

> *Medhaamaham prathamaam Brahamanavateem brahmajootaamrishishtutaam;*
> *Prapeetaam brahmachaaribhirdevaanaamavase huve.*2.

> [We invoke the intellect that created the Vedas! Intellect is possessed and revered by Brahmins, lauded by the sages as well as celibate students, to promote godliness.]

∽

Hymn CIX is composed by Rishi Atharva in praise of *Pippali*, a herbal medicine that cures the fits of madness and insanity. I quote the first verse:

> *Pippali kshiptabbheshajjoo taatividdabhwahjee;*
> *Tam Devah samakalpayanniyam jeevitavaa alam.*1.

> [Pippali heals insanity, it also heals a deeply piercing wound. The *aushadhi* was thought of by the gods. This potent medicine ensures a disease-free long life.]

Hymn CX, also composed by Rishi Atharva is dedicated to Agni. The rishi invites Agni to act as *Hota* and shower happiness, fortune and wealth. I quote the second verse.

Jeshthaghnyam jaato vichritoryamashya moolabarhanaat pari paahyenam;
*Attainam neshad duritaani vishwaa deerghaayutvaaya shatashaaradaaya.*2.

[O Agni, protect this sacrificer from the evil and fatal effects of the *Jeshtha* and *Moola* asteric constellations. Let the child born under their influence be freed from the clutches of Yama, and let him enjoy life for a hundred autumns.]

In **Hymn CXI,** composed by Rishi Atharva, prays to Agni to cure a man of madness.

Devainsaadunmaditmunmattam rakshasaspari;
*Krinomi vidvaan bheshajam yadaanunmaditoasati.*3.

[We know the cure for insanity caused by sins committed against godly or ungodly powers. We use the medicines which will restore your sanity and free you from mental unrest.]

Punastvaa durapsarasah punarIndra punarBhagah;
*Punastvaa durvishwe Devaa yathaanunmaditoasasi.*4.

[O man, the heavenly Apsaraas have freed you from your malady. Gods Indra and Bhaga and other gods have cured you of your disease.]

∽

Hymns CXIV and CXV have been ascribed to Brahma and have been addressed to Vishvedeva. In the former hymn the Adityas are requested for deliverance from sins committed unwittingly, while in the later hymn the Vishvedevas are invoked to seek their mercy for wrong acts committed in ignorance.

Hymn CXX, composed by Rishi Kaushik, seeks relief from the effects of *Karma*:

Yadantariksham Prithivimut dhyaam yanmaataram pitran vaa jihinsim;
*Ayam tasmaad gaaryapatyo no Agnirudinnayaati sukritashya lokam.*1.

[O god Agni, the sins we have committed against *Dhyu*—the firmament, the denizens of the Earth and against our parents, causing them hurt, absolve us from them, and secure a place for us in high Heaven.]

Hymn CXXI, also composed by Rishi Kaushik, is addressed to God Varuna and Nir-riti. I quote the first verse:

Vishaanaa paashaan vi shyaadhyasmd ya uttamaa adhamaa Vaaruna ye;
*Dushvapnyam duritam ni shvaasmdatha gachhem sukritashya lokam.*1.

[O Nir-riti, presiding deity of sins, free us from the high, medium and low-grade snares of Varuna. Relieve us from bad dreams and all sins and make us enter the gates of Heaven.]

∽

Hymn CXXVII aims at destroying the dreadful disease Balaasa that causes cough, consumption, etc., which we had encountered in Hymn XIV.

The mysterous **Hymn CXXIX** is also composed by Rishi Atharva; it is dedicated to Bhaga.

Bhagena ma shanshapena saakamIndrena medina;
*Krinomi Bhaginam maapa draantvaraatayah.*1.

[O Indra, endow me with conjugal felicity, make me fortunate like the luxuriant *shanshap* tree.[146] May my austere habits fly away!]

Yena vrikshaam abhyabhavo bhagen varchasaa saha;
*Tain maa Bhaginam krinvapa draantvaraataya.*2.

[O Indra, make me fortunate like the trees, by affording me the Bhaga's felicity. May my pleasureless days fly away!]

Yo andho yah punahsaro Bhago vriksheshvaahitah;
*Ten maa Bhagin krinvapa draantvaraatayah.*3.

[146]Trees are fortunate as the creepers entwine them.

[O God Bhaga, make me fortunate with the vitality and ever-increasing power. Let our enemies remain far away from us.]

Hymns CXXX, CXXXII and CXXXIII are also composed by Rishi Atharva; they are dedicated to *Smar* and eulogize love-making. The first verse of **Hymns CXXX** is reminiscent of the Rigvedic **Hymn X. 53**, about the love affair of Prince Pururuva and the nymph Urvashi. It appears to be a wild song of a love-lorn maiden.

Rathajitaam raathajiteyeenaamApasarasaamayam smarh;
*Devah pra hinuta smarmasau maamanu shochatu.*1.

[My love-lorn behaviour is like that of the chariot-riding prince who won the heart of Apsaras. O Gods, send this love-spell towards him, let him consume with love of me.]

Asau me smartaaditi priyo me smartaaditi;
*Devah pra hinuta smaramasau maamun shochatu.*2.

[Let him think of me; do let my love think of me; O Gods, send this love-spell towards him, let him consume with love of me.]

Unmaadayata Maruta udantariksha maaday;
*Agna unmaadaya tvamsau maamanu shochatu.*4.

[O Maruts, O Agni, O Sky, send me in love-frenzy! Let him consume with love of me.]

Devi Chand translates '*smar*' as 'recollection,' confusing it with word '*smaran*' probably deliberately. Actually, the two words have the same root.

Hymn CXXXI is also dedicated to Smar. It should be kept in mind that sex had an aura of spiritualtity in the Vedic age.

O Anumateunvidam manyasvaAkoote samidam namah;
*Devaah pra hinuta smarsau maamanu shochatu.*2.

[O Devi Anumati, O Devi Aakoote, assent to our prayers! O Gods, may this glorious Love remain ever fresh in my mind!]

Hymn CXXXII is again dedicatated to *Smar.*

Yam Devah smaramasinchannapsva1ntah shoshuchaanam sahaadyaa;
*Tan te tapaami Varunashya dharmanaa.*1.

[The gods bathed all creatures of the world in water so as to make them crave for mating. I appease the god of love by Varuna's power.]

YamIndrani smaramasinchadapsvaantah shoshuchaananam sahaadyaa.
*Tan te tapaami Varunashya dharmanaa.*3.

[Indrani anointed God *Kama* in water; O maiden, I appease him by Varuna's power.]

YamIndrAgni smaramasinchadapsvaantah shoshuchaananam sahaadyaa.
*Tan te tapaami Varunashya dharmanaa.*4.

[Indra and Agni anointed Kama in water; I appease him by Varuna's power.]

~

The deity of the next **Hymn CXXXIII** is *'Mekhala'*, the girdle (what in Hindi is called '*Janeoo*') made of cotton yarn worn by a celibate student—*Brahmachaari*—around his waist. The hymn is composed by Rishi Agastya.

Aahutaashyabhihut Rishinaamshyaayudham;
*Poorvaa vratashya praashnati veeraghni bhava mekhle.*2.

[O Mekhala, you are sanctified by oblations; you are the armour of the Rishis. You are worn when the vow of celibacy is taken. Do remain attached to heroic men.]

Shraadhaayaa duhitaa tapsoadhijaataa svas risheenaam bhootakritaam babhoova;
*Saa no Mekhale matimaa dhehi medhaamatho no dhehi tapa indriyam cha.*4.

[This girdle is Faith's daughter and sister of the sages, born by the power of Tapa. O Girdle, award us a keen intellect and wisdom to control the senses and learn the scriptures.]

Hymn CXXXIV is ascribed to Shukra, meaning Indra, and dedicated to Vajra, Thunderbolt, Indra's deadly weapon. It is designed to destroy the enemies by the power of mantra instead of an armed combat.

Ayam vajrastrpauataamritashyaavaashya rashtramap hantu jeevitam.
*Shrinaatu greevaah pra shraatooshnihaa Vratrashyev Shachipatih.*1.

[As Devi Shachi's husband Indra slashed the demon Vritra's throat and hands by his thunderbolt, let this prayer annihilate our foes and vanquish their country.]

Yo jinaati tamanavichchha yo jinaati tamijjahi;
*Jinto vajra tvam seemantamanvanchamanu paataya.*3.

[O Indra's thunderbolt! Go in search of our enemies, crush them and throw them at the end of the border of our country.]

Hymn CXXXV is similarly ascribed to Shachipati Indra, wishing to acquire physical strength.

Yadashnaami balam kurva ittham vajramaa dade;
*Skandhaanmushaya shaatayan Vritrasheva Shachipati.*1.

[I eat nourishing, health giving food to increase my body strength. I take the weapon in my hand and slash the shoulders of the enemy just as Shachipati Indra slashed Vritra's shoulders.]

Yada giraami san giraami samudre iva sampibah;
*Praanaanamushya sangeerya sn giraamo amum vayam.*3.

[Whatever I devour, I devour well. I swallow the enemy's *prana*, *apaana*, eyes and all. Thereafter I swallow the enemy completely.]

∽

The Atharvan poets churned out hymns to remedy all ills and problems. **Hymn CXXXVII** is composed by Sage Veetahavya; it provides an antidote even against the falling hair of women and promises the growth of luxuriant tresses:

Yaam Jamadagni khanad duhitre keshavardhaneem;
*Taan Veetahavya aabhar dasitashya grihebhyah.*1.

[The wonder herb that Rishi Jamadagni had dug up for luxuriant growth of his daughter's hair was in fact brought by Rishi Veetahavya from another rishi's house.]

Abhishunaa meya aasan vyaamenaanumeyah;
*Keshaa nada iva vardhantaam sheershanaste asitah pari.*2.

[Locks which could only be measured with fingers, become measurable with extended hands after this wonder herb is used. Let the black locks spring thick and strong and grow like reeds upon her head.]

∽

Hymn CXXXVIII is composed by Rishi Atharva; it makes a dreadful prayer to Indra:

Kleebam kridhyopashinmatho kureerinam kridhi;
*AthaashyeIndro graavabhyaamubhe bhinattvandyau.*2.

[O herb, you are the most powerful of all the herbs! You turn our foes into eunuchs and women. Let Indra crush their genital organs with his *vajra* and let long hair grow on their pate.]

Hymn CXXXIX is also composed by Rishi Atharva. It seeks to administer a magical potion to a nubile maiden making her gullet dry in longing for the yajamaan, the sponsor of the yajna-sacrifice:

Shushatu mayi te hridayamatho shushatavaashyami;
*Atho ni shushya yaam Kaamenaatho shushkaashyaa char.*2.

[Let your heart wither for my love, let your mouth go dry for my mouth. Let your lips be parched with longing for my lips.]

The last verse is aimed at uniting a man and woman:

Yathaa nakulo vichhidya sandadhatyahim punah;
*Aivaa Kamashya vichchhinna sam dhehi veeryaavati.*5.

[As the mongoose bites the snake, rends it in pieces and joins them again, O potent Aushadhi, make the separated man and woman unite again.]

The next hymn, **CXL**, is also composed by Rishi Atharva and is intended to pacify the tiger-like double-tooth of a child, which is considered inauspicious as it bites the mother's teats while he sucks milk.

Upahooto sayujau shyonau dantao sumangalau;
Anyantra vaam ghoram tanvah paraitu dantau maa
*hinshistam pitarm maataram cha.*3.

[Let both these teeth be like friends and give pleasure to the child. Let the pain that the mother and father of the child have to suffer due to the irregularity of the teeth disappear, and the parents be relieved.]

Hymn CXLI is said to be composed by Rishi Vishvamitra; it calls upon the Vedic gods to help rear the cows—the main occupation of the Rigvedic people.

Vayurenaah samaakarat Tvshta poshaaya dhriyataam.
*Indra aabhyo adhi bravad Rudro bhoomne chikitsatu.*1.

[May Vayu deva collect these cows,[147] may Tvashta nourish them. May Indra call them affectionately, may Rudra cure their diseases.]

[147]Devi Chand translates it as: 'An active teacher should collect the pupils.'

The second verse prescribes that a tattoo be etched on their ears to increase fertility:

Lohiten svadhitinaa mithunam karnayoh kridhi;
*AkartaamAshivinaa lakshma tadastu prajayaabahu.*2.

[O cowherds, with a heated bronze weapon make a *mithuna* (mating) mark on the ears of cows. May the Ashvins make a similar mark to multiply our progeny.]

~

The last sookta of Chapter 6, **Hymn CXLII,** is also ascribed to Rishi Vishvamitra. It eulogizes the plant 'yava' (barley), the principal crop of the Vedic people.

Uchchharayasva bahurbhava sven mahasaa yava;
*Mrineehi vishva paatraani maa tvaa divyaashanirvardheet.*1.

[O Yava plant, grow in abundance in multiple shoots, rise high and fill up all our storage bins. Let not the lightening from the sky strike and damage you.]

Akshitaasta upasadoakshitaah santu raashayah;
*Prinanto askhitaah santvattaarh santvakshitaah.*3.

[O Yava, let the workers who have to sit near you and tend you be healthy; let the crop gathered from you be inexhaustible; let those who bring the grains home be numberless; let those who are nourished by you be healthy and fortunate!]

~

SELECTED HYMNS FROM ATHARVA VEDA CHAPTER 7

The introductory hymn and the next seven hymns of Chapter 7 have been composed by Rishi Atharva. **Hymn I** is dedicated to *Atma* reaching out to *Paramtma*:

Hymn I

Dheetee vaa ye anayan Vaacho agram mansaa vaa yeavavadannritaani;
*Triteyena Brahmanaa vaavradhanaastureeyenaamanvat naam dhenoh.*1.

[Those who, due to their mental acumen and intellectual vigour, reach the roots of Speech and adhere to the Truth let them be absorbed into the Brahma.]

Sa veda putrah pitaram sa maataram sa soonurbhuvat sa bhuvat punarmaghah.
*Sa dhyaamaurnodantariksham sva1 sa idam vishvambhavat sa aabhavat.*2.

[Only he is really born who attains the state described in Verse 1. He realizes who are his true father and mother and achieves an inexhaustible treasure. He reigns over the Earth and the firmament, becomes identified with the universe and permeates in all existence.]

Hymn IV contains a single verse dedicated to Vayu:

Aikayaa cha te dashbhishchaa suhute dvaabhyaamishtaye vinshatyaa ch.
*Tisribhishcha vahase trinshataa cha viyugbhirvaaya iha taa vi muncha.*1.

[O Vayu, we beseech you to grace our yajna. Come equipped with one to ten, two to twenty, and three to thirty gods, to fulfill our heart's desires and release your powers for our well-being.]

Hymn VIII is a single-verse sookta composed by Rishi Uparibhrava in praise of Brihaspati:

Bhadraadadhi shreyah prehi Brihaspatih puraitaa te astu;
*Athemamashyaa vara aa Prithivyaa aareshatrum krinuhi sarvaveeram.*1.

[O man, consider the way that leads to pleasure as inferior, and the path shown by Brihaspati, leading to ultimate bliss, the most superior. Let the best and bravest men be born on the earth to keep the foes away.]

∽

Hymn X, a pretty, single-verse sookta composed by Rishi Shaunaka, is dedicated to Goddess Saraswati:

Yaste stanah shashayuryo mayobhooryah sumnayuh suhavo yah sudatrah.
*Yen vishvaa pushasi vaaryaani Saraswati tamiha dhaatve kah.*1.

[O Saraswati, the milk from your breasts is a source of joy, wisdom, peace of mind and strength. Let us have access to it with your grace.]

Hymn XII, also composed by Rishi Shaunaka, relates to the institution of Sabha and Samiti in the kings' courts:

Sabha ch maa Samitishchavataan Prajaapaterduhitarau samvidaane.
*Yena sangachchhaa upa maa sa shikshyaachchaaru vadaani pitarah sangateshu.*1.

[The Sabha and the Samiti are required to be nurtured like the daughters of Prajapati. O forefathers, afford me the wisdom to give useful suggestions and speak respectfully in these assembelies.]

Aishaamaham samaaseenaanaam varcho vigyaanamaa dade;
*Ashyaasarvashyaah sansado maamIndra bhaginam krinu.*3.

[We benefit from the knowledge and standing of the members present. We are fortunate and achieve prosperity by the grace of Indra.]

∽

Hymn XVIII is composed by Rishi Atharva and is dedicated to Prithvi and Parjanya, the Rain-God:

Pra nabhasva Prithivi bhindheeda3dam divyam nabhah;
*Udno divyasyha no dhaatareeshaano vi shaa dritim.*1.

[O Earth, become a proper receptor of rain-water after being thoroughly ploughed. O *Parjanya*, let the gathering clouds provide ample rainfall.]

∽

Hymn XX is ascribed to God Brahma and is dedicated to Goddess Anumati. We had met the Goddesses Anumati and Sinivali in Hymn XI of Chapter VI. I quote Verse 4:

Yat te naam suhavam supraneeteAnumate anumatam sudaanu;
*Tenaa no yagyam piprihi vishwavaare rayim no dhehi subhage suveeram.*4.

[O generous and fortunate Goddess Anumati, bless our yajna to achieve fruition and grant us the gift of prosperity and brave sons.]

∽

Hymn XXVI is composed by Rishi Medhatithi and is dedicated to God Vishnu.

Vishnornu kam vocham veeryaani yah paarthivaani vimase ranjaasi;
*Yo askabhaayaduttaram sandhastham vichakramaanastredhorugaayah.*1.

[Let me declare the mighty deeds of Vishnu, who had measured out the Earth and propped up the high Heaven full of stars; He pervades the Earth, the atmosphere and the Sky.]

Yashorushu trishu vikramaneshvadhikshiyanti bhuvanaani vishwaa;
*Uru Vishno vi chakrame tredhaa ni dadhe padaa, samoodhamasya paansure.*3.

[O Vishnu, you traverse the three worlds and dwell in all these three worlds. Bestow us a dwelling endowed with prosperity. Accept the ghrita offered in the yajna and grant prosperity to the organizer of this yajna.]

Instead of proper hymns, one-verse snippets abound in the Atharva Veda on themes like vanquishing of the foes, granting of long life, elimination of jealousy, protection from curses, alleviation of the effects of sins, etc. They are quickies churned out in haste, generally devoid of poetic beauty. However, there are exceptions.

Hymn XXVII, composed by Sage Medhaatithi, is addressed to Ida (Vak or Saraswati):

Idaivaasmaam anu vastaam vraten yashyaah pade punate Devayantah;
Gritapadee shakvaree Somaprishthopa yagyamasthita Vaishvadevi.

[O Goddess Ida, you are worshipped by the pious and holy men. Accept our *ghrita* oblation and the divine Soma juice, O Universal Deity, bestow knowledge and prosperity upon us.]

One may recall that Ida figures in the Rig Veda, **Hymn I. 31,** composed by Rishi Hiranyastoop Angiras:

TvamAgne prathamamaayumaayave Deva akrinvannahushashya vishvapatim;
*Idaamakrinvanmanushshya shaasaneem pituryatputro mamakashya jaayate.*11.

[Gods made Agni the first Lord of the house of Nahusha; they made Ida the teacher of the sons of men and Agni the father of the human race.]

Jai Shankar Prasad, the towering Hindi poet, in his inimitable *Kamayani,* has a chapter on Ida, wherein Manu, the progenitor of mankind, addresses Ida as follows:

Tum Ide Usha-see aaj yahan aayee ho ban kitanee udaar,
Kalarav kar jaag pademere ye manobhava soye vihanga.

[O Ida, you have come here today like the golden-hued Dawn, and are being so generous; the yearnings of my heart, un-awakened thus far, have taken wings and are joyously chirping and twittering.]

Hymn XXXVI is a one-verse wonder, composed by Rishi Atharva. It is dedicated to a magical eye lotion for lovers. It's a charm pronounced by the bridegroom to his bride:

Akshau nau madhusankaashe aneekam nau samanjanam;
Antah krinushva mam hridi mana innau sahaasati.

[Let our glances sparkle with the love-lotion, sweet as honey; Harbour me within your bosom and let our hearts throb in harmony and unison!]

Hymn XXXVII, is another one-verse composition by Rishi Atharva. It is a nuptial charm spoken by the bride:

Abhitvaa Manujaaten dadhaami mama vaasasaa;
Yathaaso mama kevalo naanyaasaam keertayaashchan.

[With this my robe that I inherited from Manu, I envelope you. May you be all mine and give no thought to other damsels.]

Hymn XXXVIII, also authored by Rishi Atharva, has five verses addressed by a wife to her husband. I quote the first and the last two:

Idam khanaami bheshajam maanpashyamabhirorudam;
*Paraayato nivartanamaayatah pratinandanam.*1.

[I dig up this aushadhi (herbal medicine); it binds my husband to me, deters him straying from me; it makes our married life felicitous]

Aham vaddami net tvam Sabhaayaamaha tvam vada;
*Mamedsastvam kevalo naanyaasaam keertayaashchan.*4.

[In the Sabhaa you alone may speak, but at home I too shall speak; listen to what I say and approve. You should remain mine alone, never think of anyone else.]

Yadi vaasi tirojanam yadi vaa nadhyastirah;
*Iyam ha mahyam tvamoshadhirbaddveva nyaanayat.*5.

[If you have to go in a forest or to travel across a river, this aushadhi (charm) will bind you and bring you back to me.]

∽

Hymn XLVI, authored by Rishi Atharva, sings the glory of Goddess Sinivaali:

Ya subaahuh svangurih sushooma bahusoovaree;
*Tashyai vishpatnyai havih Sinivaalyai juhotana.*2.

[O priests and sponsors of yajna, offer oblation to Goddess Sinivaali, endowed with lovely arms, graceful fingers and physical charm. She will bless us with prosperity and progeny.]

Ya vishpatnIndramasi prateechee sahastrastu kaabhiyanti Devi;
*Vishno: patni tubhyam raataa haveemshipatim Devi raadhase chodayasva.*3.

[O Devi Sinivaali, you are consort of the all-powerful god Indra and the beloved of Lord Vishnu. Worshipped by thousands, O graceful goddess, we offer you obalation, shower prosperity on us.]

∽

Hymn XLIV is a two-verse sookta, composed by Rishi Atharva in praise of Goddess Kuhoo (Vak), wife of Brihaspati. I quote the first verse.

Kuhoom Deveem sukritam vidmanaapasamasmin yaggye suhavaa johaveemi;

Saano no rayim vishvavaaram ni yachchhaada dadaatu
*veeram shatadaayamukthyam.*1.

[Goddess Kuhoo performs noble deeds with great wisdom and is worthy of worship; we solicit her presence in this sacrifice. May the Goddess be pleased and shower prosperity on us and bless us with charitable, heroic sons!]

~

Hymn L, composed by Rishi Angiras, is an earnest prayer of a gambler. I quote the first two verses:

Yathaa vrikshamshanirvishavaahaa hantyaprati;
*Aivaahamadhya kitavaanakshairbadhyaasamaprati.*1.

[As the flash of lightening scorches the trees, the throw of dice destroys the gambler.]

Turaanaamaturaanaam vishvaamavarjursheenaam;
*Samaitu vishvato bhago antarhastam kritam mama.*2.

[I am the first to come and the last to leave the game of dice. Let the wealth of those addicted to the game, be awarded to me by the dice.]

~

The short hymns that follow pray for harmony among people (*Saamanashya*), long life, safety on pathways from foes, alleviation of effects of snake poison, diseases, curses, sins abound. Besides, there are one-verse or two-verse quickies on Indra, Agni, the cow.

Hymn LXVII, called '*Atma Sookta*' is ascribed to Brahma and dedicated to Atma.

Punarmaitvindriumpunaraatmaa dravinam Brahamanam cha;
*Punaragniyo dhishnyaa yathasthaama kalpayantaamehaiva.*1.

[May I, after rebirth, acquire prosperity, spiritual power, riches and Vedic knowledge. May I have access to sacrificial fires, obtain wealth and become prosperous.]

Hymn LXVIII, is composed by Sage Shantaati and dedicated to Devi Saraswati. I quote the first verse:

Shiva nah shantamaa bhava sumrideeka Sarasvati;
*maa te yuyoma sandrishyah.*1.

[O Devi Saraswati, may you bestow happiness on us and save us from diseases; may we be blessed by beholding your real image!]

∽

Hymn LXXI is composed by Rishi Atharva and dedicated to Agni.

Pari tvaAgne puram vayam vipram sahashya dheemahi;
Dhrishdvarnam divedive hantaaram bhanguraavatah.

[O God Agni, appeared miraculously by rubbing of sacrificial sticks, destroy the Rakshasas who create obstacles in yajna sacrifices. Pray kill these killers!]

∽

Hymn LXXVII is composed by Rishi Angiras and dedicated to the Maruts for protection against foes.

Saantapanaa idam havirMarutastajjujushtana;
*Asmaakotee rishaadasah.*1.

[O divine Maruts, related to the Sun, come and partake of this oblation prepared for you and slay our enemies to protect us from them.]

Yo no marto Maruto durhyanaayustirashchittaani vasavo jnghasati;
*Druhah paashaan prati munchataa sastapishthena tapasaa hantaan tam.*2.

[O benevolent, wealth-giving Maruts, if some crooked man, filled with rage against us, plans to harm us, tie him in the noose of Varuna and crush him.]

∽

Hymn LXXIX, composed by Rishi Atharva is dedicated to *Amaavashya*, the dark half of the month:

> *Yat te Devaa akrinvan bhaagadheyamamaavashye savasanto mahitvaa;*
> *Tenaano yagyam piprihi vishvavaare rayim no dhehi subhage suveeram.*1.
>
> [O Amaavashye, the oblation the Gods have granted you, considering your importance; pray, accept it to conclude our yajna and reward us with competent and brave sons and prosperity.]

Devi Chand calls Amaavashyaa a 'sociable woman'!

Hymn LXXX, also composed by Rishi Atharva, is dedicated to *Poornimaa*, the full-moon night of the month:

> *Poornaa pashchaadut poornaa purastaadunmadhyatah pauranamaasee jigaaua;*
> *Tashyaam Devaih samvasanto mahitvaa naakashya prishthe samisha madema.*1.
>
> [The full-moon night, *Pooranamaasi*, shines in the east, west and in the middle. It raises us aloft in the company of the Gods in their heavenly abode.]

Hymn LXXXI, a delightful composition of six verse by Rishi Atharva, is dedicated to the Sun and the Moon. I quote Verses 1 and 5.

> *Poorvaaparam charato maayayaitau shishu krredantau pari yaatoavarnam;*
> *Vishwaanyo bhuvanaa vichashta ritoonranyo vidadhajjaayase navah.*1.
>
> [The two children (Sun and Moon), disporting under Maya's influence, chase each other and reach the ocean. One illumines the world and the other, regulating the seasons, appears in varied shapes and is born again.]

Yosmaan dveshti yam vayam dvishmastashya tvam praanenaa pyayasva;
Aa vayam pyaashisheemahi gobhirashvaih prajayaa pashubhirgrihairdhanen.5.

[O Moon, the enemies who show hatred towards us, we too detest them; you pull out their life as you move on and enrich us by horses, cows, houses and wealth.]

∽

Hymn LXXXII is composed by the Sage Shaunaka and addressed to Agni. I quote the third verse:

IhaivaAgne adhi dhaarayaa rayim maa tvaa ni kran poorvachittaa nikaarinah;
khshatrenaAgne suyamamastu tubhyamupasattaa vardhataam te anishtatatah.3.

[O Agni, do not be pleased with those having animus against us. But make us fortunate, who pay homage to you. Let your worshippers be happy, powerful and prosperous!]

∽

Hymn LXXXIII, composed by Shunah-Shepa, adopted son of Sage Vishvamitra, eulogizes Varuna, the God of morality, and makes a fervent prayer to be released from Varuna's snares and shackles.

Prasmat paashaan Varuna muncha sarvaan ya uttamaa adhamaa Varunaa ye;
Dushvapnyam duritam nishvaasmadatha gachchhem sukritashya lokam.4.

[O Varuna, release us from your upper as well as lower snares that bind us. Drive away our sins accruing from evil dreams and let us enter the righteous realms.]

∽

Hymn XC is composed by Rishi Angiras.

Api vrishcha puraanavada vratateriva gushpitam;
*Aujo daasashya dambhaya.*1.

[O Agni, just as a gardener lops off the intertwined branches of creepers, you destroy our arrogant, violent foes.]

Vayam tadashya sambhritam vasvIndrena vi bhajaamahai.
*Mlaapayaami bhrajah shibhram Varunashya vratena te.*2.

[May we attain the foe's treasure with Indra's help and devide it amongst us! May we destroy the enemy's pride with Varuna's assistance!]

Yatha shepo apaayaatai streeshu chaasadanaavayaah;
Avasthashya knadeevatah shaankurashya nitodinah;
*Yadaatatmav tattanu yaduttatam ni tattanu.*3.

[As lustful men torment women by excessive indulgence in sex, may their physical prowess diminish!]

Griffith did not translate the third verse as the word '*shepa*', meaning penis, occurs in its first line. However, Devi Chand has added a long foot note: 'Griffith has not translated this verse, taking it to be obscene. Sayana, following the application of Kaushika-Sutra has applied this verse to an immoral person. Kaushika has written that a debauchee should be stoned to death and pierced with arrows. These remarks are wide of the mark, as there is on obscenity in the verse.'

Hymn XCVII is composed by Rishi Atharva and dedicated to Indra and Agni. It contains eight verses; I quote the first three and the last verse.

Yadadhya tvaa prayati yaggye asmin hotashchikitvannavrineemaheeha;
*Dhruvamayo dhruvamutaa savishtha pravidvaan yagyamupa yaahi Somam.*1.

[O wise Hota Agni, we select you. O mighty Agni, arrive here and accept the oblation of Soma juice.]

SamIndra no mansaa nesh gobhih sam sooribhirharivantsm svastyaa.
Sam brahamanaa devahitam yadasti sam Devaanaam sumatau yaggiyaanaam.2.

[O Indra, riding greenish steeds, bless us with a reflective mind and expressive speech. O Lord, lead us to divine knowledge and divine will.]

Yaanaavaha ushato Deva Devamstaan preraya sve Agne sadhasthe.
Jakshivaansah papivaanso madhoonyasmai dhatta vasavo vasooni.3.

[O resplendent Agni, the gods, desirous of receiving oblation, whom you have invited, have received oblation; now send them to their heavenly abodes. O Vasus, lovers of ghrita and Soma juice oblations, bless the sponsor of the sacrifice with abundant wealth and fame.]

The fifth verse offers oblation to yoni, the female sexual organ, and the sixth verse to male semen. The last verse offers oblations to the Earth, the Sky and other divinitees:

Manasaspata imam no divi deveshu yagyam.
Swaahaa divi swaahaa Prithivyaam swaaha Antarikshe swaahaa Vaate dhaama dwaahaa.8.

[Lord of the Mind, lay this our sacrifice in heaven among the Gods. Hail in heaven! Hail on earth! Hail in air! In wind have I paid offerings. Hail!]

∽

Hymn CIX, authored by Rishi Badrayani, is addressed to Agni:

GhritamApsaraabhyo vaha tvamAgne paansoonakhebhyah sikataa apashchya;
Yathaabhaagam havyadaatin jushaanaa madanti Deva ubhayaani havyaa.2.

[O God Agni, Pray, carry this ghrita offering to the heavenly Apsaras. In this drama of win–lose, let those who are opposed to us, bite the dust or be drowned in water. Let all the gods receive their portion of the oblation.]

Devi Chand calls Agni as 'Brahmchari'!

∽

There is a one-verse hymn, **CXI**, attributed to God Brahma and dedicated to *Vrishabha,* in reality 'the seed-spilling Man':

Indrashya kukshirasi Somadhaana aatmaa Devaanaamuta manushaanaam;
Iha prajaa janaya yaasta aasu yaa anyatreha taaste ramantaam.

[O Vrishabha, gorge on Soma! You are the God's soul and His treasure for procreation, being the custodian and source of semen. Generate mankind here. May mankind live happily, here and elsewhere.]

∽

The next hymn, **CXII**, containing two verses and is ascribed to the Lord of moral order, Varuna, as the hymn seeks to be absolved from sins he may have committed:

Shumbhani DhyaavaPrithivi antisumane mahivrate;
*Aapaha sapta susruvurDeveestaam no munchantvarhasah.*1.

[Radiant Heaven and Earth are firm on their chosen course; they afford us pleasure and happiness from close. May the Seven celestial streams that flow here, protect us against sins.]

Munchantu maa shapathyaa3datho Varunyaa dut;
*Atho Yamashya padveeshhad vishvasmaad Devakilbishaat.*2.

[O Lord Varuna, forgive us for our habitual curses, slander and animosity; protect us from Yama's fetters. May you liberate us from sins arising out of our irreverent actions.]

Most probably, the 'seven celestial streams' in the first verse point to the 'Sapta Sindhu'—the rivers in the Indus basin.

Hymn CXVIII, consisting of two verses, is composed by Rishi Bhargava. It is dedicated to the deity *'Trishitika,'* which embodies *'Kama Trishna'* (lust for sex and greed for wealth).

> *Trishtike trishtavandan udamoon chhindhi trishtike;*
> *Yathaa kritadvishtaasoamushmai shepyaavate.*1.
>
> [O Lust for sex, O Greed for wealth, you create enmity among men and women, disrupt marital relations and create malevolence.]
>
> *Tristaashi trishtikaa vishaa vishaatakyshi;*
> *Parivriktaa yathaa sashyrishbhashya vasheva.*2.
>
> [May the craving for something not one's own be shunned as a poisonous creeper; it deserves to be abandoned like a cow unfit to be impregnated by a bull.]

Hymn CXIX, also composed by Rishi Bhargava, seeks to disable or disfigure an attractive woman who entices other men:

> *Aa te dade vakshanaabhya aa te-aham hridiyaad dade;*
> *Aa te mukhasya sankaashaat sarva te varcha aa dade.*1.
>
> [We will remove the power of attraction of your face, your breasts and other parts of your body, besides removing from your heart your evil desires.]
>
> *Preto yantu vyaadhyah pranudhyah pro ashastayah;*
> *Agnee rakshasvineethantu Somo hantu durashyateeh.*2.
>
> [Let your physical ailments vanish and you be protected against calumny. May Agni destroy the Rakshasa women and may Soma slay the Pishacha women.]

Hymn CXV, authored by Rishi Atharv-Angira, promises to remove the curse of an evil deity, Paap-Lakshmi, Evil Fortune.

Pra patetah paapi Laksmi nashetah pramutah pata;
*Ayasmayenaankena dvishate tva sajaamasi.*1.

[O Paap-Lakshmi, get thee hence to distant lands; go and lodge in our enemy's abode. We pierce you with a sharp iron rod and propel you there.]

The last hymn, **CXVIII**, also composed by Rishi Atharv-Angira seeks to equip and fortify a valiant warrior:

Marmaani te varmanaa chhadayaami Somastva raajaamritenaanu vastaam;
Urorvareeyo Varunaste krinotu jayantam tvaanu Devaa madantu.

[O valiant warrior, we cover your vital, vulnerable parts with this armour. May Soma fill you with invincible strength! May Varuna award you long life, and the other gods help you triumph over the wicked foes!]

SELECTED HYMNS FROM ATHARVA VEDA CHAPTER 8

Chapter 8 contains long hymns.

Hymn I is ascribed to God Brahma; it prays for long life and is dedicated to the deity Aayu. It contains 21 verses. I quote a few of them.

Antakaaya mrityave namah praanaa apaanaa iha te ramantaam;
*Ihaayamastu purusha sahaasuna Suryashya bhage amritashya loke.*1.

[We pay homage to the God of Death who terminates life. O man, let your inhaling and exhaling breaths continue unhindered. Let this man live here, in this sunny part of the Earth and then in the world of immortals.]

Iha te-asuriha prana ihaayuriha te manah;
*Ut tvaa Nir-Rityaah paashebhyo Daivyaa Vaachaa bharaamasi.*3.

[Here be your life, your breath, life-time, here be your mind; we bear you up from the fetters of perdition (Nir-riti) with the grace of Devi Vak.]

Tubhyam Vaatah pavataam maatarishvaa tubhyam varshantvamritaa nyaapah;
*Suryaste tanve shan tapaasi tvaam mrityur dayataam maa pra meshthaah.*5.

[O Man, let the wind, Matarishvan, be purifying for you, let the waters rain nectar for you; let the sun-beams provide health and happiness to your body; let Death be compassionate towards you—not let you die early!]

Uddhyaanam te purush naavayaanam jeevaatum te dakshataatim krinomi.
*Aa hi rohemamamritam sukham rathamatha jirvirvidathamaa vadaasi.*6.

[O Man, be upward looking, not downward, I endow you with long life and ability; ascend this magnificent chariot of your body and in old age preach to the council of men.]

*Aa roha tamaso jyotirehyaa te hastau rabhamahe.*8.

[Do not yearn for the dear departed, which leads your thoughts to the other world. Ascend out of darkness, come to light; we lift you by taking hold of your hands.]

Shyaapashcha tvaa maa shabalashcha preshitau Yamashya yau pathirakshi shvaanau;
*Aa roha tamaso jyotirehyaa te hastau rabhaamaye.*9.

[Let not the dark and brindled dogs of Yama, the two warders of the heavenly path, seize you. Proceed ahead, do not hesitate; don't sit in the world brooding over the past.]

Rakshantu tvaAgneyo ye apsvaantaa rakshaty tva manushya3 yamindhate;
*Vaishvaanaro rakshatu jaatavedaa divyastvaa maa pra dhhag vidhyutaa saha.*11.

[Let the fires that are within the waters defend you; let the fires that human beings kindle, defend you! Let Vaishvanara, Jatavedas defend you! Let not the fire of Heaven consume you by the bolt of lightening!]

Maa tva kravyaadabhi manstaaraat samkasukaachchara;
Rakshatu tva Dhyau rakshatu Prithivee Sooryashcha tva rakshataam Chandramaashcha;
*Antariksham rakshatu Devahetyaah.*12.

[Let not the flesh-eating (*Kravyada*) fire plot against you; move away from the avaricious, violent *Samkasukaa* fire. Let the Heaven and Earth defend you; let both Sun and Moon defend you; let the Firmament defend you from the Gods' missile.]

Maa tva Jambhaha samhanurmaa tamo vidanmaa jivhaa barhih pramayuh kathaa shyaah;
*Ut tvaAdityaa Vasavo bharantoodIndraAgnee svastaye.*16.

[Let not Rakshasa Jambha come near you, let not the Darkness find you, let not the *Rakshasa*'s tongue reach you; let the Adityas, Vasus, Indra and Agni raise you aloft for your welfare.]

Ut tvaa mrityorapeeparam san dhamantu vayodhasah;
*Maa tvaa vyastakeshyo maa tvaagharudo rudan.*19.

[O man, desirous of protecting life, I have saved you from the clutches of Death. Let the Gods award you long life; let not the wailing women with dishevelled hair raise a cry and mourn for you!]

Vyavaat te jyotirbhoodap tvat tamo akrameet;
*Apa tvanmrityum NirRitimapa yaksham ni dadmasi.*21.

[O man, the light of life is shining on you, all is bright for you; the darkness enveloping you has disappeared. We have driven away death, eternal damnation (Nir-riti) and consumption (yakshma) from you.]

Hymn II is also ascribed to God Brahma. Like the preceding Hymn I, it is also intended to bestow long life on man.

Jeevatam jyotirabhyehyarvaarnaa tvaa haraami shatshaardaaya;
*Avamunchan mrityupaashaanashanstim draagheeya aayuh prataram te dadhaami.*2.

[O man, come hitherward unto the light of the living, I take you to the world for enjoying a hundred autumns; loosening down the fetters of Death and invocation of curses, I award you a longer life-time.]

Jeevalaam naghaarishaam jeevanteemoshadheemaham;
*Traanmaanaam sahamaanaam sahasvatimiha huveasmaa arishataataye.*6.

[For restoring this man to health, I call hither a living, invigorating, life-infusing, unharming, efficacious disease-removing herb, *Arishta*.]

Krinomi te praanapaanau jaraam mritum deerghamaayuh svasti;
*Vaivasvatain prahitaan Yamadootaamshchartoapa sedhaami sarvaan.*11.

[O man desiring long life, we firmly establish the inward and outward breath (Praana and Apaana) in you, in order to keep away old age and Death and confer long life on you. I chase away the messengers of Death sent by Vivasvaan (Sun).]

Shive te stan DhyaavaaPrithivee asantaape abhishriyau;
Shan te Soorya aa tapatu shan vaato vaatu te hade;
*Shivaa abhi ksharantu tvaapo divyaah payasvatee.*14.

[Let Heaven and Earth be propitious to you, bringing no grief, bestowing wealth; let the Sun inject warmth into you, let the wind blow happiness into your heart; let the heavenly waters, full of sweetness of milk (*paayas*) flow for you!]

Shivaaste santvoshadhaya ut tvaahaarshamdharashyaa uttaraam Prithiveemabhi;
*Tatra tvaAdityau rakshataam SooryaaChandramasaavubhaa.*15.

[Let the herbs be propitious to you; I have raised you up from the lower to the upper part of the Earth. Let both the Adityas, the Sun and Moon, prolong your life!]

Shivao te staan vreehiyavaavabalaasavadomadhau;
*Aitau yakshma vi baadhete aitau munchato anhasah.*18.

[Propitious be rice and barley to you, free from the disease balasa, causing no burning; these drive off yakshma and make you free from distress.]

Mrityureeshe dvipadaam mrityureeshe chatushpadaam;
*Tasmaat tvam mrityorgopaterudabharaami sa maa bibheh.*23.

[Death is the lord of the bipeds, Death is the lord of quadrupeds; I protect you from Death, O master of the cows; you are not to be afraid of Death.]

Ye mrityava ekashatam yaa naashtraa atitaaryaah;
*Munchantu tasmaat tvaam Devaa AgnerVaishvaanaraadadhi.*27.

[The deaths that are a hundred and one, the eternal damnation that has to be overcome—from that let the Gods free you at the bidding of All-pervading, refulgent Vaishvanar Agni.]

Agneh shareeramasi paaryishnu rakshohaasi sapatnahaa;
*Atho ameevachaatanah pretudrunaama bheshajam.*28.

[O Putadru herb, you are powerful like Agni, you are slayer of demons and of our enemies and expeller of diseases. O Remedy par excellence, fulfill our desires!]

ᔑ

Hymn III is authored by Rishi Chaatan and is addressed to Jataveda Agni to destroy the sorcerers and demons.

Ayodanshtro archisha yaatudhaanaanup sprasha Jaatavedah samiddhah.
*Aa jihvyaa mooradevaan rabhasva kravyaado vrishtvaapi dhatsvaasan.*2.

[O Jataveda Agni of iron tusks, singe the sorcerers with your flaming tongue, sear the false-worshippers; devour the flesh-eaters in your mouth.]

TeekshnenaAgne chakshushaa raksha yagyam praancham vasubhyah pra naya prachetah;
*Hinsatram rakshaanshabhi shoshuchanam maa tvaa dabhan yatudhaanaa nrichakshah.*9.

[With your sharp eyes, O Agni, you defend the sacrifice and conduct it forward to the Vasus; O far-seeing, men-watcher Agni, you are slayers of demons; let not the fiends injure you!]

Triryaatudhaanah prasitim ta aitvritam yo Agne unnRiten hanti;
*Tamarchishaa sfoorjayanJaatavedah samakshamenam grinate ni yungdhi.*11.

[O Jataveda Agni, let the sorcerer come thrice within your reach, who slays *Rta* with untruth and falsehood. Roaring at him with your flames, O Jatavedas, trounce and trample him in front of the worshipper.]

Yah paurusheyena kravishaa samadkte yo ashvyena pashunaa yaaatudhanah;
*Yo aghnyaayaa Bharati kheeramagni teshaam sheershani harsaapi vrishcha.*15.

[O Jataveda Agni, the sorcerer who kills men and smears his face with his blood, who feeds on the flesh of cattle and of the horses, who steals the milch cows and milk; cut off their heads and burn them in your flames.]

Samvatsarneem paya usriyaayaastashya maasheed yaatudhaano nrichaksha;
*peeyooshamAgne yatamastripsaat tam pratyanchamarchishaa viddya marmani.*17.

[Whatever milk of the cows is collected during the year, O men-watcher Agni, let not the wicked Rakshasas steal and partake of it. The daredevils who would like to drink the besting (the first milk after calving), you pierce them in their vitals and scorch them.]

Tvam no Agne adharaadudaktstvam paschyaadut rakshaa purastaat;
*Prati tye te ajaraasastpishthaa aghashansm shoshuchato dahantu.*19.

[Guard us, O Jataveda Agni, from below, from above, protect us from behind and from front; let your radiant, sizzling flames consume the devilish Rakshsas.]

Hymn IV, also composed by Rishi Chaatan, targets the sorcerers and demons. The Hymn is dedicated to Gods Indra, Soma and the Maruts.

IndraSoma tapatam raksh ubjatam nyarpayatam vrishnaa tamovridhah;
*Paraa shrneetamachito nyoshatam hatam nudethaam ni shisheetmatritnah.*1.

[O Indra and Soma, burn the demons; You two bulls, destroy them that thrive in darkness. Crush and scorch down these idiots; chase and pierce the voracious fiends.]

IndraSoma vartayatam divo vadham sm Prithivyaa aghashansaaya tarhanam;
*Ut takshatama svayam1 parvatebhyo yen raksho vaavridhaanam nijoorvathah.*4.

[O Indra and Soma, hurl your dreadful bolt from the sky against the evil-minded rascals. Forge a weapon from the mountains and slay the ever-increasing foes.]

Suvigyanam chikitushe janaaya sachchaasachcha vachasee paspredhaate;
*Tayoryat satyam yataradvjeeyastdit Somoavati hantyasat.*12.

[A knowledgeable man knows that true and untrue words are at variance. Soma verily favours which has a greater measure of truth; he smites the untrue.]

Vi tishthadhvam Maruto vikshavee3chchhata gribhaayat rakshasah sm pinashtan.
*Vayo ye bhootvaa patayanti naktabhirye vaa ripo dadhire deve adhvare.*18.

[Scatter yourselves, O Maruts, among the people, seek, seize and crush the demoniacs, who becoming birds, fly in the nights or put defilements in the sacrificial fire.]

Devi Chand calls the Maruts 'state employees'! Most amusing!

Hymn V is composed by Rishi Shukra and dedicated to Devi Kritya-dushan. It wards off witchcraft with an amulet, called *Mani,* which is worn by the afflicted man.

Ayam manih sapatnahaa suveerah sahasvaan vaaji sahamaan ugrah;
*Pratyak krityaa dooshayanneti veerah.*2.

[This amulet is rival-slaying, possessing magical strength—powerful, vigorous, overpowering and formidable; it reverses the enemy's witchcraft back to him.]

Yah krityaa Angiraseeryaah kritya Aasureeryaah kritya svayamkrita yaauchaanyebhirabhritaah;
*Ubhayeestaah paraa yantu paraavato navatim navyaati.*9.

[The witchcrafts that are of the Angirasas, the witchcrafts that are of the Asuras, the witchcrafts that are self-made, and those that are brought by others—let all these go away to the distances, across ninety navigable streams.]

Svastidaa vishaam patirVratrahaa vimridho vashee;
Indro badhnaatu te manim jigeevan aparaajitah Somapaa abhayankaro vrishaa;
*Sa tvaa rakshatu sarvato diva naktam cha vishvatah.*22.

[Let Indra, Vritra slayer, the supreme lord of the people; let the Soma-drinking Bull, conqueror of foes, giver of welfare, bind the amulet to you—the Conqueror who remains unconquered, the fearless one who instills fearlessness in others; let him defend you on all sides, by day and by night, on all sides.]

Hymn VI is ascribed and dedicated to the deity of child-birth, *Matrinama.* It aims at guarding pregnant women from miscarriage. It is employed in the eighth month of a woman's pregnancy by binding an amulet.

Yau te maatonmamaarha jaataayaah pativedanau;
*Durnaamaa tatra maa gridhadalinsha uta vatsapah.*1.

[When at your birth your mother carefully cleaned and rubbed your genitive organs, let them not be harmed by the ill-named diseases, *Aalinsh* and *Vatsapa.*]

Maa sm vrito mop srip uru maava sripoantaraa;
*Krinomyasyai bheshajam bajam durnaamachaatanam.*3.

[O disease causing germs, do not creep between her thighs, nor creep down inside; we have given her a remedy—*bajam.*]

Durnama cha Sunama chobhaa samvritamichchhatah;
*Arayaanapa hanmah sunamaa strainamichchhataam.*4.

[Both the ill-named *Durnama* and well-named *Sunama* seek to approach the pregnant woman's womb. We smite away the miserly Durnama and let the well-named Sunama remain to assist the pregnant woman.]

Yah krishnah keshyasur stambaj ut tundikah;
*Araayaanashyaa mushkaabhyaam bhansasoapa hanmasi.*5.

[The Asuras who are black, hairy, tuft-born and have a snout besides—these niggards we smite away from her pudenda, from her buttocks.]

Yastvaa svapanteem tsarati yastvaa dipsati jaagrateem;
*Chhayaamiv pra tantSuryah parikraamannaneenashat.*8.

[O pregnant woman, he who surprises you while sleeping or tries to harm you while waking, let the circling Sun make them to vanish like a shadow.]

Yah krinoti mritavatsaamavatokaamimaam striyam;
*Tamoshadhe tvam naashyaashyaah kamalamajjivam.*9.

[O herb, whatsoever makes this woman deliver a dead child, whatever makes her abort, destroy such germs or diseases; let her genitals bloom like a lotus stalk.]

Paryastaakshaa aprachankashaa astrainaah santu pandagaah;
Ava bheshaj paadaya ya iman smvivritsatyapathih svapatim
*striyam.*16.

[Let the squint-eyed, lame, sightless Rakshasas who approach a pregnant woman be cast away; let a lustful man who tries to violate her in her dream be dammed.]

Uddharshinam Munikesham jambhayantam mareemrisham;
Upeshantamudumbalam tundelamuta shaludam;
Padaa pra vidhya paashnrayaa shthaleem gauriva
*spandanaa.*17.

[Let the pregnant woman trample under foot a lascivious man, an imposter who wears long hair like a sage, a violent frequent visitor who approaches her lustfully—as an angry cow kicks the milk-pan with her foot and heel.]

Ye Suryaat parisarpanti snusheva shvashuraadadhi;
*Bajashcha tesham pingashcha hridayeadhi nu vidhyataam.*24.

[As a daughter-in-law turns away seeing her father-in-law, the disease-causing germs creep away from the the light of the Sun. Let both *Bajaa* and *Pingaa* herbs pierce the germs and diseases and kill them.]

Aprajaastvam maartavasamaad rodamaghamaavayam;
*Vrikshaadviva strajam kritvapriye prati muncha tat.*26.

[Childlessness, still-birth, barrenness, guilt, crying—we attach all these to your enemies as if presenting them a garland of flowers.]

Hymn VII is composed by Rishi Atharva and is dedicated to the plants and herbs for restoration of health.

Ya babhrvo yaashcha shukraa rohineeruta prishnayah,
*Asikreeh krishnaa aushadheeh sarvaa achchhaavadaamasi.*1.

[Those herbs that are brown, bright, red and spotted, dark or sunburnt and black in colour, all of them do we invoke.]

Traayantaamim purusham yakshmaad Deveshitaadadhi;
*Yaasaam Dhaushpitaa Prithivee maataa samudro moolam veerudham babhoova.*2.

[May the herbs and plants, of which the Heaven has been the father, Earth the mother and ocean the root, save this man from yakshma sent by gods.]

Aapo agram divyaa aushadhayah;
*Taste yakshmamenashya1mangaadangaadaneenashan.*3.

[O patient, we have invoked here the water and the herbs that possess divine efficacy; have abolished from your every limb the consumption, caused by sin.]

Prastrinatee stambineerekashungah pratanvateeroshadheera vadami;
*Anshumateeh kaandineeryaa vishaakhaa havyaami te veerudho vaishvadeveerugraah purushajeevaneeh.*4.

[I address the leafy, the bushy, the single sprouted, the wide spreading herbs; those rich in shoots and have spreading branches; I call for you the powerful, efficacious plants that are gifts of God and give life to man.]

UnmunchanteerviVarunaa ugraa yaa vishadooshanee;
*Atho balaasanaashneeh krityaadooshaneeshcha yaastaa ehaa yantvoshadhee.*10.

[May the formidable, poison eradicating, balasa-dispelling herbs, that are free from the bonds of Varuna—let those herbs come here.]

Sinhashyeva stanthoh sm vijanteAgneriv vijanta aaabhritaabhyah;
*Gavam yakshmah purushaanaam veerudabhiratinuttau naavyaa aity strotyaah.*15.

[As the cows shiver at the roaring of a lion and tremble in front of raging fire, let the yakshma of kine and of men, go beyond navigable streams, driven by these powerful herbs.]

Ashvattho darbho veerudhaama Somo rajamritam havih;
*Vreehirvashcha bheshajo divasputraavaamratyo.*20.

[The *ashvattha* (holy fig tree or peepal), durva grass, the king of plants, Soma, the immortal oblation, as well as rice and barley; nourish us like the gifts of Heaven.'

Yaah suparnaa Aangiraseerdivyaa yaa raghato viduh;
Vayaansi hansaa yaa viduryaashch sarve patatrinah;
*Mrigaa yaa viduroshadheestaa asmaa avase huve.*24.

[What herbs of Angiraases and, the eagles know, what are known to swans, the crows and all the birds that fly, all medicinal plants known to sylvan beasts, we have invited them all to heal this ailing man.]

Yaavateeshu manushyaa bheshajam bhishjo viduh;
*Taavatirvishwabheshajeeraa bharaami tvaamabhi.*26.

> [I have brought to you for your benefit and well-being the many remedial herbs known to the physicians.]
>
> *Pushpavatih prasoomateeh phalineeraphalaa uta;*
> *Sammaater iva duhraamasmaa arishtataataye.*27.
>
> [The herbs that are rich in flowers, rich in shoots, rich in fruits and those that are fruitless, let all these herbs free him from disease and harm.]
>
> *Uta tvaahaarsha panchashalaadatho dashashalaadut;*
> *Atho Yamashya padvishaad vishvasmaad Devakilbishaat.*28.
>
> [I have delivered you from sufferings of five diseases, and pains of ten organs; I have saved you from Yama's shackles and from all offences committed against Gods.]

The above hymn, to my mind, reveals the essential characteristic of Atharvedic hymns in contrast to Rigvedic hymns. The Rigvedic hymns were chanted during a homa sacrifice, invoking the Vedic gods to descend and receive oblation and confer boons on the yajamaan and the rishi who composed the hymn and also the priests performing the homa sacrifice. It is indeed a natural urge in man to pray to God for blessings and boons.

The Atharvedic hymns, on the other hand, are designed to cure a person suffering from a physical ailment. It would have been acceptable if the Atharvan priest had acquired real herbs known for remedial qualities, sang their praise and applied them to the affected part of his client. But in these hymns, he only invoked the imaginary or real curative herbs and recited the hymn before the affected person. It appears there was no real herb!

Just like the imaginary Rigvedic gods, the Atharvedic herbs too were imaginary. But there is a basic difference—while the Rigvedic rishis believed that the heavenly gods came down to partake of the oblation that was offered to the living God Agni, who was the messenger of the gods, the Atharavan poet just invoked the real or imaginary herbs and hoped to drive away aches and pains and dreadful maladies of the illiterate, credulous masses.

Hymn VIII, composed by Rishi Bhrigu-Angira, is intended to conquer enemies; it's dedicated to Indra.

The opening verse is based on the Rigvedic pattern:

Indro manthatu manthitaa Shakrah Shoorah Purandarah;
*Yathaa hanaama senaa amitraanaam sahastrashah.*1.

[May Indra, the mighty hero, destroyer of strongholds, shake and destroy our enemies, and give us strength that we may slay them by thousands.]

Amoonashvattha nih shrineehi khaadaamoon khadiraajiram;
*Taajadbhanga iva bhajyantaam hantvenaan vadhako vadhaih.*3.

[O Peepal Tree, speedily crush the enemy formations; let them break like the castor oil plants or stalks of hemp. Destroy our foes with your terrible arms.]

Ayam loko jaalmaasichchhakrashya mahato mahaan;
*tenaahamIndrajaalenaamoonstamasaabhi dadhaami sarvaan.*8.

[This great world was the net of the mighty Indra; by that net of Indra, I encircle all my foes with darkness.]

Sedirugraa vyraiddhiraartishchaanpavaachanaa;
*Shramastanindreeshcha mohashcha tairamoonabhi dadhami sarvaan.*9.

[Debility, formidable failure and misfortune which cannot be exorcised away; toil, fatigue, weariness and bewilderment—with these I encircle all my foes.]

Mrityaveamoon pra yachchhaami mrityupaa shairmee sitaah;
*Mrityorye aghalaa dootastebhaya ainaan prati nayaami baddhvaa.*10.

[I deliver these my enemies to Death; with fetters of Death are they bound. Having bound them, I lead them to meet the wicked messengers of Death.]

Vishvedevaa ooparishtaadubjanto yanvojasaa;
*Maddhena ghnanto yantu senamAngiraso maheem.*13.

[Let all the gods from heaven go crowding with force; let the Angirases go slaying the enemy army from the middle flank.]

Vanaspateen vaanasptyaanoshadheeruta veerudhah;
*Dvipaachchatushpaadishnaami yathaa senaamamoom hanan.*14.

[The forest trees and their progeny, the herbs and the plants, the bipeds and the quadrupeds, I dispatch all of them to slay the enemy army.]

GandharvaApsarasah sarpaan Devaan punyajanaan pitran;
*Drishtaandrishtaanishnaami yathaa senaanaamamoom hanan.*15.

[The Gandharvas and Apsaras, the serpents, the gods, noble men, the heavenly Fathers, those seen and unseen, I dispatch them so that they slay the yonder enemy army.]

Gharmah samiddho Agninaayam homah sahastrahah;
*Bhavashcha prishnibaahushcha Sharva senaamamoom hatam.*17.

[Let both Bhava and the speckled armed Sharva drink this hot drink and this thousand-slaying oblation that I offer and slay the yonder enemy army.]

Mrityoraashamaa padyantaam kshudham sedim vadham bhayam.
*Indrashchaakshujaalaabhyaam Sharva senaamamoon hatam.*18.

[O god Sharva, pray you and Indra slay the enemy army. Let your deadly weapons, snare them unto death's burning, unto hunger and debility.]

Samvatsaro rathah parivatsaro rathopasto viraadeeshAgni rathamukham;
*Indrah savyashthaashChandramaah saarathih.*23.

[The year *(samvatasara)* is the chariot, the complete year (*parivatasara*) the chariot seat, Viraj is the pole, Agni the chariot-mouth, the Moon the charioteer and Indra the warrior.]

~

Hymn IX is a mystic poem, composed by Rishi Atharva. Its title in W.D. Whitney's translation is 'Extolling the Viraj—The Procreative Power'.

Kutastau jaatau katamah so ardhah kasmaallokaat
katamashyaah Prithivyaah;
Vatssau Viraajah salilaadudaitaam tau tvaa prichchhaami
*katarena dugdhaa.*1.

[Whence were the two born? From which half side? Out of what side was the world born; out of which the Earth? The two young *vatsa* (kids) of the Viraj rose out of the waters; I ask you about them—who milks Viraj?]

Yo akrandayat salilam mahitvaa yonim kritvaa tribhujam
shayaanh;
Vatsah kaamadudho Viraajah sa guhaa chakre tanvah
*paraachaih.*2.

[He who caused the waters from the depths of the yoni to resound and erupt, made a triangular recess there to create new bodies.]

Yaani treeni brihanti yesham chaturtha viyunakti Vaacham;
Brahmainad vidyaat tapasaa vipashchid yasminnekam
*yujyate yasminnekam.*3.

[Out of the conjunction of these three glorious beings, the fourth *Vacha* (Speech) manifests. The wise may, with the force of tapa, realize the inspired One in which the individual is merged.]

Brihatah pari Sammani shashthaat panchaadhi nirmitaa;
*Brihad brihatyaa nirmitam kutoadhi brihatee mitaa.*4.

'Out of *Brihat* were born five *Sama*, from them was created the sixth being. Brihat was fashioned out of *Brihati*; out of what was Brihati made?]

Brihati pari maatraayaa maaturmaatraadhi nirmitaa;
Maayaa ha jagge maayaayaa maayaayaa Maatali pari.5.

[Brihati, the metrical measure, was born from '*Matra*' as mother; Illusion (Maya) was born from Illusion and Matali was created then.]

Shat tva prichchhaam Rishiyah Kashapeme tvam hi yuktam yuyukshe yogyam ch;
viraajamaahurBrahmanah pitaram taan no vi dhehi yatidhaa sakhibhyah.7.

[We, these six seers ask you, O Kashyapa, you joined what was to be joined. They call Viraj the parent of the Brahma; explain it to us according to our deserts.]

Apraanaiti praanen praanteenaam viraat svaraajmabhyeti pashchaat.
Vishvam mrishantimabhiroopaam Viraajam pashyanti tve na tve pashyantenaam.9.

[O Rishis, Breathless Viraj goes by the breath of breathing ones; she goes unto *Svaraj* (the self-luminous supreme Being) from behind, and touches Him and assumes different forms.]

Ko Virajo mithunatvam pra ved ka ritoon ka u kalpamashyaa;
Kramaan ko ashyaah katidhaa vidugdhaan ko ashyaa dhaama katidhaa vyushteeh.10.

[Who understands the coupling of Viraj? Who understands the seasons and their ordering? How many times has Viraj been milked? Where is her abode; how many are the dawns of her abode?]

Ritashya panthaamanu tistra aagustrayo gharma anu reta aaguh.
Prajaamekaa jinvatyoorjamekaa rakshati Devayoonaam.13.

[Three—Fire, Sun and Moon—have come along the road of righteousness. Three heats have come after the seed; one enlivens the progeny, one the refreshment; one defends the realm of the Gods.]

Agnishomaavadadhuryaa tureeyaaseed yagyashya pakshaavrishaya kalpayantah;
*Gayatreem trishtubham jagateemanushtabham grihada brihadarkee yajamaanaaya svaraabharanteem.*14.

[She that was fourth, set Agni and Soma; the seers arranged the two wings of the sacrifice, Gayatri, Trishtubh, Jagati, Anushtubha, Brihadarkee, bringing Heaven for the sacrificer.]

∽

Hymn X is extended in six parts or *Paryaya*. It deals with the same theme of 'Extolling the Viraj' and is ascribed to Atharavacharya, Rishi Atharva. It has one-liner verses.

Paryaya I

1. Viraj verily was this universe in the beginning. Everyone was afraid when she was born, thinking 'This one will become the universe.'

2–3. She ascended and then descended in the house-holder's fire; they who know this become good householders.

4. She ascended and then descended in the southern (Dakshin) fire; those who know it become fit for sacrificial gifts.

5. She ascended and then descended in the Assembly (Sabhaa); one who knows this becomes fit for the Assembly.

6. She ascended and then descended in the *Samiti;* one who knows this becomes fit for the Samiti.

7. She ascended and then descended in the Address Hall; those who know it become fit to attend the Address Hall.

Paryaya II

1. She ascended; she stood striding the firmament in four directions.

2. Of her the gods and men said: 'She verily knows that upon which both Gods and men subsist; let us call her.

3. They called her.

4. O Goddess of nourishment and strength, come! O nourisher of the Fathers, come! O lovely Speech, come! O rich in cheer, come!

5. Indra was the young (*vatsa*) of her, Gayatri was the halter, controlling Viraj, and the cloud was the udder (of this heavenly cow).

6. Brihata Sama and *Rathantar* Sama were the two teats and *Yagya-yagiya* and Vamadevya Sama were the other two.

7. The Gods milked the Herbs and Brihata Sama milked the vast Sky.

8. Waters were generated by Vamadevya Sama and the system of yajna was evolved by Yagyayagiya.

Verses 16 and 17 repeat Verse 13.

These Viraj verses go over my head; they probably require a mystical frame of mind to fathom their elusive sense!

Paryaya III, IV, V and VI have been composed in a similar fashion.

SELECTED HYMNS FROM ATHARVA VEDA CHAPTER 9

Hymn I is composed by Rishi Atharva and is dedicated to the deity called Madhukashaa (honey-whip), the daughter of the Maruts. Bhagwati Devi Sharma defines Madhukashaa as one who inspires men to procreate and nourish the progeny.

> *DivasPrithivyaa antrikshaat*
> *samudradaAgnetvaataanmadhukasha hi jagge;*
> *Taam chaayitvaamritam vasaanaam hridbhih prajaah prati*
> *nandanti sarvaah*.1.

> [Verily from Sky, from Earth, from atmosphere, from ocean, from fire, from Vayu was born Madhukasha, the 'Honey-Whip.' When she appeared donning the garb of immortality, all creatures of the world rejoiced in their hearts.]

Mahat payo vishvaroopamashya samudrashya tvota reta aahuh.
*Yat eti madhukashaa raraanaa tat praanastadamritam.*2.

[Madhukasha's milk is 'Vishwa-roop' of various hues and qualities; she is also called the 'Ocean's seed'. She is the divine stimulator of procreation and nourishment; a river of nectar flows wherever she goes.]

Pashyantyashaashcharitam Prithivyaam prathannaro bahudhaa meemaasamaanaah;
*AgnerVaataan Madhukashaa he jagye Marutaamugraa naptih.*3.

[In sundry ways, reflecting from different points of view, the learned view Madhukashaa's character and course of action on the Earth. Verily this awe-inspiring daughter of the Maruts was born from Vayu and Agni.]

MaatAdityaan duhitaa Vasunaam pranah prajaanaamamritashya naabhih;
*Hiranayvarnaa Madhikashaa ghritaachee mahaan bhargashcharati martyeshu.*4.

[Golden-hued Madhukashaa is the daughter of the Vasus, mother and nourisher of the Adityas. Dripping with the juice of life, she is life of living creatures and bestower of immortality. Madhukasha moves among mortals emitting light.]

Madhohkashaamajanayanta Devaastashyaa garbho abhavad vishvaroopah;
*Tam jaatam piparti maataa sa jaato vishvaa bhuvanaa vi chashte.*5.

[The Gods generated Madhukasha, from her was produced an all-formed, world-embryo. This, when born, was tender and was replenished by the mother; world-embryo looks abroad on all existence.]

Kastam pra veda ka u tam chiketa yo ashyaa hridah kalashah Somadhaano akshitah;

*Bramha sumedhaah so asmin madet.*6.

[Close to the heart of Madhukasha is the unexhausted vessel filled with Soma; who knows that? Let Brahma of excellent wisdom revel in it!]

Sa tau pra veda sa u tau chiketa yaavashyaah stanau sahastradhaaraa vakshitau.
*Oorjam duhaate anapasfurantau.*7.

[Brahma knows about Madhukasha's two inexhaustible, thousand-stream breasts; they milk out refreshment unresisting.]

Hinkarikratee brihatee vayodhaa uchchayairghoshaabheti yaa vratam;
*Treen gharmaanabhi vaavashaanaa mimaati maayum payate payobhih.*8.

[Madhukasha goes about ecstatically, vigourously proclaiming herself, spreading sweetness and light, streams of milk flowing from her abundant breasts.]

Stanayitnuste vaak Prajaapate vrishaa shushmam kshipashi bhoomyaamadhi;
*Agnervaataanmadhukashaa hi jaggye Marutaamugraa naptih.*10.

[O Prajapati, Madhukasha gladdens the hearts of men as thundering clouds moisten the earth and impregnate her. Verily from Agni, from Vayu was born Madhukasha, the formidable daughter of the Maruts.]

Yathaa Somah praatah savane Ashvinorbhavati priyah;
*Eva me Ashvinaa varcha aatmaani dhriyataam.*11.

[As at the early pressing Soma is loved by the Ashvins, so, O Ashvins, let spendour be maintained in my Self!]

Yathaa Somo dviteeye savan IndrAgnyorbhavati priyah;
*Eva me Indra Agni varcha aatmaani dhriyataam.*12.

[As at the second pressing Soma is loved by IndrAgni, therefore, O Indra and Agni, let spendour be maintained in my Self!]

In this manner the hymn goes on invoking the Ribhus, Indra, Ashvins, Vak, etc. **Verse 22** particularly glorifies the Brahmins and the kings:

Yo vai kashaayaah sapta madhooni veda madhumaan bhavati;
Brahamanashcha raja cha dhenushchaandvaanshcha vreehishcha yavashcha madhu saptamam.22.

[He who knows the seven honeys of Madhukashaa becomes rich in hone—the Brahmin and the King, the milch-cow and the ox, rice, barley and honey are the seventh.]

∽

Hymn II is also composed by Rishi Atharva. He invokes the god of love, Kama, in the hymn. Strangely however, the God of Love is assigned the task of castigating the enemy!

Sapatnahanamrishabham ghriten Kaamam shikshaame havishaajyen.
Neechaih sapatnaan paadaya tvambhishtao mahataa veeryena.1.

[O the rival-slaying bull, Kama, I offer you ghrita with oblation. O mighty bull, do castigate my enemies with your power.]

Yanme manaso na priyam na chakshuso yanme babhasti naabhinandati;
Tad dushvapnyam prati munchaami sapatne Kamam stutvodaham bhidaiyam.2.

[What is not agreeable to my mind or my sight, what gnaws me, what I don't enjoy like the evil-dream—Let them all be fastened on my foes.]

Dushvapnyam Kaama duritam cha
Kaamaaprajastaamasvagataamavartitim;
Ugra eeshaanah prati muncha tasmin yo
asmabhyamamhooranaa chikistasaat.3.

[O formidable and powerful God Kama, bad dreams and hardships, want of progeny, homelessness and utter ruin which distress us, fasten these on our enemies, who seek and devise distresses for us.]

Saa te Kaama duhita dhenuruchyate yaamaahurvaacham kavayo Viraajam.
*Tayaa sapatnaan pari vringdhi ye mama paryenaan praanah pashvo jeevanam vrinaktu.*5.

[O Kama, your daughter, Vak, is a milch-cow, whom the poets call Viraj; let her avoid my rivals; let breath, cattle, life be denied to them.]

IndraAgni Kaama saratham hi bhootvaa neechaih sapatnaan mama paadayaathah;
*Teshaam pannaanaamadhamaa tamaanshAgne vaastoonyanunirdaha tvam.*9.

[O Kamadeva, by forming an alliance with Indra and Agni, riding a chariot, you make my rivals fall downward, into the lowest darkness. O Agni, burn them all, along with their houses.]

Te-a-dharaanchah pra plavantaam chhinnaa neeriva bandhanaat;
*Na saayakapranuttaam punarasti nivartanam.*12.

[Just as a boat severed from its mooring floats away downwards in the stream, let my rivals, repelled by your keen arrows, fall down; there should be no return for them.]

Chyutaa cheyam brihatyachyutaa cha vidhyuda bibharti stanayitnoonshcha sarvaan.
*UddyannaAdityo dravinena tejsaa neechaih sapatnaan nudataam me sahasvaan.*15.

[This great Earth bears the assault of lightenings and all thunderstorms; let Aditya arising with all brilliancy, thrust downward, all my powerful rivals!]

The hymn goes on in this fashion desiring to rain devastation on rivals, seeking help from God Kama and other gods.

Kaamo jagye prathamo nainam Deva aapuh pitaro na martyaah;
*Tatastvamasi jyaayaan vishwahaa mahaanstasmai te Kaama nama it krinomi.*19.

[At the creation of the universe, Kama was the first born, not the Gods, not the Fathers, nor did the mortals precede Him; You, Kama, are superior, forever great. To you therefore, O God Kama, do I pay homage!]

Na vai Vaatashchan Kaamamaapnoti naAgnih, Sooryo nota Chandramaah;
*Tatastvamasi jyaayaan vishvahaa mahaamstasmai te Kaama nama it krinomi.*24.

[Not even Vayu, nor Agni, nor Sun, nor Moon is your peer; O God Kama, superior than them all are you, always great; to you as such I pay homage!]

∽

Hymn III is composed by Rishi Bhrigu-Angira. It is a pretty poem lauding Shaalaa, the Homestead!

Upamitaam pratimitaamatho parimitaamut;
*Shaalaayaa vishvavaaraayaa naddhaani vi chritaamasi.*1.

[Of the props, the supports and the connectors of the dwelling that possesses all choicest things, we unfasten the parts that have been tied up.]

HavirdhaanamAgnishaalam patneenaam sadanam sadah;
*Sado Devaanaamasi Devi shaale.*7.

[Oblation holder, fire-place, wives' rooms and there is the seat of Gods where we offer prayers; O heavenly dwelling, you are the seat of the Gods!]

Agnimantashchhaadayasi purushaan pashubhih saha;
*Vijaavati prajaavati vi te paashaanchshritaamasi.*14.

[O wonderous *Shalaa*, You afford shelter to the householder, his family members, the household fire; we unfasten your fetters.]

Trinairaavritaa paladaan vasaanaa raatreeva shaalaa jagato niveshanee;
*Mitaa Prithivyaam tishthasi hastineeva padvati.*17.

[Covered by grass, clad with straw, the dwelling protects the men and the cattle, like the night. Built on a part of the earth, O homestead, you stand on strong feet like a female elephant!]

Brahamanaa shalaam nimitaam kavibhirnirmitaam mitaam;
*IndraAgni rakshataam shaalaammritau Saumyam sadah.*19.

[The dwelling, equipped with yagya-shala, is built by the poets. May Indra and Agni protect this seat of Soma.]

Kulaayeadhi kulaayam koshe koshah samubjitah;
*Tatra marto vi jaayate yasmaad vishvam prajaayate.*20.

[This nest nestles the bodies of living beings; in the nest of the bodies, nestles the womb, the embryo. In the embryo, the mortal man shall propagate his kind, from whom all is generated.]

Maa nah paasham prati mucho gurutbhaaro laghurbhava;
*Vadhoomiva tvaa shaale yatra kaamam bharaamasi.*24.

[O dwelling, do not tie us up in a bond or fetters; do not weigh heavy, nor be a burden on us. We shall decorate you like a bride and carry you where we go.]

In the remaining seven verses, homage is paid to the homestead from every quarter and all directions.

*Dashodishah Shaalaayaa namo mahigne svaahaa devebyah svaahebhyah.*31.

[So, from every direction and sub-direction we bow in reverence to *Shaalaa*!]

∽

Hymn IV is ascribed to Brahma, and is dedicated to Rishabha, the bull.

Saahastrastvesha rishabhah payasvaan vishvaa roopaani vakshanaasu bibhrat.
*Bhadram daatre yajamaanaaya shikshan Baarhasptya ustriyastantumaataan.*1.

[The bright Bull possessing limitless prowess, rich in sperm, bearing all forms in his bellies, desiring to accomplish what is excellent for the sacrifice, he, the ruddy Bull, Brihaspati, has extended his power over the universe.]

Somen poornam kalasham vibharshi Tvashta roopaanaa janitaa pashoonaam;
*Shivaaste santu prajanva iha yaa imaa nya1snbhyam svadhite yachchha yaa amooh.*6.

[O Vrishabha, you bear a vessel filled with Soma, O generator of cattle, you shape the forms like Tvashta; propitious to you be these pudenda of the cows that are here; confer to us your powers.]

Indrashaujo Varunashya baahoo Ashvinoransau Marutaamiyam kakut;
*Brihaspati sambhritametamaahurye dheeraasah kavayo ye manishinah.*8.

[O Vrishabha, you possess Indra's strength, Varuna's two arms, the Ashvins' two shoulders, the Marutas are your hump. They who are wise, the poets who are learned, call him Brihaspati in the form of a Bull.]

Daiveervishah payasvaanaa tanoshi tvamIndra tvam Sarasvantamaahuh;
*Sahastram sa aikamukhaa dadaati yo Brahmana rishabhamaajuhoti.*9.

[Rich in sperm you stretch unto the godly people; they call you Indra, they call you Sarasvant. You award a thousand cows to one who makes an offering of a bull to a Brahmin.]

In the process of sacrificing the Bull, it is cut up into pieces.

Paarshve aastaAnumatyaa Bhagashyaastaamanoovrijau;
*ashtheevantaavabraveenMitro mamaitau kevalaviti.*12.

[His sides are Goddess Anumati's, his flanks of Bhaga's; of his knees Mitra said: those are wholly mine.]

Gudaa aasasantSineevaalyaah Sooryaayaastvachamabruvan;
*Utthaaturbruvan pada rishabham yadakalpayan.*14.

[His intestines are Sinivavali's, they called his skin Surya's; they assigned his legs to the upstander (head-priest) of the sacrifice when they prepared the bull for sacrifice.]

Brahmanebhya rishabham datvaa vareeyah krinute manah;
*Pushtim so aghyaanaam sve goshthe-ava pashyate.*19.

[Having given a bull to a Brahmin, one displays generosity; he obtains prosperity of the inviolable cows in his own house.]

Gaavah santu prajaah santvatho astu tanoobalam;
*Tat sarvamanu manyantaam Deva rishabhdaayine.*20.

[May the Gods grant them cows, may they be blessed with progeny, may they gain physical strength, who donate a bull to the Brahmin.]

∽

Hymn V is composed by Rishi Bhrigu. It is concerned with offering 'Panchaudan–Aja', goat and five rice dishes. This sookta relates to sacrifice of *Aja*, of a goat. Devi Chand's translation of Aja—immortal soul—is misleading and evasive. Bhagwati Devi Sharma is generally steadfast in her translation, but even she hides the obvious meaning and says it probably means '*ajanmaa*'—one who is yet to be born.

Aa nayaitamaa rabhasva sukritaam lokamapi gachchhatu prajaanan;
*Teertvaa tamaansi bahudhaa mahaantyajo naakmaa kramtaam triteeyam.*1.

[Bring the goat here, take hold; let him with full knowledge go unto the world of well-being; crossing the great darknesses variously, let the goat step into the Third Heaven!]

Indraaya bhaagam pari tva nayaamyasmin yagye yajamaanaaya soorim;
*Ye no dvishantyanu taan rabhasvaanaagaso yajamaanaasya veerah.*2.

[O Goat, I lead you to the noble Yajaman for offering you to God Indra. O Goat, trample under your feet those who have ill-will towards the Yajaman and let the Yajaman be blessed with brave sons.]

Pra padoava nenigdhi dushcharitam yachchaar shudhaih shafairaa kramtaam prajaanan;
*Teertvaa tamaansi bahudhaa vipashya naakamaa kramtaam triteeyam.*3.

[O Goat, wash your feet for purification of the evil that might have stuck to your hooves; with cleansed hoofs let the goat cross the darknesses and step into the third firmament.]

Anu chchhaya shaamen tvachametaam vishastaryathaaparva1sinaa maabhi mansthaa.
*Maabhi druhah parushah kalpayainam triteeye naake adhi vi shrayainam.*4.

[O slaughterer, with a weapon of black metal remove the goat's skin, having no hostility against the goat; ensuring that the bone joints are not harmed; prepare him joint-wise and set him apart for the third firmament.]

Richaa kumbhheemadhyagnau shrayaamyaa sinchodakmava dhehyenam;
*Paryaadhattaagninaa shamitaarah shrato gachhatu sukritaama yatra lokah.*5.

[Singing a Vedic mantra, I set the cauldron upon the fire. Pouring water in the vessel, you cook it nicely; let the goat go to high heaven where the righteous dwell.]

Ajo Agnirajamu jyotiraahurajam jeevataa brahmane deyamaahuh;
*Ajastamaanshapa hanti dooramasmimanloke shraddhadhaanen dattah.*7.

[The goat is lustrous like Agni and they call the goat 'Light'. They say that the goat is to be given to a Brahmin priest; the goat given in this world by one having faith, dispels and drives far away the darknesses.]

Ajastrinaake tridive triprashthe naakashya prashthe dadovaansam dadhati.
*Panchaudano Brahmane deeyamaano vishvaroopaa dhenuh kaamadudhaashyekaa.*10.

[This goat sets the yajaman, who has offered it for sacrifice, on to the sacred space beyond Three Heavens or three firmaments. Being given with five rice-dishes to the priest, the goat is like the heavenly *Kama Dhenu*, who grants all wishes.]

Ajo vaa idamagre vyakramata tashyora iyamabhavad Dhauh prashtham;
*Antariksham madhyam disham paarshve samudrao kukshee.*20.

[The goat verily strode out here in the beginning. This Earth became its breast, the Sky its back, the atmosphere its middle, the quarters its ribs and the oceans its belly.]

Satyam chartam cha chakshushee vishvam satyam shraddha praano Viraat shirah.
*Aisha vaa aparimito yagyo yadajah panchaudanah.*21.

[His eyes are Truth and the changing seasons, the universe is its existence, Faith is its breath and Viraj its head; verily the goat with five dishes is a limitless offering!]

Aparimitameva yagyamaapnotyaparimitam lokamava rundhade.
*Yojampanchaudanam dakshinaajyotisham dadaati.*22.

[One who offers the goat and five dishes in sacrifice and also bestows enriching *Dakshina* on the priest, verily becomes the lord of the infinite world.]

Nashyastheeni bhindyaanna majjo nirdhayet;
*Saarvamenam samaadaayedamidam pra veshayet.*23.

[Do not split its bones, nor suck out its marrow; let this goat as a whole enter in the firmament here and there.]

Idmidmevaashya roopam bhavati tenainam sam gamayati;
Isham maha oorjamasmai duhe yojam panchaudanam
*dakshinaajyotisham dadaati.*24.

[This and this, verily, is the form of this sacrifice; this we integrate with the Eternal Being. It yields foodgrains, greatness and prosperity to the sacrificer!]

Pancha rukmaa pancha navaani vastraa panchaasmai
dhenavah kaamadudhaa bhavanti;
*Yojam panchaudanam Dakshinaajyotisham dadaati.*25.

[May the generous host of the sacrifice, shining in the light of Dakshina, be rewarded with five gold ornaments, five new garments and five milk-spilling cows.]

Ya poorva patim vittvaathaanyam vindate-a-param;
*Panchaudanam cha taavajam dadaato na vi yoshatah.*27.

[A woman who gains a second husband, if they together offer a goat and five rice-dishes, they shall not be separated.]

Yo vai naidaangha naamartum veda;aish vai naidaagho
naarturdajah panchaudanah;
Bhraatrivyashya shriyam dahati bhavatyaatmanaa; yo3jam
*panachaudanah dakshinaajyotisham dadaati.*31.

[This goat with five rice-dishes is a fiery weapon; he who offers a goat with five rice-dishes with the warmth of Dakshina, indeed burns out the fortune of his unfriendly foes; he thrives by himself, who gives a goat with five rice-dishes, with the light of sacrificial gifts.]

Ajam cha pachata pancha chaudanaan;
*Sarvaa dishah sammanasah sadhreecheeh saantredeshaa prati grihnantu ta aitam.*37.

[Cook ye the goat and five rice-dishes; let all the quarters in unison with the intermediate directions, accept your offering!]

Hymns VI–XII are dedicated to the 'Entertainment of Guests' and are ascribed to God Brahma. There are six Paryaya (sections).

Paryaya 1

*Yad va atithipatiratithheen pratipashyti Devayajanam prekshyate.*3.

[Seeing a guest is as auspicious to the householder as organizing a sacrifice to the Gods.]

*Yat tarpanamaaharanti ya aivaAgnishomeeyah pashurbadhyate sa aiva sah.*6.

[Offering gratification like water, milk or food to a guest is equivalent to offering animal sacrifice to Agni and Soma.]

*Yadaavasathaan kalpayanti sadohavirdhaanaanyeva tat kalpayanti.*7.

[Preparing lodgings for a guest is like preparing for sacrifice.]

*Yaduparishayanamaaharanti swargameva ten lokamava rundhve.*9.

[Preparing a bed for the guests is akin to opening the gates of Heaven.]

*Yanyulookhalmusalaani graavaana aiva te.*15.

[The pestle and mortar used to prepare a meal for the guests are sacred like the stones for extracting the Soma juice.]

Paryaya 2

*Sarvo vaa aisha jagdhapaapamaa yashaannamashnanti.*8.

[Verily every such householder has his sins devoured whose food is partaken of by the guests.]

*Praajaapatyo vaa aitashya yagyo vitato ya upaharati.*11.

[To Prajapati verily his offering extends who extends such hospitality to guests.]

Paryaya 3

*Ishtam cha vaa aish poortam cha grihaanaamshnaati yah poorvoatithershnaati.*1.

[A householder who partakes of food before serving it to the guests devours the fruits there of and is denied all credit.]

*Praajaam cha vaa aisha pashooshcha grihaanaamashnaati yah poorvoatithershnaati.*4

[The householder who eats before his guest might suffer loss of his family members and animals.]

*Aisha vaa atithiryachchhrotiyastasmaat poorvonaashniyaat.*7

[The guests are like the priests invited to offer sacrifices; it's wrong to partake of food before them.]

*Ashitaavatyatithaavashneeyaad yagyasha saatmatvaaya yagyashya vichchhedaaya tad vratam.*8.

[Only after the guests have been offered food one should partake of it himself in order to maintain the soulfulness of the act.]

Aitad vaa oo svaadeeyo yadadhigavam sheeram vaa maansam vaa tadeva naashneeyaata.9.

[The sweet dish, *ksheer*, prepared by cow's milk, or a non-vegetarian dish, should be offered to guests before the householder partakes of these.]

Paryaya 4

All the 10 verses of this Paryaaya are devoted to explaining the right way of serving food to a guest. Each item, like the milk dish Ksheer, or milk, ghrita, honey, non-vegetarian dish and even water, should be served respectfully in proper containers. By doing so the host shall obtain as much merit as by performing a highly successful Agnishtoma sacrifice held in the Spring season.

Paryaya 5

*Tasmaa Usha hinkranoti Savita pra stauti.*1.

[For the householder who knows how to honour a guest, Dawn brings a message of joy while the Sun sings his praise.]

Brihaspatiroojayod gaayati Tvasta pushtayaa parati harati
*Vishve Deva nidhanam.*2.

[Brihaspati praises him, Tvashta strengthens him and Vishvedeva expresses his commendation.]

*Tasmaa abhro bhavan hinkranoti stanayan pra stauti.*6.

[Thundering clouds and lightening bring him messages of joy.]
[Householders who honour guests in this spirit are blessed with prosperity, progeny and herds of cattle.]

Paryaya 6

Yat pariveshtaarah paatrahastaa poorve chaapare cha
*prapadyante chamasaadhvaryava aiva te.*3.

[Those who serve the guests holding food containers in their hands are venerable like the priests who assist in sacrifice.]

Yada vaa atithipatiratitheen parivishya
*grihaanupodaityavabhrithameva tadupaavaiti.*5.

[The householder who returns home after serving the guests earns the merit of having bathed in a sacred river.]

*Sa upahootah Prithivyaam bhkshayatyupahootastasmin yat Prithivyam vishwaroopam.*7–9.

[The food served to honoured guests attains the qualities of the best food available on the Earth, in the Sky and even in the high Heaven.]

*Aapnoteemam lokamaaonotyumam.*13.

[The noble householder who accords such hospitality to his guests here, receives a similar treat in the yonder world.]

*Jyotishmato lokaanjayati ya aivam veda.*14.

[Those who know and observe the rules of proper hospitality to their guests shall in after-life conquer luminous worlds!]

∽

I used to wonder why the Sanskrit word for 'guest' is '*atithi*'. '*Tithi*' means 'date' and 'atithi' means 'one who comes without a date or appointment'. They were mendicants—*sanyaasi* or sadhu—they came without an appointment and were held in high esteem. This tradition was prevalent till the modern times. I remember a Hindi couplet by the poet Vrinda, which I had read in school:

Saanyee itnaa deejiye, jyaan mein kutumb samaaya,
Mein bhee bhookhaa naa rahun, Sadhu na bhookhaa jaaya.

[O Lord, give me enough to take care of my family; let me not remain hungry and let not a Sadhu go away hungry from my door.]

But the sadhu is to be distinguished from a beggar. There was rampant poverty in those days and beggars were a common sight. The poet Vrinda had another couplet denouncing beggary as well as miserliness:

Maangana gaye so mari rahe, marey so maangana jaanhi;
Unsey pahile voh marey, hota karata jo naahi.

[Those who go abegging are as good as dead; only those that are dead, go to beg. But those who have, and yet say no to a beggar, die even before them!]

~

Hymn XIII is authored by Rishi Bhrigu Angira. It is meant for eradication of all kinds of diseases—just by chanting the verses of this hymn!

Shhershaktim sheershaamayam karnashoolam vilohitam;
*Sarva sheershanyem te rogam bahirnimantrayaamahe.*1.

[Headache, all head ailments, ear-ache, anemia, all head-diseases of yours, do we dispel out of you by incantation.]

Yashya bheemah prateekaash oodwepayati poorusham;
*Takmaanam vishwasharadam bahirnimantrayaamahe.*6.

[The takman of every autumn, whose fearful aspect makes a man tremble—we expel out of you by incantation.]

Ya ooru anusarpatyatho aiti gaveenike;
*Yaksham te antarangebhyo bahirnimantrayaamahe.*7.

[The yakshma that creeps along the thighs, goes into the groins; we expel it out of you, your limbs, by incantation.]

Aaso Balaaso bhavatu sootrambhavatvaamayat;
*Yakshamaanaam sarveshaama visham nirvochamaham tvat.*10.

[Let the Balasa become urine, let Yakshma become poison (...) I expel them by incantation.]

This magic-mantra goes on in sing-song fashion for 21 verses: out of the patient's belly, lung, navel, heart, brain, intestines, feet, knees, hips, buttock, spine, etc.

The last verse is:

San te sheeshrnah kapaalaani hridayasha cha yo vidhuh;
UddyanAdititya eashmibhih sheernorno
*rogamaneenashoangabhedamsheeshamh.*22.

In the end the poet exclaims: 'O Aditya, with your rays you have made all diseases to disappear!'

Hymns IX and X are called Atma Sookta and are ascribed to God Brahma. Hymn IX begins with quoting the celebrated Ashya Vamashya hymn of the Rig Veda (I. 164). These two long hymns have been designed on that celebrated hymn, full of mystifying riddles:

Ashya vaamashya palitashya hotustashya bhraataa madhyamo astyashnah;
*Triteeyo bhraataa ghritaprashthoashyaatraapasham vishpatim saptaputram.*1.

[We have witnessed the world protector Sun along with His seven daughtrs, His golden Rays. His second son is the voracious lightening. The third is Agni, who has ghrita at his back. I have seen the Lord of His subjects and the purifier of all.]

Dhyaurnah pitaa janitaa naabhiratra bandhurno maataa Prithibhishcharantam;
*Uttaanyoshchamvoaryonirantaratraa Pitaa duhiturgarbhamaadhaat.*12.

[Ruling over the world, the Sun is our father and brother; the Earth our mother. He is at the centre of the universe. Between the two globes of heaven the Sun impregnates the Earth and creates all living creatures.]

Viraad Vaag viraata Prithivi viraadAntariksha viraat Prajaapatih;
*ViraanaMrityuh saadhyaanamadhiraajo babhoova tasya bhootam bhavyam vashe a me bhootam bhavyam vashe krinotu.*24.

[The supremely immense Brahma is the Speech (*vaanee*), the Earth, the Firmament and Prajapati, the ruler of all and destroyer! He is the lord of the past and present; Let Him bring them under my control.]

SELECTED HYMNS FROM ATHARVA VEDA CHAPTER 10

Hymn I is authored by Sage Praty-Angiras. It is designed against witchcraft and the malady named Kritya, which we have encountered many times earlier.

Yam kalpyanti vahatavau vadhoomiva vishwaroopaam hastakritaam chikitsavah;
*Saaraadetvapa nudaam ainaam.*1.

[She (Kritya) whom the adept witchcraft practitioners bedeck like a bride at a wedding—let her go far off; we push her away.]

Sheershanvati nasvati karnini krityakritaa sambhrataa vishwaroopaa;
*Saaraadetvapa nudaam ainaam.*2.

[Having a head, a nose, ears, put together, all-formed, by the witchcraft-maker—let her go far off; we push her away.]

Shudrakritaa Rajakritaa streekritaa Brahmabhikrita;
*Jaayaa patyaanutteva kartaaram bandhvrichhatu.*3.

[Whether created by a Shudra or a king or Brahmin, let her go to her maker, like a wife expelled by her husband.]

Praticheen Angirasoadhyaksho nah purohitah;
*Prateecheeh kritya aakrityaamoon krityakrito jahi.*6.

[The pre-eminent master of the art of witchery is our purohit, Angiras. He had repelled these evil instruments against their makers and will now slay the witchcraft makers.]

Apa kraama naanadati vinadhaagardabheeva;
*Kartrin nakshaysveto nuttaa Brahmana veeryaavataa.*14.

[O Kritya, shouting like an unfastened female donkey, go away, attack your makers; I push you away by a powerful spell.]

Vaata iva vrikshaan ni mrineehi paadaya maa gaamashvam purushamuchchhisha aisham;
*Kartrin nivritetah kritye apraajaastvaaya bodhaya.*17.

[As the whirlwind uproots the trees, O Kritya, you go and destroy your makers, their cows and horses.]

Upahritamanubuddham nikhaatam vairam tsaaryanvidam kartram.
*Tadetu yata aabhritam tatraashva iva vi vartataam hantu krityaakritah prajjam.*19.

[We have found out the hostile secret magic, let it return to where it came from; let it roll about like a wild horse and slay the progeny of the witchcraft-maker.]

Greevaaste kritye paadau chaapi katsryaami nirdrava;
*IndraAgni asmaan rakshtaama yau prajaanaam prajaavati.*21

[O witchery incarnate, I will cut up your neck-bones and slice your feet, run away; let Indra-and-Agni defend us!]

Indeed, the Atharvan rishis had transformed themselves into magicians and wonder-workers. In the garb of eradicating witchcraft, they had become practitioners of witchcraft!

Hymn II is ascribed to Narayana, the god. It is modelled on the '*Ken Sookta*' in Kena Upanishad.

Kena paarshnee aabhrite poorushashya ken maansam sambhritam ken gulphau.
Kenaanguleeh peshaneeh kena khaani kenochchhalankhau madhyat kah pratishthaam? 1.

[Who formed the two heels of the first man and woman? Who formed their flesh and ankles? Who made their nimble fingers? Who designed the man's penis to expel liquid semen and who made his testicles? Who designed the woman's vulva to receive the penis? Who gave them a sense of balance, enabling them to stand firmly?][148]

Kati Devaah katame ta aasan ya uro greevaashchikyu poorushashya;
Kati stanau vyadadhuh kah kafodau kati skanadhaan kati prishteerchinvan? 4.

[How many gods were there and which one fashioned the chest and neck-bones of man? Who designed the woman's ample breasts and joined their collar and shoulder bones with the ribs?]

Ko ashya baahoo samabharad veeryam karavaaditi;
*Ansau ko ashya tad Deva kusindhe adhyaa dadhau.*5.

[What God brought together the man's two arms, saying 'he must perform heroism' and set his two shoulders upon his trunk (for shooting arrows?)]

Kah sapta khaani vi tatard sheerchani karnaavimau naasike chakshanee mukham;
*Yeshaam purutraa vijayashyashya mahyani chatushpaado dvipado yanti Yamam.*6.

Hanvorhi jivhaamadadhaat puroocheemadhaa maheemadhi shishraaya Vaacham;
Sa aa vareevarti bhuvaneshvantarapo vasaanah ka u tachchiketa? 7.

[Who bored the seven openings in the head—the ears, eyes, nostrils and the mouth? Through whose surpassing power the bipeds and quadrupeds complete the journey of life? Who set the tongue within the jaws and placed the powerful speech? He pervades the worlds and the waters. Who indeed understands it?]

Mastishkamashya yatamo lalaatam kakaatikaam prathamo yah kapaalam;

[148]Translated by Robert Van de Weyer; Van de Weyer, Robert, *366 Readings from Hinduism,* Jaico Publishing House, 2003.

Sa aa vareevarti bhuvaneshvantarapo vasaanah ka u tachchiket? 8.

[Which god produced his brain, his forehead and the skull, and then ascended to high heaven?]

Kenaapo anvatanuta kenaahara karoda ruche;
Ushasam kenaanvaindhda ken saayambhavam dade? 16.

[Who has spread the waters on the earth? Who made the days filled with light and who enkindles the dawn; who has given the gift of eventide?]

Ko asmin reto nyadadhaat tanturaa taayataamiti;
Medhaam ko asminnadhauhat ko baanam ko nrito dadhau? 17.

[Who planted the semen in men to put foetus in the female womb, saying 'let his line be extended'? Who guides children from folly to wisdom? Who urges men and women for music and dance?]

Kenemaanbhoomimaurnot ken paryabhavad divam;
Denaabhi manhaa parvataan ken karmaani poorushah? 18.

[Who has bedecked the earth? With what the sky has been surrounded? What power made the man a match for mountains in greatness? What makes him perform heroic deeds?]

Ken Parjanyamanveti ken Soma vichakshanam;
Ken yagyam cha shradhaa cha kenaasmin nihitam manah? 19.

[What makes him utilize Parjanya's showers and search for Soma, perform sacrifice and imbibe faith? By whom was he endowed with mind?]

Ken shrotriyamaapnoti kenemam pameshthinam;
BrahmeAgni poorusho Bramha samvatsaram mame? 20.

[What makes man seek the supreme Brahma? How does

he make Agni to appear and how does he measure the seasons?]

Brahmashrotriyamaapnoti Brahmem parmeshthinam;
*brahmemAgni Poorusho Brahma samvatsaram mame.*21.

[The Param Brahma inheres revelation, Parmeshthi Prajapati and Agni and measures the seasons.]

Keneyam bhoomirvihitaa ken Dhyauruttaraa hitaa;
Kenedamoordhvam tiryak chantariksha vyacho hitam? 24.

[Through whom is this Earth held down and the Sky held up? Through whom the atmosphere—the vast expanse between the Earth and the Sky sustained?]

Brahmanaa bhoomirvihita Brahma Dhyauruttaraa hita;
*Brahmedamoordvam tiryaka chantariksha vyacho hitam.*25.

[By Param Brahma is the Earth held down and the Sky above. By Param Brahma is the atmosphere, the expanse, set aloft and across.]

Ashtaachakraa navadvaara Devaan pooryodhyaa;
*Tashyaam hiranyayah koshah swargo jyotishaavritah.*31.

[This eight-wheeled and nine-door citadel of the body is the impregnable stronghold of the Gods. In that there is a golden vessel, covered with light, going heaven-ward.]

Tasmin hiranyaye koshe tryare tripatishite;
*Tasminam hiranyayeem yashsaa sampareevrittaam.*32.

[In that three spoked golden vessel, having three supports, resides a soul-possessing Yaksha, whom verily the knowers of the Brahma know.]

Prabhraajmaanaam harineem yashsaa sampareevritaam;
*Puram hiranyayeem Brahmaa viveshaaparaajitaam.*33.

[The Brahma entered into the resplendent, golden, unconquered stronghold which was all steeped in glory]

Hymn III, composed by Rishi Atharva, is dedicated to a charm or an amulet—*Varana Mani*.

1. This 'Varana' is my enemy-destroying, powerful charm. With its help you slaughter your wicked foes.

3. This Varana amulet is effective universally and heals all ailments. It is radiant like gold and has a thousand eyes; go ahead and vanquish your foes.

8. What sins my mother, my father, my brothers and myself might have committed, let this divine herb absolve us from all these.

11. I am wearing this divine Varana amulet on my breast. Let it drive away and crush my foes as Indra vanquished the barbarians, the Asuras.

12. Wearing this Varana amulet, I shall live to see a hundred autumns; may it assign to me both kingdom and authority, a large army and a herd of cattle.

14. As both Vayu and Agni destroy and devour forest trees, O Yajamaan, let the Varana amulet devour your rivals, those born before or after. May it protect you!

16. O magic Varana charm, slaughter the foes of this Yajamaan before their appointed life-time, who are intent on snatching his kingdom or strive to take away his cattle.

19. As there is glory in the Earth and in this Jataveda Agni, so let the Varana amulet sprinkle glory on me and anoint me with glory.

25. As there is immortality in the Gods and they are established in Truth, so let this Varana amulet grant me immortality and establish me in Truth.

Hymn IV, composed by Rishi Garutman, is dedicated to the mythical serpent, Takshak. It is meant to afford protection against snakes and snake poison. Since they are charms, all the verses, except the first, are disjointed words, not proper sentences.

> *Indrasha prathamo ratho Devaanaamaparp ratho Varuna's tritteeya ita.*

*Ahinaamapamaa rathah sthaanumaaradathaarshat.*1.

[Indra's was the first chariot, then of the Gods; Varuna's was the third. The chariots of serpents go slow but can enter even a tree's dried trunk.]

Darbhah shochistaroonakamashvashya vaarah parushashsya vaarah;
*Rathashya bandhuram.*2.

[Durva grass, fire of sacrifice and young shoots of grass are dangerous for the snakes; *ashvaivarah* (horse's tail-tuft) *purush varah* (tough man's tail-tuft) and chariot's droppings help remove the snake venom.]

Paidvo hanti kasarneelam Paidvah shvitramutaasitam;
*Paidvo ratharvyaah shirah sam bibheda prikvaah.*5.

[The herb *Paidva* slays the snakes, *kasarnila* and black and white snakes. Paidva has split the head of Ratharvi (snake) and of a viper.]

Sanyatam na vi shparad vyaattam na san yamat.
*Asmin kshetre dvaavahee stree pumaanshcha taavubhaarasaa.*8.

[Let not the snake open his closed mouth to bite us, nor close the opened mouth.]

Aghaashvashyedam bheshajmubhayoh svajashya cha;
*Indro meahimaghaayantamahim Paidvo arandhayat.*10.

[I have remedy for serpents called *Aghashva* and *Svaja*. Just as Indra subdues his foes, *Paidva* tames these serpents.]

Kairaatikaa kumaarikaa sakaa khanati bheshajam;
*Hiranyayeebhirbhribhirgireenaamupa saanushu.*14.

[The *Bhil* maiden of the *Kirataas* digs herbs with shovels upon the ridges of the mountains.]

Indro me-a-himarandhayatpradaakum cha pridaakvam,
*Svajam tirashchiraajim kasarneelam dashonasim.*17.

[Indra has put snakes in my power—the *Pradaku, Svaja, Tirashchiraj, Kasarneel, Dashonasi*, etc.]

Aheenaam sarveshaa visham paraa vahantu Sindhavah;
*Hataastirashchiraajayo nipishtaasah pridaakavah.*20.

[Let the poison of all snakes be carried away by River Sindhu and others; the most dangerous snakes *Tirashchiraaji, Pridaaku*, etc. have been slain already.]

Angaadangaat pra chyaavaya hridayam pari varjaya;
*Athaa vishasya yat tejoavaacheenam tadetu te.*25.

[I remove the snake's venom from your every limb, making it avoid the heart; let it move downward and go away.]

Aare abhood vishamraud vishe vishampraagapi;
Agnirvishamherniradhaat Somo niranyeet;
*danshtaaramanvagaad vishamhiramrita.*26.

[The venom has been obstructed and bound; poison has killed poison. Agni has burnt the venom; Soma has driven it out. The venom has gone back to the snake, killing the snake.]

Hymn V is composed by three rishis, Sindhu-Dweep, Kaushik and Vihavya. Verses 37–41 are ascribed to God Brahma. Some verses are metrical, some in prose. It is dedicated to various deities—*Aap* (the divine Waters), Indra, Vishnu, Varuna, Vaishwanar, Agni, Moon, Prajapati, etc. William Dwight Whitney states that 'Water Thunderbolts' mentioned in the hymn 'appears to be nothing more than a highfalutin name, well befitting the black magic of this hymn, for handfuls of water hurled with much hocus-pocus.'[149]

Indrashauja sthendrashya saha sthendrashya balam
sthendrashya veeryaam1 sthendrashya nrimnam stha;
*Jishnave yogaaya Brahmayogairvo yunjmi.*1.

[149]Whitney, William Dwight, *Atharvaveda-Samhita*, Harvard University, 1905, p. 579.

[O divine Waters, you are Indra's forces, his power, his strength, his manliness and heroism. I unite you with *Brahmayoga* for winning victories.]

The next five verses, **Verses 2–6**, are repetitive. They unite the divine Waters with Kshtra Yoga, Indra Yoga, Soma Yoga and Yoga Yoga!

Agnerbhaaga stha; apaam Shukramaapo Devivarcho asmaasu dhatta; Prajapatervo dhamnaasmai lokaaya saadaye.7.

[O divine Waters, you are Agni's portion; O sperm of waters, shower us with splendour! With the ordinance of *Prajapati*, I install you in this world.]

The next seven verses are similar to the above. In place of Agni, they substitute Indra, Soma, Varuna, Mitra-and-Varuna, Yama, the heavenly Fathers and God Savita. I quote **Verse 14**:

Devashya Saviturbhaaga stha; ApaamShukramaapo
Devivarcho asmaasu dhatta; Prajapatervo dhamnaasmai
lokaaya saadaye.14.

[O divine Waters, you are Savita's portion; O sperm of waters, shower us with splendour! With the ordinance of Prajapati, I install you in this world.]

Yo va AapoApaam bhaago3psva1ntaryajusho Devayajanah;
Idam tamami srijaami tam maabhyavanikshi;
Tena tamabhyatisrijaamo yo3smaan dveshti yam vayam dvishmah;
tam vadheyam tam strisheeyaanena brahmanaanen karmanaanen menya.15.

[O divine Waters, what portion of Waters within the Waters is for the sacrificial formula, for sacrificing to the Gods; let it strengthen me and be directed against those who hate us and whom we hate. May I slay them with this spell, this invincible weapon.]

Verses 16–21 repeat the above verse by inserting different adjectives—like 'waves of waters', 'child of waters', 'bull of the waters', 'golden embryo of the waters' and 'heavenly stone of the waters'.

> *Yadarvaacheenam traihaayanaadanritam kim chodim;*
> *Aapo maa tasmaat sarvasmaad duritaat paantvamhas.*22.
>
> [What lies and untruths we might have spoken in the last three years, O Waters, protect us against any distress from that falsehood.]
>
> *Ariprаa Aapo apa ripramasmat;*
> *Prasmadeno duritam suprateekah pra dushvapnyam pra malam vahantu.*24.
>
> [Of godly aspect are you, O Waters, free from defilement! Take away all filth and all sins from us and protect us from bad dreams.]
>
> *Vishnoh kramoasi sapatnahaa PrithivisanshitoAgnitejaah;*
> *Prithivimanu vi krame-aham Prithivyaastam nirbhajamo yoasmaan dweshti yam vayam dvishmah;*
> *Sa maa jeeveet tam praano jahaatu.*25.
>
> [O divine Waters, you are as powerful as Vishnu's strides! You are revered on the Earth; fulgent like Agni, you slay my rivals. Remove from the Earth those who hate us and whom we hate. Let them not live; let their breath quit them!]

The subsequent 10 verses, from **Verses 26 to 35**, have been spun out by interchanging the names of deities like Vayu, Earth, Surya, Atmosphere, the Quarters, Brahma, Soma, making similar prayers. These chants are a mere jugglery of words!

Verse 36 even leaves space for filling the name of the specific foes who are to be made the targets of annihilation, as follows: 'Ours is what has been conquered, ours is what has been destroyed. Now do I target for destruction the splendour, life-time and breath of the man of ——— lineage, son of ——— (father and mother).'

Verses 37 to 41 are repetitive. Let me illustrate:

Suryashaavritamanvaavarte dakshinaamanvaavritam;
Saa me dravinam yachchhatu saa me
Brahmanavarachasam.37.

[I follow the wide course of the Sun southward; let it yield me prosperity and the glory of *Brahma*-splendour!]

In the following verse 'quarters filled with light', Saptrishis, Brahma, 'myself' and the 'Brahmin' have been substituted.

Yam vayam mrigayaamahe tam vadhai strinavaamahai;
Vyaatte Parmeshthino brahmanaapeepadaam tam.42.

[Whom we hunt, whom we cut them down by our deadly weapons; through our magic spell we push them into the wide-open mouth of the Supreme God.]

Vaishwaanarashya danshtraabhyaam hetistam samadhadabhi;
Iyam tam psaatvaahutih samid devi saheeyasi.43.

[Let my magic *mantra* send my foe as an offering into the tusks of Vaishvanar Agni. Let him be devoured as divine fuel!]

Paraa shrineehi tapasaa yaatudhaanaan parAgne raksho harasaa shrineehi;
Paraarachishaa mooradevaanchharneehi paraasutripah shoshuchatah shrineehi.49.

[O Agni, crush away the *yatudhan*s by your heat; throw them far away. Scorch the rapacious rascals who feed on lives and drive them away!]

Apaamasmai vajram pra haraami chaturbhrishtim sheershabhidyaaya vidvaan.
So ashyaangaani pra shrinaatu sarvaa tanme Devaa anu janantu vishwe.50.

[O Waters, I hurl the *Chatur-bhrishti* (four-pointed) thunderbolt of waters at this man to split his head into pieces; let it crush all his limbs! Let all the Gods give assent to this my deed!]

Hymn VI, ascribed to God Brihaspati, sings the glory of the *Faal-Mani,* an amulet fabricated out of the plough-share. The first five verses of the hymn describe this magical amulet. Fashioned by craftsmen and smiths, it can split the heads, not only of enemies, but even of one's own cousins!

Araateeyorbhraatrivyashya durhaardo dvishatah shirah.
*Api vrishchaamyojasaa.*1.

[The head of the mean cousin and of an evil-hearted, hateful man, I cut off with the power of this amulet.]

Varma mahyamayam manih falaajjaatah karishati;
*Poorno manthen maagamad rasen saha varchasaa.*2.

'This wonder amulet, created out of the plough-share after a thorough churning, shall protect me like an armour.]

Yat tvaa shikvah paraavadheeta taksha hasten vaashyaa;
*Aapastvaa tasmaajjeevalaah punantu shuchayah shuchim.*3.

[O amulet, you were sliced by an expert blacksmith, and the carpenter had carefully designed you. Thereafter the vigorous, divine Waters had purified you!]

Hiranyastragayam manihi shradhhaam yagyam maho dadhat;
*Grihe vasatu noatithih.*4.

[Let this golden garlanded amulet, empowered by devotion and *yajna*, dwell in our house as an honoured guest.]

Yamabadadhanaad Brihaspatirmanim faalam
ghritashachutamugram khadiramojase;
TamAgni pratyamunchata so asmai duha aajyam
*bhooyobhooyah shvahshvastema tvam dvishato jahi.*6.

[God Brihaspati had invented and worn this bestower of abundant *ghrita;* Agni had got it fastened to himself. It yielded him *ghrita*, morn after morn. O amulet destroy my enemies!]

Yamabadadhanaad Brihaspatirmanim faalam
ghritashachutamugram khadiramojase;
TtamIndrah pratyamunchataujase veeryaaya kam;
*So asmai balamid duhe bhooyobhooyah shvahshvasten tvam dvishato jahi.*7.

[The bestower of abundant ghrita—the amulet that Brihaspati had worn for acquiring power, and Indra had fastened on for doing deeds of heroism! It gives you strength morn after morn; with that you slay your enemies!]

Verses 8 to 21 describe how God Soma, the Sun, Moon, Vayu, the Ashvins, Savitar, Varuna, Dhaataa and other gods derived benefit from this jewel. The later verses depict how it is benefitting even foodgrains like wheat and rice and honey, besides adding to our prosperity and helping us in winning wars against enemies.

~

Hymn VII is a mystical hymn composed by Rishi Atharva and dedicated to the 'Skambha'—The Frame of the Universe.

Kasminnange tapo ashyaadhi tishthati, kasminnanga
Ritamashyaa dhyahitam;
Kva vratam kva Shriddhaashya tishthati kasminnange
*satyamashya pratishthitam.*1.

[In what part of him does tapa (austerity) reside? In what part stays Rta (Order)? Where is vrata (vow) situated, where faith? In what part does Truth reside?]

Kasmaadangaada deepyate Agnirashya kasmaadagaada
pavate Matarishva;
Kasmaadangaada vi mimeetedhi Chandramaa maha
*Skambhasya mimano angam.*2.

[In what part the flames of Agni rise, from what part blows Matarishva (Vayu)? From which part the Moon rises, measuring the great Skambha?]

Kasminnange tishthati Bhoomirashya kasminnange
tishthatyaAntariksham;

Kasminnange tishthatyaahitaa Dhauh
*sasminnangetishthatyuttaram Divah.*3.

[In what part of him is situated the Earth, in what part the atmosphere? In what part is situated what lies beyond the Sky?]

Kvaarthamaasaa kva yanti maasaa samvatsarena saha samvidaanaah;
Yatra yantritatavo yatraartavaah skambham tam broohi katamah svideva sah? 5.

[Whither go the half-months, whither the months, in accordance with the year? Whither go the seasons and parts of seasons? Tell me truly where is that Skambha?]

Kva prepsanti yuvati viroope ahoraatre dravatah samvidaane;
Yatra prepasantirabhiyantaapah skambham tam broohi katamah svideva sah? 6.

[Desiring what to attain, run the two damsels, bright and dark?[150] Desiring to attain that the Waters flow? Tell me truly where that Skambha is?]

Yat paramamavamam yachcha madhyamam Prajapatih sasrije vishwaroopam;
*Kiyataa skambha pra vivesh yatra tatra praavishat kiyat tad babhoova.*8.

[What was the highest, lowest, and the middle sphere created by Prajapati? By how much the Skambha entered those regions and in how much it did not enter?]

Yasmin bhoomirantariksham dhyauryasminnadhyaahitaa;
yatrAgnishChandramaah Suryo vaatastishthantyaarpitaah skambham tam broohi katamah svideva sah? 12.

[In which exist the Earth, the Firmament and the Realm of the Gods, where the Sun, the Moon, Vayu and Agni subsist;

[150]Two damsels—Day and Night.

tell me about that Skambha.]

Yashya Brahma mukhamaahurjivhaam madhikashaamuta;
Virajomoodho yashyaahuh skambham tam broohi katamah svideva sah? 19.

[Of whom they call Brahma the mouth, Madhukasha the tongue; of whom they call Viraj the breasts—that Skambha tell me, truly, which is he?]

yatraAdityaashcha Rudraashcha Vasavashcha samaahitah;
bhootam cha yatra bhavyam cha sarve lokaah pratishthitaah skambham tam broohi katamah svideva sah? 22.

[Where the Adityas, the Rudras and the Vasus are set together; where what is and what is to be (the present and future), all the words are established—that Skambha, tell me truly, which is He?

Yasshya bhoomih pramAntarikshamutodaram;
Divam yashchakre moordhaanam tasmai jeshthaaya Brahmane namah.32.

[Of whom the Earth is the feet, atmosphere the belly and the Sky the head—to that Param Brahma we pay our homage!]

Apa tashya hatam tamo vyaavritah sa paapmana;
Sarvaani tasminjyoteeshi yaani treeni Prajapatau.40.

[One who gets to know the Skambha, his darkness disappears. He is separated from evil, in him are established all the three lights of Prajapati!]

Hymn VIII is composed by Rishi Kutsa, who also belongs to the Angiras clan. This hymn is also dedicated to Param Brahma.

Yo bhootam cha bhavyam cha sarvam yashchaadhitishthati;
Svaryashya cha kevalam tashmai jeshthaaya Brahmano namah.1.

[He who is Lord of what is and what is to be, who rules over

Heaven; to that Param Brahma we pay homage!]

Skambheneme vishtabhite Dhaushcha bhoomishcha tishthatah;
Skambha idam sarvamatmanvad yat praanannimishachcha yat.2.

[Upheld by the Skambha, both Sky and Earth stand fast. The Skambha embraces all that has a soul, that breathes and winks!]

Dvaadash pradhayashchakramekam treeni nabhyaani ka u tachchiket.
Tatraahataastreeni shataani shankavah shashtishcha kheelaa avichaachalaa ye.4.

[Twelve fellies, one wheel, three naves—who understands that? Therein are inserted three hundred and sixty pins, pegs that are immovable.]

Idam Savitarvi jaaneehi shad yamaa aika aikajah.
Tasmin haapitvamichchhante ya aishamaka aikajah.5.

[O Savita, do you distinguish them? Six are twins, one is born alone; all six seek to mingle with the Self-born!]

Aikachakram vartat aikanemi sahastraakshram pra puro pashcyaa.
Arhena vishvam bhuvanam jajaan yadashyaardham kva tad babhoov.7.

[One wheel, with one rim and a thousand syllables, moves up and down. With a half it has generated all existence; where is the other half—what has become of that?]

Prajapatishcharati garbhe antardrishamaano bahudhaa vi jaayate;
Ardhen vishvam bhuvanam jajaam yadashyaardha katamah sa ketuh.13.

[Prajapati resides within the womb; remaining unseen, yet

He is manifestly born. With his half he has generated all existence, what his other half is, who here knows?]

Doore poornen vasati door oonen heeyate;
*Mahad Yaksham bhuvanashya madhye tasmai balim raashtrabhrito bharanti.*15.

[The Mighty Yaksha dwells in the midst of existence at a distance, abandoned by the Complete and the Incomplete; to him the kingdom-rulers offer animal flesh.]

Sahastrahanyam viyataavashya pakshau harerhansashya patatah swargam;
*Sa devaantsarvaanrashyupadadhya sampashyan yaati bhuvanaani vishswaa.*18.

[When after endeavouring for a thousand days, the wings of this swan fall off, he remains established in his unbound Self. With divine light lodged wihin his Self, this unbound Self proceeds Heaven-ward surveying all worlds.]

Shatam sahastramyutam nyarbudamsankheyam svamsmin nivishtam;
*Tadashya ghnantyabhipashata aiva tasmaad Devo rochata aisha aitat.*24.

[A hundred, a thousand, a hundred million, innumerable souls have entered and been absorbed into Him! Death slays them, even as He looks on. Therefore, He shines bright.]

Poornaat poornamudachati poornam poornen sichchate;
*Uto tadabhya vidyaam yatastat parisichyate.*29.

[The Absolute was born from the Absolute and was nourished by the Absolute; we have learnt today. Whence was the Absolute poured out?]

Aishaa sanatnee sanameva jaateshaa pruraanee pari saravam babhoova;
*Mahee devyushaso vibhaatee saikenaiken mishataa vi chashte.*30.

[IT, the everlasting Power, exists from the beginning of Time and is imminent in the universe. IT illumines Usha with golden hue and looks at All in the twinkling of eye.]

Pundareekam navadvaram tribhirgunebhiraavritam;
*Tasmin yad Yakshmaatmanvat tad vai Brahmavido viduh.*43.

[The lotus-flower of nine doors is endowed with three qualities—what radiance Yaksha hides within it? That is known only to the knowers of the Brahma!]

Akaamo dheero amritam svambhoo rasen tripto na kutashyanonah;
*Tameva vidvaan na bibhaaya mrityoraatmaanm dheermajaram yuvaanam.*44.

[Free from desire, un-perturbed, immortal, self-existent, satiated with Self, free from all deficiency! Knowing that ageless, young Atma, one is not afraid of death.]

∽

Hymn IX, authored by Rishi Atharva, celebrates offering of 'a cow and a hundred rice-dices (*Shatodana*)'. Earlier we had seen a hymn offering a 'goat with five rice-dishes'.

Aghaayataamapi nahyaa mukhaani sapatneshu vajramarpayaitam;
*Indren dattaa prathmaa shataudanaa bhratrivyaghnee yajamaanashya gaatuh.*1.

[Silence the mischief-makers, let them keep their trap shut; let Indra strike our enemies with thunderbolt. Offered by Indra first of all, the cow with a hundred rice-dishes, will shower success on the sacrifice.]

Yah shataudanaam pachati kaamaprena sa kalpate;
*Preetaa hrishayrtvijah sarve yanti yathaayatham.*4.

[He who cooks the cow of hundred rice-dishes, let all his wishes be fulfilled! Let the priests who attend to sacrifice receive well-deserved rewards.]

Ye te devi shamitaarah paktaaro ye cha te janaah;
*Te tvaa sarve gopsyanti maibhyo bhaisheeh shataudane.*7.

[O heavenly cow of hundred rice-dishes, the men who have pacified you, and who are cooking you, do not get frightened by them; they will take good care of you.]

Devaah pitaro manushyaa Gandharvaapsarasashcya ye;
*Te tvaa sarve gopshyanti saatiraatramati drava.*9.

[The gods, the heavely Fathers, the Gandharvas and the Apsaras, they will all guide you; you go beyond the over-night sacrifice to the gods.]

Antariksham divam bhoomimAdityaan Maruto dishah;
*Lokaantsa sarvaanaapnoti yo dadaati shataudanaam.*10.

[Those who donate a cow of the hundred rice-dishes, obtain the Firmament, Heaven, Earth, the Sun, the Maruts and all else!]

Yat te shiro yat te mukham yau karno ye cha te hanoo;
*Aamikshyaam durhataam daatre ksheeram sarpiratho madhu.*13.

[O inviolable cow, let your head, mouth, ears and jaws yield curds, milk, butter and honey to your giver!]

This repetitive litany goes on thus offering the nostrils, horns, eyes, lungs, heart, throat, entrail and intestines, rectum, bone marrow, blood, etc., in the next 11 verses.

Ulukhale musale yashcha charmani yo vaa shoorpa tandulah kanah;
*Yam vaa Vaato maatarishvaa pavamaano mamaathaAgnishtaaddhotaa suhutam krinotu.*26.

[What in the mortar, on the pestle, on the hide, or what rice-grain kernel in the winnowing basket was left, or what the wind, *Matarishva,* shook, Let Agni as *hotra* make that well offered!]

> *Apo deveermadhumateerghritashyachuto brahmanam hasteshu praprithak saadayaami;*
> *Yatkaama idamabhishinchaami voaham tanme sarvam sam padyataam vayam shyama patayo rayinaam.*27.
>
> [I offer to the Brahmins the heavenly waters, rich in honey, dripping with ghrita. O holy Brahmins, let our wishes be fulfilled—may we be the lords of wealth!]

Devi Chand's predicament in translating this hymn can be easily imagined as he has been translating 'cow' as 'Vedic Speech'. After all, how can 'Vedic Speech' be cut up in different limbs!

Bhagawati Devi Sharma, who translated the hymn in Hindi, also has difficulty in accepting that a cow is being sacrificed. She has theorized that the Earth and the nourishing nature have also been called a 'cow' in a wider context, and asserts that 'the hymn does not relate to cow sacrifice'.

∽

Hymn X authored by Rishi Kashyap and is dedicated to '*Vasha*' Cow; it is similar to the above hymn by Rishi Atharva. In **Verses 13–15** the Vasha Cow frolics with the Gandharvas on the ocean. In **Verse 16**, the ocean came to her as a horse to mount her and so on. To my mind this hymn is an imitation of the preceding hymn by Rishi Atharva. But Sage Kashyap has made amends by showing Rishi Atharva ensconced in heaven in **Verses 12 and 17**, enjoying the company of the sanctified Vasha Cow.

∽

SELECTED HYMNS FROM ATHARVA VEDA CHAPTER 11

Hymn I is ascribed to Brahma and is dedicated to Aditi, mother of Indra and the Adityas, who is preparing a rice-dish wishing for progeny!

> *Agne jaayasvaAditirnaathiteyam brahmodanam pachati putrakaamaa;*

*Saptarishayo bhootakritasthe tvaa manthantu prajayaa saheha.*1.

[O Agni, you are invited; Aditi, desirous of begetting sons, is offering a rice-dish. The Seven Seers, being progenitors, are churning the pot.]

Devi Chand translates the verse as: 'O noble learned person, attain to fame! Just as a married, high-spirited woman, yearning for children, firmly fixes her mind in her mind God, the bestower of Vedic knowledge, food and riches, so should the seven Rishis, the doers of noble deeds, in domestic life, kindle thee with offspring.' In the footnote he mentions the Seven Rishis as: Skin, Eye, Ear, Tounge, Nostril, Mind, Intellect!

He has an aversion to disclosing the names Vedic gods as mentioned earlier. He translates Agni as 'noble learned person', Aditi as 'a married high-sprited woman, yearning for children', and *Adityas* as 'the Bestower of Vedic Knowledge, food and riches'! I have quoted him to provide some comic relief to the reader.

Agneajanishthaa mahate veeryaaya brahmodanaaya paktve Jatavedah;
*Saptarishayo bhootakritaste tvaajeejanannasyai rayim sarva veeram ni yachchha.*3.

[O Jataveda Agni, you are born for great deeds. The Seven Seers have invited you for rice-dish offering. Enrich this woman with brave sons.]

The hymn proceeds in similar fashion as the hymn authored by Rishi Atharva in the former chapter—to carry oblations to Gods and let the yajaman to ascend to high Heaven after completion of his life here; make Aditi's enemies perish and let her be blessed with brave sons and prepare for child-bearing.

Aimaa aguryoshitah shumbhamaana uttishtha naari tavasam rabhasva;
*Supatnee patyaa prajayaa prajaavatyaa tvaagan yagyah prati kumbhagribhaaya.*14.

[These maidens (Powers of Sacrifice) have come, adorning themselves; now arise, O woman, espoused by your husband, be blessed with progeny; your sacrifice has fructified—receive this vessel!]

The hymn has reached its climax with this verse, yet it goes on interminably for 23 verses more! It invites the Waters, Grains, Rice, the God of Sacrifice, Soma, *Rta*, *Nir-riti* (Destruction), etc. and the Oblation itself! The last verse is a prayer by the priests:

Yen devaa jyotishaa dhyaamudayan Brahmodanam paktvaa sukritashya lokam;
*Tena geshma sukritashya lokam svaraarohanto abhi naakamuttam.*37.

[Propelled by the power of offering oblation, the Gods ascended to high Heaven! Let us also be rewarded a place in the highest firmament for cooking the rice-dish.]

Hymn II, composed by Rishi Atharva, is dedicated to God Rudra, especially as Bhava and Sharva.

BhavaaSharvau mridatam maabhi yaatam Bhootapati Pashupati namo vaam;
*pratihitaamaayataam maa vi sraashtam maa no hinsishtam maa chatushpadah.*1.

[O Bhava and Sharva, make us happy, do not go against us. O *Bhootapati* (Lord of beings) and *Pashupati* (Lord of cattle),[151] we pay our homage to you. Do not shoot the arrow drawn at us; nor harm our bipeds and quadrupeds.]

Shune kroshtre maa shareeraani kartamliklavebhyo gridhebhyo ye cha krishnaa avishyavah;
*Makshikaaste pashupate vayaansi te vighase maa vidanta.*2.

[151]In later times, God Shiva was called Bhootapati and Pashupati.

[O violent Gods, do not (kill us and) turn our bodies into food for dogs, jackals, flies, carrion kites or vultures.]

Krandaaya te praanaaya yaashch Bhava ropayah;
*Namaste Rudra krinmah sahastrakshaayaamartya.*3.

[O Bhava, we hear your roar, fear your terrible presence, and pray for your grace; we salute you, O thousand-eyed Rudra!]

Astraa neelashikhanden sahastraakshena vaajinaa;
*Rudrenaardhakaghaatinaa ten maa samaraamahi.*7.

[O fast-moving Rudra of blue-locks and thousand eyes, destroyer of forces of the Demon *Ardhak*, may we never be your target!]

Sa no Bhavah pari vrinaktu vishvata aapa evAgnih pari vrinaktu no Bhavah;
*Maa noabhi maansta namo astvasmai.*8.

[Let Lord Bhava spare us as fire avoids water; we bow to you in reverence not to trouble us!]

Chaturnamo ashtakritvo Bhavaaya dasha kritvah Pahupate namaste;
*Taveme pancha pashvo vibhaktaa gaavo ashvaah purusha ajaavayah.*9.

[Four times, eight times, ten times we bow in reverence to you, Lord Bhava! O Lord, let these five be under your care—cows, horses, men, sheep and goat!]

Tava chatastrah pradishtava Dhaustava Prithivi tavedamugrorva antariksham.
*Tavedam sarvamaatmanvad yat praanat Prithivimanu.*10.

[O formidable Rudra, you are the Lord of four directions, the Heaven, the Earth and the firmament! Lord of all that live and breathe upon the Earth!]

Uruhu kosho vasudhaanastavaayam yasminnimaa vishvaa bhuvanaanyananyantah.

*Sa no mrid Pahupate namaste parah kroshtaaro abhibhaah shvaanah paro yantvaghaRudro.*11.

[O Lord of cattle, Lord of vast spaces where the Vasus live, our salutations to you, be gracious to us! Let these jackals, wild dogs, evil portents and the shrieking, wild-haired demonesses go far away from us.]

Namah saayan namah pratarnamo raatryaa namo diva;
*Bhavaaya cha Sharvaaya chobhaabhyaamakaram namah.*16.

[O God Rudra, we pay homage to you in the evening and morning, by night and by day! To both Bhava and Sharva, we have also paid homage.]

Sahastrakshyamatipashyam purastaad Rudramashyantam bahudhaa vipashchitam;
*Mopaaraama jivhyeyamaanam.*17.

[O Rudra, you hurl weapons in all directions, endowed as you are with a thousand eyes! May we not fall foul of your tongue that devours all evil-doers!]

Yashya takmaa kaasikaa hetirekamashvashyeva vrishanah kranda aiti.
*Abhipoorva nirnayate namo astvasmai.*22.

[Our homage to you, O Lord! Let your deadly weapons, like the neighing wild stallions assail Takman and *Kasika* (tuberculosis, fever, cough).]

Sinshumaaraa ajagaraah purikayaa jashaa matsyaa rajasaa yebyho ashyasi;
*Na te dooram na parishthaasti te Bhava sadhyah sarvaan pari pashyasi bhoomim poorvasmaadadhanshyuttarsmin tsamudre.*25.

[You rule over the dolphins, porpoise, pythons and fishes—they all testify to your glory; no creature is beyond your reach, O Bhava! You keep an eye over all, and smite across the Eastern to the Southern Ocean.]

Hymn III is dedicated to Brihaspati. It is authored by Rishi Atharva; it extolls a rice dish (*Odana*).

*Tashaudanashya Brihaspatih shiro Brahma mukham.*1.

[Of this rice-dish Brihaspati is the head, Brahma the mouth!]

*DhyaavaaPrithivi shrotre SuryaaChandramasaavakshinee SaptaRishayah pranaapaanaah.*2.

[Heaven-and-Earth are the ears, Sun-and-Moon the eyes; the Seven Seers are its breath-and-expirations.]

*Chakshurmusalama Kama ulukhalam.*3.

[Its eyes are the pestle; its mortar is Desire.]

*Diti shoorpamaditih shoorpagraahee Vatoapaavinak.*4.

[The winnowing basket is goddess Diti while Aditi holds the basket. Vayu is the winnower.]

*Ashvaah kanaa gaavastandulaa mashakaastusha.*5.

[Horses are the grains, cows the rice; the husk-straws fly like the mosquitoes.]

*Shyaamamayoashamansaani lohitamashya lohitam.*7.

[Its flesh is black like iron; its blood is red like copper.]

*Trapu bhasma haritam varnah; pushkarmashya gandha.*8.

[The grains are golden in colour and exude the fragrance of lotus flowers; the ash that remains is like tin.]

*Iyameva Prithivi kumbhi bhavati radhyamaanshaudanashya Dhaurapidhanam.*11.

[The Earth is the vessel to hold the rice-dish, covered by the Heaven!]

*Ritam hastaavanejanam kulyopasechanam.*13.

[The seasons sprinkled water on it and the rivulets moistened it.]

*Ritavah paktaara aartavaah samindhate.*17.

[The Seasons are stirring the broth; the days and nights are kindling the fire.]

*Yaavad daataabhimanasyeta tannati vadet.*25.

[Be satisfied with what the Giver has given; don't crave for more!]

*Tvamodanam prashee3stvaamodanaa3 iti.*27.

[Have you eaten the rice-dish or the rice-dish eaten you?]

*Paraancham chainah prasheeh praanaastvaa haashyantityenahaaha.*28.

[If you have eaten the rice-dish while reclining, your breath will quit you; no one tells you this.]

*Naivaahamodanam na maamodanah.*30.

[Indeed, I have not eaten the rice-dish, nor the rice-dish eaten me.]

*Odan aivaudanam praasheet.*31.

[The rice-dish itself has eaten the rice-dish!]

Devi Chand's translation for this last verse: 'God has devoured this created universe'.

Hymn IV, also authored by Rishi Atharva. The eminent sage continues extolling Odana. Unlike Hymn III which had one-liner verses, the verses in this hymn are multi-liner. However, all 18 verses are almost similar, content-wise. However, the poet gives a dire warning of dreadful consquences if while savouring the rice-dish anyone changes one's posture, the ear, the eye, the mouth, the tounge, the teeth, the stomach, etc., and warns that it would have adverse consequences. These verses issue from the Earth or the

Sky, from the eyes of the Sun or Moon, and so on. It will suffice if I quote the last verse:

Tatashchainmannyayaa pratishthayaa praasheeryayaa chaitam poorva rishyayah praashnan;
Apratishthanoanaayatano marishyaseetyenmaaha;
Tam vaa aham naarvaancha na paraancham na pratyancham;
Satte pratishthaaya;
Tayain praashisham tayainmajeegamam;
Aish vaa odana sarvaangah sarvaparuh sarvatanooh.
*Sarvaanga aiva sarvaparuh sarvatanooh sam bhavati ya aivam veda.*18.

[In earlier times the posture in which the knowledgeable Rishis had savoured the rice-dish, if these verses were not pronounced in the same posture the person would lose his status, The poet says this condition should be clearly explained to him. Besides, the one desiring to savour the rice-dish should say he has taken it having established himself in the supreme Brahma and has obtained the beneficial effects. Savoured in the correct posture and manner the Rice-dish bestows the promised boons and blessings.]

Hymn V is yet another hymn by Rishi Atharva eulogizing the rice dish. The verses become one-liners again.

*Bradhna loko bhavati bradhnashya vishtapi shrayate ya aivam veda.*2.

[Those who understand the mystic of the Rice-dish, attain the regions of the Sun.]

*Aitasmaada vaa odanaat trayastrimshatam lokaan niramimeeta Prajapati.*3.

[Prajapati created thirty-three gods by the power of the Rice-dish!]

*Teshaam pragyaanaaya yagyamsrijata.*4.

[Yagya-sacrifice was created to open the doors to the celestial worlds.]

Sa ya aivam vidusha upadrashtaa bhavati praanam runaddhi.5.

[One who reviles him who attains this knowledge is soon deprived of his vital breath.]

Na cha praanam runaddhi sarvajaanim jeeyate.6.

[Not only the loss of vital breath; he suffers total ruination.]

Na cha sarvajyaanim jeeyate purainam jarasah praano jahaati.7.

[Not only does he suffer total ruination; his vital breath leaves him before his old age.]

∽

Hymn VI is composed by Rishi Vaidarbhi Bhargava; it is dedicated to Prana (Life Force).

Praanaaya namo yashya sarvamidam vashe; yo bhootah sarvashyaIshwaro yasmintsarvam pratishthitam.1.

[Homage to the Life Force, Prana, in whose control is this whole universe, who is the Lord of all living things and pervades in All!'

Namaste Praana krandaaya namaste stanayitnave; Namaste Praana viddyute namaste Prana varshate.2.

[Homage to you, O Life Force, who roars from the sky and thunders from the clouds! You are the lightening of the clouds and waters of the rains!]

Yat Praana stanayitnunaabhikrandatyoshadheeh; pra veeyante garbhaan dadhateatho bahveervi jaayante.3.

[O Life Force, when you, through the clouds, target your thundering roar at the herbs, they are impregnated! They receive the embryo and multiply!]

*Abhivrishtaa aushadheyah praanen samavaadiran; aayurvai nah praateetarah sarvaa nah surabheerakah.*6.

[The herbs, having been fulfilled, raise their voice in accord: 'O Life Force, you have prolonged our life-span, now fill us all with divine fragrance!]

Yaa tepraana priyaa tanooryo te prana preyasi;
*Atho yad bheshajam tava tashya no dhehi jeevase.*9.

[O Life-bestowing Power, fructify us with your immortalizing life-force! Grant us a long and fruitful life!]

Praanah prajaa anu vaste pitaa putramiva priyam;
*Praano ha sarvasheshvaro yachcha praanati yachcha na.*10.

[O Life Force, may you live with us and enliven us, like a father to his son! You are the lord of all that breathes and breathes not!]

Praano Virat Praano deshtri Praanam sarva upaasaate;
Praano ha SurayashChandramaah praanamaahuh
*Prajapataim.*12.

[O Life Force, *Prana, you* are *Viraj*, all-impeller, urging to generate, worshipped by all! *Prana*, verily, is the Sun and Moon, and they all call him Prajapati!]

Apaanaati Praanati purusho garbhe antaraa;
*Yadaa tvam Praana jinvashyatha sa jaayate punah.*14.

[Life Force, Praṅa breathes life into the womb; quickened by Prana the embryo inhales and exhales within, and is born.]

PraanamaahurMatarishvanam Vato ha Praana uchcyate;
Praane ha bhootam bhavyam cha Praane sarva
*pratishthitam.*15.

[They call Life Force the *Matarishvan*, the *Vata*. In Life Force is all estabhished—what has been existing and what will be existing!]

Antargarbhashcharati Devataasvaabhooto bhootah sa u

jaayate punah;
*Sa bhooto bhavyam bhavishyat pitaa putram pra viveshaa shacheebhih.*20.

[Life Force, Prana, dwells in divinities and prevails in future as the father dwells in his son!]

Oordhvah supreshu jaagaara nanu tiryana ne padhyate;
*Na suptamashya supteshvanu sushraava kashchana.*25.

[O Life Force Prana, remain awake in sleeping beings; no sleeping being is bereft of Prana.]

Praana maa mat paryaavrito na madanyo bhavishsi;
*Apaam garbhamiva jeevase praana badhnaami tvaa mayi.*26.

[O Breath of Life, do not desert me; dwell within me as the embryo dwells within a womb!]

~

Hymn VII, '*Brahmacharya Sookta*' is ascribed to God Brahma and dedicated to Brahmachari, celibate Vedic student. The author has not revealed his name and ascribed the hymn to Brahma. One remains a Brahamachari till he abstains from sex.

Brahmacharishnamshcharati rodasi ubhe tasmin Devah sammanso bhavanti;
*Sa daadhar Prithiveem divam cha sa aachaaryam tapasaa piparti.*1.

[The Brahmachari becomes in tune with the Heaven and Earth; the gods lodge in him, becoming like-minded. He fills his teacher with fervour.]

Poorvojaato brahmano Brahmachari dharmam vasaanastapasodatishthat.
*Tasmaajjaatam brahmanam Brahma jeshtham Devaashcha sarve amaraten saakam.*5.

[As a particle of the Brahma, Brahmachari, immerses in Vedic lore and equipped with the heat of knowledge is born as the Brahma.]

Brahmachari janayan brahmaapo lokam Prajapatim parmeshthinam Virajam;
Garbho bhootvamritashya yonaavIndro ha bhootvasuraamsttarha.7.

[Nurtured in the celestial womb, the Brahmachari has access to Prajapati, the creator of Viraj; becoming Indra, he shatters the Asuras.]

Abhikrandan stanyannarunah shitingo brihachchepoanu bhoomau jabhhar;
Brahmachari sinchati sanau retah Prithivyaam tena jeevanti pradishashchatastrah.12.

[Like a roaring and thundering black-and-brown virile cloud, the Brahmachari, pours seed upon the Earth and impregnates vast level surfaces, fructifying the four quarters.]

(There is contradiction here. A Brahmachari cannot be like a 'virile cloud' and cannot impregnate.)

Aachaaryo Brahmachari Brahmachari Prajapatih;
Prajapatirvi rajati ViradIndro s bhavadvashee.16.

[Brahmachari becomes the Acharya, Brahmachari is Prajapati. Prajapati gives birth to Viraj; Indra cohabits with Viraj and rules the world.]

(This is highly exaggerated and inappropriate praise.)

Paarthivaa divyaah pashava aaranyaa graamyaashcha ye;
Apakshaa pakshinashcha ye te jaataa Brahmachaarinah.21.

[All creatures born of Prajapati individually bear breath in their bodies and are protected by the Brahma; the Brahmachari is their progenitor.]

Brahmachari, Brahma bhraajad bibharti tasmin Devaa adhi vishwe samotah;
Praanaapaanau janayannaad vyaanam Vaacham mano hridayam Brahma medhaam.24.

[Brahmachari holds in himself the radiant *Brahma*; all Gods reside in him. By Him are created Prana, Apana, Vyan, Speech, mind, heart, knowledge and it All.]

Brahmachari, the Vedic student, has been extolled in this hymn as a replica of the Supreme Brahma. By composing this hymn, the Brahmins, being Vedic students, have attempted to make for themselves and their tribe a pre-eminent place in the evolving Hindu society. But they are not entitled to be called 'Brahmachari' unless they remain celibate.

Hymn VIII, composed by Rishi Shantati, is a prayer for deliverance from sins (*Paap Mochan*). We have already encountered several hymns on the same theme. It was the main activity for which the Brahmins were employed.

Agnim broomo vanaspatinoshadiruta veerudhah;
*Indram Brihaspati Suryam te no munchantvamhasah.*1.

[We pray to Agni and to the forest trees, the herbs and the plants, Let Indra, Brihaspati and the Sun deliver us from sins!]

Broomo rajaan Varunam Mitram Vishnumatho Bhagam;
*Ansham Vivasvantam broomaste no munchantvamhasah.*2.

[We pray to King Varuna, Mitra, Vishnu, also Bhaga and Vivasvan; let them deliver us from sins!]

Broomo devam Savitaaram Dhataarmuta Pooshanam;
*Tvashtaarmagriam broomaste no munchantvamhasah.*3.

[We pray to God Savita, Dhata, the forward-going Pushan, Tvashta; let them deliver us from from sins.]

The litany goes on in this manner.

Divam broomo nakshatraani bhoomim yakshaani parvataan;
*Samudra naddho veshantaaste no munchantvamhasah.*10.

[We call upon the Sky, the asterisms, the Earth, the Yakshas, the mountains, the oceans, the rivers, the ponds—let them deliver us from sins.]

Adityaa Rudraa vasavo divi devaa Atharvaanah;
*Angiraso maneeshinaste no munchantvamhasah.*13.

[The Adityas, the Rudras, the Vasus, the Gods in Heaven; the Atharvas, the Angirases who are full of wisdom—let them deliver us from sins.]

(The poet probably belongs to the clans of the Angirases and Atharvas, as he has bracketed them with the Gods—the Adityas, the Rudras, the Vasus!)

Yagyam broomo yajamaanmrichah Samaani bheshjaa;
*Yanjooshi hotraa broomaste no munchantvamhasah.*14.

[We address the sacrifice, the sacrificer, the verses, the chants, the remedies, the sacred formulae, the invocations; let them deliver us from sins.]

Further on, the poet calls upon the darbha grass, hemp, barley, the demons, the serpents, gods from east, west, south and north and all gods collectively along with their spouses. He finally solicits:

YanMatali rathakreetamamritama veda bhshajam;
*TadIndro apsu praveshyat tadaapo datta bheshajam.*23.

[The immortal remedy brought by the chariot, known to Matali, which Indra administered into the waters; that remedy, O waters give to us!]

Hymn 9 is composed by Rishi Atharva. It extols the 'Remnant [*Uchchhishta*] of the Offering', the remains of the oblation offered in the yajna!

Uchchhishte naam roopam, chochchhishte loka aahitah;
Uchchhishta IndrashchAgnishcha vishvamantah
*samaahitam.*1.

[In the remnant are set the name and form, in the remnant is set the world; within the remnant are set together both Indra and Agni, and all else.]

Uchchhishte DhyaavaPritihivee vishwam bhooam samaahitam;
Aapah Samudra uchchhishte Chandramaa Vaata aahitah.2.

[In the remnant Heaven-and-Earth and all existence is set together; in the remnant the waters, the ocean, the Moon, the wind are set together.]

Sannuchhishte asamshchobhau mrityurvaajah Prajapati.
Laukyaa uchchhishta aayattaa vrashcha drashchaapi Shrirmayi.3.

[In the remnant are set 'being and non-being' (*sat* and *asat*), Death, vigour and Prajapati, all the worlds. Their radiance is reflected on us.]

Rik, Saama, Yajuruchhishta udageethah prastutam stutam;
Hinkaar uchhishte svarah Saamano medishcha tanmayi.5.

[The Rigvedic verses, chants of Sama Veda, the formulae of Yajur Veda, the tone and the song are all set in the remnant; let them stay in me.]

AIndraagnam Pavamaanam mahaanAgnirmahaavratam;
Uchchhishte yagyashyangaanyantargarbhaiva maatari.6.

[That relating to Indra-and-Agni, the purifying Soma, the great verses and rituals of *yajna*, they are all contained in the remnant like the embryo within a mother.]

The hymn goes on in this manner, mentioning the *Rajasuya* and *Vajapeya yajna,* the horse sacrifice, the vows (vrata), Dakshina, the one-night, six-night, sixteen-night sacrifices, the nine-part Earth (sic), oceans, skies. All these exist in the remnant!

Pitaa janituruchchhishtauasoh pautra pitaamahah;
Sa kshiyati vishwashyeshaano vrishaa bhoomyaamatighnyah.16.

[The remnant is father of the father and of grandfather as well as grand-son of breath. The remnant is the ruler of all, and dwells like an overpowering Bull upon the Earth.]

Verses 17 to 22 enumerate the qualities like truth, virtue, dominion, kingship, seasons, pebbles and herbs, clouds and lightening, success, prosperity, etc. as being part of the remnant.

Yachcha pranati pranena yachcha pashati chakshusaa,
*Uchchhishtaajajaggire sarve divi Devaa divishritah.*23.

[From the remnant were born what breathes with breath and sees with eye-sight, and all the Gods in Heaven and those residing in Heaven.]

Verse 24 claims that Sama Veda, the Puranas, Yajur Veda and all gods resided in Uchchhista, **Verses 25 and 26** hold that all the gods, happiness, mirth were born from Uchchhista!

Devah pitaro manushyaa Gandharvaapsarasashcha ye;
*Uchchhishtaajajaggire sarve divi Devaa divishritah.*27.

[The Gods, the Fathers, human beings, the Gandharvas-and-Apsaras were all born from *Uchchhishta Brahma!*]

Hymn X is composed by Rishi Kaurupathi. It expatiates on *Manyu* (Ardour, Passion, Fury).

Yanmannurjaayaamaavahat sankalpashya grihaadadhi;
*Ka aasam janyaah ke varaah ka oo jeshthavaro bhavat.*1.

[When Manyu (Ardour) brought his wife from the house of Sankalpa (ambition). who were the men from the girl's side, who the groomsmen; who were the wooers, who the chief wooer? Who was the creator?]

Tapashchaivaastaam karma chantarmahatyarnave;
*Janyaaste varaa Brahma jeshthavaro bhavat.*2.

[Penance (tapa) and action (karma) existed before Existence and they were on both sides; Brahma was the chief wooer.]

Kuta Indrah kuta Somah kuto Agnirjaayata;
kutasTvastaa samabhavat kuto Dhaataajaayat? 8.

[Whence was Indra, whence Soma, whence Agni was born? Whence did Tvashta come into being? Whence was Dhata born?]

IndraadiIndrah Somaat Somo AgneraAgnirajaayat.
*Tvashtaa ha jagge TvashturDhaaturDhaataajaayat.*9.

[From Indra Indra, from Soma Soma, from Agni Agni was born; Tvashta was born from Tvashta, from Dhata Dhata was born.]

Sansicho naam te Devaa ye sambhaaraantsamabharan;
*Sarva sansischya martya Devaah purushamaavishan.*13.

[There were Gods who poured and nourished the man's body; having fused together the man's body the Gods entered man.]

Uru paadaavashtheevantau mukham jivhaan greevashch keekasaah;
*Tvaachaa praavritya sarva tat sandhaa samadadhanmahee.*15.

[Which wise sage constructed the thighs, the feet, the knee-bones, the head, both the hands, the face, the ribs, the nipples, and both the sides?]

Sarve Devaa uppashikshan tadjaanaad vadhoo satee;
*Isha vashasya yaa jaayaa saasmin varnaabharat.*17.

[All the Gods guided and assisted in the endeavour of the creation of woman (*Jaayaa, Vadhoo, Sati*) and the divine creative power of God lent colour and lustre to her body.]

Yadaa Tvashta vyatunat pitaa Tvashtarya uttarah;
*Graham kritvaa martya Devaah purushmaavishan.*18.

[When Tvashta and other superior gods fashioned the man's eyes, ears, limbs, they made the mortal their lodging place and entered the man.]

Steyam dushkritam vrajinam satyam yagyo yasho brihat;
*Balam cha kshatramojashya shareeramany pravishan.*20.

[Theft, evil deeds, dishonesty; truth, *yajna*, power, bravery, all these then entered the man.]

Asthi kritvaa samidham tadashtaapo asaadayan;
*Retah kritvaajyam Devah purushamaavishan.*29.

[The All-pervading God, using the man's bones as fuel and semen as sacrificial ghrita, offered them in yajna and equipped the man's body with eight kinds of waters. Then the gods entered his body.]

Yaa aapo yaashcha Devataa ya Viraad Brahmana saha;
*Shareeram Brahma praavishachchhareereadhi Prajapatih.*30.

[With the waters and the deities, the Brahma with Viraj entered the human body, and remained therein as Prajapati.]

Prathamen pramaarena tredhaa vishvan vi gachchhati;
*Ada aiken gachchhatyada aiken gachchhateehaikena ni shevate.*33.

[On the release of first vital breath at the time of death, the soul goes from here to three different regions: for doing one kind of deeds to higher, different kind of deeds to lower, and is born again to enjoy the world for yet another kind.]

Hymn XI is composed by Rishi Kankayan and is dedicated to goddess *Arbudi*[152] (Destroyer of the Foes).

Ye baahavo yaa ishvo dhanvanaam veeryaani cha.
Aseen parshoonayudham chittakootam cha yaddhidi;
*Sarva tadArbude tvammitrebhyo drishe kurudaaraanshcha pra darshay.*1.

[O Arbude of powerful arms! The arrows and bows, swords, axes and other weapons that you possess, the ideas and strategy you have in your mind, let our enemies see

[152]Following Sayana, Griffith had observed that Arbudi and Nyarbudi were serpent-like demons of the air, sons of Kadru, a female serpent-demon.

them; also let them see the spectres you have under your control.]

Uttishthat sam nahyadhvam mitraa devaajanaa yooyam;
*Sandrishta guptaa vah santu yaa no mitraanyArbude.*2.

[Stand up and equip yourself, O friendly deity, and afford protection to those who are our friends and supporters.]

Arbudirnaama yo deva eeṣhanashcha nyarbudih:
yaabhyaamantAntarikshamaavritamiyam cha Prithivi mahee;
*taabhyaamIndramedibhyaamaham jitamnvemi senayaa.*4.

[O god-like Arbudi and Nyarbudi, you traverse the atmosphere as well as the Earth and are friends of Indra; with your strategy, we vanquish our enemies!]

Sapta jaataan Nyarbuda udaaraannam saṃeekshyan;
*Tebhishtavamaaje hute survairuttishtha senayaa.*6.

[O Nyarbude, we are offering ghrita ahuti to you; get ready with your army of spectres when you have received our offering.]

Aliklvaa jaashkamadaa gridrahaah shenaah patatrinaah;
Dhvaankhaa shamunayastripyantvamitreshu sameekshayan
*radite Arbude tava.*9.

[O foe-destroyer Arbudi, let the buzzards, vultures, hawks, falcons, eagles, ravens and every carrion-eater, feast on the foes slain by you.]

Pratighnaanaah sam dhaavantoorah patooraavaaghnaanaah;
Aghaarinirvikesho rudyastyah purushe hate radite Arbude
*tava.*14.

[O Arbudi! Smiting themselves on their breasts and thighs, their hair dishevelled, the wives of our foes slain by you, are wailing for their men.]

TayaArbude pranuttaanaamIndro hantu varmvaram;
Amitraanaam Shacheepatirmaameeshaam mochi
*kashchan.*20.

[O Arbudi, let the armies of our foes, terrified by your spectres, be slain by Mighty *Shachi-pati* Indra, let no one escape.]

~

Hymn XII, authored by Rishi Bhrigu Angira, is also designed for 'Conquering the Enemies'. It sings the glory of the three-jointed thunderbolt of Indra, called Trishandhi.

Uttishthat sam nahyadhvamudaaraah ketubhi saha;
*Sarpaa itarajanaa rakshaansyamitraananu dhavat.*1.

[Stand up and equip yourself with armour, O spectres, serpents, demons, holding aloft your banners, and charge against our enemies.]

Eeshaam vo veda rajyam trishandhe arunaih ketubhih saha;
Ye Antarikshe ye divi Prithivyaam ye cha maanavaah;
*Trishsndheste chetasi durnaamaana upaasataam.*2.

[Come flying your ruddy flags, armed with Trishandhi, I acknowledge your power. May the denizens of air, Heaven and Earth and all those evil-minded ones remain under your control!]

Anterdhehi Jataveda Aditya kunapam bahu;
*Trishandheriyam senaa suhistaastu me vashe.*4.

[O Jataveda Agni, O Adityas, burn the enemy corpses; let thunderbolt Trishandhi and the forces remain under my control.]

Uttishtha tvam DevajanaArbude senaya saha;
*Ayam balirva aahutastrishashandheraahutih priyaa.*5.

[Arise, O god-like Arbude, with your army; this oblation which is dear to the Lord of Trishandhi, is being offered to you!]

BrihaspatiraAngirarasa rishayo Brahmasanshitaah;
*Asurakshayanam vadham Trishandhim divyaashrayan.*10.

[Brihaspati of the Angiras clan and other seers blessed by Brahma, have set up the Asura destroying weapon—thunderbolt Trishandhi—in the sky.]

God Brihaspati has been included in the Angiras clan of sages in this and **Verses 12 and 13!**

Sarvaanllokaantsamajayan Devaa aahutyaasayaa;
*BrihaspatiraAngiraso vajram yamasinchataasurakshayanam vadham.*12.

[All worlds did the Gods conquer by means of that weapon—the *Asura*-destroying thunderbolt—which Brihaspati of Angiras clan has procured.]

VaayurMitraanaamishvagraanyaanchatu;
Indra aishaam bahoon prati bhanaktu ma shakan pratidhaamishum;
*Aditya aishaamastram vi naashayatu Chandramaa yutaamagat panthaam.*16.

[Let Vayu bend up the arrow-points of the enemies; let Indra break their arms, making them unable to shoot their arrows; let Aditya make their missiles disappear; let Moon make them lose their way.]

Trishandhe tamasaa tvamitraan pari vaaraya;
*Prishdaajyapranuttaanaam maameeshaa mochi kashchan.*19.

[O thunderbolt Trishandhi, create darkness by your magical powers and envelop all our enemies; destroy them then by your blast, let none escape.]

Ye rathino ye arathaa asaadaa ye cha saadinnah;
*Sarvaanandatu taan hataan gridhaah shenaah patatrinah.*24.

[Those riding chariots or without them, those on horse-back or on foot—let all be slain, let vultures and falcons eat them.]

Yaam Devaa anushthanti yashyaa naasti viraadhanam;
*TayIndro hantu Vritrahaa vajrena Tishandhanaa.*27.

[The endeavour that the Gods intend to perform never remains unfulfilled; let Indra, the Vritra-slayer, destroy our enemies with his three-jointed thunderbolt, Trishandhi!]

SELECTED HYMNS FROM ATHARVA VEDA CHAPTER 12

Hymn I is the celebrated *'Prithvi Sookta'*, composed by Rishi Atharva, dedicated to *Bhoomi*—the motherland.

Satyam brihadRitamugram deeksha tapo Brahma yagyah Prithivim dhaaryanti;
*Sa no bhootashya bhavyashya patnyurum lokam Prithivi nah krinotu.*1.

[Truth Supreme, formidable Rta (Order), Consecration, Penance, Brahma and yagya-sacrifice sustain the Earth; let the Earth, mistress of what is and what is to be, make available to us extensive regions to live.]

A sambaadham madhyato manvaanaam yashaa udvataah pravatah samam bahu;
*Naanaaveeryaa aushadheeryaa bibharti Prithivi nah krinotu.*2.

[There exists cordiality among the people here, though there are high and low; let the Earth that bears herbs and plants of many qualities, spread out for us and make us prosperous.]

(This assertion is not quite true. The Hindu society was deeply divided in castes, which was sanctioned by a Rigvedic sookta, as pointed out earlier.)

Yashyam Samudra uta Sindhuraapo yashyaamannam krishatayah sambabhoovuh;
*Yashaamidam jinvati praanadejat saa no bhoomih poorvapeye dadhaatu.*3.

[Where the oceans, rivers, canals, many other sources of water and the crops provide ample food and nourishment; let this land (*bhoomi*) sustain all that breathes and moves here.]

Yat te madhyam Prithivi yachcha nabhyam yaasta oorjastanvah sambabhoovuh.
Taasu no dhehyabhi nah pavasva maataa bhoomim putro aham Prithivyaah;
*Parjanyah pitaa sa oo nah pipartu.*12.

[O Earth, the great variety of refreshing fruits and food stuff that arise from your middle parts, your navel, in them let us lodge; let them be enervating for us. The Earth is my mother, I am her son; Parjanya is our father, let him fill us, fulfill us.]

*Taa nah prajaah sam durhitaam samagraa vaacho madhu Prithivi dhehi mahyam.*16.

[In concert may these people of our country advance; O motherland, afford us nourishment and the gift of sweet speech.]

Yaste gandhah pushkarmaavivesha yam sanjabhruh Suryaaya vivaahe;
*Amartyaah Prithivi gandhamagre ten maa surabhim krinu maa no dvikshata kashchan.*24.

[O Earth, the fragrance of yours that entered the blue lotus, the fragrance that wafted at Surya's wedding; make me fragrant with your fragrance at the beginning of creation; let none hate us!]

Yaste gandhah purusheshu streeshu punsu Bhago ruchih;
Yo ashveshu veereshu yo mrigeshoota hastishu;
*Kanyaamyaam varcho yad tenaasmaan api sam srija maa no dvikshat kashchan.*25.

[O Motherland, your scent is suffused in men and women, your power permeates in wild horses and elephants; the maidens exude your spendour and fragrance.]

Yatate bhoome vikhanaami kshipram tadapi rohatu;
*Maa te marma vimrigvari maa te hridayamarpipam.*35.

[Whatever herbs I dig out of you, O Earth, let those quickly grow up; let me not injure your vitals, nor your heart.]

Yasyaam gaayanti nrityanti bhoomyaa mrtyaa vyaimabaa;
Yudhyante yashyaamaakrando yashyaam vadati dunduhih;
Saa no bhoomih pra nudataam sapatnaansapatnam maa
*Prithivi krinotu.*41.

[Men sing and dance with loud music here and warriors battle with spirited shouts and war-cries as the drums resound. May the motherland drive off our enemies and rid us of our foes!]

Janam bibhratee bahudhaa guhaa vasu manim hiranyam
Prithivi yathokasam;
Sahastram dhaaraa dravinashya me duhaam dhruveva
*dhenuranapasfurantee.*45.

[May our Earth, bearing peoples of various speeches and varying customs according to the places they reside in, grant us wealth in a thousand streams, like a steadfast and unresisting cow.]

Yaam dvipaadaah pakshinamh sampatanti hansaah
suparnaah shakunaavayaansh;
Maatarishveyate rajaansi krinavamshchyaavayanshcha
vikshaan;
*Vatashya pravaamupavaamanu vaatyarchih.*51.

[Where the winged bipeds, swans, eagles, hawks fly in the winds of Heaven, where *Matarishvan* comes rushing, raising dust, uprooting trees and Vayu makes the fire kindle brighter and go hither and thither!]

Dhaushcha ma idam Prithivi chantarikshaam cha me
vyachah;
Agnih Surya aapo medhaam vishve Devaashcha sam
*daduh.*53.

[Heaven, Earth and the Firmament have given me this wide expanse; May Agni, Sun and the Waters, grant me wisdom to live!]

Upasthaate anameevaa ayakshmaa asmabhyam santu Prithivi prasootaah;
Deergham na aayuh pratibuddhyamaanaa vayam tubhyam balihritah shyaam.62.

[O Mother Earth, let the children reared in your lap be free from sickness and consumption. May we live long and pay our homage in yajna-sacrifice!]

Bhoome maatarni dhehi maa bhadrayaa supritishthatam;
*Sanvidaana Divaa Kave shriyaam maa dhehi bhootyaam.*63.

[O Mother Earth set me down in a position of honour; O Poet of the Universe, O Goddess, bestow prosperity upon me, make me fortunate!]

∽

Hymn II has been authored by Sage Bhrigu; it calls upon the *Kravyaad* (flesh-eating) Agni to devour Yakshma and give relief to the people from this dreadful disease. We have seen several such hymns earlier, attempting to cure all kinds of diseases, just by reciting these Sanskrit chants before the illiterate masses. There were no hospitals in those days and these chants probably afforded some psychological relief. People suffered fatalities stoically, taking them as the wrath of God.

1. O *Kravyaada* Agni, go and ascend the pile of reeds; there is no place for you here in this house. This piece of lead is your portion. Take away dreadful yakshma from our cattle and men; go out through the doors taking the disease along.

3. O Kravyaada Agni, we drive out from here both Death and Nir-riti (Eternal Damnation); you take away from here those who are inimical to us and devour them. We turn you towards those that are inimical to us.

8. I send the flesh-eating Agni far away; let him go, carrying evil people to Yama's subjects. Here let this Jatavedas carry the oblation to the Gods.

12. The devouring Agni has ascended high in the Sky; He has released us from sin, from all imprecation.

14. The crushing, bursting and destroying chants have made your yakshama disappear and go away.

15. The flesh-eating yakshama that is in our horses, in our kine, goats and sheep, do we thrust out.

21. Go away, O Death, along a distant road, other than the Gods go upon.

22. These living ones have turned away from the dead; our invocation of the Gods has been auspicious today. We now laugh and dance together.

29. By upward ways, full of wind, stepping over those that are lower, thrice seven times did the departed seers escape Death.

31. Let these women, not widows, well-spoused, touch themselves with ointment, with butter; Joyously, wearing jewels, without disease, let them ascend the bed to unite with their husbands.

39. When a man falls prey to yakshsma and dies, his house becomes a place of torture for his widow; a knowledgeable Brahmin should be invited then, who would pacify and remove the flesh-eating Kravyaad Agni.

45. O Agni, lengthen out the life-span of the living; let them who are dead go unto the world of the Fathers. Do assign to this good house-holder an ever-better dawn.

53. O Flesh-eating Agni, this black-colour ewe is your portion along with this piece of lead, which people call your gold; the ground black beans are your portion of oblation. Now go and seek Aranyaani, the spirit of the woods, for lodgement.

∽

Hymn III, titled 'Cremation as a Sacrifice', is ascribed to Yama, the Lord of Death. The hymn extends to 60 verses; I quote a few to convey its essence. The hymn appears to relate to a couple who lived a happy wedded life, produced sons and then travelled towards the ultimate destiny, Death.

2. Agni fastens the man's body after his death when it becomes fuel. O man and wife, when living, let your sight be clear, your powers (*veerya*) immense, your brilliancy (*teja*) great, and your energies manifold.

3. O husband and wife, enter into the world, unite as a couple and by the vigour of your procreative energies *(retas)* extend the thread of life and produce sons.

4. O Sons, praiseworthy among the mortals, enter into the waters of life and attain the purpose of life by savouring the dish which mother nature is preparing for you.

6. O husband and wife, on the Earth or in the firmament, whichever place is secured by offering this sacrifice, which is full of light, of honey, live together there with your sons till old age.

In the next four verses the couple is guided towards eastern, southern, western and northern directions.

11. This fixed quarter belongs to Viraj; we extend our salutations to the goddesss of fertility! O goddess Aditi, accept our cooked offering!

14. Let this broad, powerful pressing stone remove impurities; let this cooked rice-dish be placed on the Earth. Let not this couple suffer from sins committed by their sons.

17. O rice-dish, you are taking us to the heavenly world, let me and my wife go together. I grasp her hand, let her come with me; let not Nir-riti (Destruction) torment either of us, nor miserly people.

24. Let Agni, while cooking, prepare you on the east; let Indra with the Maruts prepare from the south, may Varuna assist on the western quarter and Soma on the north!

The hymn trails on endlessly, invoking the gods Brihaspati, Parjanya, and the instruments used in preparing the rice-dish like the pestle, the kettle, the stirring stick, spoon, etc., till the rice-dish reaches Heaven.

37. Spread the rice-dish in the bowl smeared with ghrita and pour ghrita over it to present it to the Gods in Heaven. O Gods, welcome this rice-dish as a lowing cow welcomes her calf, who is desirous of sucking her teats. (Devi Chand has translated this verse as: 'O learned preceptor, advance this deserving pupil, lead him forward to fame, let him shine with knowledge! O learned persons, elevate the soul as a lowing cow welcomes the tender calf desirous to suck milk!)

43. Let Agni burn the godless demons; let the flesh-eating pishacha not have a draught here; we thrust them out, we bar them away from us. Let the Adityas and the Angirasas fasten them.

45. This rice-dish has been received for the most exalted Gods. Anoint it with ghrita; this is the portion of Angirasas here. (This hymn has obviously been composed by a rishi of the Angirasa clan who presumes that his ancestors have not only reached Heaven, they have indeed become gods like the Adityas!)

Again, the hymn drags on, asking the various gods to accomplish the task.

55. To the eastern quarter, to Agni as overlord, the rice-dish is presented; thence to the Adityas it is commited. Let them guard it till the appointed life-time, thereafter be united with the cooked rice-dish.

56. To the southern quarter, to Indra as overlord the rice-dish is presented, etc.

57. To the western quarter, to Varuna as overlord the rice-dish is presented, etc.

58. To the northern quarter, to Soma as overlord the rice-dish is presented, etc.

59. To the fixed quarter, to Vishnu as overlord the rice-dish is presented, etc.

60. To the upward quarter, to Brihaspati as overlord the rice-dish is presented, etc.

~

Hymn IV has been composed by Rishi Kashyapa and is dedicated to the Vasha Cow—a barren cow. In this hymn, Rishi Kashyapa denounces those who fail to give their barren cow in donation to a Brahmin and applauds those who do it. It should be borne in mind that in the Vedic times beef was commonly eaten by all communities; there was no stigma attached to it. Indeed, beef was prized and considered high-quality food.

Dadaameetyeva bruyaadanu chainaamabhutsata;
Vashaam Brahmabhyo yaachadbhyastat
*prajaavadapatyavata.*1.

['I give her,' thus should everyone say—'I give the cow to the Brahmin who asks for her.' By such an act the giver is blessed by progeny and so are his descendants.]

Prajayaa sa vi kreeneete pashubhishchopa dashyati;
Ya aarsheyebhyo yaachadabhyo Devaanaam gaan
*na ditsati.*2.

[He bargains away his progeny and loses all his cattle, who is not willing to give the cow of the Gods to the sons of seers who ask for her.]

Kootayaashya sam sheeryante shlonayaa kaatamardati;
*Bandayaa dahyante grihaah kaanayaa deeyate svam.*3.

[If the cow's horn is broken its owner gets crushed; if she becomes lame the owner falls in a pit; if she is crippled the owner's houses burn down; if she loses an eye, the owner loses all his possessions.]

8. If while in the man's keep, a crow pecks at the vasha cow's hair, then the man's sons would die and he will be down with yakshama (Tuberculosis).

10. When the barren cow is born, she is born for the Gods and the Brahmins; therefore, she should be given to the Brahmins—in that way the man will protect his possessions.

12. Whoever is not willing to give such cow of the Gods, to the sons of the seers who ask for her, falls under the wrath of Gods and the fury of the Brahmins!

14. As a deposited treasure of the Brahmins is the barren cow; accordingly, the Brahmins come to ask for her in whosoever's house she is born.

17. Whosoever declares the cow not to be the deposited treasure of the Gods for the Brahmins, Gods Bhava and Sharva would both go striding down to him and attack him with their arrows.

24. The Gods asked the man for the cow when she was first born; Rishi Narada was there together with the Gods, he drove her away.

26. For Agni and Soma, for Kama, for Mitra and Varuna—for

these the Brahmins ask her; he incurs their wrath who gives her not.

28. If anyone, having overheard these verses, still keeps her in his herd, the wrathful gods would cut down his life-span.

33. The cow is the mother of the Rajanya (the ruling class) as it came about in the beginning; by giving her to a Brahmin they don't lose anything as the cow is indeed the Brahmin's safe deposit.

34. As stealing from the spoon, when the sacrificial ghrita is being offered to Agni; he who gives not the barren cow to Brahmins, incurs the wrath of Agni.

40. The cow when gifted to the Brahmins proves beneficial to other cattle. Moreover, it is a thing dear to the cow that she would be an oblation to the Gods.

The hymn goes on like this, giving all kinds of plausible, implausible, imaginary and outlandish justifications for donating barren cows to the Brahmins, fiercely denouncing those who fail to do so, threatening them with baleful and ominous consequences. The hymn reveals the shameless greed of the Brahmins!

Devi Chand simplifies the sensitive matter by translating 'Vasha cow' as 'Vedic Knowledge', and confidently asserts that it should be given to the Brahmins. He is a Sanskrit scholar and knows what a 'Vasha cow' means!

Hymn V has been divided into seven Paryayas or parts; it has been ascribed to Atharavacharya and dedicated to '*Brahmagavi*', the Brahmin's cow. The hymn asserts that not only the Vasha cow, but cows in general should be donated to the Brahmins to gain religious merit. According to Bhagawati Devi Sharma, Brahmagavi should be taken to mean the Brahmin's erudition, his speaking power or his yogic power.

Paryaya 1

*Shramenaan tapasa srishtaa Brahmana vittarteshritaa.*1.

[By toil, by penance, founded on righteousness, is the cow created, and is recognized as holy by the Brahmins.]

*Satyenaavritaa shriyaa praavrittaa yashasaa pareevritaa.*2.

[Sanctified by Truth, full of fortune, the cow is enveloped in glory.]

*Brahma padavaayam Brahmanoadhipatih.*4.

[One achieves salvation through her; the Brahmin is her overlord.]

*Taamaadadaanashya Brahmagaveem jinato Brahmanam Kshtriyashya.*5.
*Apa kraamati soonritaa veeryam punya Lakshmih.*6.

[The Kshatriya who usurps *Brahmagavi* and scathes the Brahmin, loses his happiness, heroism, good fortune and wealth.]

Paryaya 2

*Ojashcha tejashcha sahashycha balam cha Vaak chendriyam cha Shrishcha Dharmashcha.*1.
*Brahma cha kshatram cha Rashtram cha vishashcha tvishishcha yashashcha varchashcha dravinam cha.*2.
*Aayushcha roopam cha naama cha keerteeshcha praashchapanashcha chakshushcha shrotram cha.*3.
*Payashcha rasashachannadhyam chartam cha satyam cheshtam cha poortam cha prajaa cha pashavashcha.*4.
*Taani sarvaanyapa kraamanti Bramhagavimaadadaanashya jinato Brahmanam khstriyashya.*5.

[Brahmagavi embodies energy and vigour, speech and mental strength, glory and virtue, devotion and dominion, kingdom and the people, honour and property, life-span and physical charm, name, fame, breath and expiration, sight and hearing, milk and drinks, food and edibles, progeny and cattle, truth, sacrifice and righteousness. All these depart from the Kshatriya who takes *Brahmagavi* to himself and harms and injures the Brahmin.']

Paryaya 3

*Saishaa bheemaa Brahmagavya dhavishaa saakshaat Krityaa koolbajamaavritaa.*1.

[Brahmagavi is terrible, possessing deadly poison; she destroys men taking the shape of Kritya.]

*Sarvaanyashyaam ghoraani sarve cha mritavah.*2.

[She can cause horror and bring about death of the offenders.]

*Saa brahmajyam Devapeeyum brahmagavvyaa deeyamaanaa mrityoh padveesh aa dhyati.*4.

[Taken away from a Brahmin, she binds the enemies of the gods and Brahmin-killers into fetters of death.]

*Vajro dhaavantee Vaishvaanara udveetaa.*7.

[When she runs, she goes like thunderbolt; when she goes up, she goes like fire.]

*Sediroopatishthantee mithoyodhah paraamrishtaa.*13.

[She becomes a killer when someone approaches her and touches her.]

*Sharavyaa mukheapinahyaamaana ritirhanyamaanaa.*14.

[She sends a volley of arrows when her mouth is fastened and brings calamity on him who troubles her.]

*Anugachchhantee praanaaanupa daasayati Brahmagavee Brahmajyasya.*16.

[Brahmagavi goes after him who harms a Brahmin and extinguishes his vital breath.]

Paryaya 4

*Vairam vikrityamaanaa pautraadhyam vibhaajyamaanaa.*1.

[Brahmagavi is hostility incarnate when being slaughtered;

she creates discord and disaffection among sons and grandsons.]

*Visham prayasyanti takmaa prayastaa.*4.

[When assaulted, she is deadly like poison to her foe; when tormented she is like Takman (fever).]

*Aghama panchyamaanaa dushvapnyam pakvaa.*5.

[It is sinful to cook her; when cooked she becomes a tormenter like bad dreams.]

*Sharvah kruddhah pishyamaanaa Shimidaa pishitaa.*9.

[She is terrible like God Sharva when she is cooked in the cauldron; she is like demoness *Shimida* when being dissected.]

*Avartirashyamaanaa Nir-Ritirashitaa.*10.

[She is ruination when being eaten and perdition when partaken of.]

Ashitaa lokaachchhinatti Brahmagavi
*Brahmajyamasmaachchaamushmaashcha.*11.

[Brahmagavi when desecrated removes the offender from this world and the one yonder.]

Paryaya 5

Agnih kravyaad bhootvaa Brahmagavi Brahmajyam
*pravishyaatti.*3.

[Brahmagavi, having become the flesh-eating Agni, enters into the *Brahmin*-killer and devours him.]

Vivaahaam gyaateentsarvaanapi kshaapayati Brahmagavi
*Brahmajyashya kshatriyenaapunardeeyamaanaa.*6.

[Brahmagavi, when not returned by the kshatriya, scorches all his near relations and acquaintances.]

Avastumenamasvagamaprajasam karotyaparaaparano bhavati ksheeyate.7.

[Brahmagavi makes him without abode, without progeny, and his line comes to an end; he is utterly destroyed.]

Paryaya 6

Kshipram vai tashyaahanane griddhaah kurvata ailabam.1.

[Quickly after the demise of the *Brahmaghaatee,* the killer of Brahmins, the rogue vultures begin to make a din.]

Kshipram vai tashyaadahanam pari nrityanti keshineeraghnaanaah;
Paaninorasi kurvaanaah paapamailabam.2.

[Quickly at his cremation near the pyre, the wailing women gather and dance, their hair wildly strewn, beating their breasts with hands, making an indecorous din.]

Chhindhyaa chhindhi pra chhindhyhapi kshaapaya kshaapaya.5.

[O Brahmagavi, cut up and rend to pieces this Brahmin-scather, destroy him utterly.]

Vishvadevee hyuchyase Krityaa koolbajamaavrittaa.7.

[O Brahmagavi, you are Kritya and *Kulbaj*, the divine powers of destruction, who cause havoc on the earth.]

Oshantee samoshantee Brahmano vajrah.8.

[O Brahmagavi, you are the thunderbolt of God; cut off this Brahmin-scather's head!]

Aghnye padaveerbhava Brahmanashyaabhishastyaa.12.

[O inviolable Brahmagavi, you act like iron-shackles and tighten the feet and limbs of this reviler of the Brahmins.]

Tvyaa pramoorna mriditamAgnirdahatu dushchitam.15.

[O Brahmagavi, slaughtered and crushed by you, let Agni burn this malevolent character.]

Paryaya 7

Vrishcha pra vrishcha san vrishcha dah pra dah san dah.1.

[O *Brahmagavi*, rend him, cut him to bits, scorch and consume and burn him to dust.]

Brahmajyam Devyaghnya aa moolanusandaha.2.

[O inviolable *Brahmagavi*, burn this Brahmin-hater down to his roots.]

Yathaayaad Yamasaadnaat paapalokan paraavatah.3.

[O *Brahmagavi*, cut up his limbs and throw them off to far distances in evil worlds, beyond the Yama's abode.]

Agnirenam Krivyaat Prithivyaa nudataamudoshatu
Vayurantarikshaanmahato varimnah.11.

[Let *Kravyad* (flesh-eating fire) burn him up and thrust him down from the earth; let Vayu send him beyond the atmosphere!]

Surya ainam divah pra nudatam nyoshatu.12.

[Let the Sun thrust him down from the sky after burning him to ashes!]

SELECTED HYMNS FROM ATHARVA VEDA CHAPTER 13

This chapter contains three long hymns followed by six small hymns. They were composed by anonymous poets and ascribed to God Brahma. They are dedicated to the Sun, called *Rohit* (ruddy) here. These hymns were mainly used during the solar eclipse, when the sudden disappearace of the sun caused terror among the people. Indeed, they proved quite effective, as the Sun invariably came out of the grip of the demons, Rahu and Ketu, by the time the chanting of the hymns was arranged and performed.

Hymn I

Udehi vaajinn yo apsvantaridam raashtram pra vish soonritaavat;
*Yo Rohito vishwamidam jajaan sa tva rashtraaya subhritam bibhartu.*1.

[O mighty Sun, forever moving, rise up from the waters, enter into your kingdom that is full of pleasantness. O Ruddy One, may the God who has created this world enable you to serve and nourish your kingdom!]

Devi Chand ignores that the hymn is addressed to the Sun; he calls him 'Mighty King' who 'livest amongst his subjects' and addresses him to 'enter this thy kingdom equipped with fine statesmanship'!

Udvaaja aa gan yo apsvaantervish aa roha tvadhyonayo yah;
*Somam dadhanoapa aushadheergaashchatushpado dvipada aa veshyeha.*2.

[O Ruddy One, come up from the waters; may Soma help you nurture the herbs and the two-footed and four-footed beings.]

Yooyamugraa Marutah prashnimaater Indren yujaa pra mrineeta shatrun;
*Aa vo Rohitah shranavat sudaanavastrishaptaaso Marutah svaadusammudah.*3.

[O formidable Maruts, with Indra as an ally, slaughter our foes; the Ruddy One shall heed you, make him come out of the waters.]

Rooho rooroha Rohita aa roorohgarbho janeenaam janushaamupastham;
*Taabhih sanrabdhamanvavindan shadurveergaatum prapashyanniha rashtramaahaa.*4.

[The Ruddy One has ascended and has come up; he is the embryo in the women's womb and had lodged in the six wide spaces; knowing the way out, sheding lustre, he has come back to his kingdom.]

Rohito dhyaavaaprithivi adrinhat en sva stabhitam ten naakah;
*Tenontariksham vimitaa rajaansi ten Devaa amritamanvamindan.*7.

[The Ruddy One made firm the Heaven and Earth; by him was established the Sky, by him the Firmament, the spaces, were measured out; by him the Gods discovered immortality.]

Rohito yagyashya janitaa mukham cha Rohitaaya vaachaa shrotrena manasaa juhimi;
*Rohitam Devaa yanti sumanshyamaanaah sa maa rohaih saamitai rohayatu.*13.

[The Ruddy One is the generator and the mouth of yagya-sacrifice; to the Ruddy One I make oblation with my speech, my hearing, my mind.]

The long hymn goes on like this into 60 verses. I quote the last two verses.

Maa pra gaama patho vayam maa yagyaadIndra Sominah;
*Manta sthurno araatayah.*59.

[O Sun, let me never forsake the path of righteousness. I pay homage to Indra and Soma; may our foes never have a sway over us.]

Yo yagyashya prasaadhanastanturdeveshvaatatah;
*Tamaahutamasheemahi.*60.

[The adorable God, who pervades the three worlds through His subtlety; may He lead us on path of sacrifice that leads straight to Him!]

Hymn II, in similar fashion, is ascribed to Brahma and dedicated to the Sun.

Udashya ketavo divi shukraa bhraajanta eerate;
*Adityashya nrichakshso mahitavratashya meedhushah.*1.

[The shining rays of the Radiant God go across the Sky; of the *Aditya* who keeps an eye on all men.]

Dishaam pragyaanam svarayantamarchishasupkshamaashum patayantamarnave;
*Stavaama Sooryam bhuvanashya gopaam yo rashibhirdisha aabhaati sarvah.*2.

[He shines in the fore-known four quarters with his bright wings, flying swiftly across the ocean; we pay homage to the Sun, the Shepherd of Existence, whose rays traverse in all directions.]

Yat praad pratyad svadhayaa yaasi sheebham naanaaroope ahanee karshi maayayaa;
*tadaAditya mahi tat te mahi shravo yadeko vishwam pari bhooma jaayase.*3.

[O Aditya, through your Self-force you go swiftly eastward and westward and with your *maya* create night and day in different shapes; you alone possess such tremendous power in the universe!]

Vipashchitam taranim bhaajramanm vahanti yam haritam sapta bavhee;
*Srutaad YamAttridivamunninaya tam tvaa pashyanti pariyaantamaajim.*4.

[Seven luminous golden rays conduct the effulgent Sun, whom we see going around; Rishi Atri had established the Sun in the Sky from the waters.]

The composer of the hymn obviously belonging to the Atri clan, makes the preposterous claim that Rishi Atri had established the Sun in the Sky from the waters. Sage Atri was undoubtedly a celebrated Vedic sage, but the claim of fixing the Sun in the firmament, made by his descendant is atrocious.

> *Svasti te Soorya charase rathaya yenobhavantau pariyaasi sadhyah;*
> *Yam te vahanti harito vahishthaah shatamshvaa yadi vaa sapta bavhee.*7.
>
> [Mount, O Sun, your chariot, running to the two ends of the world, drawn by seven, nay, a hundred golden steeds!]
>
> *Poorvaaparam charato maayayaitau shishoo kreedantau pari yaatoarnavama;*
> *Vishwaanyo bhuvanaa vichashte Hairanyairanyam harito vahanti.*11.
>
> [The two playful kids (Sun and Moon) with their maya, go after one another; one lights the whole universe, the other rides golden steeds.]
>
> *Divi tvaAtridhaarayat Soorya maasaaya kartave;*
> *Sa aishi sudhritastapan vishwaa bhootaavachaakashat.'*12.
>
> [Flying high in the firmament we see the golden bird, whom people call Savita, the inspirer and impeller; the unfailing light of the world which Atri found.]

The nameless author of the hymn has repeated the extravagant claim of Rishi Atri 'finding' the Sun in the firmament!

Finally, the last verse:

> *AbodhyAgnih samidhaa janaanaam prati dhenumivaayateemushaasam;*
> *Yahvaa iva pra vayaamujjihaanaah pra Bhaavah sisrate naakamachchha.*46.
>
> [As the milch-cows are awakened at dawn for milking, Agni has been awakened by the kindling of sacrificial fire. The flames of sacrifice rise to the Sky like young shoots of trees going Heaven-ward.]

Hymn III is also ascribed to Brahma and dedicated to the Sun. It imprecates persons who are disrespectful towards the Brahmins, the knowers of Vedic knowledge. The verses, extending to three or four lines, are mostly of a sing-song, repetitive nature. All the following verses repeat the same refrain cursing the Brahmin-scather: 'O Ruddy One, make him quake, destroy him; fasten the Brahmin-scather by fetters!'

Ya ime DhyaavaaPithivi jajaamn yo draapim kritvaa bhuvanaani vaste;
Yasmin kshiyanti pradishah shadurveeryaah patango anu vichaakasheeti;
Tashya Devashyakruddhastaitadaago ya aivam vidvaansam Brahmanam jinaati;
*Ood vepaya Rohita pra kshneehi brahmajyashya prati munch paashaan.*1.

[He who engendered these, the Heaven and Earth, who made the worlds the mantle which He wears; in whom abide the six wide-ranging directions, which the Flying One (*Patang*—Sun) scans. He who scathes a Brahmin, the knower of Vedic knowledge, offends and makes God angry. O Ruddy One, make him quake, destroy him; fasten the Brahmin-scather by fetters!]

Ayam sa Devo apasvantah sahastramoolah purushaako attrih;
Ya idam vishvaam bhuvanam jajaana;
Tashya Devasya kruddhasyaitadaago ya aivam vidvaansam Brahmanam jinaati;
*Ood vepaya Rohita pra kshneehi brahmajyashya prati munch paashaan.*15.

[He who brought this universe into existence is the god Sun, who has thousands of roots and branches, who is free from sorrows and wants.[153] The Sun God ordains that the one who scathes a Brahmin, the knower of Vedic knowledge, offends and makes Him angry. O Ruddy One, make him quake, destroy him; fasten by fetters the Brahmin-scather!]

Ashtadhaa yukto vahati vanhirugrah pitaa Devaanaam janitaa mateenaam;
Ritashya tantu mansaa mimaanah sarva dishah pavate maatarishvaa;
Tashya Devasya kruddhasyaitadaago ya aivam vidvaansam Brahmanam jinaati;
*Ood vepaya Rohita pra kshneehi brahmajyashya prati munch paashaan.*19.

[*Maatarishvaa* Agni who is upholder of divine force, if enraged acts in eight ways. Vayu purifies the environment through sacrificial rituals. The Sun ordains that the one who scathes a Brahmin, the knower of Vedic knowledge, offends and makes Him angry. O Ruddy One, make him quake, destroy him; fasten by fetters the Brahmin-scather!]

Ya aatmadaa baladaa yashya vishwaa oopaasate prashisham yashya Devah;
Yosyeshe dvipado yashchatushpadah;
Tashya Devasya kruddhasyaitadaago ya aivam vidvaansam Brahmanam jinaati;
*Ooda vepaya Rohita pra kshneehi brahmajyashya prati munch paashaan.*24.

[The Supreme God bestows spiritual power, gives physical strength; even the gods wait upon Him for direction, who is the master of the bipeds and quadrupeds. He ordains that the one who scathes a Brahmin, the knower of Vedic knowledge, offends and makes God angry. O Ruddy One, make him quake, destroy him; fasten by fetters the Brahmin-scather.]

[153]*Dehik, Devika, Bhautika Taapa*—Physical, Spritual and Elemental calamities.

Krishnaayaa puto Arjuno raatryaa vatsoajaayata;
*Sa ha dhyaamasi rohati rooho rooroha Rohitah.*26.

[The ruddy-bright son, child of the dark mother (night) is born; He ascends upon the limitless Sky and traverses the universe!]

∽

Hymn IV is also ascribed to Brahma; it again extolls the Sun.

*Sa aiti Savitaa svardivasprishthe-avachakashat.*1.

[God Savita, the impeller, rises in High Heaven, keeping his back to the firmament.]

Sa Dhaataa sa vidhartaa sa Vayurnabha oochchhritama;
*Rashmibhirnabha aabhritam Mahendran aittyaavaatah.*3.

[He is the Creator and the Disposer, he is Vayu; brightening the worlds with his rays he advances as Indra.]

So Aryaman sa Varunaah sa Rudrah sa Mahaadevah; 4.

[He is Aryaman, Varuna, Rudra and *Mahadeva*; brightening the worlds with his rays he advances as Indra!]

Pashchaat praancha aa tanvanti yadudeti vi bhasati;
*Rashmibhirnabha aabhritam Mahendran aittyaavaatah.*7.

[He shines as he emerges, his rays surround him then; brightening the worlds with his rays he advances as Indra!]

*Tamidam nigatam sahah sa aish aika aikavrideka aiva.*12.

[All power is concentrated into Him; He is the One and One only.]

*Aite asmin Devaa aikavrito bhavanti.*13.

[All the luminous gods merge and mingle in One God!]

∽

Hymn V is ascribed to Param Brahma.

Keertishcha yashshchaambhashcha nabhashcha
Brahmanavarchasvaam chaanna channaadhyam cha.1.

[He who knows this God as the One, obtains renown and glory, water and Sky, *Brahma*-splendour, as well as food and nourishment.]

Ya aitam devamekavritam veda.2.

Na dviteeyo na triteeyashchaturtho naapuchyate;
Ya aitam devamekavritam veda.3.

Na panchamo na shasthah saptmonaapuchyate;
Ya aitam devamekavritam veda.4

Naashtmo na navamo dashmonaapuchyate;
Ya aitam devamekavritam veda.5.

[Those who know this One God, know not second, nor third, nor fourth, fifth, sixth, seventh, eighth, nineth, nor the tenth!.]

Sa sarvasmai vi pashati yachcha praanati yachcha na;
Ya aitam devamekavritam veda.6.

[They know only Him who watches over all who breathe and who breathe not.]

Tamidam nigatam sahah sa aish aika aikavrideka aiva;
Ya aitam devamekavritam veda.7.

[Into Him is concentrated all power; He is the One and Only power!]

Sarve asmin Devaa aikavritau bhavanti;
Ya aitam devamekavritam veda.8.

[All the gods become '*ek-vrat*'(One-form) in him!]

Hymn VI is also ascribed to Param Brahma; the verses are repetitive and mechanical.

*Bhootam cha bhavyam cha shrddha cha ruchishcha swargashcha svadhaa cha.*6.

[He who prays to Him would obtain the past and the future, spiritual power and lustre, self-esteem and Heaven.]

Paapaaya vaa bhadraaya vaa purushasuraaya va;
*Yadvaa krinoshyoshadheetyadvaa varshasi bhadraya yadvaa janyamaveevridhah.*7.

[He creates the sinners as well as noble men—men with godly and ungodly propensities; He sends beneficical rains and produces herbs. He verily is Death and Immortality!]

Ambho arunam rajatam rajah sah iti tvopaasmahe vayam;
Namaste astu pashyata pashya maa pashyat;
*Annaadhena yashasaa tejasaa Brahmanavarchasen.*8.

[We worship you in your various forms, O Sureme Brahma! Let the red vault of morning, the silver, shimmering day, the universal power controlling the planets; shower mercy on us, provide us with food and fame, vigour and zest for life!]

Hymn VII is again ascribed to Brahma. The verses of this hymn are a masterpiece of tautology. I quote a few verses:

18. The Sun is born of the day; the day is born of the Sun.

19. Just as the night is born of the Sun, the Sun is born of night.

(It goes on in this manner—the atmosphere, Vayu, the Sky, the quarters, the Earth, Agni, water, Vedic verses, yajna-sacrifice are born from each other!)

41. He thunders, he sends lightening and a shower of hail-stones!

43. He makes the herbs grow, sends excellent rains and increases the race of man!

44. Such O bountiful one, is your greatness, O Indra (*Maghvan*); hundreds are your forms!

45. All beings are bound by your law; you are all-pervading!

Hymn VIII

46. God Indra is greater than immortality; He transcends the cycle of birth and death!

47. O Indra, consort of Shachi, stronger than the parsimonious; O mighty, all-prevailing God, we worship you!

48. We bow down to you, O valorous God, heed us!

49. Equip us, O God, with food and fame and the brilliance of Param Brahma!

50. We worship you O Omnipotent, for your bravery, power and greatness; equip us with food, fame and the brilliance of Param Brahma!

51. Heed us, O Lord, we worship you for red, silvery and sovereign powers; equip us with food, fame and the brilliance of Param Brahma!

Hymn IX

52. We worship you, O Omnipotent, beneficent, sovereign Lord, heed us; bestow us with food, fame and the brilliance of Param Brahma!

53. O Expansive, wide and broad God, we worship you; heed us; bestow us with food, fame and the brilliance of Param Brahma!

54. We worship you, O opulence provider, benefactor of the virtuous!

55. We worship you, pray heed us, O All-seeing One!

56. O Lord, equip us with food, fame and the brilliance of Param Brahma!

SELECTED HYMNS FROM ATHARVA VEDA CHAPTER 14

Marriage Ceremonies. 1.

This long hymn containing 64 verses begins with repeating the verses from the Rigvedic hymn dedicated to the wedding of Sun's daughter, Surya, (R.V. 85). Towards the end it becomes a crude copy, almost a parody of the original hymn. It is composed by an anonymous poet and ascribed to 'Savitri-Surya'.

1. By Truth the Earth is established; by the Sun is the Sky established; by Rta (Righteousness) the Adityas stand and Soma is set upon the Sky.

3. One thinks himself to have drunk Soma when they drink crushed herbs; what Soma the priests (Brahmins) know, of that no earthly man partakes.

5. Guarded by covering arrangements, defended by watchmen, O Soma, you stand hearing the sound the pressing-stones make; no earthly man partakes of you.

6. Her heart's desire was the pillow, the dreams in her eyes were the collyrium, Heaven and Earth were her treasures, when Surya went to her husband.

20. Let Bhaga lead you hence, grasping your hand; let the Ashvins carry you by a chariot; go to your husband's house, and speak with authority to the members of the household.

(The hymn, 85.26, mentions Pushan instead of Bhaga)

21. Happily may you mingle yourself with your husband and prosper with progeny; rule over the husband's household and in old age, along with your husband, guide them.

25. Give away the *shamulya* (the bridal robes) to the Brahmins, which gets possessed by *Kritya* (evil spirit), when you begin cohabiting with the husband.

26. The bride's garments become blue-red due to Kritya's intermingling, by which the husband is bound in bonds.

27. Unlovely becomes the husband's body, glittering in evil way, when the husband's member is wrapped in bride's garment.

28. Surya's garment has carved in and is torn in places; only the Brahmin can mend it and use it now.

29. The wedding garment has turned evil and poisonous, becomes prickly and barbed like a spear, and needs to be abandoned; the priest who solemnized her marriage deserves to get it.

30. By taking the garment the Brahmin priest has made it free from evil; it becomes pleasant and enjoyable now and brings no harm to the bride.

(In the following verses the hymn goes on rambling about the selection of a bride, till it comes to Surya in Verse 55.)

55. Brihaspati first arranged Surya's hair; with this O Ashvins, we thoroughly adorn her for her husband.

61. O Surya, mount this strong-wheeled, flower-adorned bridal-chariot, glittering like gold; make your husband live a long and happy life.

64. Let Vedic verses be recited before and after, in the middle and at the end, all around the bride's chariot. Reaching the husband's house free from diseases, let her be auspicious, gentle and pleasant, and rule in her husband's house.

Marriage Ceremonies. 2.

This hymn, too, is ascribed to Savitri, Surya, like the preceding hymn. It appears to be a continuation of the preceding hymn and is patterned on Surya's wedding hymn. About a dozen verses from the Surya hymn also occur in it.

1. O Agni, Surya was brought before you as a bride; may you bless the brides to be and their husbands for progeny and prosperity!

3. O Surya, Soma was your first husband, the Gandharvas were the next; Agni was your third husband, the fourth was one of human birth.

6. O Bride, rejoicing with propitious mind, exhibit your wealth to your husband to be extolled; O husband and wife, lords of beauty and health, construct a fair ford to drink in it freely, shedding all restraint and anxiety.

10. The *yakshma* that follows the bridal chariot, let the worshipful gods send it back whence it came.

13. This comely bride has come to her husband's home, appointed by *Vidhata*; let Aryaman, Bhaga, Ashvins and Prajapati bless her with progeny!

14. As a soulful cultivated field, a woman goes to her husband's home; in her, O man, you scatter seed; she shall give birth to progeny for you from her womb, bearing your male sperm.

(W.D. Whitney adds a footnote: 'The likening of the woman to a field is very familiar in later times.' Whitney gives references to Manu, Aeschylus, Sophocles and adds: 'My colleague, Professor George F. Moore, calls my attention to Koran ii. 22, "Your women are your ploughland!"')

15. O newly wedded Bride, be firm and resolute; you are like Viraj! O Lord Vishnu, O Saraswati, O Sinivali, let her have progeny; may she be made fortunate by Bhaga!'

17. May you be pleasure-giving, O bride, loving to your husband, begetting brave sons! Be in easy control of your household, show kindness to your brother-in-law; may you all thrive together!

20. O bride, come to the hearth and pray and offer oblation to the household-fire; pay homage to Saraswati and to the Fathers.

21. Let the husband spread cozy, comfortable cushions for you to lie on; O Sinivali bless her with progeny, O Bhaga, make her fortunate!

22. Spread a soft deer-skin on a bed of grass; let this virgin (*kanya*), who has found a husband, sit on it to pray!

24. Sit on the deer-skin, O bride, to worship the homestead fire, that slays all the demons; here give birth to progeny for this husband; may this son of yours be of good primogeniture!

31. Mount the nuptial bed, O Bride, with joy and give birth to progeny for your husband; awakening to new pleasures all night, like Indrani, seeing the dawns tipped with light!

32. The Gods in the beginning of the world lay with their spouses, embracing bodies with bodies; O youthful, ardent bride, like Surya unite here with your husband!

37. O men and women, you become father and mother, mating after the woman's menstruation; let potent men unite with women to generate progeny and wealth!

38. O Pushan, rouse the woman to be eager to please, the woman in whom men sow their seed; so that she will spread her thighs in her desire, and we, in our desire, will plant our penis in her!

41. This bridal garment and the bride's dress given by the Gods together with Manu, whoso gives to a knowledgeable Brahmin, he verily slays the demons crawling in the nuptial bed.

42. This bridal garment and the bride's dress, provided at Brahma's directions to be the Brahmin's share; O Brihaspati and Indra, let these be given to a knowledgeable Brahmin!

43. Awaking out of a pleasant coupling, mightily enjoying

yourselves in merriment, may you (husband and wife) live long, seeing the outshining dawns, having good sons, kine, good houses.

44. Like a bird coming out of an egg-shell, the bride, wrapped in the fragrance of conjugal night, dresses herself in new clothes in the morning, ridding herself of the demons crawling in the nuptial bed.

45. Beautiful are Heaven and Earth, bound by divine laws, let them shower happiness on us! Let seven divine waters flow through them, let the waters cleanse us of all our sins!

46. Unto Surya and unto the gods Mitra and Varuna, who shower happiness on all beings, have I paid this homage.

48. The darkness that shines in deep blue, brown and red colours, let it go far away; she is a consuming monster, I have spotted her and fastened her on this pillar.

49. Kritya's witchcrafts that entered the bride's garments, the fetters of King Varuna, all problems in consummation, failures of conception—I hang them on this pillar.

50. This my lovely body loses its sheen by wearing the bridal dress and undergarments; O lord of vegetation, let their fiber have a soft touch; let us not suffer torture, wearing them.

52. Eager, filled with longing are these maidens, going to a husband from the father's world; Hail to their vow of wedlock!

53. The vow of wedlock ordained by Brihaspati was maintained by Gods; the splendour that entered into the kine, with that do we unite this woman!

54. The vow of wedlock ordained by Brihaspati was maintained by Gods; the *brilliancy (teja)* that entered into the kine, with that do we unite this woman!

55. The vow of wedlock ordained by Brihaspati was maintained by Gods; the fortune (Bhaga) that entered into the kine, with that do we unite this woman!

Verses 56, 57 and 58 are mechanical repetitions. **Verses 59-63** have no connection with marriage ceremonies; they are, in fact, ill-omened wailings for the dead and have been omitted by me.

64. Here, O Indra, rouse these two spouses together like two Chakravakas (legendary love-birds); let them along with their progeny, live out a full life-time.

65. During marriage, what demonic Kritya effects crept into the wedding gown, the sitting-pedestal, the nuptial bed; let them be removed in the bath.

69. We secure her every limb from yakshma; drive away yakshma from the Earth and the Heaven. Let that defilement not attain the waters, O Agni, let it not attain Yama and the Fathers!

70. O bride, I gird you with the milk of the earth; I gird you with the milk of the herbs; I gird you with progeny, with riches, with strength!

71. I am He, you are She! Chant am I, verse thou! Heaven I, Earth thou! Let two of us unite together; let us generate progeny!

75. Equipped with fine intellect, O Bride, be watchful and be the mistress of your house-hold; let Savita grant you a long life, may you live for hundred autumns!

SELECTED HYMNS FROM ATHARVA VEDA CHAPTER 15

This chapter is divided into 18 Paryayas. Rishi Atharva has authored the entire chapter and has dedicated it to *Vritya*.

The word 'Vritya' is defined as one 'belonging to a roving band of holy men'; it also means one who does not observe '*vrata*' (vows). The praise of the Vratya is an idealization of the pious vagrant or wandering religious mendicant. But a later Upanishad recognizes Vratya as among the many forms in which the Parama Brahma is celebrated in the Atharva Veda. Vratya appears to be an imaginary supernatural being like the Skambha.

Devi Chand says that Pt Jaidev Vidyalankar and Pt Khemkaran Das Trivedi have translated the word Vratya as 'God'.

Paryaya I

Vraatta aaseedeeyamaan aiva sa Prajaapatim samairaryat.1.

[There existed Vratya; He stirred up Prajapati Brahma and guided him.]

*Sa Prajaapatih suvarnamaatmannapashyat tat praajanayat.*2.

[Prajapati Brahma perceived his own form, shining like molten gold, from which He generated it all.]

*Tadekambhavat tallalaamamabhavat tanmahadbhavat tajjeshtham bhavat tad Brahmabhavat tat tapoabhavat tat satyambhavat ten praajaayata.*3.

[Vratya became unique, the sole One, like enormous Golden Star, Supreme *Brahma*, *Tapa* (holy fervor) and Truth, and created the Universe!]

*So avardhat sa mahaanbhavat sa Mahaadevo abhavat.*4.

[He enlarged Himself ever more and became Maha Deva (the Great God)]

*Sa Devaanaameeshaam paryait sa Eeshanoabhavat.*5.

[He encompassed it all and became the great Lord of the Gods, the *Isha.*]

*Sa aikavraatyo abhavat sa dhanuraadatta tadevIndradhanuh.*6.

[He became the sole Vratya; He took to Himself a bow; that was the Indra's bow, called *Indra-Dhanush.*]

*Neelamshodaram lohitam prashtham.*7.

[Blue is His belly; His back is red.]

*Neelenaivaapriyam bhraatrivyam prornoti lohiten dvishantam vidhyateeeti Brahmavaadino vadanti.*8.

[With the blue He overwhelms a hostile cousin, with the red He pierces the one hating him; So, say those who are known as the *Brahmavadin.*]

Paryaya II

*Sa oodatishthat sa pracheen dishamanuvyachalaat.*1.

[He arose; He moved out toward the eastern quarter.]

*Tam brihachcha rathantaram chadiAdityaashcha vishwe cha Devaa anuvya chalan.*2.

[After Him moved out *Brihat* and *Rathantar* and the Adityas, and all the Gods.]

Brihate cha vai sa rathantraaya chaAdityebhyashcha vishwebhyashcha Devebhya
*Aa vrishchate ya aivam vidvaansam Vratyamupavadati.*3.

[He who reviles the all-knowing Vratya, offends against the Firmament and the Earth, the Adityas and all Gods.]

*Brihatashcha vai sa rathantarashya chaAdityaanaam chavishwesham cha Devaanam priyam dhama bhavati tashya prachchyaam dishi.*4.

[Those who revere Vratya, make the eastern quarter their home; thry areloved by the atmosphere, the Earth, the Adityas and all Gods.]

*Shraddhaa punshachali Mitro maagadho vigyaanam vaasoaharushneesham raatri keshaa haritau pravartau kalmalirmanih.*5.

[Faith is His wife, Mitra his panegyrist, discernment his garment, day the turban, night the hair, sunrays are his earings, and the stars his string of jewels!]

*Bhootam cha bhavishyachcha parishkanau mano vipatham.*6.

[The Past and Future are His footmen; the mind is His war-chariot.]

*Maatrisvaa cha pavamaanashcha vipathavaahau Vaatah saarathi tathaa reshmaa pradotah.*7.

[The In-breath and Out-breath are the two horses of His chariot, the wind His charioteer and whirlwind the prodding stick.]

*Keertishcha yashashcha purahsaraavainam keertirgachchhatyaa yahso gachchhati ya aivam veda.*8.

[Fame and glory are His harbingers! Those who know this, attain fame and glory.]

Sa oodatishthat sa Dakshinaam dishmanu vya chalat.

[Vratya arose; He manifested himself in the southern quarter.]

*Tam yagyaayagyiyam cha Vaamadevyam cha yagyashcha yajamaanashcha pashavashchaanuvyachalan.*10.

[After Him followed *Yagya-Yagyiam, Vamdevyaa,* the sacrifice; the sacrificer and the cattle.]

*Yagyayagyiyaaya cha vai sa Vaamdevyaya cha yagyaaya cha yajamaanaaya cha pashubhyashchaa vrishchate ya aivam vidvaansam Vraatyamupavadati.*11.

[He offends *Yagya-Yagyiam, Vamdevya,* the sacrifice, the sacrificer and the cattle, who reviles the All-knowing Vratya.]

*Yagyayagyiyashya cha vai sa Vaamdevyashya cha yagyashcha cha yajamaanashya cha pashoonam cha priyam dhaama bhavati tashya Dakshinaayaam dishi.*12.

[Those that revere Vratya, make the southern quarter their dear abode and come to possess *Yagya-Yagyiam, Vamdevya,* the sacrifice, the sacrificer and the cattle.]

*Usha punshachalee mantro maagadho vigyaanam vaasoaharughneesham ratreem kesha haritau pravartau kalmalirmanih.*13.

[Dawn is his wife, the verses are the panegyrist, discernment the garment, day the turban, night the hair, sunrays are his earings, and the stars a string of jewels!]

Amaavashyaa cha paurnamaasee cha parishkandau mano vipathama;
Maatarishvaa cha pavamaanashcha vipathavaahau Vaatah saarathi reshmaa pratodah;
*Keerteeshcha yashashcha purahsaraavainam keertieetgachhatyaa yasho gachchhati ya aivam veda.*14.

[Amavashya (the dark, moonless night) and Poornima (full-moon night) are His two footmen, the mind is His war-chariot; In-breath and Out-breath are the two horses of His chariot, the wind His charioteer and whirlwind the prodding stick! Fame and glory are His harbingers! Those who knows this, attain fame and glory.]

The remaining half portion of the hymn goes on in similar fashion, repeating or substituting the names of gods like Varuna or Soma.

Paryaya III

Vratya stood erect for a year, practising penance; the gods asked Him why was he standing? 'Get me a settee.' He told them.

3. The gods created a settee for Him.

4. Summer and Spring were the two legs of the settee; Autumn and the Rains were the other two.

5. The Atmosphere and *Rathantar* were its length-wise joints; Yyagya-Yagyiam and *Vaamdevyaa* the cross-wise joints.

6. The verses of the Rig Veda were its warp; the verses of Atharva Veda its weft.

7. The Vedas were His cushion to lie on; the supreme Brahma is his coverlet.

8. The settee rested where Sama-chants were sung.

9. That settee the Vratya ascended.

10. The gods were His attendants, solemn vows his messengers, all living beings his courtiers.

11. Those who know this, they really know!

Paryaya IV

1–2. For Vratya, the gods made two months of Spring his guardians, and atmosphere and Rathantar his attendants.

The following verses of this Paryaya have been mechanically formulated to include the four quarters—East, West, North and South; the seasons—Spring, Summer, Rains and Winter. They became Vratya's attendants like the Earth, Agni, the Adityas, etc.

Paryaya V

1. For protecting Vratya the gods appointed god Bhava to aim arrows from the East.

2–3. Neither Bhava, nor Sharva and Isha, injure Him; they protect the cattle and the people.

4. From the southern quarter, Sharva was appointed the archer by the gods.

The remaining 12 verses have been mechanically constructed in the same fashion. W.D. Whitney calls the structure of these hymns 'very strange and obviously opposed to the sense!'

Paryaya VI

1–3. The Vratya moved out toward the fixed quarter; after Him moved out both Earth and Agni and herbs and forest trees. Verily both of Earth and of Agni and of herbs and forest trees, He becomes the dear abode of those who know this!

4–6. He moved out toward the upward quarter; after him moved out *Rta* (Righteousness) and Truth, Sun and Moon and asterisms. Verily both of Righteousness and Truth, and of Sun and Moon and of asterisms! He became the dear abode of those who knows this!

The hymn goes on like this, bringing in the verses and chants, sacrificial formulae and the Param Brahma; the Itihasa, the Puranas, Gathas and eulogies; the sacrificial fire and householder-fire, Dakshina, the sacrificer and the cattle; the seasons, months and day-and-night; Diti and Aditi, Ida and Indrani, Viraj, and all the Gods and deities; Prajapati Parameshthi and the Great-Grand Father—all following the Vratya—and He became the dear abode of them who know this!

Paryaya VII

1. The majestic Vratya went to the ends of earth; He became the ocean!

2–4. After Him followed Prajapati, Parameshthi and the Great-Grand Father, the waters, Faith (becoming the rains); those who know this, obtain water, faith and rains!

5. He who knows this, receives Faith, sacrifice, food and nourishmen!.

Paryaya VIII

1–3. The Vratya became the ruler of all and became King. He showered His grace on all tribes, kinsmen, on food and nourishment. Those tribes and kinsmen who know this, obtain food and nourishment.

Paryaya IX

1. The Vratya moved out towards the people.
2. After Him followed the Sabha, the Samiti, the Army, and Sura (wine).
3. Those who know this obtain the boons of the Sabha, the Samiti, the Army, and Sura (wine).

Paryaya X

In this hymn, Vratya goes to households for food or lodgement as an uninvited guest. In the old Hindu tradition, giving food to someone who comes to one's door is considered sacred. The Chandogya Upanishad (V. 24.4) states that if the sacrificial remnant is to be offered even to an outcaste, it is as good as if offered to the omnipresent Brahma!

1–2. So then, to the houses of whatever King the all-knowing Vratya comes as a guest, he should esteem him better than himself; the King does not diminish his kingdom, nor the royal glory by doing this!

3. Thence verily arose spiritual knowledge and heroism and valour; they asked Vratya whom shall we enter?

4–5. Let spiritual knowledge enter the gods! Thence spiritual knowledge entered Brihaspati; heroism and valour entered Indra!

6. This Earth verily is Prajapati, the Sky is Indra.

7. Verily, Agni is spiritual knowledge, the Sun is heroism and valour.

8–9. Those who regard the Earth as Brihaspati and Agni as Param Brahma, obtain the splendour of spiritual knowledge.

10–11. He who takes the Sun as embodying valour, and regards the sky as Indra, is endowed with Indra's power and becomes valorous.

Paryaya XI

1–2. In whose house resides such an all-knowing guest, he should come up to Him and say: 'Vratya, where, pray, is your abode? Here is water for you, let my family members gratify you; Vratya, be it so as you like, be it so as is your will; Vratya, be it so as you desire!

3. In that he says to him: 'Vratya, where, pray, is your abode?' he thereby gains possession of the paths that gods travel on.

4. In that he says to him: 'Vratya, here is water for you,' he thereby gains possession of the waters.

5. In that he says to him: 'Vratya, let my family members gratify you,' he thereby enhances his life-span.

6. In that he says to him: 'Vratya, be it so as is dear to you,' he thereby gains possession of what is dear to him.

7. In that he says to him: 'Vratya, may you have whatever you love,' he becomes dear to his dear ones.

8. In that he says to him: 'Vratya, be it so as is your will,' he thereby gets possession of his will.

9. Those who know the authority that Vratya possesses over all, get to possess the authority over others.

10. In that he says to him: 'Vratya, be it so as you desire,' he thereby gets possession of his desires.

11. One who acts in accord with Vratya's desire, comes to be in Desire's desire; those who know, know this!

Paryaya XII

1–2. In whose house the All-knowing Vratya comes as a guest when he is lighting the sacrificial fire, he should offer Him seat and say: O Vratya, give me permission; I am about to offer oblation.

3. If Vratya permits, the householder should offer oblation; if He does not, he should not offer oblation.

4-5. He who, being permitted by All-knowing Vratya, offers oblation, comes to know the path the Fathers go, and the path that the Gods go on.

6. The Gods take no offence against him; his oblation is duly made.

7. Oblation made by such a sacrificer enriches the Gods; his place in the world is made secure in all directions.

8–9. He who not being permitted by All-knowing Vratya offers oblation, knows not the path the Fathers go, and the path that the Gods go on.

10. He offends against the Gods; his oblation is not duly offered.

11. There is no protection or support for him in the world, who not being permitted to offer oblation, offers it.

Paryaya XIII

1–2. In whose house the all-knowing Vratya abides for one night as a guest, he thereby gains possession of the Earth's sacred places.

3–4. In whose house the all-knowing Vratya abides for second night as a guest, he thereby gains possession of the pure worlds in the atmosphere.

5–6. In whose house the all-knowing Vratya abides for a third night as a guest, he thereby gains possession of the pure worlds in the Sky.

7–8. In whose house the all-knowing Vratya abides for a fourth night as a guest, he thereby gains possession of the pure worlds of the pure people.

9–10. In whose house the all-knowing Vratya abides for unlimited nights as a guest, he thereby gains possession of the pure worlds that are unlimited.

11–12. Now into whosoever house a guest comes posing himself as the all-knowing Vratya, in reality only bearing the name, should he invite him or refuse?

13. Giving such a guest the benefit of doubt, he may invite him in taking him to be some deity. He should wait upon him, offer food and lodging.

14. To that deity his hospitality shall be deemed to have been offered.

Paryaya XIV

1–2. As Vratya moved out toward the eastern quarter, He met a troop of the Maruts. He ate food-grains with the mind of a food-grain eater, who knows thus.

3–4. As Vratya moved out toward the southern quarter, He met Indra; He ate food-grains with the mind of a valorous being, who knows thus.

5–6. As Vratya moved out toward the western quarter, He met King Varuna; with the waters as food-eaters he eats food, who knows thus.

7–8. As Vratya moved out toward the northern quarter, He met King Soma and made oblation offered by the Seven Seers as food-eater, with oblation as food-eater, he eats food who knows thus.

9–10. As Vratya moved out toward the fixed quarter, He met Vishnu and following him, made Viraj as food-eater; with Viraj as food-eater he eats food who knows thus.

11–12. As Vratya moved out toward the cattle, He met Rudra, and following him, making the herbs as food-eater, he eats food who knows thus.

13–14. As Vratya moved out toward the Fathers, He met King Yama, and following him, making '*svadha*' as food-eater, he eats food who knows thus.

15–16. As Vratya moved out toward the men, He met Agni, and following him, making '*svaaha*' as food-eater, he eats food who knows thus.

17–18. As Vratya moved out toward the upward quarter, He met Brihaspati and following him; making '*vashat*'[154] as food-eater, he eats food who knows thus.

19–20. As Vratya moved out toward the gods, He met *Isha* (the supreme Lord); following him, making Fury (*manyu*) as food-eater; with Fury as food-eater, he eats food who knows thus.

21–22. As Vratya moved out toward progeny, he met Prajapati (Lord of progeny) and following him; making breath as food-eater,

[154] 'Vashat' is an exclamation uttered by the Hotri priest at the end of the sacrificial verse on hearing which the Adhrvyu priest casts the oblation offered to the deity into the fire.

he eats food who knows thus.

23–24. As Vratya moved out toward all the intermediate directions, he met Parameshthi; following Him, making Param Brahma as food-eater, he eats food who knows thus.

Paryaya XV

1–2. Of that Vratya, there are seven breaths—seven in-breathing and seven out-breathing.

3–9. Vratya's first in-breathing is upward, that is Agni; the second is preferred, that is the Aditya (Sun); the third is inferred, that is the Moon; the fourth is mighty, that is the Pavaman (cleansing air); the fifth breath is yoni (the womb) by name, that are the waters; the sixth breath is 'deer' by name, that are the cattle; his seventh breath is 'unlimited' by name and is called '*prajaa*', that are all creatures.

Paryaya XVI

1–9. The Vratya's first in-breath is called 'Poornamaasi' (Full-Moon Night); second in-breath is called '*Ashtaka*'; the third in-breath is called Amavashya (No-Moon Night); the fourth in-breath is called Shraddha (Faith); His fifth in-breath is called Deeksha (Consecration); the sixth in-breath is called Yagya (Sacrifice); His seventh in-breath is called Dakshina (Gifts given to the Priests).

Paryaya XVII

1–7. The Vratya's first out-breath is this Earth; the second is the *Antariksha* (Firmament); the third is the Sky; the fourth are the asterisms (the stars in the sky); the fifth are the Seasons; His sixth out-breath is called '*Artava*' (products of different seasons—flowers, fruits, vegetables and cereals), His seventh out-breath is the year.

8. The divine forces go about the same purpose; thus, verily the seasons go about following the directions of the Vratya.

9. From Amavashyaa to Poornima as the Seasons go round the year, they follow the Vratya's directions.

10. Vratya is wrapped in immortality and so are the Seasons; to Him we offer oblation!

Paryaya XVIII

1–2. The Vratya's right eye is the yonder Sun; His left eye is the Moon.

3. His right ear is the Agni; His left ear is the cleansing Vayu.

4. Day and Night are his two nostrils; Diti and Aditi are the two parts of his skull; the year is his head.

5. We bow westward in homage to Vratya during the day, and eastward during the night.

SELECTED HYMNS FROM ATHARVA VEDA CHAPTER 16

Paryaya I

The hymn is authored by Rishi Atharva.

1. The potent Bull of the Waters burst forth; from him were generated the heavenly fires.

2. Breaking, bursting, killing, slaughtering;

3. Dimming, mind-slaying, uprooting, consuming, ruining body and soul.

4. All these I let go now; let them never come near me.

5. All these I let go against him who hates us, whom we dislike.

6. The beneficial part of the waters, I let you go down unto the ocean.

7. The fire that is in the waters, the dimming, uprooting, consuming, I let go.

8. O waters, the fire that has entered you; what of you is terrible, this is that.

9. May the rains, with Indra's mighty power, pour upon you.

10. Free from defilement are the waters now; let them wash defilement from us.

11. Let the pure waters wash our sins and protect us from evil dreams.

12. O Waters, look at me with benign eyes; touch my skin with your auspicious body.

13. We invite the propitious fires that dwell in the waters; let

them bless us with kingly power and splendour

Paryaya II

This hymn is also authored by Rishi Atharva and is dedicated to *Vak*, Goddess of Speech.

1. Free from the evil-eye, let our speech be sweet like honey.
2. '*Madhumatee stha madhumateem Vak mudeyam!*' Rich in honey are you, O *Vak*, may my speech be rich in honey!
3. I invoke my guardian *(Gopa)*; invoke his guidance.
4. May both my ears hear words of knowledge, praise, and what is auspicious.
5. Let my power of listening not desert me; bless me with eagle-like sight, O unfailing light!
6. Inspirer of learned seers; I bow in reverence to divine Speech!

Paryaya III

This hymn is ascribed to Brahma and is dedicated to the Adityas. It is clearly a prayer by a Brahmin priest!

1. May I be opulent in riches and be ahead of my equals.
2. Let both brilliance and aspirations not desert me; let not my intellectual power and spiritual power forsake me.
3. Let not ritual purification with water and the vessel for drinking the Soma (*chamas*) desert me; let not my patrons and supporters forsake me.
4. Let not the raining cloud and thundering lightening desert us; let not charity to the suppliant and the Fire Stick (*Matarishva* Agni) forsake me.
5. Brihaspati, the joy-giver, compassionate God, is the lord of my soul.
6. May my heart be free from torment; let the wide Earth and the vast ocean support us!

Paryaya IV is ascribed to the Supreme Brahma and dedicated to Aditya. It prays to Usha, Agni, Vayu, Yama, etc. for protection and long life.

Paryaya V is ascribed to Yama and urges him to spare the agony of bad-dreams which he controls.

Paryaya VI is also ascribed to Yama and addressed to Usha.

It prays her to carry away bad-dreams to him who hates and curses the poet!

Paryaya VII is again ascribed to Yama. The poet wants to pierce and exterminate his enemy to be pierced by the two tusks of Vaishvanara. He also desires the curse of evil-dreaming to afflict his enemy!

Paryaya VIII is a lengthy hymn containing 27 verses. It is also ascribed to Yama. The verses are all repetitive. The poet prays to let the enemy exit the world and asserts that after vanquishing the enemy, the booty, cows and all else should rightfully come into his possession. The hymn leaves the space blank for substituting the enemy's name along with his parentage by the sacrificer!

Paryaya IX

This hymn is also ascribed to Yama; it prays to several deities.

1. Ours is the booty that I have conquered and have got it in my possession. I have vanquished all my enemies, the niggards!

2. Agni and Soma have allowed it; may Pushan keep me in the society of the virtuous!

3. May we (after our demise) attain heavenly bliss; merge into the light of Sun!

4. Shower prosperity on us, O God; let yagya-sacrifice be synonymous with prosperity! Bestow wealth and prosperity upon us!

SELECTED HYMNS FROM ATHARVA VEDA CHAPTER 17

Hymn I is composed by an anonymous poet and ascribed to Param Brahma; this is a 30-verse homage to the Sun (Aditya), who is also identified with Indra and Vishnu. The verses are identical, save for a slight change in the boon that has been sought.

1. I praise the adorable god Indra, vanquishing, overpowering, the conqueror, subduer of foes! Victorious, controller of the mighty, embodiment of pleasure, O Lord of the land and cattle, owner of riches, May I enjoy a long life!

The boon sought in the next four verses are—'May I be dear to the Gods! May I be dear to living beings! May I be dear to the cattle! May I be dear to my equals!'

6. Arise, arise O Sun, arise upon me with splendour; let those I hate be subject to me; let me not be subject to them! O Vishnu, your heroisms are manifold; set me in comfort in the highest firmament!

7. Arise, arise O Sun, arise upon me with splendour; let me be favourite of those I see and do not see! O Vishnu, your heroisms are manifold; set me in comfort in the highest firmament!

8. O Sun, let not the evil spirits fetter you in the waters; subduing their curses, you have ascended the Sky! O Vishnu, your heroisms are manifold; set me in comfort in the highest firmament!

The next 3 verses are addressed to Indra.

9. O Indra, endow us with good fortune, protect us with your inviolable rays! O Vishnu, your heroisms are manifold; set me in comfort in the highest firmament!

This senseless jumbling up of the Sun, Vishnu and Indra as well as similar invocations go on till the Verse 26. Verses 27 and 28 make a mention Kashyap's *jyotish*. Rishi Kashyap was probably the seer who had composed the hymn.

27. Protected by the shield of Prajapati's light and splendour, I, Kashyap, reaching long age exhort, may I live for a thousand years!

28. Protect me, O Aditya, by your light and splendour; let not the arrows sent by Gods or men to slay Kashyap reach me.

30. Let Agni be my guardian and protect me; let the rising Sun drive away the snares of Death; let the brightly flushing Dawns and firmly-set mountains shower a thousand breaths on me!

SELECTED HYMNS FROM ATHARVA VEDA CHAPTER 18

This section of the Atharva Veda reflectes on the Funeral Ceremonies. In large part the verses of this section have been taken from the Rig Veda and the Taittiriya Aranyaka. The hymns have been composed by Rishi Atharva and are dedicated to Yama.

Funeral Verses. 1.

This section on Funeral Verses curiously begins with the Rigvedic hymn X. 10 with minor variations, in which Yami proposes to Yama to beget a son to carry their lineage. The hymn is a dialogue between Yama and Yami and has been quoted by me in the Rigvedic section, as translated by Wendy Doniger. Barring four–five verses, all other verses have been taken from that enchanting hymn as Yama is the God of Death!

Yama and Yami were twins; born of Vivasvan (Sun). According to Wendy Doniger, in the Avestan mythology the primeval incest of the twins, Yama and Yami, remains an important episode in the procreation of the human race. However, in the Rig Veda, Yama rejects the erotic solicitations of his sister, Yami.

I quote verses which give an essence of the Rigvedic hymn:

1. [Yami] Would that I might draw my friend into intimate relationship, now that he Sun, our father, has gone far across the ocean. A man of foresight should receive a grandson from father, thinking of what lies ahead on the Earth.

2. [Yama] Your friend does not desire this kind of friendship, in which a woman of his own kind would behave like a stranger. Divine spirits, supporters of the sky, see far and wide.

3. [Yami] The immortals desire this, that offspring should be left by the mortal. Let your mind unite with my mind; as a husband, you enter my body as your wife.

5. [Yami] The god Tvashta, the creator and impeller, shaper of all forms, made us man and wife even when we were still in the womb. No one disobeys his commands; Earth and Sky are our witnesses for this.

14. [Yama] Never will I mingle my body with your body. They will call a man who unites with sister a sinner. Arrange your lustful pleasures with other man, lovely lady, not with me.

15. [Yami] What a weakling you are, O Yama, I have not been able to find any mind or heart in you. Some other woman will surely embrace you, like a girdle embracing a harnessed stallion, like a creeper clinging to a tree.

After quoting the Rigvedic hymn in full, Rishi Atharva pays homage to other Gods and Goddesses—Agni, Usha, Indra, Rudra, Saraswati, Soma, Yama, Tvashta, Varuna.

20. When the Hotra kindles the sacrificial fire early in the morning, implored by the Yajaman, the dawn, lustrous, glorious and plentiful, reveals herself for man.

21. The radiant falcon, Sun, appeared after the golden Dawn; when the Aryan tribes chose the wondrous Agni as the Hotra, then emerged *Dhee* (Meditation, Devotion, Prayer).

The next nine verses are devoted to Agni, seeking immortality and riches.

28. Agni has incessantly worshipped the apex of the dawns, the Jataveda, meets the rays of the Sun at many places; Agni stretches out to meet the Heaven-and-Earth.

Verse 29–31 eulogize Heaven-and-Earth, Agni as well as the *Hotra;* **Verse 32** is in praise of the *Vishve Deva*, **Verse 33** praises Mitra, **Verse 34** Yama, **Verse 35** Vivasvan, **Verse 36** Mitra, Aditi, Savita and Varuna. **Verses 37 and 38** urge the Vritra-slaying Indra to be bounteous with bounties, **Verse 39** praises Mitra and Varuna again and **Verse 40** eulogizes the formidable Rudra. **Verses 41, 42 and 43** address Saraswati for her favours and for showering abundance of wealth. The Fathers are invoked in **Verses 44, 45 and 46.**

47. Indra was glorified by the seers, Yama by Angirasa, Brihaspati too expands with praise by poets; we invoke those, besides invoking our ancestors (Angirasas); may they protect us!

Verse 48 praises Soma and Indra, **Verses 49-50** Yama, **Verses 51-52** the Fathers, **Verse 53** invokes Tvashta, **Verse 54** prays to Yama and Varuna, **Verses 55-56** also offer oblation to the Fathers.

57. O Agni, brightly do we invoke you and enkindle you; pray bring our resplendent Fathers to eat oblation!

58. Our revered Fathers, the Angirasas, the Atharvans, the Bhrigus, who abide in heaven; may those worshipful ones, shower favours upon us!

59. O Yama, come here with worshipful Angirasas; revel here with our Fathers who were the descendants of Rishi Virupa. We invoke your father Vivasvan too; let him, too, sit on *kusha*-grass

seats and partake of the oblation!

61. The revered Fathers ascended up from here and were established in high heaven. Other Fathers too ascended the way the Angirasas have gone on.

Funeral Verses. 2.

Like the preceding hymn, this too is composed by Rishi Atharva. While the preceding hymn contained 61 verses, this has 60 verses. It also begins with verses from the Rig Veda, which form about one-third part of this hymn. The first three verses are from R.V. X.14.

1. Pour the Soma to Yama, bring to Yama the consecrated oblation; to Yama goes the sacrifice prepared and heralded by Agni!

2. Offer the oblation enriched by honey and ghrita toYama, and draw near. Let us pay homage to the path-making rishis of earlier times!

3. Offer to Yama, the King, oblation of ghrita-rich payas (kheer); may He accept our oblation and reward us a long fruitful life!

4. O Jataveda Agni, perform his funeral without unduly hurting him; do not scorch the skin, nor scatter the body. When you have done, send him forward unto the Fathers!

7. O dead man, let your eyes go the Sun, your breath to Vayu; you go to Heaven or Earth or the waters according to your deeds, or merge into the herbs and plants if there lies your welfare!

8. O Jataveda Agni, let the indestructible Self that exists in his body be purified by your tapa and be carried to the world of pure souls!

11. To the two brindled, four-eyed, dogs of Yama,[155] who keep watch over men and guard the pathway entrust this man. O King Yama and let him go to the world of pure souls!

17. The brave who died fighting in wars and those who gave dakshina in sacrifices, O Yama, let them go the world of pure souls!

30. O soul of the dear departed, the milch-cow I donate and the rice-dish I offer in shraadha (funeral rituals), let it nourish

[155]They are offspring of Sarama, the hound of Indra.

you in the world of pure souls!

33. From mortal men the Gods hid their own immortality; they made a woman-like figure and gave her to Vivasvan. Tvashtaa's daughter Saranyu mated with Vivasvan and gave birth to Ashvin brothers,[156] and then deserted both the twinned pairs of children.

37. 'I allow admittance to him who has come and become mine here,' says the wise Yama. 'Let him stay here in my abode.'

48. Watery is the lowest Heaven, full of stars is the mid-most part; the third is called *Pradhyo*, fore-heaven, in which the Fathers reside.

The next 11 verses are a repetition of what has already been said before. The last verse of the hymn is addressed to the deceased, who was probably a king. This verse has been lifted from Rig Veda—X. 18.9. The sacrificial priest removes the bow of the deceased and gives it to his grieving widow.

60. From your dead hand do I take the bow you had carried; let it confer power and glory on us. There are you, now go the abode of the dead; and here may your noble survivors overcome all foes who fight against them!

Funeral Verses. 3.

This long hymn containing 73 verses is also authored by Rishi Atharva and is dedicated to Yama. From this hymn, 33 verses have been traced to the Rig Veda.

1. O departed man, this woman, preserving faithfully the ancient dharma (moral duty), lies down beside you, choosing her demised husband's world. Bestow upon her both progeny and wealth![157]

2. Rise up, O woman, and return to the world of living, do not remain with a man from whom the breath of life has departed. In the past he took your hand, desired your body. But now he is

[156]Griffith considers Saranyu to be the daughter of Tvashta and wife of Vivasvaan; she gave birth to Yama and Yami and the twin Ashvins.

[157]Sayana's interpretation is that a woman after the death of her husband should lay herself on the pyre along with her husband and burn herself. Dhritarashtra's younger brother Pandu's wife had done that. It is likely that the *Sati-Pratha* had religious sanction in earlier times; Sayana would certainly know better.

gone. Say to him: 'You are there; I am here!'

3. I saw the youthful maiden, being led and taken for the dead; when she was enveloped with blind darkness, I turned her back and led her homeward. (The young widow was rescued from immolation; however, the meaning is not clear, as the following verse confirms her immolation.)

4. O inviolable woman, having known the world of the living, now move together with him upon the path to the gods; he was your lord and master, make him ascend to the heavenly world! (This verse gives an indication of the custom of Sati!)

6. O Agni, the dead man you have consumed, extinguish him thoroughly; let us sprinkle fragrant water on the cremation site so that the *durva* grass sprouts.

7. O departed man, passing the first light, the second light and the third light on your way, enter the highest station of the Gods!

13. The first among the mortals to die was Yama who went to the world of the dead; Vivasvan's son, King Yama gathers men together. We offer oblation in His honour!

15. Let Kanva, Kakshivan, Purumeedha, Agastya, Shavashva, Sobhari, Vishvamitra, Jamadagni, Atri, Kashyapa, Vamadeva protect us!

21. O Agni, our ancient Fathers in olden days speeded the noble task of divine worship, singing praises, they sought pure light and devotion; they dispelled darkness and revealed the ruddy Dawn!

Verses 22, 23, 24 are also addressed to Agni in similar manner.

25. Let Indra, with the Maruts, protect me from the eastern quarter, as the Earth guards the Sky. We offer oblation to the gods who prepared the path to Heaven and guide the soul!

Verse 26 urges god *Dhata* for protection from perdition in the southern quarter; **Verse 27** prays to Aditi for protection in the western quarter; **Verse 28** prays to Soma in the northern quarter.

29. O departed soul, proceed now—we offer sacrifice to the Gods who support existence, to the Sun supporting the Earth from above, to all the creators of the world, as also to the path-finders!

30. O departed soul, proceed now in the eastern quarter—we offer sacrifice to the Gods who support existence, to the Sun supporting the Earth from above, to all the creators of the world,

as also to the path-finders!

The **Verses 31 to 35** indicate the southern, western, northern, the fixed quarter and the upward quarter.

36. Dhatar art thou, maintainer art thou, Bull art thou!

37. Water-purifying art thou; honey purifying art thou; wind purifying art thou!

Verses 38 and 39 are addressed to the oblation-containers.

40. Three steps the departed soul ascended and went after the four-footed one with its vrata. Guided by the undying syllable (Akshar—Om!), the soul rests on the navel, purifying itself in the abode!

41. Why are men mortal; why the gods don't die? Brihaspati held a sacrifice and the gods achieved immortality! Yama severs the men's breath!

42. O Jataveda Agni, you have carried the offering, having made it fragrant, to the Fathers; we offer the oblation to you!

43. Let the yajaman, sitting near the golden fire, be rewarded with wealth and food-grains! Let prosperity shower on his sons and grandsons so that they hold sacrifices!

46. They, our Fathers' Father, followed after the Soma-drinking Lord Yama, sharing his gift of oblations; may Lord Yama sup with pleasure!

49. Pay homage to the wide, expanded Mother Earth, the propitious Prithvi; the Earth is soft as wool to him who offers sacrificial gifts; let her protect you on the road forward to the Fathers!

50. O Mother Earth, heave yourself, not press downward heavily; afford him easy access gently tending him. Cover him, as a mother wraps her skirt about the child!

53. O Agni, do not scald this bowl of oblation; this bowl is meant for the Gods to drink Soma to satiety. Immortal Gods and the Fathers love to sup from this bowl!

67. O Indra, give us wisdom as the sire gives wisdom to his sons. Guide us, O much-invoked God; may we, living long, attain to light!

69. O departed soul, we offer you svadha made of sesame and barley; let King Yama allow you to savour it!

73. Purifying your life, O departed soul, get out of this body, here your kindred shine with splendour; don't be left behind midway, forsake not the renowned world of the Fathers!

Funeral Verses. 4.

Authored by Rishi Atharava and dedicated to Yama, it is the longest hymn of Atharva Veda, containing 89 verses. It uses only a dozen verses of the Rig Veda. However, W.D. Whitney remarks that 'it looks as if it were made of after-gleanings from the stock material of the tradition.'

1. O Jataveda Agni, ascend the waters which gave you birth, go on the path travelled by the Fathers, carrying oblation to the Gods; carry this soul who had offered sacrifices here to the world of ethical souls.

2. The Gods, the seasons, arrange the sacrifice, the oblation, the sacrificial cake, the ladles, the implements of sacrifice; with them you go by the paths that the gods travel, by which those who have sacrificed go to the heavenly world (Svarga)!

3. You go happily along the road of righteousness by which had gone the Angirasas, performers of good deeds; spread out upon the (ultimate) third firmament where the Adityas feed on honey!

4. Three divine birds are perched at the summit of the third firmament; let the heavenly world filled with amrita yield riches and refreshments to the yajaman, the sacrificer, and fulfill his desires!

Verse 5 talks of the sacrificial spoon, **Verse** 6 of the ladle, **Verse** 7 of the fords they cross on the path.

8. The Angirasas tracked the eastern fire, the Adityas go to the householder's fire; Agni carries sacrificial oblations on the southern path.

The hymn then traverses the different quarters—east, west, north, south, in front, below, above.

15. Agni is your invoker, Brihaspati your officiating priest, Indra the supervising priest; the offered sacrifice having been completed, goes on the ancient track!

From **Verse 16 to 27**, the hymn describes the *viaticum*—holy communion—given to the dying person or one in danger of death.

16. The oblation is rich in *Pooye* made in ghrita, let it be

placed here; it is offered to the assembled Gods who paved the path to the third firmament!

Verses 17 to 27 continue the refrain of verse 16 substituting other preparations like Ksheer, Charu, flesh, grains, honey, juices, water, sesame, etc. **Verses 28 and 29**, have been borrowed partly from the Rig Veda X. 17.12 and X. 107.4

28. The drop of Soma that leaped to earth for the gods and seers and into the Sky for the Gods and this Soma, as oblation, we seven hotras offer to you as your limbs are shaken.

Devi Chand has added a footnote: According to Pt Jaidev Vidyalankar, the verse may mean: 'The semen of man, that was present before in man and then came into the womb of woman, pervades through both the splendour of man and the uterus of woman. Man offers it as oblation to *Yosha-agni* through seven Pranas (vital breaths), similarly, the Divine semen is installed in the primordial cause of the universe in the very beginning of the creation.'

29. Let Vayu of hundred streams and the Sun that brightens the universe, shower their blessings on the sacrificer (the yajaman) who has given opulent dakshina to the seven priests of this sacrifice!

31. O mortal man, God Savita has given this garment to you to wear; putting it on, go happily about in Yama's realm!

32. The parched rice is the cow and sesame seeds are her calf. Upon their inexhaustible nourishment, O departed soul, you dwell in Yama's kingdom!

34. May the variegated yellow grains and white, bluish cows; black grains and red cows; may these cows with sesame calves never perish and, unresisting, yield him nourishment!.

35. In Vaishvanara (Agni) I offer this oblation, like a thousand-fold fountain of hundred streams; it would nourish our Fathers, Grand-Fathers and Great Grand-Fathers—all our ancestors!

Verses 36–44 go on in similar manner. **Verses 45–47** invoke Saraswati to partake of the oblation and **Verse 48** invokes the Earth. Partly, these three verses have been lifted from the Rig Veda. **Verses 49–50** refer to Dakshina, so coveted by the priests!

50. This sacrificial gift (Dakshina), like a milch cow, has come to us bestowing vigour, given by the yajaman. As old age unfailingly

follows young age, this Dakshina would certainly carry all these nourishment to the Fathers in the surest manner!

56. O departed man, cover yourself with the golden garment worn by your father; and glorify the custom of offering Dakshina to the priests as you proceed towards heaven.

Verses 58, 59, 60 and 61 have also been lifted from the Rig Veda.

58. Far-seeing Soma the Bull flows, the Lord of hymns, the extender of day, of morning, and of the Heaven; mixed with the streams, he caused the waves to resound, and with the singers aid they entered Indra's heart![158]

59. O Agni, your bright smoke lifts itself aloft, and far-extended shines in Heaven; O Purifier, like the Sun you shine with your radiant glow![159]

60. Soma (*Indu*) verily goes forward to Indra's rendezvous; the comrade does not violate the comrade's agreements; Soma rushes onward like a youth after youthful maidens, and gains a course of hundred paths.[160]

61. They have eaten, they have revelled, the friends have risen and passed away. The sages luminous in themselves have praised you with their latest hymn. Now, O Indra, yoke your two bay steeds![161]

62. O Soma drinking Fathers, go back on the profound paths taken by our ancestors, awarding us long life, progeny, and abundance of wealth!

63. O Soma drinking Fathers, you go back on the dark and deep paths travelled by the Fathers to your stronghold; come back again, at the end of the month, on the dark night of Amavashya to eat the oblation, and bestow on us the progeny of brave heroes!

Verses 64–65 invoke Jataveda Agni, and **Verses 69–70** invoke Varuna.

70. Release all fetters from us, O King Varuna, with which man is bound cross-wise and length-wise; let us live for a hundred

---

[158]R.V. 86. 19.
[159]R.V. 2. 6.
[160]R.V. 86. 16.
[161]R.V. 1. 82. 2.

autumns!

Verses 71 to 85 are mini quarter-size verses addressed to various gods, the Sky and Earth, and the dear-departed. I quote **Verses 71, 72 and 85.**

71. *Agnaye kavyavaahnaaya svadha namah*. [I bow in reverence to Agni, carrier of oblation to the Fathers!]

72. *Somaye pitramate svadha namah!* [I bow in reverence to Soma of grand lineage!]

85. *Namo vah Pitrah svadha vah Pitrah*. [We bow in reverence to you Fathers; we offer energizing libation to you, O Fathers!]

The last two verses have been borrowed from the Rig Veda.

88. O radiant Agni, O effulgent imperishable God, we kindle you; your wondrous light shines in the sky (in the Sun); shower wealth on the singers of your praise![162]

89. The Moon runs within the waters (in the ocean of air), and the Golden Bird (the Sun) with beauteous wings in Heaven! You, lightenings, with your golden wheels, men cannot find where you abide. Mark this as my woe, O Heaven and Earth![163]

SELECTED HYMNS FROM ATHARVA VEDA CHAPTER 19 CONSTITUTING SUPPLEMENTARY HYMNS

In W.D. Whitney's view this chapter is a collection of discordant and superficial readings of no real importance; all these were added later on. The chapter lacks authenticity and most probably it was not a part of the Atharva Veda. I quote Hymn IX. *Shanti Sookta.*

Hymn. IX. Shanti Sookta

Shantaa Dhyuh shantaa Prithvi
shantamidmurvaAntariksham;
Shantaa udanvatiraapah shantaa nah sanvoshadheeh.1.

[Peace-giving be Heaven and Earth, the firmament and the

[162] R.V. 6.4.
[163] RV. 1. 105. 1.

ocean with high tide; blissful be the herbs and plants for us!]

I have quoted the original hymn for its magical chanting effect; it seems to sprinkle peace on the listener! The last verse of the hymn too has the same effect.

1. Let our actions in former lives and our present acts be peace-giving; let the past and future and present acts be peace-giving!

2. Let the most exalted goddess Vak, made radiant by the Brahma, absolve us from unpleasant words we might have uttered, and shower peace on us!

3. Let the mind of man made radiant by the Brahma, absolve us from unpleasant acts we might have performed, and shower peace on us!

4. Let the five senses, with mind as the sixth, made radiant by the Brahma, absolve us from any sinful act we might have committed, and shower peace on us!

5. May Mitra, Varuna, Vishnu, Prajapati, Indra, Brihaspati, Aryaman be gracious to us!

6. Let Mitra, Varuna, Vivasvan, Yama, the Earth and atmosphere, shower peace on us!

Shantir Prithvi, shantir Antariksha, shantir Dhyuh, shantir Apah, shantir Aushadhiyah, shantir Vanaspatayah, shantir Vishvedevah, shantih sarve me Devah! Shantih shantih shantih shantibhih; Tabhih shantibhih sarvashantibhi! Shamyamoaham yadih ghoram yadih krooram yadih paapam tachhantam tachchhivam sarvameva shamastu nah. 14.

[Let Prithvi, the Firmament, the Universe, all Gods, the herbs and plants, be favourable to us; let's attain something beyond Shanti. Let even our misdeeds, cruel and sinful acts be appeased and become propitious and beneficent to us!]

PART FOUR

UPANISHADS AND ARANYAKAS

Upanishads are a group of writings that make up the last section of a collection of Hindu scriptures called the Vedas. The Upanishads form a basic part of Hinduism and have influenced most Indian philosophy. The Upanishads are sometimes called the Vedanta, which means 'the summing up of the Veda'. The word 'Upanishads' means 'to sit close to'. It suggests that this sacred material was originally secret. Most of the Upanishads were composed as dialogues between a teacher and a student. The most important ones appeared between 800 and 600 BC.

Several important Hindu schools of thought, including the sankhya and yoga schools, were founded on the teachings of the Upanishads. These teachings follow two basic philosophies. One states that there is one single fundamental reality, called Brahma, or God, which corresponds to Atma, the soul. Thus, there is no real distinction between the soul and God. The other Upanishadic philosophy states that each soul is individually eternal'.[164]

Historian A.K. Majumdar[165] observes:

> Learned Brahmins retired to the forests (aranya) where they taught higher wisdom and much of the boldest speculations about *Brahma*. These teachings are known as *Aranyakas.* Learned men from distant towns and villages were invited to the royal courts, honoured and rewarded. They held discussions with the learned priests of the courts or other learned men, not only on rites and ceremonies, but on the mind soul, the future world, nature of the gods, the Fathers, different orders of beings, nature of *Brahma*, whose manifestation is all. Many of the Brahamana works and Upanishads were probably composed there ... In the epic age

[164]The World Book Encyclopedia, Vol. 20, p. 271.

[165]Majumdar, A.K., *Hindu History,* Rupa Publications, New Delhi, 2008, pp. 306–7.

the Ikshvakus of Koshala, the Janaks of Videha and the kings of Varanasi were renowned patrons of learning.

While the word 'upanishad' is said to mean 'sitting down at the feet of another to listen to his words', it really means 'setting at rest igonorance by revealing the knowledge of the supreme spirit; the mystery which underlies or rests underneath the system of things', 'a class of philosophic writings (more than a hundered in number) attached to the Brahminas; their aim is the exposition of the secret meaning of the Vedas, and they are regarded as the source of the Vedanta and Samkhya philosophies.'[166]

SELECTED THEMES BORROWED FROM THE UPANISHADS

Truth, Light, Immortality!

At the beginning of an act of worship, one should recite the words: '*Asato ma sadgamaya, Tamaso ma jyotirgamaya, Mrityotr ma amritama gamaya!* [From delusion lead me to Truth; from darkness lead me to Light; from Death lead me to Immortality!]', 'Death is delusion and Truth is immortality'. Those who have understood this maxim have conquered the world and are free from all fear.[167]

Trinity and Unity

The universe is a trinity: name, form and action. The source of all names is the word, for it is by the word that all names are spoken. The word is behind all names; and God is behind the word.

The source of all forms is the eye, for it is by the eye that all forms are seen. The eye is behind all forms, and God is behind the eye.

The source of all actions is the body, for it is by the body that all actions are performed. The body is behind all actions, and God is behind the body.

[166]Monier-Williams, Monier, *A Sanskrit-English Dictionary*, Oriental Publishers, Delhi, 1899.

[167]Brihadaranyaka Upanishad, I: 3.28.

While the universe is a Trinity, it is also a Unity; this unity is the soul, the spirit of all life.

The immortal is veiled by the real. The soul, the spirit of life is immortal. Name and form are real; and by them the soul is veiled.[168]

The Reality of Love

One day Rishi Yagyavalkya said to his wife Maitreyi: 'The time has come for me to leave this worldly life. So, I shall divide my property between you and my other wife Katyayani.'

Maitreyi replied: 'If I were to possess all the wealth in the world, would it help me attain immortality?' The sage replied: 'Not at all. You would merely live and die like any other wealthy person. No one can purchase immortality with gold.' Maitreyi said: 'What is the point of giving me something that will not make me immortal? I should prefer you to teach me all that you know about attaining immortality.'

Yagyavalkya exclaimed: 'You have always been very dear to me; and now you say something which is very dear to me. Come and sit beside me; and as I speak, concentrate hard.'

She sat at his side and Yagyavalkya spoke: 'A wife holds her husband dear, not out of love for him, but out of love for the soul within her. A husband holds his wife dear, not out of love for her, but out of love for the soul within him. Parents hold a child dear, not out of love for the child, but out of love for the soul within them. People hold religion dear, not out of love for religion, but out of love for the soul within them. People hold the entire world dear, not out of love for the world, but out of love for the soul within. Thus, we should watch and listen to the soul, we should reflect and meditate upon it. When we come to understand the soul, we understand all existence.'[169]

Salt in Water

Sage Yagyavalkya continued: 'No one can understand the sound of a drum without both the drum and the drummer. No one can

[168]Brihadaranyaka Upanishad 1: 6. 1–3.
[169]Brihadaranyaka Upanishad 2: 14–18, 20.

understand the sound of a conch shell, without understanding the shell and the one who blows it. No one can understand the sound of a lute without understanding both the lute and one who plays it. As there can be no water without the sea, no touch without the skin, no sound without the ear, no smell without the nose, no taste without the tongue, no thought without the mind, no work without the hands, and no walking without feet, so there can be nothing without the soul.

'When you throw a lump of salt into water, it dissolves, you cannot take it out again, and hold it in your hands. Yet if you sip any part of the water, the salt is present. In the same way the soul can be perceived everywhere and anywhere; the soul has no limit or boundary.

'At present there is duality. You perceive other beings: you see them, hear them, smell them, and think about them. Yet when you know the soul, and when you recognize that the soul within you is the soul of all beings, how can you perceive other beings? How can you see and hear them, smell them and think about them? How can you regard yourself as subject and other beings as objects, when you know that all are one!'[170]

The Light within the Heart

Rishi Yagyavalkya went to visit Janaka, who was king of Videha. The king asked: 'What is our light?' The sage replied: 'The Sun is our light, for by the Sun we sit, work, go out and come back.' The king asked: 'When the Sun sets, what is our light?' The sage replied: 'When the Sun sets, the Moon is our light, for by the Moon we sit, work, go out and come back.' The king asked: 'When both the Sun and the Moon have set, what is our light?' The sage replied: 'Fire is our light, for by the glow of fire we sit, work and go out and come back.' The king asked: 'When the Sun and the Moon are not there and the fire has burnt itself out, and when no one speaks, what is our light?' The sage replied: 'The soul is our light, for by the guidance of the soul we sit, work, go out and come back.'

[170]Brihadaranyaka Upanishad 2: 4. 7–9, 11–14.

'What is the soul?' the king asked. The sage replied: 'The soul is consciousness. It shines as the light within the heart. While remaining unchanged, the soul thinks and moves. The soul is in the world of waking life, and is in the world of dreams. When the soul takes on a body, it seems to assume the body's frailties and limitations; but when the soul sheds the body at death, it leaves all these behind.'[171]

State of Consciousness

Rishi Yagyavalkya continued: 'As human beings we have two states of consciousness: one in this world, and the other in the world beyond. There is a third state between these two; in this third state we are aware of both worlds, with their sorrows and their joys.

'When we die, it is only the physical body which dies; we continue to have a non-physical existence, in which we retain the effects of our past lives. These effects determine our next life. During this period between lives, we experience the third state of consciousness.

'In the third state of consciousness there are no chariots, no horses drawing them, and no roads on which they travel; we make up our own chariots, horses and roads. In this third state there are no joys no pleasures; we make up our own joys and pleasures. There are no ponds filled with lotus flowers, no lakes and no rivers; we make our own ponds, lakes and rivers. That which we make up, is determined by the effects of our past lives.'[172]

From One Life to the Next

'When a caterpillar has come to the end of a blade of grass, it reaches out to another blade, and draws itself over to it. In the same way the soul, having come to the end of one life, reaches out to another body, and draws itself over to it.

'A goldsmith takes an old ornament, and fashions it into a new and more beautiful one. In the same way the soul, as it

[171]Brihadaranyaka Upanishad 4: 3. 1–8.
[172]Brihadaranyaka Upanishad 4: 3. 9–10.

leaves one body, looks for a new body which is more beautiful.

'The soul is divine. But through ignorance people often identify the soul with the mind, the senses and emotions. Some people even identify the soul with the elements of the earth, water, air, space and fire.

'As people act, so they become. If their actions are good, they become good; if their actions are bad, they become bad. Good deeds purify those who perform them, bad deeds pollute those who perform them.

'Thus, we may say that we are what we desire. Our will springs from our desires; our actions spring from our will; and what we are, springs from our actions. We may conclude, therefore, that the state of our desires at the time of death determines our next life; we return to earth in order to satisfy those desires.'[173]

∽

In Mundaka Upanishad (Canto II. 1) there is a verse that explains '*Pranava*', the sacred syllable, Om:

> *Pranavo dhanuh sharohyAtma Brahma tallakshyamuchyate;*
> *Apramattain veddhavyam sharavattanmayo bhavet.*

> [Om is the bow; the soul is the arrow; and Brahma is called the target. It is to be hit by an unerring man. One should become one with it just like the arrow.]

Swami Gambhirananda explains it: 'Pranava, the syllable Om, is the bow. Just as the bow is the cause of the arrow's hitting the target, so Om is the bow that brings about the soul's entry into the Imperishable; for the soul when purified by the repetition of Om, gets fixed in the Imperishable with the help of Om without any hindrance, just as an arrow shot from a bow gets transfixed in the target.'

Another verse explains Brahma:

> *Hiranmaye pare kaushe Virajam Brahma nishkalam;*
> *Tatchchhubhram jyotishaam jyotistadyada Atmavido viduh.*

[173]Brihadaranyaka Upanishad 4: 4. 3–6a.

[In the supreme, bright sheath is Brahma, free from taints and without parts, It is pure, and it is the Light of lights. It is that which the knowers of the Self realize!]

The Third Mundaka, Canto I, begins with this verse:

Dva suparnaa sayuja sakhaayaa samaanam vriksham parishvajaate;
*Tayoranyah pippalam svadvattyanashnannanyo abhichakasheeti.*1.

[Two birds that are ever associated and have similar names, cling to the same tree. Of these, one eats the fruit of divergent tastes, and the other looks on without eating.]

This verse also occurs in the famous 'Ashya Vamashya' hymn of the Rig Veda, composed by Sage Dirghatam Auchathya.

Samaane vrikshe purusho nimagnoaneeshayaa shochati muhyamaanah;
*Jushtam yadaa pashatyanyameeshamashya mahimaanamiti veetashokah.*2.

[On the same tree, the individual soul remains stuck, as it were: and so, it moans, being worried by its impotence. When it sees thus the other, the adored Lord and His glory, then it becomes liberated from sorrow.]

Satyen labhyastapasaa whyesh Aatmaasamyaggyaanen Brahmacharyena nityam;
*Antahshareere jyotimayo hi shubhro yam pashanti yatayah ksheenadoshaah.*5.

[The bright and pure Self within the body, that the ascetics with (habitual effort and) attenuated blemishes see, is attainable verily through Truth, mental concentration, knowledge, and continence practiced constantly.]

Satyameva jayate naanritam Satyen pantha vitato Devayaanah;

Yenaa-akramantrishayo hyaaptakaamaa yatra tatsatyashya paramam nidhaanam.6.

[Truth alone wins, not untruth. By Truth is laid the path called *Devayaana*, by which the desireless seers ascend to where exists the supreme treasure attainable through Truth.]

Realizing the supreme importance of Truth in life, India, on her independence, had adopted '*Satyameva Jayate*' as our national emblem!

There are many Upanishads. I will briefly mention Isha Upanishad, Kena Upanishad and the Katha Upanishad from Swami Gambhirananda's translation.[174]

ISHA UPANISHAD

Om! Isha vashyamida sarva yatakincha jagatyam jagata;
Tena takten bhunjitha ma gridhah kashyasviddhanama.1.

[Om. Isha (Ishvara), the Supreme Lord, owns or covers all this—whatever moves on the Earth. Protect (your inner Self) through that detachment.]

Kurvanneveha karmani jijivishechchhata samah;
Avam tvai nanyathetoasti na karma lipyate nare.2.

[By performing ethical karma, one should hope to live for a hundred years. For a man, who lives thus, karma may not cling to him.]

Anejadekam manaso javeeyo nainaddveva aapnuvanpoorvamarshata;
Tadvaavatoanyaanatyeti tishthhattasminnapo maatarishvaaDadhaati.4.

[174]*Eight Upanishads*, Swami Gambhirananda (trans.), Advaita Ashrama, Calcutta, 1957.

[The Brahma, or God, is unmoving One, and yet goes faster than the mind. The senses cannot overtake it, since *It* had run ahead. Remaining stationary, *It* outruns all other runners. *It* being there, *Matarishva* supports all activity.]

Tadejati tannejati tvaddoore tadvaantike,
Tadantarasha sarvasha tadu sarvashaash bahyatah.5.

[*That* (Brahma) moves, *That* does not move; *That* is far off, *That* is near; *That* is inside all this, and *That* is also outside all this.]

Yastu sarvaani bhootaanyaatmanyevaanupashati;
Sarva bhooteshu chatmaanam tato na vijuguptase.6.

[He who sees all beings in the Self (Brahma) itself, and the Self in all beings, feels no hatred for anyone by virtue of that realization.]

Yasminsarvaani bhootaanyaatmaivabhoodvijaanatah;
Tatra ko mohah kah shoka aekatvamanupashatah.7.

[When to the man of realization, all beings become the very Self, then what delusion and what sorrow can there be for that *Seer of Oneness*?]

(Or—For the man of realization, who perceives all beings as parts of the *Brahma*, there is no delusion, nor sorrow for that Seer of Oneness.)

Sa paryagaachchhukramakaayamavranamanaasnavir shuddhamapaapavidvam;
Kavirmaneeshee paribhooh svayambhooryaarthaatathyatoar-thanvyadadhaachchhaashvateebhyah samaabhyah.8.

[He is all pervasive, pure, bodiless, without wound, without sinews, taintless, untouched by sin, omniscient, Ruler of mind, transcendent, and self-existent.']

(The first part of this verse defines the *Brahma*.)

Andhama tamah pravishanti yeaavidyamupaasate;
*Tato bhhooya eva te tamo ya oo vidyaaya rataah.*9.

[Those who worship *avidyaa* (rites) enter into blinding darkness; but into greater darkness than that enter those, who are engaged in *vidyaa* (meditation)].

(This, to my mind, is a riddle!)

Anyadevaahurviddyayaanyaadaahyrviddya;
*Iti shushruma veeraanaam ye nastadviçhachakshire.*10.

[They say that by *vidyaa* a really different result (is achieved), and by *avidyaa* a different result (is achieved), thus have we heard (the teaching) of those wise men who explained that to us.]

Viddyam chaaviddyam cha yastadvedobhaya saha;
*Avidhyayaa mrityum teetravaa vidyayaamrat mashnute.*11.

[He who knows these two, vidyaa and avidyaa, together attains immortality through vidyaa, by crossing over death through avidyaa.]

Andhama tamah pravishanti yeaasambhhooti mupaasate;
*Tato bhooya iva te tamo ya oo samhootyaa rataah.*12.

[Those who worship the Un-manifested (Prakriti) enter into blinding darkness; but those who are devoted to the Manifested (Hiranyagarbha) enter into greater darkness).]

Anyadevaahuh sambhavaadanyadaahurasambhavaaaaaaaat;
*Iti shushruma dheeraanaama ye nastidvichachakshire.*13.

[They spoke of a different result indeed from the worship of the Manifested, and they spoke of a different result from the worship of the Unmanifested'—thus we have heard (the teaching) from those wise men who explained that to us.]

Sambhhootim cha vinaasham cha yastadvedobhaya saha;
Vinaashen mrityum teetravaa
*sambhootyaamritamashnute.*14.

[He who knows these two, the Unmanifested and the Manifested (Hiranyagarbha), together, attains immortality through the Unmanifested by crossing death through the Manifested.]

Hiranmayen paatrena satyashapihitam mukhama;
*Tattvam Pooshannapaavrinu satyadharmaaya drishtaye.*15.

[The face of Truth is concealed by a golden vessel. (Brahmin in the Sun's orb). Do thou, O Sun, open it so as to be seen by me who am by nature truthful.]

Agne naya supathaa raaye asmaan vishvaani Deva vayunaani vayunaana vidvaana;
*Yuyodhyasmajjuhuraanameno bhooyishthhaam te namauktim vidhema.*18.

[O Agni! O God! Knowing, as you do, all our deeds, lead us by the good path for the enjoyment of the fruits of our deeds; remove from us all sinful thoughts. We offer thee many words of salutation.]

Om! Pooranmadah poornamidam poornaata poornaat pooranamudachyate;
Poorasha poornamaadaaya poornamevaavashishate.
Om! Shantih Shantih Shantih!

[Om! That (Supreme Brahma) is infinite, and this (conditioned Brahma) is infinite. The infinite (conditioned Brahma) proceeds from the infinite (Supreme Brahma). Realizing the infinitude of the Infinite (unconditioned Brahma), it remains as the Infinite!]

Om! Let there be: Peace! Peace! Peace!

KENA UPANISHAD

Om! Keneshitam patati preshitam manah
Kena Pranah prathamah praiti yuktah?

Keneshitaam Vachamimaam vadanti
Chakshuh shrotram kah u Devah yunakti?[175] 1.

[Willed by whom does the directed mind go towards its object? Being directed by whom does the vital force, that precedes all, proceed? By whom is this Speech willed that people utter? Who is the Effulgent Being who directs the eyes and the ears?]

Shrotrasha shrotram manaso mano yada Vaacho ha vacham
sa u Pranasya pranah;
Chakshushachachakshuratimuchya dheerah
*pretyaasmaallokadamritaa bhavanti.*2.

[Since He is the Ear of the ear, the Mind of the mind, the Speech of speech, the Life of life, and the Eye of the eye, therefore the intelligent men after giving up and renouncing the world, become immortal.]

Na tatra chakshurgachchhati na vaaggachchhati no manah;
*Na vidhyo na vijaaneemo yathaitadanushishaat.*3.

[The eye does not go there, nor speech, nor mind; we do not know the Brahman. Hence, we are not aware of any process of instructing about it.]

Anyadeva tadviditaadatho aviditaadadhi;
*Itishushruma poorveshaam ye nastadvyaachchakshire.*4.

[That (Brahman) is surely different from the known; *It* is above the unknown! Such was what we heard from the ancients who explained *It* to us.]

Yadvaachaanabhyuditam yen Vagabhyadate;
*Tadeva Brahman tvam viddhi nedam yadidamupaasate.*5.

[That which is not uttered by speech, that by which Speech is revealed; know that alone to be *Brahman*, not what people worship as an object.]

[175]*Kah?* Rig Veda, X. 121. 1. '*Kasmai Devaay havishaa vidhema?*' 'Who Is the God Whom We Should Worship with the Oblation?'.

Yanmanasaa na manute yenaahurmano matam;
*Tadeva Brahman tvam viddhi nedam yadidamupaasate.*6.

[That which man does not comprehend with the mind, that by which the mind is encompassed, know that alone to be *Brahman*, not what people worship as an object.]

Yachchakshushaa na pashati yen chakshoo shi pashati;
*Tadeva Brahman tvam viddhi nedam yadidamupaasate.*7.

[That which man does not see with the eye, that by which man perceives the activities of the eye, know that alone to be *Brahman*, and not what people worship as an object.]

Yachchhotrena na shranoti yen shotramidam shrutam;
*Tadeva Brahman tvam viddhi nedam yadidamupaasate.*8.

[That which man does not hear with the ear, that by which man perceives the activites of the ear; know that alone to be *Brahman*, and not what people worship as an object.]

Yatpraanena na praaniti yen praanah praneeyate;
*Tadeva Brahman tvam viddhi nedam yadidamupaasate.*9.

[That which man does not smell with the organ of smell, that by which the organ of smell is impelled; know that alone to be *Brahman*, and not what people worship as an object.]

KATHA UPANISHAD

In *Katha Upanishad,* Part I, Canto II, the boy Nachiketa meets Yama and asks him:

Anyatra dharmaadanyatraadharmaadanyatraasmaatkritaakritaat;
*Anyatra bhootaachcha bhavyaachcha yattatpashsi taddada.*14.

[Tell me, of that thing which you see different from virtue, different from vice, different from cause and effect, and different from the past and future.]

Sarve vedaa yatpadamaamnanti tappaasi sarvaani cha yadvadanti;
*Yadichchhanto brahmacharyam charanti tatte pada sangrahena braveebhyomityetat.*15.

[Yama answers: 'I tell you briefly of that goal which all the Vedas with one voice propound, which all the austerities speak of, and wishing for which people practice *Brahmacharya*: it is this: *Om*.']

Anoraneeyaanmhato maheeyaanaatmaa-ashya jantornihito guhaayaam;
*Tamakratuh pashyati veetashoko prasaadaanmahimaanmaatman.*20.

[The Self that is subtler than the subtle and greater that the great, is lodged in the heart of (every) creature. A desireless man sees that glory of the Self through the serenity of the organs, and (thereby he becomes) free from sorrow.]

Aaseeno dooram vrajati shayaano yaati sarvatah;
*Kastam mahaamadam Devam madanyo gyaatumarhati.*21.

[While sitting *It* travels far away; while sleeping, *It* goes everywhere. Who but I can know that Deity who is both joyful and joyless.]

Part I, Canto III

Aatmaan rathinam viddhi shareera rathaveva tu;
*Buddhim tu saarathim viddhi manah pragrahameva cha.*3.

[Know the individual Self as the master of the chariot, and the body as the chariot. Know the intellect as the charioteer, and the mind verily as the bridle.]

Yastu vigyaanavaanbhavati samanaskah sadaa shuchih;
*Sa tu tatpadamaapnoti yasmaadbhooyo na jayate.*8.

[That (master of the chariot), however, who is associated with a controlled mind, is ever pure; he attains that goal from which he is not born again.]

Yachchhedvaanmanasee praagyastadyachchhejgyaana aatmani;
*Gyaanmaatmani mahai niyachchhettadyachchhechhanta aatmani.*13.

[The discriminating man should merge the speech into the mind; he should merge the mind into the intelligent self. He should merge the intelligent self into the Great Soul, he should merge the Great Soul with the Self that always remains at peace.]

Uttishthata jaagrat praapya varaannibodhata;
*Kshurashya dhaaraa nishitaa durgam pathastatkavayo vadanti.*14.

[Arise, awake, and learn by approaching the excellent ones. The wise ones describe the path to be as impassable as a razor's edge, which is difficult to tread on.]

Ahabdamasparshamroopavyayam tathaa-arasam nityamagandhavachcha yat;
Anaadhyanantam mahatah param dhruvam nichaayyaa tanmrityumukhaat pramuchyate.

[One becomes freed from the jaws of death by knowing *That* which is soundless, touchless, colourless, undiminishing and tasteless; eternal, odourless, without beginning and without end, distinct from *Mahat,* and ever constant!]

Naachiketamupaakhyaanam mrityuprokta sanaatanam;
*Uktvaa shutvaa cha dedhavi Brahmaloke maheeyate.*16.

[Relating and hearing this eternal anecdote—as received by Nachiketaa and as told by Yama—intelligent men glimpse the Brahma.]

PART FIVE

CULTURE OF THE AGE OF THE EPICS: RISE OF THE BHAKTI CULT

The Rigvedic people worshipped many gods, some major, some minor; they laid the foundations of the 'Hindu' religion. Their form of worship was the yajna; igniting fire in the sacred yajna vedi, invoking the gods by chanting Vedic verses composed by sages, and offering them ahuti of ghrita and well-cooked flesh. The fumes lifted over the grove of trees into the sky and the chants echoed in the silence of the dawn.

They did not call themselves 'Hindus'. The word 'Hindu' is a variant of the river Sindhu's name—Indus—on whose banks the Rigvedic people had arrived after crossing the high mountain passes of Afghanistan. The Persians or Iranians, their fellow travellers, called them 'Indoos' as they had settled on the banks of the Indus. The River Indus also gave her name to the country they had reached—'India.' The Muslim invadors who came later, called the country 'Hindustan.'

Religion is defined as 'The expression of man's belief in and reverence for a superhuman power or powers regarded as creating or governing the universe.'

A unique quality of Hinduism is that the Vedic gods, whom the founding fathers had worshipped, holding yajna sacrifices, have been transformed in later times. Most Vedic gods have gone in oblivion, or have been superseded by other gods. In Atharvedic hymns there is a mention of 'Thirty-Three Gods'. These have evolved from the three principal Vedic gods, Brahma, Vishnu and Mahesh; Maheshwar Shiva having evolved from Rudra.

In modern times, God Brahma, too, has been eclipsed. In the whole of India, there is just one temple dedicated to him now, in Pushkar (Rajasthan). Rama and Krishna, the principal deities of Northern India, are both believed to be avatars of Vishnu. Their full-size images, along with their ethereal spouses, in resplendent jewellery and colourful costumes, abound in the sanctum sanctorum of high-rise, beautifully constructed temples.

Shiva temples abound both in North and South India. He is revered in the abstract sexual form of 'Linga-in-Yoni'. The majestic, sky-high Shiva temples of South India, where he is overwhelmingly venerated, are the most wonderful architectural and sculptural monuments of the world. Shiva's son Ganesh is a roly-poly god, possessing the head of an elephant; his large, elephantine prehensile trunk, with two tusks emerging on each side, comes down over his rotund belly. Strangely, his mount is a mouse, shown sitting near his folded feet! In South India, however, Shiva's other son Kartikeya, or Murugan, is worshipped instead of the roly-poly god Ganesh of North India.

My mother used to tell us a hilarious tale about Ganesh. When Krishna's wedding procession to marry Rukmini was starting from Dwarka, the question arose whether Ganesh, with his elephantine physical features, was to be included in the marriage party or not. Someone commented that his elephantine trunk, coming down his massive belly, would be the prime target of ridicule in the sarcastic songs of the ladies of the bride's household, and he should be better left behind. Krishna told Ganesh to stay back to guard Dwarka in his absence. In the morning, the chariots carrying Krishna's marriage party left for the bride's city. Ganesh could not stomach this insult and sent an underground battalion of rats ahead of the marriage party to make the drive-way hollow underneath. The chariot wheels got stuck; the procession halted. Only when Krishna went back to cajole Ganesh and brought him in his chariot, the marriage party could proceed further.

Krishna's story forms an important part of the Mahabharata. We will come to it after narrating the story of Shri Rama. The magnificent edifice of Hinduism was shaped by these two great epics, the Ramayana of Sage Valmiki and the Mahabharata compiled by Sage Veda Vyas.

THE RAMAYANA

Rama was born in the Ikshvaku dynasty of Ayodhya. Ikshvaku is said to be the son of Manu, the adi purusha, who survived the Flood. King Ikshvaku started the dynasty on the northern bank of the river Sarayu (Gandaka), a tributary of the Ganga. The dynasty had a long line of great kings like Sagar, Bhagirath, Dilip, Raghu, Nabhag, Aja and Dashratha. Rama was the eldest son of Dashratha. The story of his life is called the Ramayana.

The Sanskrit epic Ramayana was composed originally by Sage Valmiki, who is believed to be a contemporary of Prince Rama. It is considered to be an 'Itihas Kavya' (historical poem). However, the original story scripted by Valmiki has been superimposed by the pundits in order to transform Prince Rama into an avatar of God.

~

Rishi Valmiki lived in his ashram on the bank of the river Tamasa, a tributary of the Ganga. One day the celestial Sage Narada paid a visit to Valmiki at his hermitage. Valmiki asked Narada who was the most righteous and valorous among the kings, dedicated to the welfare of his people. Narada replied it was Prince Rama of Ayodhya and told him the story of, how, while Rama was exiled for 14 years by his father King Dashratha, his beautiful wife Sita was abducted by Ravana, King of Lanka, and how, after crossing the sea, Rama marched to Lanka with Vanara King Sugriva's army, and rescued Sita after killing Ravana and made his triumphant return to Ayodhya at the end of his exile.

Narada returned thereafter to his heavenly abode, and Valmiki went to the river for a bath, mulling over the story narrated by Narada. There he saw a pair of *kraunch*[176] birds making love, cooing and clucking in pleasure. At that instant, a hunter shot the male kraunch with an arrow and the blood smeared bird fell

---

[176]Aquatic bird like a swan or crane with a colourful plumage

into the water with a shriek. The female kept standing by her dead lover, wailing piteously and long. Valmiki's heart was filled with sorrow and compassion. This sight kindled sparks of wrath in his mind and he uttered a curse:

> *Ma nishad, pratishtha twam gamah shashwatih samah,*
> *Yat kraunch maithunadaikam wadhih kama mohitam.*

> [O fowler, May you never know peace; you have killed this kraunch, engaged in love-making.]

This spontaneous utterance from his mouth filled the rishi with wonder. It was poetic diction! He had composed a *chhanda* in a metrical order—*anushtup chhanda*—having four *pada* of eight syllables each. He returned to his cottage and recited the shloka to his disciples. They too liked it and excitedly began reciting it to each other.

While Valmiki was still musing upon the birth of poetry in his heart, Brahma, the four-headed god of creation (as he came to be depicted later on), came to visit him. Valmiki told him about the shloka he had composed. Lord Brahma smiled and replied that it had actually happened by His inspiration. Brahma wanted him to compose the story of Rama Dashrathi, who was in reality an avatar of Lord Vishnu, whose story had been narrated to him by Sage Narada that morning. Brahma added that the secret truths about all the characters in the story would be revealed to him, as to no one else. Saying this, the god departed and the story was composed by Valmiki.

~

Prince Rama of Ayodhya preceded Shri Krishna by a few centuries. Indeed, he was a historical figure like Jesus Christ and the Buddha. In fact, Gautama Buddha had traced his ancestry from the ancient Ikshvaku dynasty of Rama. However, apart from the mention of the Ikshvaku dynasty in the Puranas, no historical record or physical proof of Rama's existence exists. Even the composition of Ramayana by Rishi Valmiki is shrouded in myth, although the original text, said to be composed by him, survives.

Let me quote a part of Chapter One of Arshia Sattar's translation of *The Ramayana*[177] of Valmiki:

> One day he [Sage Valmiki] said to the eloquent Narada: 'Tell me, Great One, who is the most virtuous man in the world of humans? Who is the most dedicated to the welfare of all beings, who has conquered anger? Who is this man, whose anger frightens even the gods?'
>
> Narada, who knows the past, the present and the future, was delighted with Valmiki's question. 'There are few men with all the qualities that you have described,' he replied. 'But there is one man, O Sage, who has all these virtues. Listen, and I will tell you about him.
>
> Born into the clan of Ikshavaku, his name is Rama. He is brave and illustrious, well-versed in the science of polity. He is well-spoken and glorious. He is a skilled archer with a muscular body and long arms. He protects all the creatures of the world and he upholds dharma. This virtuous man is the son of Kausalya, the first queen of Dashratha. Rama is ready to sacrifice everything for the truth.

~

The historicity of Rama was fudged by the pundits to sanctify him as an avatar of God Vishnu. By inserting the additional first and the last chapter during the Puranic times, they incorporated fanciful stories of Rama's divine descent in Valmiki's poem, virtually turning it into 'Rama Purana'.

The story does not begin in Ayodhya in the extant version; it begins in heaven where the gods are beseeching Lord Vishnu to take human form and be born as King Dashratha's son as a mortal, as Ravan had secured a boon that he could not be killed by a god or a Rakshasa; only a 'man' could kill him!

~

[177]Sattar, Arshia (trans.), *The Ramayana, Valmiki*, Penguin Books India, 2000.

The renowned Indologist Dr J. L. Brockington, Emeritus Professor of Sanskrit at the University of Edinburgh and Secretary General of the International Association of Sanskrit Studies, researched the text of the extant Valmiki Ramayana. He found that there was a world of difference between the polished Sanskrit verses of the first and the last chapters (inserted by the pundits later on) and the verses of the original chapters in the older form of Sanskrit, composed by Rishi Valmiki. He meticulously highlighted the linguistic and poetic differences between the two sets of verses—the original form and the later additions—and submitted his thesis to the Oxford University. In 1984, the Oxford University honoured him by the award of DLit, and published his book, *Righteous Rama,* based on his thesis.

Years later, after my retirement in 2000, I happened to find Dr Brockington's *Righteous Rama*[178] in the library of the India International Centre at Delhi. It was an eye opener. Holding that the scene of Sita's *agni-pariksha* was interpolated later on, Brockington rues in his characteristic scholastic dispassion: 'Little trace remains of what was no doubt the original happy ending of the story. There is no reason to suppose that Rama and Sita were not joyfully reunited and lived happily ever after. In the version now extant, however, later qualms about Sita's virtue cause Rama to be made coldly spurn her, saying (for the first time) that he undertook the quest and combat simply to vindicate his own and his family's honour and not for her sake.'

To my mind, by proving the historicity of Valmiki's Ramayana, Brockington had, indeed, established the historicity of Rama beyond a shadow of doubt. It filled me with rapture!

The most popular rendering of the story of Rama is Tulsidas's *Rama Charita Manas* in the Avadhi dialect of Hindi. The saint-poet Tulsidas was an ardent devotee of Lord Rama. Living in a cottage on the Ganga's bank at Varanasi, he had composed this popular classic in 17 years. Like millions of Hindus, he believed

[178]Brockington, J.L., *Righteous Rama,* Oxford, 1984.

in the historicity of Rama. However, his Rama is not a man; He is the supreme God of the universe! I had read *Rama Charita Manas* during my school days. He describes the birth of Rama as follows:

> *Bhaye pragat Kripala Deendayala, Kaushalya hitkari...*
>
> [The kind-hearted Lord Rama who showered mercy on the weak, appeared before his mother in divine form. He had four arms, wore a bejewelled crown, was bedecked with ornaments and held a golden bow in his hand! Beholding his divine form, Kaushalya was over-joyed, but she asked Him to change himself into an infant.]

Every year, about a fortnight before Dashera, an itinerant *Ramalila* party came to our town and erected a stage at the town's central *chaupar* (market square). These Ramalila shows gave concrete shape to the inchoate images that had formed in my mind by reading the Ramayana.

One of the temples in our town used to organize uninterrupted recital (*akhanda paath*) of the entire Tulsidas Ramayana. The temple priest installed loudspeakers on the top of the temple and the voice travelled far, resonating in the air. I had learnt the tune in the Ramalila shows, and used to enjoy participating in it for a few hours.

Another eminent Hindi poet, Keshav Dasa, wrote his *Rama Chandrika*, which is considered a unique literary achievement. It's written in an ornate language, which tested the limits of my comprehension, and I gave up. In more recent times, Maithili Sharan Gupt, who was honoured as our poet laureate after the country's Independence, composed his masterpiece *Saket* in 1931. Saket (or Nandi Gram) was a place near Ayodhya where Rama's brother Bharata lived after Rama had gone into *vanavaas*.

The most distinguishing feature of Maithili Sharan's *Saket* is the way in which the poet depicts the meeting of Prince Bharata with exiled Prince Rama in Chitrakoot, and how his mother, Kaikeyi, repents:

> *Tadnantar baithi sabha utaj ke aage,*
> *Neele vitaan ke taley deep bahu jaage.*

[Thereafter the Assembly met in front of Rama's cottage; the blue orb of the sky was filled with twinkling stars.]

Rama asked Bharat:

Hey Bharat-bhadra ab kaho abhipsit apna.

[O noble Bharat now tell me what do you want?]

Bharat answered:

Hey Arya, raha kya Bharat abhipsit ab bhi?
Mil gaya akantaka rajya usey jab, tab bhi?

[O *Arya*, does Bharat still need to ask for anything more? Even after getting the whole kingdom to rule!]

Paya tumne taru-taley aranya basera,
Rah gayaa abhipsit shesh tadapi kya mera?

[You have got to lodge under a tree in the forest; What is still left for me to ask for now?]

Tanu tadapa tadapa kar tapt taat ney tyaga,
Kya raha abhipsit aur tathapi abhaga?

[Our anguished father quit his body, writhing in pain! What is now left for me to want now?]

Ha, isi ayash ke liye janam tha mera,
Nij Janani ke hi haath hanan tha mera.

[Alas, I was born just to get this adverse fame! I was begotten, to be slayed by my own mother!]

Ab kaun abhipsit aur Arya, vaha kiska?
Sansaar nashta hai, bhrashta huaa ghar jiska.

[Who wants more now, O Arya, and what? With my world destroyed, my household ruined!]

Mujhse mainey hi aaj swayam moonh phera;
Hey Arya, bataado tumhi abhipsit mera.

[I have turned my face from myself today; O Arya, now *you* tell me my unfulfilled desire!]

Rama got up then, took Bharata in a close embrace, and said:

Uskey aashaya ki thaah milegi kisko?
Jana kar Janani he jaan na paayi jisko!

[Who can gauge the depth of his heart, when his own Mother, who gave him birth, failed to know him?]

Kaikeyi spoke then; startling everyone:

Yeh sacha hai tau phir laut chalo ghar Bhaiya;
Aparadhin mein hoon haaya tumhari Maiyaa!

[If that's true, then you return home, O Rama! I am the culprit, alas! your Mother!]

Such heart-felt passion is rare in Hindi poetry!

∽

After reading Professor Brockington's book, I studied several famous authors of Rama's story—P. Lal's *Ramayana of Valmiki*, N.R. Narlekar's *A New Approach to the Ramayana*, H.D. Sankalia's *Ramayana: Myth or Reality*, Kalidasa's *Raghuvanash*, etc. Besides, I consulted books by historians like Nagendra Nath Ghosh, Majumdar, Raychaudhari, Kumar Suresh Singh and others. I also read archeologists like B.B. Lal and K.N. Dikshit.

N.R. Narlekar held that 'this transfiguration of history into mythology, this deification of Rama, was chiefly necessitated by the phenomenal rise and spread of Buddhism, which threatened to sweep the established Vedic religion clean out of existence.'

∽

The reason why I wanted to write my own version of the story of Rama is given in the prologue of my book, *Ramayana: Before He Was God.* [179]

[179]Varma, Ram, *Ramayana: Before He Was God*, Rupa Publications, 2010.

To me reading Valmiki's *Ramayana,*
As it existed today, was a pain.
There are exaggerations galore—
Dashratha had already lived
And ruled for eleven thousand years,
When he decided to crown Rama.
His army was a thousand million strong!
Every *pundit* appears to have added
A number of zeroes with impunity,
As his homage to Rama Almighty,
The zero, afterall, was their own invention!
Hanuman, assuming a giant shape,
Miraculously takes a jump
Over a hundred *yojana* long sea—
Turning the twenty mile long Palk Straits
Into a sea stretching to a thousand miles!
Ravana's city, Lanka, had palaces
Made of gold, set with precious stones.
A herd of elephants was made to march
Over Kumbhakarna's mountain-size belly,
When beating of drums was of no avail
In waking him, from his six-month long sleep!
When, hit by poison coated arrows,
Lakshman lost consciousness,
Hanuman flies in the dead of night
From Lanka to the high Himalayas,
And returns bringing a mountain peak
Covered with trees, shrubs and deer!
They invented fanciful tales of valour
Of Ravan and his son Meghnada,
'Fighting and humbling the mighty Indra,'
Purporting to magnify their stature,
Making them look taller than Vedic gods—
Foes worthy of an avatar of Vishnu!
The most glaring episode, however,
Being Sita's Agni-*pariksha*.
Rama refusing to accept Sita,

Asking her to prove her chastity
By an ordeal of jumping into fire!
'I did not wage the war to rescue you,
But to wash the stain on my race,'
Rama tells Sita when she meets him,
Thinking her long interminable night
Of despair was at last over,
Her face lit up in love, joy and wonder,
On seeing Rama, after her abduction.
But Rama had suddenly turned cold
And most uncharacteristically cruel.
'Your chastity is suspect', he tells her,
'Having lived so long with a lustful man.
Yet you deign to stand before me!
Your very sight is painful to me
Like a lamp's glare to a man
Suffering from infected, sore eyes.
I have no use for you, woman,
Go with whomsoever you please,
Lakshman, Bharat or Sugriva,
Or stay in Lanka with Vibhishan!'
This fake and dreadful episode,
Inserted apparently to glorify (?) Rama,
By over-zealous Brahmin moralists
Does irreparable injustice to Rama,
Putting such vile words into his mouth!
The *pundits* showed great dexterity
In painting this horrendous scene
Of Sita jumping in blazing fire.
Wouldn't Rama know he is killing her?
Yet he talks about upholding *Dharma!*
Wouldn't Agni do his *dharma* to burn?
And if Agni had miraculously rescued her
From a burning pyre in Lanka,
Why couldn't he do it again in Ayodhya?
Why couldn't the drama be staged again
To silence the doubting Thomases there?

Why was she exiled from Ayodhya then?
Pundits called Rama '*maryada purushottam*'—
'Best among men, who remains steadfast
Within sanctified walls of right action.'
Yet they made him do such dire deeds,
To defend false mores of his wife's chastity!
'Let all raped women be burnt alive then!'
My heart and soul cry out in anguish.
It's an act of perfidy against Sage Valmiki.
How filthy, ludicrous and inane
Can the *pundits* be, to so defile
The vernal stream of *Valmiki Ramayana*.
I vowed to erase the artful coats
And restore the original to the world,
Reveal the beauty of Rama's story,
Purged of all alterations and interpolations,
And let it shine in its pristine glory.

I then embarked on my project of composing the story of Rama in free verse: *Before He was God: RAMAYANA: Reconsidered, Recreated.*

∽

My daughter Vandana, an architect by profession, is also a great painter. I asked her to paint about 10 pictures illustrating Ramayana's main episodes, which could be used at the beginning of each chapter. She made about 59 paintings which greatly enhanced the book's appeal!

Dr John Brockington and Mrs Mary Brockington had rendered invaluable assistance to me in my venture. Indeed, they guided me at every step. They also obliged me by writing the book's Foreword. My publisher, Rupa, brought it out in a captivating coffee-table format in 2010.

∽

In the commonly prevelant story, Hanuman played a crucial role in Sita's rescue. He possessed superhuman capabilities. He flew into Lanka like a bird and found Sita in the Ashok Vatika. He returned to Prince Rama in Kishkindha and told him about Sita's whereabouts. During the battle, Hanuman's miraculous act of bringing the *sanjeevani* herb from the Himalayas saved Lakshman's life. Hanuman was accorded divine descent for performing these miraculous acts as the son of the Vedic god Vayu and Gandharvi Anjana.

Besides these crucial acts of Hanuman, the construction of a bridge across the ocean was necessary. It was therefore essential to make Neel possess superhuman capabilities too. Accordingly, he was said to be begotten by Vishwakarma, the creator of the universe. Even the other monkeys detailed by Sugriva in Sita's search could change their form at will and become 'mountain-sized.' They were all given divine patrimony; they were all said to be sired by gods!

∽

Even the King of Lanka, Ravana, and his son Meghnaad were shown to possess superhuman powers. Ravana and his siblings were stated to be the children of the mighty Sage Pulastya, son of God Brahma. Kuber, the Lord of Wealth, was Ravana's younger brother. Ravana had a tiff with Kuber and defeated him in battle. Kuber left Lanka, leaving his golden palaces and his Pushpak Vimana to Ravana.

After Ravana's cousin Khara's death at Rama's hands in Panchavati, Ravana had reached there in this aerial vehicle, Pushpak Vimana. Ravana's son Meghnaad too was extremely valorous; he had humbled the supreme Vedic god Indra! To vanquish such foes, Rama had necessarily to be an avatar of God!

∽

My attempt to depict Rama as a mere mortal was indeed foolhardy. The biggest problem for me, however, was—how can Hanuman cross the sea and reach Lanka?

At the time when, after his mother's assassination, Rajiv Gandhi had become India's prime minister, Sri Lanka was facing insurgency from the Tamilians living in the Jaffna area of northern

Sri Lanka. Its President, Jayavardhane, had requested Rajiv Gandhi for military assistance to quell the rebellion in Jaffna. The assistance was provided, and Rajiv Gandhi even paid a visit to Sri Lanka. At that time, I happened to read in newspaper stories that the Tamilians from Tamil Nadu had populated the entire northern Sri Lanka many centuries back, using a natural passage between India and Sri Lanka, which connected Rameshwaram and Dhanushkodi (in India) with Mannar (in Sri Lanka) and was named 'Adam's Bridge'. However, due to global warming in later times, this path had got submerged in sea water because of the rise in sea-level.

The Archaeological Survey of India had stated in an affidavit before the Supreme Court in 2010 that the 'Rama Setu', new name for 'Adam's Bridge', as it exists today is a 'natural formation made of shoals/sand-bars'.

It struck me that the story of Rama is nearly 3,000 years old. Gautama Buddha is believed to have existed in sixth century BC. He had claimed his descent from Ayodhya's royal dynasty, about eight generations after Rama. Rama should have, therefore, existed about four to five centuries before the Buddha. The sea level was considerably lower at that time, and the so-called 'Adam's Bridge' was functioning as a natural passage. The passage might have been eroded at many places, but a man with strong limbs could swim across the eroded parts. However, one had to reach the shores of Lanka before the close of day. Besides, the sea water being salty and unfit for human consumption, there was no water to drink on the way! Going across to Lanka, therefore, required extraordinary physical strength and tremendous will power.

In my retelling of the story, Hanuman did not fly into Lanka as claimed by Sant Tulsi Das. He had to foot it! Jambuwan had noticed the sea-path when the search party led by him had reached Rameshwaram:

> Jambuwan pointed to an abutment:
> Where a rocky path extended into the sea,
> Half-submerged in the heaving ocean—
> A path made of surf-washed boulders,
> Disappearing into the horizon.

They went on this weather-beaten
'Bridge' as far as they could go.
The boulders had crumbled and cracked,
Due to the Sea's fury over the years.
They went on, hopping and jumping,
To some distance, till it got dark.
As the ocean waves heaved higher
Losing their translucent hue,
They came back disheartened,
Defeated by the surging sea waves.
They huddled into a conference
On getting back to the shore,
Defeat gnawing upon their hearts.
Hanuman was crest-fallen, he hadn't
Anticipated such a colossal hurdle.
Angad said: 'Sugriva would kill us
If we returned without finding Sita,
Hadn't he said it in so many words?'
Jambuwan told him that more important
Than their own lives, was the word
Given by their king to Prince Rama,
Which had to be fulfilled at all cost.
'I've made some searching enquiries
From knowledgeable local people.'
He added: 'The path we had gone on,
Does extend right up to Lanka,
But it gets submerged at high tide,
When ocean waves go sky-high.
Even at low-tide it's not easy to cross,
Being damaged and disjointed.
Indeed, going over is most hazardous,
Only the toughest could hope to survive.
As an alternative, we could
Capture the royal barge, perhaps,
Killing the Ravana's guards,
And take it to Lanka. But the reception
We'd get there is not likely to be cordial.

The whole point is to reach incognito!'
They all agreed to what he said,
The question was who could do it.
There was an uneasy silence.
Jambuwan spoke at last, looking at
Hanuman: 'Only you could do it,
Mighty son of Anjana! You could
Subdue the ocean's rough waves,
Trample upon sharks and crocodiles,
Reach Lanka's shores by jumping,
Swimming and slithering like an ape.
Indeed, being endowed with brains,
You are stronger than an ape.
Doubtless it would require
Supreme might and will power;
A mere slip might prove fatal.
But I have faith in you, Hanuman!
Many a challenge have you taken
In the past, done the seemingly impossible,
When our survival was at stake.
This is a moment when we've to prove
Ourselves worthy of Prince Rama's trust.
We would wait here for a week,
Our eyes scanning sea waves in the evening,
Looking for your return, bringing
Glad tidings of Princes Sita's whereabouts.'

~

HANUMAN CROSSES THE SEA!

Hanuman left at the break of dawn,
When Usha's rosy tresses
Stretched across the sky's vault.
The sea was calm, in low tide,
As if dreaming, draped in a golden veil.

But soon it shed its slumber,
Regaing its blue-green hue.
The waves began to rise
As the sun rose, began breaking
Against the slippery 'bridge,'
He scampered on boulders, scrambled
Over cliffs, skipped over crevices
And fissures; swam into the gaps
Where the 'road' had disappeared.
He continued going all day long.
The words, half remembered,
Of a prayer, his mother, Ajnana,
Used to sing while doing her chores,
Kept coming to his lips:
'I have put my raft in the river,
O Lord, help me take it to shore;
Its timber is weak, the hinges creak,
And the river is deep and wide;
Eddies churn in the midstream,
And the waves rise sky high.
My hands shake, can't hold the oar,
O Lord, help me reach the shore!'

The green hump of the mainland
Which hanuman had left behind,
Had dissolved in the grey horizon,
He found himself at the dead centre
Of a vast circle of the ocean,
The horizon's rim on all sides
Being equidistant, enclosed
All around by sky's blue dome.
It was nerve-wrecking in the extreme.
Unlike travelling on road,
Where a tree, a river front, a mountain
Loomed ahead to serve as a signage,
And came nearer as one advanced.
All advance seemed unavailing here,

There being no landmark,
No indication what-so-ever to cheer
The traveller of the distance done;
Apparently, one is going nowhere!
He felt he was trapped,
Enclosed in a vast cosmic globe!

Then he noticed the Sun.
It had come up from the left,
And had gone in descent to his right.
He felt supremely reassured.
He saw schools of fish, big and small,
Jumping in the air in graceful hoops.
He spied a grey speck after a while
On the horizon, ahead of him,
And his heart missed a beat.
'Was it a grey cloud in front
Of him, or he had sighted land?'
It became larger as he advanced,
Till it looked like a green ridge
Rising from the sea's blue expanse.
All his exhaustion vanished then,
His tired legs found their spring again.
Some unseen hand with bold strokes,
Was giving finishing touches to
A painting against sky's blue dome!
'Was this the fabled Lanka of Ravana?'
He wondered, 'rising like a pinnacle,
Girdled by the choppy ocean waves?'
Kishkindha too had high ramparts,
But this jewel set in the heaving sea
Was out of this world, unique!

He was dying of thirst as he reached
The shore. He ran to a clear stream
That was flowing into the ocean,
And drank its sweet water in handfuls.
Coconut trees fringed the coast,

He saw ripe ones lying under them,
He broke a few, drank their nectar,
Then ate their milk-white flesh.
Then he saw a plantain grove,
And found a fully ripe bunch.
He gorged himself on them.

~

Hanuman spent the night under a tree in front of the fort's gate. In the morning he saw some Brahmins going in with Shiva's tilak painted on their foreheads. He too dressed like them then and went in. He found the Brahmins buying things needed for yajna-sacrifice from a shop. They asked him who he was. He told them he had come from the mainland to see Lanka. They asked him to do some work for them—carry the yajna material to the temple of Rudra Mahakaal.

Crossing the market, they passed by the royal palaces and entered a high temple. It was the King's royal temple. In an ornate hall, under a high dome, a 3-feet high black stone lingam was installed in a wide yoni. The Brahmins sat near it on the marble floor and made preparations for the yajna. He sat with them, assisting them. King Ravana entered and prostrated before the lingam and sat on a cushion. The Brahmins ignited the fire in the vedi, chanting mantras, offering ghrita ahuti and incense. Sacred smoke filled the temple hall.

Some women came escorting a bejewelled young woman, who wore strings of pearls and garlands over her shapely bosom. In the yajna smoke, she looked like an apparition. Ravana stood up then, held the woman's hand and they circled thrice around the black marble lingam. Thereafter they kept standing, facing the lingam, holding hands. The mantras being chanted by the two Brahmins resounded in the hall.

At a signal from the Brahmins, Ravana took the young woman close to the lingam. He held her hand as she bent over the lingam. She pulled up her skirts then by her other hand and lowered herself to touch the lingam. The priests offered more libations in the fire, chanting mantras.The ceremony was over and the king and the ladies departed. The priests were paid 10 gold coins each; Hanuman got five.

As they came out the priests told him it was the '*yoni-shuddhi yajna*' for the royal lady whom the king had brought some time back. One of them added in a whisper: 'We may soon have another yoni-shuddhi yajna for Sita.' 'Sita who?' Hanuman feigned ignorance. 'She is the wife of Prince Rama of Ayodhya. Our king had brought her recently.' 'Is she also ready for "yoni-shuddhi?" Hanuman asked. 'That's the problem. She is forever crying, they say.' They told him Sita was lodged in Ashok Vatika, away from the city.

Hanuman took leave of them and came back to the market. To his great surprise he saw some men dressed like Vanaras. They told him there was a settlement of Vanaras on a hillside some miles away from Lanka. He was delighted to know about it and asked them about the Ashok Vatika. 'It is a large royal garden beyond the town gates, at another end.'

Hanuman took off his Brahmin dress and changed into his Vanara outfit. He was happy to know that Vanaras were no strangers in Lanka. Feeling more comfortable now, he went towards the Ashok Vatika. The sentries at the city gate stopped him; he gave them a gold coin and they let him go towards Ashok Vatika.

Ashok Vatika was at some distance from the city gate. The sun was setting when he reached there. Fringed by tall trees, the Vatika was enclosed by a high wall. He went round some distance along the wall, climbed a tall tree near the wall and crossed into the garden by going over the entwining branches. Going from one tree to another, he saw a palace near a pretty lake. Silence reigned, save for some bird calls. He spied a woman sitting under a tree near the lake and stealthily transferred himself to that tree. She was downcast and looked famished and unkempt.

Suddenly he noticed a flurry of activity. The Vatika gates had been opened for the royal chariot. Ravana alighted from the chariot and strode towards the woman. He bowed to her and asked her to move into the palace in the Vatika. But she kept sitting there, saying nothing, looking down. He made protestations of love then, entreating her to be his Chief Queen.

Her voice was faint and feeble. She replied that she would rather die than go with him into the palace! He told her she was a fool waiting for Rama as not a bird could enter his impregnable fort. He bent down then, enclosing her into his arms. She was struggling to be free. He told her that he would have her dressed as a bride and brought to his bed. He stormed out then, stamping his feet. Sita slumped to the ground again.

Darkness was falling. There was silence, save for the bird-calls. Hanuman dropped the ring Rama had given him. She picked it up and was filled with amazement. It had Ayodhya's emblem etched on it; it was Rama's signet ring! She looked up the tree and saw Hanuman. He came down and sat before her. 'I am Hanuman, Princess; Prince Rama's messenger. He had given this ring to me, so that you'd believe me when I see you!'

'Is it a dream?' Sita wondered! Hanuman told her that Prince Rama and Lakshman were in Kishkindha, about Rama killing Kishkindha King Vali and making his brother Sugriva king. He said they would come soon, bringing Sugriva and his army, and kill Ravana. She should not despair. Sita gave him a locket she still possessed. As Hanuman went up to his tree perch, Sita went inside the Garden Palace, filled with joy.

~

The young woman whose yoni-shuddhi ceremony Hanuman had witnessed in the temple of Rudra Mahakaal was Saudamini, wife of King Mayurdwaja of Malayadesh in the north. Ravana had heard praise of her beauty and had attacked Mayurdwaja's kingdom. He killed Mayurdwaja in battle, brought his lovely queen to Lanka and had lodged her in a specially furnished suite in his palace.

That evening, after going to Ashok Vatika to meet Sita, Ravana had gone to Saudamini's suite. He called for the best palace wine and offered her a drink. He apologized to her for killing her husband and inflicting the ordeal of yoni-shuddhi on her. He said he loved her dearly and would make her his chief queen in Mandodari's place. Saudamini kept on sipping the drink, saying nothing.

Ravana showered lavish praise on her beauty and said he loved her from the bottom of his heart. Saudamini looked him straight in the face and said, 'O cruel King, you don't have to pretend you love me, for you have no notion what love is. You don't have to make me the head queen, for there could be no amends for the crime that you have committed—of killing the man I loved. You want to enjoy my body, then go ahead, strip it and take it. You could have done it the day you brought me here—a living corpse—dead in all respects but the body! You are a fiend who feeds on corpses!'

Ravana had expected sniffles and tears which required petting and cuddling; her cold resignation foxed him. He went on his knees then and said in a penitent voice: 'You are right, fair Saudamini, I am a sinner—I have sinned against you and against your husband.' He got up then and brought a black-leather lash and said: 'Here, take this lash, and punish me here and now. Strike as hard as you wish, take blood for blood; have no mercy. Kill me if you like, I will not utter a word!'

Saudamini's inner fury was awakened. She took the lash in her hand, stood up and struck him hard. Ravana winced and she struck him again, and again, till she could go no more. She was heaving and perspiring. Blood oozed out from Ravana's face and neck. But his ruddy cheeks showed a malicious grin. He got up slowly then and took her in his arms and carried her to the bed. A piercing shriek issued from her.

Hanuman was over-joyed at the success of his mission. He spent the night on a tree in the Vatika garden, and came out before dawn, jumping over trees, and rested in his tree perch outside the main gate. During the day he entered the city again and was reconnoitering Ravana's armament stores when he was arrested and produced before Ravana.

Ravana sat in full regalia in his court; his brother Vibhishan and son Meghnada were sitting on either side. The policemen told Ravana, he was a spy and was lurking in high security zone.

Hanuman admitted it and told Ravana that indeed he was

Prince Rama's messenger. Ravana was amazed. Hanuman told him that Prince Rama had killed King Vali of Kishkindha, who had thrown his brother Sugriva out of his kingdom and taken his wife Tara to bed. He told Ravana that he should return Princess Sita forthwith, else Prince Rama with his valiant brother Lakshman and King Sugriva will invade Lanka with the Vanara army.

Ravana's face was red with rage. He shouted: 'Take this monkey away and kill him!' Vibhishan intervened and told him that a messenger should not be killed. Ravana was angry at his brother's intervention. He shouted at Vibhishan and asked him to leave his court. Then he ordered his guards to set fire to Hanuman's tail, adding that a monkey loves his tail most! The guards wrapped a mock tail around his tail with strips of cotton wool and rags and drenched it in oil. Hanuman meekly submitted himself to it. They took him to the City Centre then, followed by a crowd of people, and set it on fire.

~

After attending his court where Hanuman was brought before him for reconnoitering the armament installations, and after awarding the punishment of setting his tail on fire, Ravana went to Saudamini's suite again. He found her distraught, sulking like a mauled tigress. He went close and caressed her cheeks. Saudamini was unresponsive. He gave her the lash again and said: 'Don't you want to complete the sentence, dear Saudamini?'

She took the leash and struck him hard. He fled, as if in terror. She chased him and struck again, harder, making a deep cut on his cheek. Ravana grabbed her then, snatched the lash from her and struck her. She shrieked and bolted out, howling: 'Don't touch me, you fiend, you hideous Rakshasa! Don't touch me, else the earth shall rend and devour you and your palaces. The skies shall spit fire. Look there, the sky is ablaze!'

Ravana looked out and saw the ominous blaze engulfing the city. Fire was raging over the tops of Armories. Aghast, he rushed out. His men told him it was the Vanara whose tail had been set on fire; he had jumped from roof to roof, leaving the city ablaze! Ravana saw the flames leaping up to the sky!

Hanuman had jumped up with his burning tail and entered households, making the houses catch fire. Soon the fire spread to the neighbouring households. The residents ran out, howling and shouting. The sea breeze helped spread the fire. Hanuman kept entering into other houses and setting them on fire. Soon the town became a blazing inferno. Hanuman then jumped into the sea, dowsing his burning tail. He swam towards the main gate by which he had entered the city; found a large tree with a hollow trunk and went to sleep.

He rose before dawn, broke some coconuts, drank their milk to his fill and ate the pulp. Then he went in search of the path he had come by, found it and began his return journey, skipping and singing to himself. The path seemed quite friendly now and he got to the mainland before sunset. He was hailed by Jambuwan, Angad and others, who were waiting anxiously at the shore for his return.

∽

Rama and Lakshman had lodged
On mount Rishyamook during the rains.
Six months had elapsed after Sita's abduction.
They had been paralysed by the rains,
Remained cooped up in the mountain cave.
They heard commotion on the path below,
Saw Sugriva coming up with his men.
Paying his obeisance, Sugriva said:
'My Lord, Hanuman reached Lanka,
He's brought Princess Sita's news!'

Hanuman went down on his knees,
Touched Rama's feet and gave him
The souvenir Sita had given him.
Rama held her locket on his palm
And gazed at it in wonder and joy.
Hanuman gave a brief account
Of his adventures in Lanka, and said:
'She is brave, My Lord, and unafraid;

But flickering like a candle in the wind,
Surviving against all odds, treating
Ravana's dire threats and gallant
Blandishments with equal contempt.
She said, she was sure you'd come,
Kill the monster Ravana, and rescue her.
But her strength was ebbing away,
My Lord, like the oil in the lamp!'
Rama could not hold his tears,
He stood up and hugged Hanuman:
'I marvel at your grit and courage,
Hanuman! You have achieved
The impossible; shown us the way ahead.'

Turning to Sugriva then, he said:
'Now tell me, King Sugriva,
How do we proceed from here?'
'We are all at your command, My Lord!
The entire Vanara tribe is at your service.
All able-bodied men, living in hamlets
And hills, shall heed my call,
Assemble in three days with weapons.'
Rama was gratified and added:
'Ravana has all the advantages
On his side, sitting ensconced
In his fort, guarded by the sea.
He has one crippling disadvantage,
Though; he is a coward and a thief!
On the other hand, we have men
Like Hanuman, who, overcoming
The perils of crossing the stormy sea,
Penetrated Lanka's fortified defences,
And set Ravana's citadel on fire!'

~

Sugriva's men wearing monkey and bear masks gathered in thousands, as in a festival. Sugriva formed 10 brigades commanded by Angad, Jambuwan, Hanuman, Nala, Neela and other chiefs. Before leading his army, he offered *bali* of a bison to Indra, Rudra-Shiva, Vanadevi and other gods.

It was an army marching not so much on ground as above it—jumping from one tree to another, exhibiting their skill and prowess, helping themselves to fruits, shoots, honey and all that came their way, bathing in streams and waterfalls, sleeping cooped up in tree hollows or under the rocks. They came upon the Malay mountains covered with aromatic trees where stately palms guarded the rivers meandering to the sea.

In about a fortnight they reached the sea shore and were thrilled, seeing its blue expanse; they rushed headlong into its rolling waves. Their travel fatigue was washed away by the tingling surf.

Rama and Lakshman went into the Rudra-Shiva shore-temple for worship and sought His blessings. Nala constructed huts for Rama-Lakshman, Sugriva, Angad and the other commanders. Hanuman showed them the causeway in the sea, going to Lanka, looking like an umbilical cord of the motherland.

The next day Hanuman noticed that the royal barge anchored at the jetty had left and there was no trace of the Rakshasa guards. He showed Rama, Lakshman and Sugriva the deserted outpost. Thereafter he took them on a tour of the causeway, the rocky outcrop.

∽

Ravana's mainland spy, Shardula, who wore a lion mask and roamed the Malay forests, reported to Ravana, the arrival of the Vanara army at the sea shore. Ravana summoned his council of war, his brothers Vibhishan and Kumbhakarna and his son Meghnada, besides his main generals. Kumbhakarna said: 'I stand by you, dear brother, although you have brought Sita driven by passion. Personally, I am quite excited at the prospect of war. It was getting rather dull. In fact, I feel like a seagull who sees large shoals of fish coming his way.' Ravana chuckled.

Vibhishan advised Ravana that wisdom lay in averting battle. It was still not too late to try and placate Rama by returning Sita to him. Prahastha, the Army General, intervened and said: 'Valiant Kumbhakarna and Meghnada could conquer even the gods, what to talk of a mere mortal, Rama.'

Vibhishan joined his palms and said: 'My dear brother, don't underestimate Rama's strength. Don't forget he slew our redoubtable cousins, Khara and Dushan, single-handed. Now he is joined by King Sugriva and his Vanara army. Have you forgotten the valour shown by Rama's messenger, Hanuman? Besides, I must say, kidnapping defenceless Sita was a deplorable act; it did not behove a king like you! It diminished you, diminished us all. I beg of you to return Sita and desist from punishing the whole tribe for your personal pleasure and pride.'

Ravana snarled: 'Stop it, traitor! You've crossed all limits, trying to sermonize to me! Indeed, I sense treason in your words. You are a greater enemy of mine than Rama—like a snake under my sleeve!'

Vibhishan stood up then and said: 'I am going in self-exile, quitting my motherland, Lanka. You are courting doom, dear brother; may God Rudra protect you all!'

~

The next morning, saying goodbye to his wife and children, accompanied by four of his trusted men, Vibhishan set off in a boat. The Vanara guards took him to King Sugriva. Vibhishan introduced himself and told him he had come to seek asylum. Hanuman considered it a good omen, but Sugriva went to report the matter to Rama.

Rama was intrigued and asked Sugriva to call the Vanara chiefs for counsel. When they had assembled, Sugriva said that Ravana's brother, Vibhishan, was a chip of the same block; there could be some sinister design to send him here. Angad agreed and said he should be put to a severe test.

Hanuman opined that putting Vibhishan to test, keeping him under surveillance, interrogating him, were logical suggestions. 'But I had seen him in Lanka, he had told Ravana not to harm me, a messenger of Rama. I see neither deceit nor duplicity; he has come to seek refuge.' Sugriva cautioned again: 'He might not be a spy but he abandoned his brother, my Lord, when he found himself in dire straits. We have to be careful.'

'But Vibhishan has not ditched Ravana deceitfully', said Rama. 'Believe me dear Sugriva, if even Ravana came here and asked for pardon, I would not refuse it. Call Vibhishan, I would gladly grant him asylum.'

Vibhishan bowed to Rama, introduced himself and said: 'My Lord Rama, my brother Ravana has been living a sinful life, lusting for pretty women, killing their husbands; he has become a willful tyrant. Abducting Sita was his basest crime. My sincere advice to return Devi Sita made him hurl abuses at me, and accuse me of treason. I quit in disgrace, and after taking leave of my family, have come to you, seeking refuge. My life, my destiny is in your hands!'

Rama stood up, took Vibhishan in his arms, gave him a warm hug and said: 'You are like my brother, Vibhishan, like Lakshman; as dear to me as King Sugriva!'

Then turning to Lakshman, Rama said: 'Hark Lakshman, the sea waves rise high to kiss the setting sun; a blush spreads over the sea.The time is most propitious, get the holy sea water in a pot. Let me anoint Vibhishan at this sacred spot and declare him as the new King of Lanka!'

Rama sprinkled sea water on Vibhishan's head; the Sun's golden rays touched him in blessing!

Early in the morning when Usha's rosy veil had spread over the sky, Rama prayed to the ocean to allow passage to his army to Lanka. At sunrise the work of repairing the 'Hanuman Setu' began. Sugriva divided the work among several contingents under different chiefs. He detailed one unit under Jambuwan for food-gathering for all; they stayed behind and went into the forest. The others collected stones and boulders for filling the gaps and strengthening the causeway. The corps under Nala and Neela moved with the stone-collecting units for fixing the stones in the cavities. As thousands of Vanara soldiers brought stones in their uplifted hands and hurled them in the gaps with glee, it appeared a river of stones was flowing into the sea!

During the mid-day break, Jambuwan's men brought loads of fruits and herbs for refreshments. Lakshman had gone with a battalion of bow-wielding men for hunting wild buffaloes, bisons, boars and deer. By noon they brought a huge pile for dinner. In the evening they lighted hundreds of fires and the aroma of roasting meat hung over the first day camp.

With each passing day, however, as the lead got longer, the task got tougher. Luckily the weather remained cool and breezy. In the night Rama dreamt he was standing near a deep chasm and Sita stood on a high cliff. He shouted to her: 'I'm coming, dear, I'm coming!' But his voice was drowned in the roar of the river that flowed between them.

After some days they reached a point where the land became invisible. They found themselves in the centre of a vast circle of blue-green sea. The sky's blue dome covered the vast circle of the ocean. In the following days, no matter how much they advanced, they still remained rooted at the centre of the sea. They asked Hanuman how far they had to go still? He said they had probably done more than half. Luckily the causeway had widened now, requiring less refilling and repairs. After some days they sighted a grey patch on the horizon.

'There is Lanka!' yelled Hanuman; and they all began to dance in joy.

∽

They landed at the shore at last and Rama asked Vibhishan for their next move. He told him about a camping ground at some distance from the city fort. At dawn they said prayers to God Rudra and started for the camping site. A nimble stream flowed by the side of the camping site.

∽

Rama chose Angad, Vali's son, Vanara kingdom's heir apparent, to be his messenger to Ravana. He entered Ravana's court, bowed to him, said he was King Vali's son, emissary of Lord Rama, and said: 'As you see, O King of Lanka, King Sugriva's Vanara army has surrounded Lanka. But Lord Rama has no wish to massacre your people, for no fault of theirs. He doesn't want to make Lanka a city of widows. Your brother Vibhishan has aligned with Lord Rama, supporting his right cause. Lord Rama has sent me to convey to you that even now if you return Princess Sita, you could avoid your doom.'

Ravana gave a loud guffaw of laughter and giving Angad a withering look, said: 'But you should be on my side, Angad; Rama has killed your brave father and widowed your mother. Tell Rama, Sita is living here happily as my queen. Tell him not to commit the folly of rousing the lion in his den.' Angad left, saying: 'Oh King Ravana, I see Yama Doot hordes hovering over your head!'

The next morning, the Vanara Army attacked the main gate. The Rakshasas poured burning oil on them, frustrating them. In the meanwhile, the local chief of the Vanara village, Dhumraketu, came and paid his obeisance to Rama and Sugriva. He said their forefathers had come there from Kishkindha a few centuries back.

The next day Dhumraketu brought hundreds of his men, carrying swords. He also brought a physician Sushena to look after the wounded men. He knew a spot in the fort wall, where a peepal tree had come up in its crevices and the fort wall had crumbled. He showed it to Hanuman. Hanuman led his men over the damaged portion and returned after killing many unwary Rakshasa soldiers.

The doors of the fort opened the third day. The Lankan army marched out in full regalia, led by Meghnada in a chariot, flying a pennant. He saw Angad and threw a spear at him with full force. Rather than ducking, Angad advanced and caught the spear in his iron grip and hurled it back, killing Meghnada's charioteer. The horses turned in panic, taking Meghnada back into the fort.

The next day four Rakshasa commanders, Agniketu, Yajnakopa, Rashmiketu and Suptaghna came out, riding their horses. They advanced deep in the Vanara camp and found Rama sitting by himself. They closed in on him with flaming swords. Rama stood up then, turned around swiftly, and in a flash sent four arrows from his bow; their heads rolled on the ground.

Ravana was greatly worried, learning about the demise of

his four commanders; he told Meghnada about it. Meghnada remembered he had a special set of darts, doused in deadly serpent venom, which were lethal and killed instantly. The next morning, in the darkness before dawn, slinging the quiver of poison arrows, he entered the Vanara camp and saw Rama and Lakshman standing on a small hillock, looking the other way. He stopped the chariot, invoked goddess Nikumbhila and sent a volley of shafts at them. Both brothers fell down, giving a shrill cry. He quickly came back and gave the news to his father of wounding the two princes with the deadly *Naag-paash*. Ravana was overjoyed.

There was chaos in the Vanara camp. Rama and Lakshman had dropped down, losing consciousness. Their bodies were riddled with arrows and they had gone in a deathly slumber. Sushena removed the arrows carefully. He examined the arrows and found they were laced in snake poison.

He asked Hanuman to go at once to the Vanara village. There was a Devi temple on the nearby hill. Behind the temple, on the hillside, there were herbs with brown and purple flowers which were a sure cure for snake bite. 'Take one of Dhumraketu's men along with you to show the path. Go running and bring the herbs; there is no time to lose.'

Hanuman left with a young man. By noon they were at the top of the hill at the Devi temple and they found many herbs growing behind it, just as Sushena had said. They plucked those bearing brown and purple flowers, filled a bag with them and rushed back, reaching the Vanara camp in the afternoon. Sushena made a paste and gently rubbed it on the wounds on the princes' bodies. Rama woke up at first, looking about him in amazement. Lakshman woke up soon afterwards and shouts of joy filled the camp!

Sugriva praised Hanuman's feat: 'Hanuman is like the Ashvins, healing our Heroes, like the Maruts striding far and wide and swift like Usha's golden rays!' Hanuman retorted: 'But he needs something more solid than mere praise, my lord!' Sugriva smiled and brought a basket of fruits for him.

∽

Ravana's Army Commander Prahastha saluted him in the morning and asked who would lead the army in battle that day. Ravana was confused: 'Isn't the battle over? Haven't Meghanada's deadly snake-venom arrows killed the two brothers?'

'No, my lord, the princes are alive; they had only fainted.' Ravana was bewildered. *Naag-pash* arrows were always considered fatal. The certainties were getting shaken! Prahastha suggested that Dhoomraksh should lead the Lankan army that day. Ravana assented.

Hanuman saw general Dhoomraksh's elephant coming his way; his captains were following him on horse-back. Hanuman climbed a small hillock on the way, taking a few men along. They rolled down a huge boulder which hit the tuskar. Dhoomraksh jumped down. The next instant, Hanuman was on top of him, raining fisticuffs. He lay dead; his captains fled.

On hearing the sad news, Ravana sent Vajradanshtra, who came riding a chariot. Angad hurled a huge stone on the chariot's canopy, which crashed on Vajra's head. He jumped down and attacked Angad with his sword. Angad ducked low and caught both his feet firmly in his hands. Standing up, he struck Vajra's head upon a rock, and his head burst.

Ravana sent mighty Akampan then, who came riding his chariot from the western gate. Hanuman stood there with his mace in hand. He took a high jump, going over the horses and landed on the unwary coach-man's head. The horses bolted, the coach tilted and both the warriors came down. As Akampan unsheathed his sword, Hanuman swung his mace like a thunderbolt, breaking Akampan's ribcage. He slumped on the ground and Hanuman smashed his head. The sun was setting then.

∽

The next morning Prahastha asked Ravana the same question: 'Who is to lead the army in battle today, My Lord?' His defeatist demeanour irked Ravana. 'Why don't you go yourself?' he said. Prahastha stiffened and said: 'I'm honoured, my liege!'

He called his four commanders, asked Narantaka to accompany him and sent the other three to attack from the other gates to launch a full-blast offensive from all sides.

Dwivida and Neela faced the Lankan army. Dwivida took on Narantaka. Roaring like a hungry lion, he jumped on his chariot and caught hold of Narantaka. Pulling him out of his chariot, he pummeled him with his fists. Neela confronted Prahastha but Prahastha's arrows prevented him from coming near. Disregarding the arrows, Neela made an astonishing jump and landed near Prahastha's chariot. Prahastha jumped down too, holding a lance and sliced Neela's forehead. Neela snarled like a wounded tiger, pounced upon Prahastha and made mincemeat of his head. The coachman fled with the chariot.

~

Ravana was shaken, hearing of Prahastha's demise and his army's rout. He went to Saudamini's place. Saudamini too had changed—from hating him enough to kill him, she had come to feel pity for him. She was dying of curiosity for the news. She brought him a flask, full of *sura* to drink, which he downed in quick gulps. He made love to her then but she could see his heart wasn't in it.

While coming back Ravana went to his brother Kumbhakarna's palace. Kumbhakarna was corpulent, podgy and indolent—a huge, happy-go-lucky man. He loved to eat, drink and sleep. Ravana told him about his army-commander Prahastha's demise. He then praised Kumbhakarna's valour, told him there was none in the world who could face him in battle, and asked him to lead the Lankan army the next day 'Make mincemeat of the Vanara hordes and kill the two brothers!'

~

The next morning, Kumbhakarna entered the battlefield like a tornado striking the sea coast. No boulder, no tree, no spear hindered his advance; he pulverized the Vanara hosts. His mace was like a thunderbolt and his lance a rod of flaming fire. Angad rallied the group commanders—Dwivida, Mainda, Gandhamadan, Nala and Neela, and they the attacked him jointly. But it was to no avail; they could as well have showed gumption against a volcanic eruption!

Hanuman then charged at him in anger, and challenged him to a duel. Kumbha jumped down from his chariot and they grappled, growling and grunting, their maces clanging, emitting sparks. Hanuman hit his hand that held the mace, which fell down. Kumbha then took up his lance and lunged at Hanuman, piercing his chest. Hanuman groaned, vomiting blood. Sugriva challenged Kumbha then, but Kumbha hit him with a bludgeon.

Lakshman came forward then, shooting arrows at him. Kumbha had been fighting the whole day; the day was drawing to a close. He avoided Lakshman and asked his charioteer to drive on—to meet Rama.

He saw Rama, holding his bow in his hand; Vibhishan was standing beside him. Kumbha held his lance aimed at Rama, as his horses raced towards him. Rama sent a shower of arrows at him which hit the horses.They whined in pain and lifted up their front feet. The chariot lurched and Kumbha was shaken, but he threw his lance at Rama with full force. Rama's arrow cut it in mid-air. Kumbha jumped down and charged at Rama, brandishing his mace. Rama chopped off his hand. Howling like a wounded boar, Kumbha advanced holding a huge tree branch in his other hand. Rama sliced his other hand too. Kumbha then flew at him like a fiend. Rama fired an *Agneyastra* at him. Cutting through his gold armourand his rib-cage; it pierced his heart. Kumbha fell on the earth, emitting a piercing shriek.

∽

Ravana personally supervised Kumbha's funeral. As Kumbha's sons lit the pyre, Ravana saw Agni's feisty tongues licking and greedily devouring Kumbha's ghrita-soaked body. Ravana couldn't contain his tears. Ravana's four sons, Trishira, Atikaya, Devantaka and Narantaka consoled him: 'It doesn't behove you, Sire,' Trishira said to him, 'to lament so. Uncle Kumbha has laid down his life, fighting for Lanka's honour. Have no worry, we four brave sons of yours will lead the Lankan army to victory tomorrow.' Atikaya, Devantaka and Narantaka yelled in joy at the prospect of a real fight!

Ravana repaired to Saudamini's place. She dozed off after

they had made love. But sleep had deserted him. He kept tossing and turning in the bed, then woke her up and said: 'I had always suspected Saudamini, that Yama and Agni were friends. Yet I never knew they were so cheek by jowl! It has dawned on me now that if Yama wanted to go on leave, old Agni would begin to howl!' Saudamini was puzzled, hearing him rave. 'What are you talking about?' she asked. 'Haven't you gone to sleep?'

~

The four scions of Ravana—Trishira, Atikaya, Devantaka and Narantaka—clad in glittering armour, came out the next morning followed by the rank and file of the army. Angad rolled down a huge boulder and killed Narantaka's horse. Narantaka came down and with his axe and made a gash on Angad's chest. Angad pounded his chest with his mace; Narantaka collapsed in a heap.

Trishira, Devantaka and Mahodara, their uncle, closed in on Angad. They attacked him with spears. Hanuman and Nala came rushing like wind. Hanuman landed a crushing blow of his mace on Devantaka's head. Trishira tried to hit Hanuman with a dreadful missile, who took it on his mace and broke it in pieces. Trishira unsheathed his sword then, but Hanuman snatched it and severed his head. Mahodara rained his arrows at Angad, who threw his lance at Mahodara, piercing his rib-cage, and he collapsed.

Atikaya was well-versed in archery. He moved in his chariot like a hurricane, leaving a trail of wounded Vanara soldiers. Lakshman challenged him, his arrows grazing Atikaya's forehead. But Atikaya's shafts severely wounded Lakshman. Enraged, Lakshman sent an arrow, aiming at Atikaya's neck. Atikaya's severed head, adorned with his bejewelled crown, rolled on the ground.

~

The bodies of the four princes and uncle Mahodara were laid in the royal cremation ground the next day. Their wives came beating their breasts; their shrieks rending the skies. Ravana came looking deranged, muttering: 'All my four cubs dead? How bravely had the babes babbled? And knowing full well, I hurled them into Yama's bottomless belly!'

Meghnada came forward then, wiped tears from his father's face and said: 'I'll again invoke Devi Nikumbhila tonight, offer her a special feast through Agni to propitiate her. And in the twilight hour, before daybreak, launch a surprise attack and kill Rama'.

Saudamini saw Ravana's ashen face when he came looking sick, exhausted and worn-out. Sitting by her side, holding her hand, he murmured, half in a trance: 'The kids are dead, Saudamini—all four of them!' She couldn't help sympathizing with him. She sat beside him, took his hand in hers and looked into his misty, morose eyes. Suddenly, lightening flashed in the sky. Ravana rushed out to the open terrace. There was a shattering blast of lightening. He left in falling rain, his hair flying in the wind. Saudamini sat brooding—she didn't know whether to be sad or sing and dance!

~

In the dead of night, as lightening seared the sky and wind whined, Meghnada held a solemn sacrifice in the yard of the Nikumbhila shrine, on top of the hill. A massive buffalo was tethered in a corner. A priest sprinkled holy water on the bull and applied a red tilak on its head. Meghnada held a huge axe in both his hands joined together, and brought it down on the buffalo's neck with full force. The head fell down as the bull collapsed.

Meghanada came to the vedi again after washing the blood stains and sat on a high golden seat near the vedi, and began giving grita-ahuti in the blazing fire, as the priests began chanting mantras. In the meanwhile, the ribs and other limbs of the buffalo were being prepared for oblation and were being brought to the head priest. Meghnada began offering them to Agni and to other gods through Agni. The vedi flames rose high, the sacred fumes filled the temple yard. At the end of the sacrifice, the head priest gave a portion of the havya to Prince Meghnada and then distributed the havya to the assembled men, whereafter they all left.

The midnight hour was nigh. Only the head priest and his two assistants remained in the temple yard now. They moved now into the sanctum sanctorum of goddess Nikumbhila. A man clad in black apparel was brought there. Terror was writ large on his shaven face. The head priest sprinkled holy water on his head, applied red tilak on his forehead, dropped a garland of marigold flowers around his neck and then bowed before him in reverence. Thereafter the priest covered the man's head in folds of red satin cloth.

Meghnada took a bejewelled sword in his hand then. As the head priest sounded the gong and blew the trumpet, Meghnada struck at the blind-folded man's neck. The severed head fell at the Devi's feet. It was washed clean and placed at the feet of the goddess in a gold platter. Meghnada went down on his knees and sought goddess Nikumbhila's blessing for victory.

In that dark and stormy night, as lightening rent the sky, Vibhishan came to Rama and Lakshman's log-hut and told them of the occult rites being performed by Meghnada in goddess Nikumbhila's shrine, offering human sacrifice to her and seeking victory in the battle. He stood in silence for a few moments then, and said: 'If he completes the gory rites, My Lord Rama, Meghnada would become invincible.' He advised that Prince Lakshman should raid the shrine at midnight and disrupt his sacrifice.

Rama smiled at Vibhishan's suggestion and said: 'Dear Vibhishan, we have been protecting sages, who were holding yajna-sacrifice, and were killing your tribe who came to disrupt them. Now you are asking us to disrupt a sacred rite being performed in yajna?'

Vibhishan replied, 'It is not an ordinary yajna-sacrifice, My Lord! Meghnada is performing a human sacrifice.' 'All the same,' said Rama,'we won't interfere in a religious rite. However, let's be ready for Meghnada's morning raid at us.'

After performing sacrifice at the Nikumbhila shrine on the hill, riding a chariot drawn by four white steeds, Meghnada raided Rama's camp, as the golden orb of the rising sun greeted him. The Vanara chieftains were ready but his arrows hit them hard. He wounded Angad, Sugriva, even Hanuman. Lakshman challenged him then and showered arrows at him. Meghnada had kept his Brahmastra ready for him; it pierced Lakshman's rib cage and Lakshman fell like a tree scorched by lightening. Meghnada advanced towards Rama and pinned him down with another Naag-paash. Thrilled at his achievement, Meghnada hurried back to the safety of Lanka's fort.

At the beginning of the battle when Meghnada had wounded Rama and Lakshman with Naag-paash, vaidya Sushena had asked Dhumraketu to transplant the life-saving herbs like *Vishalyakarni* and *Mrit-Sanjeevani* in a verdant patch near his hut in the camp and had assiduously nurtured them. He carefully removed the arrows from Rama and Lakshman's chests, washed the wounds and then applied a paste of the herbs on their wounds. Rama revived soon but Lakshman's wound was deeper, causing great loss of blood. Hanuman too had recovered by now; he brought the other wounded Vanaras to Sushena's hut and got them treated.

The whole night, Rama sat beside Lakshman's bed, holding his hand, minding his pulse. Indeed, it was Lakshman who had become Rama's protector, provider and chef, all rolled into one. He would keep awake in the night, guarding their hut, sleeping only in snatches. Leaving his own wife behind in Ayodhya, he had suffered untold hardships for Rama and Sita's sake. It occurred to Rama that what he and Sita did was just to tread the path of Dharma, by obeying his royal father's command, but no tenet of Dharma had ever prescribed what Lakshman did—forsaking his wife and willingly adopting a punishing lifestyle for himself undertaking such perilous tasks for their sake!

The rosy rays of Usha were streaking across the sky when Lakshman stirred. Rama called him softly and he opened his eyes, as if coming out of deep sleep. As he got up, Rama took him in his arms, pressing him close to his heart, ruffling his hair. The Vanara hordes gave a loud shout of joy!

~

Meghnada was dumbstruck when he learnt that both Rama and Lakshman had bounced back to life after being apparently dead. He was at his wit's end. He thought of a diabolical plan then. He got a pretty young woman dressed exactly like Sita in soiled garments, and after the close of fight at dusk the next day, he brought her in his chariot inside the Vanara camp.

Hanuman froze seeing Sita, recognizing her as he had seen her in Ashok Vatika. The chariot was moving at a leisurely pace, not charging in battle order. The Vanara chiefs had collected there, and Meghnada declaimed: 'Look, O Vanaras, I am killing Sita, here and now—removing the main cause of this fight.'

He caught the woman's unwashed hair in one hand, held his sword in the other, and yelling in anger, sliced the woman in two. The woman shrieked as half her body dropped down on the chariot's floor. Meghnada carried her corpse away in the fort.

They told Rama about this horrific act, who was deeply distressed at Sita's demise. But Vibhishan told him that he would rather believe in the ocean drying up than give any credence to Sita being slain. 'My Lord Rama, none can dare touch Sita, let alone harm her in any way. Devi Sita is not dead; it's Meghnada's diabolic design to dishearten and disarm you. He is a known trickster. He has mesmerized Hanuman and the chiefs in the evening shadows by killing some woman like her.' Rama's face brightened; Vibhishan's words had a ring of truth. If it was true and Sita had been slain, he thought, Meghnada would have left her dead body behind.

Vibhishan informed him that Meghnada had again gone up to Devi Nikumbhila's shrine and was performing occult rites again. 'I shudder, My Lord Rama, what havoc he might wreak on us in the morning! Do think of preventing the completion of the rites.'

Rama gave a soft smile and said: 'Dear Vibhishan, yajna is not black magic or sorcery. It's a way of saying prayers, not a deal or transaction. However, there is merit in surprising Meghnada, in engaging him in battle when he is not prepared for it. Lakshman will not interrupt the yajna. He will only challenge Meghnada when he comes out of the shrine.' He turned to Lakshman then, and said: 'Dear Lakshman, don't force Meghnada if he is resentful or is unwilling to fight. But take him on if he consents.'

~

Meghnada again organized an elaborate midnight sacrifice before the goddess and came out of the shrine at day break. He saw Vibhishan in battle armour with Lakshman. He shouted at his uncle and called him an enemy of their race. Lakshman told him, they would not fight if he was unwilling. Meghnada turned to him and said: 'Yama had twice spared your life, Lakshman; you can't escape now!'

They began showering arrows at each other. Lakshman's arrows skidded against Meghnada's golden armour and he began trying to pierce through the seams in the armour. But the sun's glare was blinding Lakshman and Meghnada's arrow brushed his forehead; blood began trickling into his eyes. Vibhishan came to his rescue by hitting the horses of Meghnada's chariot with his mace. The horses bolted. Meanwhile Lakshman had moved away from the sun's glare and fired arrows with greater precision. Meghnada hurled a spear at Vibhishan but Lakshman splintered it mid-air. Vibhishan's mace hit the charioteer, who fell down and the horses ran helter-skelter.

Lakshman steadied himself and could breach Meghnada's armour at a few places. Meghnada lost his balance and jumped down and began shooting arrows at Lakshman in desperation. Lakshman aimed an Agneyastra at his heart which hit the target, and Meghnada collapsed with a shriek. The Rakshasa commanders were aghast, seeing the prince fall. They fled in terror, carrying his blood-smeared body.

Rama saw the jubilant Vanara hoards returning. Hanuman brought Lakshman on his shoulders as he was badly bruised. But Lakshman was beaming in joy. Rama enclosed him in his arms. Vibhishan said: 'My Lord Rama, Prince Lakshman has slain Meghnada!'

Vaidhya Sushena came running and attended to Lakshman's wounds.

~

Ravana trembled like a leaf in the wind, seeing Meghnada's body. His eyes froze in horror and a hoarse, shrill cry escaped his throat. Mandodari's shrieks rent the air. 'I had told you, My Lord, to give up Sita, but you never heeded me. Now you have lost all your sons, brothers and cousins. Send her back even now, My Lord!' Ravana's blood-shot eyes glared in anger. He got up and said: 'You are right, Mandodari. Sita is the root of all this trouble. I'll dispatch her at once.'

He drove to Ashoka Vatika. Sita sat under the tree, near the little pond and saw him coming, sword in hand. She was not unprepared for death. She knew from Trijata that the battle was going against him, that he was losing his sons and brothers. But before dying she wanted to see Rama's face once and ask him to forgive her for the trouble she had given him.

Ravana's ministers ran after him and implored him to desist from the foul deed: 'You are so learned, Lord, how can you kill a woman? It's a grievous sin!' Ravana sheathed his sword and turned back.

~

Saudamini's attendants told her about Prince Meghnada's demise. She knew he'd come that night and waited. She saw footprints of grief on his mask-like face and discerned furrows of deep dread. She brought him a flask of sura, which he gulped down, and asked for something stronger. She brought him toddy, the potent local brew, which he drank in large draughts. Saudamini brought some more toddy.

Ravana asked her why was she not drinking; she filled a glass of wine for herself. Ravana took his glass to her lips, touched them and toasted effusively. 'Let's celebrate Saudamini; this might be our last night together!'

He disrobed her then and they made love.

He turned and went to sleep then, but sleep evaded Saudamini. She marvelled at her own transformation from an unruly tigress, being mated against her will, to a compliant concubine. What changed her perhaps was his reversal—when the ocean gave way to Rama's army, which laid a siege on Lanka, turning Ravana from a lion to a rat trapped in a hole. Ravana woke up after a while, softly caressed her hair, taking her to be asleep, removed his pearls and jewels, placed them on the bed and quietly left.

~

In the morning, Ravana led his army from the high northern gate. Sugriva and Angad were at the head of the Vanara army. He asked his generals to engage them and proceeded ahead. He saw Rama and Lakshman standing on a hillock and advanced towards them followed by his men mounted on tuskers and horses. It was like the malefic planets, Rahu and Ketu, going to smother the Sun and Moon.

Ravana sent a volley of specially crafted arrows in his royal smithies, with heads of lions, tigers, bears and boars, releasing a whole menagerie. Raising their ugly heads, the arrows came hissing, but Rama and Lakshman cut down most of them and they fell, shamefaced, licking the dust. Lakshman's arrows struck at Ravana's banner and another cut down his bow. Nonplussed, Ravana took up another bow from his chariot.

Vibhishan joined the fray then and began pounding Ravana's horses with his mace. Ravana's blood boiled. He hurled a formidable Shakti spear at him, but Lakshman cut it down mid-air. Infuriated, Ravana sent a more lethal Shakti spear at Lakshman, which hit him and he fell down. The Shakti had breached Lakshman's armour, wounding him. Rama's pent-up anger against Ravana welled up and he let loose a volley of sharp arrows at him. Ravana fled in terror, followed by his mounted men.

Rama turned to Lakshman then. Blood was oozing out from his chest. Lakshman had been wounded many times and Rama began to worry about him. Vaidhya Sushena came running. He washed Lakshman's wound and applied balm. He felt his pulse and saw that his facial aura was undimmed. He assured Rama that there was no cause for worry. Some time later, Lakshman revived and Rama hugged him close. Sushena gave him a fruit drink and advised rest.

Angad had killed Mahaparshva and Sugriva had slain Virupaksha. The Vanara forces were upbeat and awaited Ravana's return. They saw a chariot coming from the countryside, drawn by four black horses. Strangely, it flew Ayodhya's pennant. Rama was puzzled like everyone else. Dhumraketu alighted from it and bowed to Rama and Lakshman, Sugriva, Angad and Hanuman. He had also brought carts, loaded with meat and fruits.

He addressed Rama: 'My Lord Rama, this chariot that you see, has been made by my Vanara craftsmen. It troubled us that while Ravana and his generals fought riding their chariots, you had to fight without a mount. We know that your valour needed no accoutrements and you don't need a chariot to kill Ravana. But our craftsmen have been making the royal chariots of Lanka; they have hurriedly fabricated this chariot for you, working through nights, out of their high regard and love for you. We would feel greatly honoured if you accept it.'

Rama stood up, embraced Dhumraketu, and said: 'I am overwhelmed, dear Dhumraketu, I don't know how to thank you and your men for this wonderful gift. Indeed, I had forgotten I was a prince; you have restored my dignity. As a matter of fact, I needed the chariot—to prevent Ravana from escaping when it got too hot for him. He is going to get the shock of his life, seeing me riding a chariot. I can see, it's really a work of art! Indeed, I'm going to take it to Ayodhya, with Sita and Lakshman in it.'

Rama mounted the chariot; Dhumraketu's brother Agniketu, acted as charioteer. Rama taught him a few manoeuvers and told him not to be afraid. 'I will protect you from danger!'

Some time later, Ravana came riding another chariot. He was perplexed and greatly cut up seeing Rama riding a chariot and flying a pennant like a king. Rama sent his arrows targeting Ravana's head, while Ravana threw a three-pronged spear at him. Rama also threw a spear, which clashed with the trident mid-air and broke it. Rama and Ravana then sprayed each other with shining, flaming arrows, which looked like darts of lightening from the clouds. Achieving precision in moving chariots was hard as the two warriors were chasing each other in a circle at full speed.

Rama had been badly bruised with nicks and cuts on his face. Ravana too was bruised; blood was spilling from the vents in his armour. The sun had gone behind thick clouds in the horizon and daylight had dimmed. Twilight augured well, Rama thought, and mused: 'He is fumbling and faltering; I have to go for his neck, his jugular.'

He sent five arrows in quick succession; one grazed Ravana's temple. Ravana began sending wild shots at Rama. Rama then took out the Brahmastra gifted to him by Rishi Agastya. It went like a thunderbolt, struck Ravana's chest and pierced his heart.

Ravana gave a piercing shriek and fell down on the ground with a loud thud. Ravana's charioteer was horrified and terror striken; he bolted, taking away the chariot. Ravana's generals and the Rakshasa army deserted the battlefield.

The golden orb of the setting sun peeped out of the clouds, making Rama's face glow. Rama got down from the chariot and took Lakshman in a long embrace. He embraced Sugriva, Vibhishan, Angad, Hanuman, Dhumraketu and his brother Agniketu. Sushena came, wiped the blood stains from his face and other part of his body, applied the healing balm and gave him a drink.

Vibhishan went near Ravana's blood-smeared body, lying in dust, abandoned. He touched his brother's feet, stood in silence for a while, and returned to Rama's cottage. He sprawled on the ground then and clutched Rama's feet in reverence, happy beyond words. Rama told him to take Ravana's body home and said: 'Dear Vibhishan, let Ravana's body lie in state for people to see and pay their last respects. Perform customary rites and cremate him with full state honours.'

Vibhishan replied that Ravana was cruel, lusty and evil; he coveted beautiful wives of others and had abducted Devi Sita, inflicting such torture on her, and added: 'Although he was my brother, he had become my biggest enemy; I would not perform his last rites.' Rama smiled and said, he felt the same, but the enmity died with the man. 'Go and do as I say.'

Turning to Lakshman then, he said: 'Come Lakshman, let's bring Sita. I wonder if someone has given her the news!' He asked Hanuman to show the way. Agniketu drove the chariot.

Dusk had fallen. The guards at Ashok Vatika opened the gates for Rama's chariot. Sita sat under the tree near the pond. Ducks quaked in excitement and peacocks, roosting in trees, called in chorus, 'Piyu! Piyu!' The monkeys jumped up to higher branches. There was commotion all around.

Sita's heart missed a beat, seeing Rama emerge on her dark horizon! She ran towards him and threw herself into his open arms. She clutched him in a tight embrace, writhing uncontrollably as tears flooded her eyes. Rama squeezed her frail, trembling body to his heart. He wiped her tears, smoothed her hair, kissed her wet eyes and sunken cheeks, and said: 'I have killed him today, Seete! Your tormentor lies licking dust, in a pool of blood.' Sita clung to him, gazing at his face, her fingers exploring the contours of his face.

Her words came faltering through her sobs: 'Will you forgive me, My Lord? I gave you so much trouble! But I knew you'd come and save me.' She saw Lakshman then and said: 'Will you forgive me, Dear Lakshman? How I hurt you, by saying those cruel words to you!'

Vibhishana came then. Rama introduced him to Sita. He requested Rama to stay for a few days in Lanka. Rama thanked him and said: 'I am under a pledge of Vanavaas, as you know; I cannot stay in any city before my exile ends.'

Turning to Lakshman then, he said: 'Dear Lakshman, we are already in the month of *Magha*. After the next month of *Falguna*, in *Chaitra* the new year dawns. At the commencement of Chaitra, the term of my banishment ends. We have to hurry and head for home. We have a long way to go!'

∽

There was celebration in the camp. Vibhishana sent casks of wine from the royal stores. The Vanara hordes lighted many fires, sang songs and danced. Dhumraketu and Agniketu brought carts full of food and joined the victory festivities.

Rama held Sita's hand and led her into the cottage. She flung herself on him, clutching him tight, entwining him, moaning, sniffling, sobbing, running her hand on his body, as if trying to convince herself it was real. Rama tried to calm her by his caresses, uttering words of endearment. Her sobs would subside for a while, but soon the tide of her tears would surge afresh and she would snuggle up and press herself closer to him. Rama slipped his hand under her garments but she recoiled, turning herself into a ball. She wouldn't come close even for a kiss. She calmed down by and by; Rama went to sleep holding her in his arms.

It was still dark when Rama woke up; she had gone to sleep

in his arms. He began rubbing her back gently and softly touching her shrivelled breasts. She woke up and clung close to him, her hand going over his face, his back and his hips. He undressed her slowly, smothering her in kisses. She lifted her leg and entwined with him, and their bodies mingled in love.

∽

Ravana was cremated the next day. Rama asked Lakshman to go and install Vibhishan on Lanka's throne. King Sugriva, Angad and Hanuman, the Vanara chiefs, Dhumraketu and Agniketu, all attended the coronation ceremony. Rama and Sita stayed in the camp, relating the events to each other.

Vibhishan escorted them in the royal barge to Rameshwaram, taking their chariot along. The Vanara army walked back sprightly on the Rama Setu. On reaching the shore Rama prayed to the sea. They travelled then to Kishkindha in chariots. Vibhishan, Sugriva and Hanuman wanted to see Rama's coronation in Ayodhya and accompanied them.

∽

They sighted the new moon of Chaitra on reaching Shringaverapur. In two more days, the exile would end, thought Rama. It occurred to him that Bharat had been ruling all these years; he might be upset about the change. He asked Hanuman to go to Ayodhya and meet Bharat and gauge the state of his mind.

Hanuman went in a chariot next morning and reached Nandigram in the evening, where Bharat was staying. Dressed like a Brahmin, he went to Bharat's thatched cottage. The sentry took him in. Bharat sat on a mat of kusha grass. Hanuman bowed to him and asked: 'Are you the king of Ayodhya?'

'No. The king is away', Bharat replied. 'I am just looking after the work. What can I do for you?'

'I have come from far away to watch Prince Rama's coronation after his exile, which is ending now. But I found no signs of the impending coronation in the city, no welcome arches, festoons or buntings; it appears Prince Rama has been forgotten.'

Bharat was pained at his words and said: 'The Sarayu may

forget to flow, Vipra Deva, the Sun may forget to rise, but Ayodhya shall never forget Rama! Fourteen years ago, there were festive arches, people waited outside the palace to see his coronation. The throne was rightfully his, according to hallowed tradition. But he was exiled and he left without a word of displeasure or protest to honour his royal Sire's word.

'"Forgotten Prince Rama," did you say? Never! We are waiting for his return with baited breath. But he seems to have forgotten us, he has sent us no word, no message; he is punishing us for the sin we have committed against him!' His voice was choked with tears.

Hanuman could carry the act no further. He prostrated before Bharat and said: 'Sir, I am Hanuman, Lord Rama's messenger.' Bharat stood up and embraced Hanuman. Hanuman briefly narrated the events of Lanka to Bharat and returned in the evening to Shringaverapur.

∽

The royal charioteer Sumantra brought the state couch next morning, flying the dynasty's pennant. Bharat, Shatrughna, guru Vasishtha stood at Ayodhya's main gate in welcome. Rama bowed to Vasishtha and embraced Bharat and Shatrughna. Sita and Lakshman then bowed to Vasishtha and met the brothers, who were overjoyed. Rama introduced Sugriva, Vibhishan and Hanuman to them. Bharat could not contain his tears, though he knew it was inauspicious.

People crowded the streets, shouting in joy. The mothers, Kaushalya, Sumitra and Kaikeyi, welcomed them at the palace gates. Rama and Sita touched mother Kaushalya's feet. Kaushalya held Rama in her embrace, tears of joy flooding her eyes. Sumitra took Lakshman in her arms. He saw Urmila standing beside her and squeezed her in his arms, making her go red in the face. Rama bowed to Kaikeyi too, who placed her hand on his head in benediction.

Sage Vasishtha announced that it was time for the coronation. Bharata escorted Rama and Sita to the golden throne, carved with the Sun's emblem. Sage Vasishtha recited Rama's genealogy starting from Ikshvaku, applied tilak on his forehead and anointed him by sprinkling holy water and placed the crown on his head.

Vibhishana and Sugriva went back in a few days but Hanuman stayed on in Ayodhya.

(It struck me that Rama and Lakshman were probably the first Indians, who went on foot from Shringaverapur, on the Ganga, to Rameshwaram at the southern tip of the Indian subcontinent, after crossing the Vindhya mountains. Their father's chariot had taken them to Shringaverapur. The rest they had taken in their stride.)

Sita had become a pale shadow of her former radiant self but began to revive in the sunshine of Rama's presence and love. As she loved the outdoors rather than remaining confined in the palace rooms, Rama got a new garden with a lotus pool laid out, adjacent to the king's palace. Sita got a swing hung from a mango tree's branch. One day Rama brought a baby deer. Sita named her 'Maya' and played with her, running after her to catch her.

Mandavi and Shrutikirti came bringing their sons, Taksha and Shubha. Urmila came one day and whispered to her that she had conceived. Sita was happy at the news; how Urmila had suffered in Lakshman's absence!

In the month of Ashvin, six months after they had returned home, Sita missed her periods; she knew she had conceived. A strange gladness filled her; she felt she was soaring in the sky!

Some days later Rama told her that he was passing by the royal fields, where he had done the ceremonial ploughing in the month of *Bhadrapada*, and was happy to see that green shoots had come up in the furrows, which gave promise of a plentiful crop. Sita blushed at the mention of sowing. Playfully arching her eyes, she said that she knew of another little royal field he had been sowing assiduously. That field too was showing promise of bearing fruit and would not require any sowing for the time being.

Rama grabbed her, sensing her meaning, and rained kisses on her. 'What shall we name him?' he asked touching her belly. Sita replied, 'You know, I was found in a furrow by King Janak, who named me "Sita"—a furrow. He'll come out of the furrow, like the sacred kusha grass.' 'Yes,' said Rama, 'we'll name him "Kusha".'

∽

Rama used to wander incognito in the city in the night, dressed as a workman sometimes, after Sita had gone to sleep, to gather first-hand information about life in Ayodhya. One dark night he went to a street near the river. Most houses had put out their lights; the street was deserted. But he heard cries of a woman coming out of a house at the end of the street. From its open window, he saw a man kicking his young wife viciously and hurling abuses on her. 'Why did you go to that man in my absence?' he was questening her. She was lying on the floor, wailing piteously. Rama could make out that the man suspected her of infidelity as she had gone to another's house in his absence and she was denying the charge.'I'll kill you, hussy', he said, 'if you go near him again. Understand? I am not Rama who took Sita back after she had lived in Lanka with Ravana.'

Rama was stunned at the man's words. He walked back, greatly troubled in mind and quietly crept into his bed. Sita was in deep sleep. He drew her to himself and enclosed her in his arms. The man's words haunted him the whole night, tormenting him. Sita had told him a few days back that her pet had grown big now and had begun to trouble her a lot. She did not want to remain within the four walls of the palace; she probably missed the company of deers. Sita had added that she herself felt cramped and confined and would like to go to a rishi's ashram for a while, where she could take Rohini, a maid King Janak had brought with him one day. Rohini had earlier come to Chitrakoot with him. Sita remembered her and liked her. Rama thought Rishi Valmiki lived in his ashram on the banks of the Tamasa, beyond the river Sarayu; Sita could stay there until delivery.

He called his brothers in conference the next morning and told them there was unease in people's mind about Sita's chastity. Lakshman vehemently rubbished the report. Rama told them about his night vigil and said, 'You cannot shut people's mouth.' 'That's true, Arya,' Lakshman said, 'but you know that she is pure like

Usha's rays, which rise from the womb of darkness; like the lotus flowers emerging from slush! It'd be grossly unjust to exile her just because of such gossip.'

'But widespread public sentiment', Rama replied, 'however misinformed, cannot be ignored. She survived the ordeal of her imprisonment in Lanka; she is made of sterner stuff. She would live for the child she is carrying. Indeed, she loves outdoors and has expressed a wish to visit a rishi's ashram. You take her near Rishi Valmiki's ashram on the bank of the Tamasa, Lakshman.'

His brothers opposed it, saying it was unwarranted and most unkind. Rama was unmoved. He told them they would have a house get-together in the evening with all the mothers and kids. 'Don't give any hint to anyone about it. I'll tell Sita also only in the morning, when you should come and say goodbye to her. Lakshman would then conduct her near the ashram.'

Lakshman brought the king's chariot next morning. Sita was most excited; she was taking Maya along and held her leash. She had also brought a box full of silks and ornaments for rishi-wives and ashram inmates. Rama, Bharat, Shatrughna and the three sisters came to say adieu. Rama held her close, running his fingers through her hair, feeling the contours of her face. She blushed crimson in embarrassment. Bharat and Shaturghna were on the verge of tears.

Sita loved chariot rides, the tingling rush of cool air on her face. Maya was restive, wanting to jump out. Sita had great difficulty keeping her in control, and fastened her tight to the couch. They forded the Sarayu at a shallow spot and reached the Tamasa late in the afternoon. Two men were waiting there with a boat at the bank.

Lakshman unharnessed the horses, patted their backs and gave them grains to eat. The boatmen were hesitant to take the deer on board; they took a third man to hold her. Lakshman too got into the boat and helped Sita alight at the other bank. The boatmen placed her chest near her. Joining his hands in supplication, Lakshman begged her leave to return to Ayodhya.

She was surprised and asked, 'Aren't you coming to the ashrama? You could go back tomorrow?' He broke down, saying nothing. 'What's the matter, Lakshman?' She was puzzled. He replied: 'The King, my brother, has sent me on a cruel mission; to leave you here at the river.'

'Leave me here? What do you mean?' Sita asked.

Lakshman's voice was tremulous: 'About two years back at Panchavati, I had stood before you in like manner, unwilling to leave you. I face a similar dilemma today, forced to leave you here against my will!' He couldn't contain his tears.

Sita was beginning to understand. It dawned on her then that Rama had exiled her to the rishi's ashram. The tearful farewell by Bharat and Shatrughna and her sisters in the morning made sense now; she now understood why Rama had lingered, holding her in his arms. Lakshman bowed to her and got back into the boat. She stood there watching Lakshman go. Alighting from the boat, Lakshman harnessed the horses to the chariot. Before mounting it, he turned towards her again, joined his hands in distant salutation, bowed and drove away. The thread connecting her to Ayodhya had snapped!

~

Her mother had abandoned her at birth. She stood there holding Maya's reins. Involuntarily she felt her belly. A sudden dread struck her then; she had to take care of the unborn child and find the ashram soon. She had to take care of Maya too, who was a waif like her. She spied a plume of smoke curling up above the tree tops in the north. That must be the rishi's ashram, she surmised. Holding Maya's reins, she started going towards it. Some young boys caught up with her, they were carrying her trunk. 'Is it yours? It was lying at the river's bank.' She assented and asked them where was Rishi Valmiki's ashram. 'We are also going there', they told her.

She saw Valmiki sitting in his cottage on a deerskin. Giving Maya's reins to the boys, she bowed to him and sat on a mat in front of him. He asked who she was. All she said was: 'I am coming from Ayodhya; I need asylum.' He was amused to see the deer and asked her where had she got her. 'She is Maya; she lives with me.' He asked the boys to bring her water to wash. She washed her hands and feet, sprinkled water on her face and sat down, unleashing Maya. They brought her some fruits and gave her fresh milk to drink and readied a cottage for her. Maya was playing with the boys; Sita took the rishi's leave and went into the cottage. It was neat and tidy, cool and cozy. She dropped down on the bed and went to sleep.

In the morning she gave the gifts she had brought for the ladies residing in the ashram.

~

Janak was heartbroken hearing the news about Sita. He sent Shatananda in his royal chariot to Valmiki Ashram, asking him to bring Sita to Mithila. Rohini, Sita's nurse, took Shatananda's permission to go with him. On the fourth day they reached Valmiki Ashram. Valmiki was glad to see Shatananda and enquired about King Janak's wellbeing. Sita was glad to see he father's old Purohita.

Shatananda said King Janak had sent him to take her to Mithila. He added that the King had wanted to come himself, but his failing health did not permit it. Sita looked at Valmiki then and said: 'Baba's ashram is as good as my father's place; I receive the same love from Baba as from my father.' Valmiki nodded with a gentle smile.

Rohini greeted Sita and asked her permission to stay in her cottage and then spread her mattress on the floor near her bed.

Rohini was tired to the bone after her long, grueling journey from Mithila. But she wanted to tell Sita about the earthen pot which King Janak had found while doing ceremonial ploughing of the royal fields, which contained a newly-born babe—Sita. Indeed, she wanted to disclose to Sita that it was she who had buried the pot in the field, that she was her real mother! But Sita's even breathing indicated to her that she had gone off to sleep.

Rohini's mother Swati was a dasi (slave-girl) in Mithila's royal household. Janak's father, Hrishvaroma, was king then. Swati was very pretty; Hrishvaroma liked her and used to take her to bed occasionally. Rohini was born to her but she was not as pretty as her mother. Her mother died when she was in her teens, leaving her in the care of a senior maid, Sulochana, who was childless.

After Hrishwaroma's demise, his older son Janak ascended the throne. During Vasantotsava (Spring Festival) a young prince Kirtiratha, King Janak's distant cousin, came to Mithila. Rohini met Kirtiratha in the palace gardens. She wore a light pink dress and he was attracted to her. He threw colour on her and took her on swing rides. Swings were hanging from tall trees, young boys and girls were taking rides on them, yelling and cheering in joy, competing with each other in trying to touch high branches.

Kirtiratha took Rohini for a ride on a swing. They stood facing each other on the wooden foot-hold, holding the rope in their hands.He worked the swing, bending his feet, thrusting himself against her. She had never done a swing-ride before, but imitated him, bending her legs and thrusting herself against him, her hair flying. He was quite adept in the game and took the swing higher and higher which took her breath away. She felt dizzy; his body contact was sending her in delirium. When they got down, her cheeks were flushed, her hair dishevelled, her heart thumping. He told her she was beautiful—something no one had told her before!

Dusk had fallen. He took her into the woods beyond the lake. Late in the night, when she returned to their quarters in the palace, Sulochana was not there. She was relieved. The next evening, they again enjoyed the ride on the swing, but she refused to go to the woods. He promised to marry her next year and took her to his room. The Vasantotsava lasted a week. Swinging together and going into the woods became a routine. Kirtiratha left after the Vasantotsava.

Rohini discovered to her horror after some time that she had conceived. She told her 'mother' Sulochana about it, who was shocked, and said: 'He was a flirt and you have been very foolish. You should have never allowed it. We are slaves and they are royalty. No one will blame him for taking liberties with you.'

Rohini remained mostly indoors; keeping her secret to herself. Sulochana was proficient in midwifery. When her time came, she sat near her, massaging her. She also gagged her to muffle her cries. The baby came at midnight; it was a girl. Rohini wept inconsolably. 'How would I ever raise a girl? Her life, like mine, would be trash.' A wave of dejection overwhelmed her; tears streamed down her eyes.

Sulochana busied herself in post-natal chores, gave the baby some drops of honey to lick, wrapped her in a pink satin cloth. Then she washed Rohini clean, cleared the mess, put the baby to her breast and lay on her bed, exhausted. She had been up the whole night and slept like a log.

Rohini lay awake in the surrounding darkness, as the baby suckled her. Then she got up on sudden impulse, emptied an earthen pot, and wrapping the baby in extra cotton napkins, she put the baby in the pot and closed the lid. She came out from the servant's door, where there was no guard. It was a dark night; she went towards the fields. She saw a pit dug up for planting a sapling. She covered the pit with loose earth till about a foot, and put the earthen pot with the baby in it. A tear fell as she placed the pot in the pit. She returned to her room then, washed her hands and dropped dead on her bed.

As luck would have it, King Janak found the pot when he was ceremonially ploughing the furrows in the morning. He was childless; he brought the baby home and declared to the world that she was his daughter. He named her 'Sita', the furrow.

Rohini heard the news and thanked God. She was saved from committing an abominable sin. Her 'mother' Sulochana, who knew her secret, died the next year.

~

As Rohini lay in Sita's cottage, reminiscing about her dark deed, it struck her that she had abandoned her because she was a girl. No one ever abandoned a boy. A girl was a burden, a boy strength! Even god was unfair to girls; he made them weak in body and vulnerable. She now prayed to god to give Sita a boy. Rama might recall her then with joy.

Shatananda requested Sita again in the morning to go to Mithila. He added that the King, her father, and her mother Queen Sunayana, would be so dejected when they see him return without her.

Sita replied: 'O wise Shatananda, tell them that King Rama, my husband, had sent me here on my own wish to live in Baba's ashram for a while. But the love I have received here from Baba has made me want to linger here. Indeed, I love living in this earthly paradise! Give my father and mother my love and tell them I am... I'm very happy here; they needn't worry at all.'

Rohini came forward then and sought Sita's permission to allow her to stay there and serve her. She told her that she had no one in Mithila. Sita was happy; she asked Shatananda to leave her there.

Sita found a great companion in Rohini. But Maya had deserted her. Sita had taken Maya to the river bank, where a herd of deer came to drink water. A black buck came near her and started sniffing her. Maya was drawn to him and went with the herd, giving Sita a last, lingering look.

Sita often conversed with Valmiki, asking him about his experiences during his austerities and his meditations and about the nature of god. Valmiki too questioned her about her life experiences and the sages they had met in Dandkaranya. He had begun composing verses of the amazing story of Rama.

One night, Sita saw Maya in a dream. Sita patted her and Maya gestured her to follow her and led her to a cave. Water dripped from the cave's mouth. To Sita's surprise, she saw Rohini coming out of the cave with two baby fawns following her. Maya began to lick them. Sita also bent down to take Maya's fawns in her arms. The dream dissolved then. Sita was bathed in bliss, remembering the enchaning, vivid dream.

Dawn was breaking now; Rohini was waking up in her bed. Sita related the dream to her. Rohini said it was a good omen and asked her what did it convey to her. Sita replied: 'I really don't know, but I felt happy, dreaming it. I felt as if Maya was presenting those two kids to me, and that you had brought them in the world.'

∽

Sita's belly had bloated, stretching her skin. Rohini's gentle massage soothed her. She felt giddy sometimes and weak in the knees, or had a splitting headache. At a late hour one night forgoing sleep, Rohini was pressing her fevered temples, gently, ever so gently. Her face was faintly illumined by the wicker lamp. It soothed Sita and she said: 'How shall I ever repay your debt, Rohini? You are an angel!'

Hearing her words, Rohini broke down and replied: 'Don't call me an angel, O Queen; I am a sinner. I have sinned against you; I am only trying to atone my sins.' She began sobbing hysterically then.

'Sinned against me?' Sita couldn't understand and asked her. 'How have you sinned against me? I don't understand.'

Rohini told her the whole story then, in choked words and broken sentences. Sita got down from the bed and hugged her close, squeezed her tightly, saying: 'My Mother? O my mother; My own mother! Why didn't you tell me this before?' She wiped Rohini's tears. 'Indeed, I had a sense you were near me, keeping a vigil over me.' She crept beside her in her bed then, feeling like a little girl again, breathing in her scent.

Birds had begun chirping in the trees; a new dawn was breaking. Rohini said they had to keep pretenses and live as they had lived before, as the queen and her maid.

∽

A week later, her labour pains began. There was another lady in the Ashram, Madhavi, who knew midwifery and began attending to her. As her pain became unbearable, Sita told Madhavi that she was afraid. Madhavi gave a smile and replied: 'O Sweet Queen, we, women, are made to make children! It's our natural, God-given function. Have no worry at all, just relax; we are there to assist you. But don't you know, there are no midwives in nature. You actually don't need us.' Her words soothed Sita.

Pain simmered in her abdomen, rising in intensity and then

subsiding again. Towards midnight, there was a towering wave of pain that took her breath away. The release came in two spasms and the silence of the cottage was shattered by shrill baby-cries. She opened her eyes and saw Rohini and Madhavi both holding a baby each, proudly congratulating her: 'You have two sons; you are most fortunate!'

Sita thought of Maya and relapsed in sweet languor; a dreamy smile lingered on her face.

Rama was distraught after he exiled Sita and did not hold court for many days. Shatrughna came one evening and told him that a few days ago some sages had come from Madhura, on the banks of the Yamuna, where a daitya, Lavanasur, had created a reign of terror; they had been waiting to see him.

Rama heard them in his court the next morning. He told them that Ayodhya's territory was bounded by the Ganga, while Madhura was on the banks of the Yamuna. The sages replied: 'We know that, O mighty King, but you have earned renown in the world for exterminating Rakshasas, and the people of Madhura look up to you to safe-guard them.'

Rama looked at Vasishtha, who pleaded the sages' cause. Rama asked Shatrughna to take Hanuman and a part of the army, attack Lavanasur's fort and kill him, and rid the region of the Daitya's curse, and said: 'In the morning, I will anoint you as the King of Madhura.'

Shatrughna replied that he would leave in the morning with Hanuman and do his bidding. However, his anointing may be deferred till he returned after killing Lavanasur. Rama told him that killing of Lavanasur was not all, he had to stay on there, rebuild Madhura as a great city, establish order based on Dharma and win the confidence of people.

He anointed Shatrughna as King of Madhura next morning and they left. Hanuman came back after two months, bringing the happy news that Ayodhya's Kovidara flag now flew on Madhura, and valorous Shatrughna had extended the borders of the kingdom of Koshala.

~

In the meanwhile, after about a month of Sita's exile, Rama had sent his trusted spy, Bhadra, to go in the vicinity of Valmiki Ashram and bring Sita's news. Dressed like a wandering sage, Bhadra stayed for a couple of days at Valmiki Ashram. He came back and reported that she was living in the comfort of a cottage near Valmiki's cottage and was being looked after by the wives of other sages residing in the ashram.

~

After some time, the news of Kekaiyi's father Ashvapati's demise and crowning of her brother Yuddhajit was received. A month later Yuddhajit sent his messenger asking for help, as the wily Asuras had descended on his kingdom from the northeastern hills. Rama told Bharat to take his young sons, Taksha and Pushkal, and the army commander Jayant, and drive away the Asuras.

Bharat and his sons, assisted by a sizable part of Ayodhya's army, under the Army Commander Jayant, decimated the Asuras in a couple of years, extending the frontiers of Kekaiyadesh. Two new cities of Takshashila and Pushkalvat were established in the extended region, and in alliance with King Yuddhajit, Ayodya's Kovidara flag now flew on the icy heights of these cities.

Rama asked his chief spy Bhadra to go again to Valmiki Ashram for bringing Sita's news. He came back with the happy news of Sita giving birth to two sons and added that the babies and the mother were doing fine. On the pretext of celebrating Bharat and Shatrughna's victory, Rama called Lakshman, Urmila and the kids and had a gala celebration!

~

Kaushalya was ailing for some time. Rama went to see her one morning and put his hand on her forehead. She had gone frail and had fever. She opened her eyes and saw him; her sunken eyes beamed in joy. 'Rama, my child... I have been thinking of you... and... of Sita. You know... she has two boys.'

She remained silent for a while, as if to let it sink. 'How have you… changed… Rama?… How you… loved her once! You've … sent her… away!… What kind of… dharma… is this… my son? Bring her back… she is a Devi! She has suffered… so much… for you!'

She had a bout of coughing then. Sumitra, who was sitting beside her, rubbed her back. The Rajya-Vaidya rushed in from an anteroom; he administered some medicine which calmed her. She opened her eyes then, raised her hand and put it on Rama's head. Her eyes closed then.

That night she passed away in her sleep.

Rama's escapades for hunting in the woods came to a halt during the rains. Fourteen years ago, he had sent Sita in exile, which equalled Kaikeyi's term for his exile. It should end now, he thought. Besides, Bharat and Shatrughna had turned the kingdom of Ayodhya into an empire. A thought occurred to Rama: 'I should hold an Ashvamedha Yajna; it required the queen to slay the king's horse!'

Rishi Vasishtha had passed away; his son Suyagya Vasishtha had taken his place. Rama sought his advice about holding an Ashvamedha Yajna; Suyagya Vasishtha commended it.

Rama called Bharat from Girivraja and Shatrughna from Madhura. His black stallion was decked up in gold jewellery. The four brothers worshipped the horse at the yajna vedi. Accompanied by Hanuman, Lakshman escorted it to the northern and eastern regions, Shatrughna to the southern regions and Bharat to Girivraja in the west. Everywhere the horse went, the local kings honoured and venerated it. In the pleasant month of Chaitra Bharat brought the stallion back to Ayodhya—triumphant and unchallenged!

Suyagya Vasishtha invited celebrated rishis to Ayodhya. Rishi Valmiki came with fellow rishis; he also brought the boys Kush and Lava along with him. They stayed in cottages constructed on the Sarayu's bank along with other sages, who had arrived from far and wide.

Rishi Valmiki was composing the story of Rama. He had taught the boys, Kush and Lava, how to sing the verses. Before the assembly of the saints on the Sarayu's bank in the evening, he asked the boys to sing the verses relating to the two boons asked by queen Kaikeyi from King Dashratha, which had resulted in Rama's 14-year exile and coronation of Kaikeyi's son Bharat in his place. In the following verses Rama was called by Kaikeyi and told him that the King had awarded 14 years of exile to him and declared Bharat his successor and it was his duty to do the King's bidding. Rama replied:

Aham he vachanad Ragyah pateyamapi pavake,
Bhakshayeyam visham teekshnam pateyamapi charnave;
Niyukto guruna pitra nripena cha hiten cha,
Tad bruhi vachanam, Devi, Ragya yadabhi kankshitam;
Karishe pratigyan cha Ramo dwirnabhashte.

[At the King's command, I would jump into the fire, drink bitter poison, plunge into the sea. He is my Guru, my Father and my well-wisher. Therefore, Devi, tell me what is my father's wish; I promise, I will do it. Rama does not speak with a forked tongue!]

Sapta sapta cha varshni Dandakaranyam ashritah;
Abhishekmidam tyaktva jatacheerdharo bhava.

[For seven and seven more years, you take shelter in Dandaka forest, forgoing your coronation, wearing matted hair and bark clothes.]

Aivamastu gamishami vanam vastumaham twitah;
Jatacheerdharo Ragyah pratigya manupalayan.

[Let it be as you say, Mother, I take a pledge that I would repair to the forest, wearing sack cloth and matted hair, in accordance with the King's wishes.]

The *kil-kil* sound made by the fast-flowing waves of River Sarayu, the magic of Valmiki's composition and the musical voice of the tender-age boys, Kush and Lava, cast a spell on the assembled sages. Envelopped in the witchery of moonlight, they sat listening to Rama's words to Kaikeyi.

Rama, accompanied by his three brothers, went to the sages' camp to pay homage to them in the morning. Valmiki came out with the two boys and blessed Rama. Rama's heart missed a beat or two, seeing the boys. Valmiki told the boys: 'He is the King of Ayodhya, Rama.' They fell at his feet and he took them in his arms, one by one, pressed them close and inhaled their scent.

In the evening Rama called Lakshman to his chamber, told him to take the royal chariot in the morning, go to the Valmiki Ashram and give Sita his message: 'Even the gods make mistakes sometimes and punish an honest person for no fault; I am a mere man! Forgive me, my love, and come back home; I am eagerly looking forward to have a glimpse of your fair face!'

Lakshman started early next morning, forded the Tamasa, and reached Valmiki Ashram in the afternoon. Some boys came running towards him. He asked them about Sita, Princess of Mithila; they took him to her cottage. She had tears in her eyes when she came out. Lakshman bowed to her and asked why was she grieving. 'My mother died in the morning, Lakshman,' she told him. Lakshman couldn't understand it and asked: 'Your mother?' Sita narrated the whole story about her mother Rohini, and said: 'You have come at the right time, Lakshman. I was worried about her cremation, as Baba and others have gone to Ayodhya. Take help from these boys and take her body for cremation to the river bank.'

The coachman and the boys carried Rohini's body to the river bank, made a pyre and placed it on it. Lakshman lit the pyre and paid his homage by going around it. He bathed in the river then, and offered *jalanjali* to the departed soul. Om Shanti, Shanti, Shantihi!

The sun was setting when he returned to the ashram. Sita gave him some fruits to eat and asked him the purpose of his visit. Lakshman gave Rama's message: 'Arya Rama has asked me to convey his deep regret for the insult and cruelty he had inflicted on you. He said even the gods commit mistakes while he is just a man, and has asked your forgiveness. He has sent me to take you home, to rule over his heart and Ayodhya. He said he was dying to see you!'

A soft smile flickered on her face and she said: 'How I wish you had come yesterday, Lakshman, when my mother was alive. How happy she would have been! How ardently she had wished for it! But I can feel her presence around me; her soul would now rest in peace.'

∽

Rama waited restlessly in the evening, pacing up and down on the terrace. As the night advanced, he was worried. The hurt was too deep, he thought. 'I should have gone myself!' He couldn't sleep the whole night and set off next morning in another chariot. Midway, he saw the royal chariot returning, bringing Sita and Lakshman.

He came down, ascended in it and took Sita in his arms. Her tears came in a torrent as she clung to him like a creeper clinging a tree. She had gone frail and looked fragile. She told him about her mother, Rohini, her wasted life and her demise, and why they couldn't come yesterday.

Rama and Sita drove straight to Valmiki's cottage in the Rishis' Camp. Lava and Kush were astonished to see the king and their mother coming together in a chariot. They bowed at their feet, and Kush asked: 'You know him, Ma? He is the King!' She blushed, gave an arched look at Rama, and said: 'He is also your father, my sons! He had sent us to live in Baba's ashram.' Rama got down, embraced his sons, and asked: 'Would you like to see the palace?' They left, taking Rishi Valmiki's leave.

Lakshman had gone straight to the palace and called Bharat and Shatrughna, along with Urmila, Mandavi and Shrutikirti. They all stood at the palace gate to welcome Sita and her sons.

∽

The vedi for the Ashvamedha Yajna was erected in the spacious compound of the King's palace. Sita divined that Rama had thought of organizing the Ashvamedha Yajna for her recall. She went with her sisters in the evening where Rama's black stallion was tied. She worshipped him and offered him greens to eat.

Urmila said to her: 'Think the horse is Ravana and kill him!'

Rama walked in then; he had overheard Urmila and remarked: 'Urmila is right, dear. Although Ravana is dead, his spirit was haunting Ayodhya and had separated us. His spirit would be exorcised when you kill the horse, taking him to be Ravana. We would then live happily ever after.'

They all left then and Sita sat on a cushion near the horse, who was reclining on the floor. At midnight hour, the priest brought a bejewelled sword on a salver and presented it to her. The horse had probably sensed it and stood up. He was tethered to an ornate pillar. She took the sword in her hand, unsheathed it and mounted a stool lying near the horse's neck.

The horse was glaring at her with his red eyes and appeared like a demon. She took the shining sword in both her hands and struck at his neck with full force. It made a deep cut, the horse whined piteously as the blood gushed out. She lifted the sword to hit again. The neck hung down and blood squirted. Sita was furious now; she struck again and the neck rolled down on the floor. The horse slumped to the ground. Sita's eyes sparkled in triumph and she came down. Rama entered the hall, saying 'Bravo!' He took the blood smeared sword from her, enclosed her in his arms and took her into the palace.

Urmila later brought her back to the hall to be with the slain horse. The horse lay on the floor, washed clean, his neck had been sowed to the body.

How her world had changed all at once, she thought, as she lay down on the mattress on the floor. Dog-tired by the gruesome ordeal, she soon entered the realm of sleep.

∽

The priests made a spit near the vedi and carefully roasted the ribs and other parts of the horse's body, pouring ladleful of ghrita and sura. The aroma wafted in the morning breeze. The four royal couples sat on the four sides of the vedi. Rigvedic verses were chanted as oblations were offered by the royal couples to Agni:

The stallion with his smooth back went forth
Into the regions of the Gods, this prayer attends him;
Inspired sages exult in him, we have made him
A welcome companion at the banquet of the Gods.

The axe cuts through the thirty-four ribs
Of the racehorse, who is the companion of Gods;
Keep the ribs undamaged, place them in order,
Place them apart, calling piece by piece.

O Horse, you do not really die, nor are you harmed,
You go to the Gods on paths pleasant to go on.
The two bay stallions,[180] the two roan mares[181]
Are your chariot mates.

Let this racehorse bring us good cattle, good horses,
Male children and all nourishing wealth.
Let Aditi make us free from sin. Let the stallion
With our oblations accord sovereign power on us![182]

∽

I would like to end this narration of the Ramayana with a couplet from Sant Tulsidasa:

Dehik, Devik, bhautik tapaa,
Rama rajya kahuhi nahin vyapaa.

[During the reign of Lord Rama no one was afflicted with ailments of the body, nor tormented by spiritual anguish or troubled by physical upheavals]

Amen!

∽

[180]Of Indra.
[181]Of the Maruts.
[182]Rig Veda, 1. 162

THE MAHABHARATA

Like the Ramayana, the Mahabharata is a great Sanskrit epic of India. It tells the story of the fratricidal war, about 2,500 years ago, between the scions of the Kuru dynasty of Hastinapur, situated on the river Ganga. The city of Hastinapur existed near the modern day Garh Mukteshwar and was washed away in later times.

According to historian A.K. Majumdar, this epic was originally called 'Bharata Samhita' and contained 8,000 shlokas, which was later increased to 24,000 shlokas.[183] The Mahabharata has, therefore, been called 'a work in progress'. It is the longest poem in the world which has accumulated writings of a host of pundits who lived at various times, although it is ascribed to Rishi Veda Vyas.

The World Book says that 'its oldest parts are probably about 2,500 years old while the others can be traced to as late as AD 500. The importance of Shri Krishna as the main god of this epic developed in Hindu thought between 200 BC and AD 200. As a result, the Mahabharata can be used to trace the development of *Vaishnavite* thought (related to God Vishnu) in Hinduism.[184]

The World Book adds that the Mahabharata's main story makes up only about a quarter of the poem. It contains many other popular stories, including the tales of Nala and Damayanti, Savitri and Satyavan, Duhshant—Shakuntala and even Lord Rama. The most famous addition to it, of course, is the Bhagavada Gita, called the 'Song Celestial'. It occurs in the sixth book of the Mahabharata and is now the most widely recognized sacred text of Hinduism. It tells how Arjun had misgivings about whether it was worthwhile to be fighting his cousins, the Kauravas, in the Mahabharata battle for their share of the kingdom. Shri Krishna, who is now deemed to be an avatar of Lord Vishnu, persuaded

[183]Majumdar, A.K., *The Hindu History*, Rupa Publications, Delhi, 2008.
[184]*The World Book Encyclopedia*, Vol. 13, p. 64.

him to fight—telling him that engaging in the fight was the only right and honourable course, else people would think him to be weak-kneed.

The teachings of the Bhagavada Gita are fundamental to modern Hinduism.

I have a mega six-volume edition of the Mahabharata published by the Gita Press, Gorakhpur, with Hindi translation. It opens with a full-page colour picture of Shri Krishna, playing on his flute. In another colour picture on the next page, Goddess Saraswati is ensconced on a giant lotus flower, playing her veena, while Rishi Veda Vyasa is shown in the background, sitting in *yoga-mudra* beside a blue stream coming down the snow-covered hills. On its obverse is a stunning colour-picture of four-armed Shri Krishna, descending from the sky in a pose of benediction, against the backdrop of seven cosmic circles. In three of his hands he is holding the conch shell, the *Sudarshan Chakra* and the golden mace—*shankh, chakra,* and *gada,* while with his fourth hand, Lord Krishna is blessing a congregation of gods, including God Shiva and Brahma in the sky, and others standing below with folded hands in veneration. The caption reads: 'Prayer for Avatara!'

This *abhaya mudra* picture of Shri Krishna is followed by six more colour pictures: 1. A picture of Shakuntala's little son Bharata, sitting on a growling lion's back, holding a lion cub in his hand. 2. Bheema killing large-size snakes. 3. Ekalavya, a low caste young man, who was found practicing archery in front of a mud statue of Dronacharya, slicing the thumb of his right hand and offering it as *guru-dakshina* demanded by Rishi Dronacharya. 4. Arjun aiming an arrow at the rotating fish in princess Draupadi's *Swayamvara.* 5. Shri Krishna meeting Arjun in Prabhas Kshetra. 6. Shri Krishna in his popular 'calendar' pose playing the flute. The picture's caption reads: '*Kripasindhu Bhagavana* Shri Krishna' (The Ocean of Mercy: God Shri Krishna). Thus, four out of seven pictures at the beginning of the book are of God Shri Krishna!

Though ascribed to Rishi Vyasa, the Mahabharata has been called a 'work in progress', as innumerable stories have been strung around the main story by anonymous poets. The most important addition, of course, is the Bhagavada Gita.

ᔕ

C. Rajagopalachari, India's first Indian Governor General after her Independance, was an eminently erudite man. He took time off his official duties, and in his impeccable diction, brought out an English translation of the Mahabharata.[185] He observes that the Mahabharata 'moulded the character and civilization of India, by its gospel of dharma, which like a golden thread runs through all the complex movements of the epic; by its lesson that hatred breeds hatred, the covetousness and violence lead inevitably to ruin, that the only real conquest is in the battle against one's nature.' The following has been summarized from his book.

ᔕ

KING SHANTANU OF HASTINAPUR

King Shantanu of Hastinapur had a son, Devavrata, by his queen Ganga; the king crowned him as the heir apparent. One day while walking on the banks of the Ganga, Shantanu saw a lovely maiden, daughter of the chief of fishermen; her body emitted sweet fragrance. He was attracted by her and wanted to marry her. The girl's father laid down a condition that he would agree to the king's proposal only if he promised to make his daughter's son the heir apparent. Shantanu could not promise it and pined away in secret sorrow.

Prince Devavrata came to know the cause of his royal sire's silent sorrow and met the chief of fishers. Devavrata gave him his word of honour that he would renounce his own right of being the heir apparent in favour of the son, born of his daughter. The fisherman was highly delighted but replied: 'O great prince, I have no doubt that you would keep your word of honour, but how can I hope your children will renounce their birthright? Your sons

[185]Rajagopalachari, C., *Mahabharata*, Bhartiya Vidya Bhavan, Mumbai, 2021.

would be mighty heroes like you, and it would be hard to resist them if they sought to seize the kingdom by force. This doubt torments me.'

Devavrata realized the force of the fisherman's argument. Then, raising his hand, he took a solemn vow: 'I promise that I shall never marry and shall live a life of chastity!' Because of this terrible vow, Devavrata began to be called Bhishma! He led maiden Satyavati to King Shantanu, his father; the King was overjoyed and married her.

∽

The fisherman's daughter, Satyavati, who became the queen of Hastinapur, was deflowered before her marriage by an eminent sage. The Mahabharata contains her fascinating story.[186]

Sage Parashar met Satyavati, the nubile daughter of the boatman, when he wanted to cross the Ganga. She used to ply her father's boat. Although a fishy smell emanated from her body, a sweet smile played on her face, as she deftly rowed the boat. As the Mahabharata describes her:

> *Ateev roop sampannam, Siddhanamapi kankshitaam.*
> *Drishtev sa cha taam dheemanshachakme chauruhasinim.*
> *Divyam taam vaasveem kanyam rambjorum munipungavaha.*
>
> [She was endowed with great beauty; desire for her would arise even in the hearts of the Siddhas. Her smile was captivating and her thighs smooth like the trunk of a banana plant; the best among the Munis (Parashar) expressed a desire to mate with the dazzling virgin.]

The girl was not offended by the venerable rishi's proposal, but she pointed out to him that many sages were there on both the banks of the river, looking at them. How could they mate in such circumstances? Rishi Parashar possessed spiritual powers and created a dense fog around the boat. The girl was wonderstruck. She again pleaded that she was an unmarried girl under the

[186]Shlokas 71–85, Chapter 63, 'Aadi Parva', *Mahabharata*, Gita Press, Gorakhpur.

tutelage of her father, and added: 'If I would lose my maidenhood by uniting with you, I cannot go home then. Indeed, I wouldn't like to live after such disgrace. Pray, think about it, O great sage, and then do as you deem fit.'

The sage smiled and replied: 'Have no fear, dear. You wouldn't lose your maidenhood even after uniting with me and making me happy; I would restore it by my spiritual power. Indeed, you can even ask one more boon from me, if you like. You see, I have never been rebuffed by anyone in the past!' Satyavati asked him for getting rid of the fishy smell emitting from her body. The rishi blessed her and instantly her body began to exude a sweet fragrance, which wafted in the air!

She mated with the venerable sage then, leaving the boat to float freely in the river. Because of the sweet fragrance emitting from her body, she began to be known as '*Gandhavati*'. A son was born out of their union; he was named Vyasa. As he was dark in complexion and was raised on a small island (*dweep*) near river Ganga's banks, he was named 'Krishna Dvepayan'. Later Krishna Dvepayan Vyasa became a celebrated rishi. It was he who is said to have composed the Mahabharata.

∽

As mentioned earlier, King Shantanu's son Devavrata (Bhishma) was instrumental in getting his father married to Satyavati. King Shantanu had two sons by Satyavati—Chitrangada and Vichitravirya. Chitrangada was killed in battle with a Gandharva. Vichitravirya was still a minor and Bhishma governed the kingdom in his name.

The King of Kashi held a swayamvara for his three daughters, Amba, Ambika and Ambalika. Bhishma went there to secure brides for Vichitravirya. The three princesses went around looking at the assembled princes. They barely glanced at old Bhishma and looked away. The assembled young princes also ridiculed Bhishma, called him an 'old suitor'. Bhishma challenged them and defeated them all. He brought the three princesses to Hastinapur. Amba told him that she had mentally chosen to wed King Salva of Saubala. Bhishma sent her to Salva with proper escort. But Salva told her that Bhishma had defeated him in sight of all, and having been disgraced, he could not accept her as his wife. Amba came back and Bhishma induced Vichitravirya to accept her, but he refused to marry a maiden who in her heart had chosen another prince.

Amba then asked Bhishma to marry her. Bhishma told her about his vow and told her that he could not break his vow, although he felt deeply sorry for her. Amba's heart was seared and she resorted to severe austerities. God Subrahamanya appeared before her and gave her a garland of lotus flowers, saying that the wearer of that garland would become the enemy of Bhishma. She then went to Parashuram, a renowned foe of the kshatriyas. He came with her and fought with Bhishma but could not defeat him. She then practiced more severe austerities in the Himalayas and received a boon by the grace of Lord Shiva that in her next birth she would kill Bhishma. In order to be reborn without losing any time, she flung herself in fire and was born as a daughter of King Drupada. She wore the garland of lotus flowers given her by Lord Subrahamanya, repaired to the forest again and by virtue of her austerities was turned into a male. She was named Shikhandin.

Prince Chitrangada died young and Bhishma got Ambika and Ambalika married to Vichitraveerya. However, Vichitraveerya too died childless. Queen Satyavati then called her son, Krishna Dvepayan, to impregnate her two daughters-in-law.

Ambika was probably too terrified seeing this black complexioned bull of a man, and kept her eyes shut while uniting with him. As a result, her son Dhritarashtra was born blind. The next night, Krishna Dvepayan went to Ambalika's chambers. Seeing him, she too was afflicted and became pale when uniting with him. Her son, born after the union, had a pale complexion, and was named Pandu. When Krishna Dvepayan came again the third night, the queens were unwilling to unite with him. They sent a slave girl to sleep with him for the night. Krishna Dvepayan cohabited with her, who immensely enjoyed uniting with the sage. Her son was named Vidura.

The war called the 'Mahabharata' was fought by the grand sons of Sarasvati—the Kauravas, sons of Dhritarashtra and the Pandavas, sons of Pandu. Rishi Krishna Dvepayan Vyasa was a witness to this great battle and the story of this great war is attributed to him both as composer and compiler. In reality, he was the real grand sire of both the Kauravas and Pandavas.

The story of how it came to be written is given in the first chapter of Mahabharata, called the 'Aadi Parva'.

THE AADI PARVA

Rishi Vyasa had composed the story in his mind. He was keen to propagate it and was desirous of finding a competent scribe who could take dictation from him. God Brahma, who had helped Sage Valmiki in writing the Ramayana, divined Vyasa's problem and, suo moto, appeared before him.[187]

Vyasa was deeply beholden to the great God Brahma for appearance and joining his hands in salutation, stood transfixed before him for a while. He was in a flurry and offered a seat to the creator of the world, and at his bidding sat near him. Joy surged in his heart. He told Brahma that he had composed the poem describing the great battle in his mind but could not find anybody to write it. Brahma advised him to pray to Lord Shiva's son Ganesh for this purpose, and returned to his abode.

Vyasa now began to pray to God Ganesh, who appeared before him instantly. Vyasa received him with reverence, seated him on cushions, and then requested him to be a scribe of the poem he had composed in his mind. Ganesha agreed to do the job on the condition that the rishi maintain a continuous flow in dictation with no humming and hawing. He made it clear that he did not like his pen to stop even for a moment.

Vyasa agreed to God Ganesha'a condition but requested him that he should not begin to write the shloka uttered by him without fully understanding its meaning. After a few easy-to-understand shlokas, Vyasa cleverly composed a complex one with mixed metaphors, using words having multiple meanings. Ganesha would take some time to comprehend its meaning, which gave Vyasa time to compose the next shloka in the meanwhile.

[187]Shloka 57, Chapter 1, 'Aadi Parva', *Mahabharata*, Gita Press, Gorakhpur.

Accordingly, a combination of human and divine endeavour had gone into creating the Mahabharata.

KUNTI DEVI

King Sura of Dwarka, maternal grandfather of Krishna, was a worthy scion of the Yadava race. His daughter, Pritha, was noted for her beauty and virtue. Since his cousin King Kuntibhoja was issueless, Sura gave his daughter Pritha in adoption to him. She was therefore named 'Kunti' after her adoptive father's name. Sage Durvasa stayed at their house for a year as a guest and she served the sage with devotion. He was so pleased with her that he gave a divine mantra, and said: 'If you call upon any god repeating this mantra, he will manifest to you and bless you with a son, possessing God's glory.'

Out of her youthful curiosity, Kunti wanted to test the efficacy of the mantra and invoked the Sun God by reciting the mantra. The resplendent Sun appeared to her. Kunti was flummoxed and asked him who he was. 'Dear maiden, I'm the Sun; you have called me to have a son.' The unwed girl was aghast and told him she was not fit for motherhood. She begged him to go back and forgive her for this childish folly. But the Sun was bound by the power of the mantra to beget a son. He, however, reassured her: 'No blame shall be attached to you after bearing the son; you will regain your virginity!'

(It's interesting to note that the Sun gave Kunti a similar boon of preservation of chastiy that Rishi Parashar had given to nishada-kanya Satyavati.)

Karna was born out of this union with Sun, donning a divine armour and earrings. The child was resplendent like the Sun. Kunti could not have kept him. She placed the new-born babe in a sealed box and set it adrift in the river Ganga. A childless charioteer, Adhiratha, found the floating box and brought up the child.

There are many fables and tales attached to Karna. Once Indra came to Karna in the garb of a Brahmin and begged of him his armour and earrings. Karna cut off the earrings and the armour, with which he was born, and gave them to him. Indra was surprised by Karna's generosity; he revealed himself and asked Karna for any boon he wanted. Karna replied: 'I desire to get your infallible weapon, Shakti. Indra granted the boon but said: 'You can use the Shakti against one enemy only, whereafter it will return to me.'

Yet another fable about Karna is that he had gone to Parashurama, posing as a Brahmin, to become his disciple and to seek the Brahamastra. Parashurama was reclining one day with his head on Karna's lap when a stinging worm burrowed into Karna's thigh. Blood began to flow and the pain was terrible, but Karna bore it without shaking his thigh, lest he disturb his guru in sleep. When Parashurama woke up, he saw the blood trickling down the wound on Karna's thigh. He told Karna that he was falsely posing as a Brahmin; he had to be a Kshatriya for such physical endurance. Karna confessed and Parashurama, who was a born enemy of the kshatriyas, cursed him: 'You will forget the mantra which activates the Brahamastra when you wished to use it'.

King Kuntibhoja held a swayamvara for his three daughters, inviting princes from neighbouring states. Kunti liked the handsome prince Pandu of Hastinapur and garlanded him. Besides her, Pandu also married Madri, sister of the King of Madradesh, as advised by Bhishma.

On King Shantanu's demise, Prince Pandu became king of Hastinapur as his elder brother Dhritarashtra was born blind. Once, after he had ascended the throne, Pandu had gone hunting in the forest. He sighted a deer couple making love and his arrow killed the male. Actually, they were a sage and his wife, disguising as deer. Stricken to death, the dying sage in deer form, cursed Pandu: 'O Sinner, you will meet with death the moment you taste the pleasures of the bed.'

Pandu was heartbroken. He entrusted the kingdom to Bhishma and retreated to the forest with his wives and lived a life of abstinence. Kunti confided to him the story of the mantra that Rishi Durvasa had gifted her. Pandu was very happy; he urged Kunti and Madri to invite the gods by the power of the mantra, and beget sons. During the many years they lived in the forest Kunti gave birth to Yudhishthir, Bhima and Arjuna by the power of the mantra, while Madri gave birth to Nakula and Sahadeva.

However, once, in spring time Pandu was, overpowered by desire and cohabited with Madri, despite her earnest protests, and fell dead. Unable to contain her sorrow and her feeling of guilt, Madri also jumped into her husband's burning pyre.

(I surmise that it was probably Queen Madri's self-sacrifice that gave rise to the accursed practice of committing Sati in later times.)

Thereafter Kunti returned to Hastinapur, bringing with her the three sons of her own and two of Madri's.The eldest, Yudhishthir, was 16 years old at that time.

~

Dhritarashtra was blind but he seems to possess magical sexual potency. He produced a hundred sons with his blindfolded wife, Gandhari! Real life apart, even in the world of fiction, no one has been credited to have achieved such an impossible feat. I surmise that the pundits, who composed this grand epic, added an extra zero to glorify the incredible muscle-power of Bhima, whose main function during the Mahabharata war was to kill the hundred sons of Dhritarashtra. In physical prowess, Bhima excelled all his brothers and cousins. While playing, wrestling or swimming with them, he would easily defeat, even browbeat, Duryodhan and his brothers.

Tormented and bested by Bhima, one day Duryodhan and his brothers planned to drown this bully in the Ganga. The boys used to eat lunch together after sporting in the river for a few hours. Duryodhan poisoned Bhima's food who felt drowsy after eating and went off to sleep. Duryodhan and his brothers bound him with wild creepers and threw him in the river. The river's waves carried him downstream and left him some distance away at the bank. He regained consciousness after some time and returned to the camp late at night.

When the boys were returning, Yudhishthir asked Duryodhan about Bhima, not seeing him in their midst. He replied that Bhima had left the river before them. Not finding him in the palace, Yudhishthir and his brothers went to the river again but did not find him. They returned in great sorrow. Late at night Bhima trudged wearily back home, and narrated Duryodhan's devilish plan to kill him. Yudhishthir told him to keep it to himself and advised him not to sport with the Kaurava cousins. Needless to say, Duryodhan was greatly surprised to see Bhima alive.

∽

The Pandava and Kaurava princes learnt the practice of arms first from Kripacharya and later from his brother-in-law Dronacharya. Dronacharya was the son of a Brahmin, named Bharadwaja. He had devoted himself to learning archery and attained great expertise. Drupada, the son of the king of Panchala, was his fellow student. Once in boyish enthusiasm, he told Drona that when he became king, he would give him half his kingdom. When, after his sire's demise, Drupada became king, Drona went to him and reminded him of his promise to gift him half his kingdom. Drupada feigned ignorance and sent him away.

Drona went to live in his brother-in-law Kripacharya's house, who was then, the tutor of the princes. One day, the princes were playing with a ball near a well when suddenly the ball fell into the well. As Yudhishthir peered into the well, his ring also fell into it. Drona, who happened to come there, sent arrows around the ball to pick it up and take it out, almost magically. He similarly picked up Yudhishthir's ring too. Seeing this, Bhishma employed him and he became Kripacharya's successor.

The rebuff he had received from King Drupada rankled in Dronacharya's heart. After becoming the tutor of the princes, he sent Karna and Duryodhan to seize him and bring him. When they failed, he sent Arjuna who vanquished him and brought him before Dronacharya. But now that Drona was installed in

Hastinapur, he considered Drupada's humbling by Arjun to be sufficient revenge. He set Drupada free.

King Drupada performed tapa, observed fasts and offered sacrifices, desiring to be blessed with a son who would slay Drona and a daughter who should wed Arjuna. His wish was fulfilled; his son Dhrishtadyumna slew Dronacharya in the Mahabharat war and his daughter Draupadi wedded Arjuna.

∽

Once, a decision was taken to exhibit the proficiency of the princes in the presence of the royal family and the public. Arjuna displayed extraordinary skill with his weapons; Duryodhan was cut up with envy and hate.

Towards the end of the show, a handsome young man bearing arms strode up to Arjuna and said to him: 'Arjuna, I shall show greater skill than you have displayed.' Taking permission from Dronacharya, he easily duplicated all the feats that Arjuna had performed. Duryodhan threw his arms around him in exultation and showered high praise upon him. The young man said: 'I am Karna; I desire single combat with Arjuna.' Arjuna was filled with anger and accepted his challenge.

Kunti saw the intruding youth; she knew him to be her first born and fainted. Kripacharya intervened then and told Karna that Arjuna was a prince of the royal family and high-born princes could not engage in single combat with unknown adventurers. Duryodhan stood up then and said: 'If the combat cannot take place merely because Karna is not a prince, I hereby crown Karna as the king of Anga.' He obtained the assent of Bhishma and Dhritarashtra and performed the ceremony there and then, putting a crown on Karna's head.

At that moment the old charioteer Adhiratha walked in. Karna bowed his head to him, Adhiratha embraced him. Bhima roared with laughter and exclaimed: 'Oh, he is the son of the charioteer!' Karna's lips trembled with anguish. Duryodhan took Karna in his chariot and drove away.

∽

Bhishmaka, King of Vidarbha, had five sons and a daughter, Rukmini, who was a matchless beauty. She had heard of Krishna's renown and wished to be united to him in wedlock. However, her eldest brother, Rukma was against the idea. He wanted her to marry Shishupala, the king of Chedi. Their father, King Bhishmaka being old, Rukma's became the dominant voice and it looked as though Rukmini would be compelled to marry Shishupala.

Fearing that she would be married to Shishupala, Rukmini mustered courage and abandoning all maidenly reserve, sent an emissary to Krishna with a letter for Krishna in Dwarka.

Krishna read her letter: 'My heart has already accepted you as my lord and master. But I am going to be married to King Shishupala against my wishes. The matter cannot brook delay. You have to rescue me before Shishupala carries me away. Come to the temple of Devi Parvati where I would be going to worship in the morning (she mentioned the date).'

A Brahmin brought the letter to Krishna. Without losing any time, he left for Vidarbha in his chariot. Balarama came to know about it; he too mounted his chariot and went in Krishna's trail.

Shishupala had arrived at Kundinapur, capital of Vidarbha for marrying Rukmini, with his retinue. On the appointed day, Rukmini proceeded to the temple in the morning to offer her prayers. 'O Devi', she implored, 'You know my heart's desire. I prostrate before you. Grant that Krishna may espouse me.'

As she came out of the temple, she sighted Krishna's chariot. She fled to him straight, like a needle going to the attracting magnet, and got into his chariot. Krishna drove off with her, to the bewilderment of the ladies accompanying her to the temple and others. The charioteer who had brought Rukmini to temple hastened back and informed prince Rukma.

Rukma went after Krishna in hot pursuit with his army. In the meanwhile, Balarama had also arrived there and a great battle ensued. Rukma's forces were routed. Balarama and Krishna returned to Dwarka in triumph, where Rukmini's wedding was celebrated with great fanfare.

Duryodhan thought of another stratagem to vanquish the Pandavas. He told his father, King Dhritarashtra, that the citizens were openly praising the Pandavas and were hostile to his rule just because of his blindness, although he was older than Pandu. He added that the people were clamouring to make Yudhishthir king. 'If that happened, where would we go? After Yudhishthir his son would be king, and then the son's son. We will be perpetually subservient to them. It's most unfair.' He asked his father to send the Pandavas to Varanavata for some time so that he could create favourable environment for the Kaurava side.

A great festival in honour of Lord Shiva was going to held at Varanavata, which was a picturesque spot. The unsuspecting Pandavas were easily persuaded when Dhritarashtra told them that the people of the place were eager to welcome them. Duryodhan sent a minister Purochana to Varanavata to prepare a magnificent palace for the stay of the Pandavas. It was furnished with all conveniences and was ready before the Pandavas arrived there. However, Purochana used combustible materials like jute, lac, ghee, oil and fat in the construction of the palace.

Vidura had cautioned Yudhishthir and had given an oblique hint of Duryodhan's wicked plan by saying: 'The conflagration that devastates a forest cannot hurt a rat sheltered in a hole or a porcupine which burrows in the earth.'

The people of Varanavata gave a joyous reception to the scions of King Pandu. Vidura sent an expert miner, who secretly dug up an underground passage, which opened beyond the moat that surrounded the newly built palace. To allay all suspicion, Purochana waited a full year before setting the wax palace to fire. On the fateful day Kunti had arranged a sumptuous feast and at midnight, when the servants had gone to sleep, the Pandavas got out by the escape tunnel and Bhima set fire to the magnificent palace. Purochana, the architect, was consumed in the fire.

The townspeople came and watched the terrible conflagration; they exclaimed in sorrow: 'The wicked Duryodhan has killed the sinless Pandavas.' When the news reached Dhritarashtra he felt sorrow as well as joy: 'Just as the water of a deep pool is cool at the bottom and warm on the surface, so the heart of Dhritarashtra was at once warm with joy and chilled with sorrow'. Dhritarashtra and his sons cast off their royal garments, dressed themselves in single garments and performed the propitiatory rites at the River Ganga. No outward show of heartbroken bereavement was omitted.

Kunti and her sons, wearing simple garments, trudged for some days before reaching Ekachhatra and stayed incognito at a Brahmin's house. One day there was a great hue and cry in the Brahmin's house, they were staying in. A rakshasa had started living in a cave near the town and would come out in the night, catch hold of a man or two and devour them. The townspeople made him agree to eat one person a day, who would bring food to his cave in the night.

It was the turn of the Brahmin in whose house the Pandavas were staying, to send someone to carry the food that day. Kunti knew the prowess of her son Bhima. She asked him to take the carriage the townspeople had brought, full of many kinds of meat, delicacies, jugs of curds and intoxicating liquours. Bhima was pleased; he parked the cart in front of the Rakshasa's cave and thought: 'I must eat the food before it gets thrown in the confusion of my fight with the Rakshasa. Besides, after I have slayed him, I shall be polluted at the touch of his corpse, and would not be able to touch the food.'

Reasoning thus, he began devouring the delicacies. The Rakshasa came out, but Bhima paid him no heed till he had made short work of the eats, curds and the liquors. The Rakshasa attacked him and they wrestled with each other. Bhima caught hold of the Rakshasa then, and threw him up like a ball. He came crashing down; Bhima placed his knee on his back and broke his bones.

~

The news of the swayamvara of Draupadi reached them when they were at Ekachhatrapur. Many Brahmins from the town were going there in the hope of receiving the customary gifts and to see the pageant of a royal wedding. Kunti, with her motherly instinct, read her sons' desire to go to Panchala and win Draupadi. So, she told Udhishthir: 'We have been in this city so long. Let us therefore go to Drupada's prosperous kingdom.' They also joined the Brahmins and stayed at the house of a potter.

Drupada had wished to marry his daughter to Arjuna but he was plunged in sorrow when he heard about the burning down of the palace they were living in. He was, however, relieved by a later rumour that they had escaped.

A mighty steel bow was placed in the marriage hall. The candidate for the princess' hand was required to string the bow and shoot a steel arrow through the central aperture of a revolving disk, at a target placed at a great height.[188] Many valiant princes had gathered including the sons of Dhritarashta accompanied by Karna, as well as Krishna, Shishupala, Jarasandha and Salya. Dhrishtadyumna on horseback rode in front of his sister Draupadi, seated on an elephant. Looking pretty like a picture, she entered the hall with a garland in hand, coyly glancing at the valiant princes. Dhrishtadyumna held her hand as she walked to the centre of the hall, and he loudly proclaimed:

> O valiant princes, he who sends five arrows in succession through the hole of the wheel and unerringly hits the target, if he also be of good family and presence, shall win my sister's hand.

Young hopefuls came forward one after another, but failed; some could not even string the huge bow. Shishupala, Jarasandha, Salya and Duryodhan were among the unsuccessful aspirants. Karna's string slid back and the mighty bow jumped out of his hands. Then there arose from among the group of Brahmins a youth who advanced towards the bow. It was Arjuna. He asked Dhrishtadyumna: 'Can a Brahmin try to bend the bow?' Dhrishtadyumna replied: 'Of course, if he be of good family and shoots the target, my sister will become his life-mate.'

Arjun shot five arrows in succession through the revolving mechanism right into the target, which fell down. The crowd

[188]The story I had read in school had a tougher requirement. The shooter was not allowed to look directly at the target. He had to look into a bowl of water placed on the floor, see the reflection of a metal fish revolving on a disk placed on high, and send his arrow piercing the eye of the fish!

cheered in tumult and there was a joyous blare of musical instruments. Draupadi approached Arjuna and placed the garland around his neck.

The princes protested loudly, saying there was no system of a swayamvara among the Brahmins. Krishna, Balarama and others sought to appease the princes. Dhrishtadyumna followed them to the potter's house and could surmise that they were the Pandavas. He came back and gave the news to King Drupada, who rejoiced; he invited them to the palace. They came along with their mother Kunti. But Drupada was unhappy to know that his daughter would be the wife of all five brothers.

Yudhishthir answered: 'O King, kindly excuse us. In a time of great peril, we vowed that we would share all things in common and we cannot break that pledge. Our mother has commanded us to do so.'

Vidura gave the news to Dhritrashtra. He was surprised and asked: 'Are the Pandavas still alive? We have been mourning them as dead! So, the daughter of Drupada has become our daughter-in-law; that's good.' Duryodhan went to Shakuni and told him that Purochana had let them down.

Bhishma was very happy to learn that the Pandavas were alive and that Arjuna has won Draupadi in the great contest. He advised Dhritarashtra that the proper course will be to welcome them back and give them half the kingdom. He added that the citizens also desired such a settlement. He told Duryodhan that there was much loose talk, not complimentary to him, about the fire incident in the wax house. All blame, even suspicion, will be put to rest if he invited the Pandavas and gave half the kingdom to them. Dronacharya also gave the same advice.

But Karna flew into rage and told Dhritarashtra that Dronacharya had received wealth and high honours from the King and should not give such wrong advice. Drona was angry and told Karna that he was advising the king to go on a wrong path. He told the king to follow the advice given by Bhishma.

Dhritarashtra turned to Vidura and asked his advice, who

replied: 'The counsel given by Bhishma, the head of our race, and by Dronacharya, is wise and just and should not be disregarded. The Pandavas are also your children like Duryodhan and his brothers. You should realize that those who advise to injure the Pandavas are really bent upon the destruction of the race. Drupada as well as Krishna and the Yadavas are staunch allies of the Pandavas. It is impossible to defeat them in battle. It is bruited about that we had tried to kill the Pandavas in the wax house, and we should first of all try to clear ourselves of the blame. The citizens are delighted to know that the Pandavas are alive and they desire to see them once again. Don't go by the advice of Duryodhan, Karna or Shakuni, O King. Follow Bhishma's advice.'

Dhritarashtra agreed to give half the kingdom to the sons of Pandu. He sent Vidura to the kingdom of Panchala to fetch the Pandavas and Draupadi.

Vidura rendered due honour to King Drupada and requested him on behalf of Dhritarashtra to send the Pandavas and Panchali to Hastinapur. Drupada mistrusted Dhritarashtra, but he merely said: 'The Pandavas may do as they like.' Vidura went to Kunti and prostrated before her. Kunti gave her assent, and Vidura returned to Hastinapur with the Pandavas, Kunti and Draupadi. As had already been decided, half the kingdom was given to the Pandavas and Yudhishthir was duly crowned king.

Dhritarashtra blessed the newly crowned Yudhishthir and bade him farewell with these words:

> My brother Pandu made this kingdom prosperous. May you prove a worthy heir to his renown! King Pandu loved me and delighted in abiding by my advice. I have made this settlement so that there may be no strife or hatred between you and my sons. Go to Khandavaprastha and make it your capital. Our ancestors Pururavas, Nahusha and Yayati ruled the kingdom from there. That was our ancient capital. Re-establish it, befitting its old glory, and be famous!

~

Khandavaprastha was a dense, frightful forest area at that time, on the southern bank of Yamuna, which had crumbling vestiges of the old city. It was infested with thieves and wicked men. Krishna and Arjuna, who had gone there to clear it, decided to set fire to it and construct a new city in its place. They cleared it and fortified the area, built palaces and renamed it Indraprastha,[189] and moved in when it was completed.

The Pandavas ruled from Indraprastha in full glory. Yudhishthir thought of performing the Rajasuya sacrifice and assume the title of 'Emperor.' He sought Krishna's advice in the matter. Krishna told him about the cruel king Jarasandha, son of King Brihadaratha of Magadha, who had conquered many kings and held them in subjection; he said that he would not accept Yudhishthir's sovereignty. Besides, Krishna's maternal uncle Kamsa, son of Ugrasena, was married to Jarasandha's daughter and had become his ally.

It was Kamsa who had imprisoned Krishna's father Vasudeva and mother Devaki, and had killed their seven children. Krishna survived because immediately after his birth, in the dead of night his father had carried him away from Mathura, crossing the River Yamuna, to Nand and Yashoda in Gokul-Vrindavan.

Krishna added that he and his people had attacked Jarasandha in the distant past, but after three years of continuous fighting they had to acknowledge defeat. Krishna left Mathura then with his people and moved to Dwarka, where they built a new city.

Yudhishthir observed then, that it was mere vanity and vainglory to desire to become an emperor. But Bhima opined that ambition was a noble virtue of a king and we should subdue Jarasandha. Krishna said that Jarasandha had unjustly imprisoned 86 kings. He was cruel and unjust and indeed deserved to be slain. He added that if Bhima and Arjuna agreed, he would accompany them and help slay the wicked Jarasandha by stratagem and set free the imprisoned kings. Yudhishthir was apprehensive about the risk of losing his brothers, the main pillars of his and the

[189]The place is still called Indraprastha. The Pandava capital was probably situated where Shah Jahan's Red Fort stands now.

kingdom's strength; but Bhima and Arjuna were enthusiastic about the plan and he agreed.

Shri Krishna advised them to provoke Jarasandha to a single combat with Bhima. They disguised themselves as holy men, clad in robes of bark-fibre, and entered Jarasandha's palace unarmed. But Jarasandha saw their proud bearing of kshatriyas, and the scar marks on their hands made by bow-string. They disclosed their identity then and admitted they were his foes, and sought 'one to one' combat with him. Jarasandha said: 'Krishna, you are a cowherd and Arjuna is a mere boy. Bhima is famous for his physical strength and I would fight with him.' Since Bhima was unarmed, Jarasandha agreed to fight without weapons.

Jarasandha and Bhima were equally matched in strength and the Mahabharata records that they fought for 13 days, without taking any rest or refreshments. But that appears to be poetic license taken by the pundits to exaggerate the importance of the combat; it may have lasted a full day. In the end, the mighty Bhima lifted Jarasandha and dashed him to the earth. Then seizing his legs, he tore his body asunder in two halves, threw him down, and roared in exultation.

However, the pundits are not content with such an unglamourous, rather pedestrian, description of this great event. The text mentions that after Bhima split Jarasandha into two and threw away the two halves, Jarasandha'a two halves at once joined together, and were made whole. Jarasandha leapt up again, attacked Bhima and held him in his grip. Bhima was aghast at Jarasandha's horrible sight and was at a loss what to do. He looked at Krishna in bewilderment. Krishna picked up a straw, tore it in two, and threw the pieces in opposite directions, not together. Bhima took the hint. He again lifted Jarasandha, tore him asunder and threw the two portions in different directions. King Jarasandha lay dead.

The next morning, his son was crowned King of Magadha, and Krishna, Bhima and Arjuna returned to Indraprastha.

More than 50 years ago, when I was director of public relations and tourism for the state of Haryana, I had gone to Patna and had travelled to Rajageer (old Rajagriha), the former capital of Magadha, now in ruins, to visit the site of this famous, historic duel. The director of tourism department for the state of Bihar had sent me in a car with a guide to show the site of the wrestling arena. The tourist guide's version was that at the time of his birth, the newly born Jarasandha had slipped from the midwife's hands and fallen on a sword and was cut into two halves. However, the infant's body was re-joined by the midwife, Jara Rakshasi, and therefore he came to be called Jarasandha—'Joined by Jara'.

After reaching the site, the guide graphically described the fight and also mentioned Krishna's clever but foul deed of splitting the straw into two, thereby giving Bhima the hint to catch Jarasandha by his legs and split him into two. According to the guide, Jarasandha's officers were watching the duel. They were stunned at their king's death. They wanted to capture the three of them. But immediately after killing Jarasandha, Krishna, Bhima and Arjuna got into their waiting chariot, and swiftly got away. He added that when they fled, Lord Krishna's chariot had made deep ruts on the road, which could be seen even now. He showed me over 6-inch-deep ruts on the rocky road, made by Shri Krishna's divine chariot; these ruts in hard stony surface stretched to 2–3 furlongs.

I closely inspected the ruts. They were indeed astonishing. However, it was improbable that such deep ruts could be made by the plying of one chariot on such a rocky surface. It occurred to me then that Rajagriha was a prosperous capital city of Magadha, which had thrived for a few hundred years. There must have been many state chariots of similar axel-length and wheel-size, their wheels protected by metal sheets. Besides, many wealthy people may have owned private chariots. Those chariots had, in fact, plied on this rocky path for hundreds of years. I reasoned that the daily operation of those chariots had made the 6-inch-deep deep ruts. But the popular legend serves as a proof of Shri Krishna's divinity.

In the meanwhile, when the news of Shishupala's slaying by Krishna reached Shishupala'a friend Salva, he became very angry and besieged Dwarka with a mighty force. In Krishna's absence, old Ugrasena was in charge of the defence of the city. Dwarka was a strongly garrisoned fortress built on an island in the sea and well provided with adequate means of defence. Besides, there was abundant supply of food and weapons and the garrison had many illustrious warriors. To ward off the attack, all the bridges were demolished and even ships were not allowed entry into the ports in the realm. All entrances to the city were guarded.

Nevertheless, during the siege of the city by the forces of Salva, the residents suffered great deal. Krishna returned to Dwarka and attacked Salva's forces and defeated him.

~

King Yudhishthir was mighty pleased at the success of Krishna's mission of killing Jarasandha. He performed the Rajasuya sacrifice, inviting many neighbouring kings. It was a custom to render the first honour in the yajna to the guest who was considered most worthy of taking precedence over all others. Bhishma advised that Shri Krishna, the king of Dwarka, should be honoured first of all; Yudhishthir was of the same opinion. Accordingly, prince Sahadeva requested Shri Krishna to accept the honour, and he was duly honoured.

Shishupala, King of Chedi, who hated Krishna, laughed aloud in derision and told Yudhishthir in the assembly: 'How ridiculous and unjust! This dotard Bhishma has proposed the name of one who was a fool by birth, and a cowherd by breeding. His father Vasudeva was a servant of Ugrasena. He is not of royal blood and no ruler; he doesn't even have the merit of age. There are many mighty princes present in the assembly—there is Duryodhan and there is Karna, disciple of Sage Parashurama, and several others. Besides, there were learned men like Drona and Kripa. Leaving them all, you chose Krishna who is neither royal, nor heroic, nor learned, nor holy, nor even hoary. It is like offering a beautiful maiden to a eunuch!'

Shishupala walked out after saying such harsh words, calling upon other kings to join him. Many of them rose to follow him. Yudhishthir ran after him, trying to appease him, but he was hurling insults on Krishna. In the melee, there ensued a terrible fight between Krishna and Shishupala; he was slain by Krishna and his body was taken away by his supporters. The Rajasuya was duly celebrated thereafter and Yudhishthir was recognized as Emperor.

~

Duryodhan had come to attend the Rajasuya sacrifice and saw the new capital city of Pandavas and its unprecedented wealth. Their palaces had sight-eluding crystal doors and Yudhishthir's Court Hall was of exquisite beauty. Indeed, in our High School course, there was a chapter on this episode of the Mahabharata, in which Duryodhan's visit to the crystal palace of the Pandavas was decribed. It was mentioned that while going round in the palace Duryodhan fell down in a pool of water, as he could not judge its depth due to the transparency of water filled in it. Draupadi, who was watching from her chamber, burst into loud laughter seeing him fall and remarked: 'The progeny of the blind is also blind!', She had referred to Duryodhan's royal sire, the blind king Dhritarashtra. Duryodhan took it to heart!

~

On his return to Hastinapur, Duryodhan told Shakuni: 'Surrounded by his brothers, Yudhishthir was looking like Indra. Before the very eyes of the assembled kings, Shishupala was slain by Krishna and not one of them had the courage to come forward to avenge him. I wish to engage the Pandavas in battle and drive them out of Indraprastha.'

Shakuni answered: 'No. That will not be easy. But I know a way to drive Yudhishthir and the Pandavas out of Indraprastha without any fight or bloodshed. Yudhishthir is fond of the game of dice, you know, but is altogether ignorant of its tricks. If you invite him, he will not refuse, following the royal tradition. I can play with him on your behalf and win his kingdom and wealth for you, without shedding a drop of blood.'

Duryodhan had to make his father agree to invite Yudhishthir to a game of dice. He told him about the prosperity he had seen in the capital city of the Pandavas and told him frankly that he was green with envy. Dhritarashtra replied: 'Is not the Pandavas prosperity ours too? Why should you be jealous of your brothers?' Duryodhan retorted: 'But the kshatriya's duty is a constant seeking of victory over others.'

Shakuni was also present there. He intervened to say that inviting Yudhishthir to a game of dice was an infallible plan. 'You have only to send him an invitation.' Dhritarashtra wanted to take Vidura's advice but Duryodhan told him: 'He will only give us platitudes of morality. Moreover, Vidura does not like me and is partial to the Pandavas. You know this as well I do'. Dhritarashtra said: 'The Pandavas are strong. I do not think it wise to antagonize them. The game of dice will only lead to enmity.'

After they had gone, Dhritarashtra called Vidura and told him about it. Vidura said: 'O King, this will undoubtedly bring about the ruin of our race by raising up unconquerable hate.' Dhritarashtra over-ruled Vidura and asked him to go and invite Yudhishthir. Vidura went to Indraprastha and told him he had come on behalf of King Dhritarashtra, to invite him and his brothers to Hastinapur and play a game of dice in the beautiful, newly erected hall like theirs.

It had become a matter of etiquette and honour, according to Kshatriya tradition, not to refuse an invitation to a game of dice; indeed, it was considered a king's dharma. As Gurcharan Das observes: 'Dharma, the word at the heart of the epic (Mahabharata), is in fact untranslatable. Duty, goodness, justice, law and custom all have something to do with it, but they all fall short. Dharma refers to 'balance'—both moral balance and cosmic balance. Dharma derives from the Sanskrit root 'dhr', meaning to sustain. It is the moral law that sustains the society, the individual and the world.'[190]

Accepting the invitation, Yudhishthir went with his brothers and asked Duryodhan who would play with him. Duryodhan replied that in his stead his uncle Shakuni would cast the dice.

[190]Das, Gurcharan, 'Prelude', *The Difficulty of Being Good*, Penguin India, 2012. p. xi.

Yudhishthir had been sure of defeating Duryodhan, and said: 'I think it's not customary for any man to play on behalf of another.'

Shakuni retorted tauntingly: 'I see that you are forging an excuse for not playing.'

Yudhishthir flushed and casting caution to the winds, replied: 'Well, I shall play.'

The hall was filled to capacity. There were Bhishma, Dhritarashtra, Drona, Kripa, Vidura, witnessing what they could not prevent.

At first, they wagered jewels, gold and silver, then chariots and horses. Yudhishthir lost continually. Yudhishthir pledged his elephants and armies and lost them too. The dice thrown by Shakuni seemed, every time, to obey his will. Cows, sheep, cities, villages, all his possessions were soon lost by Yudhishthir.

Shakuni asked: 'Is there nothing else that you can wager now?'

Yudhishthir thought for a moment and said: 'Here is the handsome Nakula; he is one of my riches. I place him as wager.'

Shakuni was surprised and said: 'Is that so? We shall be glad to win your beloved prince.' He cast the dice and won. The assembly trembled. A kind of madness had overpowered Yudhishthir. He then wagered Sahadeva and lost him.

The wicked Shakuni was afraid that Yudhishthir might stop there. So, he lashed out at Yudhishthir with these words: 'To you Bhima, Arjuna, being your full brothers, are no doubt dearer than the sons of Madri. You will not offer them, I know.'

Yudhishthir was stung to the quick and said: 'I offer as wager the ever-victorious Arjuna. Let's play.' He lost him. With tears in his eyes, he said: 'Bhima is our leader in battle. He strikes terror in the hearts of demons; he is equal to Indra. I offer him as a bet.' He lost him too.

With a mischievous grin Shakuni asked: 'Anything else you can offer?' 'Yes, I offer myself. If you win, I shall be your slave.'

Shakuni won. He stood up in the assembly then and shouted the names of the five Pandavas and loudly proclaimed that they had all become his lawful slaves. He then turned to Yudhishthir and said: 'There is one jewel still in your possession, your wife Draupadi! What about her?'

Yudhishthir despairingly said: 'I pledge her', and trembled.

Shakuni cast his dice and shouted: 'I have won.'

As for the game of dice, Gurcharan Das adds:

> I tried to picture the look of shocked incomprehension on Yudhishthir's face when he loses his kingdom and his wife in the dice game and this happens at the very moment of his greatest triumph when he is consecrated 'king of kings'. He could only suppose that his world had gone awry. Gradually, I begin to realize that the dice game may be symbolic of the quixotic, vulnerable human condition in which one knows not why one is born, when one will die and why one faces reverses on the way. The only thing certain, the Mahabharata tells us, is that *Kaala* (Time) is always cooking us! 'In this cauldron fashioned from delusion, with the Sun as fire and day and night as kindling wood, the months and seasons as the ladle for stirring, Kaala (Time or Death) cooks all beings: this is the simple truth (*Kalah pakati bhootani sarvani*).'[191]

~

Duryodhan turned to Vidura and said: 'Go and fetch Draupadi. She must henceforth sweep and clean our house'. Vidura exclaimed: 'Are you mad?' Then turning to the assembly, he said: 'Yudhishthir had no right to stake Panchali as by then he had already lost his freedom and lost all rights.' Duryodhan was angry at these words of Vidura and told Pathikami, his charioteer: 'Go forth and bring Draupadi immediately.'

Pathikami went to Draupadi and said: 'O revered princess, your husband Yudhishthir had wagered you in the game of dice and lost you; now you belong to Duryodhan. I have been sent by him to take you to serve in his household.' Pathikani then told her the whole story.

Draupadi was dumbfounded. Regaining her fortitude, she told him to go back and ask the prince who played the dice if he first lost himself or his wife. Pathikani went to the assembly and asked

[191]Das, Gurucharan, *The Difficulty of Being Good*, Penguin Book, India, 2012, XVII.1.3.

Yudhishthir what answer he should give her. Yudhishthir remained speechless and Duryodhan bade Pathikani to bring Panchali to the assembly to ask the question herself. He went to her again and humbly said: 'Princess, the mean-minded Duryodhan desires that you go to the assembly and ask your question yourself.' Draupadi answered: 'No. Return to the assembly and put the question and demand an answer.'

The charioteer returned and Duryodhan turned to his brother Duhshasana and said: 'Go and fetch Draupadi, even if you have to drag her here.' Duhshasana went to her and said: 'Come, lovely lady, why do you delay? You are now ours. Make yourself agreeable to us, now that you have been won by us.'

Panchali rose trembling and started to run for refuge towards Dhritrashtra's queen's chamber. Duhshasana darted towards her, caught her by the hair and dragged her to the assembly. Controlling her anguish, Draupadi appealed to the elders gathered there: 'How could you, who are experts in the game, consent to my being staked by the king, who was trapped into the game and cheated by wicked persons? Since he was no longer a free man, how could he stake anything afterwards? If you believe in God and Dharma, forsake me not in this horror which is crueller than death!'

The elders hung their heads in grief and shame. A roar of wrath escaped Bhima and turning towards Yudhishthir, he said: 'Even vagabond professional gamblers would not stake the harlots who live with them, and you, worse than them, have left the daughter of Drupada to the mercy of these ruffians!' Arjuna gently remonstrated Bhima.

Vikarna, son of Dhritarashtra, could not bear the sight of Panchali's agony and standing up he said: 'O kshatriya heroes, why are you silent? I am a mere youth but your silence compels me to speak. Yudhishthir was enticed to this game by a deeply plotted invitation and he pledged this lady when he had no right to do so, because she does not belong to him alone. For that reason alone, this wager is illegal. Besides, Yudhishthir had already lost his freedom; how could he offer her as a stake? Moreover, it was Shakuni who suggested her as a pledge, which is against the rules of the game, under which neither player may demand a specific bet. We must admit that Panchali has not been won by us.'

Karna got up then and upbraided him, calling him a stripling, who was injuring his family by his ignorance. He said even the clothes the Pandavas and Draupadi were wearing were now Shakuni's property. Looking towards Duhshasana he said: 'O Duhshasana, seize the garments of Pandavas and the robes of Draupadi and hand them over to Shakuni.' Hearing Karna's searing words, the Pandavas flung off their garments.

Duhshasana went to Draupadi to seize her clothes by force. She raised her hand and wailed: 'O Lord of the World, abandon me not in this dire plight. Protect me!' She fainted then and dropped on the floor. As Duhshasana tugged at her clothes, a miracle occurred. In vain Duhshasana toiled to strip off her garments by pulling them off, but fresh garments were seen to clothe her body, and soon a heap of resplendent clothes was piled up before the assembly. Duhshasana was tired and sat down in sheer fatigue. The assembly marvelled at the miracle.

Bhima, with quivering lips, loudly uttered a terrible oath. 'May I never go to the blest abode of my ancestors, if I do not rend the breast and drink the heart's blood of this sinful Duhshasana, this shame of the Bharata race!'

Dhritarashtra called Draupadi to his side and attempted to soothe her with affection. He turned to Yudhishthir then and said: 'You are so blameless that you can have no enemies. Forgive in your magnanimity the evil done by Duryodhan and dismiss all memory of it from your mind. Take back your kingdom and riches and everything else and be free and prosperous. Return to Indraprastha.'

The Pandavas left that accursed hall, bewildered and stunned and left Hastinapur in the morning. Duryodhan upbraided his father. He made his doting father send another invitation to a game of dice. The messenger reached the Pandavas midway and invited Yudhishthir to another game of dice. Yudhishthir exclaimed: 'Good and evil come from destiny and cannot, in honour, be refused. If we must play again—we must, that is all. A challenge to dice cannot in honour be refused. I must accept it.' They retraced their steps.

Truly, as the composer Vyasa says: 'There never was and never can be an antelope of gold! Yet, Rama went in vain pursuit of what seemed one: surely, when calamities are imminent, the judgement is first destroyed.'

Yudhishthir returned to Hastinapur and had a game of dice with Shakuni again, though everyone in the assembly tried to dissuade him. The stake played for was that the defeated party would go with his brothers into exile to the forest and remain there for 12 years and spend the thirteenth year incognito. If they were recognized in the thirteenth year, they should go again in exile for 12 years.

Yudhishthir met with defeat on this occasion also, and the Pandavas took the vows of sanyasis and repaired to the forest. All the members of the assembly bent down their heads in shame.

Krishna was filled with righteous indignation when he heard of Duryodhan's perfidy. Draupadi approached him and, in a voice drowned in tears and broken with sobs, told him the story of wrongs done to her: 'O Madhusudana, I was dragged to the assembly when I had but a single garment on my body. Bhishma and Dhritarashtra sat mutely. Even my husbands did not protect me; Bhima's bodily strength and Arjuna's Gandiva were of no avail, when I was dragged by my hair. I, the wife of five great heroes, was dishonoured, and even you had deserted me!' She stood trembling before him, convulsed by grief.

Krishna was deeply moved. He consoled the wailing Draupadi and said: 'Those who tormented you shall lick the dust in the battle. Wipe your tears. I solemnly promise that your grievous wrongs shall be amply avenged. I will help the heroic Pandavas. Take my word; you shall become an empress.'

Dhrishtadyumna also consoled his sister and told her that the end of the Kauravas was near. Krishna told her: 'I was in Dwarka at that time, fighting with Salva who had besieged my city. If I was here, I would not have allowed the fraudulent game of dice.' He took her leave and returned to Dwarka with Subhadra, Arjuna's wife and their child, Abhimanyu. Dhrishtadyumna went back to Panchala taking with him the sons of Draupadi.

~

At the beginning of their stay in the forest, Bhima and Draupadi used to argue with Yudhishthir. Bhima would tell him that it scorched him and Arjuna, day and night, how these miscreants had seized their kingdom by fraud and were enjoying it. Besides, after the 12 years of exile in the forest, how can they remain incognito for a year? 'Can the Himalayas be hidden under a handful of grass? Can Draupadi walk about unrecognized by others? Even if they somehow lived in hiding, the wicked sons of Dhritarashtra will find out through their spies. Then we again go into vanavaas for another 12 years!' But Yudhishthir maintained that they should abide by the promise they had made.

Arjuna went to the Himalayas to practice austerities in order to obtain special weapons from the gods. Bhima told Yudhishthir that they owed all this calamity to that mad game of dice, and added that while they were suffering, the strength of their foes was growing.

Towards the end of their exile an interesting encounter with a Yaksha happened at an enchanting pool. Yudhishthir's brothers had fallen unconscious on drinking its water. Then, dying of thirst, Yudhishthir also entered the pool and was about to drink its water when he heard a voice without form: 'Your brothers died because they did not heed my words. You have to answer my questions first and then quench your thirst. The pool is mine.'

Yudhishthir said to the bodiless voice: 'Please ask your questions.'

The voice put questions rapidly one after another. It asked: 'What makes sun shine every day?'

Yudhishthir replied: 'Power of Brahman.'

'What rescues man in danger?'

'Courage is man's salvation in danger.'

'By the study of which science does man become wise?'

'Not by studying any shastra does man become wise. It is by association with the great in wisdom that he gets wisdom.'

'What is more nobly sustaining than the earth?'

'The mother, who brings up the children she has borne, is nobler and more sustaining than the earth.'

'What is higher than the sky?'

'The father.'

'What is fleeter than the wind?'

'Mind.'

'What is blighter than a withered straw?'

'A sorrow-stricken heart.'

'What befriends a traveller?'

'Learning.'

'Who is the friend of one who stays at home?'

'The wife.'

'Who accompanies a man in death?'

'Dharma. Dharma alone accompanies the soul in the solitary journey after death.'

'Which is the biggest vessel?'

'The earth, which contains all within itself, is the biggest vessel.'

'What is happiness?'

'Happiness is the result of good conduct.'

'What is that, abandoning that man will be loved by all?

'Pride—for abandoning pride man will be loved by all.'

'What is the loss that yields joy and not sorrow?'

'Anger—giving it up, we will no longer be subject of sorrow.'

'What is that, by giving which up, man becomes rich'

'Desire—getting rid of it, man becomes wealthy.'

'What makes one a real Brahmin? Is it birth, good conduct or learning?'

'Birth and learning do not make one Brahmin. Good conduct alone does. However learned a Brahmin may be, he will not be a Brahmin if he is slave to bad habits. Even though he be learned in the four Vedas, a man of bad conduct falls to a lower class.'

'What is the greatest wonder in the world?'

'Every day, men see creatures depart to Yama's abode and yet, those who remain, seek to live for ever. This verily is the greatest wonder.'

Thus, the Yaksha posed many questions and Yudhishthir answered them all.

In the end the Yaksha asked: 'O King, one of your dead brothers can now be revived, whom do you want survived? He shall come to life.'

Yudhishthir thought for a moment and then replied: 'May the cloud-complexioned Nakula arise!'

The Yaksha was pleased at this and asked Yudhishthir: 'Why did you choose Nakula in preference to Bhima who has the strength of a thousand elephants? I have heard that Bhima is most dear to you. And why not Arjuna, whose prowess of arms is your protection? Tell me why you chose Nakula rather than either of these two?'

Yudhishthir replied: 'O Yaksha, Dharma is the only shield of man not Bhima or Arjuna. If Dharma is set at naught, man will be ruined. Kunti and Madri were two wives of my father. I am surviving, a son of Kunti, and so, she is not completely bereaved. In order that the scales of justice may be even, I asked that Madri's son Nakula may revive.'

The Yaksha was pleased with Yudhishthir's impartiality and granted that all his brothers would come back to life.

VANA VAAS

Having lived for 12 years with the Brahmins, they chose King Virata's Matsya *Desha* for living incognito for a year. Arjuna had suggested it and Yudhishthir knew that King Virata was virtuous and strong and would not be won over or frightened by Duryodhan.

Arjuna asked Yudhishthir what job would he seek. He answered that he would like to be the king's courtier, delighting him with his conversation in the garb of a sanyasi. Bhima said he would like to be a cook in the king's kitchen. Arjuna wanted to be a eunuch—braiding his hair like a woman, dressing in female attire to entertain the ladies of the king's court by dancing. Nakula said he would work in the king's stable while Sahadev decided to tend the king's large herd of cows.

Yudhishthir looked at Draupadi then; it seemed like sacrilege asking her to serve. 'O best of kings,' she said, 'have no anxiety about me; I shall be an attendant employed in royal female apartments in the court of the queen of Virata, be her companion and attendant, braiding her hair and humouring her with titbits. I'll tell her that I had been serving Princess Draupadi.'

They dressed themselves to suit their roles and went to King Virata. He could see the nobility of their mien and hesitated at first but yielded to their urgent solicitations. Yudhishthir became the king's companion and spent his days playing dice with him. Bhima became the chief of the cooks. Arjuna assumed the name of Brihannala and taught dancing, singing and instrumental music to King Virata's daughter, Princess Uttara, and other ladies. Nakula and Sahadeva looked after the king's horses and cows and bulls.

Draupadi began serving Queen Sudeshna and lived in inner royal apartments. Queen Sudeshna's brother Kichaka was the commander-in-chief of Virata's army. He was smitten with Draupadi's beauty, and taking her to be a mere maid-servant, made amorous overtures to her and sought to seduce her. She complained to queen Sudeshna and implored her protection. But Kichaka had greater influence over her and shamelessly confided to her. Sudeshna saw nothing wrong in it.

The next evening, the queen gave a golden jug to Draupadi and said: 'Sairandhri, go to my brother's house and bring me wine.' Draupadi requested her to send some other maid, but the queen insisted that she go herself. Kichaka began pestering her with urgent entreaties and solicitations. Draupadi told him it did not behove him, as he belonged to a noble royal family while she was of a low-caste and a married woman. When he persisted, she told him he would perish if he took undue liberties with her, as she was protected by the Gandharvas, who were her husbands. He seized her by the arm but Draupadi wrenched herself free and fled to the court, wailing loudly. But Kichaka followed her, hurling abusive words. No one could say a word against the commander-in-chief.

She went that night to Bhima, woke him up, and told him how brutally Kichaka had pursued her and insulted her in front of everyone. They decided that Kichaka should be beguiled, to come alone at night to a solitary spot in the dancing hall, where

Bhima would be waiting for him, disguised as a woman.

Kichaka renewed his baleful attention next morning and said: 'Sairandhri, I am the real sovereign here. Don't be a fool, and enjoy life with me.' She replied that she could no longer resist his solicitations, but he must keep it a secret. Kichaka was greatly delighted at this and agreed to come alone in the dancing hall at night where she would be waiting for him.

He perfumed and decked himself and at night entered the empty dancing hall. In the dim light he saw a woman lying on a couch, dressed in festive clothes. He gently laid his hand on her. Bhima gripped it in his iron grip and lept forth on him like a lion on its prey, and hurled him to the ground. Kichaka fought for dear life and they wrestled grimly. But he was no match for Bhima. In the end Bhima killed Kichaka, pounding and kneading his body into a shapeless lump of flesh. Draupadi then woke up the guards and said to them: 'Kichaka came here to molest me, but I had warned him that the Gandharvas, my husbands, would not spare him.'

Queen Sudeshna was deeply grieved at her brother's death and was also afraid of her maid's occult powers. She told her to leave. Members of the royal household had also requested the queen to send her away. Only one month was left for living incognito; she earnestly begged Queen Sudeshna to let her stay for just a month, when her Gandharva husbands would take her away.

∽

The spies of Duryodhan were making all out efforts to search for the Pandavas right from the beginning of the thirteenth year. After several months of futile search, they reported their failure and added that they had probably perished. Then came the news that the Army Commander of Matsya, Kichaka, had been killed in single combat on account of a woman in the Queen's court. Duryodhan surmised it was probably Bhima who had killed powerful Kichaka. He decided to invade Virata's city and carry his cows. If the Pandava's were there, they would have to live for another 12 years in the forest, otherwise nothing was lost.

He asked his ally King Susharma to attack Matsya from the

south while his Kaurava army would later launch an attack from the north, which would be relatively less defended. King Virata was deeply distressed. He thought that if Kichaka had been there, he would have made short work of the raiders. He shared his anxiety with Kanka (Yudhishthir's assumed name). Yudhishthir told him: 'O King, don't worry. Though I am a hermit, I am expert in warfare. I shall put on the armour, go in a chariot and drive away your enemies, taking your stable keeper and cowherd along with me. I have heard that they too are great fighters. Kindly give orders so that the chariots and weapons be given to us.'

King Virata was delighted. The Pandavas, except Arjuna, went out with King Virata and his army to oppose Susharma. Susharma surrounded Virata's chariot, compelling him to get down and fight on foot, and captured Virata. Virata's army lost heart and began to scatter in all directions. Yudhishthir told Bhima to attack Susharma, release Virata and rally the scattered Matsya forces.

At these words of Yudhishthir, Bhima was about to uproot a tree, to crush Susharma's chariot, but Yudhishthir stopped him and said: 'No such tricks, dear, and no battle cry; else your identity will be revealed. Fight from the chariot with bows and arrows.'

Bhima attacked Susharma, captured him and set Virata free. The dispersed forces of Matsya rallied into a new formation and defeated Susharma's army.

~

In the meanwhile, Duryodhan attacked from the north and began despoiling the cattle ranches on the outskirts of the city. The Kaurava army marched in strength and rounded up countless cows. The leader of the cowherds ran to the city and told Prince Uttara about it. The prince wanted to have a charioteer. Draupadi heard this and went to Princess Uttara and told her that Brihannala, who taught her dancing, had been the charioteer of Prince Arjuna and had even learnt archery from him.

The Princess ran to her brother and conveyed the information to him. He asked her to send Brihannala to him. Brihannala drove the chariot expertly. But the young prince felt diffident, sighting the huge Kaurava army and said: 'How can I, single-handed, attack this great army? Let the Kauravas march off with the cows. I don't care. What a fool I was to brag!' Arjuna allayed the Prince's fears and said: 'Be not afraid, Prince Uttara, I shall fight the Kauravas. Help me by taking the reins of the chariot, and I shall do the rest. We will rout the enemy and recover your cows. You will have all the glory in our victory.'

Reluctantly the Prince agreed, and took up the reins of the chariot. Arjuna took him to a tree near the burial ground, where he had hidden the special weapons he had brought after doing penance and praying to the gods. He brought down the leather bag he had hidden there and took out the gleaming weapons. The Prince was amazed. Arjuna removed the conch-bangles from his hands and put on leather gauntlets. He twanged his bow Gaandiva and blew his conch Devadatta.

The grandsire Bhishma recognized the sounds of Arjuna's conch and bow and told Duryodhan: 'Indeed, dear Duryodhan, the stipulated period of 13 years of exile had ended yesterday. Reflect before deciding on a battle with Arjuna. If you want to make peace with the Pandavas, now is the time for it.' Duryodhan replied that he shall not give even a village to the Pandavas, and said: 'Let us fight.'

Then Dronacharya said: 'Let Prince Duryodhan take away a fourth of the army and return to Hastinapur. Let another quarter of the army surround the cows and seize them; if we return without seizing the cows, it would amount to an acknowledgement of defeat. With the rest of the army, the five of us will give battle to Arjuna.' The Kaurava forces arranged themselves accordingly in battle array.

Arjuna was keenly observing all this and said: 'O Prince Uttara, I do not see Duryodhan in their army formation; I think he has turned back, taking the cows with him. Let us pursue him and recover the cows.' While going after Duryodhan, he reverentially sent arrows towards Bhishma, Dronacharya and Kripacharya, making the arrows fall at their feet.

Seeing Arjuna going in pursuit of Duryodhan, Bhishma and other Kaurava warriors turned to give Duryodhan cover. Arjuna continued fighting all alone. First, he attacked Karna and drove him away. He attacked Drona then, but his son Ashwatthama joined him and attacked Arjuna. Kripacharya too joined them. However, Ashwatthama was tiring and Kripa was routed by Arjuna. Arjuna then reached Duryodhan. Bhishma and others surrounded Duryodhan and they all rode away towards Hastinapur, leaving the cows.

Arjuna said: 'O Prince Uttara, turn back the horses now. Our cows have been regained; our enemies have fled. Now return to your kingdom, adorning your person with sandal paste and flowers.' On the way back he deposited his weapons on the tree, dressed himself as Brihannala and sent messengers in advance to proclaim that Prince Uttara had won a glorious victory.

King Virata returned to his capital after killing Susharma amidst the acclamation of the citizens. Not finding Prince Uttara, he asked about him. The queen told him that he had set out to conquer the Kauravas who had invaded the city from the north. Yudhishthir, disguised as *sanyasi* Kanka, told him not to worry as Brihannala had gone as his charioteer, and added 'Whoever fights from a chariot driven by her, can be sure of victory.' They began playing their game of dice then.

Meanwhile the message had been received that Prince Uttara had defeated the Kaurava army. Virata sent out his ministers to welcome his son, returning in triumph. The king was full of his son's prowess and told Yudhishthir: 'See the glory of my son, Kanka, he has put the famed Kaurava warriors to flight.' 'Yes,' replied Yudhishthir with a smile, 'your son is indeed fortunate to have secured Brihannala to drive his chariot.'

Virata was angry at this persistent glorification of Brihannala at the expense of his son Uttara and growled: 'While I am talking about my son's victory, why do you go on expatiating on the charioteering skill of the eunuch?' Yudhishthir replied: 'O King, I know what I am talking about. Brihannala is no ordinary person. The chariot she drives can never see defeat.' King Virata could stand it no longer. He threw the dice in Yudhishthir's face and gave a blow on his cheek.

The gatekeeper announced the arrival of Prince Uttara and the charioteer Brihannala. 'Bring him in. Bring him in.' Yudhishthir whispered to him to send Prince Uttara alone. Uttara entered and paid due homage to his royal father. When he turned to do obeisance to Kanka, he was horrified to see his bleeding face, for now he knew that Kanka was the great King Yudhishthir. He asked his father who had caused hurt to him.

Virata said: 'I hit him because when I gave him the news of your glorious victory, this Brahmin extolled your charioteer, the eunuch. I am sorry I struck him, but it's not worth talking about.'

Uttara was overwhelmed with fear and said: 'Alas! You have done a grievous wrong, Father. Fall at his feet right now, and pray for forgiveness, otherwise we will be destroyed.'

Virata stood with a puzzled frown but Uttara fell at Yudhishthir's feet asking for pardon. Virata then embraced his son and said: 'My boy, you are truly a hero. Tell me how did you defeat the great Kaurava army?'

Uttara answered: 'I conquered no army, rescued no cows. All that was the work of a godlike Prince. He took up our cause, rescued me from destruction, put the Kaurava soldiers to flight, brought our herd back, and has now gone away. I only acted as his charioteer.' Uttara spoke thus because Brihannala had asked him not to reveal his identity to his father.

The king could hardly believe his ears. 'Where is that godlike Prince?' He asked and added: 'I must see and thank the hero who rescued my son and beat back my foes. I will give my daughter, Uttaraa, in marriage to him.' Uttara told his father that the Prince had promised to come the next day.

The next day, in Virata's hall of assembly, leading citizens had gathered to celebrate the King's and Prince Uttara's victory. Kanka the courtier; Valala the cook; Brihannala the dancer; Tantripala, the stable hand; and Dharmagranthi, the cowherd, also arrived, but to everyone's surprise, they sat among the princes and nobility. King Virata entered the court then. He lost his temper seeing them occupying the high seats and gave vent to his displeasure. When they felt they had enough fun, the Pandavas disclosed their identity to the amazement of all.

Virata was overwhelmed with joy to think that the Pandava princes and Panchali had been ministering to him all these days in disguise. He embraced Yudhishthir in gratitude. He also insisted on giving his daughter in marriage to Arjuna. But Arjuna said: 'No, that would not be proper, for the princess had learnt dancing and music from me. I, as her teacher, am in a position of father to her.' However, he gladly agreed to accept her for his son, Abhimanyu.

Having completed the thirteenth year of their exile without being discovered, the Pandavas began to live in Upaplavya in Matsya territory and sent emissaries to summon their friends. Shri Krishna and Balarama came from Dwarka with Arjuna's wife Subhadra and their son Abhimanyu, accompanied by many Yadava warriors. King Virata went to receive the Pandavas, amidst loud and long blare of trumpet conches. The King of Kashi, as also the Saibya ruler, arrived with their forces. King Drupada of Panchala arrived with three divisions of his army, bringing his sons, Dhrishtadyumna and Shikandin, and daughter Draupadi and her sons. Besides them came many others princes who were attached to the Pandavas.

Abhimanyu's marriage with princess Uttara was solemnized according to Vedic rites before this illustrious gathering of friendly princes. After the wedding celebrations were over, they met in conclave in King Virata's hall of assembly.

'You all know the story of deceit,' said Krishna to the hushed assembly, 'how Yudhishthir was cheated at the game-board and deprived of his kingdom and was exiled with his brothers and Draupadi to the forest. For 13 years, the brave Pandavas have patiently borne this torture, in redemption of their pledged word. Ponder well and counsel a course in consonance with Dharma. The noble Yudhishthir wishes good to the sons of Dhitarashtra. In giving your counsel, bear in mind the honourable magnanimity of the Pandavas and the meanness of the Kauravas. We do not know what Duryodhan has in his mind. I personally feel we should send an able and upright emissary to persuade him to a peaceful settlement by restoring half the kingdom to Yudhishthir.'

Balarama then rose and, while endorsing Krishna's suggestion, emphasized that the emissary should be a man who has weight and ability to bring about a peaceful settlement. In his view Duryodhan was not going to accept giving half the kingdom to the Pandavas.

Satyaki, the Yadava warrior, said Duryodhan had shamelessly deceived Yudhishthir and if he now refused to part with half the kingdom, let there be no delay in getting on with the preparations for a fight.

Drupada's heart was gladdened by Satyaki's resolute words. He stood up and opined that soft words will not bring Duryodhan round to reason. He advised to send word instantly to their friends Salya, Dhrishtaketu, Kekeya for support. He added that his priest, Sanjay, can be sent to Hastinapur with proper instructions about what he should say to Duryodhan and how should he convey the message to Bhishma, Dhritarashtra and Dronacharya.

Krishna rose then and agreed to Drupada's suggestion. He added that Balarama and he were bound to the Kauravas and the Pandavas with equal ties of affection. Addressing Drupada then, he said: 'Dhritarashtra holds you in high esteem and Drona and Kripa were your boyhood friends. You should properly instruct your Brahmin envoy on his mission of peace. But if he fails to persuade Duryodhan out of his error, prepare for the inevitable conflict and send word to us.'

Drupada called his head priest Sanjay and said to him: 'Duryodhan deceived the Pandavas with the connivance of his father, King Dhirtarashtra, who would not listen to the sane advice of Vidura. Show the old weak king, who is misled by his son, the path of Dharma and wisdom. You will find in Vidura a great ally in this task. You should try to take support also from Bhishma and Drona, to bring Duryodhan on the right path.'

∽

After Sanjay left for Hastinapur, the Pandavas sent word to the kings likely to favour their cause, to collect their forces and hold themselves in readiness for war. Arjuna went to Dwarka himself to obtain Krishna's support. Duryodhan got to know about it and he too sped towards Dwarka in his chariot.

They reached Dwarka the same day and went to Krishna's palace. Krishna was sleeping in his bedroom. They were both his close relations and could go into his bedroom. Duryodhan entered earlier and occupied a decorated chair at the head of the bed; Arjuna sat on a seat at Krishna's feet. When Krishna opened his eyes, he saw Arjuna first. Arjuna stood up, folded his hands in salutation, and bowed to him. Krishna saw Duryodhan then. He asked them what they wanted.

Duryodhan said: 'It looks as though war would break out between us soon. If it does, you must support me. We both claim equally close relationship with you. Since I came first, you have to be on my side.'

Krishna replied: 'You may have come before, but I saw Arjuna first. So even in this respect, your claims on me are equal and I am therefore bound to render assistance to both sides. In distributing favours, the traditional usage is to begin with the junior-most among the recipients. The Narayanas, my tribesmen, are my equals in battle, and our army is large and almost invincible. In my distribution of assistance, our army will be on one side, and I, individually, on the other. But I shall wield no weapon and take no part in actual fight.'

Turning then to Arjuna, he said: 'Partha, think it over well. Would you want me, alone and weaponless, or would you prefer the prowess of the Narayana army? Exercise the right of the first choice which custom gives you as the younger man.'

Arjun replied with reverence and without hesitation: 'I would be content if you are with us, though you may wield no weapon.'

Duryodhan could hardly contain himself for joy at what he thought was Arjuna's imbecile choice. He gladly chose Vasudeva's army and his request was granted. He went to Balarama and told him the story and asked for his support. Balarama told him, it was impossible for him to side with one whom Krishna opposes, and added that he would not be able to support him against Krishna.

Duryodhan returned to Hastinapur in high spirits. Krishna then turned to Arjuna: 'Dhananjaya, why did you choose unwisely, preferring me alone and un-armed, to my fully equipped and heroic forces? I had given you the first option, thinking you would ask for my army, as I had foretold that I would not take part in the fight at all.' Arjuna answered: 'Janardana, I wish to win the battle with you driving my chariot, unarmed.' Krishna assented with a soft smile.

Salya, King of Madradesh, was brother of Madri, the mother of Nakula and Sahadeva. When he heard the Pandavas were camping at Upaplavya, making preparations for war, he collected a big army and set off to join the Pandavas at Upaplavya. News of Salya marching to join the Pandavas reached Duryodhan, who thought Salya should be persuaded to join his side. He sent his officers, instructing them to provide King Salya and his extensive army all help at camping sites on the way, and offer them sumptuous hospitality. Several rest houses and camping sites were accordingly erected by them, serving food and drinks. Salya was exceedingly pleased and assumed that all that was done by his nephew, Yudhishthir.[192]

He called the officers and told them that he was very pleased with their dedicated service and wanted to reward them. He desired that they should convey it to their boss and take his permission to allow it.

Duryodhan, who was following them unobserved, at once took this opportunity to present himself before King Salya. He told him how honoured he felt at Salya's acceptance of his hospitality. Salya was greatly moved and exclaimed: 'How noble and kind of you! How can I repay you?'

Duryodhan replied: 'You and your forces should fight on my side. O King, this is the reward I ask of you.'

Salya was stunned. Duryodhan added: 'You are the same unto us both. I mean as much to you as the Pandavas. You must agree to come to my aid.'

Salya answered: 'Be it so. But I have to meet Yudhishthir and tell him that I have given you my word of honour.'

The Pandavas received him with great éclat. Nakula and Sahadeva were joyous beyond words to see their uncle. The

[192]They were so unlucky; they did not have mobile phones in those days!

Pandavas narrated to him their hardship and suffering. When they started talking about obtaining his help in the impending war, Salya related the story of his promise to Duryodhan and found himself on the horns of a dilemma. Yudhishthir said to him: 'Great warrior, you are bound to keep the promise you have made to Duryodhan'.

Salya replied that he had been tricked into giving his word to Duryodhan and added: 'I have acted wrongly. Bear with me.'

Sanjaya, Drupada's chief priest, reached Dhritarashtra's court. He submitted that he was the emissary of the Pandavas and addressed him thus: 'O great king, you and Pandu were sons of King Vichitraveerya, and according to our tradition, equally entitled to the father's property. Your sons have taken possession of the whole kingdom, while Pandu's sons are without their share of the common inheritance. There can be no justification for this. The Pandavas are prepared to forget the sufferings they have undergone and to let bygones be bygones. They are unwilling to resort to war, because they fully know that war never brings any good, only destruction.

O great King, render unto them what is due to them. This would be in accordance with justice and with the agreement previously reached. Let there be no delay.'

Bhishma was in agreement and said that restoration of half of the kingdom to the Pandavas was the right thing to do. Karna angrily broke in and told Sanjaya: 'How can Yudhisthira claim the property that he had lost at the game board? If he wants anything, he must beg for it as a gift.' Bhishma interposed: 'Son of Radha, you speak foolishly. If we do not do as this messenger tells us, war will be upon us and Duryodhan and all of us are doomed to destruction.'

Dhritarashtra called Sanjay aside and sent him back to convey his affectionate regards to the Pandavas and tell them that he also wanted the avoidance of war. Sanjay returned and gave Dhritarashtra's message to Yudhisthira. He added that while Bhishma was agreeable to his pleadings of peaceful settlement,

Karna had intervened and said: 'Yudhisthir should come and beg to get what he had lost in the game of dice.'

Yudhisthira sent him back again to King Dhritarashtra to give his message thus: 'Was it not through your generosity that we obtained a share of the kingdom when we were young? You, who made me a king once, should not deny us our share now and drive us to make us beggars living on the charity of others. There is enough room in this world for both us and the Kauravas. Let there be no antagonism between us.'

Dhritarashtra spent a restless night after he had sent Sanjaya back to Yudhisthira. In the morning he called Vidura for his advice. 'To give the Pandavas their share in the kingdom is the safest plan,' Vidura said. 'Only this can bring good to both sides. The right course is to treat the Pandavas and your own sons with equal affection.' He counselled him in this manner at great length.

The next morning Sanjaya returned and gave him Yudhisthira's message. Bhishma counselled Dhritarashtra against opposing the combined might of Arjuna and Krishna. He said: 'Karna, who boasts repeatedly that he will slay the Pandavas, cannot equal Arjuna's might. Your sons are heading for destruction, listening to his words. What was Karna able to do when Arjuna singlehandedly beat back your son's attack on Virata's capital?'

Duryodhan stood up then and said: 'Father, do not worry about our safety. That we will win the war is certain. Yudhisthira knows it; he, therefore, begs now for only five villages. He is scared of our eleven divisions.'

Sanjaya took the message back.

KRISHNA GOES AS EMISSARY

Krishna had come to Upaplavya. Yudhisthira told him that Dhritarashtra was trying to secure peace without giving them any territory. 'There is none but you to protect us; none who can advise us in this crisis. Only you can guide us in Dharma and statesmanship.'

Krishna said in reply: 'For the good of you both, I have decided to go to Hastinapur to Dhritarashtra's court myself to make a last-ditch effort to avert war and try to secure your rights without war.' Yudhisthira was worried about Krishna's safety; Duryodhan, he thought, was perverse and will not stop at anything. Krishna smiled and told him not to worry about him in the least.

Draupadi had overheard this conversation. She came and stood before Krishna, holding her locks in her hand, and said in a voice quivering with grief: 'Madhusudana, look at these tresses of mine and do what honour requires be done. Even if Arjuna and Bhima are against war, my old father will go and fight, supported by my children. With Subhadra's son Abhimanyu at their head, my children will fight the Kauravas.'

She began sobbing then. Krishna told her: 'Don't weep, Draupadi, Duryodhan will not listen to my words of peace. Take my word, the Kauravas are all going to fall and their bodies would be food for wild dogs and jackals. You will be fully avenged, and that too, soon.'

Dhritarashtra gave Krishna a rousing welcome, getting welcome-arches erected at city's gates. He got Duhshasana's palace vacated for him, which was bigger and more beautiful than Duryodhan's, and placed chariots at his disposal. Krishna first went to Dhritarashtra's palace and then to Vidura's house. Kuntidevi met him there, and thinking of the suffering of her sons, she wept. Krishna comforted her and taking her leave, went to Duryodhan's palace. He gave him a warm welcome and invited him for dinner. Krishna smiled and said: 'Emissaries eat only after their mission is fulfilled.'

He went to Vidura's house then to rest. Vidura told him that Duryodhan's arrogance was based on his confidence that no one can defeat him as long as Bhishma and Drona stood by him. He advised him against going to Duryodhan's palace; the wicked man might plot against his life. Krishna smiled and told him not to worry about his life.

The next morning Duryodhan and Shakuni came to Krishna and informed him that Dhritarashtra was waiting for him in his court. Krishna went, taking Vidura along. As Dhritarashtra entered,

Krishna too rose and told Dhritarashtra what the Pandvas wanted and said: 'O King Dhritarashtra, do not bring ruin to your people. It is your duty to restrain your sons. The Pandavas are prepared for war but they desire peace. Treat them also as your sons and devise an honourable solution.'

Dhritarashtra said: 'Madhava, I desire precisely what you say, but my wicked sons do not listen to me. I entreat you to advise Duryodhan.'

Krishna turned to Duryodhan then and said: 'You are the descendant of a noble line. Pursue the path of Dharma. This famous line is in danger of being destroyed. Make peace with your cousins by giving them half the kingdom.' Bhishma and Drona also pressed upon Duryodhan to heed Krishna's advice.

Duryodhan stood up then and said: 'Madhusudana, you wrong me out of love for Arjuna. The Pandavas, of their own volition, staked their kingdom and being defeated, forfeited it. How am I responsible for it? I will not give the Pandavas an inch of land, not even a needlepoint of it.'

Krishna laughed and said: 'The dice game was fraudulently arranged by you and Shakuni and you afterwards insulted Draupadi in an assembly of princes and yet you have the impudence to say that you have committed no wrong.' He also reminded him of the other iniquities he had perpetrated against the Pandavas.

Duhshasana stood up then and told Duryodhan: 'These people have bound you with ropes; let's get away from here.' Duryodhan walked out of the hall with his brothers.

Krishna went to Kunti and told her what had happened. 'May you protect my sons!' she said. Krishna got into his chariot and sped away towards Upaplavya.

KUNTI MEETS KARNA

Kunti was greatly perturbed, realizing that war had become a certainty. She was sure that grandsire Bhishma would not want to kill her children, nor Dronacharya, perhaps, they being his own disciples. But Karna was the chief enemy of the Pandavas. Her heart was consumed with agony like a faggot in the fire. She thought of seeking Karna out and tell him the truth about his birth; he might abandon Duryodhan's cause then.

She went to the river in the morning, where Karna offered his daily prayers and meditated. He was standing facing east, offering prayers. She stood behind him quietly.

He was greatly amazed and puzzled to see the mother of the Pandava princes waiting patiently for him to finish his prayers. He made a deep bow and said: 'The son of Radha and the chariot-driver Adhiratha bows to you. I am at your service, O Queen; what can I do for you?'

'O Karna,' she said, 'you are not Radha's son, nor is the charioteer your father. Know that you are the Sun god's son, born out of my womb.' She then narrated to him the story of his birth and how she had to abandon him as she was still unwed then.'You have joined Duryodhan, not knowing that the Pandavas were your real brothers, and have come to hate them. My son, living in dependence on Dhritarashtra's sons does no befit you. Join your brothers now, and being the eldest, rule the kingdom.'

Karna's mind was in a whirl after hearing Kunti's revelation. He stood in silence for a while. With great effort of will, he controlled the temptations of self-interest and the promptings of natural affection, and said: 'What you have said, dear mother, is contrary to Dharma. You deprived me of all that was my birthright when you threw me away. You have revealed the truth of my birth now, thinking of your other children's welfare. I have eaten the salt of Dhritarashtra's sons, and now, when the battle is about to begin, you want me to be untrue to my salt. I have myself urged them into this war. How can I now desert them? Could there be a blacker treachery and baser ingratitude? Mother dear, I must discharge my debt—with my life, if necessary.'

'But yet,' he continued, 'I cannot have my mother plead completely in vain. You have to part with Arjuna or me; either he or myself must die in this war. I will not kill your other sons, whatever they might do unto me. Mother of warrior sons, you will still have five sons. Either I or Arjuna will survive in this war, and with the other four sons, you will still have five sons left.'

∽

Krishna reached Upaplavya and told the Pandavas what took place at Hastinapur. They formed the army in seven divisions and appointed Drupada, Virata, Dhrishtadyumna, Shikhandin, Satyaki, Chekitana and Bhimasena at the head of each division. Arjuna suggested that Dhrishtadyumna, who was born to bring about Dronacharya's end, should be made the Supreme Commander. Indeed, the choice was between Dhrishtadyumna and Shikhandin, whose name was suggested by Bhima and who was born to kill Bhishma. Krishna was in favour of Dhrishtadyumna, who, for 13 long years, had been brooding over the insult of his sister Draupadi in Duryodhan's court. Dhrishtadyumna was appointed the Supreme Commander.

∽

Bhishma stood in command of the Kaurava army. Duryodhan bowed reverently to him and said: 'May it please you to lead us and achieve victory and fame even as Kartikeya led the gods. We will follow you as calves follow the sire-bull.'

'So be it,' said the grandsire. 'But you should understand that the sons of Pandu are to me the same as you, sons of Dhritarashtra. I shall lead the army and discharge my duty. But I cannot kill the sons of Pandu. This war does not have my approval. Short of killing the Pandavas, none else shall I spare in the Pandava army. One thing more: Karna, whom you hold dear is opposed to my leadership. If you like you may ask him to take over the leadership of the army and conduct the battle from the outset. I shall not object.'

Bhishma was appointed the Generalissimo of the Kaurava forces which rolled like a great flood into the fields of Kurukshetra.

∽

THE WAR BEGINS

The war was fought under some inviolable rules. The fight commenced with sunrise and ended at sunset. After sunset the warriors on both sides mixed freely with their friends and enemies. Single combat was only between equals. During the fight, those who left the field or retired would not be attacked. A horse rider could only attack a horse rider. Similarly, charioteers, elephant troops and infantrymen could engage themselves in battle only with their counterparts in the enemy ranks. Those who sought quarter of surrender were safe from slaughter. It was wrong to slay one who had been disarmed or was retreating or had lost his armour. Non-combatant attendants, drummers or conch blowers were not attacked. It was unlike modern times, when all is fair in love and war. However, even in the Mahabharata war occasional transgressions occurred.

When the battle was about to begin, Yudhisthir doffed his armour and walked unarmed towards the Kaurava army. He went to Bhishma's chariot. Bending low, he touched his feet in salutation and said: 'Grandsire, permit us to begin the battle. We have dared to give battle to you; we seek your benediction before beginning the fight.' Bhishma blessed him putting his hand on his head. Yudhisthir went to Dronacharya then, his preceptor, touched his feet and sought his blessings. Drona blessed him too, and Yudhisthir walked back to his side.

Seeing his grandfather, his Guru Dronacharya, his brothers and cousins, their sons, their fathers-in-law and friends on both the sides, Arjun was suddenly filled with doubt and deep anguish. He told Krishna that his limbs were getting benumbed, mouth drying up and shivers going down his spine. 'My bow is slipping from my hand; my skin is burning and my mind is wavering. There are evil omens and I see no point in killing my own people for the sake of the kingdom. Blinded by greed, my cousins don't perceive any evil in the destruction of their own race, but why we who clearly see the sin involved in it, shouldn't turn away from this crime? Let them kill me, Krishna, I'm not prepared to kill my kinsmen even for winning the three worlds.'

Speaking thus, he cast away his arms and sat down, dejected, in the hinder part of the chariot.

Krishna disapproved of his oration and asked him whence this weakness had arisen in his heart. It did not behove an Arya like him. He said, 'It would neither lead you to heaven nor fame, Arjun. Don't yield to such un-manliness, it doesn't become a brave man like you. Cast off this base faintheartedness. Get up and fight.'

But Arjun did not get up, and pleaded: 'How can I fight Bhishma and Drona and kill them? They are worthy of deepest reverence. It's better to live on alms in this world than slay these noble elders. We don't know whether we will win or they will conquer us. I am bewildered and don't know what is my duty. O Krishna, guide me, I am your disciple, I have taken refuge in you!'

Thereupon Shri Krishna is said to have delivered to him the philosophic discourse, called the Bhagavada Gita, containing, 18 chapters. Obviously, Krishna couldn't have delivered the whole book in the battlefield, when the two armies were standing face to face, rearing for battle. To my mind, the Bhagavada Gita is an imaginary discourse composed by learned pundits with a view to projecting Shri Krishna as God. Needless to say, they have eminently succeeded in their venture.

I had read the Bhagavada Gita years ago. It's an uplifting poem and has received universal acclaim from prominent philosophers of the world. It was Mahatma Gandhi's constant companion. Its central message of '*nishkaam karma*' has charmed mankind, cutting across religious and language barriers.

S. Radhakrishnan in his edition of Bhagavada Gita observes: 'The Bhagavada Gita is later than the great movement represented by the early Upanishads and earlier than the period of the development of the philosophic systems and their formulations in sutras. From its archaic constructions and internal references, we may infer that it is definitely a work of the pre-Christian era. It was probably composed in the fifth century BC, though the text may have received many alterations in subsequent times.'[193]

Dr Radhakrishnan goes on to argue that 'Krishna could not have recited the seven hundred verses to Arjuna on the battlefield. He must have said a few pointed things which were later elaborated... into an extensive work.' He adds that according to Garbe, the Bhagavada Gita was originally a samkhya yoga treatise with which the Krishna-Vasudeva cult got mixed up and in the third century BC it became a part of the Vedic tradition by the identification of Krishna with Vishnu.

Dr Radhakrishnan also mentions that Ramanuja admitted that while the paths of knowledge, devotion and action are all mentioned in the Gita, he holds that its main emphasis is on devotion. Similarly, referring to Madhva (AD 1199–1276), Radhakrishnan holds that devotion is the method emphasized in the Gita.

In sum, Radhakrishnan believes that Shri Krishna persuaded Arjun to engage in battle by saying a few pointed things and the Gita is a later production by the pundits. It is clear that Shri Krishna had nothing to do with this great philosophic treatise, although it has been literally put in his mouth. It was composed solely by the pundits. It's not of divine origin, as an average Hindu is led to believe.

As stated by Radhakrishnan, what Shri Krishna might have said to Arjun at the field of war is reflected in the second and third verse of Chapter II:

Kutas tva kashmalam idam vishme samupasthitam?
Anaryajushtam asvargyam akeertikaram Arjun.
Klaibyam maa sma gamah, O Partha, nai 'tat tvayy upapadyate,
Kshudram hrydaya daurbalyam tyaktavo, uttishtha O Parantapa.

[Whence has come to thee this dejection of spirit in this hour of crisis, O Arjun? It is unknown to men of noble mind; it does not lead to heaven; it only causes distress.

[193]Radhakrishnan, S., *Bhagavadgita*, George Allen & Unwin, Great Britain, reprinted by Blackie & Son, India, p. 14.

> Yield not to this unmanliness, O Partha, for it does not become you. Cast off this petty faintheartedness, O Oppressor of the foes!]

In other words, Shri Krishna told him that people would not understand this nobility of heart on his part; they would only say that he had got frightened. Krishna used the word '*klaibyam,*' meaning 'unmanly' or 'impotent', which was enough to spur Arjun to action.

THE BATTLE

I now propose to give a day-to-day summary of the 18-day battle, called Mahabharata and then summarize the Bhagavada Gita from S. Radhakrishanan's celebrated translation.

The First Day

Duhshashan was leading the Kaurava force and Bhimsena the Pandava army. The noise of the battle filled the air. The kettledrums, trumpets, horns and conches made the vault of heaven ring with their clamour. Horses neighed, charging elephants trumpeted and the warriors roared like lions.

Bhishma's chariot was raining havoc on the Pandava army. Abhimanyu could not bear it; he attacked the great-grandsire, showering him with his arrows, many of which reached the target, wounding the grand old patriarch. One of his shafts brought Bhishma's flag down. He faced Kripacharya then and broke his arrow. The Kaurava warriors were enraged and made a combined attack on him. Bhimasena was overjoyed at Abhimanyu's performance and yelled in admiration. Even Bhishma was struck with the boy's valour and unwillingly used his full strength against him.

King Virata, his son Uttar, and Dhrishtadyumna, son of Drupada, came to relieve Abhimanyu. Uttar rode an elephant and led a fierce charge on Salya's chariot-horses and trampled them, but Salya hurled his javelin which pierced the young prince's chest.

Uttar's elephant charged at Salya, who cut off its trunk. His arrows pierced the elephant and it dropped dead, uttering a shrill cry.

Virata's son Shveta was furious at his brother's demise. He attacked Salya but seven chariot warriors came to protect Salya. Shveta defended himself marvellously, parrying their shafts, cutting down their javelins. Duryodhan sent more warriors to attack Shveta, but he put them to flight and attacked Bhishma and cut down his flag-post. Bhishma's arrows killed Shveta's horses and charioteer. Shveta took a mace and threw at Bhishma's chariot to smash it. Bhishma had anticipated it, he jumped down instantly and putting his bow on the ground, pulled its string to his ear, and sent an arrow at Shveta, who fell dead. Virata lost both his brave sons that day.

The Second Day

Arjuna was unhappy at the losses on the first day. He told Krishna that their army would soon be destroyed if the grandsire was not removed from the scene. Krishna immediately took the chariot in front of Bhishma's. Both the chariots were drawn by white steeds. Arrows crashed with arrows and a few arrows of Bhishma hit Arjuna's and Krishna's breasts. Arjuna was angry seeing blood flowing from Krishna's breast. Their chariots were moving so fast and so close that it was not possible to say where Arjuna was and where Bhishma. Only the flags could be distinguished.

While this action was taking place in one arena, in another arena a fierce battle was being fought between Dronacharya and Dhrishtadyumna, son of the king of Panchala and brother of Draupadi. Drona was able to inflict wounds on his challenger's body, while Dhrishtadyumna hurled heavy maces and sharp missiles at Drona. But Drona broke them into pieces. Then Drona's arrows killed Dhrishtadyumna's charioteer. Dhrishtadyumna jumped down, holding a mace in his hand and advanced menacingly towards Drona. Drona's arrows smashed his mace. He took a sword in hand then and rushed at him, but Drona disabled him. Bhima saw Dhrishtadyumna's predicament. He sent a shower of arrows at Drona and carried Dhrishtadyumna to safety.

Duryodhan sent Kalinga forces against Bhima. Bhima killed

many Kalinga warriors, moving about like Yama incarnate. Bhishma came in support of the Kalingas, while Satyaki and Abhimanyu came in support of Bhima. One of Satyaki's shafts hit Bhishma's charioteer and he dropped down. The horses carried Bhishma out of the field. Arjuna also inflicted heavy casualties on the Kaurava army that day.

The Third Day

The Kaurava army was arrayed in eagle formation; Arjuna and Dhrishtadyumna decided in favour of crescent formation for their forces. Bhima was on the right horn of the crescent and Arjuna on the left.

Bhima and his son Ghatotkacha attacked Duryodhan's division. Bhima's shafts hit Duryodhan and he lay in swoon in his chariot. Duryodhan's charioteer quickly drove his chariot away. Bhima took advantage of the fleeing Kaurava army and wreaked havoc on it. Drona and Bhishma came up quickly and restored the army's confidence. Krishna asked Arjuna to go for the grandsire as he was the main pillar of the Kaurava forces. Arjun sent three shafts which broke the grandsire's bow. He picked up another but it too met with the same fate.

However, Krishna could see that Arjuna was not going for the grandsire's life; he was just playing games. Krishna jumped down, taking his discuss to attack Bhishma. Arjun ran after him and entreated that he return to the chariot.

The Fourth Day

As the battle commenced on the fourth day, the principal Kaurava warriors, Ashawatthama, Bhurishrva, Chitrasen and others surrounded Abhimanyu. Arjuna saw this combined attack and came to his son's rescue. Dhrishtadyumna also joined him. Chitrasen was killed. Duryodhan and his brothers joined in and they attacked Dhrishtadyumna. Bhima came in then and attacked Duryodhan's brothers. Duryodhan charged against Bhima with a large force of elephants. Seeing the elephants coming to attack him, Bhima got down from his chariot, holding his massive mace and attacked the elephants. The elephants scattered in a wild stampede, throwing the Kaurava ranks into disorder. The slaughtered mammoths lay dead in the field like black hillocks

Bhima returned to his chariot and sent arrows at Duryodhan but his armour saved him. However, he succeeded in killing eight of his brothers. Duryodhan was enraged and fought Bhima fiercely. One of Duryodhan's arrows struck Bhima's chest and he reeled and sat down. Ghatotkachha saw his father sitting dazed in the chariot; he fell upon the Kaurava army and started killing them mercilessly. The sun was setting and they called it a day.

The Fifth Day

Bhima stood at the head of the advance lines as usual. Dhrishtadyumna, Satyaki and Shikhandin stood behind him followed by other generals. Yudhishthir and the twin younger brothers held the rear. Bhishma was in his elements and Arjuna retaliated fiercely. Then Bhishma, Drona and Salya made a combined attack on Bhima. Seeing this Shikhandin came forward and Bhishma turned away. Shikhandin was born a girl and had later turned into a man. Bhishma's code of honour did not permit attacking a woman. Drona attacked Shikhandin and compelled him to withdraw.

Duryodhan sent a large force against Satyaki, but Satyaki destroyed it and advanced to attack Bhurishrava. Bhurishrava was a powerful fighter. Satyaki was weary after his fight with Duryodhan's force. He pressed on Satyaki fiercely, putting him in distress. Satyaki's 10 young sons, seeing their father's plight, launched a combined attack on Bhurishrava. Bhurishrava was undaunted by numbers. His arrows broke their bows and all the 10 sons of Satyaki were slain by him. Satyaki went wild, seeing his sons killed, and attacked Bhurishrava in his chariot. The chariots of both warriors dashed against each other. They jumped down, holding their swords and shields and engaged in single combat. But Bhima intervened and took Satyaki away in his chariot; he knew that Bhurishrava was an unrivalled swordsman.

The Sixth Day

Bhima pierced the Kaurava army's lines to seek out Duryodhan's brothers and kill them. Eight of them rushed on him in a combined attack, surrounded his chariot from all sides and showered their shafts at him. Bhima faced them bravely, but lost his patience and jumped down from his chariot, holding his mace in hand.

In the meanwhile, when Dhrishtadyumna saw Bhimasen's chariot disappear in enemy lines, he was alarmed and rushed after him to prevent disaster. He reached Bhima's chariot and asked the charioteer where Bhima was. He told him that asking him to stay there, he had gone, holding his mace in his hand. Dhrishtadyumna drove his chariot into the enemy lines. He found Bhima surrounded by enemies in their chariots, grievously wounded. He took him in his chariot and picked out the arrows that had pierced his body. Duryodhan, grieved by the killing of his brothers by Bhima had reached there along with Dronacharya. But in the meanwhile, Abhimanyu also came there with a force of 12 chariots.

Drona killed Dhrishtadyumna's charioteer, so Dhrishtadyumna got into Abhimanyu's chariot. Bhima had regained his strength by this time and in that indiscriminate fight, found himself facing Duryodhan. Duryodhan was hit by a sharp shaft fired by Bhima and fell unconscious in his chariot. Kripacharya extricated Duryodhan with great skill and took him away in his own chariot. The sun had set and the day's fight ceased.

The Seventh Day

In the battle between Drona and Virata, Virata was bested and his chariot was destroyed; he then got into the chariot of his son Sanga. Sanga too was killed by Dronacharya, and Virata withdrew; he had earlier lost his sons Uttara and Shveta.

Kritavarma fiercely attacked Bhima but was defeated by him, losing his chariot. He ran for his life towards Shakuni's chariot. With Bhima's arrows sticking all over his body, he looked like a porcupine speeding away in the forest.

Salya attacked his nephews Nakula and Sahadeva, killing Nakula's horses. Nakula went up in Sahadeva's chariot. They both continued fighting from the same chariot. Salya was hit by

Sahadeva's arrow and swooned. His charioteer skillfully drove him away.

Three of Duryodhan's brothers jointly attacked Abhimanyu, who inflicted a heavy defeat on them. But he spared their lives as Bhima had sworn to kill them. Thereupon, Bhishma attacked Abhimanyu. Arjuna asked Krishna to drive towards Bhishma. The other Pandava brothers also joined him. But the grandsire held his own against their combined might. The sun was setting at that time and they called it a day.

The Eighth Day

Bhima killed eight of Dhritarashtra's sons early in the battle. Duryodhan sent the rakshasa Alambasa to kill Iravan, Arjuna's son by his Naga wife. Iravan was killed after a fierce fight. At this Bhima's son Ghatotkacha uttered a loud war-cry and fell upon the Kaurava army. Duryodhan and the King of Vanga jointly attacked Ghatotkacha. Ghatotkacha hurled a javelin at Duryodhan. The Vanga king brought his elephant forward to save Duryodhan. The missile hit the elephant instead of Duryodhan.

Bhishma was worried about Duryodhan and sent Drona to support him.They all attacked Ghatotkacha together. Yudhishthir sent Bhima to protect him. Bhima faced them all together. Indeed, he went wild and killed eight more of Duryodhan's brothers.

The Nineth Day

Duryodhan was heart-broken at the slaughter of so many of his brothers by Bhima. He spoke to grandsire Bhishma in the morning and gave vent to feelings of disappointment over the way the battle was going. Bhishma said: 'You are now reaping the harvest of the hatred you deliberately sowed. I am pouring my life out for you like ghrita on sacrificial fire. But I have two limitations. I cannot fight Shikhandin; he was born a woman and I cannot raise my hand against a woman. Nor can I kill the Pandavas; my mind revolts against it. I will do everything else, barring these two factors.'

Duryodhan told Duhshasana to ensure that the grandsire was not exposed to Shikhandin.

In the Pandava camp, Krishna told Arjuna that he should not have any qualms of conscience in killing grandsire Bhishma. Arjuna replied: 'I would much rather have continued to be in exile in the forest than kill the grandsire and my teachers, whom I love. But I shall obey you.'

Bhishma and Arjuna confronted each other. Arjuna's shafts hit Bhishma's bow and shattered it many times, but he took another and the fight continued. Krishna told Arjuna: 'Dhananjaya, you are not fighting as you should.' Saying this, Krishna jumped down from the chariot, taking his discuss and advanced towards Bhishma. Arjuna too jumped down then, caught hold of Krishna and cried: 'Stop, Krishna, don't break your pledge. This is my duty, I'll do it. Pray, mount the chariot and take the reins.'

The Tenth Day

In the morning, before sunrise, Arjuna told his brothers and other chiefs fighting on their side, that he would be fighting the grandsire Bhishma that day. He advised them that they should engage all other leaders of the Kaurava army, and not allow them to come to defend the grandsire.

Arjuna attacked Bhishma, keeping Shikhandin in front of him. Bhishma did not retaliate when Shikhandin's arrows pierced his breast. The old warrior's eyes glared as if to consume Shikhandin. He knew his end was near and calmed himself. Standing behind Shikhandin, Arjuna aimed arrows at the weak points in Bhishma's armour. Bhishma could feel which were Shikhandin's arrows and which Arjuna's. He took up a javelin and hurled it at Arjuna, who cut it to pieces.

Bhishma decided to come down, holding his sword and shield but Arjuna cut his shield to pieces. Bhishma then fell headlong to the ground from his chariot, arrows sticking all over his body with no space left. His body did not touch the ground on account of the arrows sticking out all over his body. Both armies ceased fighting and all warriors came running and crowded around the great hero, lying on his bed of arrows, their heads bowed in reverence.

'My head hangs down, unsupported', said the grandsire. Princes ran and brought cushions. Bhishma rejected them and looking at Arjuna said: 'Partha, give me a cushion befitting a warrior.' Arjuna took out arrows from his quiver and so placed them that Bhishma's head rested on the quills.

Bhishma said then: 'Now, I must lie until the sun turns northward.'[194] Looking at Arjuna again, he said: 'I am tormented with thirst. Get me some drinking water.' Arjuna raised his bow, drew it to his ear and shot a shaft down into the earth on right side the grandsire. A gentle trickle of water gushed out from the opening made by his arrow and came within the reach of his mouth, to quench his thirst.

Looking at Duryodhan then, the grandsire said: 'Make peace with them, dear. Let the war cease with my exit.' Duryodhan looked away, without saying a word.

The Eleventh Day

Duryodhan held counsel with Karna and they decided to make Dronacharya the Supreme Commander of the Kaurava army. Duryodhan asked Drona to capture Yudhishthir alive. The Acharya was greatly pleased. The Pandava spies carried the news to them. They arrayed their forces to ensure that Yudhishthir was never left unsupported.

Kripacharya fought with Dhrishtaketu and worsted him. Abhimanyu gave a grand demonstration of his valour when he fought Paurava, Kritavarma, Jayadratha and Salya single-handed and made them withdraw. There was a great combat between Salya and Bhima in which Bhima defeated Salya, and he was made to retire.

Drona led an attack on Yudhishthir. He cut down Yudhishthir's bow. Dhrishtadyumna tried to intercept Drona but in vain. Arjun came up then and sent a shower of sharp arrows at his revered preceptor. Drona retreated.

[194]Dying when the Sun is southward was considered inauspicious. Because of his remarkable vow of celibacy, Bhishma had received the boon of choosing his time of death. He lay on the bed of Arjuna's arrows till the end of the battle.

The Twelfth Day

Drona told Duryodhan that it was not possible to capture Yudhishthir so long as Dhananjaya (Arjun) was nearby. The chief of Trigartadesh made a plan of taking the Sampataka oath and challenging Arjuna to battle and draw him away from Yudhishthir's side. Sitting before the fire, dressed in matted grass, they took the sampataka oath after going through funeral ceremonies for themselves, as if they were already dead.

They challenged Arjuna in the morning. Arjuna said to Yudhishthir. 'Susharma's men are calling me to battle, I cannot refuse. I shall destroy them all and return. Permit me to go.' He asked the Panchala prince Satyajit to protect Yudhishthir and left. The Trigartas fell in the fire of Arjuna's wrath in swathes.

Drona then gave orders for a violent assault on the Pandava forces. He avoided Dhrishtadyumna and went towards Drupada, inflicting heavy casualties. Satyajit made a fierce charge on Drona's chariot but he was too good for him. Satyajit and Vrika, a prince of Panchala, fell dead. Virata's son Shatanik too suffered the same fate.

Bhima, Satyaki, Nakula, Drupada, Virata and Shikhandin then came to protect Yudhishthir. Duryodhna led a large elephant division against Bhima, who cut down his flag. The king of Anga marched against Bhima; Bhima killed him. King Bhagadatta of Pragjyotishpur then charged against Bhima. Arjuna returned in the meanwhile to fight Bhagadatta. He hurled shafts at him, breaking his bow and piercing the joints of his armour. He sent an arrow which entered the head of Bhagadatta's giant tusker. The elephant stood rigid for a while and sank down giving an agonized squeal. Arjuna then sent a sharp crescent-headed shaft which pierced Bhagadatta's chest.

Shakuni's brothers Vrisha and Achala attacked Arjuna, who dashed their chariots to pieces and they both lay dead. Shakuni came forward and attacked Arjuna fiercely but had to leave the field in face of Arjuna's shafts.

The Thirteenth Day

The Samsaptakas again challenged Arjuna and he had to engage in a do-or-die battle with them. In Arjuna's absence Drona had arranged his army in a lotus formation and waged a fierce battle. Yudhishthir called Abhimanyu and told him that his valiant father was away and if we got defeated in his absence, he would be grieved beyond measure. No one amongst us has been able to break Drona's array. 'I can do it,' Abhimanyu said. 'My father had instructed me to penetrate this formation. I can do it. But after forcing my way in, I shall be at a loss to come out, not having been instructed as yet by my father.' Yudhishthir told him that they would all follow him and enter in his wake, and defeat the Kaurava army. Bhimasen too supported the proposal and told Abhimanyu that he would be immediately behind him, like the other chiefs.

Abhimanyu was greatly pleased to lead the Pandava army. He asked his charioteer to drive fast. However, Jayadratha, King of the Sindhus, Dhritarashtra's son-in-law, ensured that the breach was closed immediately after the young man's entry, before the other Pandava warriors could enter. Yudhishthir hurled a javelin at Jayadratha, cutting his bow, but he took up another and sent unerring shafts at Yudhishthir. Bhima's arrows crashed down his canopy and flagstaff. Jayadratha re-armed himself and killed Bhima's chariot horses. Bhima got into Satyaki's chariot. But Jayadratha succeeded in preventing the Pandavas' entry.

Abhimanyu went ahead, unafraid. Duhshashan faced him but was struck senseless in his chariot by Abhimanyu. Karna attacked him then but Abhimanyu broke his bow. Indeed, he disabled all those who confronted him. Duryodhan's son Lakshman charged on him; Abhimanyu's swift shaft pierced him and he lay dead. Duryodhan yelled, seeing his son fall, and the six warriors, Drona, Kripa, Karna, Ashwatthama, Kritavarma and Brihatbala, all closed upon Abhimanyu, surrounding him on all sides, violating the rule of face-to-face combat.

Drona asked Karna to aim at the reins of his horses and cut them off. 'Disable him thus and then attack him from behind' he added. Karna broke his bow by a shaft discharged from behind him. His horses and the charioteer were killed. Abhimanyu now stood on the ground with his sword and shield. Drona's shaft broke Abhimanyu's sword and Karna's sharp arrows tore his shield into bits. Standing in the ring of his enemies, Abhimanyu took one of his chariot wheels in his right hand and began whirling it like a discus. However, the combined onslaught of the warriors from all sides overpowered him. The chariot wheel was shattered to pieces and a son of Duhshasana then struck him with a mace from behind and killed him. The Kaurava warriors exulted and danced in frenzy.

While there was blowing of conches and cries of victory by the Kaurava army, Yuyutsu, a son of Dhritarashtra who was there, did not approve it. 'This is ignoble', he angrily cried. 'You have forgotten your code. Verily, you should be ashamed, but you shout brazen cries of victory. Having committed a most wicked deed, you revel in joy, blind to the danger that is imminent.' He threw his weapon away in disgust and left the battlefield.

Yudhishthir was plunged in grief at Abhimanyu's demise. 'I pushed him to the battle front! What words of comfort can I offer to Arjuna now? What shall I say to Subhadra, quivering like a cow who has lost her calf? He overcame Drona, Duryodhan, Ashwatthama, he made Duhshasana flee in fear. Indeed, I have killed Arjuna's beloved son!'

After defeating and slaying the Samsaptakas, Arjuna and Krishna were proceeding towards their camp at evenfall. Arjuna had a premonition of disaster. There was mournful silence in the camp and they came to know about Abhimanyu's demise. Arjuna cried in grief: 'Alas, has my dear boy become Yama's guest? Subhadra's brave son slain? What comfort shall I give to Subhadra?'

Shri Krishna spoke to his stricken friend: 'Dear Arjuna, do not give way to grief. Born as kshatriyas we have to live and die by weapons. Warriors must be ever ready to die. If you give way to grief, your brothers and other kings will lose heart. Stop grieving and infuse courage and fortitude into their hearts.'

Yudhishthir related the whole story: 'I incited Abhimanyu to enter the enemy's formation; I knew that he alone could do it among all of us. I told him we shall follow immediately behind him, adding that this great deed of yours will please your father and your uncles. He broke the great formation and we went behind according to plan. But just then the wicked Jayadratha came, began fighting with us, effectively stopping us from entering. A whole bunch of redoubtable warriors surrounded Abhimanyu and slayed him.'

Hearing it, Arjuna fell in swoon. When he recovered, he took a solemn pledge: 'Before the sunset tomorrow, I shall slay Jayadratha who caused my son's death!' He twanged the Gandiva string then and Krishna blew his conch Panchajanya with full force. Bhima said: 'This twang of Arjuna's bow and this blare of Krishna's conch shall be the summons of Death unto the sons of Dhritarashtra!'

~

Sanjaya briefed Dhritarashtra in the night: 'Subhadra's son, like a young elephant in a lily pond, single-handedly worked havoc in the Kaurava army. He was thus overpowered by numbers and killed cruelly. And having killed him, your people danced around his dead body like savage hunters exulting over their prey. All good men in the army were grieved and tears rolled down their eyes.'

~

The Fourteenth Day

Jayadratha came to know about Arjuna's vow. He went to Duryodhan in fear and trepidation and said: 'I do not want to be in this battle any longer. Let me go back to my country.' 'Do not fear', replied Duryodhan, 'O King of Sindhu, all our veterans and warriors shall stand between you and danger. Karna, Bhurishrava, Salya, Chitrsena, Vikarna, Durmukha, Duhshasana, Drona, Shakuni and myself, we are all here and you cannot be in danger. The whole of my army will have but one task today—to defend you against Arjuna.' Jayadratha went to Dronacharya then who told him: 'You will be placed behind a strong force that Arjuna cannot pierce. Discard all fear and fight.'

Durmarshana, brother of Duryodhan, stood with a large force. He challenged Arjuna. Arjuna beat his army like clouds driven about by gale. Duhashasana came forward then leading a huge force of elephants. He fought fiercely but withdrew defeated.

Dronacharya came forward and challenged Arjuna. Arjuna told him he was grieving for his son and asked him to let him pass. He also sought his guru's blessings for fulfillment of his vow. Drona replied he must fight and defeat him before he could reach Jayadratha. He discharged a shower of arrows at Arjuna, cut his bow-string. Krishna drove the chariot to the left of Drona and proceeded forward. Kritavarma and Sudakshina, who opposed their passage, were defeated. The King of Kamboja then led his army against Arjuna but after a fierce fight he lay dead. Shrutayu and his brother Ashrutayu attacked Arjuna then, from both sides but Arjuna was able to slay both brothers and their two sons.

Duryodhan was greatly agitated when he saw Arjuna's chariot advancing triumphantly towards Jayadratha and asked Drona why he was not stopping him. Dronacharya answered: 'In fact our plan has borne fruit. Yudhishthir is unsupported by Arjuna now. I would rather go for him, take him prisoner and deliver him to you. You go and oppose Arjuna.'

In the meanwhile, the brothers Vinda and Anuvinda attacked Arjuna who slew them both. Duryodhan challenged Arjuna then. Arjuna killed his horses and broke his bow, disarming him. He sent needle-sharp arrows to pierce the parts of his body not covered by armour. Duryodhan turned and fled. Krishna blew his conch, celebrating it.

Seeing Drona's chariot advancing towards Yudhishthir, Dhrishtadyumna attacked him but Drona was dominating and dodged him. Satyaki intervened then and they sent sharp shafts at each other. Yudhishthir called Satyaki and asked him to go and help Arjuna fulfill his vow. Satyaki replied that Arjuna had given him firm instructions to guard and protect him from Drona. But ordered by Yudhishthir, he left leaving him in Bhimasena's charge.

Yudhishthir told Bhima that he could hear the sound of Krishna's conch but not the twang of Arjuna's Gandiva. He feared that Arjuna had been slain and Krishna was fighting the Kauravas. He sent Bhima also to go and save Arjuna. Bhima could not disobey him; he asked Dhrishtadyumna to guard Yudhishthir and left. The Kauravas opposed Bhima with full force. Bhima killed 11 sons of Dhritarashtra but Drona stopped him. Bhima threw his mace at Drona's chariot which crumbled to pieces and Drona had to take another chariot.

Bhima advanced, mowing down all opposition and reached where Arjuna was fighting Jayadratha and his supporters. As soon as he espied Arjuna, Bhima roared. Krishna and Arjuna were exceedingly pleased and raised yells of joy. Karna wanted to stop Bhima from going in support of Arjuna. Bhima began to destroy his chariots. Duryodhan sent his brother Durjaya to render assistance to Karna. Durjaya attacked Bhima who killed his horses and sent Durjaya to the abode of Yama, and turned towards Karna again. Duryodhan sent his brother Durmukha then. Bhima licked his lips with gusto and sent nine shafts in succession at him; Durmukha's armour was broken and he fell down, lifeless. He attacked Karna then whose arrows wounded Bhima all over. However, seeing Duryodhan's brothers dying for his sake and the physical pain of his own wounds made him lose his courage and he turned away defeated. Bhima stood in the battlefield, red with wounds all over like flaming fire; emitting a triumphant yell and marched ahead to support Arjuna.

Krishna saw Satyaki coming and said to Arjuna: 'There comes the valorous Satyaki! Your disciple and friend is marching up triumphantly breaking through enemy lines.'

Arjuna did not like Satyaki to have left Yudhishthir unguarded as Drona was seeking an opportunity to capture Yudhishthir and he expressed his displeasure to Krishna. In the meanwhile, Bhurishrava saw Satyaki and challenged him. There was an old enmity between the two. Satyaki's grandfather, Sini, had rescued Krishna's mother Devaki, when she was a maiden, and was forcibly being taken away by Bhurishrava's grandfather Somadatta. Sini had done this on behalf of Vasudeva, whom Devaki liked, and they were later married.

Bhurishrava challenged Satyaki. Their chariots dashed against each other and they were in a deadly embrace without weapons. Krishna knew about the family feud and was concerned about Satyaki's fate. 'Dhananjaya' said Krishna, 'Satyaki is exhausted;

Bhurishrava is going to kill him now.' But Arjuna was following only Jayadratha's movements. Krishna told him that Satyaki had come after an exhausting battle with the Kauravas and was forced to accept Bhurishrava's challenge. 'It is a most unequal battle; unless we help him, he will be slain.' Bhurishrava lifted Satyaki and brought him crashing down.

Again, Krishna importuned: 'Satyaki is lying almost dead on the field, the best among the Vrishni clan. One who came to help you is dying before your eyes and you are looking on, doing nothing.' Bhurishrava had put his foot on the prostrate body of Satyaki and was about to slay him with his sword, when Arjuna shot an arrow which chopped off his arm holding the sword. Bhurishrava complained against this unethical act and said: 'You must have been instigated by the son of Vasudeva.' Arjuna replied: 'Don't I know, you cheered the man who killed my weaponless boy Abhimanyu?'

Bhurishrava then spread his arrows on the ground with his left hand and made a seat for meditation. Satyaki had recovered now. He picked up a sword, advanced towards Bhurishrava, sitting in yoga posture on a seat of arrows, and with one stroke beheaded him.

∽

'The decisive hour has come, Karna', said Duryodhan. 'If before sunset, Jayadratha is not slain, Arjuna would commit suicide. With him gone, the destruction of the Pandavas is certain, and the kingdom will be ours. We must ensure that Partha does not reach Jayadratha in time. You, Ashwatthama, Salya, Kripa and I must guard Jayadratha.' 'My King,' Karna replied, 'I have been wounded all over by Bhima; my limbs have no power in them. Still, I'll do all I can.'

Krishna called another charioteer, Daruka, and sent Satyaki in it to attack Karna. Satyaki killed his four horses, his flag staff was cut asunder and the chariot smashed. Karna ran and climbed into Duryodhan's chariot.

Arjuna broke through the Kaurava opposition and reached Jayadratha and fought with him. Jayadratha was no mean foe. The battle raged long. Both were looking westwards, for the day was nearing its end. Suddenly, the sun sank and the horizon reddened, but the battle did not cease. Then a cloud covered the sun and it became dusky and dark; the Kaurava army shouted in joy: 'The sun has set. Jayadratha has not been killed. Arjuna has lost! Hurray!'

The next instant the Sun came out of the cloud cover and Krishna said: 'The sun beckons Dhananjaya! Shoot your arrow now.' Jayadratha was looking towards the horizon when a shaft flew from the Gandiva and carried away Jayadratha's head.

The Fifteenth Day

Bhima's son Ghatotkacha, by his rakshasi wife, was a brave and indefatigable fighter and had performed several acts of heroism during the war. On the fifteenth day, fighting did not cease at nightfall. The Kaurava army went on a rampage and killed the men of the Pandava army. Ghatotkacha and his troop of Asuras, who are strongest at night, found darkness an additional advantage and violently attacked the Kaurava army camp. Duryodhan's heart sank when he saw thousands of his men killed by Ghatotkacha and his demon army. He told Karna to kill Ghatotkacha at once. Karna was himself angry and bewildered having just been wounded by the Asura's arrow. He had the spear obtained after his penance. He hurled it at the young giant; Ghatotkacha, Bhima's beloved son, dropped dead.

Dronacharya was raining havoc on the Pandava army. 'O Arjuna', Krishna said, 'there is none that can defeat Drona. There is but one thing that will make him fumble. If he hears that Ashwatthama is dead, he will lose all interest in life. Someone must tell him that Ashwatthama has been slain in battle.'

It was strange. But when the ocean was churned at the beginning of the world and the dreaded poison arose, threatening to consume the gods, did not Rudra come forward to swallow it and save them? To save his friend Sugriva, who had wholly depended on him, Rama was driven to kill Vali from behind a tree, disregarding the rules of fair play. So also, now Yudhishthir decided to bear the shame of it, for there was no other way.

There was an elephant named Ashwatthama in the Pandava

army. Bhima lifted his iron mace and brought it down on the huge tusker, Ashwatthama, and it fell dead. After killing the elephant Ashwatthama, Bhimasen drove his chariot near Dronacharya and roared: 'I have killed Ashwatthama; Ashwatthama is dead!'

Dronacharya came near Bhima and asked, 'Is it true? Is Ashwatthama dead?' Bhima replied: 'Yes, it's true! I have killed Ashwatthama; Ashwatthama is dead.' He then whispered in a feeble voice—'*Naro va Kunjara*' (Man or Elephant). However, this qualifying clause was drowned in the din of cheering drums.

When Drona heard his beloved son had been slain, he threw his weapons away and sat down in the yoga posture on the floor of his chariot. Dhrishtadyumna, with a drawn sword, climbed his chariot and cut off his head. The Pandava army gave a great shout of victory.

The Sixteenth Day

Duryodhan installed Karna as the Chief of the Kaurava Army. Arjuna led the attack on Karna, supported by Bhima. Duhshasana launched a concentrated attack on Bhima, who chuckled seeing him, and proceeded to redeem his promise to Draupadi. Jumping down from his chariot, Bhima ran towards Duhshasana's chariot and leapt upon Duhshasana like a tiger on its prey. He hurled him down and broke his limbs. 'Wicked beast, is this the wretched hand that held Draupadi's hair? Here, I tear out its root from your body.' He tore Duhshasana's arm out and threw it away. Then he opened his rib cage and drank his blood like a beast of prey, fulfilling the terrible oath he had taken 17 years ago. He danced then, raising his blood smeared hands and roared: 'I have done it! Draupadi, I have done it!'

This horrific scene made everyone shudder. Even Krishna was shaken as he saw Bhima in this ecstasy of wrath.

Karna came face to face with Arjuna and sent a dazzling arrow at him; it hit Arjuna's helmet. Arjuna was red in the face with anger. Suddenly the left wheel of Karna's chariot sank in bloody mire. Karna jumped down from his chariot to lift the wheel from the mud. 'Wait a minute', he shouted, 'let me take out my chariot's wheel.'

Krishna retorted: 'Now you remember the rules of fair play! But when you and Duryodhan asked Duhashasana to drag Draupadi in the Hall of Assembly and he began to strip her, you were enjoying her disgrace. And when a mob of you surrounded Abhimanyu and shamelessly slew him, you were enjoying it!'

Karna bent his head in shame, got back in his sunk chariot and sent an arrow at Arjuna with unerring aim which stunned Arjuna for a few moments. He jumped down again to take out his wheel.

'Waste no time, Arjuna', Krishna said: 'Slay your wicked enemy now.' Arjuna was hesitating, but obeying Krishna, he sent an arrow which severed Karna's head.

The Seventeenth Day

Duryodhan chose Salya to be the Supreme Commander of his army and Yudhishthir led the Pandava attack that day. The battle raged for a long while. Then Yudhishthir hurled his spear at Salya, which went straight and struck him; Salya lay dead in the field.

The surviving sons of Dhritarashtra joined together and attacked Bhima from all sides. Bhima went after them, one by one, and slew them all, and said to himself: 'I have not lived in vain! Yet Duryodhan still lives!'

Shakuni led the attack on Sahadeva's division. Sahadeva discharged a sharp-edged arrow at him, saying: 'You are the root cause of bringing this calamity on us. Here is your reward.' It sliced off Shakuni's head.

Left leaderless, the Kaurava army scattered and fled in all directions. In vain, Duryodhan tried to rally his defeated army. Carrying a mace, he walked towards a pool of water and entered it to cool himself.

The Pandavas came after him. Yudhishthir exclaimed: 'After destroying the whole family and the tribe, can you escape death concealing yourself in a pond?'

Stung to the quick, he replied: 'I have not come here as a fugitive for my life. I stepped into the water to cool the fire that is raging within me. I have no fear of death. But why should I fight? My desire for the kingdom is gone; you enjoy it now.'

'That's generous indeed! Especially after you had said you

would not allow us even a needle point of land.'

Duryodhan came out, took the mace in hand and said: 'I am single; you come one by one.' Yudhishthir retorted: 'Tell me, how was Abhimanyu killed? Did you not consent to many commanders of your army combining and attacking that boy? But I accept your request; Bhima would fight with you.'

The combat began between Bhima and Duryodhan. Sparks flew when their maces clashed. The two were equal in strength and skill, and the battle raged long. Bhima leaped like a lion holding his mace and as he came down, he broke Duryodhan's thighs. Duryodhan fell on the ground. Bhima jumped on his prostrate body, stamped on his head with his foot and danced.'

'Cease Bhima', Yudhishthir said, 'you have paid off the debt.'

~

Krishna's brother Balarama came to Kurukshetra after completing his tour of holy places. He saw Bhima breaking Duryodhan's thighs and was enraged by this cruel act. Krishna told him it was the duty of a kshatriya to fulfill the vow he had taken. Bhima had taken the vow when Draupadi was disgraced by Duryodhan and his brothers.

Duryodhan half raised himself on his arms in spite of his excruciating pain and said to Krishna: 'Your father Vasudeva was a servant of Kansa. You are no prince!' He then hurled a long diatribe on Krishna.

'Son of Gandhari,' Krishna replied: 'It is your own misdeeds that have brought about your end. Do not attribute it to me. Bhishma and Drona had to die on account of your sins; you are the main cause of the death of Karna and others and are guilty of committing wrongs against the sons of Pandu. What punishment can be too severe for the outrage which you inflicted on Draupadi?'

The Eighteenth Day

Dronacharya's son Ashwatthama heard that Duryodhan lay mortally injured and that he was stricken down against all rules of chivalry. He went to where Duryodhan was lying. Seeing Duryodhan's pitiable condition, he took an oath that he would kill the Pandavas that night. Duryodhan, who was in the last physical agony of departing life, was transported with joy and ordered his men who stood nearby to install Ashwatthama as the Supreme Commander of what remained of the Kauarava army.

Ashwatthama woke up Kripacharya and Kritavarma and informed them of his plan. Kripacharya remonstrated him: 'It is wholly wrong. How can men who have gone to sleep be attacked? Duryodhan, for whose sake we fought this war, is on his last breath. Let us go to Dhritarashtra and take counsel of wise Vidura.'

Ashwatthama retorted: 'The Pandavas killed my father through a lie, telling him I was dead. I can only repay my debt by carrying out this plan. I have to kill Dhristadyumna and the Pandavas when they are asleep. My noble father was killed when he had thrown away his weapons and had sat down in prayer.'

Ashwatthama found Dhristadyumna sleeping without his armour. He leapt on him and kicked him to death. Similarly, he killed all the sons of Draupadi. He came out then and set fire to the whole camp. He then went to the dying Duryodhan and told him: 'I have killed all the Panchalas as also the all sons of the Pandavas.' Hearing this, Duryodhan slowly opened his eyes and, gasping for breath, said: 'Ashwatthama, you have done for me what the great Bhishma and the valiant Karna couldn't achieve! You have gladdened my heart and I die happy.' Saying this, Duryodhan gave up the ghost.

Seeing the devastation caused by Ashwatthama's foul deed, Yudhishthir lamented: 'At the very moment of victory we have been totally defeated.' Draupadi was overwhelmed by inconsolable grief. She came to Yudhishthir, weeping bitterly, and said: 'Is there no one to avenge my children's slaughter by slaying this sinner Ashwatthama?'

Bhima went out in his search and killed Ashwatthama. He prised out the shining jewel which was part of Ashwatthama's head, and going to Draupadi, said: 'Angel of spotless purity, this jewel is for you. The man who killed your innocent sons, has been killed. Duryodhan has been destroyed. I have drunk the blood of Duhashasana. I have avenged the great outrage and discharged my debts.

Draupadi took the jewel from Bhima, went to Yudhishthir, and said: 'Faultless King, it befits you to wear this jewel in your crown.'

HASTINAPUR GETS ITS KING

Yudhishthir was duly crowned King at Hastinapur. He went to where Bhishma lay on his bed of arrows awaiting his death, and took his blessing and instruction on Dharma. The instructions grandsire Bhishma gave to Yudhishthir are contained in the famous Shanti Parva of the Mahabharata. After giving his discourse, the great Bhishma passed away. King Yudhishthir went to the Ganga and offered libations for the peace of the departed souls. Dhritarashtra also came there and joined in.

Yudhishthir performed an Ashwamedha Yajna after being crowned. He would issue orders after taking Dhritarashtra's consent, making him feel that the kingdom was being ruled on his behalf.

Gandhari was looked after by Kuntidevi and Draupadi. After some years Dhritarashtra and Gandhari went to live in the forest. As Gandhari kept her eyes covered, Kunti too decided to accompany them to the forest. Yudhishthir was upset and requested her not to desert them. She replied: 'I shall be with Gandhari and go through the discipline of forest life and would soon join your father.'

They had spent three years in the forest when a fire broke out. The three of them sat down on the ground, facing eastward in yoga posture and calmly gave themselves up to the flames.

SHRI KRISHNA PASSES AWAY

Krishna ruled at Dwarka for 36 years after the Kurukshetra battle was over. The Vrishnis, Bhopas and other branches of the Yadavas of Krishna's tribe spent their days in unrestrained self-indulgence and luxury, losing all sense of discipline and humility.

One day, they had gone to the beach and spent the whole day in dance and drink and revelry. The liquor began to work. At first merry, then pugnacious, and then they began to talk without restraint, raking up old offences against each other and began quarrelling with one another. Kritavarma who had fought on the side of the Kauravas and Satyaki on that of the Pandavas began to argue with each other, accusing each other of gross misconduct and treachery.

Kritavarma cited the killing of Bhurishrava against Satyaki and Satyaki accused Kritavarma of going with Aswatthama to set fire to the Pandava camp, killing sleeping soldiers. A number of revellers joined them and soon all of them came to blows. It soon developed into a fierce fight. Satyaki drew his sword and beheaded Kritavarma. Others fell upon Satyaki and rained blows on him. Pradyumna, Krishana's son, joined the fray to rescue Satyaki and in the melee both Pradyumna and Satyaki were killed. Balarama later passed away in grief.

Shocked and bewildered by this tragic brawl, and seeing the passing away of his brother Balarama, Krishna roamed about on the wooded beach and lay down on the ground among the shrubs. A hunter, looking for game and taking him to be a wild animal, shot an arrow at the prostate figure which pierced him and proved fatal.

RETREAT TO THE HIMALAYAS

The sad tidings of the death of Krishna and the destruction of the Yadavas reached Hastinapur. The Pandavas were plunged in grief. They placed Parikshit, son of Abhimanyu and Uttara on the throne, and the five brothers, accompanied by Draupadi, went on a pilgrimage. After visiting holy places, they finally reached the Himalayas. A dog joined them somewhere on the way and kept them company.

The seven of them toiled up the mountain path that was covered with snow. Their feet were benumbed, their bodies exhausted, but their spirits were high, seeing the snow-covered peaks sparkling against the blue sky. They were unaware of the crevasses—deep fissures caused by the warming of the earth in the upper reaches, which were hidden by fresh snow. Draupadi was the first to fall in a crevasse, and in an instant disappeared in its deep depths. Nakula and Sahadeva fell after going up for some time. Arjuna and Bhimasen, too, fell into crevasses after a while.

Yudhishthir was left alone; he was tired to the bone but the dog kept him company. They trudged on. God Indra appeared then in his celestial chariot. Yudhishthir paid him reverence and Indra said: 'Your brothers and Draupadi have arrived before you. You have lagged behind, burdened by your body. Ascend my chariot, I have come to take you. I will take you with your body.'

When Yudhishthir ascended in Indra's chariot, the dog also climbed up. 'No, no.' said Indra: 'There is no place for dogs in heaven!' He pushed the dog away. 'Then there is no place for me either', said Yudhishthir, and added: 'He has kept me company all the way.' He began to get down from the chariot. Indeed, Dharma, in the form of a dog, had come to test Yudhishthir and vanished.

Indra disappeared when they reached the celestial abode. Yudhishthir saw Duryodhan sitting on a beautiful throne, but not his own brothers or anyone else. He was astonished, and said aloud: 'Where are my brothers? This evil man is sitting here; I don't see my great brothers. We were driven by this man's hostility and envy to kill our friends and relatives!' The celestial sage Narada appeared before him then, and said: 'O Renowned prince, this is not right. Here, in swarga, we harbour no ill-will against any one. Do not speak in this manner about Duryodhan. He has attained his present state by the power of Kshatriya Dharma.'

Yudhishthir replied: 'O noble sage, this man, Duryodhan, did not know right from wrong; he was an ace sinner and had caused untold suffering to numberless people. He is here, not my brothers. I long to see them and be with them all. What good is heaven, without them?'

A messenger appeared beforeYudhisthira then and he followed

him. He had to wade through hell, going over slippery slime of blood and offal. The path was strewn with mutilated human bodies, carrion and bones, and there was an insufferable stench in the air. He thought of returning but he heard human voices: 'O *Dharmaputra*, do not go back. Be here for some time at least. Your presence has given us momentary relief from extreme torture. You have brought a whiff of fresh air, fragrant and pleasurable, giving us some relief from our intolerable agony.' The voices were of Bhima, Arjuna, Nakula, Sahadeva, Draupadi and Karna.

Yudhisthira was overwhelmed by deep sorrow. He turned to his angel-attendant and said; 'You go back. I shall stay here with my people.'

After some time, Indra and Yama appeared before him. On their arrival, the darkness rolled away and the horrid sights disappeared. A fragrant breeze began to blow. Yama smiled and said to him: 'This is the third time I have tested you. You chose to remain in hell for the sake of your brothers. However, it is inevitable that kings and rulers must go through hell for a while. Neither Bhima, nor Arjuna or Karna are in hell. It was an illusion designed to test you.'

The next instant Yudhisthira's mortal frame was gone. With the disappearance of the human body, all traces of anger and hatred also disappeared. He saw Draupadi and all his brothers. Karna and the sons of Dhritarashtra were also there, serene and free from anger. In this reunion, Yudhisthira found peace and real happiness.

~

Chaturvedi Badrinath, in the introduction of his award-winning book, *The Mahabharata*,[195] observes:

> The direction the Mahabharata takes is a continuation of the one that Upanishdas had taken. The latter had broken away from Vedic ritualism and its belief in the magical efficacy of 'acts,' and had turned human attention to the *inwardness* of the self instead. The Mahabharata is even more steadfast on its path. The Vedic idea of Rta, the cosmic order out

[195]Badrinath, Chaturvedi, *The Mahabharata*: *An Inquiry in the Human Condition*, Orient Blackswan, 2007, pp. 15–17.

> there, is replaced with the idea of Dharma as the foundation of life. The yajna or sacrificial act is replaced with self-understanding. Gaining punya (merit) is replaced with giving and sharing, with no eye on 'reward'. Tapas or austerity is given an inward, ethical meaning. Tirtha or pilgrimage is not to some geographical place but to one's inner self in relation with the other. Thus, daya or kindness, or compassion is a tirtha. The focus radically shifts from 'acts' to relationships. The Mahabharata radically changes the meaning of yajna, tapas, karma, and tirtha; and in making them relational, it gives them a deeply ethical meaning. The word Rta is heard only rarely, and dharma becomes the dominant sound. The chanting of mantras is replaced with the sound of inquiry into the foundations of the relationships of *the Self with the Self, and of the Self with the Other*.

Chaturvedi Badrinath adds: 'The Mahabharata systemically confronts one reality with another, one truth with another, when one is clearly the opposite of the other, but both are manifest in life simultaneously. For example, the necessity of "*kshma,*" forgiveness and reconciliation, is shown to be fundamental to human relationships, and is spoken of in the highest terms.'

BHAGAVADA GITA

The Bhagavada Gita is stated to be the essence of India's Vedic wisdom and is considered a spiritual and philosophical classic of the world. Indeed, Henry David Thoreau had paid a rare compliment by saying that 'in relation to Bhagavada Gita our modern world and its literature seem puny and trivial.'

The Bhagavada Gita is written in the form of a dialogue between Shri Krishna and Arjuna. In **Chapter II,** Krishna develops his argument by saying that according to the Gyan-yoga, man's body is mortal but the soul is immortal, which takes birth in another body and that the body is unreal while the soul is real. Wise men do not grieve over death of near and dear ones. While the body is slain the soul is not; it is everlasting, eternal. It sheds the body like worn-out garments and adorns itself with new ones:

Nainam chhindanti shashtraani, nainam dahati paavakah,
*Na chainam kledayantyaapo, na shoshayati maarutah.*23.

[Weapons do not cleave the Self, fire does not burn, waters do not make wet, nor does the wind dry the Self.]

Shri Krishna says that a person's station in society determines his or her duty. He tells Arjuna that being a Kshatriya, it's his bounden duty to fight. It would be contraty to his dharma, if he refused to fight and he would incur sin. **Verse 32** says, 'Happy are the kshatriyas, O Parth, for whom such a war comes of its own accord as an open door to heaven.'

He adds that even according to karma yoga (the yoga of selfless action) which applies to all persons, one's right is to perform one's duty sincerely, without caring for the fruits of action:

Karmaneyv aadhikaaraste, maa phaleshu kadaachana;
*Maa karmaphala hetur bhoor, maa te sango astva karmaami.*47.

[To action alone hast thou a right and never at all to its fruits; let not the fruits of action be thy motive; but this should not lead one to inaction.]

However, as regards the Vedas, contrary voices are heard in the Gita in different chapters. In Chapter II itself, **Verses 42, 43 and 44** appear to be critical of the Vedas:

Yaamimaam pushpitaam vaacham pravadantya vipashchitaha,
Vedavaadarataah Partha naanyad asteeti vaadinah.
Kaamaatmaanah svargaparaa janma karma phala pradaam,
Kriyaa vishesh bahulaam bhogaishvarya gatim prati.
Bhogaishvarya prasaktaanaam tayaapahritaa chetsaam.
Vyavasaayaatmikaa buddhih samadhaanau na vidheeyate.

I quote below S. Radhakrishnan's translation of these verses:

'O *Partha*, the undiscerning who rejoice in the letter of the Vedas, who contend that there is nothing else, whose nature is desire and who are intent on heaven, proclaim these flowery words that result in rebirth as the fruit of actions and (lay down) various specialized rites for the attainment of enjoyment and power. The intelligence which discriminates between right and wrong, of those who are devoted to enjoyment and power and whose minds are carried away by these words (of the Veda) is not well-established in the Self.'

45. 'The action of the three-fold modes is the subject matter of the Veda; but do thou become free, O Arjuna, from this three-fold nature; be free from the dualities (the pairs of opposites), be firmly fixed in purity, not caring for acquisition and preservation, and be possessed of the Self.'

46. 'As is the use of the pond in a place flooded with water everywhere, so is that of all the Vedas for the Brahmin who understands.'

S. Radhakrishnan had commented on these verses: 'The Vedic Aryans were like glorious children in their eager acceptance of life. They represent the youth of humanity whose life was fresh and sweet... They had also the balanced wisdom of maturity. The Gita's author, however, limits his attention to the *karma-kand* of the Veda, which is not its whole teaching. While the Veda teaches us to work with a desire for recompense whether in a temporary heaven or in a new embodied life, *Buddhi-yoga* leads us to release.'

Earlier, in **Verse 38**, the spirit of equanimity finds a beautiful exposition:

> *Sukhaduhkhe same kritva, laabhaalaabhau jayaajayau,*
> *Tato yuddhaaya yujyasva naivam paapam avyaapsasi.*38.
>
> 'Treating alike pleasure and pain, gain and loss, victory and defeat, then get ready for battle. Thus, thou shall not incur sin.'

Arjuna then asks Krishna what were the qualities of a person who is *sthitapragya.* Krishna answers that one who casts off all cravings of the mind, who remains unperturbed amidst sorrows, who is free from passion, fear and anger, is called sthitapragya. However, Shri Krishna adds that one who was devoted to Him would be equally entitled to be called sthitapragya:

> *'Taani sarvaani samyamyah yukta aaseeta mataparah;*
> *Vashe hi yasyndriaani, tasya pragyaa pratishthitaa.*61.
>
> [Therefore, having controlled all the senses and concentrating his mind, he should sit in meditation, devoting himself, in heart and soul, to Me. He whose senses are under his control is known as *sthitapragya.*]

My own study of Bhagavada Gita gives me an impression that its composition was a combined venture, undertaken by many pundits, as the same philosophic points are developed over and over again in different chapters. That would also explain why on important question of Vedic philosophy, different points of view have been expressed in different chapters. According to S. Radhakrishnan, in the verses that are critical of the Vedas, true karma is distinguished from ritualistic piety.

Reacting to Krishna's espousal of gyan yoga and karma yoga, Arjun asks him at the beginning of **Chapter III**: 'If you consider Knowledge superior to Action, why are you urging me to this dreadful action?'

Krishna tells him that one cannot avoid performing his allotted duty and adds that he should do it in the spirit of a yajna-sacrifice. He goes on to explain that in ancient days Prajapati, the Lord of creatures, created men along with yajna (sacrifice) and had said: 'By this shall ye bring forth and this shall be unto you that which will yield the milk of your desires.' Indeed, here Krishna becomes a votary of Vedic sacrifice, and tells Arjuna:

Devaan bhaavayataanen te devaa bhaavayantu vah;
*Parasparam bhaavayantuh shreyah param avaapsyatha.*11.

[By this (Yajna sacrifice) foster ye the Gods, and let the Gods foster you; thus fostering each other you shall attain to the supreme good.]

Ishtaan bhogaan hi vo devaa daasyante yajnabhaavitah;
*Tair dattaan apradaayaibhyo yo bhunakte stena eva sah.*12.

[Fostered by sacrifice the Gods will give you the enjoyments you desire. He who enjoys these gifts without giving to them in return is verily a thief.]

Yajnashishtaashinh santo muchyante sarvakilbishaih;
*Bhunjate te tvagham paapaa ye pachantyaamakaarnaat.*13.

[The good people who eat what is left from the sacrifice are released from all sins but those wicked people who prepare food for their own sake—verily they eat sin!]

Annaad bhavanti bhootaani parjanyaad annasambhavah;
*Yajnaad bhavati parjanyo yajnah karmasamudbhavam.*14.

[From food all creatures come into being; production of food is dependent on rain; from sacrifice rain comes into being and yajna-sacrifice is rooted in prescribed action.]

Karma brahmodbhavam viddhi brahmaksharsamudbhavam;
*Tasmaat sarvagatam brahma nityam yajne pratishthitam.*15.

[Know that prescribed action has its origin in the Vedas, and the Vedas proceed from the Indestructible!. Hence the all-pervading Infinite is always present in yajna-sacrifice.]

The phrase 'prescribed action has its origin in the Vedas' obviously refers to the division of the society among the four varnas of the society.

In these verses Shri Krishna is made to offer a whole-hearted commendation of Vedic sacrifices while he was critical of them in Chapter II. He speaks in different voices which cofirms my impression that many pundits had contributed to the writing of the Bhagavada Gita.

Besides, it needs to be explained that the Vedic sacrifice offered by Prajapati above pertains to the celebrated hymn 'Purusha Sookta' (R.V. 10. 90), which I have quoted in the Vedic section earlier. This hymn appears to have been interpolated when the hymns of the Rig Veda were reduced to writing. The pernicious concept of varna (caste) was inserted in this hymn, although no such social divisions existed at that time.

Shri Krishna dons the mantle of God after six verses and declares:

> *Na me Paarthaasti kartavyama trishu lokesh kinchana;*
> *Naanavaaptam avaaptavyam varta eva cha karmaani.*24.
>
> [O Partha, there is no duty in all the three worlds for Me to perform, nor is there anything worth attaining, unattained by Me; yet I remain in action.]
>
> Utseedeyur ime lokaa na kuryaam karma ched aham;
> Sankarashya cha kartaa shaam upahanyaam imaah prajaah.
>
> [If I ever cease to act, these worlds would perish. I might prove to be the cause of confusion and of the destruction of people.]

After five verses Shri Krishna advises Arjuna:

> *Mayi sarvaani karmaani sannyasyaadhyaatmachetsaa;*
> *Niraasheer nirmamo bhootvaa yudhyasva vigatajvarah.*30.
>
> [Therefore, dedicating all actions unto Me, with your mind fixed on Me, who is the Self of all; freed from desire and of the feeling of *meum*, and cured of mental agitation, fight.]

Probably the biggest boast that the *pundits* make Shri Krishna propound is at the beginning of **Chapter IV**. He declaims:

> *Imam vivasvate yogam proktavaan aham avyayam;*
> *Vivasvaan manave praah, Manur Ikshvaakave abraveet.*1.

[I revealed this immortal *yoga* to Vivasvaan (the Sun); Vivasvaan conveyed it to (his son) Manu; and Manu imparted it to (his son) Ikshvaaku.]

Sa evaayam mayaa te-adya yogah proktah puraatanah;
*Bhako-asi me sakhaa cheti rahasyam hyetad uttamam.*3.

[The same ancient *yoga*, which is the supreme secret, has this day been imparted to you by Me, as you are my devotee and friend.]

Arjuna gives expression to his doubts about it and says:

Aparam bhavato janma, paramam janma Vivastatah;
*Katham etad vijaaneeyam tvam aadau proktavaan iti.*4,

[But you are of recent origin, while the birth of Vivasvaan dates back to remote antiquity. How then am I to believe that you imparted this *yoga* at the beginning of creation?]

Shri Krishna is unfazed and replies:

Bahooni me vyatitaani janmaani tava cha-Arjuna;
*Taanyaham veda saarvaani na tvam vettha Parantapa.*5.

[Arjuna, you and I have passed through many births; I remember them all; you do not remember, O chastiser of foes!]

Ajo'api sannavyaatmaa bhootaanaam Ishvaro'api san;
*Prakritim svaam adhishthaaya sambhavaamyaatmamayayaa.*6.

[Though I am'birthless', I am immortal. I am the Lord of all beings. I manifest Myself through My own *Yoga Maayaa* (divine potency), keeping My nature (*prakriti*) under control.]

And then Shri Krishna utters the most quoted verse:

Yadaa yadaa he dharmasya glaanir bhavati Bharata,
Abhyutthaanam adharmasya tadaatmaanam
*srijaamyaham.*7.

[O Bharata (Arjuna), whenever righteousness is on the decline and unrighteousness in the ascendant, then I create Myself!]

Paritraanaaya saadhunaam vinaashaaya cha dushkritaam;
*Dharma samsthaapnaarthaaya sambhavaami yuge yuge.*8.

[For the protection of the virtuous and destruction of the wicked; for establishing dharma, I manifest Myself from age to age!]

After four verses, the pundits make Shri Krishna assert that it was He who had created the division of the Vedic society into four varnas:

Chaatur varnayam mayaa srishtaam gunakarma vibhaagashah;
*Tashya kartaaram api maam viddhyakartaaram avyayam.*13.

[The four orders of society (viz. Brahmin, Kshatriya, Vaishya and Shudra) were created by Me; classifying them according to the *gunas* (qualities) predominant in each and apportioned appropriate duties to them. Although I am the originator of this creation, know me to be a non-doer.]

(The composers of Bhagavada Gita make Shri Krishna proclaim that He had created the four orders of society.)

Verses 31 and 32 applaud the Vedas:

Yajnashishtaamritbhujo yaanti brahma sanaatanam;
*Naayam loko'astyayajnasya kuto'anyah kurusattama.*31.

[Yogis who enjoy the nectar that has been left over after the performance of a sacrifice, attain the eternal *Brahmin.* To the man who does not offer sacrifice even this world is not happy; how, then, can the other world be happy for him?]

Evam bahuvidhaa yajnaa vitataa brahmano mukhe;
Karmajaan viddhi taan sarvaan evam jnaatva
*vimokshyase.*32.

[Many such forms of sacrifice have been set forth in detail in the Vedas; know them all as actions of mind, senses and the body. Thus, knowing the truth about them you shall be freed from the bondage of action through their performance.]

Sankhya yoga and karma yoga are explained in **Chapter V.** It asserts that only the unwise say that these two forms of yoga lead to divergent results. However, they are identical, as far as their result goes. The true yogis are not touched by their actions.

Brahmanyaadhaaya karmaani sangam tyaktvaa karoti yah;
*Lipyate na sa paapena padmapatram ivaambhasaa.*10.

[He who acts offering all actions to God, and shaking off attachment, remains untouched by sin, as the lotus leaf by water.]

However, there is a refreshing verse that transcends not only the four-fold division of the society, but regards even the beasts with equanimity.

Vidyaa vinaya sampanne, brahmane gavi hastini;
*Shuni chaiva shvapaake cha panditaah samadarshinah.*18.

[The wise look with equanimity on all, whether it be a learned Brahmin, a cow, an elephant, a dog or even a dog-eater (outcastes like the Chandals).]

Referring to this verse, S. Radhakrishnan remarks that 'the Eternal is the same in all, in animals, as in men, in learned Brahmins as in despised outcastes. The light of the *Brahman* dwells in all bodies and is not affected by the differences in the bodies it illuminates.'

In **Chapter VI, Verse 29, the** same idea is reiterated:

Sarva bhootastham aatmanam sarvabhootaani chaatmani;
*Ikshate yogayuktaatmaa sarvatra samadarshanah.*29.

[The *Yogi* who is united in identity with the All-pervading Infinite consciousness, whose vision everywhere is even, beholds the Self existing in all beings and all beings as dwelling in the Self.]

In the next two verses Shri Krishna asserts his identity again:

Yo mam pashyati sarvatra, sarvam cha mayi pashyati;
*Tashyaaham na pranashyami sa cha me na pranashyati.*30.

[He who sees Me present in all beings, and all beings existing within Me, he is never lost in Me, nor am I ever lost to him.]

Sarva bhootasthitam yo maam bhajatyekatvam aasthitah;
*Sarvathaa vartamaano'api sa yogi mayi vartate.*31.

[The *Yogi* who is established in union with Me, and worships Me as dwelling in all beings as their very Self, whatever activities he performs, he performs them in Me.]

In the last verse of this chapter Shri Krishna again proclaims:

Yoginaam api sarveshyaam madgatenaantaraatmanaa;
Shraddhaavaan bhajate yo maam sa me yuktatamo
*matah.*47.

[Of all *Yogis*, he who devoutly worships Me, with his mind focussed on Me, is considered by Me to be the best *Yogi*.]

I quote a few verses from **Chapter VII**:

Mayyaasaktamanaah Partha yogam yunjan madaashrayah;
Asamshayam smagram maam yathaa jnaasyasi tach
*chhrunu.*1.

[O Partha, now listen how, with the mind attached to Me, and practising *Yoga* with absolute dependence on Me, you will know Me as the repository of all power, strength and glory and other attributes; I am the Universal soul in entirety, without a shadow of doubt.]

Shri Krishna goes on recounting His glory:

Raso'aham apsu Kaunteya, prabhaasmi shashisooryayoh;
*Pranavah sarvavedeshu shabdah khe paurusham nrishu.*8.

[O Son of Kunti, I am the sapidity of water, and the radiance of the moon and the sun; I am the sacred syllable *Om* in all the Vedas, the sound in ether, and virility in men.]

Shri Krishna goes on to say that He is the subtle odour in the earth, the brightness in fire, the life in all living beings, the austerity in the ascetics and the sexual desire in all beings, but in my human form the ignorant people do not recognize me.

Avyaktam vyaktim aapannam manyante maam abuddhayah;
*Param bhaavam ajaananto mamaavyayam annuttamam.*24.

[Not knowing my Supreme nature, unsurpassable and undecaying, who am the Supreme Spirit beyond the reach of mind and senses, and the embodiment of Truth, Knowledge and Bliss; the ignorant persons regard me to have assumed a finite form through birth, as an ordinary human being.]

Naaham prakaashah sarvasya yogamaayaa samaavritaah;
*Moodho'ayam naabhijaanaati loko maam ajam avyayam.*25.

[Veiled by *Yoga-Maya*—my divine potency—I am not manifest to all. Hence these ignorant folks fail to recognize Me, the birthless and imperishable Supreme Deity.]

Chapter IX, Verse 11, 17 and 18 repeat the same assertion:

Avajaananti maam moodhaa maanushim tanum aashritam
*Param bhaavam ajaannto mama bhootamaheshvaram.*11.

[Not knowing My Supreme nature, fools deride me. (I am) the overlord of the entire creation, who has assumed the human form through my *Yoga-Maya,* for deliverance of the world as an ordinary mortal.]

Pitaaham asya jagato maataa dhaataa pitaamahah;
*Vcdayam pavitram omkaara rik saama yajur eva cha.*17.

[I am the sustainer and ruler of this universe, its father, mother and grandfather, the one worth knowing, the purifier.

I am the sacred syllable OM, and the three Vedas—Rik, Yujus and Sama.]

Gatir bhartaa prabhuh saakshi nivaasah sharanam suhrit;
*Prabhavah pralayah sthaanam nidhaanam beejam avyayam.*18.

[I am the supreme goal, sustainer, lord, witness, abode, refuge, well-wisher, seeking no return; I am the origin and end, resting-place, store-house, to which all beings return at the time of universal destruction, and I am the imperishable seed.]

However, a verse in a different meter has been inserted which is mildly critical of the Vedas, although Shri Krishna had owned them in **Verse 17** above. It anticipates the Karma-Yoga theory that was developed later.

Te tam bhuktvaa svargalokam vishaalam
Ksheene punye martyalokam vishanti
Evam trayeedharmam anuprapannaa
*Gataagatam kaamakaamaa labhante.*21.

[Having enjoyed the extensive heaven-world, they return to this world of mortals on the stock of their merits being exhausted. Thus, devoted to the ritual with interested motive, recommended by the three Vedas as the means of attaining heavenly bliss, and seeking worldly enjoyments, they repeatedly come and go (i.e., ascend to heaven by virtue of their merits and return to earth when the fruit of the merit has been enjoyed.)]

The chapter ends with the punch line: Worship Me!

Manmanaa bhava madbhakto madyaajee maam namaskuru;
*Maam evaishasi yuktvaivam aatmaanam matparaayanaah.*34.

[Fix your mind on Me, be devoted to Me, worship Me and make obeisance to Me! Thus, linking yourself with Me, and entirely depending on Me, you shall come to Me!]

In **Chapter X**, Shri Krishna dwells at length on his manifestations. He claims himself to be Vishnu among the Vedic gods, and Vasuki among serpents, Rama among the wielders of arms, the Gayatri Mantra among Vedic hymns, and so on. The list is endless. The chapter ends with Shri Krishna's declaration that He holds this entire universe by a fraction of his yogic power!

∽

In **Chapter XI,** Arjun requests him to show him His imperishable form. Shri Krishna obliges by showing his His Virata Swaroop, transforming himself into the Supreme Deity, surpassing the effulgence of a thousand suns, possessing infinite faces, wearing divine ornaments and wielding divine weapons. Arjun sees Him, devouring in his flaming mouth Dhritrashtra, Bhishma, Drona and all others. Arjun is terrified by this spectacle and requests him to take back his pleasing, four-armed form. Thereupon, Krishna assumes his four-arm figure, and tells him that neither by studying the Vedas, nor by performing austerities or giving donations, etc. any person can see this form of his.

∽

In **Chapter XII**, Shri Krishna proclaims: 'I consider them to be the real Yogis, who endowed with supreme faith, ever united through steadfast devotion to Me, worship Me with their minds centred on Me.' (12. 2). He tells Arjun that He loves such devotees who neither rejoice nor hate, nor grieve, nor desire; who deal equally with friends or foes and are the same in honour and ignominy, and are free from all attachment.

∽

In Chapter XIII, Shri Krishna explains the concepts of the '*kshetra*' and the '*kshetragya*' and says:

> *Idam shareeram Kaunteya, kshetram ityabhidheeyate;*
> *Etad yo vetti tam praahuh kshetragya iti tadvidah.*1.

> [This body, O son of Kunti, is termed as the kshetra (Field)

and its knower is called kshetragya (Knower of the Field) by the sages.]

Kshetagyam chaapi maam viddhi sarvakshetreshu Bharata;
*Kshetraskshetragyor gyanaam yat taj gyaanam matam mama.*2.

[O Bharata, know Myself to be the kshetragya of all kshetras. That is the truth about the kshetra and the kshetragya.]

The following verses are probably the best expression of the Universal Spirit that pervades the universe:

Jneyam yat tat pravakshyami yaj jnaatvaamritam shnute;
*Anaadimat param Brahma na sat tan naasad uchyate.*12.

[Let me tell you about the knowledge, knowing which one attains supreme bliss. The Supreme Brahma, who is the Lord of Prakriti and Jiva, is said to be neither Sat nor Asat.]

Bahir antashcha bhootaanaam acharm charam eva cha;
*Sukshmatvaat avijneyam doorastham chantike cha tat.*15.

[The Supreme *Brahma* exists both within and without all beings, and constitutes the moving as well as the unmoving creation. And by reason of the subtlety of Param Brahma, Param Brahma is incomprehensible. He is close at hand and yet stands far.]

Dhyaanenaatmani pashyanti kechid aatmaanam aatmanaa.
*Anye saankhyena yogena karmayogena chaapre.*24.

[Some by meditation behold the Supreme Spirit in their heart with the help of their refined and sharp intellect; others realize it through the discipline of knowledge, and still others, thorough the discipline of action. i.e. Karma-Yoga.]

Anaaditvaan nirgunatvaat paramaatmaayam avyayah;
*Shareerastho'api, Kaunteya, na karoti na lipyate.*31.

[O son of Kunti, being without beginning and without attributes, this Supreme Spirit, though dwelling in the body, in fact does nothing, nor gets tainted.]

In **Chapter XIV**, Shri Krishna again asserts that He is the supreme Spirit and exhorts Arjuna to take the path of devotion.

Idam jnaanam upaashritya mama saadharmyama aagataah;
*Sarge'api nopajaayante pralaye na vyathanti cha.*2.

[Those who, by practising this knowledge, have entered into My being, are not born again at the cosmic dawn, nor feel disturbed even during the cosmic dissolution (*pralay*).]

Mama yonir mahad Brahma tasmin garbham dadhaamyaham.
*Sambhavah sarvabhootaanaam tato bhavati Bharata.*3.

[O Bharat, my primodial Nature, known as the Supreme Brahma, is the womb of all creatures; in the womb I place the seed of all life. The creation of all beings follows from the union of Matter and Spirit.]

Sarvayonishu, Kaunteya, moortayah samvhavanti yaah.
*Taasaam Brahma mahad yonir aham beejapradah pitaa.*4.

[O son of Kunti, of all embodied beings that appear in all the species of various kinds, *Prakriti* (Nature) is the receiving Mother, while I am the seed-giving Father.]

Shri Krishna then goes on to explain the Gunas—Sattava, Rajas and Tamas.

In two memorable verses Shri Krishna then sums up the Gita's philosophy:

Samaduhkhasukhah svasthah samaloshtaashmakaanchanh;
*Tulya priya-apriyo dheeras tulyanindaatmasamstutih.*24.

[He who is ever established in the Self, taking pain and pleasure alike; who regards a clod of earth, a stone and a piece of gold, as equal in value, he, verily, is possessed of wisdom; who accepts the pleasant as well as the unpleasant in the same spirit, and views censure and praise alike.]

Maanaapmaanayos tulyas tulyo mitraaripakshyah;
*Sarvaaranbhaoarutyaagu gunaateetah sa uchyate.*25.

[He who is equipoised in honour or ignominy, is alike towards a friend or a foe and has renounced the sense of doer-ship in all undertakings, is said to have risen above the three Gunas.]

Shri Krishna ends this chapter emphasizing on His worship in the last two verses.

Mam chayo'avyabhichaarena bhaktiyogena sevate;
*Sa gunaan samateetyaitaan Brahmabhooyaaya kalpate.*26.

[He who, transcending these three Gunas, constantly worships Me through the Yoga of exclusive devotion. He becomes eligible for attaining the Supreme Brahma.]

Brahmano he pratishthaaham amtitashyaavyayasya cha;
*Shaashvatasya cha dharmsya sukhashyaikaantikasya cha.*27.

[For I am the substratum of the imperishable Brahma, of immortality, of the eternal Dharma and of unending bliss!]

~

In **Chapter XV**, Shri Krishna begins this chapter with a riddle-like verse about an imperishable ashvattha (peepal) tree, which has its roots upward in the sky, its branches below in the earth and its leaves in the Vedas. He adds that one who knows this tree is the knower of the Vedas!

Oordhvamoolamadhahshaakhamshvattham praahuravyayam;
*Chhandaasi yashya parnaani yastam vedah sa vedavit.*1.

[They speak of an eternal Ashwattha tree, which is rooted above and branching below, whose leaves are the Vedas. He who knows it knows the Vedas.]

The riddle probably means that our soul comes from high heaven and the body from the earth. There are references to such a tree in the Katha Upanishad and the Mahabharata.

In **Verse 12**, Shri Krishna reverts to singing his own glory:

Yad aadityagatam tejo jagad bhaasayate'akhilam;
*Yach chandramasiyach chaagno tat tejo viddhi maamkam.*12.

[The radiance in the sun that illumines the entire world and that which shines in the moon and that which shines in the fire, know that radiance to be Mine.]

He makes another astounding claim in **Verse 14**.

Aham vaishvaanaro bhootva praaninaam deham aashritah.
*Praanaapaaansamaayuktah pachaamyannam chaturvidham.*14.

[I take the form of Vaishvanara, which is the fire lodged in the body of all creatures, and digest and assimilate the four kinds of food by uniting with the Prana (exhalation) and *Aprana* (inhalation) breaths.]

In the next verse Shri Krishna says, He is the 'indweller' in all creatures, and adds that He is the only object worth knowing through the Vedas and adds that He is also the origin of Vedanta!

Sarvashya chaaham hridi sannivishtomatah smritigyanimapohanam cha;
*Vedaishcha sarvairahameva vedhyovedantakridvedavideva chaaham.*15.

[I am seated in the hearts of all beings. From Me alone comes memory, wisdom, and also the loss thereof. I am that which is known in all the Vedas. Verily, I am the Author of Vedanta, and the knower of the Vedas am I.]

I am quoting a few verses from **Chapter XVI:**

Tejah kshmaa dhritih shauchamdroho naatimaanitaa;
*Bhavanti sampadam daiveemabhijaatashya Bharata.*3.

[Vigor, forgiveness, fortitude, purity, absence of hatred and pride, these O descendant of Bharata, belong to one born with the divine property.]

Pravrittim cha nivrittim cha janaa cha ciduraasuraah;
*Na shaucham naapi chaachaaro na satyam teshu vidhyate.*7.

[The demonic people know not how how to follow right or how to refrain from wrong; there is neither purity, nor good conduct, nor truth in them.]

Aatmasambhaavitaah stabdhaa dhanamaana madaanvitaah;
*Yajante naamayagyaiste dambhenaavidhipoorvakam.*17.

[Self-glorifying, haughty, filled with vanity and intoxication of wealth, they perform yajna sacrifices only for name out of hypocrisy, disregarding the scriptural injunctions.]

Tasmaachchhaastram pramaanam te
karyaakaryavyavasthitau;
*Gyaatvaa shastravidhaanoktam karma kartumihaarhasi.*24.

[Therefore, let the Scriptures be your authority in ascertaining what ought to be done and what ought not to be done. Having learned the injunctions declared in the Scripures, you should act here in the world.]

In **Chapter XVII,** Shri Krishna distinguishes the *Satvika, Rajasika* and *Tamasika pravritti* and explains that men of Satvika disposition worship gods; those of Rajasika temperament worship demigods and the demons; while others, who are of Tamasika disposition, worship the spirits of the dead and ghosts.

Abhisandhaaya tu falam dambhaarthamapi chaiva yat;
*Ijjyate Bharatshreshtha tam yagyam viddhi raajasam.*12.

[O best of the Bharatas, the yajna-sacrifice which is offered for the sake of mere show and even with an eye on the fruit is of Rajasika nature.]

DevaDvijaGurupragyapoojanam shauchamaarjavam;
*Brahmacharyamahinsaa cha shaareeram tapa uchyate.*14.

[Worship of the Gods, of the twice-born Brahmins, the spiritual teachers and wise men; purity, simplicity, continence, non-injury: these are called the austerities of the body.]

Om tatsaditi nirdesho Brahmanastrividhah smritah;
*Brahmanaasten Vedaashcha yagyaashcha vihitah puraa.*23.

[OM, Tat, and Sat are the triple appellations of the Supreme Brahma, by which in olden times were created the Vedas and the Brahmanas as well as yajna sacrifices.]

Ashraddhyayaa hutam dattam tapastaptam kritam cha yat;
*Asadityuchyate Paarth na cha tatpretya no iha.*28.

[An oblation which is offered, a gift given, an austerity practiced, and whatever good deed is performed, if it is without faith, it is termed as naught, i.e. '*asat*'; therefore, it is of no avail here or hereafter.]

∽

In **Chapter XVIII,** Arjun wants to know the true nature of *Sanyasa* and *Tyaga*. Shri Krishna answers:

Kaamyaanaam karmanaam nyaasam sannayaasam kavayo viduh;
*Sarvakarmaphalatyaagam praahus tyaagam vichakshynaah.*2.

[Some sages understand Sanyasa as the giving up of all actions that are motivated by desire, while the wise declare that Tyaga consists in relinquishing the fruit of all desire.]

Tyaajyam doshavad ityeke karma praahur maneeshinah;
*Yajnaadaantpahkarma na tyaajyam iti chaapre.*3.

[Some wise men declare that all actions contain a measure of evil, and are, therefore, worth giving up; while others say that yajna-sacrifice, charity and penance are not to be given up.]

Shri Krishna replies that acts of sacrifice, charity and penance should not be given up as these acts are indeed purifiers, and adds:

> *Etaanyapi tu karmaani sangam tyaktvaa phalani cha;*
> *Kartavyaaneeti me Partha nishchitam matam uttamam.*5.

> [O Partha, these acts of yajna-sacrifice, charity and penance and all other acts of duty must be performed without attachment and expectation of reward: this is my well-considered and supreme verdict.]

S. Radhakrishnan observes that the Gita insists not on renunciation of action but on action with renunciation of desire. In these verses sanyas is meant as the renunciation of all works and tyaga for renunciation of the fruits of all works. Not by karma, not by progeny or wealth, but by tyaga or relinquishment, is release obtained.

Verse 6 reaffirms what has been enunciated earlier and is probably the essence of the Song Celestial:

> *Etaanyaapi tu krmaani sangam tyaktcaa ohalaani cha;*
> *Kartavyaaneeti me Partha nishchitam matamuttamam.*

> [All these actitvities of *yajna* sacrifice, charity and penance, and all other acts of duty too, must be performed without attachment or expectation of result or reward; they should be performed as obligatory duty, O son of Pritha. This is my well-considered and final opinion.]

Verse 17 addresses Arjun's problem of being unwilling to kill for acquiring the kingdom:

> *Yasya naahankrito bhaavo buddhir yasya na lipyate;*
> *Hatvaapi sa imaal lokaan na hanta na nibadhyate.*17.

> [He who is not motivated by false ego of being a performer, whose mind is free from the sense of doer-ship, and whose reason is not affected by the objects to be achieved, does not really kill; for even after having killed all these people no sin accrues to him.]

Niyatam sangarahitam aaaraagadveshah kritam;
*Aphalaprpsunaa karma yat tat saattvikam uchyate.*23.

[That action which is prescribed by the scriptures but is not accompanied by the sense of doer-ship, and has been done without any attachment or aversion by one who seeks no return, is called *Sattvika*.]

Muktasango'nahamvaadi dhrityutsaahasamanvitaah;
*Siddhyasiddhyor nirvikaarah karta satika uchchatey.*26.

[Free from attachment, un-egoistic, endowed with firmness and zeal and un-swayed by success and failure—such a doer is said to be Satvika.]

∽

Out of the verses quoted above, the following verses are my favourite:

Nainam chhindanti shashtrani, nainam dahati pavaka;
Na chainam kledyantyapo, na shoshyati marutah. II.23.

[The soul can never be cut to pieces by weapons, nor can fire burn it; neither can it be moistened by water, nor withered by wind.]

Sukkha duhkhe same kritva, labha-labhau jaya-jayau;
Tato yuddhaya yujysva, naivam paapam vapshasi. II.38.

[Treating alike pleasure and pain, gain and loss, victory and defeat; get ready for the battle, fighting thus you will not incur sin.]

Yada yada hi dharmasya glanir bhavati Bharat;
Abhyutthanm adharmasya, tadatmanam sryjamyaham. IV.7.

[O descendant of the race of Bharata, whenever and wherever there is a decline of *Dharma* (righteousness) and *Adharma* is predominant, I incarnate then and take birth.]

Although this verse is uttered by Shri Krishna, and its purport evidently was to declare him as an avatar of God; it might have a deeper meaning. It may also mean that at an appropriate time in the history of a nation, a person imbued with high sprituality might emerge, like Gandhi, who is not afraid of death, and provide leadership.

> *Vidya vinay sampanne Brhamane gavi hastini;*
> *Shuni chaiva shvapaake cha panditah samdarshinh.* IV.18.
>
> [The wise and humble sages, by virtue of true knowledge look upon with equanimity on all—whether a learned Brahmin, a cow, an elephant, a dog or a dog-eater (outcaste).]

When the brahmins inserted the clause of 'four varnas' in the *Purush Sookta* of the Rig Veda, they also violated this verse of the Bhagavada Gita.

> *Jitatmanah prashantasya parmatma samahitah;*
> *Sheetoshna sukh duhkheshu tatha manaapamanyo.* VI.7.
>
> [The Supreme Self (*Parmatma*) dwells in the '*Jitatman*' (who has conquered the mind), for he has attained tranquility. To such a man happiness or distress, heat or cold, pleasure or pain, honour or dis-honour are much the same.]
>
> *Yo mam pashayti sarvatra, sarvam cha mayi pashyati;*
> *Tasyaham na pranashyami, sa cha me na pranashyami.* VI.30.
>
> [For one who sees Me (God or the Supreme *Brahma*) present everyehere, in all beings, and believes that all beings exist within Me, I am never lost to him, nor is he ever lost to Me.]
>
> *Sama duhkha-sukhah, sva-sthah, sama loshtaashma-kaanchanah;*
> *Tulya-priyaapriyo dheeras, tulya-nindaatma-samstutih.* XVIII.24.
>
> [He who is established in the Self, who regards alike happiness and distress, who looks upon a clod of earth, a stone or a piece of gold as of equal worth, who accepts the pleasant and unpleasant, desirable or undesirable in the same spirit and views censure and praise alike.]

> *Brahmabhootah prasannatma, na shochati na kankshyati;*
> *Samah sarveshshu bhooteshu madbhaktim labhate paraam.*
> XVIII.54.
>
> [One who is thus transcendentally situated realizes the *Supreme Brahma* and becomes jouful in spirit, who neither laments for losses nor desires to have anything. He is equally disposed towards every living being. In that state he attains Me in pure devotion.]

The pundits make Shri Krishna specify varna-specific duties. He prescribes study and teaching of the Vedas and other scriptures to Brahmins, remaining dauntless in battle for the Kshatriyas, agriculture, rearing of cows and trading to the Vaishya and service of the other classes to Shudras. Shri Krishna adds that remaining devoted to his own natural duty, man attains perfection and God realization.

∽

It is evident that the main purpose of composing the Gita was to enshrine Shri Krishna as the Almighty God! S. Radhakrishnan throws light on this issue: 'We do not know the name of the author of the Gita. Almost all the books belonging to the early literature of India are anonymous. However, the authorship of the Gita is attributed to Vyasa, the legendary compiler of the Mahabharata.'[196]

Radhakrishnan quotes Farquhar who said: 'It is an old verse Upanishad, written rather later than the Svetashvatara, and worked up into the Gita in the interests of Krishnaism by a poet after the Christian era.' I would like to mention that while the publication by the Gita Press boldly adds *'Sri Bhagvana Uvach'* on the shloka sattributed to Shri Krishna, Radhakrishnan, in his commentary, refers to the speaker of the verses as 'The teacher.'

[196]Radhakrishnan, S., *The Bhagavadgita*, Blackie & Son (India) Ltd. 1977, p. 12.

PART SIX

INDIAN CULTURE AND CIVILIZATION IN SOUTHEAST ASIA

In the Southeast Asia, Indian missionary activity was followed by commercial enterprise which resulted in founding of royal Hinduised kingdoms. This paved the way for complete cultural conquest of Southeast Asia by the Hindus and made for emergence of another India outside India in Southeast Asia. In ancient Indian literature, these countries are referred to as *Suvaranabhoomi* and *Suvarnadweep*—'The Land and Island of Gold.' This colonial and cultural expansion of India had proceeded to these countries through land route and by the sea. We are familiar with a trade route by land through Upper Burma and Yunnan. The Burmese chronicles also refer to a more direct route between Eastern India and Burma through Arakan. Direct voyages from South India might have also been made to these countries. The two famous ports on the eastern and western coasts around that time were Tamralipti and Bhrigukachchaa. The geographical names given to these parts by Indians refer to artilcles of trade and commerce, for example, Rupyakadvipa, Tamradvipa, Karpuradvipa, Narikeladvipa, etc.

In the wake of trade and commerce came political authority and cultural relations. With the increasing circulation of Indian commodities in Southeast Asia, the Hindu culture firmly established its roots over all the area. Hindu Princes of blue blood sought fortune in these far-off lands, married among native chieftains and laid foundations of great centres of Indian culture and authority. Priests and missionaries popularized Indian religious doctrines. Emperor Ashoka sent Sona and Uttara as Buddhist preachers to these parts, as we learn from his inscriptions, and thus augmented the cultural revolution in and Indianisation of Southeast Asia.

In the lower valley of the Mekong River we get the evidence of the earliest Hindu kingdom which in the Chinese texts goes by the name of Funan. It was during a few centuries preceding and succeeding the Christian era, that the colonizing movement gathered fresh momentum and Hindu rule was established in some of these parts. The city of '*Vyadhapura*'—of Hunters—emerged where K'ang Tai, a Chinese 'ambassador' came in the third century AD. He records the victory and subsequent marriage of Kaundinya I, a Brahmin, with the Naga princess, Soma. Kaundinya I became the founder of a dynasty. His successors ruled upto the opening decades of the third century AD. After the demise of the last king, the people elected the general of the deceased king, Fan-Che-man, as the ruler. He entered into diplomatic relations with India and China. Kaundinya II emerges thereafter, who established himself as a ruler by matrimonial and political alliances. These Funan rulers adopted Sanskrit names. Kaundinya II was succeeded by Shreshthavarman, who was followed by 'Ch-ye-pa-ma' or Jayavarman. Jayavarman had friendly diplomatic relations with China and had also established trading relations. However, in his demise, his legitimate heir, Gunavarman was removed by Rudravarnam. No clear line of rulers seems to emerge thereafter.

R.C. Tripathi mentions liberation of the kingdom of Kambuja by Shrutavarman and Shreshthavarman in his book.[197] Kambuja comprised portions of Cambodia, Cochin–China and parts of Laos and Siam. King Bhavavarman ruled about the middle of the sixth century AD; Jayavarman I came to the throne of Kambuja towards the close of the seventh century AD. In AD 802, Jayavarman II occupied the throne of Kambuja. He adopted the title of 'Chakravartin' and made his capital in the Angkor region, which became the future nerve centre of the political and cultural life of Kambuja. He freed the people from the Javanese rule. Under the guidance of the Brahmin Hiranyadama, he performed some Tantric ceremonies lest Kambujia should become a dependency again. The Chinese and Arab writers record the greatly augmented prestige of the Khmer Kingdom in the days of Jayavarman II. His successor Jayavarman III was overthrown by Indravarman, whose successor Yashovarman is credited with numerous victories which

[197]Tripathi, R.C., *India—Heritage, Culture, Polity*, Bharat Book Centre, Lucknow, 2020.

greatly enhanced the glory of his empire. He built a new capital, which is called after him as Yoshodhoropura. Rajendravarman is another great ruler of this dynasty. By the tenth century, Kambuja transcended its original limits. The northward expansion resulted in the full consolidation of Kambuja power in the upper valley of the Mekong River. A large portion of Siam was conquered towards the West. In the south, it extended into Malay Peninsula beyond the isthmus of Kra. Thus, Kambuja was now an empire embracing Cambodia, Cochin–China, Laos, part of Yunnan, the greater part of Siam, the whole of Menam Valley and northern portions of Malaya. It bordered on Burma towards the west and touched the fringes of Champa in the east.

However, in 1001 when Jayavarman V died, internal troubles began. But the rise of Suryavarman II in 1113 put them to rest. The Kambuja inscriptions record in eloquent language his victories over hostile kings. But it was only when Jayavarman VII, the 'Grand Monarch' arrived on the scene the old order was restored. He defeated the Cham army in a naval engagement, and made Champa, a province of his empire. Thai principalities of Laos accepted his suzerainty and the frontiers of his kingdom ran along the Chinese empire. He took laurels for his wars as well as for peace. His public welfare measures remind us of Ashoka, says R.C. Tripathi, the benevolent enlightened monarch of India. He constructed temples and public buildings and built the city of Angkor Thom. He was Buddhist by faith and received the posthumous title of *Paramasaugata*.

Though the worship of the Puranic Trinity was widely prevalent in Southeast Asia, the place of honour was accorded to God Shiva. Among the various images of the three gods of the Trinity, the largest numbers belong to Shiva and his family and the majority of the temples are dedicated to him. The dominant cult in Funan is that of Maheshvara. In Champa, the worship of Shiva became a national cult and the temple of 'Bhadreshvara Swami' (another name of Shiva) acquired the character of a national sanctuary. Lord Shiva is conceived of possessing the same attributes which are assigned to him India. Such appellations of Shiva as Maheshvara, Rudra, Gireesha, Tyrambaka, Shambhu, Shankara, Siddheshvara,

Pashupati, etc. were quite common. His dual aspect is known. He is not only the destroyer but also the preserver of the universe. The benevolent and terrible facets of the creator and destroyer of the world are represented in the iconic form in the names of 'Mahadeva' and 'Mahakala' and destruction of the Cupid and Tripura Shiva were quite familiar. Shiva worship as Linga Puja is popular in Cambodia and Champa. Corresponding to this, was the worship of Shakti, Shiva's consort. She is known as Devi, Parvati, Gauri. A particular form of Durga or Mahishamardini is the same as in India. In her Mahakala aspect, she was known as Mahakali. Besides, we find in the Shiva pantheon, the potbellied, elephant headed god of wisdom, Ganesha and Kartikeya, the six-headed peacock-rider, god of war and Nandi, the bull of god Shiva.

Vishnu never acquired so prominent a place as Shiva. But under certain rulers and dyanasties, he enjoyed preference. Suryavarman II was a worshipper of Vishnu and Angkor Vat was Vishnu's temple originally. The Belehan statue of Airlangga from Java shows the king in the form of Vishnu, riding Garuda. Kerterajas, the founder of Majapahita, is deified as Vishnu. Goddesss Lakshmi is represented as four-armed, noted for her fickleness. Numerous images of Trimurti are frequent. Mahayaan Buddhism, with the rise of Sailendras, became the dominant religion of Malaya Penunsula. They made viharas at Nalanda and Negapattana.

Great strides in temple building were made in Kambuja, where great temples arose not out of popular faith, but to house the personal deity of the king or his ancestor who was generally apotheosized. The Angkor region and the period of its greatness are noted for the outstanding advances made in the field of art and architecture. The additional features of this age are the spacious galleries, the pyramidal structure with high central towers rising into several stages and the human faced towers, richly figures and ornamental designs and cornices with the base reliefs. The Angkor Vat and the Bayon temples are the chief works of Indian chisel in those lands. According to Brian Harrison, Angkor Vat is the greatest of funerarary mountain-temples whose spirit is one of 'aloof majesty'. In all appearance a Vaishnava pantheon, it is a funerary temple of King Suryavarman II. It was planned on a grand scale and its moat measured 650-feet wide. A two-and-a-half mile long wall ran round the temple. This massive grand monument is one of the finest creations of the artistic and technical skill of the colonists.

The Angkor Thom city, the Bayon temple (formerly attributed to Yashovarman I) and the Batei Chamr (ascribed at one time to Jayavarman II) are, in the opinion of most critics, the realization of the dreams of the 'Grand Monarch', Jayavarman VII of Kambuja. He rebuilt the city Angkor Thom with a 'monument of victory' (the city wall) and the 'Sea of Victory' (the moat) around it. The Bayon is his chef d'oeuvre of pyramidal structure and the great faces on its towers, representing Avalokiteshvara, may, according to Coedes, portray the features of the king himself, who dominates in silence the magnificent ruins of Ankkor Thom. The Bantei Chmar belongs to the Bayon School of architecture.

The monuments of Java too are unique. Chandi Kalasan is a landmark in the Javanese Buddhist architecture whereas the impressive and beautiful Lara Jongran Chandi is the finest example of Hindu architecture. But undoubtedly the finest monument of Javanese art in the Buddhist mountain-temple of Borobudur 'a fruit matured in the breathless air'. A hill has been terraced in nine stages and supports a small stupa at the top. The lower terraces depict in the wall of the galleries the well-known Budhist stories. The central stupa is encircled by 72 perforated stupas, each containing a Buddha image. Hoening once believed that its plan was of a nine-storied pyramid. But in the opinion of most of the scholars, it was intended to be a stupa whose terraces are 'a constructional necessity' rather than an innovation of style. Built in the late eighth century when the Sailendra Empire was at its acme of glory, Borobudur, a hill carved into a stupa, reveals the calm balance and serene dignity of the age.

From another part of Southeast Asia, we get the famous Ananda temple, most remarkable in some aspects. The sublimity of architectural effect, finely achieved in the Burmese pagodas, inspires wonder and surprise. Fergusson finds in no Asian country the existence of such a form of art. Painting was not unknown and this art was largely used as a decorative form in secular and religious buildings. The Buddhist birth stories, life-episodes of Gautama, the Buddha, and the Hindu mythological stories found full expression in the various huge structures of Southeast Asia which abound the whole land. Thus, the Indian colonists accomplished almost a complete cultural victory in Southeast Asia. This brilliant chapter of Indian history is rarely rivalled in the annals of the world. But the Muslim conquest of Java meant a death-blow for Indian culture in those regions. However, the Islamic population of the Southeast Asian countries looks at Rama and Krishna as their heroes and the stories of the Ramayana and the Mahabharata figure prominently in their life and literature. Indeed, the narrative of the 'rise of an India outside India' is a fascinating tale of epic grandeur.

THE RISE OF BUDDHISM

In the sixth century BC, there was a phenomenal rise of Buddhism in India. Vedic sacrifices were in vogue those days. The Buddha strongly criticized and condemned them, saying there were no such gods as Indra, Brahma, Rudra, etc. who came to eat the well-cooked flesh of the ribs of a bull or horse in the yajna; only the pundits gorged on them. The Buddha travelled on foot and preached his new faith based on morality and drew large crowds to his congregations.

According to Paul Deussen,[198] 'Only in small measure did Buddhism owe its success to the originality of its ideas, for almost all its essential theories had their predecessors in the Vedic and epic (the Ramayana and the Mahabharata) periods. The fundamental idea of Buddhism, laid down in the four holy truths is this—that we can extinguish the pains of existence only by extinguishing our thirst for existence. The same idea is put forth in the 12 Nidanas, which by a series of steps go back from the pains of life to the thirst for life and from this to ignorance, as the ultimate cause of thirst and pain altogether. We see in these and many other Buddhistic ideas only a new form of what Yajnavalkya teaches in *Brihada-aranyaka* Upanishad.'

On the other hand, historian John Keay observes,[199] 'The Sanskrit texts evoke a mostly agrarian way of life in which the states play a minor part and status is governed by lineage and ritual observance. Buddhist and Jain texts, on the other hand, portray a network of functioning states, each of which an urban nucleus heavily engaged in trade and production. Here wealth as well as lineage confers status. Indeed, the Buddhist concept of "merit" as something to be earned, accumulated, occasionally transferred and eventually realized seems inconceivable without a close acquaintance

[198]Deussen, Paul, *Outlines of Indian Philosophy*, Crest Publishing House, New Delhi, pp. 32–3.

[199]Keay, John, *India a History,* Harper Collins, India, 2000, pp. 63–6.

with the moneyed economy. By interleaving between these two societies a further century, Buddhism's newly revised or 'short chronology' allows the more gradual and credible evolution of state and city without unduly taxing the archeological record.

Similarly, it allows room for the evolution of a tradition of heterodoxy and dissent. Buddhist texts in particular portray a society that was already in religious ferment when the Buddha was born. Rival holy-men swarmed across the countryside performing feats of endurance, disputing one another's spiritual credentials and vying with one another for followers and patronage. That this was not simply the impression of partisan hotheads is shown by the dispassionate Kautilya, whose compendium on statecraft, the Arthashastra, recognizes such renunciates as an important constituent of any state; they are to be given legal protection and free passage; special forest areas are to be allotted to them for meditation and special lodging-houses in the city. Saints or charlatans, they evidently mirrored a society to which the paranormal, the supernatural and the metaphysical had a strong appeal. Many of them went naked or unwashed and they cheerfully flouted the taboos of caste status. Defying social convention, they yet enjoyed society's indulgence. Renunciation had become an accepted way of life in which ascetism was seen as a prerequisite to spiritual enlightenment.

The philosophies on offer from this rag-tag army of reformers ranged from mind-boggling mysticism to defiant nihilism and blank agnosticism, from the outright materialism of the Lokayatas to the heavy determinism of the Ajivikas, and from the rationalism of the Buddha to the esotericism of Mahavira. Most, however, agreed in condemning the extravagance of Vedic sacrifice, in sidelining the Vedic pantheon, and in ignoring Brahminical authority.

Moreover, many, including the Jains, Buddhist and Ajivikas recognized an assortment of antecedents whose teachings or experiences had in some sense anticipated their own. In other words, Mahavira, the Buddha and Gosala of the Ajivikas acknowledged well-established traditions of heterodoxy; as one might infer from their own reception, they were able to capitalize on an already existing thirst for spiritual and moral guidance, as well as an abiding credulity. Clearly the new sources of wealth and authority associated with state formation and urbanization had plunged society into a crisis which the rigidities of varna-ashram-dharma (the organization of society into caste-varnas and into social vocations) could scarcely accommodate, and to which the ritual oblations of the Vedas seemed irrelevant as well as widely extravagant.'

Gautama Buddha (564 to 487 BC) was a scion of the Sakya clan, a minor branch of the solar dynasty of Ayodhya. Claiming their descent, from the mythical Ikshvaku, from Rama, they were late Aryan migrants (into India) of fair colour. Buddha's father Shuddodhana, is designated as Raja or chieftain of a 'republic' Kapilvastu, in Nepalese Terai, straddling the common border of India and Nepal. This fertile valley of gurgling streams, lush sal forests, mango and tamarind groves and golden rice fields nestled against the Himalayan foothills between the rivers Rapti and Rohini. The 'Republic' of Kapilvastu was subject to the overlordship of the King of Koshala.

According to John Keay, these alternative state systems were variously interpreted as oligarchical, republican or even democratic. The term now used for them is '*Gana Sangha*'—'*gana*' meanta 'clan' or 'horde' which, qualified by '*sangha*' or 'organization', would mean a 'government by discussion,' or more commonly, 'republics.'

That a clan-based society should opt for a constitution which was more egalitarian and less autocratic than monarchy seems perfectly logical. Actually, the 'republics' merely institutionalized the monarchical traditions of consultation among the leading clansmen, which goes back to the Vedic times. There was a tradition of the open *Samiti* as well as the more respected and specialized *Sabha*.

Most of the mid-millennium republics of Bihar and Uttar Pradesh—those of the Licchavis, Sakyas, Koliyas, Videhas, etc.—came into being as a result of the process of segmenting off from a parent clan.

Prince Siddartha's mother, Maya Devi, is said to have had a dream during her pregnancy, that she was carried by angels to a lake, given a bath and taken to a mansion. A white elephant, with a pink lotus flower in his trunk, approached her and penetrated her. She narrated this dream to her husband, Shuddodhana. He consulted seers who said, it signified that the child would become either a great ruler or a sage. He was named Siddhartha, loosely meaning 'child of destiny.'

Maya Devi died a week after her son's birth at Lumbini Park. The child was nursed by Gautami, his mother's sister, who was also married to Shuddodhana, and the child was also called 'Gautama.' At 19 he married the fair Yashodhara. When Siddhartha Gautama was 29, a son, Rahul, was born. When the young prince was told about his son's birth, he thought: 'A son is born to me; a fetter has been forged on me. If I allow paternal love to bind me, it would mean a life-long bondage.' He made up his mind to break free.

One night, as Yashodhara and the child slept, he roused his servant, Channa, and asked him to saddle his horse. He rode out of the palace at dead of night, followed by Channa. Towards day-break, he reached the woods. He left the horse then, removed his princely garments and ornaments and donned saffron robes, and asked Channa to return with them to the palace.

In a poem composed by Maithili Sharan Gupt, independent India's 'poet-laureate', the grief-stricken Yashodhara opens her heart to her female attendant:

> *Sakhi, ve mujhase kaha kar jaate!*
> *Kah tau kya mujhko ve apni path badha hi paate?*
>
> [O my friend, He should have told me before going away! Why did he pre-suppose that I would only be an obstacle in his path?]

Clad like an ascetic, Siddartha journeyed to Rajagriha (Rajagir), where he met two sages, Arada Kalama and Rudrak Ramaputra.[200] He had philosophical discourses with them for a

[200]Eraly, Abraham, *Gem in the Lotus*, Viking, Penguin Books, Delhi, 2000, p. 251.

few months. Afterwards, he went to village Uruvela, on the bank of the River Niranjana, 16 kilometers south of Gaya, to practice austerities.

Here he was joined by a group of five ascetics. He lived with them for about six years. He began a severe course of penance, outdoing his fellow ascetics. It is said that he used to forgo to eat many times and even went without clothes. He began living on millets, ground sesame, even grass. He also tried to remain standing all the time, without sitting, and became a bundle of bones without flesh.

One day he went to the river to bathe and while returning accepted a meal of milk-rice from the daughter of a cowherd. Thereafter he kept staying at Uruvela, no longer at war with his body. He regained his health and his physical and mental equanimity. He now sought enlightenment with cool deliberation. His fellow ascetics left now, thinking he was giving up his spiritual quest.

Sitting cross-legged in yogic posture, facing east, in a grassy meadow near a pond at a solitary spot under an old peepal tree, he sank in deep meditation. For 49 days he continued with this daily routine 'like a flame in a windless spot,' According to traditional Buddhist accounts, which are fictional, he was repeatedly assailed by the devil Mara. Mara even sent his three lovely daughters, Desire, Unrest and Pleasure, to tempt and seduce him!

On a full-moon day in May 528 BC at day break, after a night of deepening ecstasy and insight, Siddhartha Gautama attained enlightenment. 'My mind was emancipated,' he would later tell his followers. 'Ignorance was dispelled, true wisdom dawned; darkness vanished, light arose.' He became *Buddha* (One who Knows) or 'the Awakened'. His followers called him '*Tathagata*,' the Emancipated One. The peepal tree, under which he attained is revered now as the Tree of Wisdom. A majestic, seven-storeyed temple, dedicated to the Buddha, stands at the site now.

The Buddha remained at Uruvela for seven weeks after his enlightenment, reflecting on the insight he had gained and elaborating its implications. Although he did not claim to have received any divine light, he formulated a radically new doctrine. 'This noble truth concerning the mitigation of sorrow was a light he ignited himself,' he asserted. He added that 'men who are overpowered by passion and lost in darkness cannot see this truth.'

He came to the Dear Park in Varanasi where his five former ascetic companions were lodging. He delivered to them his first sermon, expounding the doctrine of the 'Four Noble Truths'. They were:

1. Belief in the immortality of the soul.
2. Rejection of all rites and rituals, the caste system and the popular idea of God.
3. Culture of love, truth, charity, forgiveness, absolute purity of life in thought, speech and action.
4. Following the Golden Mean between an ostentatious, pleasure-seeking life and an austere life.

The five ascetics were his first converts. He told them: 'Following these four Noble Truths leads to removal of sorrow and of craving, so that no passion remains.'

Later, he evolved the 'Noble Eight-fold Path' of right views, right aspirations, right speech, right conduct, right livelihood, right effort, right mindfulness and right contemplation.

The Buddha set up communities of dedicated *bhikshus* and *bhikshunis* (alms-seeking monks and nuns) and created a large following. It was a faith created by the charisma of the Buddha's personality. The appeal of Buddhism was enhanced by the breaking down of the rigid caste system prevalent in Hinduism. The Buddha rectified the grave wrong done by the pundits, bowdlerizing the Purusha Sookta, in the Rig Veda. By including the great masses of the Shudras and the down-trodden in the common fraternity of the Rajanya, Brahmin and Vaish, he revolutionized the Hindu society.

Some time later, the Buddha converted Sage Kashyapa and his 500 disciples. It was to them that he preached the Fire Sermon:

> All things, O brethren, are on fire; the eye is on fire, the impressions received by the eye are on fire, and the sensations arising out of these impressions are likewise on fire!

> And with what are these on fire?
>
> With the fire of passion, say I, with the fire of hatred, with the fire of infatuation; with birth, old age, death, sorrow, lamentation, misery, grief and despair are they on fire!
>
> The ear is on fire, sounds are on fire, the nose is on fire, the tongue, the body, the mind, the ideas are on fire. And with what are these on fire? With the fire of passion! Say I.
>
> Seeing this, O Brethren, the true disciple conceives an aversion for the eye and for the impressions received by the eye, and for the sensations arising therein. So also, for the ear and sounds, for body and tangible things, for the mind and its sensations. And in conceiving this aversion, man becomes divested of passion. By the absence of passion, he becomes free! When he is free, he becomes aware that he is free, and he knows that there is no rebirth for him. He is no more of this world!

The conversion of Sage Kashyapa was of great advantage to the Buddha, for Kashyapa was a renowned sage in his own right. The public acknowledgement of the Buddha as his guru by Kashyapa enhanced the stature of the Buddha in the eyes of people.

Among the kings who patronized the Buddha's new teaching were Prasenajita of Koshala and Bimbisara of Magadha. King Bimbisara, though not initiated, shared his faith and made the gift of *Velu-Vana* (Bamboo-grove) to the Buddhist Order. In the Koshalan capital of Shravasti, the Buddha delivered numerous discourses and, since his own Sakya republic had been overrun by Koshala and remained under its suzerainty, he may have felt some allegiance to King Prasenajita.

The Buddha next visited his home, Kapilvastu, and converted the royal family. His son Rahul, his brother Ananda and brother-in-law Devadatta were converted to the new faith.

From Kapilvastu, the Buddha returned to Rajagriha and then went to Shravasti, the capital of Koshala. A rich merchant Anathapindika presented to him the monastery he had built for the Sangha in the Jetavana grove in the city. It became the

Buddha's favourite monsoon retreat. Vishakha, the munificent wife of another wealthy merchant became his shishya. Yasa, a young wealthy merchant of Varanasi and his wife were also among his first lay followers. Several of Yasa's friends entered the order and many others became lay devotees.

∽

A sober, down-to-earth realist, and no ethereal visionary, the Buddha was primarily concerned with the problems of life on earth, not of life after death. Buddha's teachings are characterized by compassion and practical wisdom and psychological insight, not high metaphysics. This is poignantly revealed in the haunting parable of the Mustard Seed, told in *Anguttara Nikaya*:

> In the town of Shravasti there was a poor, frail, simple-minded woman named Kisa Gotami, whose sole consolation in life was her only child, a son. Unfortunately, he died in infancy, and this drove her out of her mind with grief, and she kept wandering around the town carrying the child's corpse, imploring everyone: 'Give me medicine for my son!' Someone sent her to the Buddha, saying he alone would have such medicine.
>
> Gotami then hastened to the Buddha's hermitage and pleaded: 'Give me medicine for my son!' The Buddha in his compassion took her hand and said to her: 'You did well, Gotami, in coming here for medicine.' He told her to go back to the town and fetch some mustard seeds for the medicine from a family where no one had died.
>
> She set out immediately, excited with the thought that she would now be able to revive her son. She went from house to house asking for mustard seeds, hoping to find a household in which no death had occurred. It was an impossible mission. Gradually, the awareness dawned on her that there was no such household and what she was doing was absurd. She then left her son's body in a cremation-ground and returned to the hermitage.
>
> 'Gotami, did you get the grains of mustard seeds?' The

> Buddha asked her and she replied: 'I did not find the mustard seeds; O Swami, Grant me refuge!'

Compassion—dispassionate compassion—marked every act of the Buddha. There was no hell-fire in his sermons, only gentle ministry. Buddhism, unlike Hinduism, was a proselytizing religion, 'one of the greatest missionary religions on earth', as Weber had observed.

As the number of monks grew, the Buddha sent them off to different parts of the land to work as his missionaries, telling them: 'Go my brethren, travel from place to place.' What began as the lonesome private quest of an individual for release from the ordeal of life turned into a public religious movement![201]

According to the Buddha, the human condition became bearable by restraining indulgence and accumulating merit, whereby release (*moksha* or *nirvana*) might eventually be attained. Buddhism was not a rival faith but more a complementary discipline. He offered merely heightened insight, not divine revelation. It was his followers in the generations to come who would elevate the Buddha and other enlightened ones (*Boddhisatvas*) into deities, thus claiming for Buddhism the authority and the supernatural paraphernalia of a religion.

~

The noblest thing about the Buddha was that he welcomed men of all classes and castes to his Sangha, unlike the Vedic prejudice against the Shudra and the untouchable menials. The Buddha found it ridiculous that Brahmins should claim special sanctity for themselves, simply because they could recite the compositions of Vedic sages! He was equally scornful of their blind acceptance of Vedic tenets as immutable wisdom. Thus, the spread of the Buddha's non-ritualistic sect threatened the very profession and livelihood of the Brahmins; his rejection of the caste system imperilled the dominant social position of the Brahmins.

The Buddha's questioning of Vedic sacrifice finds place in the Jatakas:

[201]Eraly, Abraham, *Gem in the Lotus*, Viking, Penguin Books, Delhi, 2000. Pages 263–7.

The Vedas have no hidden power to save...
None, however zealously he (the Brahmin) prays,
Or feeds fuel to the sacrificial fire,
Or gains merit by his mummeries...
The greedy liars propagate deceit,
And fools believe the fictions they repeat!

Often the Buddha derided the very concept of God as an omnipotent entity. He also exhorted against 'the fatal craving of men for women' and said: 'Brethren, I know of no other single form by which a man's heart is enslaved as it is by that of a woman... I know of no other single scent ... savour ... touch, by which a man's heart is enslaved as it is by the scent, savour and touch of a woman.'

He allowed unwed minor boys to be admitted as a lama, and said: 'I allow you to give ordination to lads.'

To my mind, this was fraught with cruelty to the innocent kids. It robbed the innocent boys of their natural function of propagation of life. My heart bleeds when I see child lamas swarming in the monasteries at Manali, Lahoul and Spiti!

Buddhism remained a relatively minor sect for about two and a half centuries after its founding and did not thrive in India. But it flourished in a greater part of Asia in a modified form. About one-third of the people of the world profess Buddhism now. However, historian A.K. Majumdar says that 'the Buddha consciously set himself up not as the founder of a new religion, but as an ardent Hindu reformer. He believed to the last that he was proclaiming only the ancient and pure form of Hinduism, corrupted at a later date.'[202]

~

In the Buddha's last days, there were clear signs of physical decline. On his last tour, he travelled north from Rajagriha and proceeded to Vaishali, the capital of the Lichchhvis. Vaishali was a rich city those days, rich and fun-loving, and was the home of the renowned courtesan Ambapali. The Buddha camped in Ambapali's mango

[202]Majumdar, A.K., *Hindu History*, Rupa Publications, New Delhi, 2008, pp. 372

grove. She hastened to pay him homage and invited him and his monks to dine at her mansion. Lichchhvi nobles then arrived there and invited the Buddha, but he declined even though they offered large sums of money as inducement. Ambapali served the Buddha with her own hands. After dining, the Buddha delivered a discourse which gladdened her, and she presented to the *Sangha* the grove in which the Buddha was camping. However, in a Hindi film made on the Buddha, Ambapali sings a song, in Lata Mangeshkar's inimitable voice, while entertaining the Buddha in her palace: *'Yeh bhoga bhi aik tapashya hai, tum tyaga ke maare kya jaano!'* (This 'enjoying life' is also a kind of 'burning oneself', of which people like you, who have been ruined by Tyaag, know nothing!)

The Buddha spent the rainy season at village Beluva. After his health recovered, Ananda requested him to lay down rules to guide his followers. The Buddha refused to do so, saying his teachings did not constitute the final and definitive truth and added: 'Be to yourselves, O Ananda, your own light and your own refuge. Whosoever, after my departure, shall be his own light, his own refuge and shall seek no other refuge, shall be my true disciples!'

After the rains, the Buddha proceeded towards Kushinara. At Pava, his disciple, the metal-smith Chunda, invited him for a meal. Next morning, he dressed and taking his outer robe and the bowl, reached Chunda's place. Chunda served him pork with rice porridge boiled in milk. Probably the pork meat had spoiled, so the Buddha told Chunda to bury the remaining meat in the ground. Chunda did as the Buddha advised, and went and sat near the Buddha, who then delivered a discourse to him.

The Buddha was affected by dysentery and went to Kushinara (now called Kasia), a small town on the river *Chhoti* Gandak, 130 kilometres east of Kapilvastu. They crossed the stream by a boat and reached the Sal grove at the outskirts of the town.

The Buddha lay down on his right side, with one foot resting on the other. It was the full-moon day of the month of *Vaishakha* (May), strangely coinciding with the day of the Buddha's birth. As he lay dying, Ananda began to weep. The Buddha is said to have told him, and the brethren who had accompanied him: 'Everything that comes into being, passes away. Strive without ceasing!'

As he passed away, his disciples almost deified him by pronouncing: 'The earth quaked and thunder rolled!' records the Mahaparinibbana Sookta.

∽

The Buddha had not given any instructions what was to be done with his mortal remains. Ananda had asked him: 'How, Lord, are we to deal with the body of the Tathagata?' The Buddha had replied: 'Worry not about the body-rites of the Tathagata. O Ananda, strive for your own welfare, remain heedful, ardent and resolute! There are many discreet nobles, discreet Brahmins and heads of households, who are believers in the Tathagata—they will see to the body-rites of the Tathagata!'

It was King Bimbisara's patronage that proved crucial. Bimbisara's Magadha made good its claim to most of his hotly contested relics. Immediately afterwards, it was in the Magadhan capital of Rajagriha, that the first Buddhist council was convened. Magadha's fast growing economic prosperity provided the social ambiance particularly favourable to Buddhism.

A number of chieftains of the local tribe of Mallas had gathered as Kushinara. After wrapping the Blessed One's body in several folds of new cloth, they placed it on a bed of flowers on the ground and decorated it with garlands. For six days, they paid their reverence, chanting hymns, playing music and dancing. On the seventh day, eight chieftains, after bathing and putting new clothes on the body, carried it into the city in a procession from the northern gate of the town, as the populace paid their homage, and went out by the eastern gate.

They built a funeral pile, showered perfumes and placed the body of the Tathagata on it and set it on fire. The next day when the ashes were collected, other chieftains and kings had also gathered. They wanted to share the relics of the Blessed One. The Mallas were reluctant, but a venerable Brahmin, named Bona, reminded them about the Buddha's message of peace and forbearance. The relics were then divided into eight portions and each of them built monuments in their kingdoms to place the relics in their domain.

∽

Reading the elaborate description of the Buddha's funeral rites, I was reminded of Socrates, who was charged with corrupting the morals of the youth of Athens and was sentenced to death by drinking hemlock. Many of his friends and pupils were sitting by him in the hall, when he began sipping from the chalice full of hemlock. They conversed with him about his philosophy for some time, and when they sensed that the poison had started affecting him, asked him how would he like his body to be disposed off—by cremation of burial? Socrates replied: 'I would have gone away then! I have no concern what happens to the body.'

Another incident, the death of Mahatma Gandhi, comes to my mind. Gandhi had come down for his morning prayer-meeting, which was attended by hundreds of people. Nathuram Godse came forward and bowed before him, folding his hands, as if in salutation. He had a pistol enclosed in his hands. He straightened up then, aimed the pistol at Gandhi and pumped three bullets into his bare chest. Gandhiji saw the pistol aimed at him but did not duck when Godse fired. Gandhiji collapsed on the ground, an involuntary sound '*Ahaa!*' escaped his throat. The Mahatma showed a rare equanimity in the face of death!

Godse, his killer, also made no move to run away after commiting this heinous crime. He kept standing there, raising his hand and holding the pistol skyward, and waited for the guards to come and arrest him. He left an honest account of why he committed this dreadful deed and cheerfully went up the gallows!

∽

The ideology of *Dhamma* died with the death of Ashoka in 231 BC. According to John Keay: 'The spirit of humanity embodied in Ashoka's Edicts that crossed the barriers of sect, caste and kin, and pointed to "the community of India", would be revived by a host of other reformers, not least by Guru Nanak of the Sikhs and eventually by Mahatma Gandhi.'[203]

---

[203]Keay, John, *India: A History,* Harper Collins, India, 2000, p. 100.

Abraham Eraly holds that 'the Buddha never claimed that he was expounding a divinely revealed final wisdom. Rather he saw himself as a questing mortal, a guide who removed mental blinkers and pointed out new avenues for gnostic exploration... "A man must take medicine to be cured," the Buddha is quoted by Ashvaghosha as saying. "Likewise, the mere sight of me ennobles no one to conquer suffering; he will have to meditate for himself about the gnosis I have communicated."... the Buddha was really a counsellor in the garb of a prophet.'[204]

The Dhammapada says: 'Abstention from sin, doing good works, and purifying one's own mind, this is the teaching of Buddhism.' The Jatakas proclaim: 'Well now, watch and guard the three avenues of the voice, the mind, and the body; do no evil whether in word or thought or deed.'

'There were no class or caste distinctions in the Sangha; all were brothers and comrades to each other, and all freely mingled and ate together, in total disregard of the conventional social taboos. The monks, having renounced the world, were not concerned with worldly institutions and hierarchies. Said the Buddha: "Just as, brethren, the great rivers Ganga, Yamuna, Asirvati, Sarabhu, and Mahi, on reaching the mighty ocean renounce their former names and lineage and one and all are reckoned as the mighty ocean, even so, brethren, do the four classes—Kshatriyas, Brahmins, Vaisyas and Shudras—go forth from home to the homeless life under the Dharma discipline of the Tathagata and renounce their former names and lineage."'[205]

~

It was Emperor Ashoka's imperial patronage that transformed the Buddha's religion into an all-India religion, and set it on the path of a world religion. Ashoka had converted to Buddhism in the third century BC. He collected the Buddha's relics and distributed them to innumerable stupas which he had built throughout the

[204]Eraly, Abraham, *Gem in the Lotus*, Viking, Penguin Books, Delhi, 2000, pp. 288–90.
[205]Ibid. 308.

country. Hsuan Tsang recorded that he saw more than 80 stupas and monasteries built by Ashoka. The original Sanchi stupa built by Ashoka was expanded about a century later to double its size. However, none of the stupas built by Ashoka exists now in its original size. With the passage of time the stupa changed from being funerary monuments to sacred objects of veneration.

After Ashoka's conquest of the bloody Kalinga war, the 'Beloved of the Gods,' as Ashoka called himself, erected rock edicts on many sites in the country like Giranar, stating that 'only the conquest by 'Dhamma' was a true conquest.' He equated Dhamma with 'mercy, charity, truthfulness and purity.' In his message, Askoka laid emphasis upon non-violence, preserving life in all forms and 'right conduct' toward one's fellow human beings.

The third Buddhist Council is supposed to have met under Ashoka's patronage at his capital, Pataliputra. His injunctions implied a ban on sacrificial extravaganzas, and thereby the Emperor provocatively swiped at the Brahmins, who derived their prestige from conducting yajna-sacrifices.

Ashoka also built pillars and erected them at many places in the country. They are the finest works of Mauryan art. 'A good number of them have survived the ravages of time and the vandalism of men,' says Abraham Eraly.[206] Eraly quotes Vincent Smith: 'In these pillars the skill of the stone-cutter may be said to have attained perfection, and to have accomplished tasks which would, perhaps, be found beyond the powers of the twentieth century. Gigantic shafts of hard sandstone...were dressed and proportioned with the utmost nicety, receiving a polish which no modern mason knows how to impart to the material. Enormous surfaces of the hardest gneiss (coarse-grained metamorphic rock) were burnished like mirrors.'

Describing the Sarnath pillar, Eraly says: 'The pillars are beautifully proportioned, and crowned with animal sculptures of outstanding artistic merit. The most renowned of them is the Saranath pillar, its capital of four snarling lions being the emblem of

[206]Eraly, Abraham, *Gem in the Lotus*, Viking, Penguin Books, Delhi, 2000, pp. 415–416.

the Republic of India. The lions are set back-to-back on an abacus, which in turn is mounted on an inverted bell-shaped lotus... The abacus is adorned with fine bass-relief carvings of animals—an elephant, a horse, a bull, and a lion, with wheels separating them.'

Eraly also quotes John Marshall who had called them 'the finest carvings that India has yet produced, unsurpassed...by anything of their kind in the ancient world.' He mentions that 'When Firuz Tughluq moved one of these pillars from near Ambala to Delhi, it was carried to the Yamuna in a cart of 42 wheels, drawn by 8,400 men, and then down the river to Delhi in a raft made of a large number of boats.' A later descendent of Ashoka replanted the sacred peepal tree at Bodh Gaya in the seventh century AD.

King Bimbisara had died before the Buddha. He was enamoured by the beauty of Amrapali, the official courtesan of the Lichchhavi Republic of Vaishali. Amarapali was supposed to bestow her favours only on the Rajas of Vaishali, who ruled over thousands of small principalities of Vaishali. A desultory fight had been going on for some years between Bimbisara's kingdom of Magadha and the Republic of Vaishali. In the midst of this desultory fighting, it was discovered that King Bimbisara had entered Vaishali in disguise and, undetected, enjoyed a week's dalliance in Amrapali's delectable company. Bimbisara had to be made to pay for this indiscretion, and thereafter the Lichchhavi's had duly multiplied their attacks on Magadhan territory.

Besides the on-going fight with Vaishali, Bimbisara's son Ajatashatru got involved in warfare with the kingdom of Koshala over a piece of land in the vicinity of Varanasi, which had come to Bimbisara as the dowry of his Koshalan bride. Her father, King Prasenajit of Koshala resumed control of this land after the demise of his daughter. Old Prasenajit's son usurped the father's throne and launched an attack on Rajagriha. Koshalan army was camping in the dry bed of river Rapti and was overwhelmed by a flash flood. Due to this happenstance Ajatashatru easily over-ran the Koshalan army. Besides the land near Varanasi, Ajatashatru annexed the entire kingdom of Kashi.

JAINISM

A.K. Majumdar states that the first *Tirthankara* of Jain religion was Adinatha Rishabhadeva and adds that the Jain merchants of Rajasthan, who built a splendid temple in marble at Mount Abu, had dedicated it to Rishabhadeva. The tenets of Rishabhadeva were:

1. Salvation can be achieved without the idea of God.
2. Creation is self-evolved and is eternal.
3. Man should have extreme regard for life in any form.
5. Evolving Moral self-culture, and
6. Living in state of nature.

Life lived according to these tenets led to *Kevalya Gyana* (Pure wisdom), which led to moksha (salvation). *Yetis* among men alone were entitled to have the enviable 'pure wisdom'—a sure step to salvation!

However, Rishabhadeva admitted the authority of the Vedas partially, although he could not approve of animal slaughter. His religion was pure, sublime and natural and as such it was meant for the wise alone, though afterwards it was introduced amongst laymen in suitable forms. Rishabhadeva is said to have renounced the world and undertaken penance in the Himalayas, where he received enlightenment. He came back from the mountains and declared himself as *Jina* and expounded his tenets mentioned above. His followers came to be called Jains.

It is evident that the stoical severity of the religious tenets was suitably modified for the masses. Jainism is a thriving, living religion professed by millions of Indians. They admit all Hindu gods, worship some of them but consider them inferior to their *Arihants* (saints) who had followed the original tenets. The Jains worship 24 Tirthankaras for the past, 24 for the present and 24 for the future. Parshvanatha and Vardhamana Mahavira are the twenty-third and twenty-fourth Tirthankaras. Surprisingly while

Hindus have only one Indra, they have as many as 64 Indras. Besides, they have 22 Devis (Goddesses). They have no caste divisions among themselves.

∽

Preceding the Buddha by over two-and-a-half centuries, Tirthankar Parshvanatha (820 to 750 BC) was a son of Raja Ashvasen and queen Bamadevi of Varanasi. Like the Buddha, he refused royalty and lived as an ascetic. He attained Enlightenment at Varanasi, and began to preach. The districts of Maldah and Bogra in north Bengal were great centres of his faith. His converts were mostly from the depressed classes.

Tirthankara Vardhaman Mahavira (597 to 527 BC), was a contemporary of Gautama Buddha and had undertaken penance in the hills of Rajagriha in Bihar. His father was Raja Siddartha of Pawana and mother Queen Trishala. He renounced the world at the age of 30 and attained enlightenment after performing self-mortification for 12 years. He went to Kaushambi later on, where King Satanika honoured him. He had 11 chief Brahmin converts.

Vardhaman Mahavira's sect is called *Digambar* (Clad in sky!—no clothing). The Jain saints who are his followers just minimally cover their body. They are differentiated from the Jain saints who are followers of Tirthankar Parshvanatha, who wear white cotton clothes and are called *Shwetambara*.

∽

It appears from the foregoing that Buddhism and Jainism arose mainly because of two reasons: First, against the offering of flesh in Vedic sacrifices; and second, as a revolt against the creation of the degraded fourth category of the lowly 'Shudra' in Hinduism. People belonging to these lower classes gladly embraced the new religions in large numbers.

While Jainism thrived in India, Buddhism spread in China, Tibet, Japan and Korea. Southward it covered Sri Lanka, Thailand, Burma, Cambodia and Vietnam, adapting itself to various cultures, developing distinctive forms in different countries.

∽

SAINTS AND GURUS

GURU NANAK

Guru Nanak, a saint, phosopher, poet, reformer and guide, was born in 1469 at village Talwandi near Lahore. Right from his childhood he devoted himself to meditation, to look within, forgoing school education. He was the progenitor—the founder—of the *Sikh Panth*—Sikhism. His basic tenet, the *mool mantra,* is:

> *Ikk Onkaar,*[207] *Sat-naam, Karta Purakh, Nirabhau,*
> *Niravair, Akaala Moorat, Ajooni saibhan.*
>
> [There is one Supreme Reality—*OM*! His name is Truth—the One who created All, and resides in All creations! He has neither dread nor fear, nor any animosity! The One True One is the only Truth! He is Timeless, Self-Illumined and All-Pervasive!]

Guru Nanak would tell people '*Vand Chhakko!*'—'Eat by Sharing with others'. Give a portion of what you earn to unknown strangers and thereafter eat yourself. Give with love and compassion! Give what you can give without any expectation! Share the *Dasvaandh* (one-tenth) of what you earn with others. For, according to Guru Nanak: 'Giving is Receiving!'

His constant companion was Bhai Mardana, a Muslim. For him there was no Hindu, no Musalman—all were children of God!

> Rama and Rahim are One—like flowers upon a bower;
> Only there is *Ikk Onkar*—One omniscient pervasive power!
> And every person is this world is equal before the True One!
> The alternate meandering paths reach the same God—
> The All-pervasive God, or whatsoever name you use!
> Whichever path you choose

[207] *Ikk Onkar* is similar to the concept of *Param Brahma* in the *Rigveda,* which Guru Nanak had never studied.

At the journey's end you reach—
Ikk Onkaar—Satnaam! God's true name!

He had gone to the temple of Jagannath Puri on the sea-shore, with Bhai Mardana once. It was a full-moon night. He was enchanted by the Moon's reflection in the ocean. He began chanting a prayer:

Ikk Onkar!
O luminous stars, I offer this prayer to the True One:
The Cosmos is thy abode, Sun and Moon are radiant lamps,
The stars, the planets are like offerings of pearls;
Thy incence is the aroma of sandalwood,
The mountain winds are tender like breeze,
The Earth offers all the plants in the woods.
Fragrant blooms flower and fall at your feet,
A veneration exquisite, majestic and sweet!
You have a thousand forms—and still you are formless!
The universe is illumined and thou art the Light!
Thy light radiates and lights all within!
Like a thirsty song-bird I yearn for thee!
Let thy name be my abode, my resting place;
Let thy name guide me down a path that leads to You!
Your name rings true across the ether, beyond the stars!
Your name is but one though people call You by a thousand names!

~

Accompanied by Bhai Mardana, Guru Nanak had gone to Mecca once, undertaking a long and arduous sea-journey. He was tired and went to sleep on the open terrace of the sacred Mosque in Mecca. In the morning, he was found sleeping with his feet towards Mecca. Qazi Rukn-ud-Din objected to it, saying: 'It is disrespectful to point your feet in the direction where God resides.' Nanak replied: 'But please tell me, if there is any place on the earth where God does not reside! God is everywhere! He dwells in every nook and corner, in each leaf and every drop of the ocean!' The Qazi was silent.

Folding his hands, Nanak told the Qazi: 'The True One is ubiquitous, omniscient, All powerful and ever-loving! Endlessly Infinite, extremely vast, Unlimited and Unbound! The True One resides everywhere!'[208]

SANT KABEER

Sant Kabeer lived in the same age. He explained the Vedic concept of all-pervading *Brahma* to the simple, un-lettered masses of India in a couplet:

> *Jyon til maaheen tel hai, jyon chakmak mein aag;*
> *Teraa Saanyee tujjha mein, jaag sakey tau jaag!*
>
> [As there is oil in the tiny oil-seeds and there is fire in the flint stone; in the same way God, your Master, lives in you! Wake up, if you can!]

He composed innumerable such couplets in simple language used by common people, to give his message:

> *Matee kahe kumhaar se, tuu kyaa rondey moye;*
> *Aik din aisaa aayegaa, mein rondoongi toye!*
>
> [The soil says to the potter: Beware, just as you are kneading me ruthlessly, A day shall dawn, when I will be kneading you!]
>
> *Paani keraa bud-budaa, asa maanas kee jaat;*
> *Dekhat hee chhip jaayegaa, jyon taaraa parbhaat.*
>
> [Like the water bubble is the nature of man; in a wink, it shall disappear, like the stars at the break of dawn!]

[208]I have borrowed the above material on Guru Nanak from 'The Guru, Guru Nanak's Saakhies' by Rajni Sekhri Sibal, published by Story Mirror Infotech Pvt. Ltd., Mumbai.

Enigmatic sprituality of Kabeer is reflected in this tiny couplet:

Bhalaa huaa meri mataki phooti re;
Mein tau paniyaa bharan se chhooti re.

[He imagines himself to be a *panhaarin*—a woman drawing water from a well, and says: It was good happenstance that my earthen pot broke down; now I am relieved of this tiresome chore of drawing water from the well.]

To my mind, he means to say: 'When this earthen pot of my life breaks, I would be free from the cycle of birth and death.'

Another self-effacing gem:

Buraa jo dekhan mein chalaa, buraa na miliyaa koye;
Jo dil khojyaa aapanaa tau, mujhase buraa na koye.

[When I went in search of a bad man, I could find no one. When I searched within my own heart, I found that there was none as bad as myself!]

He sings a ditty in praise of his lifestyle:

Mana laagyo mero yaar fakiri mein!
Jo sukha paayo bhajan karan mein,
Vo sukha nahin ameeree mein!
Haath mein toombaa, bagal mein sotaa,
Chaaron dishaa jaageeree mein.
Prem Nagari mein rahani hamaari;
Bhali bana aayee saboori mein.
Aakhir yaha tana khak milega,
Kaahe phire magroori mein?
Kahe Kabeer suno bhai saadho,
Sahab mile saboori mein!
Mana laagyo mero yaar fakeeree mein!

[O my friend, my mind and heart are happy and contented in this life without possessions'—*faqiri.* The pleasure I get in singing hymns, cannot be experienced in a life of prosperity and wealth. Holding in my hand the hollow shell of gourd and a staff under my arm, all four directions are in my ownership! I reside in the City of Love, where all is well in a life of contentment. Ultimately, this body shall merge into dust; then why remain puffed up in vainglory? Listen O wise men, says Kabeer: you will find the Lord in contentment! My innermost Self is happy in a life of non-possession! Indeed, Less is More!]

Kabeer composed many songs. Here is one that points to his attaining the state of ultimate bliss:

Mana masta hua phir kyon boley?
Heeraa paayaa baandh gatharia,
Baar baar vaako kyon kholey?
Hansaa nahaave Maansarovar,
Taal talaiyaa kyon doley?
Halkee thee jab chadhee taraaju,
Pooree bhayi phir kya toley?
Kahat Kabeer suno bhai saadho,
Saahab mil gayaa til oley!

[When the heart is filled with bliss, no words can utter it! You have found a rare diamond; enclose it in a pouch! Why do you open the pouch to see it again and again? The swans bathe in the Mansarovar; why should they go to lakes and ponds? (The next couplet, '*Halkee thee jab chadhee taraaju, Pooree bhayi phir kya toley?*' is too deep for me.) It was light—not heavy—when I tried to weigh it; Now it's full! Then why do you weigh it?' It probably refers to a person's state of awareness, which when it was faint and feeble, he was curious to know its depth. But when it has reached fullness, there remains no need to measure its depth now; it's become immeasurable! Says Kabeer, listen O my brother, holy men, I have found the Lord hiding behind a tiny oil-seed!]

Most of Kabir's songs express a passionate desire to meet and mingle with the Lord:

Jaa kaaran hum deha dhari hai, milibo anga lagai;
Yahu aradaasa daasa ki suniye, tana ki tapan bujhaai.

[Kindly heed my prayer—the reason why I was born, getting the human form, was to mingle with your Self! Heed this prayer of your servant—Cool my body's heat!]

Supane mein Saanyi mile, sovat liya lagaaya;
Aankha na kholoon darapataan, mata sapanaa ho jaye.

[In my dream did my Lord come to me! I woke up to his tender touch! I did not open my eyes fearing it might only be a dream!]

Kabiraa yeh ghar prem ka, khaalaa kaa ghar nahin;
Seesa utaare bhunyi dhare, taba paithe ghar maahin.

[O Kabir, this is an abode Love, not the dwelling house of your aunt, in which you can enter at your will! You can enter in this house only if you sever your head and lay it at His feet!]

Samajha dekha mana meeta piyaare, aashik hokar sonaa kya re?
Kahe Kabeera prem kaa marag, sira denaa tau ronaa kya re?

[O my mind, my friend, do ponder! When you have fallen in love, why crave for sleep? Says Kabir—unique is the path of love! When you have to sever your head, why cry?]

I love this lovely song:

Ghoonghat ke pata khol, re tauhe Piyaa milenge!

Remove the veil, You will meet your gracious Lord!

Ghata ghata mein vohi Saayeen ramate,
Katuka vachan mata bole, re tauhe Piyaa milenge!

[In the heart of every being does He reside; Never say a harsh word to anyone! Your gracious Lord will meet you!]

Sunna mahal mein diyaa baar le, Aashaa se mata dole, re tauhe Piyaa milenge!

[Light the lamp in the void of your heart; never lose hope! Your gracious Lord will meet you![

Joga jugata saun rangamahal mein, Piyaa paaye anamole, re tauhe Piyaa milenge!

[By the power of Yoga and and constant remembrance, in your heart's grand palace, you shall meet your precious Lord!]

Kahe Kabir aananda bhayo hai, baajat anahada dhole, re tauhe Piyaa milenge!

[Says Kabir, you shall experience supreme pleasure by lending your ear to the music coming from the celestial drum!]

In another unique love-song, Kabir sings:

Haman hai ishka mastaanaa, hamko hoshiyaari kya?

[I am drunk with the love of the Lord; why should I be care-worn?]

Hamaara Yaara hai hamamein hamana ko intazaari kya?

[My Love dwells in me; I don't have to wait for him!]

Haman Hari naam raacha hai, hamana duniya se yaari kya?

[I am always chanting His name; why should I befriend the world at all?]

MIRA BAI

Mira Bai was a princess of the state of Chittor; its capital was later moved to Udaipur where the Rana built a new palace. Mira took *sanyaas* after the demise of her husband, Prince Bhojaraj, and became a devotee of Shri Krishna. She wrote haunting poetry singing Krishna's praise, deeming Him as her husband!

Mero tau Girdhar Gopal doosaro na koi.
Jaake sir mor-mukut, mero pati soi.

[Only Girdhar Gopal[209] is my own! There is no other! The One who wears a peacock crown on his head, is my Husband!]

Mirabai composed hundreds of songs in praise of Shri Krishna:

Hey ree main tau prem diwaani, mero darda na jaane koy;
Ghayal ki gati ghayal jaane, jo koi ghayal hoye.

[I am madly in love; no one understands my pain. Only one who gets wounded, can understand the acute pain of the wounded person.]

Sooli oopar sej Piya ki, sovan kis vidhi hoye;
Gagan mandal par sej Piyaa ki, kis vidhi milano hoye?

[My husband sleeps on a hangman's board; how can I sleep with him? My beloved sleeps in the star-sudded firmament; how can I ever meet him?]

Darad ki maari bana-bana doloon, vaidya milyaa nahin koye;
Meera ki Prabhu peer mitegi, jada Vaidya Sanwaria hoye.

[Tormented by pain, I wander in deep dense forests, searching for the healer, whom I never met! O my Lord, Meera's pain will be healed only when *Sanwaria* (Krishna of dark viasage) becomes my healer!]

Elsewhere, she sang ecstatically in praise of tiny rain drops. She was born in the dry desert area of Rajasthan, where rainfall is scanty and the occasional showers were like heavenly blessing:

Nanhi nanhi boondan meha barase;
Bhanak suni Hari aavan ki.

[Tiny rain drops are falling from the sky; in their soft whispers, I hear intimations of Krishna's advent! (Krishna is also known as *Hari.*)]

[209]'Girdhar Gopal'—one who hold a hill on his hand and rears the cows. Shri Krishna was reared by Yashoda. He used to take the family cows to the grass-lands for grazing. One day there was an execcive downpour. Krishna is said to have lifted up a hillock, under which he and his fellow cowherds shelterd with their cows.

In another song, Mira asks the *Rana* (King of Mewar; here meaning Shri Krishna) to employ her as a servant in his palace:

> *Ranaji mhaane chaakar raakho ji;*
> *Chaakar rahashyaan, baag lagaashyaan,*
> *Nitta ootha darshan paashyaan.*
>
> [O Ranaji, employ me as a servant in your palace! I would create a garden for your dalliance, and have the pleasure of seeing your benign form every morning as you come out to saunter in the garden!]

SWAMI YOGANANDA PARAMAHANSA

Swami Yogananda Paramahansa was born in 1893 and learnt meditation and yogic samadhi from Yogi Yukteshwar Giri who was a disciple of Yogi Lahiri Mahashaya, an acclaimed sage.

I have Swami Yogananda's Autobiograhy.[210] He narrates the astonishing story of his life. His original family name was Mukunda—one of the many names of Krishna! His parents were disciples of the aforesaid sage, Lahiri Mahashaya. His father, Bhagbati Charan Ghosh, was a high officer in the Bengal–Nagpur Railways, posted at Gorakhpur. Abinash Babu, a junior employee of the Railways, working under him, requested him for a week's leave to visit his guru, Lahiri Mahashaya, in Banaras (Varanasi). Bhagwati Charan Ghosh refused to grant him leave and told him sternly not to waste time meeting religious fanatics.

Later, Abinash Babu met Bhagbati Charan Ghosh on his evening walk on a woodland path, where he was again advised by his boss to strive for worldly success rather than wasting time in meeting sadhus. It was a tranquil evening suffused with golden rays of the setting sun. As they walked together, they saw the form of Abinash Babu's guru Lahiri Mahashaya just a few yards away

[210]Paramhans, Yogananda, *Autobiography of a Yogi*, Jaico Publishing House, Bombay, 1977.

from them! In his evanescent form Lahiri Mahashaya reprimanded Bhagbati Charan Ghosh: 'Bhagabati, you are too hard on your employee!' Abinash Babu went down on his knees, exclaiming: 'Lahiri Mahashaya! Lahiri Mahashaya!' The saint vanished as mysteriously as he had appeared!

Bhagbati Charan Ghosh stood motionless for a while, seeing this apparition and said: 'Abinash, not only do I give you leave, but I give myself leave to start for Banaras tomorrow. I must know this great Lahiri Mahashaya, who is able to materialize at will to intercede for you. I will take my wife and ask this master to initiate us on his spiritutal path. Will you guide me to him?' They called on the rishi Lahiri Mahashaya who initiated Bhagbati Charan Ghosh and his wife in the spiritual practice of Kriya Yoga.

Abinash Babu had narrated this episode to Yogananda, the author of the book I possessed, when Yogananda was studying in school and had added: 'Lahiri Mahashaya had taken a definite interest in your birth. Your life shall surely be linked with his own! The Master's blessing never fails!' However, Yogi Lahiri Mahashaya had died one year after Yogananda was born.

~

When still a student, the boy Yogananda had a powerful urge to go the Himalayas and had fled to Naini Tal, in the foothills of the Himalayas. His elder brother Ananta chased him and brought him back. Later, Ananta told him that their mother had taken him as a new-born babe to Sage Lahiri Mahashaya, who had predicted that the child will be a yogi in his later life. Their mother expired some time after his brother made this revelation to Yogananda.

Even before completing formal education, Yogananda had spiritual leanings, as the incident of going to Nainital indicates. He had been going to meet Sage Yukteshwar Giri who was living in their vicinity. Yukteshwar Giri told him to complete his degree course from the Calcutta University 'as some day you would be going to the West and they would be more receptive to India's ancient wisdom if the strange Hindu teacher has a university degree.'

Yogananda began living in Benaras where Shri Yukteshwar

Giri, diciple of Lahiri Mahashaya, resided and learnt Kriya Yoga from him for 10 years.

Swami Yogananda's book is full of prophetic statements and miraculous events. It mentions many miraculous events foretold by his gurus to him. Many of them, however, look like common happenings which have been given the garb of a miracle. It is rather unfair to say this about a world-famous spiritual guru, but he appears to have a knack of presenting events and incidents of his life in the garb of prophetic revelations.

'All creation is governed by law.' Sage Yukteshwar told Yogananda once. 'The principles that operate in the outer universe, discoverable by scientists, are called natural laws. But there are subtler laws that rule the hidden spiritual planes and the inner realm of consciousness; these principles are knowable through the Science of Yoga. It is not the physicist but the Self-realized master who comprehends the true nature of the matter. By such knowledge Christ was able to restore the servant's ear after it had been severed by one of the disciples.'

Yogananda reaveals that in 1915, shortly after he entered the Swami Order, he 'clearly perceived the Unity of the Eternal Light behind the painful dualities of Maya! The vision descended on me as I sat one móning in my Father's Gurpar Road home.' He had been thinking of the countless deaths that had occurred in the First World War. He suddenly saw the vision of the dead body of the commander of a ship while canons and guns were shooting. Then he saw a vision of himself bring hit by a bullet in his chest and he fell down groaning. His eyes opened then. He found himself seated in the lotus posture in his Gurpar road home. Then he beheld a vision of light and heard a voice, saying: 'In the image of my light I have made you. The relativities of life and death belong to the cosmic dream! Behold your dreamless being! Awake, My child, awake!'

His mentor Sant Yukteshwar had told Yogananda that he would be creating three institutions—'a sylvan retreat in the plains, another on a hilltop and still another by the ocean'.

This prophecy came true. In 1918, Shri Yogananda set up the first institution, the Yogoda Satsang Brahmacharya Vidyalaya in the premises of the Kasimbazar Palace in Ranchi which the Maharaja of Kasimbazar had donated to him. Later, in 1925, the International headquarters of 'Self-Realization Fellowship' atop Mt Washington in Los Angeles was established, and in 1938, the Yogoda Math, at Dakshineshwar on the Ganga was started. Besides these, 'Shri Yukteshwar Seaside Ashram' was set up in Puri.

Yogananda's Meeting with Mahatma Gandhi

Mahatma Gandhi had identified himself with the poor and lowly millions of India, whom he called '*Daridra* Narayan,' the 'Godly Poor!' All his life he worked tirelessly for removal of inequality, oppression and social injustice against them, particuraly the *Shudra*. Many a times he lodged in a *Bhangi Basti* (colony of the scavengers) with a view to to eradicating the curse of untouchability from India by his personal example. In his ashram in South Africa, he and his wife, Kasturba, were cleaning the toilets of the residents of his ashram.

Shri Yogananda gives a charming description of his visit to Wardha Ashram to meet the Mahatma in 1935. He was accompanied by Miss Bletsch and Mr Wright from the USA. Mahadev Desai, Gandhiji's secretary received them. Ten years back, in 1925, Gandhiji had paid a visit to the Ranchi school that was being run by Shri Yogananda. Shri Yogananda observes that 'no other leader in the world has attained the secure niche in the hearts of his people that Gandhi occupies for India's unlettered millions.'

It happened to be Gandhiji's weekly Day of Silence! They had lunch with Gandhiji together with 25 bare-footed *satyagrahis*,[211] squatting before brass cups and plates. After a community chorus prayer, a simple meal of *chapatis*[212] sprinkled with ghee[213] and boiled and diced vegetables was served, besides lemon jam. Gandhiji gave Yogananda a spoon of neem-paste which the Swami gulped down with water, recollecting his childhood days when his mother made him swallow some neem-paste. Neem-paste is

[211]Volunteers for Truth.
[212]Common wheat bread made on house-hold fire-place.
[213]Clarified butter.

considered a notable blood cleanser. Gandhiji himself was licking it with relish.

In the afternoon, Shri Yogananda chatted with Madeleine Slade, Gandhiji's disciple known as Mira Behn, who told him about her visit to villages in the morning to teach villagers simple hygiene, showing them how to clean their latrines. She told him that the illiterate villagers cannot be educated except by example. 'I looked in admiration at this highborn Englishwoman,' observes Swami Yogananda, 'whose true Christian humility enables her to do scavenging work, usually performed only by "untouchables".'

At eight o'clock in the evening, Gandhiji's *'maun vrata'* ended; then he greeted Yogananda: 'Welcome, Swamiji!' (as if meeting for the first time!) They discussed America and Europe and the world's condition in general. Gandhiji told Mahadev Desai: 'Make arrangement for Swamiji to speak on Yoga tomorrow at the Town Hall.' Then he handed Yogananda a bottle of citronella oil, saying: 'The Wardha mosquitoes don't know a thing about *ahimsa*, Swamiji,' and chuckled with a twinkle in his eyes.

∽

Shri Yogananda's book also carries a photograph of '*Mahavatara*[214] *Babaji*', Guru of Shri Lahiri Mahashaya. Shri Lahiri Mahashaya used to go occasionally into snow-clad caves of the higher Himalayas to pay obeisance to his guru, simply called Babaji. Shri Yogananda states that 'Babaji's mission in India had been to assist prophets in carrying out their special task.' He had stated that Babaji had given yoga initiation to Shankaracharya and even to Sant Kabeer. He added: 'Babaji is ever in communion with Christ!'

However, Yogananda adds an explanation about this mysterious Babaji: 'That there is no historical reference to Babaji, need not surprise us. The great guru has never openly appeared in any century; the misinterpreting glare of publicity has no place in his millennial plans. Like the Creator, Babaji works in humble obscurity, as the sole but silent Power!' He narrates a story of a man who approached

[214]Great incarnation.

Babaji on a hill top, and requested him to take him as his disciple. On Babaji's refusal the man jumped down the cliff. Babaji later got his mangled body retrieved and restored him to life!

BHAGWAN OSHO

Another famous Indian spiritual leader who made an ashram in Pune and later in the U.S. is popularly known as **Bhagwan Osho.** I have his book, *Tantra Vision: Beyond the Barriers of Wisdom*,[215] which describes him as: '*OSHO*, Never born, Never died; Only visited this planet from December 11, 1931 to January 19, 1990.'

A poem is printed at the beginning of the book:

For the delights of kissing the deluded crave
Declaring it to be the ultimately real!
Like a man who leaves his house, and standing at the door,
Asks (a woman) for reports of sensual delights.
The stirring of biotic forces in the house of nothingness
Has given artificial rise to pleasures in so many ways.
Such *yogis* from affliction faint, for they have fallen
From celestial space, inveigled into vice!
As a Brahmin, who with rice and butter
Makes a burnt offering in blazing fire,
Creating a vessel for nectar from celestial space,
Takes this through wishful thinking as the ultimate!
Some people who have kindled
The inner heat and raised it to the fontanelle
Stroke the uvula, with the tongue in,
A sort of coition and confuse
That which fetters with what gives release!
In pride they will call themselves *yogis*!

[215]OSHO, *Beyond the Barriers of Wisdom*, Diamond Pocket Books, Delhi.

'*Tantra* is freedom: freedom from all mind-constructs, from all mind-games: freedom from all structures; freedom from the other. Tantra is a space to be! Tantra is liberation!'

Tantra is not a religion in the ordinary sense. Religion again is a mind game; religion gives a certain pattern. A Christian has a certain pattern, so has the Hindu, so has the Muslim. Religion gives you a certain style, a discipline. Tantra takes the disciplines away!

When there is no discipline, when there is no enforced order, a totally different kind of order arises in you. What Lao Tzu calls '*Tao*', what the Buddha calls dharma—that arises in you! That is not anything done by you. Tantra simply creates space for it to happen. It does not even invite, it does not wait; it simply creates a space. And when the space is ready, the whole flows in!

Tantra says: If you are in order, then the whole world is in order for you. when you are in harmony, then the whole existence is in harmony for you. when you are in disorder, then the whole world is in disorder. And the order has not to be a false one, it has not to be a forced one. When you force some order upon yourself, you simply become split; deep down the disorder continues!

You can observe it: if you are an angry person, you can force your anger, you can repress it deep down in the unconscious, but it is not going to disappear. Maybe you become completely unaware of it, but it is there—and you know it is there. It is running underneath you, it is in the dark basement of your being, but it is there. On top of it you can sit smiling, but you know it can erupt any moment. And your smile cannot be very deep, and your smile cannot be true, and your smile will be just an effort that you will be making against yourself.

A man who forces an order from the outside, remains in disorder. Tantra says there is another kind of order: You don't impose any order, you don't impose any discipline; you simply drop all structures, you simply become natural and spontaneous. It is the greatest step a man can be asked to take. It will need great courage because society will not take it; society will be dead against it. Society wants a certain order. If you follow society, society is happy with you. If you go a little bit astray here and there, society is very angry. And the mob is mad!

The Tantra is a rebellion. I don't call it revolutionary because it has no politics in it. And I don't call it revolutionary because it has no plans to change the world: it has no plans to change the state and the society. It is rebellious but it is individual rebellion. It is one individual slipping out of the structures and the slavery! But the moment you slip out of the slavery, you come to feel another kind of existence around you, which you have never felf before—as if you were living with a blindfold and suddenly the blindfold has become loose, your eyes have opened, and you can see a totally different world.

This blindfold is what you call mind; your thinking, your prejudices, your knowledge, your scriptures—they all make the thick layer of a blindfold. They are keeping you blind, they are keeping you dull, they are keeping you 'un-alive'. Tantra wants you to be alive—as alive as the trees, as alive as the rivers, as alive as the sun and the moon. That is your birthright. You don't gain anything by losing it; you lose all. And if everything is to be lost in gaining it, nothing is lost. Even a single moment of utter freedom is enough to satisfy. And a long life of a hundred years, yoked like a slave, is meaningless.

To be in the world of Tantra needs courage: it is adventurous. Up to now only a few people have been able to move on that path. It is not a fight against society, remember; it is just going beyond society. It is not anti-social; it is asocial. Your whole life is just a nightmare. Have a look at it! There is no poetry, and no song, and no dance, no love, and no prayer. (Italics mine!)

You should begin meditating at orgasm, when your male centre (*muladhar)* is meeting with your female centre (*svadhistan)*, forgetting the woman you are making love to, and vice versa for women. Close your eyes and begin meditating. When orgasm happens your whole body-energy is throbbing with dance. A door opens at this moment and an inner bliss flows into you. It is coming from your innermost core. You can use that love-wave to go far inside. In that moment of thrill, things are not on the earth: you can fly. That is when you move into prayer.

After one such experience, a second chance for another such meeting would suddenly appear, for the energy released from the first meeting creates the possibility for the second meeting. And when energy is created by the second meeting, it creates the possibility for the third meeting. At the fourth such meeting, there is no male female. Man has become the woman, the woman has become the man; all division disappears. This is the absolute! The Adam and Eve have disappeared into each other; the divide dissolved. This is what Hindus call *sat-chit-ananda*. This is what Jesus calls the Kingdom of God.

Six *chakra*s you will have to work in; with the seventh you disappear as part of duality. Matter is no more matter; mind is no more mind. You have gone beyond. This is the transcendental space the Buddha calls *nirvana*.

The first meeting between muladhar rand swadhistan is like sleep; the man and woman have met inside you, but they have met in the unconscious. However, you will feel a new radiance, a new glow. The second meeting is like a dream. The third meeting is like re-awakening in full-moon light.

When the Buddha became enlightened, he wanted to go to Yashodhara and talk to her, to express his gratitude to her. She saw a luminous aura around him; she fell at his feet and asked to be initiated.

Summing up, Osho says that sex is not ultimate in pleasure; it is just the beginning, the alpha. It is not the bliss supreme, just an echo of it. Because of this delusion even in the twentieth century, the Nizam of Hyderabad had five hundred wives!

In India, the Brahmins have been doing yajnas. They have been offering rice and butter into the blazing fire, and imagining that this offering is going to God. Sitting around a fire, fasting for many days, doing certain rituals, repeating certain scriptures, you can create a state of autohypnosis. You can be fooled by yourself and think that you are reaching to God.

Offering ghee to fire is not going to help. You have to burn your inner fire. And sexual energy moving upwards becomes fire. It becomes a flame. It is fire. Sex energy is the most miraculous thing. It is through sex energy that life is born. While making love to a woman, the fire is going out. When you throw your seeds of desire, of thought, of ambition and greed, they are burnt.

Finally, you throw your ego—the most purified dream, that too is burnt. That is real yajna, real ritual, real sacrifice. The fire has to move inwards, then it gives rebirth to you, it rejuvenates you.

The fifth chakra, *visuddha*, is in the throat. It is the last chakra from which you can fall. With the sixth chakra your third eye opens. The fifth chakra, visuddha, is male. The throat becomes almost a genital organ, having more finesse than the genital organ. Just a little tickle with the tongue you enjoy greatly, real sex is nothing compared to it. That is the last temptation, like Satan coming to tempt Jesus or Mara tempting the Buddha. It is very difficult to avoid it; it is infinitely more pleasurable than sexual pleasure. You have to move beyond it; not succumbing to desire at the last post.

Tantra is not against love making. It is all for it. Sex is the first rung of the ladder, a seven-runged ladder. Man is the ladder. The first rung is sex and the seventh is *Sahasrar*—Samadhi!

FLOWERING OF VERNACULAR POETRY

Besides the anonymous authors of the Ramayana, Mahabharata and the Gita, Sanskrit produced great poets like **Bhasa, Bhavabhuti and Kalidasa.**

Kalidasa's *Megh Doot* (Cloud Messenger) portrays a Yaksh who dwells in the divine city of Alakapuri in the Himalayas. He had offended his master Kubera and was banished for a year to the hill of Ramagiri, in the modern Madhya Pradesh. He suffered pangs of separation from his beautiful wife, whom he had left behind.

At the beginning of the rainy season, he sees a large cloud heading northward to the mountains and pours out his heart to it. Yaksh (in reality—Kalidasa) tells the Cloud the route to the mountains, describes the lands, rivers and the cities over which the cloud had to pass. On this pretext, Kalidas describes the beauty of the Narmada River and the forests on its banks. Then the Cloud is told to turn westward and visit the splendid city of Ujjayaini (modern Ujjain):

> Where the wind from the River Shipra prolongs the shrill melodious cry of the cranes, fragrant at early dawn from the scent of the opening buds of lotus, and like a lover, with flattering requests, dispels the morning languor of women, and refreshes their limbs.
>
> Your body will grow fat with the smoke of incense from open windows where women dress their hair. You will be greeted by the palace peacocks, dancing to welcome you, their friend. If your heart is weary from travel, you may pass the night above the mansions fragrant with flowers, whose pavements are marked with red dye from the feet of lovely women.

Then as the Cloud nears the Himalayas, it sees the magic city of Alkapuri: 'Where Yakshas dwell with lovely consorts in white mansions, whose crystal terraces reflect the stars like flowers. They drink the wine of love distilled from magic trees, while drums beat softly, deeper than your thunder.'

Then the Yaksh describes his home, and his lovely wife, weak from sorrow and longing. He gives the Cloud a message for her—that his love for her is constant and the time of reunion is approaching:

'I see your body in the sinuous creeper, your gaze in the startled eyes of the deer, your cheek in the moon, your hair in the plumage of peacocks, and in the tiny ripples of the river I see your sidelong glances. But alas, my dearest, nowhere do I find your whole likeness!'

As in English literature so in Sanskrit, the greatest poet was also the greatest dramatist. Three of the plays of Kalidasa have survived but *Abhijnaan Shakuntala* (The Recognition of Shakuntala) has won universal renown and would remain unsurpassed in world literature.

~

Writing about the beauty of the Sanskrit language, the great litterateur and the first Vice President of India, S. Radhakrishnan opines that 'no translation of the Gita can bring out the dignity and grace of the original (Sanskrit verses). Its melody and magic of phrase are difficult to recapture in another medium.'[216] The philosophy of the Gita had charmed Schopenhauer, one of the world's greatest philosophers!

~

While Sanskrit ceased to be a spoken language in India, it gave birth to several vernacular languages like Bengali, Oriya, Marathi, Hindi, Punjabi, etc. Owing to the extensive reach of vernacular languages, poets vied with each other in composing poetry in the vernaculars, particularly the Bhakti poetry.

Tulsidas's Ramcharitmanas has emerged as the most popular retelling of the story of Lord Rama. It took him 17 years in

[216]Radhakrishnan, S., Preface, *Bhagavadgita*, George Allen & Unwin, Great Britain, reprinted Blackie & Son, India, p. 7.

composing it, living in a cottage on the bank of the Ganga in Varanasi. I surmise that by calling his retelling Ramcharitmanas, he was probably likening it to the Manasarovar Lake, at the foot of Mount Kailash, considered as the abode of Lord Shiva, which reflects the snow-clad massif in its sparkling blue waters.

As mentioned earlier, in Valmiki's original Sanskrit composition, Prince Rama was not an incarnation of Lord Vishnu. The pundits added the episode of Brahma meeting Valmiki in his ashram and telling him the story of Prince Rama of Ayodhya. (Similarly, Brahma had a meeting with the composer of the Mahabharata, Rishi Veda Vyasa, briefing him about the divine origin of Shri Krishna!) The '*Bala Kaanda*' and the '*Uttar Kaanda*' were added to the original story composed by Valmiki, weaving the myth of Rama's divine incarnation into it.

I like the shower of poetic imagery in Tulsidasa's description of the rains, when Rama and Lakshman are held up in a cave in Kishkindha, while they were going in search of Sita.

Ghana ghamand nabh garjat ghora;
Priya-heen darpat maan mora.'

[Rama tells Lakshman: The arrogant, fierce clouds are thundering in the sky and my heart trembles in the absence of my beloved.' Note the alliteration of '*ghana, ghamand and ghora.*]

Damini damak rahi ghana maanhi;
Khal kee preet jatha thir naahin.

[Lightning blazes across the sky just as a rogue's friendship is not stable.]

Barsahin jalad bhoomi niyaraaye;
Jatha navahin budh vidya paaye.

[Clouds come down near the earth for showering rain, as wise men bow down after gaining knowledge!]

Boonda aghat sahahin giri kaise;
Khal ke bachan sant saha jaise.

[The mountains bear the lashing by the showers of rain, as holy men suffer a rogue's words in silence.]

Bhoomi parat bha dhabar paani;
Jani jeevahi maya laptaani.

[The rainwater gets soiled as soon as it falls on the earth; as the soul is smeared by *Maya* instantly at man's birth.]

Dadur dhun chahun disa suhayee;
Veda padhahin janu batu samudai.

[Sonorous music of frogs is heard from all directions as if student groups are reciting the Vedic *richas*. (This verse is reminiscent of the charming hymn on frogs in the Rig Veda.)]

While Tulsidas worshipped Shri Rama, Saint-poet **Soordasa,** so called as he was born blind, was a devotee of Shri Krishna. He composed thousands of lyrical songs describing child Krishna's antics in Brij *bhasha* (dialect) spoken around Mathura, the birth-place of Lord Krishna. Krishna's parents, Vasudeva and Devaki, were lodged in jail by King Kansa, who had heard a prophecy that he would be killed by their progeny.

He had already killed seven of their new-born babes at birth. Krishna was the eighth; born in the dead of night. His father Vasudeva put him in a basket and swam across the Yamuna, carrying the basket on his head, undetected by the royal guards in darkness, and returned after leaving the baby in the care of the cowherd Nanda and his wife Yashoda. Soordasa describes Yashoda rocking the crib:

Yashoda Hari paalane jhulave
Hulraave, dulraave, jhulaave; joi soi kuchh gave

[Yashoda rocks the child Krishna in a crib. She hums and caresses him and sings whatever comes to her mind.]

When still a small boy, Krishna used to take the family's herd of cows to graze, along with other kids of the village taking their cows to the grassy, forest areas and bringing the cows home in the evening. One day, when he came home in the evening, he found his mother absent. He was hungry and raided the butter-pot, hanging from the ceiling, in which Yashoda used to collect butter. He reached up, placing a stool or something on the floor, and avidly lapped up the butter, which he loved. Yashoda came back and discovered his misdeed. She upbraided him but he vehemently denied doing it:

> *Mein nahin maakhan khayo, Mayya meri, mein nahin maakhan khayo.*
> *Chaar pahar Bansibut bhatakyo, saanjh pare ghar aayo*
>
> [I haven't eaten the butter, O my Mother, I haven't done it at all. I roamed after the cows in the bamboo forest for full four *prahars*,[217] and have just returned home, gathering the cows after dusk-fall.]
>
> *Mein baalak bahiyan ko chhoto, chheenko kehi vidhi paayo?*
>
> [I am a child with puny arms; how could I reach the pot hanging high from the ceiling?]

Thereupon, Yashoda points to his butter-smeared mouth. But he invents a defence:

> *Gwal-baal sab bair pare hain, barbas mukh laptaayo.*
>
> [All my fellow cow-herds are inimical to me; they have forcibly smeared my mouth with butter!]

Yashoda was unwilling to accept this explanation. So, Krishna tells her:

> *Yeh le apni lakuti kamaria, bahut hi naatch nachayo.*
>
> [Okay then, take back this little stick and this blanket you have given me; I have had enough of dancing to your tune!]

---

[217]*Chaar Prahar*: One *prahar* equals about three hours—so 'four *prahar*' means practically the whole day.

Soordasa taba vihansi Yashoda, le urr kanth lagayo.

[Soordasa says, 'Yoshoda smiled then and taking him in her arms, pressed him close to her heart!']

The *Soor Sagara* is verily an ocean of poems. Soor Dasa would sing them aloud. He was reckoned to be the towering poet of the age. There is a famous couplet, composed by some critic that compares the relative merit of the principal poets of Hindi literature:

Soor Soor, Tulasi Shasi, Udugan Keshav Das,
Ab ke Kavi khaddyota sum, jahn-tahn karata prakash.

[Soordasa holds the pre-eminent position among the Hindi poets, like the dazzling Sun in the universe, followed by Tulsidasa who shines like the Moon. Keshav Das (who wrote *Rama-Chandrika* in a sophisticated, scholastic diction) shone like bright stars, while the later poets are like moths, twinkling here and there.]

This sweeping summation is most unfair to many Hindi poets of high eminence like **Jaishankar Prasad, Maithili Sharan Gupt, Mahadevi Varma, Nirala** and others.

A Muslim poet in Emperor Akbar's court, **Abdur Rahim Khanekhana,** is a unique phenomenon in the world of Hindi poetry. He composed excellent poems in praise of Krishna in the *Brij* dilect which became highly popular. He took up the '*lakuti* and *kamaria*' from the above song of Soordasa on child Krishna, and sang:

Ya lakuti aru kamaria par, raaj tihun pur ko taji daroon,
Aathahun siddhi navo nidhi ko sukh, Nanda ki gai charai bisaroon

[I would gladly abdicate as the ruler of three worlds in exchange of the stick and the blanket of Krishna! I would forgo the enlightenment afforded by the eight *Siddhis* as well as enjoyment of nine treasures, in lieu of taking the cows of Nanda (Yashoda's husband) for grazing.]

Abdur Rahim Khanekhana was deeply troubled by the poverty of the masses and used to give liberal alms to the poor, who lined up every morning outside his house in Agra. People observed that he sat with downcast eyes as he gave charity, a picture of humility, not in a proud posture. They asked why did he show such humility. He wrote a beautiful couplet in answer:

Denhaar koi aur hai, daita rahata dina-rain;
Log bharam ham par karen, taason neecho nain.

[The Giver is someone else, who goes on giving, day and night! But people wrongly believe that I am the giver. Therefore, I assume a humble demeanour, keeping my eyes downcast.]

He composed several couplets. My daughter Jyotsana has sent me a few, which I quote below:

Rahiman dhaagaa prem kaa mata todo chatakaaya;
Toote se phir naa jude, jude gaantha pari jaaya.

[O Raheem, do not break the thread of love; for the thread will never be whole again. When joined again, the joint will ever remain as an uncomfortable reminder.]

Roothe sujan manaaiye, jo roothe sau baar;
Rahiman fir-fir poiye, toote muktaa haar.

[O Raheem, if noble men are displeased, go all out to please them, even if they get displeased a hundered times. Just as a garland of pearls is joined again and again, whenever it gets disjointed.]

Rahiman dekh badain ko, laghu na deejiye daari;
Jahan kaam aave suee, kahaa kare tarvaari.

[O Raheem, do not throw away a small thing when you find something big. Where a needle is required, what use will be a sword?]

Rahiman paani raakhiye, binu paani saba soon;
Paani binaa na oobare motee, maanus, choon.

[O Raheem, always keep and preserve water, for it's all barren and lifeless without water. Without water there will be no pearls, no mankind and no bread from flour.]

Taruvar phal nahin khaata hai, sarvar piyata na pani;
Kahi Raheem par kaaja hita, sampati sanchahin sujaan.

[The trees don't eat their fruits; the ponds don't drink their water. Raheem says that noble, benevolent persons accumulate wealth for benefitting others.]

Rahiman nij mana ki vyathaa, mana hee raakho goya;
Suni athilehein loga saba, baanti na lehoo koya.

[O Raheem, keep your mental anguish, perturbarion or pain hidden in deep recesses of your heart. For people will just laugh away; no one would share them with you.]

It's indeed remarkable that an important Muslim noble of Emperor Akbar's court, coming from a Muslim country, could write such pithy poetry in Hindi, which would be readily understood by the common, even illiterate people.

ART AND ARCHITECTURE: GODS ENSHRINED IN TOWERING TEMPLES

Apparently, the main cause of the rise of the powerful liberal religions, Buddhism and Jainism, which cost Hinduism a large following, was the offering of animal sacrifice in Hindu religious rites. Yet another reason for decline was that there were very few patrons who could afford the elaborate Vedic sacrifices. The householders maintained *Grihyagni* in their homes for worship.

The pundits too had the predicament of not finding many patrons. They, therefore, set about revising the Ramayana and the Mahabharata, supplanting their historicity and converting them into the holy books of Hinduism like the Bible or the Koran. In the revised versions of these two epic poems of India, they conferred divinity on Shri Rama and Shri Krishna.

Godhood eminently fitted Shri Rama. His traversing almost the entire length of the Indian sub-continent on foot, forging a rag-tag army of primitive people who dressed like monkeys or bears, reaching the southern tip of Indian subcontinent and going over the cliffs partially submerged in the ocean, reaching Lanka and rescuing his wife, Princess Sita, from the confinement of the fortified castle of the King of Lanka who had abducted her from Chitrakoot, was nothing short of miraculous. He richly deserved the halo of divinity, although he had deviated from the ethics of chivalry in the manner in which he killed the king of the monkey tribe, Vali. But there were extenuating circumstances. Vali had driven out his younger brother Sugriva and taken his wife, Tara to bed. In a manner of speaking, Sugriva was in similar plight as Rama, and had sought Rama's help.

Shri Krishna was born in a prison; his parents were imprisoned by the cruel king Kansa. His father, Vasudeva, carried the new-born infant in the dead of night in a basket on his head, going across River Yamuna to a hamlet of cowherds a few miles downstream, and leaving his new-born baby in the care of a childless couple.

Krishna grew up in lowly surroundings but regained his princely stature and regal mien, and set up his kingdom in Dwarka, near the sea-shore.

He was closely related to both the Pandavas and Kauravas. However, he did not like the scheming and selfish Duryodhan. Yet, he gave his army to him and gladly became Arjuna's charioteer in the fratricidal battle, Mahabharata. However, in later times the pundits composed the Bhagavada Purana, describing the miraculous acts of Krishna's childhood, like lifting a hill on his finger, or dancing on the hood of a serpent in a pool, etc. The pundits also composed the universally acclaimed Srimad-Bhagavada Gita in 18 chapters, wherein Krishna proclaims himself as God. The Gita was supposedly recited by Shri Krishna to Arjuna, when the two armies were standing face-to-face on the battle-field at Kurukshetra, and when Arjun expressed his aversion to killing his cousins and venerable gurus to regain his kingdom. Apart from reciting the Gita, Krishna also revealed to Arjuna His celestial Viraat Svaroop, His sky-high form establishing His divinity.

The publication of these two books, the Ramayana and the Mahabharata had a miraculous effect on the public mind. While the Vedic sacrifices were esoteric, confined mainly to the rulers and the wealthy people; the temples that came up enshrining Rama and Krishna as God Almighty had an exoteric effect. They were within the reach of millions of common people and opened the new path of Bhakti, affording them darshan (glimpse) of their dazzling gods and goddesses.

The temples were built in cities and villages, even on the road side. People flocked to them in the morning and evening. Kings built magnificent temples with ornate carving and captivating statues. They were mostly dedicated to Rama, Krishna and Shiva (Rudra) and their consorts. These temples created limitless employment opportunity for the pundits and their progeny. They had been rendered jobless after the eclipse of the Vedic culture as there were not many sponsors of the elaborate yajna sacrifice.

A.L. Basham observes that 'it is the full and active life of the times which is chiefly reflected in the art of ancient India. The tendency of the Indian art is diametrically opposite to that of medieval Europe. The temple towers, though tall, are solidly based on earth... Gods and demigods alike are young and handsome... Occasionally they are depicted as grim or wrathful, but generally they smile, and sorrow is rarely depicted. With the exception of the dancing Shiva the sacred icon is always firmly grounded, either seated or with both feet flat on the ground.'

It needs to be highlighted that Indian temple structure, Hindu, Buddhist and Jaina alike, made full use of the female form as a decorative motif... The colossal rock-cut image of the Jaina saint **Gomateshvara** at **Shravana Belgola** in Mysuru stands upright in the posture of meditation, a faint smile on his face. The artist seems to have tried to express the soul set free from the trammels of matter. Gomateshvara is shown to have stood for so long in meditation that creepers twined round his motionless legs. The inspiration of Indian art seems to be to depict delight in the world. The exquisite marble statues of the temple at Khajuraho even show uninhibited coupling, *Maithuna*.

The Buddhist stupa began as an earthen burial ground, which was revered by the people. They were large hemispherical domes, containing a central chamber, in which the relics of the Buddha were placed in a small casket often beautifully carved in crystal. The core of the stupa was of unburnt brick, covered with a thick layer of plaster. The stupa was crowned by an umbrella of wood and stone, and was surrounded by a wooden fence enclosing a path for the ceremonial clockwise circumambulation (pradakshina), which was the chief form of reverence paid to the relics within it.

In the second century BC the old Sanchi Stupa was enlarged to twice its original size, becoming a hemisphere of about 120 feet in diameter. Towards the first century BC, four glorious gateways (torana) were added at the four cardinal points. The Stupa at Amaravati, completed in AD 200 was even larger than the one in Sanchi.[218]

---

[218]Basham, A.L., *The Wonder That Was I*ndia, Rupa & Co, 1967, pp. 347.

The whole of Southeast Asia received most of its culture from India. Early in the fifth century BC colonists from Western India settled in Ceylon, which was finally converted to Buddhism in the reign of Ashoka. By this time a few Indian merchants had found their way to Malaya, Sumatra, and other parts of Southeast Asia. Gradually they established permanent settlements, marrying native women. They were followed by Brahmin and Buddhist monks, and Indian influence gradually leavened the indigenous culture.There arose great civilizations, capable of organizing large maritime empires, and of building such wonderful memorials to their greatness as the **Buddhist stupa of Borobodur in Java,** or the **Shaivaite temples of Angkor in Cambodia.**

The most pervasive influence in Southeast Asia during the fifth to seventh centuries seems to have been exercised by the Pallavas of Kanchipuram.[219] In mainland Southeast Asia, an important new kingdom had begun to emerge in the sixth century. Based in Cambodia, it would soon absorb Funan, the Indic kingdom, on the lower Mekong from which it had probably broken away, and would eventually emerge as the great Khemar Kingdom of Angkor. Its kings, like many of Funan and Champa (another Indic state in Vietnam), almost always bore names ending in 'varman' just like the Pallavas.

Indian settlements in Malaya were presumably engaged in trans-shipment activity. Thanks to the trade and missionary activity, the first signs of Indianised cultures in Southeast Asia emerged. Early Chinese texts indicate the existence of 'petty Indian states from the second century AD' on the Malay peninsula. One such, called Tun-Sun by the Chinese, had five hundred families from India, which also included a thousand Brahmins to whom the native population gave their daughters in marriage.

They claimed descent from the union of a local princes with a certain Kambu, whose descendants were known as 'Kambujas'. From this word came 'Cambodia' and 'Khmer.' Later on, such exchanges were established with the Khmers of Angkor.

Another tradition indicates that a Brahmin, Kaundinya, crossed

---

[219]Keay, John, *India: A History*, Harper Collins, Delhi, 2000, p. 174.

the Gulf of Thailand to the mouth of Mekong. There the local queen Liu-ye (Willow-Leaf) wanted to seize his ship. But when Kaundinya fired an arrow which holed her ship, she changed her mind. Frightened, she gave herself up, and Kaundinya took her for his wife. He governed the country and passed power on to his descendants. Thus, according to Chinese sources, was the Indic kingdom of Funan founded in about 100 AD.

This kingdom would survive for five centuries, providing the impetus for other Hindu-Buddhist trading kingdoms on the Vietnamese coast (Champa, Lin-i) before becoming incorporated into more famously 'Hinduised' kingdom of the Khmers of Angkor.[220]

Angkor Wat was 'discovered' by a French expedition. It had been deserted for centuries when Henry Mouhot found it, and was overgrown by trees. There is no local recollection of either site having ever been otherwise.

In the seventh and eighth centuries, there arose in central Java the kingdoms of Sailendra and Sanjaya. These dynasties are given credit for the glorious phase of Javanese temple-building which began in AD 780. The temples are all clustered within a small area of the city of Jogikarta. They conform to the layout and elevation plans at Pallavan and Chalukyan sites.

The sculptural colossus, Stupa of Borobodur, in Java, built in the eighth century AD is the largest of the stepped pyramids which were developed in Burma and Indonesia. Beginning in about AD 775, it assumed final shape in AD 840, with frequent redesigning in the interim. It was probably begun as a Hindu shrine and was later transformed into a Buddhist place of worship after the second stage of construction. The ground-plan of Borobodur represents a classic mandala of Hindu architecture; its four sides, as long as a football pitch, are rounded at the corners. The three topmost, or innermost stages, are turned circular. However, each tier is accessible only by flights of steps located in the middle of each side. A similar design can be detected in the base-plan of contemporary temples, as opposed to stupas, in both Java and India.

∽

[220]Keay, John, *India: A History*, Harper Collins, Delhi, 2000, p. 124.

Little more than the inner core remains of the tall stupa of Sarnath near Banaras, where the Buddha delivered his first sermon. It was once a most imposing structure of beautifully patterned brickwork with a high cylindrical upper dome rising from a lower hemispherical one, and the larger images of the Buddha set in gable ends at the cardinal points. The stupa at Nalanda was enlarged seven times. In its present ruined state, it gives an impression of a brick pyramid.

Cave Temples in places like Karli near Mumbai, with a Chaitya Hall, were created at the beginning of the Christian era. The Chaitya Hall is 124 feet deep into the rock with ornate columns. As the cave monastery became too small for its inhabitants, a new cave was excavated nearby and a complex of caves grew over the centuries. The most famous of these groups is that of **Ajanta,** in the north-west corner of Hyderabad. 27 caves, some going 100 feet deep in the rock, were excavated in the horseshoe curve of a hillside. The earliest caves date from second century BC while others are as late as seventh century AD. The splendid sculpture and lovely paintings with which they are adorned make them one of the most glorious monuments of India's past.

Cave Temples of Ellora, near Aurangabad, some 30 miles from Ajanta, were constructed from the fifth to the eighth centuries AD. There are no less than 34 caves, most of them Hindu and some Buddhist and Jain. The crowning achievement of Ellora is the great **Kailashnath Temple,** excavated from the top of a giant rock, on the instructions of the Rashtrakuta emperor Krishna I. (AD 756 to 778). It's a temple carved like a gigantic statue from the hillside.

The construction began at the top of the cliff, working down to the base. It is the most stupendous single work of art executed in India, unique in the world! The entire rock face was cut away from the top and a splendid temple was carved from the hillside, complete with shrine room, hall, gateway, votive pillars, lesser shrines and cloisters—the whole structure is adorned with divine figures and scenes, large and small, of a grace rarely seen in Indian art. The ground plan of Kailashnatha Temple is of about the same size as the Parthenon but its height is one-and-a-half times of the Parthenon.

However, Kailashnatha Temple is not the earliest temple hewn from a single rock. At Mamallapuram, on the sea-coast some 30 miles south of Madras, 17 small-size temples were carved from outcropping hillocks of granite under the patronage of the Pallava kings. The most famous of these are the 'Seven Pagodas'. Near them is the most ingeniously carved frieze, **Gangavatarana,** showing the descent of River Ganga on the earth. Those who came to watch the spectacle are monkeys and a horde of majestic elephants with their kids trailing behind them!

The latest cave-temples of importance are those of Elephanta, a beautiful little island off Mumbai. These,. in the same style as those of Ellora, are famous for their sculpture, especially for the majestic Trimurti figure of Shiva.

The most famous of Kashmir's early temples, dating back to the eighth century, was dedicated to Martanda (the Sun); it was demolished later on and never re-built. The place is now called 'Mutton' by local people who are mostly Muslims.

India's largest concentration of temples is at Bhuvaneshwar, the capital of Odisha. They were constructed over many centuries and by a succession of dynasties. Some of them date from the seventh century, others as late as the thirteenth. They display a remarkably consistent style of pineapple-shaped *shikharas*. The colossal **Lingaraja Temple** probably belongs to late eleventh century. At **Khajuraho**, the ceremonial capital of the Chandelas in central India, the 20 intact temples were constructed between tenth to twelfth centuries. They show explicit sexual postures.

Bhuvaneshwar, Puri and Konark happened to be sufficiently remote from Muslim attention. When five hundred years later, the British antiquarian Captain Burt stumbled upon 'the finest aggregate number of temples congregated in one place to be met in all India,' he found the site choked with trees and its elaborate system of lakes and watercourses overgrown.

At **Konark** the Ganga kings of Odisha had created one of the most elaborate and ambitious temples ever conceived. The **Sun Temple,** dedicated to the Sun-God Surya, It incorporated the idea, also associated with Apollo, of the Sun being drawn by a chariot.

Colossal stone wheels, each intricately carved, were positioned along its flanks and a team of massive draft horses, also stone-cut, reared seawards, apparently scuffing and snorting under the strain. Even in the partially reconstructed state, the conceptual scale of this temple is overwhelming, and so too the rich variety of its sculptural ornamentation, which as usual includes many mithuna (intertwined couples), busy making ingenious love!

The **Cholas** had occupied the region of the Kaveri delta since prehistoric times. However, during the long **Pallava** supremacy over the Tamil south, from sixth to ninth centuries, they had acted as tributaries. In a decisive battle in AD 897, the **Chola king Aditya** withstood a Pandyan invasion. Thereafter he secured the Pallava heartland around modern day Chennai (Madras), which included Kanchipuram and Mamallapuram. He called himself *Madurai-konda*, 'Conqueror of Madurai.'

Meenakshi Madurai

The towering temples of South India are unique structures of mankind and have an ambiance of their own. I have visited most of them. To me they are among the most wonderful creations of man. William Dalrymple gives a superb description of the towering Meenakshi temple of Madurai and its presiding deity, Meenakshi, the Goddess of procreation, as well as of the worshippers who throng her court annually. I would shamelessly borrow from his vivid account.[221]

'The temple is "a town within a town", accessed by four sky-kissing gate-ways, called *Gopuras*. These *Gopuras* are astounding multi-storied structures which rise into a tapering, wedge-shaped pyramid. Each layer is swarming with brightly coloured, colossal images of gods and demons, heroes and *Yakshi*. They rise up to three-fourth height of the tower and terminate in a crown of cobra heads, tipped with a pair of cat's-eared demon finials. The astounding complexity and elaboration of the gopuras' decoration

---

[221]Dalrymple, William, *The Age of Kali*, Penguin Books, India, 2004, pp. 177–84.

is something one can see from far away, long before one is able to visualize the complexity of their detail.'

'The temple, the Brahmins tell you, is a *tirtha*', William Dalrymple says, 'a crossing-place linking the profane to the sacred...it is doorway to the divine...I passed under the Gate of Eight Goddesses and into a forest of carved pillars—on closer inspection lines of heavy breasted Hindu caryatids: *Yakshis,* courtesans, goddesses and dancing girls. Everything about the architecture was deeply, and consciously, feminine: heading towards the innermost sanctuary of the presiding goddess, one sunk deeper and deeper in the darkness, down a long, straight, womb-like passage.'

He adds: 'There is a reason for this all-pervading femininity. This temple at Madurai is one of the few in India, containing both male and female deities, where the goddess is always worshipped *before* the god (Lord Shiva or Sundareshvara)... For it is because of Meenakshi, not her consort, that the temple is famous throughout India. The conscious fecundity of the temple is evident in every aspect of its decoration.'

William Dalrymple goes on with his vivid description. 'The cavalcade, ringing gongs and bells with a caparisoned elephant and a third *rath* carrying a huge golden horse, a temple band, banging cymbals and drums move out of the temple and into the streets, cheered on by the crowds of waiting pilgrims. At the end the procession goes to the temple pond where goddess Meenakshi, Lord Sundareshvara and their son Murugan are taken for the boat ride on the holy waters.'

(Murugan is Katikeya and Lord Sundareshvara is Shiva.)

A pilgrim tells William Dalrymple that he walked there from his village in Kerala just to see this sight. It took him 9–10 days to reach. 'On this day, if you ask anything of the goddess you are sure to get success', the man tells him.

'Is there anything in particular that you will be asking for?' questions William Dalrymple.

'We all want children.'

'You have no children?'

'I have three sons. But I want six.'

'How many does your wife want?'

'She wants only three. So, she has stayed in Kerala.'

'The temple of Madurai,' says William Dalrymple, 'is contemporary with those of ancient Greece and Egypt; yet while the gods of Thebes and the Parthenon have been dead and forgotten for millennia, the gods and temples of Hindu India are now more revered than ever before... Indeed, it is only when you grasp the astonishing antiquity and continuity of Hinduism, that you realise quite how miraculous its survival has been.

'Madurai is one of the most ancient holy temples in India, a Benares of the south, and long before its existence was first noted in the West in the fourth century BC, it was already an important centre. For Madurai was a major terminus of the Spice Route from the very earliest period, linking the pepper groves of India with the groaning tables of the Mediterranean.' William Dalrymple reminds the reader that the English word 'pepper' is a loan from Tamil—'*pippali*'.

~

King Aditya's son Parantaka suffered a crushing defeat at the hands of Krishna III, the last king of Rashtrakutas. Now it was the Rashtrakuta who called himself 'Conqueror of Kanchipuram' and even of Tanjore, the Chola capital. For the next 40 years Chola endeavours were directed towards recovering lost ground. The finest creation of the Chola dynasty (tenth to twelfth centuries) is the impressive **Shiva temple at Tanjore**, built by King Rajendra I, son of Rajaraja. It had taken 15 years to build. A monumental lingam is established in the main shrine beneath the 65 metre shikhara.

In AD 1020 King Rajendra's general was completing his campaign in Andhra, when he received instructions from the king to continue north to obtain water from the Ganga River with which to sanctify the Chola land. He must have followed the east coast and crossed many rivers, his elephants being lined up to breast their currents and to form bridges for his infantry to march over. He crossed Odisha and '*Vangala desa* (Bengal) where the rain never stopped.'

The main trophy of this campaign, according to the inscription was the water of the sacred Ganga, 'whose flow, strewn with fragrant flowers, had splashed against the places of pilgrimage.' The water jars were presented to King Rajendra who waited on the banks of the Godavari River. He poured it into the ceremonial tank about five kilometers long and called it **Chola-Ganga!** The city he founded was called 'Gangai-konda-Cholapuram' (The city of the Chola, who conquered the Ganga). Indeed, the Ganga is venerated in South India. The Rigvedic people knew the Indus, her tributaries and the Saraswati, which dried up in later times. Ganga is the spine of India's socio-cultural fabric.

His successor King Rajendra I built the temple near **Kumbhakonam,** at his new capital of Gangai-konda Cholapuram. It was probably the most magnificent temple built in India. The comparatively modest tower of Pallava style was replaced by a great pyramid-sized tower, rising from a tall upright base and crowned by a domed finial, the whole being nearly 200 feet high. This set the style of Dravidian shikhara, which has continued with some variation in later years. Both these temples contain elaborate pillared halls and beautiful decoration.

In the next phase of Dravidian architecture, the emphasis shifted to the entrance gateway of the surrounding wall on the four sides. The new style is often called Pandyan, from the name of the dynasty which supplanted the Cholas in the Tamil country. Unlike the earlier *Shaivite* dynasties, the Pandyans were *Vaishanavites*. The culmination of this style are the temple complexes of Madurai and Shrirangapatanama. The outer wall of Shrirangama temple measures 2,475 by 2,880 feet. The gateway towers have gopuramas covered with massive sculptured figures.

The Hoyshala dynasty had its capital at Halebid. The temples built by them at Halebid and Belur have no towers but they are most ornately and delicately carved.

The Cholas lost their hold on Anuradhapuram in Sri Lanka in AD 1070, but in AD 1077 a seventy-two men Chola mission reached China and diplomatic exchanges took place. The Nataraja Temple at Chidambaram took the Cholas almost hundred years, from AD 1150 to 1250, for completion as their resources diminished.

There have been two kings named Bhoja—the nineth-century Pratihara king Bhoja of Kanauj and the more distinguished eleventh century 'philosopher king Bhoja' of Dhar, now a small town between Ujjain and Mandu in Madhya Pradesh, beside River Shipra. King Bhoja ascended the throne of Dhar in 1010 and reigned for about 50 years. He happened to be an exact contemporary of the Chola King Rajendra I. In scholastic attainments, he outshines even Harsha's intellectual genius as portrayed in Bana Bhatta's *Harsha-Charita*. King Bhoja's scholarship ranged over subjects as varied as philosophy, poetics, phonetics, yoga, archery, medicine and veterinary science. His palace rooms at Dhar served as venues for intellectual discourses and the temples of Dhar as colleges of higher education. A pro-Chalukya chronicle, *Prabandha Chintamani*, says: 'Among poets, gallant lovers, enjoyers of life, generous donors, benefactors of the virtuous, archers, and those who regard Dharma as their wealth, there is none who can equal Bhoja!'[222]

---

[222]Keay, John, *India: A History*, Harper Collins, Delhi, 2000, p. 230.

DEBATE ON ADVAITA VEDANTA PHILOSOPHY

Despite the spread of the Bhakti-cult from Kashmir to Kanya Kumari, and building of magnificent, 'sky-kissing' temples, particularly in South India, the debate on Advaita Vedantic Philosophy continued till the ninth century, when **Adi Shankaracharya,** acknowledged as the greatest religious leader and philosopher, formulator and codifier of Advaita Vedanta philosophy—the non-dualistic system based upon the Upanishads—was born in AD 788 in a poor Brahmin family, in village Kaladi in Kerala, near Alwaye. He was taught Vedic verses in a Gurukul.

The word 'advaita' essentially refers to the identity of the Self (Atman) and the Brahma. '*Ekameva Adviteeyam Brahma*' (The Absolute is One, not two). The essence of Shankaracharya's philosophy is: 'The Brahma alone is real; this world is an illusion' (*Brahma Satyam Jagat Mithya, Jeevo Brahmaiva Na Aparah*'. 'Brahma is the only Truth, the world is unreal; there is no difference ultimately between *Brahma* and individual Self!' His masterpiece is the *Brahma-Sutra-Bhashya*—the commentary on the Brahma-Sutra, which is a fundamental text of the Vedanta school.

I have a book, *Outlines of Indian Philosophy* by Paul Deussen, German Indologist and Professor of Philosophy at the University of Kiel,[223] who was strongly influenced by Arthur Schopenhauer. He observes that: 'Indian philosophy through all the centuries of its development has taken its course uninfluenced by West-Asiatic and European thought'.I will sum up the discussion by quoting Dr Paul Deussen, who was a friend of Friedrich Nietzsche, and Swami Vivekananda:.

'Modern European philosophy has sprung from the scholasticism of the Middle Ages whereas medieval thought is a product of Greek philosophy, on the one hand, and of the

[223]Deussen, Paul, *Outlines of Indian Philosophy*, Crest (Jaico) Publication, Delhi, 1996.

Biblical dogma, on the other. The doctrine of the Bible has again its roots in part in the oldest Semitic creed and in part in the Persian religion of Zoroaster, which, as an intermediate link between the Old and the New Testament, has exercised more influence than is commonly attributed to it. In this way the whole of European thought, from Pythagoras and Xenophanes, from Moses and Zoroaster, through Platonism and Christianity down to the Kantian and post-Kantian philosophy, forms a complex of ideas, whose elements are variously related to and dependent on each other. On the other hand, Indian philosophy, through all the centuries of its development, has taken its course uninfluenced by West-Asiatic and European thought; and precisely for this reason the comparison of European philosophy with that of the Indians is of the highest interest. Where both agree the presumption is that their conclusions are correct, no less than in a case where two calculators working by different methods arrive at the same result; and where Indian and European views differ it is an open question on which side the truth is to be found.'

The esoteric Vedanta does not admit the reality of the world nor of the Samsara, for the only reality is the Brahma, seized in ourselves as our own Atman. The knowledge of this Atman, 'Aham Brahman asmi' does not produce moksha (deliverance), but is moksha itself.

Then we obtain what the Upanishad say:

> *Bhidyate hridyaygranthih, chhidyante sarvasanshayah;*
> *Ksheeyante chasya karmaani, tasmindrishte paravare.*

> [When realizing the *Brahman* as the highest and the lowest everywhere, all knots of our heart open, all sorrows split, all doubts vanish, and our works become nothing. Certainly, no man can live without doing work, and so also the *Jeevanmukta*; but he knows, that all these works are elusive, as the whole world is, and therefore they do not adhere to him nor produce for him a new life after death.]

The Gospels fix, quite correctly, as the highest law of morality: 'Love your neighbour as yourselves.' But why should I do so, since by the order of nature I feel pleasure and pain in myself, not in my neighbour? The answer in not in the Bible (this venerable book being not yet quite free from Semitic realism), but it is in the Veda, in the great formula *'tat tvam asi'* which gives in three words metaphysics and morals altogether. You shall love your neighbour as yourselves—because you are your neighbour, and mere illusion makes you believe, that your neighbour is something different from yourselves. Or in the words of the Bhagavada Gita: 'He, who knows himself in everything and everything in himself, will not injure himself by himself, '*na hinasti atmana atmanam*'.

'The *Samsaara* is just so far from the truth,' says Shankara, 'as the *Saguna vidya* is from *Nirguna vidya*. 'In reality there is no Samsaara, the manifold world, but only Brahman, and what we consider as the world is a mere illusion (Maya), similar to a *Mrigtrishnika*, which disappears when we approach it, and not more feared than the rope, which we took in the darkness for a serpent.' There are many similies in the Vedanta, to illustrate the illusive character of this world, but the best of them is perhaps, when Shankara compares our life with a long dream: 'A man, while dreaming, does not doubt of the reality of the dream, but this reality disappears in the moment of awakening, to give place to a truer reality, which we were not aware of whilst dreaming.' The life is a dream! This has been the thought of wise men from Pindar to Sophocles, but nobody has better explained it than Shankara. And the moment when we die may be similar to the awakening from a dream; it may be that heaven and earth are blown away like the nightly phantoms of the dream, and what then may stand before us? Or rather in us: *Brahman*, the eternal reality, which was hidden to us till then by this dream of life!

This world is Maya, is illusion; is not the very reality, that is the deepest thought of the esoteric Vedanta, attained not by *tarka* (argument) and by *anubhava* (experience), but by returning from this variegated world to the deep recess of our own self (Atman). Do so, if you can, and you will become aware of, and experience a reality very different from empirical reality—a timeless, spaceless, changeless reality. One may then realize that whatever is outside of this true reality, is mere appearance, is Maya, a dream!

Plato had come to the same truth, that this world is 'world of shadows', and that the reality is not in these shadows, but behind them. There is astonishing accord here between Patonism and Vedantism!

This is the sum and tenor of all morality, and this is the standpoint of a man knowing himself as a particle of the Brahman. He enters into Brahman, like the streams into the ocean:

> *Yatha nadyah syandamanah samudre,*
> *Astam gachchhanti naamroope vihaya;*
> *Tatha vidvaan naamroopaadvimuuktah*
> *Paraasparam purushmupaiti divyam.*

> [He leaves behind him *naama* and *roopam*, leaves his *individuality*, but he does not leave behind his *Atman*, his Self. It is not the falling of a drop in the infinite ocean, it is merging into the ocean, becoming free from fetters of ice, as it were, and returning from the frozen state to that what it is really and has never ceased to be, his own—the all pervading, eternal Brahma!]

And so, the Vedanta, in its pure and unfalsified form, is the strongest support of pure morality, is the greatest consolation in the sufferings of life and death. Indians keep to it![224]

Explaining the philosophy of the Upanishads, Deussen says:

> The two terms, *Brahman* and *Atman*, form almost the only objects of which the Upanishads speak. Very often they are treated as synonyms, but when a difference is noticeable, *Brahman* is the philosophical principle, as realized in the universe, and *Atman* the same, as realised in the soul. Having presupposed this, we might express the fundamental thought of all the Upanishads by the simple equation:
>
> *Brahman = Atman*
>
> *Brahma,* the power from which all worlds proceed, in which

[224]Deussen, Paul, *Outlines of Indian Philosophy*, Crest (Jaico) Publication, Delhi, 1996.

> they subsist, and into which they finally return, the eternal, omnipresent, omnipotent power is identical with our *atman*, which is in each of us which we must consider as our true Self, the unchangeable essence of our being, our soul. This idea alone secures to the Upanishads an importance reaching far beyond their land and time; for whatever means of unveiling the secrets of Nature a future time may discover, this idea will be true for ever, from this mankind will never depart. If the mystery of Nature is to be solved, the key of it can be found only there, where alone Nature allows us an interior view of the world, that is ourselves.

Paul Deussen adds that:

> 'In the *Yajnavalkya* chapters of *Brihada Aranyaka* Upanishad, and therefore in the oldest texts of the Upanishads, we find as the point of departure of the Upanishad- doctrine a very bold idealism comparable to that of Parmenides in Greece, and culminating in the assertion that the *atman* is the only reality and that nothing exists beyond it. The whole doctrine may be summed up in three statements:
>
> 1. The only reality is the *Atman*;
> 2. The *Atman* is the subject of knowledge in us;
> 3. The *Atman* itself is unknowable.
>
> All things in heaven and earth, gods, men, and other beings exist only so far as they form a part of our *Atman*.'

Paul Deussen then quotes *Chandogya Upanishad*: 'The *Atman* is my soul in the inner heart, smaller than a barley corn, smaller than a mustard-seed, smaller than a grain of millet; and *Atman* again is my soul in the inner heart, larger than the earth, larger than the atmosphere, larger than the heavens and all these worlds.'

Talking about Adi Shakaracharya, Paul Deussen says: 'He constructs out of the materials of the Upanishads two systems, one esoteric, philosophical (called by him *Nirguna Vidya*, or *Paramarthic Avastha*) containing the metaphysical truth for the few ones, rare in all times and countries, who are able to understand it; and another exoteric, theological (*Saguna Vidya*, *Vyavaharik Avastha*) for the general public who want images, not abstract truth; worship not meditation.'

∽

Shankarachaya had travelled the length and breadth of India, having religious discourses with well-known theologians of the day, including the Buddhists. He had travelled right up to the mouth of the Gangotri glacier and had set up a monastery at Joshi Math. He had also built a Shiva temple atop a hillock at Srinagar in Kashmir.

Shankaracharya exhibited great philosophical astuteness by distinguishing an esoteric system (*Paravidya*) containing a sublime philosophy, and an exoteric system (*Aparavidya*) embracing under the wide mantle of a theological creed, all the fanciful imaginings which spring in course of time.

However, the greatest exponent of *Nirguna Bramha* finally burst into song: '*Bhaj Govindam, Bhaj Govindam, Bhaj Govindam moodha mate!*' [O foolish man, worship Govinda!] and cheerfully joined the ranks of Meera and Soordasa.

∽

PART SEVEN

THREAT TO HINDUISM FROM ISLAM

The Hindu Kush peak in the Himalayas defined the extent of *Aryavarta*, as India was called in olden days. The northern kingdom of Gandhara straddled the north-west frontier and extended deep into Afghanistan. A Hindu dynasty known as the Shahi's had risen there in prominence in mid-nineth century. Al-Biruni links the Shahi's with the great Kushana emperor **Kanishka.** Hsuan Tsang in the seventh century had found the kings of Kabul region to be devout Buddhists. The Buddhist King's brahmin minister, Lalliya, who belonged to the Shahi clan, had staged a palace coup. Historian Kalhana's chronicle of Kashmir praises 'the mighty glory of the Shahis'. In Afghanistan the feudatories of the Shahis ruled over considerable territories to the south and east of Kabul.[225]

However, in AD 870, the Shahi king lost Kabul. In Afghanistan they only retained Lamgan, a part of the Kabul River valley, west of Jalalabad. They made their capital near Attock on the Indus then. **Sabuktigin**, a Turkish general, who had seized Ghazni in 977 came into conflict with the Shahi King, Jayapala. The Muslim historian Ferishta records that 'girding up his loins for a war of religion, Sabuktigin ravaged the provinces of Kabul and Panjab in 986.' Jayapala sued for peace and settled for an indemnity of a few fortresses, elephants and money.

Sabuktigin was recognized by the Baghdad caliph as governor of vast territories of northern Afghanistan. He died in Balkh in AD 997 and was succeeded by his son **Mahmud**. Mahmud continued the God-given duty of every Muslim to root out idolatry by trouncing his infidel neighbours and appropriating their fabled wealth, and resolved to make yearly incursions to serve both God and Ghazni.

He made 16 yearly raids on India, starting from the year

[225]Keay, John, *India: A History*, Harper Collins, Delhi, 2000, p. 203.

1000. Jayapala lost 15,000 men and again paid an indemnity of 50 elephants. He abdicated in favour of his son Anandapala and then climbed into his own funeral pyre. In 1008 Mahmud overran the whole of the Punjab and took the great citadel and temple of Kangra in whose vaults had been stored the accumulated wealth of Shahi kings. The haul of gold ingots was 180 kilos, besides two tonnes of silver and 70 million silver coins. In 1012 he attacked Thanesar, Harsha Vardhana's original capital, and returned with plunder that is impossible to count.

In 1018 he attacked Mathura. The main Krishna temple impressed even Mahmud. His secretary al-Utbi found it simply 'beyond description'—though not beyond desecration. After tonnes of gold, silver and precious stones had been prised from its images, it shared the fate of the Mathura city's countless other shrines—'being burnt with naphtha and fire and levelled to ground'.

Kanauj was sacked then, and Mahmud at last reached the Ganga. The Pratihara ruler seems to have left his capital, with its 'seven forts and ten thousand temples' almost undefended. From this campaign Mahmud returned with booty valued at 20 million dirhams, 53,000 slaves and 350 elephants.

In 1025 he targeted Somnath, another temple-city and place of pilgrimage. Somnath's fort looked more formidable. It seems, though, to have been defended not by troops but by the temple keepers, the Brahmins, and hordes of devotees. Unarmed, they placed their trust in blind aggression, and the intercession of the temple's celebrated lingam. With ladders and ropes Mahmud's disciplined professionals scaled the temple walls and went about their business of loot and mayhem.

'The dreadful slaughter' as one chronicler calls it, was much worse outside the temple. 'Band after band of the defenders entered the temple of Somnath, and with their hand clasped round their necks, wept and passionately entreated before the Shiva lingam. Then again they issued forth until they were slain and but few were left alive...the number of the dead exceeded fifty thousand.'

Twenty million dirhams worth of gold, silver and gems was looted from the temple. But what rankled even more than the loot and the appalling death-toll was the satisfaction which Mahmud took in destroying the great gilded lingam. After stripping it of its gold, he personally struck it with his sword—which must have been more like a sledge-hammer. The bits were then sent to Gazni and incorporated into the steps of the new Jami Masjid (Friday Mosque) there, to be humbled and defiled by the feet of the Muslim faithful.

After one more assault into southern Sind, Mahmud died in 1030. He would not be forgotten. 'Mahmud was a king who conferred happiness upon the world and reflected glory of Mohammedan religion,' declaims Ferishta. The historian goes on to admit that Mahmud was sometimes accused of 'the sordid vice of avarice' but concludes that this was all for a noble cause; for 'no king ever had more learned men at his court, kept a finer army, or displayed more magnificence.' The great scholar al-Biruni enjoyed his patronage; so did Firdausi, the poet. Ghazni city, which they adored, was indeed transformed into a worthy capital. Yet for Hindus, this paragon of valour and piety would ever be but a monster of cruelty and iconoclasm.[226]

∽

In 1191 **Muhammad of Ghor** came down from Ghazni and raided the Sirhind or Bhatinda forts and had taken them. At that time **Prithviraja Chauhan**, was the ruler of the extensive kingdom of Ajmer, which extended into modern Punjab. He was a descendent of King Ajayaraja, who in early twelfth century, had established the capital city, 'Ajayameru', which came to be called Ajmer in later times. Prithviraja had ascended the throne in 1177. Shaikh Muinuddin Chisti had founded the famous *dargah* at Ajmer just a few months before Prithviraja's accession.

Prithviraja hastened to rescue the fort at Sirhind taken by Ghori. They met at a place called Tarain, near Thanesar (in modern Haryana), about 150 kilometres from Delhi. Muhammad Ghori came face to face with Govind Raj, Prithviraja's Army commander. Ghori's lance scraped Govind Raj's face, taking away his front teeth. Govind Raj took his revenge with a spear that

[226]Keay, John, *India: A History*, Harper Collins, Delhi, 2000, pp. 206–10.

struck Ghori's upper arm. Ghori was about to fall off his mount, when a young warrior leapt up behind him and took him away from the battlefield. His soldiers followed him, breaking off the encounter. Prithviraja did not give chase; he mistook retreat for an admission of defeat. The Muslim forces were allowed to withdraw in good order. Prithviraja proceeded towards Sirhind/Bhatinda fort occupied by Ghori and seized it.

Muhammad withdrew to Ghazni to convalesce and assemble more troops. By mid-1192 he was back at the head of 120,000 horse. Prithviraja was a young man in his mid-twenties and returned to the fortunate field of Tarain, his army comprising 300,000 horses. To his support had come the Guhila ruler of Mewar (Udaipur).

According to Ferishta, Muhammad had sent an ambiguous letter to Prithviraja suggesting truce. Prithviraja and his troops spent the night in revelry. The battle began early in the morning when the Indian forces, due to late night revelry, were waking up and were in urgent need of ablutions. Govinda Raj of Delhi, the hero of the first battle of Tarain, was slain, his body was recognized by its missing teeth. Slain too was the Guhila king, Sammat Singh. In all about 100,000 men are said to have been sent to death. Prithviraja was taken prisoner and taken to Ghazni.[227]

Historian John Keay does not give credence to Col Tod's account of the battle at Tarain (present-day Taravadi) between Muhammad Ghori and Prithviraja Chauhan. Col Tod was the agent of the British government at Jaipur. Tod had relied on the poem, *Prithiviraja Raso*, composed by Chand Baradai, the bard of Prithviraja Chauhan who claimed that he had accompanied Prithviraja Chauhan to Ghazni.

Chand Baradai, in his heroic poem, gives a graphic account of what happened at Ghazni in Muhammad Ghori's court. He describes that Prithviraja was brought blind-folded in the King's court and was given a bow to exhibit his prowess at shooting arrows for the amusement of King Muhammad and his courtiers.

Chand Bardai was standing beside Prithviraja and gave him

[227]Keay, John, *India: A History*, Harper Collins, Delhi, 2000, p. 231–239.

a message in a couplet that he composed:

Chaar baans chaubees gaza, angul ashta pramana,
Taa oopar Sultan hai, mata chooke Chauhana.

[The Sultan is sitting (on his throne in the attic) at a height of four bamboo poles plus twenty-four yards and eight digits. O great Chauhan, don't miss the target. (Let your arrow pierce the Sultan!)]

Col Tod was an admirer of the Rajputs and had accepted the bard's version that Prithviraja's arrow had killed the Sultan.

Historian John Keay observes: 'Tod was wrong in imagining that the bard "Chand" was a contemporary eye-witness, let alone Prithviraja's friend, his herald, his ambassador.' John Keay did not accept Chand Bardai's 'poetical histories' as reliable evidence. Indeed, how could a blinded man, standing on the ground below, measure the height of the Sultan's palace balcony where he sat, down to inches, and shoot him?

John Keay maintained that 'the rout of the *rajputs* at Tarain was arguably the most decisive battle in history of India.'

~

The gates of Delhi were now wide open for Muslim invasion. Within a year of victory at Tarain, Muhammad Ghori's forces had taken Delhi, Meerut, Kol (Aligarh) and Barab (Bulandshahar). Ajmer was already in Ghorid control; in another three years the forts of Ranathambhor, Gwalior and Narvar fell. To the east, Kanauj and Varanasi had been overrun. Muslim forces pushed into Bihar, Bengal, even Assam. In the south-west, the Gujarati capital at Patan was sacked and so was the Chandela province. Ghori's Indian empire was larger than Harsha Vardhana's.

The assaults were rarely made by Muhammad Ghori himself; his conquests in India had been principally achieved by his Turkish commanders. In 1206, Ghori suppressed a revolt at Lahore but he was killed by a hill-tribe of Ghakkars in Punjab, who penetrated his camp in the night.

Ghori had no sons; his commander **Qutbuddin Aibak** eliminated his rivals and became the Sultan of Delhi. He built the Qutb Minar and the adjacent mosque at Delhi. These were constructed from re-assembled components—pillars, capitals, lintels of 27 Hindu and Jain temples existing there.

Ferishta records that at Varanasi, Muhammad Ghori and Qutbud–din Aibak demolished the idols of a thousand temples and then rededicated these shrines 'to the worship of the true God, Allah'. They also carted away treasures from the temples on camels—1,400 camel-loads according to one estimate. At Ajmer Qutbuddin Aibak built a grand mosque of high-ceiling, by stacking three squat temple pillars on top of one another.

But after four years, in 1210 Qutbuddin Aibak died while playing polo. He fell off his pony, the pony fell on top of him, and the pommel of the saddle cut into his chest. Probably the Hindu sacred law of Karma was his undoing!

John Keay observes that the Muslim chroniclers chose to portray the occupation of northern India as a religious offensive and to paint its principals as religious heroes; but such a view cannot stand the test of historical scrutiny.

∽

Muhammad Ghori was succeeded by **Shamshuddin Iltumish**. During the 26 years of his reign, he was almost continuously in the field, engaged against fellow Muslims, not against Indian 'idolators'. East of Delhi he had to reconquer much of what is now Uttar Pradesh and then face Muslim rivals in Bihar and Bengal. His son Nasiruddin killed the Khilji ruler of Bengal but later he fell sick and died.

Iltumish died in 1236 leaving an ineffectual and licentious son but a redoubtable daughter, **Razia**. Razia toppled her brother in seven months and became the **Sultana of Delhi**. She dispensed with the veil, dressed in mannish garb of coat and cap and appointed Jamaluddin Yakut, an Abysssinian, as her personal attendant. As she was bravely dashing to douse a revolt at Bhatinda, conspirators from her own army isolated Yakut and killed him. Razia ended as a prisoner in the fort she had come to redeem. However, she managed to win the backing and affection of one of the conspirators. She married him, but on their return to Delhi, they were captured by Hindu forces and killed. Her successor, the ineffectual Sultan Nasiruddin reigned for 21 years guided by **Ghiyasuddin Balban,** another Turkish slave. In 1265, Balban poisoned Nasiruddin and became Sultan. He reigned till 1287.

Balban's forces put down insurrection in the Ganga–Jamuna Doab and cleared the region around Delhi of both the marauding Mewatis and the scrub jungle in which they found sanctuary. A major expedition into Bengal, whose governor was again in revolt, took three years and was distinguished by more fearful reprisals. But on Bulban's return, his most capable son and preferred successor was killed in a skirmish with the Mongols. Balban never recovered from this blow. He was in his eighties and spent his nights howling with grief.

Balban's grandson, who succeeded him, spent his time in revelry. Ferishta records that the young Sultan 'delighted in love and in the soft society of silver-bodied damsels with musky tresses.' Delhi welcomed the change: 'Every place was filled with ladies of pleasure and every street with music and mirth.' This excessive indulgence reduced the young Sultan into a 'gibbering wreck' and his three-year old toddler was made Sultan!

Bulban dynasty was replaced by **Jalaluddin Feroz Khilji,** a grey-haired patriarch, who started the Khilji dynasty in 1290. He displayed clemency unheard in the annals of the sultanate. Conciliating rivals and forgiving enemies, he 'weaned the citizens of Delhi from their attachment to the old family', says Ferishta. In 1296, Jalaluddin Feroz Khilji's nephew, **Alauddin Khilji,** who was also his son-in-law, succeeded him.

ASSAULT IN THE SOUTH

In 1296, Alauddin Khilji led a plundering expedition from his base at Kara, near Allahabad, and pushed as far south as Bhilsa, near Bhopal in Madhya Pradesh. He had kept it secret from his uncle Jalaluddin Feroz Khilji. He secured high-value booty from this ancient capital and the neighbouring Buddhist centre of Sanchi. He then proceeded to Devagiri, which was an impregnable citadel protected by a moat. Alauddin was in a hurry. After a week's siege, he negotiated a settlement with King Ramachandra and parted with a Seuna bride and treasure beyond his wildest dreams.

The Sultan, his uncle, sent a message of congratulations and bade him to return to Delhi. But Alauddin went back to Kara on the Ganga, and inveigled his uncle into paying him a visit. The unsuspecting Feroz sailed down the river with unarmed attendants and was cut down as he stepped ashore. Alauddin went to Delhi after quickly disposing his fellow conspirators.

From 1297 to 1303 Alauddin faced almost annual Mongol onslaughts. He not only stemmed the tide but reversed it. Sind and Panjab were regained and he began raiding Ghazni, Kabul and Kandhar in Afghanistan. He possessed a Turkish cavalry in combination with a solid Indian elephant-phalanx. He invaded Gujarat in 1298 and attacked the rebuilt Somnath temple, hammered the replacement lingam and brought enormous quantities of gold and precious stones. He invaded Malwa in 1299 and Chittor in 1303. He appointed a Hindu captive, who was a eunuch and had quickly espoused Islam, who was called **Malik Kafur**. Malik Kafur attacked Belur and Halebid in 1310. The Hoysalas of Karnataka had built spectacularly ornate temples at Belur and Halebid which were robbed. He reached right up to the temple cities of Madurai, Srirangam and Chidambaram and stripped the magnificent temples of solid gold idols and emptied their gold-filled temple cavities and obtained much other portable wealth. Malik Kafur turned for home laden with 241 tonnes of precious booty.

Alauddin planned a prodigious minaret near Qutub Minar. But it never reached much above the current stump height. He assumed the title of 'The Second Alexander' on his coinage. He succumbed to sickness and then death in 1320.

In the space of four years, two of his sons and a Hindu convert occupied the throne and were killed, and so was Kafur who briefly acted as king-maker. Alauddin's son Mubarak was a 'monster in the shape of a man' in Ferishta's words. Among the other grossly unmentionable indecencies, he led 'a gang of abominable prostitutes, stark naked, along the terraces of the royal palaces, and obliging them to make water upon the nobles as they entered the court.'

Such unspeakable obscenities apart, the Hindus, their religion and their temples, had never before suffered such devastation.

THE TUGHLAKS

In 1320 **Ghiyasuddin Tughlak,** the son of one of Balban's slaves, emerged victorious from the five-year power struggle that followed Alauddin Khilji's death. His eldest son, Muhammad bin Tughlak who was sent to the Deccan to deal with the rebellious Kakatiya king, Pratap Rudra of Warangal, was successful in his second attempt. He was recalled to Delhi in 1323 to act as viceroy while Ghiyasuddin himself had to go to Bengal for a successful campaign and to Tirhut in north Bihar to sort out recalcitrant Hindus.

Ghiyasuddin Tughlak built the Tughlakabad fort to the east of Qutb Minar in the early 1320's. To prepare for his ceremonial entry into his new citadel of Tughlakabad, he had asked his son Muhammad to construct a timbered pavilion at a place called Afghanpur on the banks of the Jamuna. **Muhammad** and other notables received the Sultan there in the rainy month of July. After dining, when Muhammad and other notables had retired, lightning struck the pavilion and the roof of the pavilion fell down, crushing Ghiyasuddin and his other younger son Mahmud, besides other five to six men.

Ibn Batuta, a distinguished scholar from Morocco, who had visited Delhi after eight years of Afghanpur tragedy, opines in his *Travels* that the pavilion was designed to collapse; that it collapsed as Muhammad had ordered ground-stumping elephants to make sure that it did fall down.

Ibn Batuta was appointed Chief Justice of Delhi by **Sultan Muhammad** and then one of his ambassadors. Ibn Batuta was fascinated by his master's personality, unable to decide between reverence and revulsion, seduced by the royal benevolence and appalled by the royal callousness. He says Muhammad was pre-eminent for two things, 'giving presents and shedding blood', and adds: 'At his gate there was always to be seen some poor persons becoming rich or some living condemned to death.'

In 1333, Muhammad took the decision of taking his capital from Delhi to Devagiri, 1,400 kilometres from Delhi, where Allauddin Khilji had defeated the Seuna king Ramachandra. He must have done it due to its being a fortress on a hill, safe from enemy attack. He renamed Devagiri as Daulatabad. Delhi was deserted. However, the whole scheme was soon abandoned.

Muhammad remained on the throne till 1351. During this period Bengal slipped away from his control and Rajput princes in Rajasthan were reasserting their autonomy. In both Andhra and the Tamil Nadu, Muslim commanders established independent dynasties. Historian Barani has listed 22 major rebellions. Yet in Delhi his authority seems never to have been seriously challenged. He was comparatively free of religious and ethnic bigotry. He died while pursuing rebels into the wastes of Sind.

Feroz Shah Tughlak, his cousin, took over in 1351. His two expeditions into Bengal were largely fruitless and his six-year campaign in Gujarat and Sind was disastrous. But he routed the temple-building Ganga dynasty of Odisha in 1361, desecrated the great shrine of Lord Jagannath of Puri and massacred the local population. However, the local king was reinstated later.

He extended the *jizya* tax to all non-Muslims, including the hitherto-exempt Brahmins. He got an Ashoka pillar standing near Ambala to be laboriously shipped down river and fixed in Tughlakabad. His tomb, an austere, plain block of grey sandstone stands in Hauz Khas.

After his demise in 1388, there was a long and bloody succession crisis. The city was overturned when Mongol forces under **Taimur the Lame**, fresh from the conquests of Persia and Baghdad and now firm adherent of Islam, crossed the Jamuna just below Ferozshah Kotla. With little difficulty, the Mongols defeated the incumbent sultan and for three days indulged in an orgy of rape and killings. According to Taimur's personal record, the gold, silver, jewels and precious brocades defied accounting. Exclusively Muslim quarters were spared; everywhere else was sacked, and the entire Hindu population was either massacred or enslaved. Hypocritically, Taimur wrote in his memoir: 'Although I was desirous of sparing them, but I could not succeed, for it was the will of Allah that this calamity should befall the city.'

Taimur soon withdrew; the Tughlak sultan returned to his devastated capital. Two subsequent dynasties, the **Sayyads,** from 1414, and the **Lodhis,** from 1451, both Afghan in origin, continued to rule amidst the ruins, throughout the fifteenth century. However, their authority barely extended beyond Delhi. Large scale Muslim immigration of artisans, scholars, merchants and administrators was taking place. India had become a land of opportunity for Muslims from Turkey, Persia and Afghanistan. The Delhi regime became totally alien to Indians. Most infiltrators stayed on, prospered, married and settled.

KAFTAN AND LOINCLOTH

Marco Polo landed at a Tamil port in 1290. He was trying to get a coat made. To his surprise he found that in Peninsular India there were no tailors or seamstresses. In fact, there was very little clothing at all, and what there was, was neither cut nor sewn. A single length of cloth was simply tied or wrapped about the person, a custom which still survives in the wearing of the sari, the shawl, the lungi and the dhoti. Bespoke apparel may not have been a Muslim innovation, but it came from the colder north. Indeed, in many parts of India tailoring remains a Muslim preserve.

Sailing on to Quilon in Kerala, Polo noted how Hindu kings were as scantily dressed as their poorest subjects; even soldiers, when riding in battle, wore next to nothing. 'Men and women, they are all black, and go naked, all save a fine cloth worn about the middle.' Even to one coming from the East, so many bared chests and unbodiced breasts were a novelty. Like the international set who in the 1930s would be so charmed by the topless fashions still prevailing in Bali, the last outpost of Hindu society in Southeast Asia, Marco Polo drew his own questionable conclusion: 'They look not on any sin of the flesh as a sin.'

The Russian merchant, **Athanasius Niktin**, a native of Tver (Kalinin) on the Volga, reached India in 1470. He landed at a port south of Bombay (Mumbai) and noted in his memoir:

'People go about naked, with their heads uncovered and their breast bare, the hair tressed into one tail... They bring forth children every year and the children are many... When I go out many people follow me and stare at the white man. Women who know you willingly concede their favours for they like white men.'

Abdu-r-Razzak, another fifteenth century visitor to the Deccan noted that only Muslims wore trousers and kaftans (long coats). Heading an embassy from Shah Rukh of Samarkand, who was Taimur's son and successor, Abdu-r-Razzak's royal audience in India was a severe trial. The Zamorin of Calicut, another major port in Kerala, or the king of Vijayanagar would be coolly seated, wearing little but pearls and a dazzling ensemble of gold jewellery while he, 'in consequence of the heat and the great number of robes in which he was dressed, drowned in perspiration.' Whether admiring the intricate sculpture of the great Hoysala temple at Belur or ogling courtesans of Vijayanagar, ambassador Razzak showed unusually Catholic tastes... 'The veil and the zenana concealed Islam's womenfolk; the copious jewellery and the waist-level lungi merely advertised Hindu femininity.'

Hindus adopted a modified version of the Muslim pardah (*ghoonghat*, the veil) to screen their women; Muslims adopted something approaching Hindu caste distinctions.

NEW MUSLIM CITIES FOUNDED

Sultan Ahmad Shah of Gujarat founded Ahmadabad on a site beside the Sabarmati River, close to the gulf of Cambay (Surat) in 1411. It has many mosques and tombs of Gujarati sultans and their usually Rajput queens. Remarkably, elements and motifs from both Jain and Hindu traditions have been incorporated in them. They transformed *mihrab* and *minaret* into splendidly ornate features as they did with the moghal *jail* and *chhatari*. The Jami Masjid of Ahmadabad is considered the most aesthetically satisfying in India.

The new capital of Malwa was established by **Dilawar Khan** upon the rugged heights of Mandu, near Dhar, the one-time capital of Raja Bhoja. Dilawar Khan constructed airy palaces, echoing courtyards and the lotus lakes so beloved of the Rajputs and the later Mughals. It became famous as a wildly romantic site due to the love affair of Rani Roopmati and Baz Bahadur. John Keay observes that it was here and in the contemporary Man Singh palace at Gwalior that India's secular architecture began to stake its claim as a serious rival to the religious tradition of temple, tomb and mosque.

∽

Rana Kumbha of Udaipur, who reigned from 1433 to 1468, established another towering fort, Kumbhal Garh, ringed with battlements, which was named after him. The Sisodias of Mewar, unlike the kings of Jaipur, never succumbed to the might of the Mughals. At the other extremity of Rajasthan, **Raja Jodha** (reigned 1438–89), a Rajput of Rathor clan, who had been instrumental in securing Rana Kumbha's throne, established his own hill-top stronghold at what became Jodhpur.

∽

THE MAKING OF THE MUGHAL EMPIRE

Sikander Lodi, the great Sultan of Delhi, designated Agra as his alternate capital. He had been hammering at Raja Man Singh Tomar of Gwalior and was successful in taking his Narwar fort. But his siege of the superbly fortified palace-citadel of Gwalior remained fruitless. In the meanwhile, Zahiruddin Muhammad, otherwise known as **Babur** (the Tiger), had been making forays into India from Kabul. He was a distant descendant of Ghenghiz Khan on his mother's side, and on his father's side he was a fifth-generation descendant of Timurlang. When Babur was barely 15 years of age, he had occupied Samarkand, but was quickly dispossessed. Twice more he would take the city, but lose it again.

In 1504, Babur crossed the Oxus River, then the Hindu Kush, and seized Kabul. He spent the next 14 years securing his position in Afghanistan and chasing his dream of attaining sovereignty of Samarkand. To Babur, success was an ultimate certainty and failure but a temporary inconvenience.

In 1525, Babur set out towards Delhi with 12,000 horse. **Daulat Khan** meekly surrendered to him near Lahore in 1526. Babur then confronted Sultan **Ibrahim Lodhi** at Panipat. Ibrahim Lodhi is said to have marched from Delhi with 100,000 horse and 1000 elephants, about 10 times Babur's forces. Babur had made a carefully chosen formation with the close-packed walls of Panipat on one flank. He had commandeered 700 carts from the neighbourhood, which were lashed together and sheltered his match-lock men, keeping a gap for his cavalry to charge from. Besides, he had also kept additional 'flying columns' in reserve, which swung round the enemy's flanks after the battle was joined, and pressed hard from the rear.

Ibrahim had no room to manoeuvre. Despite repeated charges by his elephant and horse brigades and foot soldiers, he failed to break through the cordon of carts and was unable either to advance or withdraw. By mid-day about 15,000 of his men were slain, amongst them was the Sultan himself. The successor of Raja Man Singh of Gwalior, Vikramaditya, who had surrendered to Ibrahim Lodi in 1519, also died in Panipat.

Babur went in hot pursuit of the survivors to Delhi and sent his son Humayun to Agra, to secure the Lodi capital and the treasury. Humayun found Ibrahim's mother and Vikramaditya's family in Agra. To curry favour with the conqueror, the families of Vikramaditya and Ibrahim made a 'voluntary offering' to Humayun of a mass of jewels and valuables. Babur noticed among these the famous diamond **Koh-i-Nur**, 'the mountain of light', its weight was about 186 carats. He gave it to Humayun.

In early 1527, Babur had to face **Rana Sanga** of Udaipur. Unlike the fight against Ibrahim Lodi, the battle against Rana Sanga was a battle for Islam, since the rajputs were infidels. Babur, therefore, designated the encounter as *jihad—Dharma-yuddha*! Death in war was martyrdom! He made the Lodi retainers take oath on the Quran to fight till they fell. Babur, too, conscientiously abjured alcohol. Decanters of goblets were dashed to pieces and wine-skins emptied.

The battle was joined at Khanua near Fatehpur Sikri. Rana Sanga had a larger force. But Babur was able to receive reinforcements from Kabul in the meanwhile. He deployed his cavalry to encircle the enemy. The battle lasted the whole day and the Rana was obliged to retreat. After his victory in Khanua, Babur, the Mughal, was supreme in the heartland of northern India.

Babur had sent Humayun back to Afghanistan to make another bid for Samarkand. He himself struck south and took the fortified town of Chanderi, whose Rajput garrison re-enacted the suicidal ritual of *jauhar*. Humayun failed in his bid for Samarkand. He returned to Agra in 1529, alerted by news of his father's failing health. However, he himself fell seriously ill after reaching Agra.

Babur was distraught at Humayun's illness; he supposedly prayed by his sickbed that his own life be forfeited for his son Humayun's recovery. To a man who traded abstinence for victory at Khanua, such dealings with the divine were second nature, and once again his piety was rewarded: the father faded as the son convalesced. In 1530, **Humayun** was 22 when Babur was laid to rest in a garden in Agra which he had himself planned and landscaped. Later, in accordance with his wish, his body was removed to a retreat amidst the melons and vines of Kabul.[228]

Though Humayun reigned for 26 years, Babur ruled for barely 10. This was the only period when Mughal rule in India seemed to be threatened. Ferishta says 'Humayun was for the most part disposed to spend his time in social intercourse and pleasure.' He

[228]Keay, John, *India: A History*, Harper Collins, Delhi, 2000, p. 760 onwards.

was indulgent and indolent; his familiar solace were his playmates and the pipe (*hooka*).

Humayun committed the mistake of trusting his three brothers; he appointed each of them to command a part of the empire. He gave Kabul to Prince Kamran who promptly added Punjab to it. The brothers would support Humayun when it suited them; when it did not, each would make a bid to the throne.

The Lodi warlords had seized Kalinger in the east; Humayun proceeded towards it. In the meanwhile, **Sher Khan Suri** from Afghanistan had followed the Lodis into India and was carving out a kingdom for himself, basing himself in the fortress of Chunar. Humayun abandoned his siege of Kalinger to confront Sher Khan. However, in the meanwhile, **Ahmad Shah,** the sultan of Gujarat was threatening Agra. Humayun had to suspend his operation against Sher Shah. Ahmad Shah was defeated and Humayun installed his brother Askari there. That was a mistake. Askari allowed Ahmad Shah to reoccupy his kingdom and headed for Agra to occupy the throne. Humayun forestalled him but forgave Askari's transgression.

In July 1537, Humayun took Chunar, but Sher Shah was not there. He was strengthening himself by victories in Bihar and Bengal. In 1539, there was a decisive battle at Chausa, between Varanasi and Patna, where Sher Shah defeated Humayun's forces. Humayun's ungrateful brothers refused him refuge. Humayun had to flee, crossing the deserts of Rajasthan and Sind, sought shelter in Iran in the court of Shah Tamasp, the Safavid ruler, who was immensely pleased with the diamonds Humayun presented him.

∽

Sher Khan assumed the royal title of **Sher Shah** and entrenched himself in the Mughal territories. He made successful campaigns in the Punjab, Sind and Malwa. Thereafter he humbled the Rajput bastions of Jodhpur and Chittor and proceeded to Kalinjar.The venture had almost succeeded, but a rocket aimed at the fort rebounded off its walls and ignited the pile of rockets lying near Sher Shah. He was burnt to death. What a fateful death at the peak of glory!

Sher Shah had added to the complex begun by Humayun on the site of Indraprastha, the capital of the Pandavas, now known as Purana Qila, and had built a mosque there. Only parts of the Qila built by Sher Shah have survived, they show rich but restrained decoration. His magnificent five-storey tomb at Sasaram, midway between Varanasi and Gaya, which contains his charred remains, exhibits a palace-like grandeur.

~

As mentioned earlier when **Humayun** met **Shah Tamasp** of Iran, he gave him the glittering gifts of the jewels of India. But their friendship was fraught with religious misgivings. The unbridgeable gulf of Sunni and Shi'ite faith lay between them. Without much a-do, Humayun embraced Shi'ite faith of his royal host.

With 12,000 Persian troops plus what remained of his own following and a train of Persian courtiers and artists, he entered Afghanistan in the summer of 1544. He was opposed by his own brothers; one of whom held Kabul, the other Kandahar. It took him eight years to sort them out.

Humayun's son **Akbar** (the name means 'Nursling of Divine Light') was born during his flight from India; he was 12 years of age in 1554. Sher Shah was succeeded by his son Islam Shah Sur. Humayun defeated the Sur ruler of the Punjab at Sirhind. By August 1555, Humayun was back in Delhi. But unfortunately, in January 1556, he tripped descending down the stairs in Sher Shah's palace and died, leaving his minor son, Akbar, to the care of Bayram Khan.

~

AKBAR'S REIGN

Akbar's reign outshines that of all Indian sovereigns. He was an exact contemporary of Queen Elizabeth I of England.

Soon after Humayun's demise, **Hemu**, prime minister of one of the principal Sur claimants, stormed Delhi and put its Mughal garrison to flight. The Mughal commanders favoured a speedy retreat to Kabul. But child Akbar's guardian Bayram Khan stoutly opposed it.

In November 1556, the two armies met at Panipat, the site of Babur's great victory. Hemu, who had several victories to his credit, was commanding the operations. Mounting a gigantic elephant, named '*Hawai*', Hemu led a formidable elephant corps of 1,500 beasts. The Mughal army was led by horses. Horses would not face the elephants and victory looked to be going the way of the elephants. However, an arrow hit Commander Hemu in the eye and he collapsed. His force ran helter-skelter. Hemu was captured and brought before the young victor, Akbar, and was beheaded. Next day, the Mughal army entered Delhi in triumph yet again.

Bayram Khan, as regent, defeated the Sur rivals in Panjab, Awadh and Gwalior. He had accompanied Humayun to Iran. However, **Adham Khan**, belonging to a coterie around the nurse of Akbar's son, got Bayram Khan dismissed, then provoked into rebellion and killed.

In 1561, Adham Khan commanded an invasion of Malwa where **Baz Bahadur**, the last and most memorable of its sultans, had revived the Malwa tradition of Muslim-Rajput amity. Baz Bahadur had serenaded Rani Rupamati, a Rajput princess. This idyl now ended. Baz Bahadur was routed and put to flight. Rupamati put a chalice full of poison to her lips rather than submit to Adham Khan's attentions. Baz Bahadur's followers, Muslim as well as Hindu, were callously massacred.

Akbar took exception to Adham Khan withholding the booty. Adham Khan again made similar infringement in Awadh and later made a fatal attempt on the life of the prime minister. Akbar was enjoying his siesta and was aroused by this tumult. He came out and struck the miscreant with his sword who fell down.

~

Akbar was 19 now; he dispensed with the office of the prime minister and assumed supreme civil and military authority. He used to slip out from the royal apartments and mix and mingle with the bazaar folk incognito. He also consorted with *jogis*, *sanyasis* and *qalanders*. It dawned on him then that Indians were not uncultured infidels; whatever their religion, it was his duty not to oppress them. He lifted the detested *jizia* tax and began celebrating the Hindu festivals of Diwali and Dussehra.

When Akbar was 21, he married Jodha Bai, daughter of Raja Bharmal of Amber. The marriage was partly a reward for the family's loyalty to Humayun and partly a way of securing loyalty to himself and his heirs. Besides, Raja Bharmal had provided a sizeable cavalry for service in the imperial forces. Later, his son, Raja Man Singh had personally headed a campaign to Kabul.

Rajasthan had been a thicket of opposition to the Muslim invaders. This changed with the house of Amber (later Jaipur) becoming an ally. But **Udai Singh,** the **Sisodia Rana of Mewar,** successor of Rana Sanga who was Babur's opponent at Khanua, remained hostile. He had afforded sanctuary to Baz Bahadur, fugitive of Malwa. In 1567, Akbar himself marched south and laid a siege to Chittor. The operation dragged into 1568. In the meanwhile, Udai Singh had founded a new capital in place of Chittor, on the bank of Pichhola Lake, which was named Udaipur in his memory.

Meanwhile, Akbar was also founding a new capital. Hitherto the court had been at Agra, where the walls of the great Red Fort had been completed by 1562. Other fortified complexes at Lahore, Allahabad and Ajmer were underway. Together with Agra, they framed the core of Mughal empire in northern India. Akbar made a pilgrimage to the dargah of the Sufi saint Muinuddin Chisti at Ajmer and then he paid homage to the living member of the Chishti community, **Shaikh Salim Chishti** at Sikri near Agra. Shaikh Salim Chishti had predicted the birth of three sons to him.

Akbar was now 26 and was concerned for the succession. Although not for want of brides, he was still without an heir. His earlier two queens had failed to deliver. He had married his third queen Jodha Bai in 1562. She had given birth to Hasan and Hussain, who unfortunately died in a few months of their birth. However, in 1569, she gave birth to Salim (Jahangir). Thereupon, Shaikh Salim Chishti was heaped with honours.

In 1571, Akbar began to construct his new capital at Sikri, which was renamed **Fatehpur Sikri.** John Keay calls it 'the wildest and weirdest folly.'[229] In 1571, he had completed the construction of the Humayun Tomb at Delhi. Both his father's tomb at Delhi and the new capital at Fatehpur Sikri are of monumental scale. Humayun's Tomb was designed by a Persian architect who had previously worked at Bukhara. Its great white marble dome was quite unlike anything built in India. The dome swells from a narrow 'neck' into the bulbous hemisphere, typical of Samarkand and Iran. At Fatehpur Sikri, Akbar constructed a mosque with a *Bulanda* (lofty) gateway besides a palatial complex.

Akbar also invited holy men from all religions and sects at Fatehpur Sikri and launched into a thorough investigation of their tenets and beliefs. He presided over their heated debates. To the Quranic arguments of Sunni, Shia and Ismaili, were added the more mystical and populist appeals of numerous Sufi orders, the bhakti flavour of Shaiva and Vaishnava devotees, the fastidious logic of naked Jain saints, and the varied insights of numerous wandering ascetics who were disciples of Sant Kabir and Guru Nanak. He even invited the Portuguese padre of Goa. Akbar sought to create a faith, ***Deen-e-Ilahi***, which would satisfy the spiritual needs of his far-flung realm as well those of his conscience.

To the third guru of the Sikhs, Guru Amar Das, Akbar is said to have given the land at Amritsar on which the great Golden Temple would eventually be built.

To the orthodox, the *ulema*, of whom Akbar was especially dismissive, it looked as if Islam was under threat. Thus in 1579-80 there materialized a serious challenge to his reign, when a *fatwa* was issued during the Friday congregational prayers in Jaunpur, enjoining all Muslims to rebel, naming Akbar's half-brother Hakim, the governor of Kabul, as the legitimate sovereign. Raja Man Singh of Amber held Lahore against the invasion of Hakim. Todar Mal, another Hindu commander, was sent east to deal with the Afghans in Bengal. In 1581, Akbar himself hastened to the Panjab and continued on to Kabul. Although Bengal would continue to be troublesome, the revolt was over.

Four years later, in 1585, Akbar forsook Fatehpur Sikri and

[229]Keay, John, *India: A History*, Harper Collins, Delhi, 2000, p. 315.

shifted his court and government to Lahore. He imposed his authority on the restless tribes of the frontier, then conquered Kashmir and next Sind. Kabul too was secured. Kandhar, which had been awarded to the Shah of Persia as Humayun's rescue package, was resumed in 1595. Akbar returned to Agra in 1598.

In the last years of his reign, there was assault on Ahmadnagar. This conflict became inextricably confused with the struggle for succession and the manoeuvres of his eldest son Salim. Possibly because of the threat posed by Salim, Akbar now preferred the security of Agra's Red Fort to the comparative isolation and vulnerability of Fatehpur Sikri. He died in 1605.

STRUGGLES AND FIGHTS FOR SUCCESSION

The Mughal rule was notorious for struggles and fights for succession from siblings and their own progeny. Distrust between father and son, as also between brothers, was a recurring theme of the Mughal period.

Akbar's eldest son **Salim (Jahangir)** had attempted to siege Agra during Akbar's absence in the Deccan. In 1602, Jahangir proclaimed himself emperor and got Akbar's able finance minister Abul Fazal killed. Jahangir's own son Khusrau had laid siege to Lahore; Jahangir had him captured and blinded. In his memoir Jahangir wrote: 'A king, it is said, should deem no man as his relation.'

In 1622, Prince Khurram, Jahangir's second and best-loved son, on whom he had just bestowed the title '**Shah Jahan**' (King of the World) killed his elder brother, Khusrau, who had been blinded earlier by his own father. In the field or on the run, Shah Jahan led the imperial forces a merry dance for four years. However, 18 months before Jahangir's death in 1627, the father and son were reconciled. More blood-letting followed as Shah Jahan made good his claim to the throne by ordering the death of his one more bother, Shaharyar, and sundry cousins.

'It has to be said in defence of the chaotic Mughal successions', observes John Keay, 'that only the fittest could hope to survive.' From the filial free-for-all, there emerged some of the ablest, most charismatic and most long-lived rulers India has ever known. Humayun and Jahangir, the one addicted to opium the other to alcohol, yet had the sense to select extremely capable consorts and advisers.

In 1611, Jahangir had married the 31-old widow of one of his Afghan *amirs*. Her father, the Persian born Itimad-ud-Daula, became Jahangir's closest advisor cum minister. Her brother Asaf Khan was one of the most successful generals; and the lady herself, eventually known as **Nur Jahan** (Light of the World), acted as co-ruler and, during periods of imperial incapacity, as the supreme sovereign.

Her brother Asaf Khan had stood by Shah Jahan during rebellions and had become his closest advisor when he succeeded. Moreover, Asaf Khan's daughter, the famous **Mumtaz Mahal**, was Shah Jahan's beloved consort.[230] She had shared his troubled years on the run. She had died in 1631, while giving birth to their fourteenth child. Shah Jahan was distraught. He decided to construct a memorable and magnificent tomb for her at Agra.

THE TAJ MAHAL

The site on which the Taj Mahal stands was provided by Raja Jai Singh of Jaipur, successor of Raja Man Singh. Besides, from the Kachhawaha quarries of Makrana in Rajasthan came the acres of white marble. Construction began in 1632 and was completed in 1643. Bernier thought it to be one of the wonders of the world. For Kipling it was 'the ivory gate through which all dreams pass'. Robindra Nath Tagore called it 'a tear on the face of eternity!'

Historian John Keay too goes poetic: 'Combining the bulb-like dome of Humanyun's tomb and the marble and inlay of Itimad-ud-Daula's with the theatrical staging of Akbar's and the landscaping of Jahangir's gardens, it represented a triumphant summation of

[230]Keay, John, *India: A History*, Harper Collins, Delhi, 2000, pp. 332–333.

Moghal taste. Its symbolism, with a setting evocative of paradise and the great white tomb as an image of the Throne of God, is purely Islamic. But in its sculptural conception and its execution many have recognized an essential Indian aesthetic and ancient Indian skills.'[231].

Some years before the Taj Mahal was built, in 1659, Bijapur's Gol Gumbaz (Round Dome) was built. Muhammad Adil Shah II of Bijapur rests in it. The Sultans of Bijapur and their neighbour in Golconda had been building mosques and tombs since the 1570s. The Gol Gumbaz dome is larger than the Taj Mahal's; it is second only to that of St Peter's in Rome. The design of Gol Gumbaz displays a refreshing simplicity, combined with extraordinary technical expertise. It's a square tomb with pagoda like seven-storey towers on four corners. The towering dome emerges from that height.

'If the Taj, as befits the tomb of a queen, has feminine delicacy, the Gol Gumbaz, the tomb of a Sultan, is all masculine virility.' Observes John Keay.

Prior to the Taj Mahal, Nur Jahan had taken keen interest in building the tomb for her father Itimad-ud-Daula in Agra. This stately tomb of white marble, inlaid with semi-precious stones, is filigree in marble. It looks like a dream congealed and ushers in the classic period of Mughal architecture.

While the work on the Taj Mahal was going on, Shah Jahan had undertaken to build a 'New Delhi' in 1639. It was built to the north of Tughlakabad and was designed to supersede Agra as the imperial capital. It was completed in 1648 and was called Shahjahanabad. It enclosed about 6,400 acres and had a population of about 400,000 people. Ironically, it is now known as 'Old Delhi' as the British built 'New Delhi' in later times.

Shah Jahan had also built the Red Fort in Delhi and the great Jama Masjid, which was the largest mosque in India then. The Red Fort, though ravaged by subsequent occupants, including the British, is still a focus for state occasions and political announcements. Indian Prime Ministers address public gatherings

[231]Keay, John, *India: A History*, Harper Collins, Delhi, 2000, p. 336.

from its ramparts on special occasions. Besides, Shah Jahan re-built the Red Fort at Agra, its pillard-hall of *Diwan-i-Aam* and the white marble chambers. Shah Jahan would shuffle away his final years in Agra Fort as his son Aurangzeb's prisoner and gaze at the Taj Mahal, where he would be entombed beside his beloved Mumtaz.

The official language of the Mughal court was Persian. But a hybrid tongue, 'Urdu' (meaning 'camp'), developed in the military encampments of the empire and gained wide currency. Written in the Perso-Arabic script, much of its syntax and vocabulary was borrowed from the local languages of North India, the daughters of Sanskrit. Poetry, painting and music benefitted from the same synthesis and flourished under Mughal patronage.

AURANGZEB

In due course, each of Shah Jahan's four sons, Dara Shikoh, Shuja, Aurangzeb and Murad would mobilize separately against their father as also against one another. When Aurangzeb won this contest and in 1658, he deposed his father Shah Jahan (eight years before his demise), imprisoning him in Agra fort for the rest of his days. He justified his conduct on the grounds that he was merely treating Shah Jahan as Shah Jahan had treated his father Jahangir, and as Jahangir had treated Akbar. He zestfully revived discrimination against the Hindus and active promotion of Islamic values.

In 1652, Shah Jahan had appointed Aurangzeb the Governor of the Deccan. Aurangzeb did not like the Shi'ite Sultan of Golconda and the large Shi'ite communities, nor the Hindus. He began intriguing against the Sultan with Mir Jumla, a Persian adventurer in the service of the Golconda sultanate. In 1656, Mir Jumla joined Aurangzeb on a two-pronged attack on Golconda. Hyderabad was taken and the Sultan was besieged behind the great walls of Golconda fort.

The Golconda Sultan appealed to Delhi where Dara Shikoh, Aurangzeb's eldest brother and his deadly rival, persuaded Shah Jahan to abort the campaign against the Sultan. However, Aurangzeb extracted large territory and hefty indemnity from the

Sultan. Next year, Aurangzeb invaded Bijapur. Mir Jumla's forces ravaged Bijapur's northern cities and were poised to take over Bijapur. But once more came Shah Jahan's order to desist.

In 1657, Shah Jahan was suddenly taken ill. Prince Shuja, governor of Bengal, and the fourth brother Murad, governor of Gujarat, rushed towards Delhi. Shuja suffered defeat near Varanasi from the imperial army led by Raja Jai Singh of Jaipur. The youngest Murad, hoping for support from Aurangzeb went to Surat and waited for Aurangzeb to move north.

Dara Shikoh, who was in Agra with the Emperor, was the front-runner at this stage. He was also Shah Jahan's favourite, being the eldest son. But he inspired deep suspicion among orthodox Muslims, especially the religious *ulema*. A scholar of some repute, Dara had translated some Upanishads into Persian; he even advanced the view that the essential nature of Hinduism was identical with that of Islam. This was heresy by any orthodox standard. 'The contest was therefore as much about ideology as power,' opines John Keay.[232]

Commandeering Mir Jumla's troops, Aurangzeb met up with Murad near Ujjain and defeated the imperial army sent by Shah Jahan. Barely eight miles short of Agra, he encountered Dara in which the Rajput contingent was prominent. Dara was no match for the resolute Aurangzeb and fled north through Delhi to Lahore. Aurangzeb then occupied Agra, imprisoning Shah Jahan in the Fort.

But he knew that his victory would not be complete unless the other contenders were eliminated. At Mathura, while heading north in pursuit of Dara, he lured Murad to his camp and took him prisoner; he was beheaded later. Shuja, emerging from the east was defeated again and sent fleeing back. Dara was engaged near Ajmer. He fled and was captured, and after being carried through the streets of Agra in chains, was cut to pieces. Shuja fled from Dhaka by ship to Burma and was killed there.

Mir Jumla was appointed governor of Bengal and he made Dhaka his capital. In 1659, **Aurangzeb** was formally crowned Emperor at a grand assembly in Diwan-e-Aam of Delhi's Red Fort.

---

[232]Keay, John, *India: A History*, Harper Collins, Delhi, 2000, p. 339.

He adopted the title ***Alamgir*** (Universe Conqueror). He appointed a *Muhtasib* (Censor), a guardian of public morality, and prohibited gambling, alcohol and opium, and re-imposed the jizia tax on the Hindus. Besides, he rescinded revenue endowments enjoyed by Hindu temples and Brahmins. Hindu merchants were penalized by higher duties; the provincial administrations were instructed to replace Hindu employees with Muslims.

He ordered all newly built, or rebuilt temples to be destroyed. Among the temples razed were the great **Vishvanath temple of Varanasi** and the new Keshava Deo temple of Mathura; they were replaced with mosques.

Shahjahanabad (Delhi) erupted in protest against the imposition of jizia. They barred the emperor's short passage from the Red Fort to the Jama Masjid. A herd of elephants was brought and directed against the mob. Many were trodden to death. For some days the Hindus continued to assemble but at length they submitted to jizia. (This has been consulted from Khafi Khan's Muntakhab-al Lubab.) Apart from improving the economic strength of his treasury, Aurangzeb had probably wanted the Hindus to convert to Islam to improve their status.

In 1678 the Rathor Maharaja of Marwar (Jodhpur) died without heir. Pending the selection of a successor, Aurangzeb resumed the Marwar jagir. He sent Mughal troops to oversee the takeover. They indulged in gratuitous iconoclasm of Marwar's temples. In the meanwhile, two of the deceased Maharaja's widows gave birth to male heirs. One of the infants died but the other, Ajit Singh, immediately became a focus of anti-Mughal sentiment.

Aurangzeb conferred Marwar on an unpopular nephew of the deceased Maharaja, revolt flared. In an incident beloved of the Rajput bards, the infant Ajit Singh was whisked away by his mother, who was a Sisodia princess of Mewar, to the Rana of Udaipur. Mughal army sacked the city of Udaipur and vandalized its temples. The Rana's forces scored some notable victories; he maintained Mewar's proud record of never making personal submission to the emperor.

One of Aurangzeb's sons, named Akbar, was at the head of the Mughal forces in Udaipur. Aurangzeb now demoted Akbar to the Marwar command at Jodhpur. Prince Akbar felt slighted. Indeed, he had been contemplating to challenge his father for some time. The Rajput promises of support emboldened him. In 1681 he proclaimed himself emperor and marched against his father, who was at Ajmer at that time. But he became suspicious of his Rajput allies and fled to the Deccan, where he was warmly welcomed by the Marathas. He became their protégé.

Aurangzeb soon followed him. He was in his sixties now. The entire imperial court also went with him, and most of the Mughal army. Shahjahanabad was partially vacated. The Deccan campaign proved unending; it lasted for 26 years, right up to the emperor's demise.

During Aurangzeb's 24-year absence, besides the Golconda and Bijapur sultanates, the Marathas had created an independent homeland in the Western ghats, under Shivaji's inspirational leadership.

In the meanwhile, Sultan Muhammad Adil Shah of Bijapur acknowledged Mughul supremacy and also made the Nayaks of Madurai and Tanjore to acknowledge Mughal suzerainty. Aurangzeb found compensation in conquests in Mysore and Tamilnadu. His rule now stretched to the Konkan and Malabar coasts in the west to the Coromandel coast in the east. The tactical skills of the Maratha units of **Shahji Bhonsle** were instrumental in securing victory over the Coromandel coast. But his son **Shivaji** had other ideas.

SHIVAJI

Shivaji was just 17 years old when he had begun subverting the authority of Bijapur in the north-west of the state. He first stormed and tricked his way into the difficult terrain of the nearby forts of Western Ghats, creating an independent Maratha zone around Pune (Poona). It was previously under Ahmadnagar but was transferred to Bijapur when the Sultan of Bijapur accepted Mughal suzerainty. Shivaji played off the Islamic superiors against each other.

Shivaji had captured 40 forts in the Western Ghats and the

Konkan coast. However, there was no chance of the Marathas driving them off the from there. So Shivaji met Afzal Khan, Bijapur's best general, as a supplicant and killed him in a dramatic subterfuge in the hill-fort of Pratabgarh near Mahabaleshwar.

The local scribe, Khafi Khan, describes the fateful encounter: 'As soon as that experienced and perfect traitor [Shivaji] neared Afzal Khan, he threw himself as his feet, weeping. When he [Afzal Khan] wanted to raise his [Shivaji's] head and put the hand of kindness on his back to embrace him, Shivaji with perfect dexterity thrust a hidden weapon into his abdomen in such a way that he [Afzal Khan] had not even time to sigh, and was killed.' Shivaji had a *Bagh-nakha* on his right hand, a small iron finger-grip with four curving talons of iron, each as long and as sharp as a cut-throat razor.

Shivaji then gave a signal to his men who were hiding in the surrounding scrub. They captured the stores, treasure, horses and elephants and enrolled into his army the men Shivaji captured. Khafi Khan adds: 'Shivaji made it a rule…not to desecrate mosques or the Book of Allah, nor to seize women. Muslims as well as Hindus could comfortably serve under his standard.'

~

In 1660, Aurangzeb sent a large army to the Deccan under Shaista Khan, the brother of Shah Jahan's beloved Mumtaz Mahal, to secure the territories ceded to the empire by Bijapur in 1657, which included the Maratha homeland in the Ghats. Shivaji now faced a much more formidable foe. The Mughal army was relentlessly harried and every fort took heavy toll of the Mughal blood. Yet Pune fell where Shaista Khan resided.

Shivaji entered Pune in a 'marriage party'. They were joined by a group of Marathas who were captured by the Mughal army. In the dead of night, the bridegroom and members of the marriage party as well as those captured, entered Shaista Khan's residence by breaking a kitchen window and killed the persons sleeping inside. Shaista Khan had a lucky escape. His thumb was sliced by an attacker's sword; he swooned and fell down. His maids carried him to a safe place. However, his son and one of his wives were killed. No plunder was taken; the raiders withdrew as silently as they had arrived. Shivaji himself was not in the wedding party; he had probably secured collusion of a Mughal general.

In 1664, breaking out of the hills, Shivaji led his forces north into Gujarat and headed for the great port of Surat. They ransacked the place for 40 days. Only the well-defended English factory was spared. A Mughal army commanded by Raja Jai Singh, who had vanquished Prince Shuja, arrived in 1665. He secured fort after fort and cornered Shivaji near Purandhar. Shivaji sued for terms and agreed to surrender 20 forts. However, he retained 12 forts. He was then made to attend the Emperor in person and was detained. However, he escaped in a basket of confectionary, as per popular myth.

Several forts were recaptured by Shivaji, and in 1674, the port of Surat was pillaged again. Later on, Maratha forces struck deep into Khandesh and Berar. Pune was liberated along with much of the Konkan coast. And to top it all, Shivaji elevated himself to kingship. He invited a renowned pundit from Varanasi and got his chronology prepared, which linked his Bhonsle predecessors to the Sisodia Rajputs of Mewar, declaring him to be a kshtriya.

An elaborate Vedic yajna was organized by the pundit from Varanasi and Shivaji was anointed as a sovereign lord. Lavish donations to Brahmins were given and Shivaji set off on a token *digvijay* and raided a Mughal encampment and some more forts in Khandesh and Berar. Then in alliance with the Golconda sultanate, he made a joint attack on Bijapur territory. His last campaign, conducted entirely by Maratha forces, resulted in capturing the forts of Vellore and Jinji, south-west of Madras. When in 1680 Shivaji breathed his last, he left a Maratha kingdom, although its territories were not contiguous and were not clearly defined.

In 1681 **Shambhaji,** one of Shivaji's two competing sons, gained the upper hand and had himself crowned. It was to Shambhaji's court that Prince Akbar, Aurangzeb's rebellious son, made his way after the failure of his Rajput intrigues.

However, the conjunction of Maratha and Rajput resistance which Prince Akbar had hoped against his father never materialized. In despair Prince Akbar took a ship for Persia in 1687 to seek the Shah's support. In 1688 Aurangzeb captured Shambhaji who heaped insults on him and the Prophet Mohammad. He was dismembered, limb by limb.

Yet the Maratha bands continued their raids on the forts in the Western Ghats occupied by the Mughal army. Emperor Aurangzeb, well into his eighties, continued to lead his weary armies against them. Where the forts were recaptured by the Mughal army, the Marathas would sue for peace, offering best terms. After the Mughal army left, they would renounce their pledges, resume their lands and reoccupy the forts. Each Maratha chief was now acting independently.

In 1700 Satara, where Shivaji had moved the Maratha capital, came under siege and was surrendered to the Mughals. At about the same time Shambhaji's successor Rajaram had died. Rajaram's senior widow, **Tarabai,** assumed control in the name of his son, **Shambhaji II.** In the same year the Maratha raiders crossed the Narmada River and entered Malwa.

Two years later they ransacked Hyderabad, one of the richest cities in the peninsula. The port of Machchlipattam suffered the same fate. Maratha activities now extended to virtually the entire peninsula. Taradevi as regent began realizing 25 per cent of revenue collected in the Deccan. She also levied additional tolls on vital trade routes. Non-payment, whether by zamindars or traders would result in forcible expropriation by further raids. Indeed, she began operating a parallel revenue collections system. Shivaji's legacy had fructified.

Aurangzeb's extreme old age and the resentment stirred by his religious policies, the strain imposed on military and financial resources by the insistent Maratha campaign, and the growing discontent amongst Mughal *mansabdars* whose Deccan jagirs failed to yield their expected revenue, were all taking a toll on Mughul authority.[233]

In 1705 Aurangzeb fell seriously ill. He was carried in a palanquin to Ahmadnagar. 'I am forlorn and destitute, and misery is my ultimate lot.' he wrote. He died in 1707, his ninetieth year,

[233]Keay, John, *India: A History*, Harper Collins, Delhi, 2000, p. 359.

and was buried in a simple grave in Khuldabad, near Aurangabad.

~

Aurangzeb was survived by 17 sons, grandsons and great-grandsons. The two main contenders, Prince Muazzam (also known as Shah Alam), previously governor of Kabul, defeated and killed Prince Azam Shah, from the Deccan. He assumed the title of **Bahadur Shah** (or Shah Alam I).

Prince Ajit Singh of Jodhpur, the infant who had been sneaked out of Delhi in 1678 was about 30 years of age now. He was waiting for the death of Aurangzeb to avenge the earlier desecration of Marwar. Supported by the Kachhwahas of Amber and the Sisodias of Mewar, he rose in rebellion against the Mughals. Bahadur Shah attacked Marwar again and reached a compromise solution with Ajit Singh. A year later Ajit Singh combined with Jai Singh Kachhwaha of Jaipur and they attacked the provincial capital Ajmer, but could not succeed in defeating the Mughal army. However, 10 years later they succeeded in extending the territories of Jaipur and Udaipur to Surat in the south.

~

BIRTH OF SIKHISM

The Sikhs had fallen foul of Jahangir when they supported Prince Khusrau in 1605 during the succession crisis. **Guru Arjan Singh**, the fifth Guru, was martyred by Jahangir as a result. Guru Arjan Singh had collected and compiled the hymns of his predecessors, including compositions by non-Sikh Sufis and saints like Kabir, besides adding his own compositions. As a result, Sikh Gurudwaras had become as much a target of imperial iconoclasm as Hindu temples.

Again, in the 1658 succession crisis, Aurangzeb was enraged by the Sikh hospitality to Prince Dara. He persecuted the followers of Guru Nanak with a heavy hand. **Guru Teg Bahadur**, the nineth Guru, was condemned for blasphemy and was beheaded in 1675 in a gurudwara in Delhi near the Red Fort.

The cruellest episode was the assassination of the last (tenth) **Guru Gobind Singh** of the Sikhs in 1708. He had added his own compositions to the holy book of the Sikhs, and later, the whole became known as the Adi Grantha. The tradition of a Guru in human form was discontinued after his demise; the Adi Grantha itself was deemed to be the Supreme Guru.

Guru Gobind Singh had been hoping to win back a Sikh base which he had recently established in **Anandpur Sahib** (near Bilaspur in Himachal Pradesh) and get redress against the local Mughal commander, Wazir Khan of Sirhind, who had been hounding the Sikhs. This Mughal commander had in fact got the Guru's two sons, Jorawar Singh, aged eight years, and Fateh Singh aged five years, cruelly killed. The kids were made to stand in line and were entombed in the wall that was constructed around them. It was ghastly!

At that time, emperor Bahadur Shah was camping at Nanded on the Godawari River in the Deccan. He called Guru Gobind Singh there, apparently for reconciliation. After the Guru reached there, two Afghans—Jamshed Khan and Wasil Beg—entered the Guru's tent in the night and stabbed him to death. He was eliminated by gross treachery. Three of the ten Sikh Gurus and two innocent kids were sacrificed in the fire of Islam.

The Sikh Panth had been originally a movement for religious and social reform. However, under Guru Gobind Singh it had undergone a radical transformation; it was transformed into a political and military formation. Guru Gobind Singh had introduced a rigid standard of orthodoxy. The Sikhs must henceforth be induced through a baptismal ceremony into the *Khalsa* (the pure). They must leave their hair uncut, carry arms and adopt the epithet of '*Singh*' (Lion). Clearly recognizable, more cohesive, more territorially aware, and much more militant, the panth under the leadership of Guru Gobind Singh was readying itself to join the contest for power in the late Mughal period.

Within a year of Guru Gobind Singh's death, in 1709, **Banda Bahadur,** the Sikh General, began systematically storming the Muslim towns of the region. Although finally defeated in 1715, he left a legacy of defiant protest and sectarian militancy.

In 1799, a young Sikh military leader, **Ranjit Singh**, who had been prominent in repelling Afghan attacks from the North, had occupied Lahore. By 1805, he had secured Amritsar as the centre of Sikhhism. He blossomed into the Maharaja of the Panjab and ruled for the next 30 years!

Emperor Bahadur Shah died in 1712. He was succeeded by a debauch, Jahandah Shah. Farrukhsiyar, son of one of the unsuccessful brothers, with a sizeable army, then launched an attack on the imperial army from Bihar. Jahandah Shah's army melted away. Order was temporarily restored. In 1713, **Farrukhsiyar**, who was responsible for the bloody repression of Banda Bahadur and his Sikh army, indulged the ambitions of the English East India company and signed a firman to trade in India.

Farrukhsiyar's bid for power and his rule depended heavily on his two brothers known as the Saiyids, one of whom had been the governor of Allahabad and the other of Patna. They were now rewarded with highest offices, but they soon fell out with the emperor. Finding the Saiyids over-bearing, indispensable and intolerable, Farrukhsiyar sent the younger brother, Hussain Ali Khan, to the Deccan to keep him out of the way. Simultaneously, he gave instructions to the governor of Gujarat to get him killed. But it was Hussain Ali Khan who deposed the governor of Gujarat, and began planning his revenge on the emperor.

He conspired with the Maratha Peshwa Balaji Vishvanath, whose brother was in Farrukhsiyar'a court. They made a secret plan to kill Farrukhsiyar and in a surreptitious encounter in Delhi in 1719, Maratha Peshwa Balaji Vishwanath and Saiyid Hussain Ali Khan killed Farrukhsiyar.

Peshwa Balaji Vishvanath's son, **Baji Rao I**, succeeded him in 1720 and was considered the most charismatic and dynamic leader in Maratha history after Shivaji. Under his leadership the Marathas would raid north, south, east and west with impunity, for the next two decades.

∽

A surprising discovery of my perusal of this part of Indian history is Diwan **Murshid Quli Khan.** He was born a Brahmin in the Deccan. He was purchased, converted, adopted and renamed, and then inducted into Mughal service by one of Aurangzeb's Persian *amirs* in the Deccan. It was Aurangzeb who named him Murshid Quli Khan, impressed by his exceptional ability in increasing the state revenues and made him *Diwan*, or minister of Hyderabad. In 1701 he was sent to boost the revenues of Bengal, when apart from official duties, he founded the city of Murshidabad on the Ganga, south of Patna.

Like Sher Shah and Todar Mal before him, Murshid Quli Khan compiled new revenue rolls and established an efficient system of collection run largely by Hindus, and ruthlessly enforced it. He also transferred most existing *jagirs* from the richer parts of Bengal to less-easily taxed regions in Odisha. What are now West Bengal and Bangladesh, thus became predominantly *Khalsa*, their land revenue, in other words, being due directly to the emperor via the person of his *Diwan*.

∽

In the meanwhile, **Muhammad Shah**, the third emperor in a year, was installed on the throne by the Saiyads. By eliminating his two brothers, he had an unexpected long reign from 1719 to 1748,. In 1720, Muhammad Shah murdered his younger Saiyid brother and defeated and killed the older Saiyid in battle. Having freed himself from his minders, the young and handsome emperor began enjoying a life of pleasure. During his reign, catastrophic raids took place on Delhi not only by the Marathas. Nadir Shah of Persia devastated India in 1737 and the Afghan, Ahmad Shah Abdali, some time later. Nothing would galvanise the Emperor into action.

Nadir Shah had usurped the throne of Persia, and sieged Kandhar and Kabul. He thereafter swept across the Punjab and routed an imperial army at Karnal in 1739. He entered Delhi then and ordered general massacre—*katle-aam!* Twenty thousand men may have been butchered in a single day. Further carnage followed as the Persians concentrated on the extortion of family heirlooms and hidden treasures.

Muhammad Shah, the long-reigning emperor, celebrated for his inactivity and indulgence in pleasure, was *re-crowned* by his vanquisher, Nadir Shah. After 50 days of loot and plunder, Nadir Shah left Delhi with coins valued at eight or nine million sterling plus a similar hold in gold and silver. This does not include the jewels which were inestimable. Among them were Shah Jahan's Peacock Throne and the Koh-i-Nur diamond. However, the Koh-i-Nur was soon on its way back, having already passed from Nadir Shah's grandson to Ahmad Shah Abdali.

In 1750, **Ahmad Shah Abdali** found the imperial treasury somewhat bare. But Delhi was plundered, and its unhappy people were again subjected to pillage and their daughters ravished. The city of Mathura was devastated in like manner. Confirmed in the possession of Sind as well as Kashmir and the Punjab, Ahmad Shah Abdali had retired to Afghanistan. However, in 1760-1, he was back for more and inflicted a crushing defeat on the Marathas at Panipat.

∽

OPENING DOORS TO WESTERN MERCHANTS

Emperor Farrukhsiyar had issued the imperial firman to 'The Honorable Company of the Merchants of London trading into the East Indies' in 1719. Ever since the days of Akbar the European trading companies had been petitioning the Mughal emperors for firmans (imperial directives) to avoid the variety of vexatious exactions and demands imposed by local Mughal officials in the ports and provincial capitals. Unlike the Muslims who came to destroy the most prominent temples of India and rob them of their wealth, the Western companies ostensibly came for trade. Indeed, from ancient times Indian traders had been going all over Europe, bringing prosperity and fame to India as the 'Golden Bird of the East.'

The East India Company had received a royal charter from the English sovereign in 1600. But they needed a firman from an Indian emperor for monopoly of Eastern trade, as a reciprocal authorization guaranteeing favourable access.

More notably, in 1610 Captain William Hawkins had journeyed from Surat to Agra to petition Jahangir. Sir Thomas Roe, the first official ambassador from the Court of St. James, had also attended on Jahangir, carrying lavish gifts, for such a firman.

The British had acquired Madras (now Chennai) from the local Nayak in 1640 and had constructed Fort St George. Bombay (now Mumbai) too had passed to King Charles II as part of the dowry of his Portuguese bride, Catherine of Braganza, and was leased to East India Company. Curiously. the lease deed described Bombay as being 'in the Manor of East Greenwich in the County of Kent.'

During Aurangzeb's rule, when Shaista Khan was appointed governor of Bengal after his escape from Pune (minus a thumb), in 1684, the Company sent two ships to Hughli but they were thrashed by Mughal forces. The English withdrew down the river and landed at a spot that came to be called Calcutta (now Kolkata). In 1688, the Company official, Child, moved from Surat to Bombay and began attacking Mughal shipping. In early 1689, Sidi Yaqub, commanding a west coast fleet, besieged the Bombay Castle built by the Company for most of the year. Eventually, the British capitulated.

They journeyed up to where Aurangzeb was camping and pleaded for pardon, prostrating before him. In a spirit of forgive and forget, the emperor agreed to the restoration of their trading privileges and allowed the Company's Bengal establishment to return to the Hughli river. In 1690, the Company made a permanent settlement at Calcutta and began to construct Fort William. As a result, both Madras and Calcutta prospered.

The dynamic of the Mughal political economy was as much about troops as money. Similarly, the East India company, though a trading venture, had maintained regular troops. Through its employees it was indirectly involved in the hire and maintenance of troops by neighbouring zamindars and revenue collectors. Encouraged by the firman's confirmation of local revenue rights, the Company had also significantly increased the number of troops deemed necessary to defend its own establishments.

Thomas Pitt, once an interloper, then a Member of Parliament, had returned to Madras as governor of Fort St. George. He stayed there for 12 years, amassing a fortune, which included the 'Pitt diamond, which was bought for 45,000 Pound Sterling and sold to the Regent of France for 135,000 Pound Sterling. This money would comfortably sustain the political careers of his grandson, Chatham and great-grandson, William Pitt the Younger.

In 1746, 30 years after the Company had received the firman from Farrukhsiyar, **Robert Clive** would justify his advance to Plassey and overthrow the Bengal's Nawab. The trading company had transformed into a political force!

∽

Napoleon had contemptuously called the English, 'shopkeepers' by saying: '*L'Angleterre estune nation de boutiquiers.*' (England is a country of shopkeepers.) The English had come to India as traders. They had set up the East India Company to contest the Portuguese monopoly of spice trade. Vasco da Gama had landed at Calicut in Kerala to find a sea route around Africa to the Indies. The Portuguese had acquired some islands which afforded good shelter for their shipping. Amongst the coconut groves on one of the islands they had made a small fort. They called it 'Bon Bahia', which later became Bombay. The place was transferred to King Charles II as part of his Portuguese wife's dowry.

To the south, Goa remained in Portuguese hands while Cochin, an important entrepot for spice trade, had been wrested from them by the Dutch in 1660. The Mughal port of Surat became the main maritime outlet of northern India.

∽

For the Europeans the Hindus were infidels. The Company's charter was renewed in 1813 and it was allowed to let Christian missions operate in India. William Wilberforce, the anti-slavery champion, told the House of Commons in 1813: 'Our religion is sublime, pure and beneficent, while theirs is mean, licentious and cruel.' Indeed, even James Mill, author of *The History of British India,* had made a rather unfair comment when he said that Hinduism was 'the most enormous and tormenting superstition that ever harassed and degraded any portion of mankind.' He might have in mind the enslavement of Dasas and degaradation of the Shudras, who probably accounted for more than half of India's population.

Lord William Bentinck, as Governor General (1828–33) made a start on India's 'Reformation' with legislation to outlaw the practice of widow-burning (*suttee, sati).*

Later, in the 1850's, under Governor General Dalhousie, the process of reform and modernization was resumed. Meanwhile public works of undoubted utility, like surveys, roads, railways, telegraph lines and irrigation schemes were bringing government into direct contact with the rural masses and demonstrating its power as an agency for change. On the map it looked as if India was about to be ensnared in a steel tangle of wires and railway tracks.

∽

However, the **doctrine of lapse** that Lord Dalhousie introduced was most unfair, mean and self-serving. It held that the paramount power might assume the sovereignty of a state whose ruler was either manifestly incompetent or who died without a direct heir. In Dalhousie's words, the paramount power was 'bound to take that which was rightly its due.' He annexed seven states in seven years. They included Satara where Shivaji's direct descendants had long ruled and Nagpur and Jhansi of the Bhonsles. The Raja of Jhansi had died without a direct heir and **Rani Laxmi Bai** had adopted a son, according to Indian tradition.Similarly, Nana Sahib, the heir adopted by Peshwa Baji Rao II, found himself title-less and pensionless. In addition to these states, he annexed Awadh in 1856, on the eve of his departure from India.

Awadh was nearly the largest, probably the richest state, and the Nawab of Awadh was the most senior ruler, besides being the most loyal of all the native states. The state had been providing much of the manpower to the Company's Bengal army, about 40,000 men. Lucknow's 'Bara (Great) Imambara', 50 metres long and 15 metres high, may have been among the greatest vaulted halls. British troops not only guaranteed Awadh's security, they also helped enforce the state's revenue demands. Loans extracted from the Awadh government had part-financed several of Company's battles. The annexation of Awadh was most unfair and indefensible. These annexations had dire consequences.

INDIAN MUTINY—1857

What the British termed 'Indian Mutiny' has been called by Indian historians 'the National Uprising' or the 'First War of Independence'.

It began as an uprising in the Company's Bengal army for a different reason. A new rifle was issued to Bengal soldiers for which the cartridges, which had to be rammed down the barrel, were greased with a tallow probably containing both pigs' and cows' fat. These cartridges required to be bitten open with the teeth. To the cow-reverencing Hindus and the pig paranoid Muslim soldiers, the ammunition could not be more disgusting had it been smeared with excrement. The rebellion had taken place in February 1857 but was suppressed. Eighty-five soldiers were court-marshalled in Meerut. However, the next day the soldiers rose as one man to free the arrested soldiers. They began by attacking the British community living in the cantonment. The thatched roofs of the officers' mess were torched.

The conflagration lit in Meerut spread like wild fire in the month of May. The insurgents then headed for Delhi. Old King Bahadur Shah Jafar reigned nominally from the Red Fort, with neither subjects nor troops. The British officers were quickly evicted from the city. Bahadur Shah had little choice but to endorse the insurgents' cause. However, the Sikh soldiers rallied to the British cause.

In the meanwhile, Awadh had erupted and Kanpur had fallen. Agra, Allahabad, Varanasi and Gwalior seethed with discontent. However, a force comprised of British, Sikh and Gorkha units controlled the rebellion in Delhi in September. Two of Bahadur Shah's sons and a grandson were shot dead while in custody. The emperor was exiled to Rangoon where he died later on.

Kashmir's new Maharaja supported the British. But Awadh, where the Nawab was recently dispossessed, became the epicentre of the revolt. Lucknow became the focus of the uprising, and Nana Sahib, the adopted heir of the last Peshwa, emerged as its figurehead. After a three-week siege, he took the surrender of four hundred British people in Kanpur. He also rescued some British women who were abducted during the ensuing chaos.

The Bengal troops stationed at Jhansi had also mutinied. As in Kanpur, the small British community had sought refuge in the Jhansi fort. They were evacuated by the mutineers, and as they straggled out, were promptly massacred. However, Laxmi Bai had played no part in this massacre. The mutineers then marched off to Agra, leaving Laxmi Bai defenceless. She soon found herself challenged both by a rival claimant to her husband's defunct title and by the neighbouring Rajput Rajas of Datia and Orchha. She began raising troops and herself led them in repulsing the assault in September–October 1857. It is notable that the Rani's considerable military reputation was first acquired fighting not the British but local rivals although her force was drawn largely from elements who had aligned themselves with the rebels.

The situation changed in early 1858 with the northward advance of a section of the British Bombay army. The Rani and her advisors rightly presumed that her assertion of sovereignty was threatened and her own safety in danger. Now she definitely became reconciled to rebellion and established contact with Tantya Topi on the Jamuna. When the British laid siege to Jhansi in March, Tantya came to her aid but was repulsed. She led a ferocious resistance but Jhansi fell. She escaped in disguise with a trusty band of followers and rode hard to Kalpi.

In June 1858 Laxmi Bai and Tantiya Topi responded with the boldest move of the whole rebellion. Just when the British thought they had finally dislodged them from Bundelkhand, they seized Gwalior. Scindia himself, while remaining loyal to the British, had been pretending sympathy for the insurgents as a way of detaining the large body of mutinous troops based in Gwalior. Even an appeal in the name of the Peshwa, who was Scindia's superior in the Maratha hierarchy, failed to sway him, but it did serve to disabuse his troops. With their collaboration, Tantya Topi and the Rani entered the city and paid their forces from the accumulated riches.

Unfortunately, after barely three weeks, when the Rani was going round the ramparts of the fort on horseback, she was hit by a spray of bullets as the British launched their assault. She was cremated nearby, 'the only man among the rebels', as one of her British adversaries described her.

During our school days, we used to joyously sing a poem celebrating her bravery: '*Bundele harbolon ke mukh hamane suni kahaani thi/ Khoob lari mardani voh tau Jhansiwali Rani thi.*'

Three days later, the citadel fell and with it the last attempt at concerted action by the insurgents. Tantya roamed through Rajasthan with his followers, but was betrayed and executed.

~

The situation in Lucknow was different. At the end of June 1887, Lucknow had fallen to the insurgents. About 750 European soldiers plus the same number Indian soldiers, besides some 1,400 women, children and servants, had taken refuge in a fortified area around the British Residency on the outskirts of the city. The siege lasted nearly five months, till the fires of rebellion were doused.

William Dalrymple[234] mentions that on the eve of the Great Mutiny of 1857, Lucknow, the capital of the Kingdom of Awadh, was indisputably the largest, most prosperous and most civilized pre-colonial city in India. Its spectacular skyline—with its domes and towers and gilded cupolas, its palaces and pleasure gardens, ceremonial avenues and wide maidans—reminded travellers of Constantinople, Paris or even Venice. The city's courtly Urdu diction and baroque codes of etiquette were renowned as the most subtle and refined in the subcontinent; its dancers were admired as the most accomplished; its cuisine famous as the most flamboyantly elaborate. **Nawab Wajid Ali Shah** was a great author, poet and dancer!

The Bara (Great) Imambara complex was created by **Nawab Asaf-ud-Daula** in 1784 for *Shi'ite* religious discourses. One of the largest vaulted halls in the world, it was actually built in order to create employment during a famine. The whole complex surrounded by the Great Mosque and the Rumi Darwaja exudes a bold, reckless and extravagant self-confidence.

In 1764, before the Nawabs had even established their capital at Lucknow, their armies had already been defeated in the battle by the East India Company. **General Claude Martin**'s great palace-mausoleum, now the La Martiniere school, is perhaps the most gloriously hybrid building in India, part Nawabi fantasy and part Gothic colonial barracks. His mausoleum mixes Georgian colonnades with the loopholes and turrets of a medieval castle; Palladian arches rise to Mughal cupolas; inside, brightly-coloured Nawabi plasterwork encloses Wedgewood plaques of classical European gods and goddesses... The eighteenth century was an anarchic and violent time in India, General Claude Martin had to defend his residence with a pair of cannons filled with grapeshot.

In 1856, a year before the Mutiny, the British had forcibly deposed the last Nawab. Lucknow struck back in 1857, besieging the British in their fortified residency. After nearly two years of siege and disparate hand-to-hand fighting in the streets of Lucknow, the British defeated the Mutineers and wreaked their revenge on the conquered city. Vast areas of the capital of the Nawabs were bulldozed.

[234]Dalrymple, William, *The Age of Kali*, Penguin Books, India, 2004, pp. 26–37.

As noted earlier, unlike the Europeans who came as traders, the Muslims had come to India as invaders—to destroy the ornate temples, break the enshrined diamond-studded idols, loot the fabulous treasures of jewels and gold, and forcibly convert the Hindu infidels to Islam. Unlike them, the British, the Dutch and the Portuguese had come as traders. However, besides doing flourishing trade, the British also succeeded in setting up a powerful Indian empire.

Hordes of evangelists had come in their train. They made beautiful churches in India and were eager to convert, but not forcibly. Indeed, they found many willing converts, due to the basic infirmity at the heart of Hinduism—the *Varna-Ashram Dharma*—which forbade a sizeable section of Hindu population, the *Shudras*, from entering the temples.

SWAMI VIVEKANANDA

After losing her independence and becoming a British colony, even her religion was under threat by the zestful conversions being undertaken by foreign churches. A World Parliament of Religions was to be held in 1893 in Chicago. Swami Vivekananda came to know about it when he was travelling in Gujarat. He had been contemplating to go to the West to raise money for his project of ameliorating the lot of the poor in India. The large-scale conversions of the poor and the down-trodden by foreign missions were causing a turmoil in his mind.

In his view the West needed India's spiritual wealth to solve the existential problems of life and make life meaningful, while India needed to learn science and technology from the West to overcome the rampant poverty of the masses.

Swami Vivekananda was the first of India's *gurus* to address the World Parliament of Religions in 1893. By his inspirational lectures in several of its sessions he earned tremendous prestige for India's religion and culture in the Western world.

Known as Narendranath Datta in his pre-monastic life, he was born on 12 January 1863 in an aristocratic family of Calcutta. His father Vishwanath Datta was a medical practitioner. He studied western philosophy and history and graduated from the Calcutta University.

When he was about 18 years of age, he met **Ramakrishna Paramahansa**, priest of the Kali Temple, on the bank of the Ganga at Dakshineshwar. Sant Ramakrishna had no formal education worth the name, but had a passionate longing for God right from his childhood. He had practiced various spiritual disciplines of Hinduism and even of Islam and Christianity later on. Through direct transcendental experiences, he arrived at the conclusion that the Ultimate Reality, though one, was known under different names.

In December 1881, when Narendranath met Swami Ramakrishna, he asked him: 'Sir, have you seen God?' Ramakrishna replied: 'Yes, I see Him as clearly as I see you—only in a more intense manner!' Their meeting was like the East meeting the West. Ramakrishna was a living embodiment of the ancient sages of yore, representing ancient India characterized by asceticism; Narendranath represented the modern world, characterized by skepticism, rationalism and activism. Young Narendra was instantly won over by Ramakrishna Paramahansa!

He became a frequent visitor to Dakshineshwar. Under the guidance of the Master, he began to take rapid strides on the spiritual path. In July 1884, Narendra Nath's father died unexpectedly, leaving the family in strained circumstances. Some years later even Swami Ramakrishna developed cancer of the throat. His young disciples, including Narendra nursed him. Swami Ramakrishna instilled in these young pupils the spirit of renunciation and brotherly love for one another.

One day, he initiated the process of taking Narendra and some other young men into a monastic brotherhood, giving them ochre robes and sent them to beg food. But the Master passed away in August 1886. Under the leadership of Narendranath, 15 of these young men took formal vows of sanyasa, assuming new names; Narendranath became Swami Vivekananda. The reliquary containing the mortal remains of Sri Ramakrishna was preserved in the new monastery, called the Ramakrishna Math. The monastery has branches all over the world now.

In July 1890 Swami Vivekananda set out on a tour of India, living like a mendicant, begging for food, sometimes having his meal cooked by a cobbler or sharing a smoke with a sweeper, simutaneously living in the palaces of kings on other occasions, discovering the soul of India and trying to find out why she had lost her former glory and grandeur. He was deeply anguished by the abject poverty and backwardness of the masses. It was clear to him that the exploitation of the masses by the upper classes was the main cause of India's downfall.

Owing to the centuries of prejudicial priestcraft and the caste tyranny, the poor masses had lost the sense of individual worth and faith in their inherent powers. They were like helpless bullocks carrying the wheel of exploitation set in motion by the upper classes and castes.

Vivekananda came to understand that their miserable condition was not due to 'religion' in the true sense of the term. For the essence of true religion consisted of eternal truths, discovered by the sages of ancient India, collectively known as Vedanta. The degradation of India took place because these life-giving principles of Vedanta had not been applied in practical life to solve social and national problems and the poor masses had been denied access to these enlightening principles. He gained the conviction that if these spiritual principles were spread among the poor masses, it would awaken the dormant powers in them, and then they would solve their problems themselves.

He realized, however, that what the masses immediately needed was food, and it was not possible to produce enough food by following primitive methods of agriculture. Indians must master western science and technology and methods of organization. He saw the necessity of spreading both spiritual and secular knowledge among the masses, which could be done through a proper system of education. As may be gathered from his letters, he wanted a mass awakening effected through an intensive educational programme.

When he reached Kanya Kumari, the southern-most tip of India, he swam to the huge rock that juts out of the ocean at some distance from the shore, and meditated there for three days and nights. He got a deep conviction that he was destined to play the role of a messenger and pathfinder in the inauguration of a new epoch in the history of mankind by Shri Ramakrishna, the prophet of the modern age. In April 1893, he went to his devoted disciple, the **Raja of Khetri** in Rajasthan to obtain help for his passage to America.

The World Parliament of Religions was held in Chicago to mark the four hundredth anniversary of the discovery of America by Columbus. It was held under the chairmanship of Rev. John Henry Barrows, a distinguished clergyman of the First Presbyterian Church of Chicago. At its inaugural session when the tall and handsome Swami from India, clad in ochre robes, began his address with the words: 'Sisters and Brothers of America', he struck an instantaneous chord with the audience; they cheered him long and lustily during his spirited discourse. He became a celebrity.

He delivered as many as six lectures on Hinduism in the main sessions, on divinity of the soul, on self-realization as the highest fulfillment and lasting peace, and on the principle of harmony of religions. He also addressed the auxiliary sessions in the Scientific Section eight times. Besides, he gave a talk on women in oriental religion.

Margaret Noble (who became his disciple and changed her name as **Sister Nivedita**) made a pithy comment on his addresses: 'Of the Swami's addresses before the Parliament of Religions, it may be said that when he began to speak, it was of the religious ideas of the Hindus, *but when he ended, Hinduism had been recreated.*' (Emphasis added.)

His addresses served to alert international opinion about the subjugation of India by Britain. He returned to India in January 1897 and delivered lectures in different places, from Colombo in the South to Almora in the North, instilling pride in the people in their cultural heritage and reminding them of their duty to the masses.

He founded the Ramakrishna Mission to spread the message of Sage Ramakrishna and Vedanta and shifted the monastery to a new site at Belur in Howrah. In June 1899, he visited the western part of the USA for a year and half. On 4 July 1902, this great son of India breathed his last.

∽

Swami Vivekananda was an apostle of the equality of man and was deeply anguished by man's inhumanity towards man, treating man as a mere cog in the wheel in the industrialized West, and reducing a vast humanity to a servile state of Shudra in India. His exposition of Vedantic doctrine restored the potential divinity of the soul of every man. It later manifested in Gandhiji's concept of Daridra Narayan.

Around the same time in 1882, **Bankim Chandra Chatterjee** published his immensely influential novel, *Ananda Math,* which depicted Muslim tyranny during their rule against the Hindus and Hinduism.

Rabindranath Tagore, the celebrated poet, writer, painter, playwright, philosopher and social reformer reshaped Bengali literature and music. He was an exponent of the Bengal Renaissance and founded the Vishva-Bharati University at Shanti Niketan. He denounced the British Raj and advocated independence from Britain.

His *Gitanjali* (Song Offerings) in Bengali was published in 1910. He then translated it into a prose–poem in English. It was published in 1912 with an introduction by William Butler Yeats. Love is its principal subject; some poems detail the internal conflict between spiritual longings and earthly desires. He was awarded the Nobel Prize for Literature in 1913. He became the first non-European and the first lyricist to win it.

∽

The British had come as traders and modernized India in their own self-interest. They laid out a vast network of roads, railways, telegraph lines to serve the twin ends of efficacy in governance and promotion of trade. The 250 kilometres of railway track laid out by 1856 had become 6,400 kilometres by 1870. In recognition of the fact that the mutineers in 1857 had genuinely feared conversion to Christianity, the British curtailed missionary activity and the funding of missionary schools.

In January 1877, in a vast tented city around the Ridge, where British forces had recaptured Delhi 20 years earlier, the new imperium was solemnized at an Imperial Assemblage. The official attendance of 80,000 celebrities in this grand show included nearly all of India's '63 ruling Princes' and 300 titular chiefs and native gentlemen. **Lord Lytton**, the presiding viceroy, in his address provided a blueprint for all future imperial durbars. He took some delight in listing those present in the durbar—the Princes of Arcot and Tanjore, the principal Talukdars of Oudh, Alor Chiefs of Sindh, Sikh Sardars, Rajputs and Marathas, Arabs from Peshawar, the Maharaja of Cashmere and Jammu, the grandson of Tipu Sultan, the son of the last Nawab of Awadh and 'members of the ex-Royal family of Delhi'.

Lord Lytton read out **Queen Victoria's proclamation of 1858** which specifically disclaimed any 'desire to impose our convictions on any of our subjects' and ordered British officials to abstain from interfering with Indian beliefs and rituals 'on the pain of Our highest displeasure'.

The fiction of Company rule ended then. Queen Victoria was proclaimed the Empress of India; the Governor General became her Viceroy. The doctrine of lapse was abandoned and teaching of English in Indian schools and colleges was introduced to have cheap Babus for running government offices; bringing office staff from Britain was a costly business.

Viceroy Curzon also established the Archeological Survey of India for recording, reviving and preserving what in his opinion was 'the greatest galaxy of monuments in the world.'

With tacit British encouragement the Muslim deputies elected to official bodies, demanded that any future reforms should include separate electorates for Muslims. In 1907 the All-India Muslim League headed by **Aga Khan** was formed. In 1909 **Minto Morley Reforms Act** came into being and Legislative Councils were created in Bombay, Agra and Lahore. However, they had no power to initiate or frustrate legislation; they could merely question and criticize. India remained a British autocracy. Separate electorates for Muslims, who were about 20 per cent of the whole population, were created. This measure ultimately culminated in the bifurcation of India and creation of Pakistan.

Forty-six-year-old Mohandas Karamchand Gandhi returned to India after working as a lawyer for 26 years at Natal in South Africa. He had been working mostly for end-of-indenture settlers and had developed a form of protest which he called *Satyagraha* (Truth-force). To most observers it was 'passive resistance'. He had indeed elevated personal suffering and self-denial into a quasi-religious force. He went to remote north Bihar to win redress for its wretched Indigo cultivators. Later, he led a satyagraha in Gujarat in support of farmers unable to meet the revenue demand. Similarly, he worked for the underpaid textile mill workers. Not all his ventures were successful but it greatly enhanced his reputation and following.

The **First World War** began in 1914. Not only the sycophantic princely states but the Congress and Muslim League gave positive support to Britain. Over 20 lakh Indian soldiers were recruited. British hearts warmed at such massive all-out support.

In 1917, Viceroy Lord Chelmsford and the Liberal Secretary of State, Edwin Montague, came out with a new reform package which came into force in 1921. It promised 'the gradual development of self-governing institutions with a view to the progressive realization of responsible government in India as an integral part of the British Empire.'

SLOW MARCH TO FREEDOM

Lord Lytton's 1877 Imperial Assemblage in Delhi had coincided with the worst famine of the century in India which claimed over 5 million lives in South India. Around this time Swami Dayananda Saraswati's movement of 'Arya Samaj' was making spectacular advances in the Punjab, rekindling the flame of freedom from bondage. He also initiated the process of translating the Vedas in Hindi, while scholars like Max Muller, the Oxford Professor of Sanskrit,[235] began translating them into English. Other renowned scholars from European countries also translated them in their languages.

Even devotional gatherings and fairs contributed to the awakening of national spirit. In Maharashtra the allegiance of Pune's Brahmins would see their festivals transformed into political protest gatherings and their cults being promoted as nationalist propaganda. The novels of Bengali writers and other literary creations led to Hindu renaissance which often bracketed British rule with that of the Muslim emperors.

In John Keay's opinion 'it was the mainstream political groupings of Calcutta, Bombay and Pune, heavily influenced by **Dadabhai Naoroji** and his associates, which first urged the need for a national congress. Naoroji had become a Westminster MP and had represented Indian opinion in London.[236] The organization of a 'National Congress' had come into existence at the time of Lord Ripon's send-off demonstrations in the winter of 1884, and Allen Octavian Hume was regarded by the British authorities as the prime instigator.

Founded by Allen Octavian Hume, who had served as Agriculture Secretary in Calcutta government, the first meeting of the **Indian National Congress** was held in 1885. Most of the actors of the independence movement from Dadabhai Naoroji, Mohandas Karamchand Gandhi, Mohammad Ali Jinnah, Jawaharlal Nehru were educated in Britain's educational institutions and were 'returnees' to India. The power base of Ferozeshah Mehta and Gopal Krishna Gokhale was amongst the Bombay intelligentsia. Meanwhile radicals like Bal Gangadhar Tilak gravitated towards it from his power base around Pune.

Hindu politics emerged from the corporate urban life of the later nineteenth century, in the guise of Hindu Mahasabha of 1930s or

---

[235]Keay, John, *India: A History*, Harper Collins, Delhi, 2000, p. 458.
[236]Ibid. 455.

indeed the 'Jana Sangh' in the 1970s and its later transformation into Bhartiya Janata Party (BJP). Similar links are traced between Muslim associations of service gentry and membership of the later Muslim League. All these movements and associations would endow the political struggle with strong spiritual, cultural and social undertones.

~

The Indian National Congress existed as an annual gathering in the first decade. It met over the Christmas break, thereby ensuring that the professional careers of the lawyers, journalists and civil servants who attended, were not unduly disrupted. Its resolutions focused on national, as opposed to local or communal, issues around which delegates could be expected to unite. Its hopes lay with the London lobbying of the likes of Dadabhai Noaroji.

In 1893 the Westminster Parliament acceded to Indian National Congress demands for entrance examination into the elite Indian Civil Service to be held in India as well as England. However, the decision was aborted later on.

Gokhale, a lecturer at Bombay University, and Mehta, a Parsi lawyer, accepted the need for patience and moved easily between presidency of Congress and membership of Viceroy's Council. Tilak, on the other hand, from the same Brahmin community that had furnished the Maratha state with its Peshwas, experimented with a variety of mass-focus appeals through his editorship of his Marathi newspaper. They included the politicization of fairs and festivals associated with the local cult of Ganapati (Ganesh) and a patriotic crusade based on the defiance of Shivaji. He was imprisoned for his extreme rhetoric and came into the limelight.

~

PARTITION OF BENGAL

The **partition of Bengal** in 1905 by Lord Curzon had sparked the first nationwide protest movement. Bengal was the most populous and most troublesome administrative unit in British India. With population twice that of the Great Britain, it was predominantly

Hindu in the west and Muslim in the east. Curzon divided Bengal for ease of governance. Hindu dominated West Bengal was joined with Odisha and Bihar and Muslim dominated East Bengal was merged with Assam. He actually wanted to separate the highly vocal critics of Bengal. Simultaneously he announced that Delhi was to replace Calcutta as British India's capital.

He did not realize that the bond of the sonorous Bengali language transcended the religious divide in Bengal. Besides, in West Bengal, joined with Odisha and Bihar, the Muslims would be a linguistic minority. Similarly, in East Bengal, joined with Assam, they would also be a religious minority.

Mass rallies clogged the thoroughfares of Calcutta, Dacca and other Bengali towns. Import of British textiles was boycotted. Those on sale were publicly destroyed. Indian mills prospered and handloom weavers rejoiced. Disaffection was created even between 'extremists' like Tilak and 'moderates' like Gokhale. The extremists were famously known as 'Lal, Bal and Pal'—Lala Lajpat Rai, the militant Arya Samaj leader from Panjab, the fiery Maratha crusader Bal Gangadhar Tilak and the radical Bengali leader Bipin Chandra Pal.

Bipin Chandra Pal edited the journal *Bande Mataram*, named after the patriotic Bengali anthem written by Bankim Chandra Chatterjee and set to music by Tagore. Lala Lajpat Rai was deported to Mandalay without trial in 1907, followed by Bal Gangadhar Tilak, which brought Bombay's industries to a standstill. Even Aurobindo Ghose was brought to trial but he found a sanctuary from British rule in Pondicherry, which was under French rule and where he would set up 'Auroville'. Clandestine revolutionary groups headed by Vir Savarkar, Rashbehari Bose, had also cropped up later on.

Gopal Krishna Gokahale protested against the division of Bengal: 'The scheme of partition, connoted in the dark and carried out in the face of the fiercest opposition that any government measure has encountered in the last half-a-century, will always stand as a complete illustration of the worst features of the present system of bureaucratic rule—its utter contempt of public opinion, its arrogant pretensions of superior wisdom, its reckless disregard of the most cherished feelings of the people, the mockery of an appeal in its sense of justice, and its cold preference of Service interests to those of the governed.'[237]

Mass rallies clogged the thoroughfares of Calcutta, Dacca and Bengali towns. Protest against imported products like British textiles took the shape of boycott; Lancashire manufacturers fumed. Japan's sensational victory over a major European power in the 1905 Russo-Japanese war fanned the movement. In the 1906 session of the Congress under Dadabhai Naoroji's chairmanship one resolution boldly called for *Swaraj* (self-rule).

Curzon had resigned as viceroy within days of the Bengal partition. In 1907, All India Muslim League was formed, headed by Agha Khan. It raised its voice against the under representation of Muslims among those Indians already elected to official bodies and raised a demand for separate electorates for Muslims. They also wanted a weighted system of representation in proportion to the Muslim population. This demand had British encouragement.

Morley–Minto Reform Indian Councils Act of 1909 was brought in to extend the principle of representative institutions. The so-called Legislative Councils were formed. But they were not legislatures and had no power to initiate or frustrate legislation; they could merely question and criticize. They had made a provision for reservation of 20 per cent seats for Muslims.

~

When the **First World War** began, both the Congress and the Muslim League offered enthusiastic support to Britain. Over two lakh Indian troops and support staff would serve overseas. At that time M.K. Gandhi had landed in India from South Africa. He went to north Bihar to win redress for the poor indigo cultivators, who reminded him of Natal's indentured labourers. In 1917, he led a satyagraha on behalf of farmers who were unable to meet the revenue demand, and thereafter organized another satyagraha on behalf of the underpaid mill-workers in Ahmedabad.

During his Bihar campaign he was joined by a lawyer, Rajendra Prasad, the future president of India. In Ahmedabad, Gandhiji met

[237]Keay, John, *India: A History,* Harper Collins, India, 2000, p. 465.

a Gujarati landlord and lawyer, Vallabhbhai Patel, India's future deputy prime minister. Gandhiji, in his simple dress of home-spun khadi that barely covered him, and his austere lifestyle, resembled a religious sadhu. Rabindranath Tagore coined the epithet of 'mahatma' (Great Soul) for him, which aptly suited him.

JALLIANWALA BAGH

At the end of world-war, the government brought out the Rowlatt Act which resumed the power of preventive detention and summary trial. It belied the spirit of imminent reforms. Gandhi declared his first satyagraha against it. On 6 April 1919, nationwide *hartal* (lock-out) was observed which had mixed results.

In Amritsar, the holy city of the Sikhs, two local leaders had addressed a public gathering on the day of the hartal; they were arrested for incitement. On 11 April 1919, their supporters came out in the streets. When they were fired on by the troops, the crowd went rampant and took revenge in an orgy of arson and violence which left five Europeans dead. Sir Michael O'Dwyer, Lieutenant Governor, sent for more troops. Sir Michael and Brigadier General Reginald Dyer stationed pickets throughout the city and issued orders prohibiting all meetings and demonstrations.

On 13 April, a Sunday, which also happened to be the feast day of Baisakhi, several hundred people had assembled in the Jallianwala Bagh—which was an open space hemmed in by houses—to celebrate this popular Spring Festival. Dyer probably knew nothing about this important Hindu festival. He suspected treason. His armoured vehicle couldn't enter the arena because of the narrow passage. He therefore marched in with his troops and ordered them to fire upon the crowd. He ordered cease fire only after exhausting all ammunition. Then he withdrew.

Dyer had given no warning before firing and the army was occupying the only exit. The people had no escape. The wounded were left unattended, the dead uncounted. The official inquiry concluded that 1,650 rounds were fired, over 1,200 men, women and children were seriously wounded and 379 had died. An equally reliable but unofficial source gave the count of the dead as 530.

The massacre had happened before imposition of martial rule. When Dyer was later questioned, he seemed proud of his action. His intention, he said, was to exact revenge for the previous killings and make an example which would deter further defiance anywhere in the Punjab. Dyer's family ran a brewery near Shimla. Although relieved of his command, he was never formally punished. In England he was rewarded as 'the saviour of the Punjab!'.

The Jallianwala Bagh massacre proved to be a turning point in the freedom movement. Rabindranath Tagore renounced his knighthood. Motilal Nehru stripped off European furniture from his palacial residence in Allahabad, and abandoning his Savile Row suits, took to wearing clothes of homespun cotton recommended by Gandhiji. The suits, dresses, ties, boas and homburgs were thrown in a bonfire.

GHADAR PARTY

Ghadar (Mutiny) was the title of a weekly newspaper which had been circulating widely among expatriate Indians in the Far East and North America. It was being published by an outfit named 'Ghadar Party'. The organization was founded in the USA but was now operating from the British Columbia. The subtitle of the paper was 'Enemy of the British Government'.

When the World War broke out, a Singapore business man, who was an adherent of the Gadhar Party, had chartered a Japanese steamer to carry 300 passengers, mostly Sikhs, to Vancouver. But the Canadian authorities did not permit it to land, and the steamer was diverted. It disembarked at Budge Budge, a port on the Hooghly River below Calcutta, in September 1914. The British authorities got suspicious. British Troops escorted the passengers ashore and, when some attempted to reach Calcutta, they opened fire. 22 persons were killed; the rest were sent by train to the Punjab and were kept under surveillance.

By 1916 about 5,000 Ghadrite activists had been rounded up. Of those who stood trial in the Panjab, 46 were hanged and 200 transported or jailed. Their sympathizers in Indian troops in

Singapore were court-marshalled in 1915, and 37 of them faced a firing squad. These lowly Ghadar peasant and sepoy heroes have been much less remembered than the Bhadralok Bengal terrorists—yet surely they deserve a better fate.[238]

A Punjabi boy, Bhagat Singh, born in a family of freedom fighters a few years before, remembered the Ghadrite heroes, like Kartar Singh Saraba, who was hanged at the age of 19. The Ghadar Movement had left a deep impression on his mind. Bhagat Singh was just 12 years old when the mass-massacre of Jallianwala Bagh happened. He went there, kissed the earth sanctified by the martyr's blood, and brought back a handful of the blood-soaked soil. He used to wonder why the millions of Indians could not drive away a handful of invaders.

He met Sukhdev and Rajguru, and with the help of Sukhdev's brother Chandra Shekhar Azad formed the Hindustan Socialist Republican Party. The aim was not only to make India independent but also to create a Socialist Republic.

Chandra Shekhar Azad was born on 23 July 1906 as Chandra Shekhar Tewari. He was admitted to Kashi Vidyapeeth, Banaras. In 1921, when the Non-Cooperation Movement was at its height, Chandra Shekhar, a 15-year-old student then, joined it. He was arrested and produced before the Parasee District Magistrate. He gave his name as Chandra Shekhar '*Azad*' [Free] his father's name as '*Swatantra*' [Freedom] and his residence as 'Jail'. The angered district magistrate ordered him to be detained in jail for 23 weeks and ordered him to be punished with 15 lashes a day.

~

Gandhiji had suspended the Non-Cooperation Movement in 1922, which disappointed Chandra Shekhar Azad. He met a young revolutionary, Manmath Nath Gupta who introduced him to Ram Prasad Bismil. Bismil had formed the Hindustan Republican Association (HRA). Azad started to collect funds for Bismil's HRA, mostly through robberies of banks and government properties. He was involved in the Kakori Train Robbery of 1925. He avoided

[238]Sarkar, Sumit, *Modern India*, Laxmi Publications, 2008, p. 148.

capture but his fellow comrades, Ashfaqulla Khan, Thakur Roshan Singh and Rajendra Nath Lahiri were caught and sentenced to death.

In 1928 Chandra Shekhar Azad was involved in the murder of John P. Saunders at Lahore to avenge the brutal killing of Lala Lajpat Rai at an anti-British procession. Azad was also involved in an attempt to blow up the Viceroy of India's train in 1929.

On 27 February 1931, the CID head of the police at Allahabad (now Prayagraj), Sir J.R.H. Nott-Bower, was tipped off by some one, that Chandra Shekhar Azad was at the Alfred Park with a fellow revolutionary, Sukhdev Raj. Bower arrived with a large police contingent and surrounded the Alfred Park (also called the Company Bagh). Thakur Vishweshwar Singh, the DSP, entered the park armed with rifles and the shoot-out began. Azad's companion had escaped, uninjured. Azad hid behind a huge mango tree and began to fire at the police from behind it. Both Bower and DSP Vishweshwar Singh received injuries. Azad then aimed the last bullet of his pistol at his own head and collapsed. The DSP recovered Azad's body and cremated it secretly at Rasulabad Ghat without informing anyone.

∽

In 1928, **Bhagat Singh** had made a dramatic escape from Lahore to Calcutta and from there to Agra, where he established a bomb-making factory, which was prohibited by the British government under the Trades Dispute Act. It was to protest against the passing of this 'Act' that he, Sukhdev and Rajguru threw bombs in the Central Assembly Hall in New Delhi (now called Lok Sabha Bhawan) when the Central Assembly was in session. The bombs did not hurt anyone, but the noise they made was enough to wake up an enslaved nation from deep sleep.

After throwing the bombs, Bhagat Singh and his friend did not try to escape; they deliberately courted arrest. They had also thrown printed leaflets in the Assembly Hall, which said: 'We are sorry that we, who attach such great sanctity to human life, we, who dream of a glorious future when man will be enjoying perfect peace and full liberty, have been forced to shed human blood. But sacrifice of the individuals at the altar of the Revolution will bring freedom to all, rendering exploitation of man by man impossible.

Inquilab Zindabad! [Long Live Revolution!]'

During his trial, Bhagat Singh refused to employ any defence counsel. They were awarded the death sentence and hanged in the early hours of 23 March 1931. When standing at the gallows, the three friends were smiling and chattering, their faces lit up in the morning glow. I remember the opening verse of a song they used to sing in those days:

> *Mera rang de Basanti chola;*
> *Maa-ye, mera rang de Basanti chola!*
>
> [Drench my shirt in the festive colours of Spring, O my Mother!]

It was composed by Pundit Ram Prasad Bismil, a fellow freedom fighter. After Bhagat Singh's supreme sacrifice, some lines in his memory were added:

> *Jis chole ko pahan Bhagat Singh khela apni jaan par!*
>
> [Wearing which colourful shirt, Bhagat Singh played with his life!
> Drench my shirt in the festive colours of Spring, O my Mother!]

Later on, in films on Bhagat Singh, another sacrificial song composed by Bismil Azimabadi, was used:

> *Sarfaroshi ki tamanna ab hamare dil mein hai,*
> *Dekhna hai zor kitna bazuai kaatil mein hai.*
>
> [In my heart I cherish the desire to get my head chopped off!
> Let us see how much strength is there in the Slayer's hand!]

~

THE STIRRING SAGA OF SUBHAS BOSE

Subhas Chandra Bose was the most lustrous star of India's freedom movement. His father Janakinath Bose was a leading lawyer and government pleader at Cuttack, headquarters of the Odisha Division of Bengal Province of British India. Subhas was a brilliant student;

he had secured second position in the matriculation examination conducted under the auspices of the University of Calcutta. After securing high marks in the Intemediate examination, he joined the Presidency College, Calcutta to study philosophy.

In the class, Professor E.F. Oaten made some rude remarks about Indian culture and collared and pushed some students. A few days later, Professor Oaten was accosted on a stairway by some students and thrashed. A college servant testified to seeing Subhas among the fleeing boys. He was expelled from the Presidency College, but was allowed to join Sottish Church College. He did his BA honours in Philosophy, graduated with first class and was placed second in the merit list of the University.

His father sent him to England in 1919 to prepare for and appear in the Indian Civil Service (ICS) examination. Subhas wanted to study at the University of Cambridge, but his application was past the deadline for admission. He therefore joined the Non-Collegiate Students Board and began studying for Mental and Moral Sciences Tripos of Cambridge University.

There were six vacancies in the ICS that year. Subhas took the open competitive examination in 1920 and was placed fourth in the merit list. This was the first step. Still remaining was a final examination in 1921 on more topics on India, including the Indian Penal Code, the Indian Evidence Act, Indian History and an Indian language.

The goal appeared achievable, but he was assailed by doubts about entering the ICS. He wrote to his father about it: 'It is not possible to serve one's country in the best and fullest manner if one is chained on to the civil service.' Afterwards, in April 1921, he wrote to the Secretary of the State for India to remove his name from the list of probationers in the ICS. He took his Cambridge BA final examination, cleared it and returned to India.

He met Gandhiji who was leading the non-cooperation movement at the time, in Bombay. He differed with Gandhi on the question of means to achieve independence. For Gandhi, only non-violent means were acceptable for achieving anti-colonial ends. Gandhiji sent him to C.R. Das, in whom Subhas found the leader of his choice. Das was more flexible than Gandhi and more sympathetic to extremism, that attracted idealistic young men like Subhash. C.R. Das launched him into nationalist politics. Subhash would work within the ambit of the Indian National Congress politics for nearly 20 years even as he tried to change its course.

Subhas started the newspaper *Swaraj*; his mentor, Chittaranjan Das, was a spokesman of aggressive nationalism in Bengal. Chittaranjan Das was elected as mayor of Calcutta Municipal Corporation and Subhash became its CEO. However, in a round up of nationalists in 1925, Subhash was arrested and sent to prison in Mandalay. He contracted tuberculosis there.

After his release he became general secretary of the Congress and worked with Jawaharlal Nehru. In December 1928, he organized the meeting of the Indian National Congress in Calcutta, and acted as the General Officer Commanding (GOC) of the volunteer corps, donning a military dress. The famous Bengali writer Nirad Chaudhuri wrote about it in the newpapers: 'Bose organized a volunteer corps in uniform, its officers wore steel-cut epaulettes ... His uniform was made by a firm of British tailors in Calcutta—Harman's. A telegram addressed to him as GOC was delivered to the British General in Fort Williams. However, Mahatma Gandhi as a sincere pacifist did not like the strutting, clicking of boots and saluting and he afterwards described the Calcutta session as a "circus", which caused a great deal of indignation among the Bengalis.'

Some time later, Bose was again arrested and jailed for civil disobedience. After his release in 1930, he became the Mayor of Calcutta. In mid-1930s, he travelled in Europe and met Benito Mussolini. He observed Mussolini's party organization and saw communism and fascism in action. Later he published a book in London in 1935, *The Indian Struggle*, covering India's independence movement in the years 1920–1934. The British government banned it out of fears that it would encourage unrest.

In 1939, Subhas Bose agreed to accept nomination as Congress President. Gandhi opposed it; his preferred candidate was Pattabhi Sitaramayya. Subhas was elected president against Gandhi's wishes. Muthu Ramalinga Thevar had mobilized all South Indian votes for Bose.

However, Subhas resigned as president later on, and organized **All**

India Forward Bloc, a faction within the Congress fold. At Muthu Ramalinga Thevar's invitation, he visited Madurai. Thevar had organized a massive rally for his reception. After meeting Mussolini, Subhas had come to believe that after achieving independence, India needed socialist authoritarianism for at least two decades.

On the outbreak of World War II, Subhas Bose advocated a campaign of mass civil disobedience to protest against Viceroy Lord Linlithgow's decision to declare war on India's behalf without consulting the Congress leadership. But Gandhi was against the idea. Bose organized mass protests in Calcutta. He was thrown into jail but was released following a seven-day hunger strike by him in the jail.

On the night of 16 January 1941, Subhas Bose escaped to Germany, dressed as a *Pathan*, via Afghanistan and Soviet Union. He was advised by his Afghan friends to act as deaf and dumb as he could not speak a word of their language, Pashto. From Moscow, he reached Rome on an Italian passport of an Italian nobleman. The German ambassador in Moscow, Count von der Schulenburg flew him on to Berlin in a special courier aircraft.

Subhas founded the 'Free India Centre' in Berlin, and created the Indian Legion (consisting of 4,500 soldiers) out of Indian prisoners of war who had fought for the British in North Africa prior to their capture by Axis forces. Its members swore allegiance both to Hitler and Bose: 'I swear by God this holy oath that I will obey the leader of the German race and state, Adolf Hitler, as the commander of the German armed forces in the fight for India, whose leader is Subhas Chandra Bose.'

Schenkl, wife of Subhas, came and joined him in the luxurious residence provided to him by Hitler. In November 1942, she gave birth to their daughter. In February 1943, Bose left Schenkl and their baby daughter and boarded a German submarine to travel, via transfer to a Japanese submarine, to Japanese-occupied Southeast Asia. He had been disheartened to know that the German army was retreating now, and Hitler's tanks were rolling across the Soviet border. It meant that the German army would be in no position to offer him help in driving the British from India.

In July 1943, expatriate nationalist leader Rash Behari Bose met Subhas in Singapore to hand over control of the disbanded Indian National Army (INA), which was revived by Subhas. At a rally of the 'Azad Hind Fauj' in Burma in July 1944, he gave his most famous call in Hindi: '*Tum mujhe khoon do; mein tumhen azadi doonga!*' [You give me blood; I shall give you freedom!]

The Japanese had taken possession of the Andaman and Nicobar Islands in 1942. After reaching there Subhas came to know that the Japanese had no intention of handing over their possession to him; they wanted to retain it. Indeed, at that time they were torturing Dr Diwan Singh for his 'Indian Independence League' in the cellular jail, who later died there.

Subhas Chandra Bose died on 18 August 1945 when his overloaded Japanese plane crashed in Japanese-ruled Formosa (now Taiwan). There was wide speculation that it was a conspiracy engineered by the Japanese. The bomber aircraft, with Bose on board, had taken off at around 2.30 p.m. During take-off, it strayed from the standard path taken by aircrafts and the mechanics on the tarmac saw something falling out of the plane. It was the portside engine of the plane, or a part of it, and its propeller. The plane swung around wildly to the right and plummeted, crashing and breaking into two, and exploding into flames.

Inside, the chief pilot, the co-pilot and Lt General Tsunamas Shidei, Vice Chief of Staff of the Japanese Kwantung Army, who was to have made the negotiations for Bose with the Soviet Army in Manchuria, were instantly killed. Bose's assistant Habibur Rahman who was accompanying him, had also passed out. Subhas, although conscious and not fatally hurt, but soaked in gasoline. As he exited, his gasoline-soaked clothes instantly ignited, and he looked like a human-torch as he came out of the plane. His face was badly burnt but he was conscious.

At the hospital, the doctors applied ointment on his burnt body and bandaged it, gave him injections and blood transfusion. But he soon went into coma and passed away in a few hours. A memorial to him was created in the Rankoji Temple, Tokyo; his ashes are stored in a golden pagoda in the temple.[239]

[239]I have sourced the story through a Google search.

PARTITION OF INDIA

MURDER OF MAHATMA GANDHI

Independence dawned on 15 August 1947. India was partitioned to create a new country, Pakistan, for the Muslims. Pakistan had two parts, in the East and West of India, and was inaugurated in Lahore on 14 August by viceroy Lord Mountbatten. Mohmmad Ali Jinnah was sworn in as the president of Pakistan. Mountbatten had wished to be accepted as Governor General of both successor states. This was not acceptable to Jinnah, who called himself *Quaid-i-Azam* (Supreme Leader). He assumed the role of Pakistan's first governor-general as well as the president of its Constituent Assembly.

Early next morning, on 15 August 1947, Jawaharlal Nehru unfurled the tricolour at Delhi and was administered the oath of office of the Prime Minister of India by Governor General Mountbatten. Nehru delivered a poetic speech:

> Long years ago, we made a tryst with destiny, and now the time comes when we shall redeem our pledge, not wholly or in full measure but substantially. At the stroke of midnight hour, when the world sleeps, India will awake to life and freedom. A moment comes, which comes but rarely in history, when we step out from the old to the new, when an age ends, and when the soul of a nation, long suppressed, finds utterance. It is fitting that at this solemn moment we take the pledge of dedication to the service of India and her people and to the still larger cause of humanity.

Sardar Vallabha Bhai Patel was sworn in as deputy prime minister.

∽

The new boundary of India and Pakistan, drawn up in great haste under an English judge, Sir Cyril Radcliffe, was not announced until after the Independence celebrations were over. The Sikhs had demanded that the line of partition make an exception for sites and shrines important to them by virtue of religious or historical associations. They wanted that Lahore, Maharaja Ranjit singh's erstwhile capital, should not simply be allocated to Pakistan because its population was predominantly Muslim. That was not considered. The announcement regarding the new boundaries came on 17 August. The flow of refugees, of the Sikhs and Hindus from the newly created Pakistan to what remaind of India, and of Muslims from India to Pakistan became a flood. As the violence escalated, ghost trains chuffed silently across the new frontier carrying nothing but corpses.

East to west and west to east, about 10 million people fled for their lives in the greatest exodus in recorded history.

~

British India had many princely states which were governed by local pinces. Serious problems of integration arose only in respect of three such states.

Junagarh in the Saurashtra peninsula of Gujarat was predominantly Hindu. It proudly possessed the Ashoka rock at Girnar but its ruler was Muslim who kept a large kennel of about 800 prized species. To the nuptial of a favourite golden retriever, he had invited 50,000 guests. Being Muslim, he opted for union with Pakistan. But seeing an Indian army unit at his border, he flew to Pakistan with only four canine companions plus a few occupants of his royal harem. Pakistan protested but was unwilling to go to war over Junagarh.

An identical situation, but of vastly greater import, developed in **Hyderabad**. The Nizam and his court were Muslim but its population was largely Hindu. The Nizam prevaricated over joining Pakistan or India or to opt for independence. Delhi offered him a year's grace to decide. It proved to be but a stay of execution. In September 1948, Indian troops unceremoniously rolled across the state borders. Pakistan protested but the Nizam signed the merger document on the dotted line.

Jammu and Kashmir was a princely state ruled by the Dogra

(Hindu) Maharaja. The Jammu region was mainly inhabited by Hindus while the Kashmir region was over-whelmingly Muslim. Besides some parts of the state like Ladakh were predominantly Buddhist. Immediately after the creation of Pakistan, armed Muslim tribals bordering Jammu and Kashmir had launched a nefarious attack on the state. Armed by Pakistan and openly assisted by the Pakistan Army, they were advancing towards its capital, Sri Nagar.

The Hindu Maharaja of Jammu and Kashmir requested India for help and the Indian army along with the state army began resisting their advance. The Muslims in Pakistan were saying: '*Hans ke liya hai Pakistan; lad ke lainge Hindustan!*' (We have taken Pakistan with a smile; we'll take Hindustan by fighting.) Units of Indian army were sent to sort out the intruders.

At that time the issue of the payment of cash balance of ₹55 crores rupees due to Pakistan was under discussion and negotiation with Pakistan. In those days ₹5 = £1; ₹55,00,00,000 was a considerable sum. Inevitably, the issue had got linked with Pakistan's aggression on Kashmir. Pakistan would use the money in procuring sophisticated arms from foreign countries for equipping and mobilizing its forces against India. In a press statement on 12 January 1948, deputy prime minister Sardar Patel had put forward India's case in unequivocal terms:

'We are fully justified in providing against aggressive actions in regard to Kashmir by postponing the implementation of the agreement. The agreement does not bind the Government of India to any fixed date for payment. Pakistan would not be justified in any way in insisting on our paying the cash balances at this juncture. I have made it clear that we would not agree to any payment until the Kashmir affair was settled.'

~

Gandhiji was staying in Delhi's Birla House in those days. On the day Sardar Patel's statement appeared in newspapers, Gandhiji said in his prayer meeting in the evening that he had tried to persuade the Government of India to revoke this decision and make the payment to Pakistan but had failed. He added: 'But a time comes when a worshipper of Ahimsa is forced to start fast in order to express his opposition to any injustice to the society. He does so because he being a worshipper of Ahimsa has no other course open to him. Such a critical moment has come for me!'

He went on a fast unto death. His condition was deteriorating and on 17 January, the Indian government issued a Press statement agreeing to pay the money to Pakistan: 'In view of the appeal made by Gandhiji, the Government has decided to remove the cause of friction...and implement immediately the financial agreement with Pakistan in regard to cash balances.'

Thirteen days later, on 30 January 1948, Gandhiji was brutally murdered by Nathuram Godse in his prayer meeting at Birla House in Delhi, plunging the whole nation in grief. I have got the book, *Why I Assassinated Gandhi*, by Nathuram Godse. It has actually been put together by his brother Gopal Godse.[240]

The editor's note at the beginning of this book states: 'In the late Nineteen Seventies I came across a book "*Murder of the Mahatma and other cases from a Judge's Note Book*" written by Justice G.D. Khosla. He was one of the three judges who pronounced death sentence to Nathu Ram Godse. It was a fascinated narrative by a Judge who had interrogated the main accused to find out his real motive and had witnessed the reaction of the audience. According to him (Justice G.D. Khosla) if the audience of the court were entrusted with the task of deciding Godse's appeal, they would have brought in a verdict of not guilty by an overwhelming majority. Such was the powerful defence, that Godse moved the audience in his favour.'

Godse did not engage any lawyer in his defence; he had pleaded his own case. 'I have nothing but the purest interest of our nation at my heart in taking the extreme step against the person of Gandhiji, who was the most responsible and answerable person

[240]Godse, Nathuram, *Why I Assassinated Gandhi*, Surya Bharati Prakashan, Delhi, 2014.

for the terrible event culminating in the creation of Pakistan.[241]

'Even after the establishment of Pakistan if this Gandhian Government had taken any steps to protect the interests of Hindus in Pakistan it could have been possible for me to control my mind which was terribly shaken on account of this terrible deception of the people... Every day that dawned, brought forth the news about thousands of Hindus being massacred, Sikhs numbering 15,000 having been shot dead... Thousands and thousands of Hindus had to run away for their lives and they had lost everything of theirs.

'A long line of refugees extending over the length of 40 miles was moving towards India... Gandhiji did not even by a single word protest and censure the Pakistan Government or the Muslims concerned. The Muslim atrocities (were) resorted to in Pakistan to root out the Hindu culture and the Hindu society...now Gandhiji has started his fast unto death...

'Had Gandhiji maintained his opposition to the creation of Pakistan, the Muslim League could have had no strength to claim it and the Britishers also could not have created it in spite all their utmost efforts for its establishment... The people of this country were eager and vehement in their opposition to Pakistan; the Muslim League could have had no strength for the creation of Pakistan. Gandhiji failed in carrying out his duties as the Father of the Nation. He has proved to be the Father of Pakistan. It was for this reason alone that I, as a dutiful son of Mother India, thought it my duty to put an end to the life of the so-called Father of the Nation, who had played a very prominent part in bringing about the vivisection of the country—Our Motherland!'[242]

Nathuram Godse also thought that a sovereign government was being prevented by Gandhiji from taking policy decisions in national interest; it was therefore imperative to eliminate him.

∽

On 30 January 1948, when Gandhiji was coming for his prayer meeting in the evening, accompanied by two young girls, in the

---

[241]Ibid. 112–19.
[242]Ibid. pp. 115–17.

compound of Birla House, Nathuram Vinayak Godse fired three shots at point blank range. Gandhiji fell to the ground, with a faint '*ahh*', losing consciousness and breathed his last in a few minutes. After firing the shots, Nathuram made no attempt to escape; he raised his hand that was holding the pistol, and called the police guards and voluntarily surrendered to the authorities.

He was taken to the police station on Parliament Street, and was pacing up and down in the lock-up. Several people had gathered there. On catching sight of a person, Nathuram came near the bars and asked him: 'You are Shri Devadas Gandhi, I suppose?'

It *was* Devadas Gandhi; he was surprised and asked: 'Yes, but how did you recognize me?'

Godse replied: 'We had gone together very recently at a press-conference. You had gone there as the editor of *The Hindustan Times*.'

'And you?' Devadas asked.

'I am Nathuram Vinayak Godse, editor of a daily, *Hindu Rashtra*. I too was present there. Today you have lost your father; I am the cause of that tragedy. I am greatly grieved at the bereavement that has befallen on you and your family. Kindly believe me. I was not prompted to do this due to any personal hatred or any grudge or with any ill intention towards you.'

'Then why did you do it?'

'The reason is purely political.'

The police did not allow further discussion.

~

In his long written-statement, Godse emphasized upon the sympathy Mahatma Gandhi had for the Muslims, who had got the country divided. But Gandhiji was still interfering on their behalf. He referred to the State of Hyderabad, which had been amalgamated in India in the meanwhile: 'The problem of the State of Hyderabad which had been unnecessarily delayed and postponed has been rightly solved by our Government by the use of armed forces after the demise of Gandhiji.'

He added: 'I am prepared to admit that Gandhiji had undergone sufferings for the sake of the nation. He did bring about an awakening in the minds of people. He also did nothing for personal gain but it pains me to say that he was not honest enough to acknowledge the defeat and failure of the principle of non-violence for all our problems... It should be realized that it will never bring prosperity to India with a State (like Pakistan) founded on fanatically blind religious faith and basis for its creation'.

He ended his written statement by reiterating: 'It is a fact that in the presence of a crowd numbering 300 to 400 people, I did fire shots at Gandhiji in open daylight. I did not make any attempt to run away. In fact, I never entertained any idea of running away. I did not try to shoot myself, it was never my intention to do so, for it was my ardent desire to give vent to my thoughts in an open court.'

The arguments of the prosecution and the defence commenced on 1 December 1948 and continued day to day. Nathuram Godse argued his own case. At the trial Nathuram Godse had said, 'the two bullets that killed Gandhiji were from his pistol', while the medical report had found three bullets. C.K. Daphtary, the prosecution lawyer, submitted that the argument of 'two bullets' was being put forward by the accused (Nathuram) in order to make ground for 'benefit of doubt'.

Nathuram promptly stood up and replied: 'The pistol was automatic. The trigger was pressed once. Whether two bullets passed or three, is immaterial, for even one was sufficient, and that one was fired by me. If on this discrepancy any "benefit of doubt" accrues, the same may be granted to the prosecution.'

Again, in the midst of his arguments, C.K. Daphtary referred to the incident of the assassination as an 'immoral act'. Nathuram Godse stood up, taking strong exception to it and deposed:

> At least as far as this case is concerned, the Prosecution has no right to discuss the morality of the act; nor does this court, I humbly submit, have any jurisdiction to decide that issue. The concepts of morality would be seen to be

> changing from society to society, from country to country and from century to century. In a particular society it would be considered immoral for women not to use the veil (*parda, naqab*), but not in others. In some countries drinking liquors would not be considered immoral at all, in others it might be otherwise. In a certain century teaching Vedic lore to the non-Brahmins might have been looked upon as highly immoral, but today it is not. Such is the way concepts of morality go on changing. Nobody, therefore, will be able to determine any standard norm for judging morality or immorality for all times, irrespective of country or climate.
>
> The court only has jurisdiction to decide the legality or otherwise of my action but, in so far as morality is concerned, it is a matter of my conviction that what I did was wholly moral and upon those convictions this Court has no jurisdiction.

At the very outset Nathuram Godse had said: 'I do not desire any mercy to be shown to me. I do not also wish that anyone on my behalf should beg for mercy towards me.'

The only false statement Nathuram Godse had given in his lengthy written statement was that there was no conspiracy for this act among his fellow comrades who were also prosecuted. He had stated: 'Several persons are arrayed along with me in this trial as conspirators. I have already said that in the act I did, I had no companions and I alone am solely responsible for my act. Had they not been arraigned with me I would not have even given any defence for me as would be clear from the fact that I desired and enjoined upon my counsel not to cross-examine any of the witnesses connected with the incident of the 30 January 1948.'

This falsehood was in the hope of saving his friends from indictment.

'VANDE MATARAM!'

The day 15 November 1949 was fixed as the date of **execution of Nana Apte and Nathuram Godse**. They carried in their hands a map of undivided India, the saffron coloured flag and a copy of the Bhagavada Gita. Apte was delighted to see the golden glow of sunlight at 8 a.m. and exclaimed with joy: 'Pundit, see how charming and bewitching is this early morning sunlight!'

'Most pleasant and charming!' Godse had replied.

They stood on their planks and began singing at the top of their voices:

Namaste Sada Vatsale Matribhume,
Twaya Hindubhume Sukham Vardhitoham,
Mahamangale Punyabhume Twadarthe
Patatawesh Kayo, Namaste, Namaste!
Vande Mataram!

[I bow to Thee, O my Ever-loving Motherland!
I rejoice in having been brought up by Thee,
O Land of the Hindus! O most sacred and holy Land,
May this my body fall for Thy sake!
I bow to Thee! Forever and Evermore!]

As they bowed their heads in unison, the hangman pulled the rod of the planks from under their feet.

I had set out to trace the evolution of Hindu religion since the advent of the Rigvedic people into India at the dawn of history. The Muslim invasions and infiltrations from across Afghanistan had posed a serious threat to Hinduism but the flame of religion remained undimmed, undiminished.

THE CONSTITUTION OF INDIA

If Mahatma Gandhi was the main founder of India's freedom, Dr Bhimrao Ambedkar was the principal architect of the Constitution of India. A Constituent Assembly was formed to formulate and enact the Constitution of India. Dr Bhimrao Ambedkar was the chairman of the Drafting Committee of the debates of the Constituent Assembly.

He belonged to the Mahar caste, which was considered a lower caste of untouchables. His father was a subedar in the Indian Army. He studied in a high school in Mumbai and in 1912, graduated from Elphinstone College, Bombay, in Economics and Political Science. He was later awarded a Baroda State Scholarship for three years, under a scheme established by Sayajirao Gaekwad III, and went for post-graduation studies at the Columbia University in New York. There he had presented a paper titled 'Castes in India: their Genesis, Mechanism and Development'. Afterwards he joined the London School of Economics (LSE) and in 1923 was awarded the degree of Doctor of Science. He was also trained in the law at the Grey's Inn.

Jawaharlal Nehru invited him to join his cabinet as India's law minister. Two weeks later he was appointed chairman of the Drafting Committee of the Constitution for the new Republic of India.

AMBEDKAR'S VIEWS ON HINDUISM

Democracy is based on the principles of Liberty, Equality and Fraternity. It may be supposed that at India's Independence, Liberty was accorded to all her citizens. But as regards Equality, Ambedkar says that the Hindus who were the main community were governed by Manusmriti.[243]

'In the scheme of *Manusmriti,* the Brahmin is placed in the first rank. Below him is the Kshatriya. Below the Kshatriya is the *Vaishya*. Below the *Vaishya* is the *Shudra* and below the *Shudra* is the *Ati-Shudra* (the Untouchable). This system of rank and gradation is simply another way of enunciating the principle of inequality so that it may be truly said that *Hinduism does not recognize equality*. Manu has introduced and made inequality a vital force of life. I will illustrate it by taking a few examples such as slavery, marriage and rule of law.

'Manu recognizes slavery. But he confined it to the *Shudras*. Only *Shudras* could be made slaves of the three higher classes. But the higher classes could not be the slaves of the *Shudra*.

'As for marriage, Manu is opposed to inter-marriage. His injunction is for each class to marry within his class. But he does recognize marriage outside the defined class. Here again he is particularly careful not to allow intermarriage to do any harm to his principle of inequality among classes. Like slavery he permits inter-marriage but not in the inverse order. A Brahmin when marrying outside his class may marry any woman from any of the classes below him. A Kshatriya is free to marry a woman from the two classes next below him, namely the *Vaishya* and *Shudra*, but must not marry a woman from the Brahmin class, which is above him. A Vaishya is free to marry a woman from Shudra class which is next below him. But he cannot marry a woman from the *Brahmin* and Kshatriya class, which are above him. Why this discrimination? The only answer is that Manu was most anxious to preserve the rule of inequality, which was his guiding principle... Fraternity is another name for fellow-feeling. In the graded caste system of Manu, fraternity can only exist among people of one's own category, not in the whole society.'[244]

Ambedkar, in his undelivered speech written in 1936, Annihilation of Castes, explains the working and implications of

[243]Manusmiriti or Manava Dharmashastra was composed in second or third century AD. It was written by a pundit and ascribed to Manu.

[244]Balchandra, Mungekar (ed.), *The Essential Ambedkar*, Rupa Publications, Delhi, 2017, p. 81.

the caste system: 'Although caste may lead to conduct so gross as to be called man's inhumanity to man, yet *Hindus observe caste because they are deeply religious*. People are not wrong in observing caste. In my view, what is wrong is their religion, which has inculcated this notion of caste. If this is correct, then obviously the enemy you must grapple with is not the people who observe caste, but the *Shastras* which teach them this religion of caste... The real remedy is to destroy the belief in the sanctity of the *Shastras*. Reformers working for the removal of untouchability, including Mahatma Gandhi, do not seem to realize this fact.

'You must take the stand that the Buddha took. You must take the stand which Guru Nanak took. You must not only discard the *Shastras*, you must deny their authority, as did the Buddha and Nanak. You must have the courage to tell the Hindus that what is wrong with them is their religion—the religion which has produced in them this notion of sacredness of caste.

'The Hindu social order is based primarily on class or *varna* and not on individuals, although like the Christians and the Muslims they also believe that all men are created by God. But while the Christians and the Muslims accept this as the whole truth, the Hindus believe that this is only part of the truth. According to them, the whole truth consists of two parts. The first part is that all men are created by God. The second part is that God created different men from different parts of his divine body. The Hindus regard the second part as more important and more fundamental than the first. (As we have seen, the Brahmins mutilated the *Purush Sookta*, to inject the poison of inequality!)

'The Hindu social order is based on the doctrine that men are created from the different parts of his divine body. The Hindus regard that the *Brahmin* is no brother to the Kshatriya because the former is born from the mouth of the divinity, while the latter is born from His arms. The Kshatriya is no brother of to the *Vaishya* because the former is born from the arms of the divinity and the latter from His thighs.

'As no one is brother to the other, no one is the keeper of the order. The doctrine that the different classes were created from different parts of the divine body has generated the belief that it ust be divine will that they should remain separate and distinct. is this belief which has created in the Hindu an instinct to be ifferent, to be separate and to be distinct from the rest of the llow Hindus. The most extensive and wild manifestation of this pirit of isolation is, of course, the caste system. The castes are gain divided into sub-castes. Their number is legion.'

Dr Ambedkar is talking about Hymn 10. 90 of the Rig Veda, alled the 'Purush Sookta', in which the divinity called Purush is acrificed and the four categories of men are created. I have quoted ie hymn in the Rigvedic section of this book. 'In this famous ymn,' explains Wendy Doniger, 'the gods create the world by ismembering the cosmic giant, Purusha, the primeval male who the victim in a Vedic sacrifice. The underlying concept is quite ncient; yet the fact that this is one of the latest hymns of the ig Veda is evident from its reference to the three Vedas (**Verse 9**) nd to the four social classes or varnas (**Verse 12**) the first time iat this concept appears in Indian civilization, as well as from s monistic world-view.'

While discussing the 'Purush Sookta' in the Rigvedic part, I have lready brought out that this hymn has been bowdlerized by the rahmins at the time the Rigvedic hymns were reduced to writing. hey added two spurious verses, 11 and 12, which contradict the riginal verses. I quote the spurious verses, 11 and 12, as well as ie original verses, 13 and 14, which they dared not omit!

11. When they divided *Purusha*, into how many parts did iey apportion him? What do they call his mouth, his two arms nd thighs and feet?

12. The Brahmin was his mouth, both his arms were made ito *Rajanya*. His thighs became the *Vaishya*, and from his feet ie Shudra were produced.

13. The moon was born from his mind; from his eyes the in was born. Indra and Agni came from his mouth and from is vital breath Wind was born.

14. From his naval the middle realms of the space arose; from is head the sky evolved. From his feet came the earth, and the uarters of the sky from his ear. Thus, they set the worlds in order.

HINDUISM: THE JOURNEY SO FAR

The Rig Veda—the most ancient text of the Hindus—comprise ten mandalas, which are essentially compositions of seve principal rishis including Vishvamitra, Vasishtha, Bharadwaj Atri, Gritsmada and their descendants. The origins of Hinduisr are rooted in the hymns of Rig Veda. These hymns invoke god like Indra, Varuna, Rudra, Soma, Marut, Agni and others, wh rule all natural elements. These hymns were chanted whil performing yajna, which was the main cultural ritual tha developed during the Rigvedic period. Several of these hymn celebrate the life-giving sun and the sunrays. Others find subject as diverse as fire, *vani* (speech), the night, the forest, the rive Saraswati, demons, specific rituals and offerings, the universe, th wind, the sky and earth, cattle and horses, to name some. Th god Indra appears as the predominant protector in the Rigvedi hymns. The god Brahma, or Brahman, is the all-pervading entit The god Rudra is also mentioned, who later takes the form c the god Shiva in the post Rigvedic period. The god Vishnu i mentioned briefly.

The Rig Veda is appended with Bahamanas, which are commentary on the hymns, while the Sama Veda is the guide fo reciting the hymns or the verses with music.

The Yajur Veda suggests detailed methods to perform ritual which are also appended with Bahamanas detailing constructio methods for making the fire altar or the *havan vedi*.

While the Rig Veda is '*parlokik*' (other wordly), Atharva Ved is '*aihalokik*' (this worldly). It contains hymns with formulae fo healing from diseases and antidotes against malicious enemie Herein gods are portrayed as destroyers of demons and huma enemies, both internal and external. It also propogates a 'Hind way of life'.

The Dharamshastras—like the Manusmriti—also provide a important layer in the transformation of Hinduism as the cast system became more structured.

The Upanishads, which are the last section of the Vedas, have influenced the practice of Hinduism and elaborate upon the thought of the Vedas. Of the two distinct philosophies that emanate from them, one states that the Brahma or the supreme God corresponds to the soul or the atma. The other states that each soul is individually eternal and propagates truth, light and the immortality of the soul. The Upanishads are named Mundaka, Isha, Kena, Katha, etc.

Hinduism is rooted in the vedic gods of the Rig Veda and the Atharva Veda, who have transformed over the years. These Vedic gods were Brahma or the Brahamna, who was all pervading; Vishnu; and Rudra, who later transformed into Shiva. In the contemporary world, Brahma has almost been eclipsed while, along with Vishnu, Rama and Krishna are venerated as his avatars. Shiva is venerated in his lingum form.

The Sanskrit epic, the Ramayana, which is the story of god Rama, was composed by Sage Valmiki and later translated by Tulsidas in Khadi Boli, a local dialect, as Ramcharitamanas, has become a relevant text of Hinduism in contemporary times. The Mahabharata is another Sanskrit epic, which depicts a war that was waged about two and a half thousand hundred years ago, wherein the god Krishna appeared as a main god of the Vaishnavite thought. His teachings in the form of the Bhagavada Gita are fundamental to modern Hindu philosophy.

The religions Buddhism and Jainism, according to many, were versions of Hinduism sans rituals. They became popular in the sixth century AD. Based on the teachings of the Buddha and Mahavira, they propagated 'ahimsa' shunning rituals of animal sacrifice and advocating severity in religious tenets. These changes, in turn, moderated and modified Hindu practices.

Many saints, gurus and philosophers propagated modified paths for leading a pious life that created varied sects. Guru Nanak founded the Sikh panth (or way). Kabir explained the vedic concept of the all-pervading God through his compositions. Mirabai devoted her life to Lord Krishna in her bhajans or devotional songs. Swami Yogananda propagated the idea of Kriya

Yoga, which we glimpse in his autobiography. The vernacular poetry by poets like Bhasa, Bhavabhuti and Kalidasa were rooted around vedic characters and storylines. In ninth century AD, Adi Shankaracharya codified the Advaita Vedanta philosophy, which is a non-dualistic system based on the Upanishads. According to him, 'Brahma alone is real. This world is an illusion.' He wrote the *Brahma-Sutra-Bhashya*, which forms one of the main aspects of Hinduism today. With the annexation of India by the British, many of our ancient texts were translated into German and English and became accessible to the Western world. Swami Vivekananda addressed the World Parliament of Religions in 1893 and brought attention to the basic tenets of Hinduism and its philosophy. He was a disciple of Saint Ramakrishna Paramahansa.

The art and architecture of the temples all over India were the stage where rituals were performed. These temples varied in expression from the north to south and from the east to west of the country because of contextual differences in material, artisans, local techniques and traditions. Yet the basic planning of all temples was rooted in the Vedas like the Atharva Veda as well as later texts like the Mansara. Hinduism spread to the Southeast Asia and East Asia as trade and commerce connections spread. Its gods, beliefs and traditions amalgamated with alien cultures to create a modified version of Hinduism.

Over the ages, all religions have physically manifested themselves in the form of architecture as the political or the ruling class supported tangible expression of faith. Hindu rulers have also built temples that housed Hindu deities from the Rigvedic to Pauranic to Bhakti period. These temples were destroyed with the onslaught of Islamic invasions from time to time, and later in the Mughal period, to superimpose the sites with structures of their faith.

This was a setback to the Hindu canvas in India as invaders razed to the ground many temples across North India. Even as there were efforts for restoration by many Hindu kings and queens like Ahilyabai, who rebuilt many fallen temples, religion became one of the main reasons for political strife in the country. The British also manipulated this rift to their gain (through their infamous doctrine of divide-and-rule), leading to the partition of the country on religious lines with the Independence in 1947, giving birth to both India and Pakistan. After Independence, democracy was instituted in the country and the polity saw religion in this context of a Hindu dominant nation with a few minorities. Gandhi was assassinated by Godse, who believed that the motherland was the land of Hindus, and Gandhi was not helping in the cause by being partial to Muslims. The State started protecting the minority communities by making policies for their inclusion in the mainstream.

The Constitution of India, which was drafted by Ambedkar, gives all citizens equal rights irrespective of religion and caste. The law righted the wrong of caste-based discrimination in the Indian society, entrenched in the ancient divisions of varna. This aspect of the Hindu texts and their interpretation was rethought, with equality afforded to all by the Indian Constitution.

Today, there is a surge in the ritualistic and manifested aspect of Hinduism and the urge to rebuild temples. Consequently, there is an undercurrent in the Hindu psyche to fortify their belief through symbols and rituals that are rooted in ancient texts. The right-leaning party in power today has embarked on the revival and restoration of Hindu temple complexes like Kashi Vishwanath at Varanasi, Ram temple at Ayodhya and Jyotirlinga at Ujjain.

Hinduism is rooted in the Vedas and Upanishads, layered by the storylines of the Puranas, influenced and modified by subsequent epics like the Ramayana and the Mahabharata, reimagined by philosopher saints like Budhha, Mahavira, Gurunanak, rendered in colloquial colours by many seers, and has charted its course in a land that has seen many rulers, who tried to change it and who were changed by it. So, Hinduism, as we know it today, is a culmination or, one can say, a palimpsest of all these layers and has consequently become a way of life. It encourages the seeker to look within for what Sir Mark Tully, in his book *India's Unending Journey*, calls 'the balance between the material and the spiritual, between reason and other means of perceiving reality...'